THE GOD BREAKER

She padded to the window and pulled the shutters back. Sure enough, the sun was shining down from the north-east, and there were no thunderheads in the sky, merely high, wispy white streaks, like lines of spray on the ocean. The thunder that was not thunder had stopped, as suddenly as it started. Had she imagined it? She was certain she was already awake when she heard it, and that it was not the tail end of a dream. An old man of the clan when Saana was young had often complained of noises no one else could hear, but he had described a whine, not thunder, and—

There was no mistaking it this time. It was deeper and louder than before, and Saana knew in her heart that it was not thunder.

By Mike Brooks

The Black Coast
The Splinter King
The Godbreaker

MIKE BROOKS

THE GOD BREAKER

orbitbooks.net

ORBIT

First published in Great Britain in 2021 by Orbit

3 5 7 9 10 8 6 4

A CIP catalogue record for this book
is available from the British Library.

ISBN 978-0-356-51394-2

Typeset in Apollo MT by M Rules
Printed and bound in Great Britain by
Clays Ltd, Elcograf, S.p.A.

Papers used by Orbit are from well-managed forests
and other responsible sources.

MIX
Paper from
responsible sources
FSC® C104740

Orbit
An imprint of
Little, Brown Book Group
Carmelite House
50 Victoria Embankment
London EC4Y 0DZ

An Hachette UK Company
www.hachette.co.uk

www.orbitbooks.net

This book is for everyone who's come with me on this journey, and found something of themselves in Narida or the City of Islands.

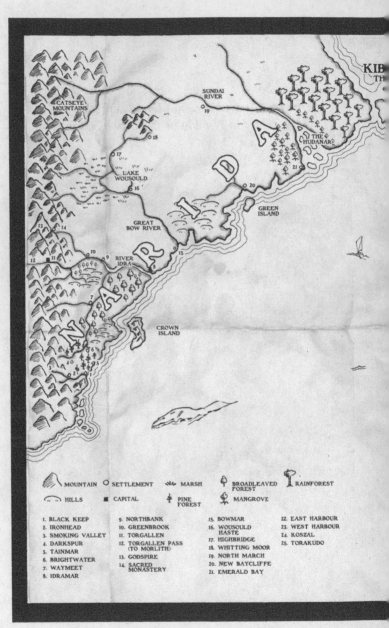

KIB
TH

SUNDAI
RIVER
19

18

17

LAKE
WOUSOULD
16

THE
HUDANAR
21

20

GREEN
ISLAND

GREAT
BOW RIVER

13   14

10
12   11   9   RIVER
IDRA
15
8

7

CROWN
ISLAND

6

3
2   1

MAP LEGEND

⛰	MOUNTAIN	○ SETTLEMENT	～ MARSH	♠ BROADLEAVED FOREST	♣ RAINFOREST
～	HILLS	■ CAPITAL	♣ PINE FOREST	♣ MANGROVE	

1. BLACK KEEP
2. IRONHEAD
3. SMOKING VALLEY
4. DARKSPUR
5. TAINMAR
6. BRIGHTWATER
7. WAYMEET
8. IDRAMAR

9. NORTHBANK
10. GREENBROOK
11. TORGALLEN
12. TORGALLEN PASS (TO MORLITH)
13. GODSPIRE
14. SACRED MONASTERY

15. BOWMAR
16. WOUSOULD HASTE
17. HIGHBRIDGE
18. WHITTING MOOR
19. NORTH MARCH
20. NEW BAYCLIFFE
21. EMERALD BAY

22. EAST HARBOUR
23. WEST HARBOUR
24. KOSZAL
25. TORAKUDO

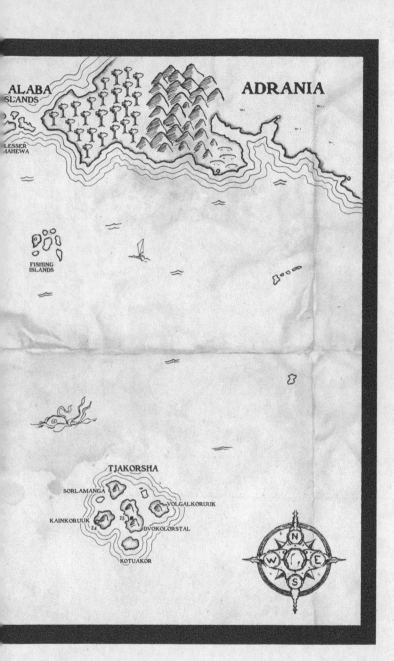

What Has Gone Before

In THE SPLINTER KING, Darel Blackcreek, *newly confirmed as the thane of Blackcreek by the Southern Marshal* Kaldur Brightwater, *leaves his home of Black Keep. He travels with Brightwater to Idramar, Narida's capital, to explain to the God-King* Natan Narida, *also known as* Natan III, *why he has let the Brown Eagle clan of the Tjakorshi settle in Black Keep despite their history as raiders. On the journey their ship is attacked by pirates, which Darel helps to fight off.*

Black Keep is left in the hands of Daimon Blackcreek, *Darel's younger brother, and his new wife* Saana Sattistutar, *chief of the Brown Eagle clan. Daimon tasks the town's new reeve* Evram *to find the witch Daimon believes lives among them. However, Saana's daughter* Zhanna Saanastutar *wishes to lead a group into the mountains to find out why the people of the Smoking Valley did not come to trade with Black Keep in the spring, as they normally would. She takes a small party with her, including* Amonhuhe of the Mountains, *a woman of the Smoking Valley who settled in Black Keep,* Menaken *of the Black Keep guard, and her friend* Tsennan "Longjaw" Jelemaszhin.

Tila Narida, the Divine Princess and younger sister of the God-King, arrives back in Idramar and discovers that her brother's sickness is a ruse, performed to head off any rash action from those who might wish to depose him now rumours are gaining strength of their divine ancestor Nari being reborn in the west. With Tila back to help control the Divine Court, Natan agrees to start "recovering", and when Tila calls the Inner Council it is agreed that they will send troops westward to find the man claiming to be Nari reborn. The stated purpose is to escort him to the monastery at Godspire, the sacred mountain, where the prophecies of Tolkar the Last Sorcerer say the reborn Nari will be proclaimed by the monks who live there. However, Tila intends to use her contacts from her double identity as Livnya the Knife, the head of Idramar's underworld, to send assassins to kill the man she views as a pretender.

Master Temach, the Master of Learning on the Inner Council, suspects that Princess Tila has ulterior motives, and discloses this to his colleagues in the Cupbearers, a secret society of academics, of whom Marin of Idramar is one. Marin agrees to persuade his husband Sar Alazar of White Hill, also known as Alazar Blade, to enroll in the army so they can go west and try to ensure the safety of the reborn Nari. On his way back from the meeting Marin runs foul of Idramar's Keepers, who recognise him from previous thefts and incarcerate him. A healer called Ravi is placed in the cell next to him, and Marin realises that she has been blamed and arrested for a theft he committed a couple of days previously.

In East Harbour, on Grand Mahewa in the City of Islands, Jeya and Galem the Splinter Prince are trying to find out who killed Galem's family, the line of exiled Naridan monarchy known as the Splinter King. Galem reveals to Jeya that thëy are not in fact male, and had only been pretending in order for thëir family to still be valued by the Hierarchs who rule the City of Islands. Thëy adopt the name Bulang, and Jeya begins to hear about deaths among the street orphans that shé knows. Unbeknown to hér, hér friend Nabanda is the culprit, and is still looking for Galem/Bulang, under threat of death from the Shark Kurumaya.

In Black Keep, Saana and Daimon are visited unexpectedly by Yarmina Darkspur, *the daughter of* Odem Darkspur. *Thane Odem's cousin* Sar Omet *offers Yarmina's hand in marriage to either Darel or Daimon. With Darel absent and Daimon already married, Daimon refuses for both of them. That night, Yarmina visits him and Saana in secret and discloses that if the offer was refused her father intended her to seduce either Daimon or Saana to damage their alliance: something Yarmina has no interest in doing. She, Daimon, and Saana agree that she will stay for a while and then return to tell her father that Daimon was a polite host, but her efforts came to nothing. However, a few days later the reeve* Evram *discovers that the fisherman* Old Elio *has marks of witchcraft in his house. Old Elio attacks Evram and flees, but the revelation angers Sar Omet, who accuses Daimon of harbouring witches. He, Yarmina, and their escort leave the next day.*

Zhanna's party reach the Catseye Mountains, but one of their number is eaten by a kingdrake that attacks their campfire at night time. As they progress higher into the pass that leads to the Smoking Valley, they encounter a girl named Kakaiduna, *who is fleeing the enslavement of her people. Zhanna and the Brown Eagles with her ambush the men pursuing Kakaiduna, and learn that they are from Darkspur, and are seeking the gold in the Smoking Valley's river.*

In Idramar, the Lord Admiral Kaled Greenbrook *attempts to blackmail Tila by confronting her alone with knowledge of her other identity. Tila kills him, but is forced to claim that it was in self-defence: a claim that Kaled's cousin* Adan Greenbrook, *the Lord Treasurer, challenges. Eastern Marshal* Einan Coldbeck *declares that it will be settled through trial by combat, and Tila realises that Coldbeck is now keeping her brother imprisoned in his quarters under pretence of continuing sickness in order to seize power for himself. She refuses the supposedly impartial champion nominated on her behalf and reaches out through her criminal* contacts to Alazar Blade, offering him a deal: if he fights for her and clears her name, she will arrange for his husband Marin to be freed. Alazar, not realizing that Tila is the same woman as Livnya — with whom Marin and he traveled to Idramar from the City of Islands — reluctantly agrees. During their conversation, Alazar learns he was only given command of Natan II's guard twenty years ago because of his relationship with Natan III, and Tila learns that her father died because he fled from combat, and Alazar only took the blame to spare her brother's feelings.

Jeya and Bulang visit a Hierarch during open court day, but as soon as the Hierarch realises Bulang's true identity they try to have thëm arrested. Jeya and Bulang manage to get away and try again at the Festival of Ashes, when all the Hierarchs will be present. However, they see a new Splinter King and family — masked as always — presented to the public, and Bulang flees in shock. Bulang realises the Hierarchs have simply replaced their "pet" family, and now questions whether thëy were even truly of Nari's line, or if this has happened before. Jeya takes Bulang to Ngaiyu, who took hér in when shé was a child, but finds Ngaiyu murdered. Shé leaves Bulang at a temple and goes with hér friend Damau to give the news to Nabanda, who has no work on the docks as the main cargo coming ashore is slaves picked up from the Fishing Islands by Zheldu Stonejaw, a survivor of the failed attack on Black Keep in THE BLACK COAST, whose ships came to the City of Islands instead of returning across the ocean to The Golden. Nabanda goes off with Damau.

Yarmina Darkspur writes a letter in secret to Daimon and sends it to Black Keep with a pedlar, warning him that her father intends to march on Black Keep and take it for his own, claiming that they harbor witches. Daimon and Saana prepare as best they can by sending out calls for aid, including a ship to go north up the coast to Thane Gilan Tainbridge and then on to Idramar to alert the Southern Marshal.

Alazar Blade accepts Tila's offer, on condition that she also frees Ravi, which Marin has requested. Tila agrees, and Alazar defeats the sar sent against him without drawing his sword. Tila takes advantage of being proven innocent in front of the public by ordering the door to her brother's chambers unlocked, and advises Marshal Coldbeck to flee before her brother can reach him. Alazar and the newly freed Marin then enrol in the Eastern Army, along with Ravi, and head upriver from Idramar.

Darel arrives in Idramar and finds it in uproar after Coldbeck's attempted coup. He meets Hiran Threestone *and his sister* Yae, *and begins a romance with Hiran. He is finally called to give an account of himself before the God-King, during a feast at which Adan Greenbrook is raised to the rank of Eastern Marshal, but Darel's explanations are not heeded and he is stripped of the rank of thane, with his lands to be awarded to Darkspur. Later that night Darel and Hiran find murdered guards, and Darel sends Hiran to get help while he follows the trail to the God-King's chambers. He finds Kaldur Brightwater and his men trying to gain access and kill Natan and Tila, on the grounds that Nari has been reborn and the current Divine Family are foolish, and trying to cling to power. Darel pretends to join Brightwater, but turns on him once the door has been broken down. Between Darel, Tila, and Natan, Brightwater and his sars are killed, and Natan restores Darel to thane and names him the new Southern Marshal for his loyalty and bravery.*

Zhanna and her crew find that the people of the Smoking Valley have indeed been enslaved by Darkspur, with their children held as hostages. They pick off a couple of the Darkspur men, then launch a night attack to help the slaves free themselves. Menaken dies, but the appearance of the huge flesh-eating dragon known as a thundertooth helps swing events in their favour, and Darkspur's men are either killed or driven off. Some members of the Smoking Valley set off with Zhanna and her crew to come back down to the lowlands to trade for food.

In Black Keep, Yarmina's warning is borne out when the forces of Darkspur arrive. Saana strikes a deal with the thralls, the warriors of The Golden who surrendered after their attack on Black Keep failed: their thralldom will be revoked if they take up arms and fight for Black Keep, which they agree to do.

Jeya and Bulang find Damau murdered as well, and Jeya realises it can only have been Nabanda killing the people shé knows. Shé arranges an ambush by passing word around to all the other people who Ngaiyu had helped, and confronts Nabanda. However, Nabanda brings hîs thugs with hîm, and is about to kill Jeya when Bulang draws hîm off. Nabanda pursues Bulang over a bridge, but Bulang and Jeya had rigged it to give way under hîs weight. Nabanda falls into the water of the Narrows, which Bulang and Jeya had previously chummed in order to draw in sharks, which then eat the already-bleeding Nabanda. Bulang and Jeya take over Ngaiyu's old house with the intention of continuing its use as a shelter for those who need it, but are found by Kurumaya. Kurumaya demands to know why they should not kill Bulang to fulfil the contract that Nabanda failed to complete: Bulang, encouraged by Kurumaya's hatred of the Hierarchs, and with no other option, reveals that thëy are the Splinter Prince.

Marin, Alazar, Ravi, and a few other soldiers narrowly escape from a riot in the city of Northbank and desert from the army to find the reborn Nari. They encounter a priest named Mordokel who leads them to a camp on the shores of the Greenwater river. While passing through the crowd Marin is briefly confronted by an old man with a staff, who then disappears. The youth Tyrun, Nari reborn, welcomes them all except for Elifel, one of Tila's assassins. Marin grapples with Elifel when he draws his knife, and his attempt on Tyrun's life fails. After they withdraw from Tyrun's presence Ravi seems overwhelmed at being welcomed and told that her heart is pure, and asks Marin if he has ever lived in fear of something his whole life only to find that it is not true.

Zheldu Stonejaw has decided to make a final run to the Fishing Islands for slaves, and then will take her ship through the Throat of the World into the northern oceans. She and her crew go to sleep on a shore, and wake up to find themselves surrounded by other Tjakorshi. The Golden has prophesied the doom of Tjakorsha and brought the entire nation across the ocean with it, and Stonejaw has to explain why she never returned after her failure. She buys her life with news that she heard in the City of Islands — that the God-King of Narida is sick — the suggestion that the Tjakorshi could conquer it and live there, and that she has someone who can guide them. The Golden accepts this information and declares that Stonejaw still has a use to it . . . for now.

Prologue

T he dreams still came.

The dreams still came, and there were no fires aboard the ships to chase them away upon waking.

Night was the hardest time, when darkness ruled. He thought that perhaps the dreams would have stopped now: in the moments after he regained consciousness, he prayed to the Dark Father and all the other gods he had encountered that they might take the dreams from him, but his prayers always went unanswered. At least, unless the continued presence of the dreams was its own answer.

Rock splitting.

Ash spewing.

Great spirits of fire awakening from slumber.

He groped for a skin of water, unstoppered it, and took a shaky swig. The door of the deckhouse was shut, and so even the faint illumination of the stars and the moon was denied to him, save through chinks in the walls. It was the price he paid so that no one might see him like this.

Memories sleeted through him, half-broken and displaced. The tall pines of what had once been home, standing stark on the eastern shore against the rising sun, then overlaid with fire and screams: the same place, at different times. His brother Kozhan, named for the hero who had set the moons in the sky, and Kozhan's friend Angorzhem: not heroes, either of them, just bullies. The look on his mother Ynga's face when the witches said that his sister Tumeszha hadn't returned from the bone walk around the crater of Volgalkoruuk, the Dawn Mountain. She would not rejoin the clan as an adult: her body would lie at the summit for ever.

Standing on the shore of the largest harbour he had ever seen, watching his mother sail away without a backward glance, with enough iron around his wrists to make him rich back home, had it not been imprisoning him.

His own bone walk, years after he should have done it, with no witches left alive to mark it. He did not find Tumeszha's body, but he did find something else. Something that even now was uncoiling within him, and fighting its way back to the surface. Something stronger than he was. Something . . . stranger.

The last memory was not the most recent, but it was always the same.

The hole.

Arms trapped at his sides by the rock of Volgalkoruuk enclosing him. The mocking voices of Kozhan and Angorzhem, who had first tricked and then forced him in. His feet flailing helplessly, his lungs choking on the strange air of the mountain's depths, and his eyes staring into nothing because his body was blocking all the light. He cried, and he screamed, and nothing did any good.

That was when the dreams had begun, and that was when his need for fire began. He saw the hole every time his eyes could see nothing else, so he closed them as little as possible. In time, fire became more than just a shield against the darkness. It had become a tool.

He shuddered, and closed his eyes.

Something else opened them, and reached for its mask.

PART ONE

PART ONE

Saana

Saana was already awake when the thunder that was not thunder came.

She was lying in the bed she now shared with Daimon Blackcreek and staring at the ceiling while he breathed in and out, his chest moving in the slow, deep rhythms of sleep. Their night together had been a hot and urgent one, markedly different to the cautious, early affections when Saana needed to subtly guide her earnest but inexperienced young husband through what she expected of him. Perhaps the uncertain future heralded by the hostile army outside the town's walls had removed his inhibitions somewhat. Saana was not displeased by the change, although she would have preferred a different cause.

She thought the noise actually was thunder at first, but something about the distant, hollow booming sounded wrong, and the weak rays of morning sun striking through the gaps in the wooden shutters were undimmed by clouds. Daimon's breathing remained unchanged, so she left him undisturbed. Who knew whether Odem Darkspur would call for an assault today? If so, Daimon would need all the rest he could get. If not, there was no need for him to wake just yet.

She rolled out of bed and slipped on a robe. Saana had spent all her life wearing wool and furs, and the smooth, cool fabric worn by Naridan nobles was still foreign to her. Nonetheless, it was pleasant on the skin, and adequate for the weather here. Tjakorsha sweltered under the long sun at the height of summer, but for much of the year it was bone-chillingly cold. Narida was warmer, even this far south, and a noble's robe was sufficient when she was merely looking out of the window.

Besides, it was good to adopt some of her husband's customs, and the fact she was both rather taller and broader than many Naridans, particularly the women, meant the robe was not quite as modest as it would have been on some. Daimon had said nothing, but his eyes had told their own story. Given that Daimon was over ten summers younger than Saana, being the object of his desire was somewhat gratifying. Their marriage had been one of necessity, not love, but it was good that her options for intimacy were not limited to her own hands.

She padded to the window and pulled the shutters back. Sure enough, the sun was shining down from the north-east, and there were no thunderheads in the sky, merely high, wispy white streaks, like lines of spray on the ocean. The thunder that was not thunder had stopped, as suddenly as it started. Had she imagined it? She was certain she was already awake when she heard it, and that it was not the tail end of a dream. An old man of the clan when Saana was young had often complained of noises no one else could hear, but he had described a whine, not thunder, and—

There was no mistaking it this time. It was deeper and louder than before, and Saana knew in her heart that it was not thunder. It lacked the rolling quality, and was not either the distant growl or the sudden hammer blow that followed a nearby lightning flash, then tailed off afterwards.

"What is that?" Daimon asked from behind her. Saana turned to see him sitting up in bed, the cover fallen away from the lean, hard lines of his chest. He would freeze in a Tjakorshi winter, and Saana had never thought of herself as one to be attracted to scrawny men, but the world had a way of surprising you.

"Your wife does not know," she replied, pushing aside the memory of the previous night, when flickering candlelight had cast interesting shadows as it played over her husband's ruddy skin. "She thought it was thunder at first, but it is not."

"What can it be, then?" Daimon asked, rising from the bed and approaching her. "It is no herd of dragons!"

Suddenly, something in Saana's head slotted into place, and she stared out of the window again as though seeking confirmation, even though she knew there was none to be had. "Do you have mountain spirits here? That sleep poorly?"

Daimon was staring at her in incomprehension, and Saana inwardly cursed the fact that her grasp of Naridan still was not good enough to make herself properly understood all the time. Then again, perhaps it simply had no direct translation. She tried again. "A mountain, that . . . coughs? The spirits inside make noise, send up smoke?"

Daimon shook his head. "Not near here, that your husband knows."

"Tjakorsha is made of such mountains," Saana told him. "They can sound like thunder, sometimes. But if there are none near here . . . "

"We have problems enough outside our walls, without mountain spirits bothering us," Daimon said grimly. "Let us hope it is not instead some sort of sorcery brought by Darkspur. Your husband should get dressed and inspect the defences."

"Your wife will come with you," Saana said. "We should see how the thralls are settling in."

*

It was midmorning, and the Darkspur lines had not moved. There were a few hundred soldiers out there, but they had not decided to try their luck against Black Keep's relatively modest walls. However, Saana noticed that some trees on the edges of the Downwoods had been felled.

"For fires?" she asked, pointing.

"Perhaps," said Sagel, scratching his chin. He was one of Daimon's original household guards, although Saana privately considered that any one of them was less of a warrior than many of her own clan. Sagel had some experience with weapons, though, and had been doing his best to impart that knowledge to the many townsfolk who had never held anything more offensive than a scythe. "If you want s'man's opinion, though, he'd say they're making a ram for the gates, or ladders for the walls. Or both."

"A ram?" Saana asked, confused by the Naridan word.

"Aye," Sagel replied. "Take a tree trunk, hack the branches off and make one end into a point. Sling it between four dragons, probably, and run it at our gate to knock it in." He sucked his teeth. "Black Keep's gate is a sturdy thing, but a decent ram might make real trouble for us. Especially if they're trying to come over the walls on ladders at the same time."

Saana grimaced. Tjakorshi raids did not besiege walled towns as Darkspur's forces were doing: any attack on such a target would be quick, with the intention of taking the defenders by surprise. Naridans, however, lived in these towns, and when they fought among themselves – as seemed more common than they would generally admit – they had developed ways of neutralising their enemies' defences. It made sense that those who were protected by such structures would also know the best tools for breaching them.

Saana was going to ask Sagel if they could hold the town against such an attack, but thought better of it. She was not only the chief of her clan, she was Daimon's wife, and while he might not be the thane of Blackcreek, he held authority here. Saana was officially Lady Saana now, and the Naridan "lowborn", as Daimon insisted on calling them, expected certainty from their nobility.

Saana was not sure if the fact Daimon had been adopted into the Blackcreek family after his own lowborn parents had died made him more or less aware of the differences in his society. She thought that perhaps he felt he had to be flawless, in order to prove his adoption had not been a mistake. This was despite many Naridan nobles being quite obviously flawed, including Daimon's adoptive father Lord Asrel, who had broken the rules of an honour duel with Daimon that he had requested himself, simply in order to try to kill Saana.

"This man is sure we will see them off," she said as confidently as she could manage, and Sagel grunted in what was probably agreement. At least sounding certain was something that Saana had some practice at. Most of the Naridans had even got used to her referring to herself as "this man" now. In the constructs of their strange, formal language, acknowledging yourself as a woman automatically meant claiming a lower status than any man who was speaking, and Saana had decided from the moment that she started learning the language that she would be having none of that.

"Aye, lady. After all, we only need to hold out until the thane of Tainbridge arrives," Achin said. He was a Naridan fisherman, but he held the spear in his hands as firmly as he might a ship's line or a net.

"Assuming he comes," Sagel said. "There's nothing to say he'll side with us, or even take one side over another. Might be he'll just sit in Tainbridge and mind his business."

"No need for that sort of down-talking," Achin protested. "S'man was just trying to be positive!"

"Aye, but we can't rely on others to get us out of this," Sagel replied, reasonably. "We've got to watch our own backs, not be waiting for someone else to——"

"*Chief!*"

That voice was not male, nor speaking Naridan. Saana looked up sharply and saw the crow-haired form of Akuto Wavechosen advancing along the top of the wall towards her.

Formerly a ship's captain, Akuto had been a thrall of the Brown Eagle clan until the day before. She had been one of Rikkut Fireheart's raiders, but surrendered when the battle had turned against them: Tjakorshi laws said she had to serve her captor clan for a year and a day, after which she would be free to return to her own, but Saana had offered a different path. It had been Akuto to whom she had first spoken, and Akuto who had first accepted. Once she took up her weapon to help defend Black Keep against Darkspur she became a free member of the town, bound to it by a new oath.

Somehow or another, Akuto appeared to have found her old war gear; the shirt of sea leather she was wearing looked to be fitted to her, and the wooden head of the blackstone axe in her right hand bore a carved wave design that well suited her warrior name. The few quick questions Saana had found the time to ask among Fireheart's former followers confirmed that the Wavechosen was indeed reckoned to be one of the finest sailors since Lodzuuk Waveborn, and widely respected.

In fact, Saana could not help feeling that Akuto looked rather more the part of chief than she did herself, but there was nothing to be done about that. At least the woman was not making any bones about acknowledging her authority.

"Wavechosen!" Saana replied. "What news?"

She was anticipating some manner of report on the readiness of the former thralls, perhaps an account of an argument between one of them and one of her own clan, or a Naridan:

maybe even a sighting of Darkspur soldiery making an approach. She was certainly not expecting the wide eyes, nor the breathless tone of alarm in the captain's voice.

"The sea's gone."

Saana resisted the urge to call her a liar or a fool. Her limited interactions with Akuto Wavechosen so far had shown the other woman to be sharp and smart, not to mention probably more knowledgeable about the ocean than Saana would ever be. If Akuto said the sea was gone, it was safe to assume that it was gone.

Saana looked towards the ocean, but she was on the west side of the town, and the buildings blocked her view. She thought she could make out the distant sparkle of sunlight reflected on water, away to the east, but not clearly.

"Show me," she told the Wavechosen, who turned and hurried away without another word. Saana followed her, doing her best to look calm and confident to any onlookers, despite the fact that moving at pace was rarely an encouraging sign, unless it was directly towards a routed enemy. Sure enough, she attracted several turned heads and curious looks as they descended stone steps off the wall and half-ran across the town, but no one fell in behind her, or demanded to know what was wrong. It was not until they reached another set of steps and climbed them to reach the eastern wall – in fact, Saana realised, the same place where she and Daimon had first seen Akuto and the rest of Fireheart's raiders bearing down on the town – that she noticed the gathering of people at the top.

It was a mix of Naridans and Tjakorshi, and both Brown Eagles and former thralls were represented. Worried faces turned towards her, and as Akuto pushed through them and Saana followed in her wake, she saw why.

The sea . . .

Well, to say that it was gone was not true. Not quite.

However, the sea was certainly a lot farther from the shore than Saana had ever seen it before, and she had been in Black Keep long enough now to see all the rhythms of the tides, as the long moon and the short moon worked their magic from the heavens above. The ribbon of the Blackcreek still wound down through the dark mud of its small estuary, but the beach beyond was laid bare to an extent Saana could have barely conceived.

"I've seen the sea here often enough," Akuto said bluntly. "This isn't normal. Even these Flatlanders seem to agree, although I can barely understand a word they're saying."

"It's not normal," Saana agreed absently, still staring at the distant waves. She tried to think. Had she seen the sea earlier? Had she looked at it at all that day? "How long has it been like this?"

"Not sure," Akuto replied. "I mean, Rodhnjan first shouted me about it, but I swear it's got a bit lower since I came to find you."

Saana chewed her lip. "So it's still moving?"

"Faster than a normal tide, by my guess."

An uneasy hollow settled in Saana's stomach, despite the fact she had eaten that morning. This did not sit right at all. She looked over at the knot of Darkspur men closest to the shore, well out of bowshot from Black Keep's walls, with Daimon's words about sorcery echoing in her head. From what she could see, they were staring towards the ocean as well, but what did that mean? Were they as surprised as she was? Even if it was some magic of unimaginable power – a Naridan witchcraft of malice, not the benign foretelling of a Tjakorshi witch – how would it aid Darkspur to pull the sea back? How would a Flatlander even manage to overcome Father Krayk? Something bubbled up from her memory. It had been close on thirty years since she had uttered it herself, but some things stuck in the mind and only needed the right prompting to return.

The tides, they rise and fall, my sweet
When the Dark Father snores
But when Father Krayk breathes in deep
Be not too near the shore.

For he will suck the waves away
And show their gleaming bed
But when Father Krayk breathes in deep
He will breathe out again . . .

"What are you humming that children's rhyme for?" Akuto asked, looking at Saana oddly.

"Father Krayk has breathed in," Saana said, and certainty crept into her mind with each word. "He *will* breathe out again. And when he does . . . "

She looked at Black Keep. Next to the river, a mile from the shore at most, with nothing but flat land to the east, west and north, and with the river diverted through the town to form the moats of the castle. The town's houses were on stilts, but their floors still stood below the height of her head when she was standing on the ground. Only the beginnings of the southern moorlands, rising on the other side of the Blackcreek, or the narrow tower of the Black Keep itself, provided any sort of height that was not a tree.

She looked over at the sea again. How long had she got? How certain was she that she was correct? If she was wrong, what she was about to command would see their home fall to enemies who wished to burn them alive.

If she was right . . . Well, then it was going to be a lot worse.

"Get to the River Gate!" she barked in Tjakorshi. Her people knew ships better than the Naridans did, so she would have to rely on them. "I want a bridge across the river, *now*! Lash the yolgus together, but be ready to cut them loose when you have to, and believe me, you'll know when that is! Don't just stand there gaping, go! Go!"

Saana was no thane of Narida, to be obeyed without question by her inferiors, but something about her urgency transmitted itself. The knot of Tjakorshi, Akuto included, turned and pelted down the steps. The Naridans who remained looked at her, their unease rapidly turning to alarm.

"Get everyone together!" Saana told them, shifting languages with an effort. "The sea is coming! *The sea is coming!* And for the love of the Dark Father," she added, as they began to move, "someone bring this man's husband to her!"

Daimon

The sea was coming.

"Move! Move!" Daimon yelled down from the walls, abandoning all the dignity of a Naridan nobleman. Aftak the priest was ringing the bell on the shrine of Nari, and the people of Black Keep were flooding out of the River Gate, heading for the southern shore across the bridge of taughs and yolgus that had been hastily lashed together by desperate Tjakorshi. Beyond, the land began to rise in the first of the moors; his people might be able to take shelter there, but only if they were fast enough. He did not want anyone to fall into the water, but neither could they afford to dawdle. Saana was already across, and coordinating efforts on the far side.

At least there were no enemies over there with her. Darkspur had no boats, and the nearest bridge was miles upriver, so the besieging forces had not bothered to cross the Blackcreek itself and set up a camp. After all, there were no settlements farther south, and no route for help to reach Black Keep. Thane Odem had groups stationed upstream and near the river's mouth who could shoot at any boat leaving or arriving at the town: making camp on the southern shore would have meant getting his men soaked and dispersing his forces, to no real purpose.

"What of the enemy?" Daimon asked, turning away from the stream of bodies making their way towards hoped-for safety.

"Still confused as to what we're doing, lord," the closest archer replied, pointing. "But they daren't approach close enough to take shots at our folk; we'll have the range on them if they do."

Sure enough, the Darkspur men upstream were watching the egress from Black Keep, but were not attempting to harass them. However, Daimon could see running figures heading towards the main bulk of the Darkspur camp, where Thane Odem's banner of a white kingdrake flew above his tent. Odem would learn soon enough that his enemies were abandoning their town. Daimon just had to hope he would not be able to organise an attack until they were gone.

Behind him, carried on the wind from the sea, came a throbbing note that had held terror for the people of Black Keep for generations. Daimon stiffened involuntarily: that noise had haunted his dreams as a child, for it was the shell horn of the Raiders. It was still difficult for him to disassociate it from the pale-faced demons who came in the dark with fire and blackstone, even though he was now married to one of those demons, and he knew that the person sounding the horn was an old woman with a mere handful of remaining teeth, and the sort of lecherous attitude that would have shamed a full-blooded youth in the throes of desire.

Today, at least, his fear was still well-placed, because Tsolga's sounding of her shell horn meant that the returning sea had been sighted, and time was running out.

"Go!" Daimon ordered the warriors on the wall with him, and they wasted no time hastening for the steps that led down to ground level, and the somewhat dubious promise of safety. Tsolga's horn had called the other guards away from their stations as well: the pockets of armed men and women dotted around the walls to mislead the forces of Darkspur for as long as possible were now fleeing. Daimon looked down and saw, to his relief, Abbatane and her stable hands running through the streets towards the River Gate.

"Are the dragons loose?" Daimon called down.

"Yes, lord!" Abbatane shouted back up to him, and the tightness around Daimon's heart eased a little. He could lead his people to safety across the river, perhaps, and his pet rattle-tail Rattler was at his side, but there was no way the makeshift bridge would have held the weight of his family's war dragons. Abbatane had taken Quill, Silverthorn, and the rest to the town's gate and set them free, where at least they could take their chances with the water rather than being trapped inside while it rose around them.

He looked to the north-west and saw the small group of longbrows cantering towards the Darkspur lines as though they had sensed what was coming. Perhaps they had; even before word had come from Saana that the sea had withdrawn, and would be coming back in force, Daimon had noticed that the castle gardens were lacking the usual songs of wind drakes rasping challenges at each other. It seemed the wild denizens of Narida knew a storm of sorts was about to break over them, and were either hunkering down or had already fled.

"Over the bridge!" Daimon called down to the stable hands, who made haste to obey. He glanced towards the sea, but the roofs of the town and the trees of the central pine grove and castle gardens got in the way, not to mention the dark, brooding presence of the Black Keep itself.

The bell of the shrine fell silent. Aftak had abandoned his post when he heard Tsolga's horn, then: that was good, since Daimon had been worried the stubborn old fool would have kept going, just in case there was still someone abed who somehow had not been roused.

"Lord!" one of his men shouted, from halfway down the steps that led towards the River Gate. "Are you not coming?"

"This lord will be the last to abandon his town," Daimon replied. "He must make sure everyone else is safe first!"

Duty. Such a strange thing, to pull you in different directions. With his elder brother Darel gone to plead for their town's survival with the God-King in Idramar, perhaps Daimon should have been first over the bridge, to give him the best chance. He was the only one who had any potential of treating with Odem Darkspur on anything like an equal footing; he was the one to whom the Naridans of the town automatically looked for leadership.

And yet, while it was the lowborn's duty to serve their nobles, it was the duty of a sar and a nobleman – and Daimon was both – to face dangers and die for their lowborn. While he could not hold rising water back with his longblade, he could at least make sure none of his folk were left behind, either to drown or to fall victim to Odem Darkspur's forces if they breached the gate.

There was Aftak, hurrying along with his staff in his hand, and his breaths puffing out his moustaches. The priest had always sported a beard almost Tjakorshi-like in its length and thickness, in contrast to the bare faces of most Naridans, but what had been seen as an eccentricity no longer seemed out of place in a town where at least half the men did the same.

The last of the gate guards were coming now, and Daimon stepped back to let them run past him. A hissing noise rose in his ears, and he cast another glance at the channel of the Blackcreek. This time his chest tightened a little in fear.

A wave was coming up the river.

When Saana hurriedly explained to him what she thought was going to occur, Daimon had a vision of a massive, foaming thing, like one of the countless storm waves that would break on the black coast in winter, only far higher. This was not that; it looked like the very front of a wave, the rush of water that rolled up the beach to wash your toes, except it was many times the size, and it was already a long way upriver. It had not yet reached the boat bridge, nor had it yet filled the Blackcreek even to the level of a high tide, but it also showed no signs of stopping.

There was Tsolga Hornsounder, bringing up the rear of the last few people fleeing the town, waving her arms and shouting in a language only half of them at best could understand. The old woman looked to be made of leather wrapped around twigs, and had a laugh that could cut stone, but Daimon knew she was highly regarded within his wife's clan and had marshalled their battle lines for decades. He could see why: even without being able to understand her, the force of her personality came through strongly as she railed at those in front of her to move faster. She even, to Daimon's amused horror, slapped Aftak on his backside as though he were a recalcitrant frillneck needing encouragement to pull a plough.

"Aftak!" Daimon shouted, as the priest whirled around with a face like thunder. "Over the bridge first!"

" . . . Aye, lord!" Aftak replied after a moment, settling for giving Tsolga a glower from beneath his bushy eyebrows, to which she responded with a suggestive waggle of her own.

That was it: no one else was coming. Daimon took one last look towards the encircling Darkspur encampment. There was far more activity there now, but he could not make out its nature or cause. Had they spotted the rapidly rising water, or were they simply trying to make sense of his people abandoning their home?

If the water only rose a little further, Daimon's folk were doomed: Black Keep would be taken and held against them, and they would be hunted down. Daimon had staked everything on the Tjakorshi's knowledge of the sea. When he married Saana they each agreed to defer to the other in matters where their spouse held the greater knowledge, and for all that Black Keep was a fishing town, no one argued that the Tjakorshi understood the ocean in a manner few Naridans did.

It occurred to Daimon, as he finally clattered down the steps towards the River Gate, that there was no outcome for today that would not be a disaster for Black Keep. The question was only whether their enemies would be struck in the same manner.

The Tjakorshi did not normally moor the yolgus, their great ocean-going rafts, at Black Keep's River Gate: they were huge, and would generally be left pulled up on the beach. However, none of the captains wanted to leave their precious vessels within easy reach of a besieging Darkspur force, so the river immediately to the south of Black Keep had become a bobbing platform of decks that already reached well out into the current even before Saana had enacted her desperate plan. Now Daimon stepped on to the nearest – the first time he had set foot on a Tjakorshi vessel since he helped Saana give Ristjaan the Cleaver to the waves on the morning after the Brown Eagle clan's arrival, which felt like a lifetime ago – and began to hurry across.

The yolgu's deck was barely less stable than Black Keep's walls, and he swiftly caught up with Aftak and Tsolga. They hopped over the narrow gap between the first vessel and the second, but there were still five to go before they reached the other side of the channel, and the wavefront—

It hit hard enough to knock the line of ships sideways. Daimon staggered, Tsolga stumbled, and Rattler hissed in alarm. Aftak actually fell with a muffled curse, until Tsolga dragged him back upright again a moment later with a strength that belied her spare build. The line of rafts, which had been bowing slightly downstream in the Blackcreek's gentle current, now began to sway back the other way.

"Keep going!" Daimon yelled, suiting actions to words and hurdling a fishing net that had been left on the deck from whenever this yolgu had last put to sea. He could see more and more people making it off the far end of the line of decks, and running on towards the rising ground of the southern moors, but a sizeable number were yet to make it to the opposite bank. He cast a hasty look downriver, and grimaced at what he saw.

The water was still rising, as though all the month's high tides had decided to come at once in a rush of greenish-grey, cut across with white crests. The deck shifted upwards beneath him, and the water was now threatening to overtop the Blackcreek's banks. On the far side, the townspeople grimly holding the last yolgu in place were being waved away by someone: almost certainly Saana, judging by the figure's height and build, and the flash of straw-blonde hair.

Cold gripped Daimon's gut. Had they managed to anchor the yolgu in any other fashion? If not, the makeshift bridge would be swept away at the far end, while the near end would hold, at least unless the Black Keep jetty itself gave way. The bridge would swing around in the current, and be pushed up against the near shore, where Darkspur's archers lurked.

Daimon glanced back and saw a knot of them standing near the bank. They had approached a little closer to the bridge and the town, perhaps realising there was no longer any threat from Black Keep's walls, but at least half seemed more interested in the river's rapid rise than in the remnants of the population trying to get away from them.

That still left several who were not, however.

"Arrows!" Daimon shouted, as the first shafts were loosed in his general direction. It was a long shot, and most fell short, but one splashed into the water not far from him, and another struck the wooden wall of the deckhouse behind him.

"Ignore them, lord!" Aftak shouted. The priest was

struggling along with Tsolga Hornsounder, each supporting the other, and Aftak also using his staff to brace himself where necessary. "We can be out of their range soon!"

"Aye, but for how long?" Daimon replied uneasily. A new lurch of the deck sent him stumbling again, but the next yolgu was only a few strides away. He hopped across the gap, then turned to offer his hand to Aftak. The priest allowed himself to be hauled over to the next deck, and Daimon reached out to Tsolga, whose grip felt more like callous than skin, and brought her across as well. The moment after both her feet made contact, however, the Hornsounder spat out something in her own language that could only be a curse.

Daimon turned and saw the far end of the bridge beginning to curve away from the shore. Either the first people across had been unable to anchor it, or their efforts had been insufficient to cope with the floodwater. The Blackcreek's banks were now being submerged: a few desperate folk jumped off the further-most yolgu as it began to swing around and started to splash towards the safety of the first hills, but they were already some way behind the majority of those who had already got across. Daimon said a quick, silent prayer to Nari that the water would rise slowly enough that everyone who had made the shore would find safety, but he had a nasty feeling that the current master of these waters was not the God-King who had died centuries before. Daimon knew enough about Father Krayk, the black-scaled sea god of the Tjakorshi, to know that mercy was not among his traits.

The bridge was still swinging around to come in line with the current. One of the Darkspur archers, heedless of the water starting to lap at the toes of his boots, sent another shaft aloft that fell some yards to Daimon's right, but the rest were backing away from the river in alarm. All the same, they were still too close, and if they decided to hold their ground then they would have some of the easiest live targets they could have ever seen.

The yolgu shuddered again from a new pulse of water. Nari save them all, was there no end to this? Saana had spoken briefly of old tales of the sea flooding the land, but even so, Daimon had not expected anything quite so . . . relentless.

"What do we do, lord?" Aftak asked hoarsely. The old priest had been a steady if slightly eccentric presence throughout Daimon's youth, but he looked thoroughly shaken.

Daimon had an idea, but wished he was able to consult with Tsolga, who had been sailing across the ocean on these vessels for at least twice as long as he had been alive. However, there was nothing for it. He would have to take this decision on his own, and hope he did not doom everyone relying on him.

On the other hand, he had made several such decisions so far this year, and the number of times he had *actually* doomed everyone stood at nil. His elder brother Darel, who was not only his thane but also the most intelligent man Daimon had ever known, had left Daimon in charge of Black Keep. If Darel believed in Daimon's decision-making abilities, Daimon should as well.

He drew his longblade and, before he could second-guess himself any further, cut through the rope that attached it to its neighbour on the Black Keep side. Freed of this constraint, the yolgu jerked free, and the entire string of rafts began to float upstream with the rush of water, rather than swinging around to lie parallel with the northern shore. The jerk also, however, knocked Daimon from his feet. He clawed wildly and hopelessly at the air, felt the momentary catch on his sleeve as the tips of Aftak's reaching fingers brushed against the cloth without finding enough purchase, and then the foaming, chilly water leaped up to meet him.

Jeya

Anaka rattled the dice and slammed them down onto the wooden step, then cautiously tilted the wooden cup to see what they had rolled. Jeya could have probably made something out if shé wanted to, but that was not the point of the game.

"Hnh," Anaka grunted noncommittally, and pushed two leaves forward. Jeya matched them. The game was traditionally played for money, but Jeya certainly did not have much to spare, and if Anaka did, they had not pushed the issue. They each started with fifteen leaves and gambled until one person had them all.

"Let's see it, then," Anaka said, and removed the cup completely to expose their dice: two twos, two fours, and a single six. Jeya lifted hér own cup to reveal three fives, which allowed hér to take Anaka's leaves into hér own pile.

"I swear you must have some kind of magic in that cup," Anaka muttered, shaking their head. "You sure you're not part Morlithian?"

"No, but I've never met a Morlithian who can do magic anyway. Besides, if I could do magic, I wouldn't be sitting here playing dice for leaves," Jeya pointed out. *Or be anywhere near you*, shé added silently. Anaka was not unpleasant company — they were fairly amiable, as thugs went — but the fact remained that they were sitting on the steps that led down from Jeya's front door because Kurumaya had ordered them to be here, and Jeya had no say in the matter. Not many people did, when it came to what Kurumaya wanted: they were a Shark, a head of the criminal underworld, and they controlled the fighting pits and most of the hired muscle in East Harbour.

Bulang was out earning a living as an assistant to the scribe Skhetul, down on the waterfront – although judging by the sun, thëy should be on their way back by now – but Jeya had no such employment. Shé was watching the house, and the cookpot bubbling away inside it, ready for whoever showed up later. This had been Ngaiyu's house once, and Jeya had found refuge here from the day shé was orphaned, so now shé and Bulang were continuing that work. Any youngster without a place to sleep could use their floor and get a bowl of something from the pot, in exchange for a copper or two. Jeya could think of nothing else shé would rather be doing.

The only problem was the reason why Ngaiyu's old house was no longer occupied by Ngaiyu. Nabanda, one of Kurumaya's thugs as well as Jeya's friend, had killed thëm.

Anaka had never attacked anyone within Jeya's sight, nor even threatened to. Neither had any of Kurumaya's other toughs. So far as anyone else knew, Jeya and Bulang just had some large, intimidating friends who would hang out at their house to make sure no one caused trouble overnight: after all, the previous owner had been murdered, for reasons still unknown to the community in general. The truth of the matter, that Kurumaya wanted to keep Bulang safe until they knew exactly what they intended to do with thëm, had never been spoken after that first night when Kurumaya had tracked them down.

"You don't *think* you've met a Morlithian who can do magic, but how do you know?" Anaka asked, in what they clearly thought was a shrewd manner. "Why would they tell you? Everyone knows they only do magic when they have those masks on, and—"

"What's that?" Jeya interrupted them, holding up a hand.

"What's what?" Anaka looked annoyed at being cut off.

"Listen!" Jeya hissed, and for a miracle, the other person did. It was a dim and distant roaring noise, like nothing Jeya had ever heard before. Shé had no idea what it could be, but it was coming from the direction of the harbour. A quick look at Anaka's face showed that they had heard it too, now they had stopped talking.

They both got up and hurried through the mud which served as a road until they got to a bend where a yangyang tree spread its branches, from beneath which they were able to look down the slight hill towards the harbour.

"What in the name of all the Hundred ...?" Anaka began softly.

East Harbour was a three-quarter circle, as though a giant had taken a huge bite out of the eastern shore of Grand Mahewa. The side open to the ocean had been further narrowed by levees until the entrance was navigable by only a few ships at once. Mighty ballistas watched this channel, ready to protect the capital of Kiburu ce Alaba from an attack by sea, and it meant the harbour as a whole was sheltered from the storm waves that could sweep in across the ocean.

It was through this gap that the ocean was now pouring, as though it had only just realised that it had been denied free access for so long, and was seeking to make up for lost time.

Jeya was unable to properly comprehend what shé was seeing. Shé had lived in East Harbour all hér life: what had changed in the ocean that had lapped at the borders of hér world all these years to make it flood in so hungrily now? Was this the end of all things? Would the waters keep rising and rising until the entire island was submerged, up to the mountains' very tops, and Jakahama of the Paddle would come and take everyone on to the Garden?

"Mushuru's ashes," Akana swore. "Will you look at that?"

Great rivulets of water were spilling over the levees and running down into the harbour. Jeya had only ever seen them overtopped by the mightiest of storm waves before, and even then only by the spray: this was a continuous deluge. The sea on the other side must have been on a level with the tops, and that was a terrifying thought.

"Oh no," shé breathed. "The Narrows!"

The Narrows were the fractured northern shoreline of East Harbour, where multiple natural and artificial channels cut through to the Mahewan Straits. They were too small and crooked to provide any sort of route for a sea invasion to occur, unless it was to be conducted with the world's largest fleet of rowboats, but the sea would care nothing for such constraints.

The words had barely left hér mouth when the first fingers of dirty water began pouring in on the far, northern side of the bay. They brought with them filth and wreckage and boats, and undoubtedly, although they were mercifully too far away to see, the bodies of people swept along as the rising water barrelled through the narrow channels and tore up whatever was in its path. Many of the buildings in the Narrows were sturdily built – warehouses and the like, intended to stand up to the ferocious tropical storms that could lash Kiburu ce Alaba – but many were not. Roofs were being borne out into the bay now, and doors, and everything else besides.

And still the water came.

"Oh no," Anaka murmured, and Jeya looked up to see them staring at the Narrows. Jeya did not know where Kurumaya lived, as such, but the Narrows seemed to be the Shark's stronghold, where many of their enterprises were based. That meant it was also where many of their underlings could be found; people who were undoubtedly known to Anaka. Maybe it was even where Anaka lived. Jeya felt a momentary pang of sympathy for them, unwanted intrusion into hér life though they were, but that was swiftly subsumed by a rising panic of hér own, because the water still kept coming. The bay was huge, but the amount of water flowing into it was incredible, and the waves on the quays already seemed to be lapping higher than they had been.

Please notice, shé thought desperately in the direction of Bulang, somewhere down near the waterfront. *Even if yöu're still in that little attic, please notice, and run inland and uphill as far and as fast as yöu can!*

"We've got to do something!" Anaka said desperately. Their fingers had curled into fists, and they were almost vibrating with urgency.

"What can *we* do?" Jeya asked. "It's the sea. We can't hold back the sea!" Shé gestured downhill. "Look, people have noticed, they're running!" Sure enough, those close to the water's edge were already beginning to flee towards the nearest area of higher ground; some with a few hastily grabbed possessions, and many with nothing other than themselves.

"But we've got to do *something*!" Anaka insisted. Older and larger than Jeya though they were, they did not seem to comprehend that this was something about which nothing could be done. Perhaps that was a side-effect of being a thug for a powerful person like a Shark: you came to believe that there was nothing in the world that could not be influenced if you tried hard enough.

Jeya had been orphaned as a child, and had survived ever since by sneaking, and thieving, and staying out of the way of those more dangerous than hér, which was most people. Shé was very used to the notion of bad things about which shé could do nothing at all, except to try to be somewhere else. It did not yet look like shé definitely needed to be somewhere else for this one, but shé would keep her options open.

"If you want to do something useful then go back to the house, keep an eye on the pot, and make sure no one steals anything," shé told Anaka. "And be ready to leave if the water gets this high."

"Where are we going to go if the water gets up to here?!" Anaka demanded, rounding on hér.

"I don't know!" Jeya snapped back. Ngaiyu's house — hér house — was nowhere near as high up as the homes of East Harbour's rich, such as the one in which Bulang used to live, but its floor was above the height of the roofs near the water's edge. "We'll start thinking about that if it looks like we need to! But if we don't, then we're still going to need a place to sleep and a meal tonight, and I think a few other people will as well!" Anaka hesitated, and Jeya flapped an irritated hand at them. "Go on, I promise I'll come and find you if the water's getting close."

Anaka was in no way Jeya's to command, but they seemed to take some comfort in receiving instructions, since they turned and made their way back to the house. Jeya stayed under the yangyang tree, and watched the water rise.

It was flooding up over the docks now, and still rising. Ships moored there were bobbing upwards, and tiny figures were busying themselves loosening ropes and anchors, to prevent them from dragging the vessels under if the water did not stop. Some of Jeya's neighbours were coming to join hér now, gasping in horror or crying out at what they saw, as the first refugees from the waterfront reached them. Others were following, but Jeya could not see Bulang anywhere. That in itself meant nothing: there was no reason why thëy would have taken this road, given that Skhetul's place was halfway around

East Harbour. Bulang might have headed inland at any point between Skhetul's and the house thëy shared with Jeya, even without the rising water. Thëy would change their route if the streets near the docks were particularly busy, or to pick up a small treat for Jeya like a honeycomb, or some tamar fruit.

The only treat Í want today is for yöu to come back safely.

Shé wanted to go searching for Bulang, but that was foolishness: as shé'd said to Anaka, there was nothing that could be done. So shé stayed and watched as the water washed higher, nudging hér neighbours aside to ensure shé could still see.

The water did not hit most of East Harbour with the force with which it had torn through the Narrows, because it had been slowed by the comparatively narrow access points it had to the bay, but that did not stop it from rising quickly. Jeya reckoned that the shadows of the yangyang's branches had barely moved a handsbreadth on the ground by the time the flood was lapping at the eaves of the houses lower down. East Harbour's lowest streets now looked like the channels of the Narrows, and some of the smaller boats which had either been freed or come loose from their moorings had been carried into those channels as the sea claimed them for its own. Now dirty waves were breaking a stone's throw from where shé stood, instead of half a mile. A great crowd of people had gathered, most of whom were watching the fate of the city below with wails and cries as their homes or livelihoods were flooded.

"It's still coming," someone said beside hér. "We'd better get away!"

"No, look," another voice replied. "It's not rising as fast now. I think we're safe here."

"Safe?! How can we be *safe*, when the ocean is behaving like this?"

Jeya looked over at the Narrows, and the channel that formed the entrance to the bay. It was hard to tell, but it did not look as though there was still a great volume of water flooding in, in excess of what the harbour already contained. Shé had no idea if what was already there was going to disappear or not, but the second speaker seemed to be right: for now, at least, it did not look as though the water was going to rise any higher, for which shé was profoundly grateful. A pressure in hér chest began to ease, just a little. Shé would always have been scared by what had happened, but it was a strangely new fear to also be concerned about a building. Shé had never had a place of hér own until recently, and it was surprising to realise how quickly shé had become attached to it.

Now shé just had to hope that—

"Jeya!"

Shé turned with relief, and most of the remaining worry in hér chest vanished as shé saw Bulang slipping through the crowd.

"Í'm so glad yöu're safe!" shé said with delight, pushing between two of hér neighbours and catching thëm into a hug. "Í was worried yöu wouldn't have made it away from the water in time!"

"Ï finished a little early today," Bulang said into hér ear, in a way that made it tickle. "Ï was already halfway up the hill by the time the water started to rise, so Ï went by the First Level canal and came back along the ridge. Ï went to the house, but Anaka was there, and said yóu'd be here." Thëy pulled back from hér and looked down at the flooded streets of East Harbour, worry in thëir eyes. "Ï hope Skhetul got out. The water must be on a level with hìs attic. Is it still rising? Do we need to find higher ground?"

"Í think we're safe for the moment," Jeya replied, checking back over hér shoulder. The water did not seem to have risen farther, and no one around was panicking, so shé took that as a good sign.

"Thank the Hundred," Bulang said. The phrase still sounded a little artificial on thëir lips, but until recently Bulang had believed thëy were the descendant of Nari, the ancient man-god of Narida. Thëy were still adapting to fitting in with the general population of East Harbour, who, although enormously varied as befitted the greatest port in the world, did not tend to consider themselves divine.

The thing was, of course, that Bulang *might* be the descendant of Nari, or thëy might not. No one could really be sure, least of all Bulang. Thëir importance to Kurumaya did not even hinge on whether thëy were or not, only on the fact that the Hierarchs had replaced Bulang's family with imposters.

Jeya tried to push Kurumaya out of hér head for the moment, as it struck hér again how very lucky shé was to have caught the interest of someone so beautiful. Bulang had the long, straight dark hair so common in those with Naridan ancestry, which hung down on either side of thëir face and helped the early evening sunlight cast interesting shadows across the full lips and deep, liquid eyes that had so entranced Jeya months before. It was a great shame that shé could not spend a lazy evening kissing that face, but even if the water in the harbour drained right away, half the city was going to be waterlogged. Those who had their own homes would be struggling to find a comfortable place to sleep: for the street kids, matters would be even worse.

For a wonder, Jeya found hérself hoping that Anaka would stick around. It might be handy to have someone to enforce order tonight, when the whole city was likely to be in upheaval. On the other hand, even the threat of Kurumaya might not be enough to keep Anaka at the house if they had their own people to check on. Besides, Kurumaya themself could have been drowned, which was a possibility over which Jeya would shed no tears at all. The Shark was ultimately responsible for the murder of both Bulang's family and various of Jeya's friends, including Ngaiyu.

"Come on," Jeya said, taking Bulang's hand. "We'd best get back. Í think we're going to have a lot of guests tonight."

Marin

The thunder came from the south in the early morning, despite the sky being clear of clouds, and Marin knew it was a sign.

The realisation sent him scurrying through the Divine One's camp on the banks of the Greenwater, the river that ran down from Narida's most sacred mountain, Godspire. So excited was he that he scarcely bothered with the niceties of excuse or apology to the people he disturbed: at least, until he approached the great tent where the Divine Tyrun dwelled. Once there his pace had to slow, mainly because of the four white-robed guards pointing spears at him.

"S'man needs to speak with the Divine One," he puffed breathlessly, eyeing the spear points nervously.

"The Divine One is breaking His fast," one of the guards said, looking at Marin with roughly the same sort of affection as he would something he had scraped off the sole of his boot.

"Then s'man will happily wait," Marin replied, folding his arms and attempting to present a front of determination.

"You can't just walk up and demand an audience with the Divine One!" one of the other guards said in exasperated tones. "Do you have any idea how many people in this camp want the exact same thing?"

Marin decided to chance it. "And how many of them saved the Divine One from a knife intended for His throat last night?"

The first guard's eyes narrowed as though this was some sort of outrageous claim, instead of a completely accurate representation of the truth, but the second speaker sighed. "Told you he'd be back."

"Of course s'man is— Look, did you not hear the sky just now?" Marin demanded.

"What, thunder? Don't you have thunder in Idramar?" the first guard retorted, who had apparently decided to be contrary for the sake of it, so far as Marin could tell.

"*There are no clouds!*" he practically shouted, moderating his tone only through the presence of so much sharp steel that still had its business ends pointed towards him. "Do none of you know the Foretellings?"

"What—"

"The Foretellings of Tolkar! The prophecies?" Marin gritted his teeth at the complete lack of comprehension on the faces in front of him. "Nari's blood, s'man—"

He cut himself off rapidly as two spear points jerked forward to very nearly prick his throat. "Forgive s'man. Figure of speech."

"Mind your tongue, city boy," the first guard growled. "We'll not have you blaspheming here."

Behind him, the flaps of the tent opened and a bald man wearing a priest's robe, but with the longblade of a sar on his belt, stepped through. He had a lit pipe clenched in his teeth, which he shifted from one side to the other upon seeing Marin. One of the guards looked over his shoulder at the new arrival, then back at Marin with an expression that clearly communicated the thought, *Now look what you've done.*

"Marin of Idramar," Mordokel said, out of the side of his mouth. "You're up early. This priest supposes it was you he heard shouting just now, disturbing the Divine One?"

Marin swallowed, but forced himself to meet Mordokel's eyes. The priest had a truly alarming stare, and looked every inch the fanatic. He was quite clearly enough to worry the men entrusted with guarding the Divine One's tent, which was an indication of the man's demeanour.

"S'man apologises most humbly if he disturbed the Divine One," Marin said, stepping back from the spear points so he could bow without opening his own throat. "However, some things cannot wait."

"The Divine One will be the judge of that," Mordokel replied instantly.

"Indeed," Marin said, straightening. "Did He hear the heavens speaking with nary a cloud to mar their face?"

Mordokel's own face dropped into a guarded expression which was, if anything, even more intense than it had been a moment before. "What did you just say?"

"You know the Foretellings," Marin persisted. "You quoted a line of them to s'man the night we met. Did you not hear the heavens speak just now?"

"No," Mordokel said thoughtfully. "Did anyone else?"

"We heard thunder, honoured Mordokel," the first guard said. "Just distant thunder, nothing more."

"Thunder with no clouds," Mordokel murmured. He sucked on his pipe, blew a cloud of smoke out of his nose, then jerked his head at Marin. "Fine. Let him through."

Marin had only arrived at the Divine Tyrun's camp the previous night and had not yet worked out what sort of hierarchy existed there; if indeed there was one at all, since Mordokel himself had made statements to the effect that all men were equal beneath Tyrun. However, it seemed Mordokel had authority over the guards, because they stepped back and grounded the butts of their spears without any form of protest. Marin followed Mordokel into the tent's interior, and for the second time in as many days, into the presence of his god.

Tyrun was not on the carved throne He had occupied when Marin met Him the night before. Instead, He was sitting on a cushion on the ground, and eating bread and salted meat out of a wooden bowl with His fingers. He looked up as Marin approached, and the gaze of those surprisingly old eyes in a young face caused Marin's breath to catch in his throat once more.

"Marin of Idramar," Tyrun said, a faint smile crossing His lips. "Welcome."

Marin did not need to be warned by the hard stares of the two other guards who stood behind the reborn god: he halted several strides away and prostrated himself.

"Please, rise," Tyrun bid him. "This god suspects you would not seek to speak with Him unless your business was important."

"Your servant believes so, Divine One," Marin replied, bringing himself back up to his knees. He took a deep breath. "Are you familiar with the Foretellings of Tolkar, the Last Sorcerer?"

"This god is not," Tyrun said, biting down on a piece of salted meat. He raised His eyebrows at Marin's expression. "You are surprised? Disappointed?"

"S'man . . . " Marin fumbled for words. He took pride in being a scholar, especially given his humble origins. If he was honest with himself, he sometimes looked down on those without his breadth of knowledge. The notion of knowing something his god did not was . . . confusing.

"This god is familiar with their broad concept," Tyrun elaborated. "Even if He had not been already, Mordokel has mentioned them. They are, as this god understands it, prophecies of events that will come to pass when He comes into His power. Is that so?"

Even facing his god, Marin could not take refuge in a partial falsehood. "To an extent, Divine One. They are signs that you will have returned; signs that the wise can read and know your claim is true."

"And do *you* need these events to know this truth?" Tyrun inquired mildly, and Marin became suddenly aware again of the spearmen watching him.

"Of course not, Divine One!" he protested. "But these events coming to pass can show the truth to those who have not had it confirmed to them by entering your presence and seeing you for themselves. One line refers to 'the heavens speaking with nary a cloud to mar their face', and this just occurred. A sound like thunder, with no clouds to be seen, let alone thunderclouds."

Tyrun raised His eyebrows. "This god heard no such sound, but . . ." He waved a hand. " . . . the canvas of this tent can block many noises. What is the import of this event?"

"Divine One, according to the Foretellings, the sky speaks in this manner shortly before Nari Reborn . . . that is, you . . . present yourself to the monks of Godspire and your claim is officially recognised," Marin explained. "In all honesty, it was excitement as much as anything else that brought your servant here."

Tyrun sighed, and looked up at Mordokel. The priest said nothing, but Marin thought he could detect a hint of satisfaction on his face.

"If your servant might ask, Divine One," Marin ventured, hesitant to see how far he could push his luck, but unable to resist in case he was never honoured with such an audience again. "Why is it that you are not aware of the Foretellings?"

Mordokel's expression darkened, but he clearly did not wish to speak out of turn, and settled for placing one hand on the hilt of his longblade while Tyrun looked consideringly at Marin.

"This god has no memories of His former life," Tyrun said finally. "He knows who He is, and what He must do, but He cannot recall the events that occurred centuries ago. He was always a man first and foremost, you understand. And these Foretellings were, in any case, written after His first death?"

"That is the case, Divine One," Mordokel murmured before Marin could reply.

"This god has not sought out these prophecies, despite His priest's urging to the contrary," Tyrun continued, with another glance up at Mordokel. "If this god should learn of what they say, would that not devalue their contents in some manner if He then knows what He is expected to do? Surely, this god should simply proceed as He sees fit, and in so doing, fulfil these prophecies? If they are in fact truthful."

Marin nodded. It was a perfectly reasonable explanation.

"The issue of Godspire is a separate one, Divine One," Mordokel put in. "The support of the monks is . . . "

"You were going to say 'essential', were you not?" Tyrun asked with mild amusement.

"This priest was," Mordokel admitted, "and he would have been in error. He will content himself with saying 'useful'. Once the news spreads that the monks have accepted your claim, the country will fall behind you with few further objections."

Marin, who had some knowledge of the Divine Family in Idramar, had his doubts about that. However, Tyrun now knew that Tila Narida had sent assassins after Him to try to end His life, so He could surely draw His own conclusions. Besides, even the Divine Princess and her shadowy tactics would find it hard to rally much support against the true heir of Nari, proclaimed as such by the monks of the sacred mountain.

Tyrun sighed again. "It seems there is little use in wishing it otherwise. Although this god is loath to dance to the tune of men long dead, His duty is to His land and His people. If His rule can begin most efficiently and quickly by gaining the support of these monks, then perhaps that is indeed the place to start. Very well, Mordokel, you have your way. Pass out the word: we make for Godspire."

Tyrun got to His feet, with a friendly nod to Marin that made his heart skip a beat in delight. More surprising, at least to Marin's way of thinking, was the small smile that Mordokel flashed him as well.

Daimon

The water was shockingly cold, and Daimon had a sudden image of the talons of the ocean's frigid depths reaching up into the Blackcreek to sink into his chest. The breath was sucked out of his lungs before he clawed his way back up to the surface, but even that provided little respite: the robes of a nobleman were thick and cumbersome, and threatening to drag him down. He would have fumbled with his belt to loosen them, but it was all he could do to keep his head above water. He realised, between one desperately snatched breath and the next, that he still clutched his longblade in his right hand: even the imminent threat of drowning was not enough to break *that* habit. He should have long been past the point where he would cling to his responsibilities under the Code of Honour ahead of his own survival, but he could not quite loosen his fingers—

A dark shape appeared above him in his water-blurred vision, and he felt something seize the front of his robes. Had a krayk been borne upriver by this sudden flood? Was he about to be dragged away to his death by one of the servants of the Tjakorshi's sea god? But he was pulled *upwards*, not downwards, and as something hard collided with his ribs, enough water drained out of his ears for him to hear the sound of virulent Tjakorshi swearing.

Things resolved: he had hit on the edge of the yolgu, and

what had seized him was not the jaws of a krayk, but the hands of Tsolga Hornsounder. The old woman was laying down on the ship's deck, held in place by Aftak's arms around her waist, and was delivering a spiel of consonant-edged invective in her own tongue as she tried to haul Daimon out of the water, while Rattler paced anxiously behind them. Daimon grabbed a breath, his head now far enough above the water that he did not take any down with the air, then succeeded in flailing his robe-swathed arms free enough from their encroaching sleeves to grab on to the yolgu himself. He tossed his longblade onto the deck, and with Tsolga's help, managed to heave one leg up, then levered himself aboard.

Daimon coughed and spat to rid himself of the taste of salt and dirt, and reached up to tickle Rattler reassuringly as the young rattletail shoved its muzzle into his face. Then, although Daimon's robes felt like they weighed as much as a longbrow, he forced himself up to his knees. He looked directly at Tsolga, from whom Aftak had hastily detached himself as soon as Daimon was safe, and bent forwards in a deep bow.

It was not the bow of a nobleman to a lowborn, even one who had performed a great service. That was, after all, what the lowborn were supposed to do: they served their lords, who had been set over them by the will of the God-King. A nobleman might acknowledge that a lowborn had performed admirably, but actual gratitude was a rarity. The most usually conveyed by such a gesture was that the lowborn had not actually disappointed on this occasion.

Daimon bowed as low to Tsolga Hornsounder as he had to the Southern Marshal, and the Unmaker take the propriety of it. It was very unlikely she would appreciate the difference, but that was not the point. He had not thought to change out of his robes before attempting to cross the river, and so she had needed to save his life. The whole point of the robes of nobility was to be impractical; the longer and more ostentatious they were, the more obvious it was that you had servants to do everything for you. Looking at Tsolga's practical garb of skin leggings and woollen shirt, Daimon considered that perhaps wearing clothing that could endanger you should be reserved for those who lived in palaces.

Palaces. His mind flashed briefly to Darel as he straightened, but Daimon had no time to think about his law-brother's exploits in the capital at the moment. Tsolga was looking at him oddly, but ducked her own head in acknowledgement of his bow, then grinned at him with more gum than teeth.

"Alive. Good," she said in Naridan. She got back to her feet and patted Aftak companionably on the shoulder as he came past her with Daimon's longblade in his hands, then deliberately bumped her hip into his. The priest looked appalled, but held the sword out to Daimon rather than shout at her.

"Thank you, Aftak," Daimon said, taking the blade from him, then bowed just as low as he had to Tsolga. Aftak, irreverent though he could sometimes be, looked as though Daimon had just danced a jig in front of him.

"Do not look at this lord like that, Aftak. You just saved his life," Daimon told the priest. He considered his longblade for a moment, but his scabbard needed to dry out, else he would just be sheathing the blade in salt water, which would do it no good at all.

"Even so, lord, this priest—"

"This lord thinks that Tsolga likes you," Daimon interrupted him, getting to his feet and moving farther from the edge of the yolgu. The deck was far from steady, but it was a great improvement on being in the water. "You might want to think on that, should we survive this." He ignored Aftak's impersonation of a freshly landed fish at that pronouncement, swung his longblade to bury it in one of the beams of the yolgu's deckhouse so he had both his hands free, and looked about him.

The water was still rising.

It was already higher than Daimon had ever seen it, even in the one spring in his youth when the snow had come down hard and heavy for much of the winter. The sun had melted it in the mountains, and the Blackcreek had burst its banks to spread across its plain, leaving sodden fields in its wake.

There was no longer any sign of the Blackcreek's channel at all, just a tide of brown-grey water sweeping across the land. To the south-east, Daimon could see figures scrambling higher into the first rises of ground where the southern moors came down close to the river. The chain of yolgus of which he was on one end was still being borne inland, with its cargo of Black Keep folk who had not made it across. And to the north . . .

The Darkspur camp was in disarray. The water was up to thigh-height now, and the northern soldiers were flailing about trying to find some sort of high ground, but there was none. A few were struggling towards Black Keep, but Daimon did not fancy their chances. Others had mounted dragons and were making for the Downwoods, where the ground did indeed rise a little, but many dragons had fled without any rider. Besides, this was not just a flood; it was a *tide*. Daimon saw one man struggling to cling to the end of a wall, then lose his grip and be swept off his feet to disappear under the merciless water.

"Poor wretch," he muttered.

"Lord?" Aftak asked, confused. "They were here to take our home, and perhaps burn us all!"

"This lord is aware," Daimon said. "And had they come at us with blades bared, he would have shown no mercy. But having nearly drowned, it is not a fate he would wish on them."

"You have a noble heart, lord," Aftak replied uncertainly.

"But drowning is a better fate than that with which they threatened us, and this priest feels no pity for them."

The knot of bowmen who loosed arrows at them had been broken apart by the water. Half a dozen or so were clinging to each other's shoulders, clearly determined not to lose each other, but Daimon could see others who had been separated. One disappeared as he watched, either tripping over some unseen obstacle or being pulled under the water by a sudden current. Another man nearby lunged clumsily through the flood to where his fellow had disappeared and dived below the surface, but when he surfaced again he was still alone.

"One comes," Aftak said, pointing behind them. Sure enough, there was a struggling figure floating in the wake of the yolgu bridge, flailing at the water. Perhaps Darkspur children did not learn how to swim like Black Keep ones did — even Daimon had played in the waves by the shore on calm summer days, or jumped off the jetty by the River Gate when the tide had been high — but the man was just about keeping himself afloat, although Daimon did not think he would be able to manage it for much longer. The Darkspur man's eyes lit on the yolgus, and Daimon saw them widen in desperate hope.

"Perhaps you should ready your blade, lord?" Aftak said quietly.

"No," Daimon said, determination sweeping through him. "We have lost no one to Darkspur; in fact, we killed one of their sars to no loss of our own. That man has not *harmed* us, Aftak, nor is he one of Thane Odem's sars, who would have helped organise this attack. He has done nothing except obey the orders of his liege lord, which he could have gone against only if he wished for punishment and disgrace."

"You wish to fish him out of the water, lord?" Aftak asked, his tone already resigned.

"We made peace with the Tjakorshi," Daimon reminded

him. "Why should we not be able to make peace with Darkspur? We never had any wish for conflict."

"The Brown Eagle clan came to us offering peace," Aftak argued. "Darkspur came seeking war!"

"And this lord's father sought to greet the Brown Eagle clan's peace with violence, and yet they still spared our town," Daimon said firmly. He shook his head. "He is one man, Aftak; the rest of Odem's force must fare as they will, but if that man can reach us, we pull him out. This lord has to believe that Naridan hearts can be won through good deeds, or what is the use of . . . of *anything*?"

"By your will, lord," Aftak said. He sucked his teeth. "Although it may not be an issue; the water might claim him yet."

"Tree!"

The shout came from behind them, and Daimon turned to see Tsolga Hornsounder darting towards the yolgu's deckhouse. Beyond her, and looming up fast, was what had caused her alarm: a large, sturdy conifer, one of the lonely sentinels of the Black Keep farmland, still standing firm against the flood. Its lowest branches would normally have been above Daimon's head, but the onrushing water had brought the yolgu up to a height with them now.

"Inside!" Daimon barked, quickly seeing that Tsolga had the best idea, and he and Aftak bolted for the deckhouse with Rattler on their heels. They barely made it into shelter before the current threw the yolgu into the branches with a tremendous cracking noise, and Daimon and Aftak were knocked from their feet to collide with the timber wall. Tsolga, who was already curled up protectively in a corner, tutted at them.

"Nari's teeth!" Daimon swore, scrambling back up and clawing his way out of the door. He wrenched his longblade from the beam in which he had left it, and took in the situation.

The yolgu was, for the moment at least, wedged in the big tree's branches, but the deck juddered beneath Daimon, and he looked to his left to see the rest of the former bridge stretching around into the current once more. Would they hold here, or be tugged loose at any moment? He turned back towards the sea, just in case there was a new bulge of water on the way, and saw the Darkspur man frantically paddling towards him.

He did not even think about it. He walked to the edge of the deck, went down to one knee, and reached out with the hand which was not holding his longblade. The other man's fear of drowning was clearly greater than any fear he had of Daimon's sword, because he reached out desperately. Daimon caught him by the wrist and heaved, dragging him onto the yolgu, whereupon the Darkspur man behaved much as Daimon had in terms of coughing and spluttering.

The deck jerked again, and Daimon looked up. The yolgu had shifted slightly, as the onrushing current began to drag it around and through the tree's branches. The Darkspur man yelped in fear, clearly terrified that his newfound safety had been an illusion.

"Get up," Daimon told him, suiting his own actions to his words. "This lord is Daimon Blackcreek. What is your name?"

"Mer, lord," the man stammered, staggering into something that was more or less upright. Bearing in mind how long he had been in the chill water, Daimon was not surprised at his body's lethargy. "Mer of Darkspur."

"This lord assumes that you wish to live, Mer of Darkspur," Daimon said, prompting a desperate nod.

"Yes, lord, very much."

"Then give the dagger on your belt to Aftak the priest." Daimon gestured to Aftak, who had now emerged from the deckhouse. "And be ready to do whatever we may need of you."

Mer made no argument and unbuckled the dagger's

scabbard with shaking hands. He passed it to Aftak, who glowered at him sternly from under bristling brows but made no move to throw him back into the water. However, the priest's stern visage rapidly gave way to one of alarm. "Lord! Look there!"

Daimon peered past Mer's shoulder, back towards Black Keep, and his knees nearly gave way. There was a new surge of water coming, a white-tipped roil of grey-brown that crested and broke *over* the town's walls: not over them by much, but, by Nari's blood, was that not enough? The walls were near-on twice the height of many a man, and now that new wave was already passing Black Keep, leaving the town inundated behind it, and was coming for them.

"It will swamp us if we are still stuck in this tree!" Daimon barked. "Get us loose! We must ride it out!"

He dashed to the branches and began hacking at them, heedless of the impact of the resinous wood on his longblade's edge. Shouts of alarm from the next yolgu along, on which he could see some half a dozen Black Keep folk, alerted him that they were also aware of the impending peril.

He was through one branch, and moved on to the next. He had no idea if he could do enough to get them free before the wave hit them, but perhaps the impact would knock them loose. His longblade felt as light as a feather in his hand, and for once he would have welcomed the heft of an axe. As though summoned by his thoughts, Tsolga appeared next to him with her own blackstone axe in hand, with which she attacked the branches as viciously as he was himself. The old woman was puffing and blowing furiously, but her weapon still bit deep into the wood. Blackstone's edge was even keener than that of Naridan steel when sharpened properly: its disadvantage was that it was brittle, and prone to splintering if it struck something hard and resilient, like metal.

Another two branches came free, and the yolgu jerked. Daimon steadied himself, looked back, then reached out and dragged Tsolga down to the deck before she could swing again.

The wave hit them.

It swept over the deck, and Daimon's scrabbling fingers could not find enough purchase to prevent himself from starting to slide towards the tree, where the sheer force of the water might impale him on the stumps of the very branches he had just cut . . .

. . . and then the yolgu jerked, and with a mighty scraping noise, came free of the tree's clutches. It immediately rose slightly higher in the water now it was no longer being held in place by the branches, because the Tjakorshi knew how to build their ships to allow the mighty waves of the ocean to spill over and off and through their decks where necessary. Daimon reached out and grabbed Tsolga, hauling the Hornsounder more firmly back onto the yolgu, then staggered up again.

"What do we do now?" Aftak demanded. The priest was soaked to the waist, clinging on to the side of the deckhouse, and looked thoroughly miserable.

Daimon sheathed his longblade. What with salt water and resin the edge was likely doomed in any case, and at least this way he would still have it on his person, and not be at risk of taking someone's hand off if he turned too quickly. "Mer! Check inside the deckhouse, see if there are any paddles!"

"Aye, lord!" Mer replied obediently, and disappeared. Daimon turned to Tsolga, who was trying to wring her sleeves out, without much success, and pointed in the direction the flood was taking them. "We must try to steer for the river channel! No trees!"

Tsolga looked at him, looked at where he was pointing, looked back at him again, then nodded. "River, no trees. Good!" She began to sing out in her own language, and

Tjakorshi heads further down the line of yolgus looked up at the familiar sound of her shrill voice yelling instructions.

"Paddles, lord!" Mer exclaimed, re-emerging with the broad wooden blades, polished bright with use. Daimon took one from him, and passed another to Aftak.

"We steer where we can," he told the priest, "and trust to Nari."

"Trust to Nari." Aftak's eyeing of the flood waters showed what he thought of that at the moment, but his grizzled head nodded in weary agreement. "Aye."

Zhanna

Zhanna liked the broad, wild expanse of the Catseye Mountains, which were so much bigger than any landscape she had known before. She had grown up on the shore of Kainkoruuk, and although its summit had reared far above her home at Koszal, it was one lone mountain rising out of the ocean. The Catseyes were a chain, peak after giant peak, and, if stories were to be believed, they ran up the entire western edge of Narida. Zhanna had already struggled to comprehend the distances involved in Narida, at least in terms of there being that much land in one place, but to think that a chain of *mountains* ran that far? It was almost beyond belief.

All that said, however, she was not unhappy to sight Ironhead when her party rounded the last bend of the valley.

"Do you think we can get use of a bed?" Tsennan Longjaw asked wistfully. He was probably the biggest warrior of the Brown Eagle clan, which meant he was probably the biggest warrior anywhere on Blackcreek lands. He was a couple of summers older than Zhanna, but had accepted her leadership despite having been on raids before coming to Narida.

"I'd also like to eat something that's not dried fish," Zhanna agreed ruefully. The people of the Smoking Valley had provisioned their party with what they could spare: mainly dried fish, since most of their stores had been eaten by the men of Darkspur who enslaved them. It kept them all going, but Zhanna dearly wished for some variety.

"How are you feeling about heading back to Black Keep?" Tsennan asked, picking his way across a rock in the path. It was shiny and smooth, and a slip on it would have potentially sent him tumbling down a steep slope of bracken and into the valley's bottom. "Are you going to miss being in charge?"

"Ugh, no, I am *not*," Zhanna said. "I can't wait to have Mama and Daimon dealing with everything for a while. Anyway," she added, glancing backwards at where Amonhuhe of the Mountains was striding along with her bowstave, "I'm not *really* in charge."

"If it came to it, I think she'd back down from you," Tsennan offered. It was safe for them to be conversing about such things, since Amonhuhe did not speak Tjakorshi, but Zhanna glared at him anyway as a warning to keep his voice down.

"I think you're exaggerating," she told him. Amonhuhe had been a forceful presence in the mountains, which was hardly surprising, given what they found there.

"If she didn't, I could always loom," Tsennan laughed. "It worked well enough for your mother and Ristjaan."

"Yeah, until Ristjaan *died*!" Zhanna snapped. Daimon killed her mother's best friend on the night the Brown Eagle arrived in Black Keep, in an honour duel over a Naridan Ristjaan had slain a decade earlier, which had not made for a welcoming environment. Tsennan was not Ristjaan the Cleaver, but Zhanna still shied away from the comparison. She had already lost Menaken, the good-looking guard of Black Keep castle, when he was killed enacting her plan to free the Smoking Valley captives and help them take their home back. Ingorzhak Avljaszhin died even earlier, on the way to the Smoking Valley: snatched up and eaten alive by an enormous kingdrake, a winged beast that still haunted Zhanna's dreams.

She blamed herself for both deaths, despite the others telling her that she should not. Should she have seen Ingor's plan to attack the kingdrake coming, and warned him off? Should she have distracted it? Should she have ever sent Menaken to the building closest to Winterhome? He was a guard, and had trained with weapons, but he was never a *warrior* like Tsennan, or Tamadh, Ingor's older brother. The last thing she needed was to start thinking of Ristjaan's dead body whenever she looked at Tsennan: a reminder of how sometimes even the best decisions could cost lives.

Zhanna rubbed the thick tattooed line that ran down her brow to the bridge of her nose. It was the mark of a Blooded fighter, the sign that she was an adult by Brown Eagle reckoning. She had earned it when she called on other young people to pick up weapons and fight back against Rikkut Fireheart's warriors, and cut Fireheart down herself with the sword of Daimon's father. That blade now rode on her hip and had given her the nickname "Longblade", in the same way as Tsennan was the Longjaw.

She had yearned to be Blooded, not for the thrill of battle, as such, but to become an adult. Now, she very much hoped she could slip away from adulthood for a while, and stay quiet for a bit so it didn't notice.

"The advantage I have over Ristjaan is that I'm not as annoying," Tsennan said, and Zhanna could not argue with him there. It was probably a good idea they were still speaking Tjakorshi, though: the Naridans thought you should not speak ill of the dead, or at least not do it loudly. The spirits of Naridans hung around, apparently, and could be called upon to guide their descendants, but might also get angry if they were disrespected. The spirits of Tjakorshi dead ended up with

Father Krayk, and so far as Zhanna was aware, that was quite enough to keep them too busy to trouble the living.

Apart from Ingor. He was the first Tjakorshi Zhanna knew of who would have died out of reach of the sea. Still, presumably his body could not have been possessed by a draug, one of the body-snatching spirits that could creep up from the underworld, given that he was swallowed by a kingdrake. All the same, Zhanna was not looking forward to explaining to Nalon and Avlja – mainly Avlja, if she was honest – why she had taken two of their sons into the mountains and returned with only one.

She suspected Tamadh was not, either. Ingor had been Blooded, had been an adult, but Tamadh would have been expected to keep his little brother safe. "Safe" was not always possible, but it could be hard to explain that to a parent.

Zhanna clucked her tongue, and her two rattletails came bounding up from behind her, prompting cries of momentary alarm or frustration from the rest of the party whose legs they wove through to get to her. She tickled each of them around the jaw and gave them a small piece of dried fish to chew on as a reward for coming when called. Thorn, who had always been hers, had at least started returning the favour; he had brought back a mountain hare two days before, which had been stringy and lean, but had provided a bit of variety in their diet. Talon, who had originally belonged to Tavi the stable master, had not yet caught anything larger than a bug, and he was welcome to keep them.

"There's nothing like the sight of home," Danid the hunter said, coming up behind them both. He was Naridan, and Zhanna switched into his language before replying.

"This warrior thought you liked being in the mountains."

"S'man does," Danid said. "You'll not catch him down one of those holes." He nodded towards the buildings that marked the mineshafts, where the people of Ironhead dug out the ore than gave the village its name. "All the same, this is the longest s'man's been away, and he's looking forward to seeing his wife and sleeping in his own bed."

Zhanna slowed a little and let Danid go first as they approached. He seemed to want to lead them in, and she was happy enough with that: she had attracted more than her fair share of odd looks the last time they came through. Danid walked a little straighter and taller as he greeted the people working in the fields, and she got an idea he wanted to be seen as the local hero who had ventured into the mountains with these strangers, and led them out again.

Fair enough. It might not be the whole truth, but she was not hungry enough for glory and renown to begrudge Danid his share. Besides, he *had* been useful, especially in the lands between Ironhead and the Smoking Valley.

A few cries of greeting went up, and more people began to emerge; straightening up from behind hedges, or coming out of houses to see what the noise was about. Danid greeted them eagerly with laughs and waves, but as they walked on into the middle of the village, Zhanna noticed something that bothered her.

"The sar's house," she said, pointing to Sar Benarin's stronghouse. "Why is it shut?"

The stronghouse was a miniature version of the Black Keep itself: a sturdy stone building on a raised buttress. When they had previously come through Ironhead, the shutters on the windows had been open, and Sar Benarin greeted them on the steps. Now the shutters were closed, despite it being the middle of the day.

"The sar's not here," someone said. Zhanna looked around and saw a woman who looked like she could have come from the Smoking Valley, strings of wooden beads and all. She enveloped Danid in a hug – his wife, presumably – but her expression was sober when she pulled back again. "Word came with a pedlar: Darkspur was marching on Black Keep. Sar Benarin took ten men and went downriver to help."

"Darkspur marched on Black Keep?!" Danid's mouth had dropped open in shock, and a pit opened in Zhanna's stomach.

"How is that possible?" Amonhuhe demanded, as much of Zhanna as of Danid's wife. "There's no way the Darkspur men could have got back in time for Thane Odem to hear news and order an attack, let alone for word of it to get here!"

"He must have been planning it anyway," Zhanna told her grimly. "You saw him at the feast: he wanted Daimon killed by the marshal!"

"Nobles," Amonhuhe muttered, in the same tone of voice as one would utter a curse. "We have to do something!"

"We will," Zhanna assured her. It looked like adulthood was not ready to release her just yet. She raised her voice. "This warrior needs a boat!"

Darel

The flood devastated the land.

Darel had watched it come in, safe from the top of Eight Winds Tower in the Sun Palace of Idramar. The ocean rose like some vast, ancient predator, and swallowed the coast. Idramar was inundated: homes were destroyed; ships in port were wrecked; thousands had been found dead afterwards, while thousands more were still missing. The water swept back out to sea as hungrily as it rushed in, dragging much of what it destroyed or killed with it. Bodies were still being brought in with each new tide. Only the higher areas of the city, of which the Sun Palace was one, escaped unscathed.

However, the damage to Idramar was not, Darel had come to realise, the most troubling thing about the flood.

"It is the same story from all the messengers," Kavran Downglade said wearily. "The waves struck with incredible force, and penetrated inland wherever the coast is flat, for miles in some places. Huge areas of farmland have been destroyed." He was the new Lord of the Treasury, having replaced Adan Greenbrook after the latter had been awarded the rank of Eastern Marshal. Downglade had been in his role for two weeks and, Darel thought, had possibly not slept properly since. Not that Darel had been doing much better.

"Can the fields be resown?" Adan Greenbrook asked. Heads around the Inner Council table turned towards Darel.

"It is somewhat late in the year," Darel found himself saying. "Besides which, if the sea's waters have soaked into the soil, the salt may prevent new crops from growing properly. There is a salt marsh next to this marshal's home," he elaborated, seeing the confused expressions. "The crops that grow in our fields farther from the shore will not grow there. Although you would be best served to speak to farmers on this matter."

"What need have we for farmers, when Marshal Blackcreek is on this council?" Meshul Whittingmoor said, with an icy smile that gave his words just enough sting to register, but stopped short of being outright disrespectful to a man who was now a Hand of Heaven.

"Plenty, this marshal would imagine," Darel retorted. "Or does the venerable Law Lord tend his own garden, and grow his own produce?" He did not wait for Whittingmoor to snap back, but instead continued on. "Lords, Idramar and the lands around it have warm summers and mild winters; that is not so in the south, where a late frost or snowfall can wither the crops, or an early one ruin them before they are ready for harvest. This marshal knows you might consider him to be an unlearned, rural thane, but believe him when he tells you that his people know *hunger*. The coastal farms, the fishing towns, wherever this wave struck, it has destroyed not only our people's ability to feed themselves, but also to feed others. There will be famine across the east, unless we take action."

"And what would you suggest?" Adan Greenbrook asked. The Eastern Marshal had been in his role for only a few hours more than Darel had held his, but he already wore his authority like a second skin. Greenbrook had been on the Inner Council for years, and navigated the murky waters of palace politics with a smoothness and fluidity of which Darel could only dream.

Were they truly so blinkered? Darel could barely believe it, but many of his illusions regarding the nature of nobility had been shattered since arriving in Narida's capital. He once believed the God-Kings were infallible, but how could that be, when two marshals appointed by a God-King had tried to stage coups in quick succession? Coldbeck, appointed by Natan Narida's father, had confined the current God-King to his chambers in the aftermath of an illness; Brightwater, appointed by Natan III himself, had tried to kill him outright.

In the end, it was irrelevant. Darel had been granted the office of Southern Marshal, one of the four most powerful men in the kingdom under the God-King, and he was going to do his best to honour that appointment.

"We must send word to the western thanes," he said, trying to sound assured. "Some of their stores must come east, to help those in need here. When harvest comes, the same thing must happen."

The smirks that met his statement were in many ways more crushing than outright mockery would have been. *You are a child, playing at being a marshal*, was the unspoken sentiment in the room. Whittingmoor, Greenbrook, and Sebiah Wousewold, the Lord of Scribes, all came from lands a long way from the ocean, which would have been unaffected by the great wave. Of course they would not wish to see their own domains bled to help others: he might as well have expected Darkspur to aid Blackcreek.

Darel swallowed at the thought of his home. He had prayed to Nari every morning and evening that Black Keep and its lands had been spared the wave's destruction, but how likely was that? What might cause a wave to hit here but not elsewhere? And yet, what possible force could have created a wave that would strike so many hundreds of miles of coastline? Darel could not even begin to imagine, and his lack of his comprehension scared him.

Most of all, however, he was scared for his brother, and everyone else he had left behind. Black Keep had no high ground within its walls, so there would have been little chance of escape. *Perhaps Daimon made it to the top of the Black Keep itself: that should have been high enough ...*

"How practical is such a suggestion?" asked a new voice, one that had barely spoken at the meeting so far. Heads turned again, as the assembled councillors looked at Natan, third of his name, God-King of Narida.

"Your Majesty, it is not a question of practicality," Lord Downglade said. The Lord Treasurer was a role of power, but Darel did not think he had yet found his feet, and was wary of crossing the council's longer-serving members. "It is a question of—"

"Given that this king has asked of its practicality, Lord Treasurer, you may be assured that it *is*, in fact, a question of practicality," Natan interrupted him. "If you do not know, then you need to find out. The Southern Marshal is correct: if there is the capacity to do this, it should be done."

"Your Majesty, such an order will not sit well in the west," Lord Whittingmoor said in a tone of concern. "We are at risk of sparking greater unrest than already exists."

"Lords," Master Temach of the universities spoke up, before the God-King could respond. Much of Idramar's various colleges had been destroyed by the wave, to Darel's great grief, but Temach's position on the council remained. "We are, begging your forgiveness, missing the most important point of what has occurred."

"And what is that?" Adan Greenbrook said testily.

"The Foretellings of Tolkar specifically mention the ocean

rising and swallowing cities!" Temach replied, and Darel took note of the hardness in the man's eyes. "This is surely incontrovertible evidence that the Divine Nari has been reborn!"

"Who are you to proclaim such a thing?" demanded Morel of Godspire. "This priest's brethren at the sacred monastery have not yet—"

"Look around you, Morel! Use your eyes! The signs are all there! People in the city are starting to speak of His return—"

"Then *where is He*?" Natan thundered, and the burgeoning argument between the high priest and the master of learning dissipated as swiftly as it had formed.

"If this king's divine ancestor is indeed reborn, how does this fact assist us?" Natan demanded, biting off every word. "*He is not here*. Were He to present Himself, this king would be only too happy to let the Divine One assume power and heal the land. Can He reverse the damage of the flood? Can He provide food enough for all?" He paused for a moment, but Morel offered no immediate assurance that this was the case. "We still have only rumours, that He is somewhere in the west. General Goldtree's forces appear to have managed little other than putting down a rebellion in Northbank which may have been sparked by their own conduct." The God-King knocked his empty goblet off the table in frustration. "Until such time as this king's divine ancestor is found, actually *found*, we can make no plans based upon His presence!"

There was silence in the council chamber. Darel had only met Natan III in the aftermath of Marshal Coldbeck's attempted coup, but he got the distinct impression that the God-King had been neither this quick-tempered nor this directly involved in the running of his kingdom prior to it. He was also fairly sure he was not imagining that the more senior councillors were none too happy about this change in their monarch.

"Lord Downglade," Natan said, his voice slightly more level.

"Unless we have definite and immediate assurance that the provisions available to the coast are sufficient, measures are to be taken to redistribute food from farther west. If necessary, we must take food from the nearest unaffected lands, and then they get assistance from those farther west of them, and so on, until the load is spread. This king's rule began with a plague in the aftermath of his father's death: he would not see it blighted by a famine as well. And who knows," he continued, with a mirthless grin. "If the western thanes object too bitterly, perhaps they will throw their support behind this king's divine ancestor, and we may finally see His face."

Darel noticed that neither Greenbrook, Wousewold, or Whittingmoor met the God-King's gaze. Marshal Greenbrook in particular hailed from lands where support for the supposedly reborn Nari was rumoured to be high. Darel's friend Hiran had guessed that Greenbrook's promotion was in part as hostage against his home's good behaviour, as well as a sop against the killing of his brother by Natan's sister Tila, for all that she had been acquitted of wrongdoing through trial by combat. It would be interesting to see how Greenbrook's tenure as Eastern Marshal played out, although Darel had a nasty feeling it was the definition of "interesting" that might involve someone's death at some point.

Darel came to Idramar to plead for understanding for his home's decision to accept settlers from across the ocean. He never intended to get mixed up in the cut and thrust of palace politics, let alone become a Hand of Heaven and be responsible for the entire South. However, it seemed that if you saved the life of your monarch and his sister, you were rewarded, even if that reward was something you felt ill-equipped to actually *do*.

Not for the first time, Darel wondered if the God-King's apparent poor decision-making when it came to appointing High Marshals now extended to him.

"This council is concluded," Natan stated. "Marshal Blackcreek, would you accompany this king?"

They all stood, and Darel followed the God-King from the chamber. He could feel the eyes of the other councillors on him, wanting to know for what purpose he was being called away, and dearly wished that he knew himself.

"Tolkar's arse, but this king hates those meetings," Natan grumbled, folding his arms on the parapet of Eight Winds Tower and looking west, towards the setting sun. "They are necessary, though, which is something he should have learned years ago."

Darel remained silent. He had no idea how to comment on the wisdom of your divine ruler, let alone a self-declared historic lack thereof.

"Are you regretting accepting your new rank yet?" Natan asked, looking over at him. Darel panicked for a moment, then took refuge in honesty.

"Your Majesty, your servant was not aware that he could have refused it."

"Of course you could have refused. What would this king have done? Executed you?" Natan barked a laugh, but it was a sour one. "That would have been poor reward for saving his life. If you wish to, you may renounce your rank and become nothing more than the thane of Blackcreek once again. Although that would give you considerably less influence in your dealings with the thane of Darkspur," he added, not a little slyly.

Darel could not help but smile. "Your Majesty makes a convincing case. Your servant does not imagine that Thane Odem will take the news of your servant's elevation well, and your servant admits this thought gives him pleasure." He schooled his expression and tried to appear sober and reflective.

"However, it would be remiss of him to accept such rank and responsibility merely for personal advantage."

Natan raised an eyebrow at him. "Would you like to tell that to the rest of them? Most men do not seek power for any purpose other than to serve themselves: that is why the line of Nari is so important, for how can one be corrupted by the lure of power when one already has it?" He sighed. "Or so this king's father and his teachers used to tell him." He laced his fingers together and stared westwards once more, and Darel felt that he was waiting for something.

"Do you disagree?" he ventured.

"This king has not always been a good king, Lord Blackcreek," Natan replied. "Recent events brought that to his attention, and he is trying to make amends. Other men seek power for their own gain, and they can do great harm without the God-King to keep them in check. No man can rule alone, but neither can a king leave all things to others. Even to his sister," he added, with a wry grin.

"Your sister, Your Majesty?" Darel said. The power and influence wielded by Tila Narida, the Divine Princess, was a matter of much whispered conjecture and absolutely no outright speech within the court.

"Tila is clever and cunning," Natan said. "And mark this king's words, those are two different things. This king relied on his sister for guidance for too long; he placed too great a responsibility on her shoulders, when she had to fight through the razorclaws on the council to achieve anything. It was a great disservice to her."

"The Divine Princess was not in the council meeting today," Darel observed, still somewhat uncomfortable with such self-critical statements. "Is she well?"

"This king believes so," Natan replied, turning away from the western sky and crossing to the eastern side of Eight Winds

Tower, which looked out over the bulk of Idramar. In times past, it would have been a magnificent view: for the last two weeks, it was a grim picture of destruction. "She will have been in the city."

"The city?" Darel tried to think of any reason why Tila Narida would go into the city, or indeed why he was unaware of such a thing taking place. Surely he would have heard the procession leaving, the guards or the trumpets or something? "Is that safe?"

"No, but . . . " Natan sighed, then winced. "Darel, please assure this king that you will not repeat what he just said to anyone, *especially* his sister."

Darel swallowed. This conversation was becoming more and more unusual, not to mention uncomfortable, with every passing second. His monarch using Darel's first name to address him was not even the strangest thing about it, although it provided a certain gut-twisting fear all of its own. "Of course, Your Majesty." He paused, trying to collect his thoughts. "Your Majesty, *why*—"

"Darel," the God-King interrupted him, straightening up from his slouch against the parapet and squinting into the distance. "Do there seem to you to be an awful lot of sails on that sea?"

Something in Natan's voice immediately alerted Darel that this was not just an idle question. He turned and followed his monarch's gaze.

There was no doubt about it. The sun was behind them, and dipping downwards, but the eastern sky was not yet truly darkening. The eastern *sea*, however, was filled with black specks near the horizon.

"Nari's blood," Darel whispered, heedless of the man standing beside him. There was no making out details yet, of course, but he had a nasty feeling that he knew what shape the sails were on those ships, and the language that would be spoken by their crews.

"That does not sound promising," Natan commented, his voice tight.

"I-It must be the Tjakorshi," Darel said, trying not to sound as scared as he was, and failing abjectly.

"The Raiders from your home?" Natan said, looking at him quizzically. "This king had no idea there were so many of them."

"No, Your Majesty, not those Tjakorshi!" Darel said. Could he put his hands on the God-King to usher him towards the steps? Was that allowed? "It must be the rest of them. And The Golden," he added as an afterthought. He had heard only the barest of tales of the demon-thing that had driven Saana's clan from their homeland, since none of them had seen it, but what he had heard was enough. By the mountain, Darel had seen Saana and her people, and he knew it would have taken something fearsome in the extreme to push them from their ancestral home.

Natan was still frowning. "What—"

"We must go," Darel said, interrupting him. Interrupting the God-King! "Your Majesty, we must leave *now*; leave the city! There is no way . . . " He looked again at the horizon, tried to count the ships there, and gave up. "There is no way we can stand against what is coming. Even if the city was whole, we would likely be outmatched. As it is, it will be a slaughter. We must sound the alarm and get everyone to flee! Idramar has an alarm?" he asked, seeing Natan's confused expression. "Your Majesty, tell me that there is a signal for your people to flee the city!"

"Of course not!" Natan snapped back, to Darel's mounting horror. "This is Idramar! This is not the south, Darel: we have barely seen a single Raider ship in this king's lifetime! Why would we ever need to flee the city?"

Of course, it was too much to expect the northerners to be sensible, Darel thought bitterly, as all his father's diatribes about the pampered, coddled thanes of the warmer lands flooded back to him.

"Then, Your Majesty, we must do what we can," he said firmly. "We will warn as many as possible, but you *must* leave, now!"

For a wonder, Natan did not object, and headed for the stone steps that led down into the Sun Palace's interior. Darel followed him, already wondering how much time they actually had. The ships were only on the horizon, but Tjakorshi vessels were famously swift, and the city was not likely to put up significant resistance. On the other hand, the palace guard was still present, and what were the chances that a strong force of invaders would head straight for the Sun Palace, or after the God-King? No, Darel thought, even with the time it would take to ready a carriage and an escort, they should be able to get clear.

And then what? Head west, of course, but—

"Tila!" Natan cried, coming to a halt on the stairs and turning around to stare back up at Darel with stricken eyes. "Tila! She is still in the city!"

"Then she must fend for herself," Darel said grimly, fighting down the nausea in his stomach at the notion of leaving the Divine Princess for The Golden and its forces. "Your Majesty, you said yourself that she is both clever and cunning: perhaps that will serve her well. We can even command men to go and search for her, but if we delay then we risk losing you both!"

Natan's face twisted in agonised indecision, morphed into guilty acceptance, then hardened again. "The Queen Mother," Natan said stubbornly. "We will not leave without this king's mother, at the very least!"

"We will make it work, but we! Must! *Go!*" Darel bellowed

at him. Natan flinched and drew in breath as though to shout back at Darel, then ground his teeth, turned, and fled downwards.

Darel exhaled and ran after him, wondering if his heart was going to jump out of his chest before he reached the bottom.

Stonejaw

T ry as she might, Zheldu Stonejaw had been unable to slip
away from The Golden's war fleet.

That was her hastily constructed plan: set the draug on
course for the Flatlands, or Narida as it was apparently called,
then make a break for it when attention was off her. Swing
back north, head for the City of Islands, then straight through
the Throat of the World and on to the mysterious northern
ocean, to leave golden-masked, body-snatching spirits and
their dreams of death and conquest far behind.

Unfortunately, the *Storm's Breath* had never been in a position where it could do any such thing. By accident or design,
Stonejaw's yolgu had been kept fairly central in the fleet, and it
would have aroused far too much suspicion to peel off. Kullojan
Sakteszhin and his ship the *Firelight* had always been lurking
to starboard, too, and Stonejaw got the distinct impression that
the other captain was keeping an eye on her.

They were perhaps a week out from the Fishing Islands
when they heard the roars, as loud as a storm wave thundering
onto a beach in front of you. Every head turned, looking back
across the ocean. Stonejaw was not the greatest navigator –
she was a fighter first and foremost, and left the finer points
of sailing the *Storm's Breath* to others better suited to it – but
even she could work out from where those noises had come.

The only thing she knew of that lay in that direction, weeks of sailing away though it was, was Tjakorsha.

"The mountain spirits," Stonejaw whispered.

"What?" asked Korsada the Dry, who had come to stand next to her. She had one hand on the narrow sword of Drylands steel from her mother, as though that would help against whatever was happening.

"The mountain spirits," Stonejaw repeated. "The Golden said they were going to break free and kill our home. According to Sakteszhin, anyway."

Korsada exhaled through her nose. "The draug sees the truth in its fires, it seems. It always has." She shook her head. "We were fools to think we could escape it."

"Then let's hope it saw victory for us all in the Flatlands," Stonejaw muttered. "I don't fancy taking those dragons on again."

"Maybe we can let Sakteszhin go first," Korsada suggested, and the thought of Kullojan Sakteszhin shitting himself in terror as a gigantic monster bore down on him did at least bring half a smile to Stonejaw's face. She had never had much issue with the man before, but he was the one who had found her, woken her, and brought her at axe-edge to The Golden, so she had pinned the death of her dream of freedom on him.

A few hours after they heard the roars of the mountain spirits, Stonejaw nearly fell from her feet when the *Storm's Breath* lurched unexpectedly beneath her. "Krayk!" someone shouted, and everyone drew back from the yolgu's edges in case the fearsome, scaled shape of one of Father Krayk's true-born children appeared, ready to snatch an unwary crewer down in its huge jaws.

"That was no krayk!" Zhazhken Aralaszhin called, pointing. Stonejaw followed his gesture and saw what he meant: the crew of every ship in sight were reacting in the same manner as hers. Either an entire swarm of the sea beasts had all decided to bump into a yolgu at once, or it had been something else.

"Watch the sea!" she instructed, warily. Every Tjakorshi knew the rise and fall of the ocean swell, but there were stories of rogue waves that swept out of nowhere to drag ships and their crews down to the depths. So it was that when the next bulge of water appeared from the south-east, a slight change in the ocean's profile that she would never have noticed had she not been looking for it, she had time to shout "Brace!" before it hit them.

Another jolt, more severe than the first, but still nothing that would cause a yolgu any issues. A little fishing tsek might have foundered, but the huge, fifty-ell bulk of the *Storm's Breath* took the hit with only a slight creak of its timbers and a few crew members knocked sideways. Stonejaw watched the sea for another hour, but nothing else came for them; at least, nothing notable above the normal pitching and yawing of the ocean's surface. By the time darkness fell that evening, she had put the entire thing out of her mind.

When they reached the Flatlands, some two weeks later, she got an idea what those jolts of water had grown into once they reached the coastline.

She did not notice the damage at first, because the sun was setting ahead of them, silhouetting the land and turning the sky behind it a rich orange. Tajen, the translator of Tjakorshi blood that Stonejaw had brought with her from the City of Islands, had clearly saved both his skin and hers by doing what she told The Golden he could: take them to the main city of this land. If the rumours Stonejaw had heard were true, their God-King was ill. Even if he was not, that barely mattered now. The Golden had come here for conquest, and it was going to get it.

The fleet released its crows as thanks to Father Krayk for

the safe passage, as was tradition, and the black cloud went croaking towards the shore ahead of the ships. It was not until they were approaching the stone quays, with the warriors of the *Storm's Breath* taking up blackstone axes and alder roundshields in preparation for the landing, that Stonejaw realised things were not as she would have expected. The water through which they were now cutting was choked with debris and swollen-limbed bodies, above which crows were circling as though hoping they would soon wash up on land. Even the stone buildings on the shore were damaged, and those spaces which looked to have once housed structures built of other materials now contained little more than wreckage, or makeshift shelters put together from salvage.

"Looks like Father Krayk got here first," Korsada said, awestruck.

"Let's hope he left us something, or The Golden won't be pleased," Stonejaw remarked. The frontrunners of the Tjakorshi fleet were making landfall, bumping up against the quays, or simply riding the breakers up the beach where the Flatlanders had left it unaltered. To her left, some ships were sailing into what had to be a huge estuary, the largest she had ever seen, to hit the city from the south. The *Storm's Breath* veered north instead, and made landfall alongside the *Firelight*.

"Where are these monsters you claim you fought, Stonejaw?" Kullojan Sakteszhin bellowed, jumping off his yolgu and wading through the waves. "Or was that just a story you made up to excuse your failure?"

"If you don't believe me, you go right on ahead!" Zheldu shouted back to him, gesturing to the streets ahead of them. By the Dark Father, but she was not eager to head in there and potentially meet a dragon and its rider coming the other way. It had been bad enough seeing her fellows ridden down and trampled on open ground; at least you could scatter and dodge there, assuming there were not too many of the bastards coming at you. Going up against one without room to move sounded like the worst sort of nightmare imaginable.

The waterfront was deserted, and the Tjakorshi swept over it like a new tide of sea leather and blackstone. Not everyone in the great fleet was a warrior, by any means – The Golden had brought with it every soul left in the islands, so far as anyone could reckon – but more than enough could swing a weapon. Grizzled raiders who might not normally have set sail again for distant lands rubbed shoulders with fresh-faced Unblooded, full of fire and eager to prove themselves under the draug's eye. Stonejaw even thought she caught sight of Ludir Snowhair, the ancient former chief of the Seal Rock clan over whose shield wall she and Rodhnjan of Kotuakor had propelled Rikkut Fireheart, what seemed like years ago now. Rikkut had captured Snowhair and made him yield, and that victory persuaded The Golden to give Fireheart command of the raid that set off in pursuit of Saana Sattistutar and the Brown Eagle clan.

Zheldu decided to steer clear of Snowhair, just in case he was still harbouring any grudges. Even the oldest arm could stick a spearfish-bill dagger in your back if your attention was elsewhere.

Shouts ahead of her signalled that the first wave of Tjakorshi had finally encountered some Flatlanders. Stonejaw and her crew pressed on, eager not to look like they were dallying, for The Golden would surely be watching for reluctance as well as valour. They found the bodies not long after: three people, no weapons evident, with great, bloody rents cut into them by blackstone. They had been fleeing with their possessions, judging by the sackcloth nearby, but any items of value had already been taken, and anything left was indistinguishable from the other debris in the street.

"Where's the glory in that?" Zhazhken asked, nudging one

of the mutilated bodies with his boot. "This wasn't a fight. This is just butchery."

"Don't pretend you were never Unblooded, Zhazhken," Korsada chided him. "You remember what it's like, being so eager to claim adulthood that you'd take any kill and call it a fair one." She her had her narrow steel blade out, and was looking around at the buildings on either side of them. "Let the young ones run on ahead looking for a warm body to cut; I think there might be something worth our time here. The locals can't have taken *everything* valuable with them as soon as they saw our sails."

Zheldu chewed her lip, thinking. Could they get away with it? Go searching for loot, maybe circle back towards the ships, then take the *Storm's Breath* and disappear before their absence was noticed? She knew it was a flawed plan even before she finished the thought. The Golden's fleet had needed most of its provisions and water to get here: setting off again without restocking was foolishness, and the act of restocking would take too long, and be too obvious.

"No," she said. "We'll push on." Another crew was already hurrying up behind them, whooping and shouting war cries. "The Golden has little reason to trust our loyalty. Let's not give it an excuse to order us killed for dawdling."

Heads nodded grimly. Stonejaw had been worried her crew would blame her for bringing them here, but they had simply been grateful she had found something for The Golden to focus its terrifying attention on, rather than their failure to fulfil the task it had given them, or the fact they tried to escape it afterwards.

"Let's get on, then," she muttered, striding forwards with her blackstone axe ready. "And by all the heroes, sing out if you see a fucking dragon."

Saana

S aana held the people of Black Keep back from going down
off the moors, even once the water had receded, just in case
it came back. To her astonishment, even the Naridans listened;
it seemed her accurate prediction of the disaster had made
even the least friendly heed her words. They spent the night
huddled up together like sea bears on a beach, trying to keep
warm through the press of each other's bodies. Thankfully
there was no rain, and the year had advanced enough that,
despite being up on the moor, the night's chill was nothing
more than uncomfortable.

"What about those swept away on the bridge?" Nalon asked
her quietly, as everyone had been trying to settle down. Saana
was extremely glad to have him with her, as he was the only
other person who spoke both languages fluently.

"They'll be safe," Saana had said firmly. "We'll see them
tomorrow."

The one thing she had taken a fierce pleasure in was the
water washing over the Darkspur camp. The crows descended
before sunset, and the location of the bodies could still be
made out in the morning as the distant, tiny black specks of
Father Krayk's sacred birds hopped and fluttered from one to
the other.

The Blackcreek itself was the first barrier, when the folk of

Black Keep descended in the morning: it was too wide for most to swim at high tide, while the thick black mud that made up its shores at low tide could swallow even the strongest person up to their knees and hold them there. The nearest bridge was miles upstream, if it had survived the flood at all, so Saana sent Akuto Wavechosen and a crew to see what they could find. They returned some hours later, floating downstream on a taugh that had been stranded on the near shore and which they had been able to wrestle back into the river, and bearing rough paddles hacked out of broken, fallen branches.

"It's not the biggest, but we can get people across on it," Akuto called out to Saana when they pulled onto the southern bank to the cheers of tired and hungry, but relieved and grateful townsfolk. "And I've got some other news you might be interested in."

"Well?" Saana demanded.

"Saw that Flatlander husband of yours," Akuto said with a sly grin, and Saana felt like she could breathe freely for the first time in a day. "Him and a bunch of others were making their way back over the fields, though they weren't moving that quickly. I don't know what they did with the yolgus; I guess they're stranded farther inland. Reckon they'll be here in a couple of hours, give or take."

"Then let's get over there and start sorting things out," Saana said. She was already anticipating the likely problems they were going to face. Even assuming that most people's houses had survived the flood more or less intact, firewood would be sodden, the wells might be undrinkable so they would have to send people back across the river with barrels to collect fresh water from the moor's streams, food stores would be ruined, the crops in the fields had been destroyed . . .

It was going to be hard, but at least they were alive to experience that hardship. Father Krayk had reached out for all the souls of Black Keep, and most had eluded his grasp. That, at the very least, was something to be thankful for.

One trip across the river later, courtesy of Akuto's salvaged taugh, and Saana walked back in through the River Gate with the stench of salt and rotting vegetation filling her nostrils. The midday sun was drawing the moisture out of the sodden earth and the timber of the buildings, and the air was thickly humid, almost hard to breathe. Puddles lay everywhere, along with great clumps of seaweed and even the occasional stranded fish. Saana caught sight of a blackstone axe, half-buried in mud: presumably the owner had not had time to take it with them across the bridge, or had prioritised something else instead. Saana's own weapon was still on her belt, since she had been armed and on the walls when Akuto had first drawn her attention to the missing sea.

She hastily readied it when she heard someone cough ahead of her. Saana and those with her – Inkeru, Nalon and Avlja, Evram the reeve and his reevesmen, and two dozen others – were the first to re-enter Black Keep. For someone else to be here either meant that they had somehow survived the entire town flooding, or . . .

"Who's there?" she shouted in Tjakorshi, then repeated the same words in Naridan.

"S'man heard it too," Evram said, stepping forward with a grim expression on his face and clutching the staff that was both his symbol and his tool of office. The three reevesmen shadowed him.

"If they were friends of ours, wouldn't they have shown themselves already?" Nalon said.

Saana raised her voice in Naridan. "Whoever you are, come out now and this man swears you will not be hurt!"

"That's a bold statement," Nalon commented in Tjakorshi.

"Nalon, shut up," Saana told him absently, in the same

language. "We've got more important things to do than hunting whoever this is through the houses. I'd rather they just came out, so we can get this over with."

"That's long enough," Evram said firmly, and started forward towards the nearest house with his reevesmen at his back. Saana briefly consider calling him back, then decided against it. This had been their home for far longer than it had been hers, and if whoever was hiding away decided to make trouble then they would almost certainly find themselves severely outnumbered.

It seemed the mysterious cougher agreed: Evram had barely taken three steps when a door two houses farther down the street banged open, and four men stumbled out into the sun.

They were Naridans, Saana could tell instantly. What was more, one of them was a sar, and although it was wet and stained, the fabric of his coat-of-nails bore the design of Darkspur.

"We yield!" the sar called, holding out his scabbarded blades in one hand with the other extended empty in front of him. Beside him, one of the others let out the racking cough that had first alerted Saana to their presence.

The simplest thing would be to kill them. Four against two dozen would be no contest at all. Dig a hole in the mud; throw the bodies in; forget about them. They had come to drive her and her people out of their new home, and their lord had threatened to burn the entire town alive.

However, they had yielded, and killing warriors who had yielded was one of the most craven acts someone could commit. Practically the only thing worse was to pretend to yield in order to then gain an advantage. Father Krayk despised both these things, and given how close the Dark Father had come to sweeping them all away, Saana had no interest in provoking him.

"Why are you here?" she demanded, playing for time.

"The sea came," the sar said, sounding almost helpless. "We managed to get atop the walls, then when the water went down, we spent the night in that house. Gavrel swallowed a lot of water." He gestured to the man who had coughed, who looked about as miserable as anyone Saana had ever seen. The sar himself was in his middle years, by Saana's estimation, and . . .

"This man knows you," she said, pointing at him with her axe. "You came with Yarmina." She searched her memory. "Sar Lahel. You spoke with Daimon about rattletails."

"Your ladyship is correct," Sar Lahel replied, with a bow in which he maintained the position of his longblade and shortblade. His arm was starting to shake a bit, Saana noticed, and part of her briefly wondered how long she could make him stand like that.

"He's a sar, and a Darkspur one at that," Nalon said flatly. "We can't trust him."

"Are you disputing this sar's honour?" Lahel barked, his brows lowering.

"Given that Omet said you were going to burn us as witches? Yeah, s'man's disputing it!" Nalon shot back. "The Code of Honour always means exactly what you bastards want it to mean, and nothing else!"

"Nalon!" Saana snapped, before Lahel could retort. "You're not helping," she added tightly in Tjakorshi.

"Aren't I?" he replied, in the same tongue. "If you play nice with them now, they'll take it as a favour."

He might be right, but Saana's patience was already stretched. If she had better things to do than hunt people through the town, she *certainly* had better things to do than bandy words with this four.

"This man does not know your code, so she will use hers," she said, speaking Naridan once more. "When warriors yield, they become thralls. They give up their weapons, live and work as a member of the clan that captured them for a year and a day. After that, they go back to their own home. Swear to *that*."

"Oh shit," Nalon muttered quietly.

"What if we don't swear?" the man named Gavrel asked Saana, between more rasping coughs.

Saana shrugged. "There are less mouths to feed." She was not sure if she would go through with it, or whether she would just send them out into the Downwoods and let them take their chances with the night and any predators that might have survived the flood, but she was done with the delicate dance of Naridan niceties.

Gavrel considered her words for a moment, then nodded. "S'man swears to it."

"Gavrel!" Sar Lahel gasped, but the soldier shook his head stubbornly.

"Forgive s'man, goodsar, but he came close enough to dying yesterday to know he don't want no part of it today. Even if they let us go . . ." He broke off as another cough shook him. "Even if they let us go, the only place s'man is likely to find food and a fire anywhere nearby is here. S'man's hungry, and he don't want to take this cough out into the woods for the night."

One of the others nodded gloomily. "Gavrel's right. S'man swears to it, too."

"Aye, and s'man," added the third. Sar Lahel still looked torn, as though he was seriously considering drawing his longblade and laying about him until he found an honourable death – and that was not a reaction that was out of the question, given how determined Asrel Blackcreek had been to do the same thing – but finally he bowed his head and lowered his blades to his side.

"Very well. This sar also swears."

"Good." Saana stepped forward and held out her hand. "The swords." Lahel hesitated, and she sighed. "We will keep them for you, but thralls do not have weapons. If you touch a weapon when you are not being attacked, you die."

Lahel hesitated, and Saana had a momentary understanding of what she was asking of him. As a sar, he was a warrior: and unlike a Tjakorshi fighter like Inkeru, or Tsennan Longjaw — and how Saana dearly hoped that *he* was healthy and well, along with her daughter — Lahel's sense of identity was caught up in that and, as Saana understood it, pretty much that alone. What would he be, if he was not a warrior?

He would be a thrall, is what he would be. Perhaps he would even be good at it.

Reluctantly, Lahel handed his blades over. Saana took them from him as respectfully as she could manage under the circumstances, then turned and gave them to Evram. "Find a place for these, and . . ." She waved a hand vaguely. "Get them to help?"

"Yes, chief," Evram replied, and Saana did her best to suppress a smile. She doubted she would ever like being called "Lady Saana" or "Your ladyship", but most of the Black Keep Naridans — *her* Naridans, as she had come to think of them — had ended up calling her "chief", much like her own clan did. At least, apart from Osred the steward, and the Dark Father only knew where *he* was now. Somewhere with Otim Ambaszhin, and the others who had sailed off up the coast to seek help before Darkspur had arrived to lay siege to Black Keep. She just hoped they had not been sucked under by the great wave, or drowned and thrown up on the shore, or any number of other potential fates.

With the intruders dealt with, Saana and her party investigated their home in more detail. The situation was not hopeless, but remained grim: many houses had escaped serious damage, but had been flooded high enough that there was nowhere dry to lie, sit, or even lean. Bedding and clothes were sodden and ruined, and had often floated away from where they had been left. The town could still provide shelter in the long term, but it needed things in the short term – food, water, preferably some dry sleeping places – that it did not have, at least not in sufficient quantity. The top floors of the Black Keep itself had remained clear of the water, and Saana was already organising for the young and old to spend the night there in conditions that would be cramped, but dry, when a shout came down from the walls.

"Lord Daimon! Lord Daimon is back!"

It turned out that Black Keep's gates of white maple had swollen in their stone frame, and even with the bars removed, it took the combined efforts of those both outside and in to get one of them open enough to admit the weary line of mud-caked walkers. Daimon was first through, and Saana caught him in an embrace, then released him again when she realised how damp he was.

"You fell in?" she asked, and then mentally kicked herself for her first words not being something about how glad she was to see him.

"Yes," Daimon admitted ruefully. "When your husband cut the lines keeping us tethered to the shore. He surely would have drowned, had it not been for Aftak and Tsolga. Yes, and you as well," he added to Rattler, who had decided to wind about the legs of them both. He sighed, and looked down at his own clothing. "And this is after a night of sleep and half a day of walking."

"At least you are back," Saana told him. "How far did the water take you?"

"A couple of miles, perhaps?" Daimon said. "We tried to

ground the yolgus when the water began to recede, for we feared we would be swept out to sea. A walk in the morning seemed the safer option, but the ground was not forgiving." He grimaced. "Not everyone made it; some few fell in, but only a few, thank Nari. And we acquired a man of Darkspur, who swore to do us no harm so long as we did not leave him to drown."

Saana snorted. "There were four in this town when we came back; one of them was Sar Lahel, who came when Yarmina Darkspur visited."

Daimon's face fell. "What happened?"

Saana shrugged. "Your wife made them swear to serve as thralls."

"You . . . You made them *thralls*?" Daimon stuttered, in utter disbelief.

"It seemed like a good idea at the time," Saana said, aware that she was sounding slightly defensive. "Perhaps we do not need to keep them thralls, but it served for the moment. Your wife suspects Thane Odem will not be pleased, however."

Daimon sucked his teeth. "Thane Odem will not be a further problem for us. We found his body, some way to the west. He drowned in the flood. The crows have him now."

"Good," Saana said immediately.

"Your husband agrees wholeheartedly," Daimon said, with feeling. "Odem is far from alone, too. Your husband does not know exactly how many men of Darkspur there were here, but we must have seen half of them dead. When we think that others may have been taken out to sea by the water retreating, it seems likely that most of their force is destroyed. Your husband does not believe we have anything to fear from them in the near future."

"That is good to hear," Saana said. She drew Daimon slightly farther to one side, away from the other reunions that were taking place just inside the gate, so that they might not so easily be overheard. "But we have another problem. The town is not fit for us to live in; not yet."

"Your husband suspected as much," Daimon replied. "He was considering this on the walk back. Much of Black Keep's farmland has been destroyed. The other Blackcreek lands farther from the sea will not have been affected, but will be overtaxed to have to feed us as well."

Saana nodded. "It will be hard."

"But perhaps there is a solution."

Saana looked at him, then folded her arms. "Your wife knows that expression. It is when you have a plan you think might anger people."

"You are not wrong," Daimon muttered. "But think about it. We have most of our people, by the grace of Nari and your quick-thinking, but little usable land. Darkspur still has its land, untouched by the sea, but a lot of its able-bodied men have been drowned."

"Less mouths to feed," Saana said slowly, turning it over in her head.

"And fewer hands to work the harvest," Daimon pointed out.

"What is your plan?"

"We march on Darkspur," Daimon said, as though it were the most obvious thing in the world. "We leave some people here with what we can spare, to take care of those who cannot travel, and to begin to put the town back into order. The rest of us head for Darkspur and see how interested they are in an alliance with terms that benefit us both."

"An alliance?" Saana said in surprise. "Why would Darkspur agree to an alliance?"

"Because Thane Odem is dead, and if his cousin and steward Sar Omet did not die from the arrows we put in him, he surely will not have escaped the flood," Daimon said baldly.

"That means Darkspur is now ruled by Lady Yarmina, who is nineteen years old, clearly well-disposed enough towards us to warn us of her father's plans, and, if your husband does not miss his guess, unlikely to take kindly to the forceful offers of marriage that are about to come her way." He spread his hands. "It is not unheard of for neighbouring thanes to take matters of marriage into their own hands by means of threats and a biddable priest, if it is not possible for a young, unmarried lady to prevent them. Having us on her land might actually be Yarmina's best option."

Saana thought about it. Yarmina had seemed genuine enough, and her warning about her father had certainly been borne out. Everything Daimon said about their respective situations felt like it would be accurate, and he surely knew better than she did about how Yarmina might be forced into a marriage by a thane who wanted his son to take possession of the Darkspur lands.

"Very well, husband," she said. "Let us march in search of an alliance."

Tila

Tila Narida, the Divine Princess, was nowhere in the Sun Palace when the Raiders arrived. Nor, officially, was she anywhere in the city of Idramar.

Livnya the Knife, on the other hand, who as the head of Idramar's criminal underworld was very much not the same person as Tila Narida, was expressing her considerable displeasure to a small group of thieves. Tila had made it abundantly clear to her underlings that all resources were to be put in to making sure the city held together, since none of their livelihoods would endure without it. The Keepers were charged with maintaining the peace, but they were primarily concerned with making sure the properties of the nobility and richer merchants remained unpillaged. For everyone else, Livnya the Knife and those under her command were, somewhat surprisingly, the only viable option of redress.

"And we know these men took the coins?" Tila asked Kradan, the scar-faced ruffian who still held authority over most of the city's rougher gangs, despite his influence diminishing somewhat in the aftermath of the Eastern Army's recruitment drive to push westwards in search of the allegedly reborn Divine Nari. Some of his men had been swept up anyway, while others had been encouraged to join in order to put a knife into any imposter claiming the title. Tila had rarely encountered a more devout group of people than her city's knot of thieves and criminals; at least, for a certain value of "devout".

"One of them talked," Kradan assured her. "There's always one that will."

Tila nodded. "Very well." She stepped past him to stare down at the group of five men on their knees with their hands bound, and dirty sackcloth over their heads.

"This lady thought she'd been clear," she said. "We do our best to make sure everyone's provided for, and in return, no one preys on those weaker than themselves." Her voice held a note of easy command, but was still inflected with the twang of Idramar's streets. Alazar of White Hill might not be in Idramar any longer, but Tila had been careless to ever let "Lady" Livnya's voice overlap with that of the Divine Princess.

The men on their knees did not reply or answer back. They knew better than to risk even greater displeasure.

"Did they hurt the woman?" Tila asked Kradan.

"Pulled a knife on her, but never hurt her," Kradan replied.

"No sticks, then," Tila instructed, and Kradan's men put down the cudgels they carried. "Let's get this over with."

The beating was swift and efficient, and while hardly merciful, it was not exactly cruel. No fingers were broken, and there were no blows to the head. The thieves were pummelled in the ribs and legs enough that they would find movement painful and rest elusive for a few days. Times were hard enough; the key was to make such transgressions not worth the offender's while, rather than instil a reign of terror so brutal it sparked mass retaliation. Tila had been dealing with the Inner Council for years, from a position of little more than respect for her bloodline and wariness of her mysterious resources, so she thought she could strike an appropriate balance with the people of Idramar.

It was when the last thuds of fist and feet on flesh had died away, and cries of pain had faded to whimpers, that she realised the sound of the city had changed.

"What's that?" Kradan asked, turning to face the mouth of the alley in which their "business" was being conducted.

Tila listened intently. Her skin felt clammy, and she was terrified she was going to hear the roaring sound that preceded the great wave, when the sea rose from its bed and swallowed whole chunks of her city. To her great relief, she could not hear any such thing, but there was no mistaking the sound of many voices raised in alarm.

"Could it be a fire?" asked Barach, her bodyguard.

"Most of the city's still too wet to burn," Kradan muttered.

"Don't be a fool," Tila told him sharply. "That's not a chance we should take." She gestured to the still-groaning men. "Set them loose, and let's see what's going on."

The thieves' bonds were cut, and they were left to stagger away as best they could. A young girl working for Kradan disappeared off with the recovered coins to return them to their rightful owner – Kradan did not issue threats of what would happen if any went missing, since anyone who had spent time in his company would be able to work that out for themselves – and the rest of them went in search of the disturbance.

It was not hard to find.

They headed in the general direction of the harbour, but never got there: as soon as they emerged from a side street onto Baker's Way, they were engulfed by a scrum of people fleeing towards the palace.

"What's happening?" Tila yelled, grabbing someone's sleeve.

"Let go!" the other woman shouted, flailing desperately at her, but stopped resisting when Barach took her other arm.

"Answer the question!" he ordered, and while it was not a shout, it was not far off.

"Raiders!" the woman gasped desperately. "In the harbour! Now let s'woman *go*!" This time, when she pulled away, Tila did not resist, and, seeing her release her hold, Barach did likewise.

"Raiders?" Kradan asked incredulously, knocking aside a man who barged into him in his desperation to get past. "This far north? That can't be right."

Tila thought for a moment of the thane of Blackcreek, Narida's new Southern Marshal, and his unlikely allies. Could they have sailed to Idramar? But why would they do so, and why would it spark such a general panic? There surely could not be *that* many of them, to set so much of the city running?

"Get your people together, as many as you can quickly," Tila told Kradan. "This lady doesn't know what's going on, but she means to find out. The Eastern Army left a garrison here, but there's no harm in having a few blades out to watch our own people."

"As you say, your ladyship," Kradan replied with a nod, and he and his men disappeared.

"Where are we going, your ladyship?" Barach asked her. He had drawn his heavy knife and was ready to intercept any threat that might present itself.

The palace, for me, Tila thought. She needed to find her brother, but there was no way she could take Barach with her. She had managed to maintain the fiction of her double life so far – through a combination of great care, a relatively small need for sleep, and putting a knife into the throat of the only man who had ever figured it out – but there was no way that Livnya the Knife would be going to the Sun Palace.

"You go and find your family," she told Barach. "Make sure they're well."

"Da can look after them," Barach said firmly. "S'man's place is with you."

Old Barach had been Livnya's bodyguard before his son, and he was still a very unwise man to provoke into a fight. Tila nodded briskly: she would just have to find another way to get rid of Barach before her destination became too obvious. "Fine. This way, then."

They had not got more than a hundred yards when the attack came. Tila heard whooping war cries, and then a small knot of figures barrelled out of a side street just ahead of them.

Raiders.

None were the size of Barach, but none were small. They lacked the savage facial tattoos with which Tila had heard they decorated themselves, and were without the long, unkempt beards so often associated with them, but there was no mistaking the pale skin, the round wooden shields, or the crude but deadly blackstone axes with which they laid about themselves. The crowd recoiled like a flock of startled gulls, but not all were quick enough, and Tila saw red wounds open as blackstone bit into flesh. Nari save her, but this was no misunderstanding caused by an unexpected arrival: these were killers, loose in her city! And how many more must there be, for this small group to have made it this far?

"That way!" she shouted at Barach, pointing to an alley on the opposite side of the street, then stuck her hands into her sleeves and drew a throwing knife from each. She had no illusions about taking the savages on, but it was better to have a weapon to hand if she needed it.

Whether they heard her shout or not she would never know, but it was at that moment that two of the Raiders looked in her direction. They charged, one of them knocking an older woman sprawling out of their way with a swipe of their shield.

Tila reacted instinctively: she set her feet, judged the distance, and flung a knife with all the force she could muster. A flicker of surprise crossed her target's face as he registered that she had thrown something, but not quite in time to duck or dodge. The blade struck his throat and sunk in, and he stumbled to a confused halt, reaching up as horrified realisation dawned. He was young, Tila realised in a flash; young enough to be her child, had she had one. They were all young, in fact. The lack of long beards was because none of the Raiders had more than the fuzzy cheeks of youth, and some lacked even that.

She took that in within a split-second, then turned to run before the other warrior could get to them. Barach was already moving: he might take his duties as her bodyguard seriously, but that usually meant making sure she was unbothered by disrespectful ruffians, or footpads who failed to realise whom they were intending to rob. He clearly had no intention of facing down a fully armed Raider with his knife, which was exactly the sort of good sense and lack of hubris that made him such an asset.

Tila sprinted away from the whooping warrior behind her as best she could. Livnya's dresses allowed her greater freedom of movement than the multi-layered affairs worn by the Divine Princess, but she was acutely aware of the drag of fabric on her legs and what felt like the massive expanse of her unprotected back. How fresh was this Raider? Had they fought their way up from the harbour? Was their breath already coming hard, or would they run her down with ease?

"Left ahead!" she shouted to Barach, seeing the alley branch. At least she knew the streets; that was an advantage over their pursuer, albeit a slim one. She and Barach knew what turnings to take ahead of time, while the Raider would have to react to their movements. She desperately tried to bring the layout of streets and alleys in this area to mind: was there anything they could use?

Barach cut left; Tila feinted to go right, as though they were splitting up, then followed him. A frustrated shout, a clatter of footsteps and the *swoosh* of a weapon through the air behind her told her that her gamble had wrong-footed the Raider, at least for a moment. Moments were critical, but how many more would she have?

They're carrying a shield and a weapon, she told herself. *They're slower than they would be otherwise. You can do this.*

Ahead, past Barach's rolling shoulders, she saw the end of the alley. It came out into a small square, in the centre of which was a shrine to Nari. Space was good; space meant room to duck and dodge, and maybe enough distance between her and their pursuer to put a knife into them.

"Go left again!" she screamed at Barach. Now they *would* split up, and perhaps one of them could take the Raider in the back . . .

Barach tripped.

Tila did not see what caused it, but her bodyguard stumbled over something at the mouth of the alley and, running at full speed as he was, fell headlong to the ground. Tila tried to jump over him, but his leg caught on hers and suddenly she was falling too, the sky and the cobbles abruptly shifting their position in relation to her.

She hit hard on her right shoulder and arm and skidded over onto her back. The jolt knocked breath from her lungs, but she began to scramble up to her knees with an urgency borne of desperation. She still had one knife out, in her left hand, perhaps she could—

The Raider was on them. Barach had not managed to get back to his feet either, but he raised his long knife to ward off the blackstone axe that was already raised to cut down at him.

The Raider altered the angle of their blow, and the weapon took Barach where his neck joined his shoulder.

"*No!*" Tila screamed, as Barach howled in pain, and his

knife fell from his hands. He clawed at his killer, hands latching onto the shield, and pulled it down and to the side. Even with his life's blood leaking out, Barach was big and strong, and the Raider leaned backwards to try to drag the shield out of his grip. In doing so they raised their jaw, giving Tila an unprotected angle on their neck.

Grief and rage gripped Tila, but her fury had always been a cold thing. She saw her opening and took it, before tears could blur her vision. Her left hand was not her stronger one, but she had always had a good eye, and enough practice over the years that she was nearly as good with it as with her right. At this range, even from her knees, it was barely a challenge.

Her knife struck the Raider under the jaw, punching up into and through their mouth. The killer staggered backwards with a muffled cry of pain, hands flying to their face. Tila scrambled to Barach's side and grabbed for his knife, but it skittered away from her grasping fingers. She reached out again, managed to close her hand around it, raised it—

The Raider collapsed forwards. Tila brandished Barach's knife at the figure that had replaced them, but it was a Naridan man carrying a wood axe, with which he had just staved in the back of the Raider's head. His eyes were wide and panicked, but the Raider was no longer moving.

It was a woman, Tila noticed numbly as she wrenched her throwing knife free, since she had no idea how many she would need before this day was out. Not even a woman: a girl. Tall and long of limb, but even someone unfamiliar with Raider features could see the marks of youth in her now-slack face. What could drive this child over so many miles of ocean to fall upon the city of a foreign land?

"Lady Livnya?" the man with the axe blurted. "That's you, isn't it?"

Tila had to swallow before she could speak. "Yes." She

looked up at him, but did not recognise his face. "You know this lady?"

"Know of, p'raps," the man said. He seemed to have calmed slightly, although he still looked on edge, and Tila realised with a flash of alarm that he was calmer because he had recognised *her*. "Would have been a harder couple of weeks without your people making sure the bad sorts weren't taking what weren't theirs."

Tila ignored him. Barach was sprawled on his back, in a rapidly spreading pool of his own blood. She took his hand in hers, and now tears blurred her vision. Barach had not been loyal to her because of who her far-distant ancestor was. Perhaps some of it had been instilled in him by his own father, but when it came down to it, he had served and guarded her because he wanted to. They were not friends, as such, but then, Tila had no friends. She had never been able to trust anyone with the secret of her double life, save for her brother and, more recently, her mother. A friend had always been someone who might expose her, and thereby put her and, through her, the entire kingdom at risk.

Barach was possibly the closest thing she had to a friend, though, and so she held his hand, and cried as he died.

However, neither Livnya nor Tila could afford to waste time on personal grief; there was too much depending on them both. As Barach's last breath rasped out of him along with a final pulse of blood, Tila forced herself back to her feet and faced the loose semi-circle of worried faces that had gathered around her. Lowborn people; people who owed Tila Narida their obedience due to her birth, but who looked to Livnya the Knife as an unexpected source of order in these confusing times. The square was free of other Raiders for the moment, but that situation would not last.

She should try to get to the Sun Palace, and her brother, but what guarantee did she have that she could make it? Her body-guard was dead, and savages were loose in the streets. Natan was surrounded by guards, and behind the walls of one of the most formidable defensive structures in the known world. He would be safe without her, and her counsel would undoubt-edly be overridden by the Eastern Marshal in any case. Never mind the Veiled Shadow; as soon as she returned to the Sun Palace, she would be nothing more than a veiled afterthought.

Out here, however, she could potentially make a difference.

"The Raiders think they can rampage through the streets of our home unchecked!" she declared to those watching her. "This lady thinks otherwise! The garrison will turn out to send them back into the sea, but we can help! One of the main routes towards the palace is behind us, but if we hold these three streets," she said as she pointed to the three seaward entrances to the square, "the Raiders won't be able to use it, and our troops will have an unimpeded route out to aid us!"

"But lady, we're not fighters!" someone objected. Tila snarled, and kicked the dead Raider over onto her back.

"They're sending *children* at us!" she shouted, pointing downwards at the dead features, to shocked and increasingly angry murmurs. "The fear is as much their weapon as black-stone! Get barricades across the streets; use furniture from buildings, wagons, anything you can! Find whatever you can use as a weapon and be ready to fight for your homes! We are not," she added, picking up Barach's knife, "going to wait to be saved at the Hand of Heaven's convenience!"

That shocked some of them into taking a step back from her, and for a moment Tila wondered if she had gone too far. She might have her own opinions of the High Marshals, but to the lowborn they were only one step down from the God-King himself. If anyone was expecting some form of divine judge-ment to manifest itself, however, they were left waiting; and as the moments passed expressions began to shift from uneasy to determined. Then, without any overt signal or communication, the people gathered around her broke away and began to do her bidding, shouting at the others milling uncertainly in the square to join them.

Tila swung Barach's knife experimentally a couple of times. It was more like a short sword in her hands, and she had never had any training in how to use such a weapon, but at least it had a bit more reach than her throwing knives if an enemy got close enough to strike at her. It seemed that, perhaps not for the first time, Livnya was able to have much more of an immediate effect on Idramar than Tila.

All she had to do now was remain alive long enough for it to matter.

Marin

Marin had expected the journey to Godspire to be an easy one, simply following the Greenwater's course up into the mountains. Unfortunately, the Pilgrim's Road was nowhere near as well-maintained as he expected, and as the terrain grew higher and more rugged it had to take wide diversions to find passable ground.

"Pilgrimages aren't supposed to be easy," Ravi said, when he complained about it one evening, as they sat around their fire. "Otherwise it wouldn't be holy, I guess."

"S'man isn't sure that makes much sense," Bones commented. The young man had remained with their group more by default than anything else. Marin was not entirely happy about it, but given Tyrun Himself had stated that Bones was welcome, Marin did not want to be the person to tell the young man to go away. At least his story seemed genuine: he came west at the urging of Livnya the Knife to kill an imposter, but had now realised that Tyrun was no imposter, and so renounced that mission.

"It doesn't have to make sense if it's holy, either," Ravi said, with a smile. "Not to us." Bones was not the only one whose attitude had changed after the audience with Tyrun; Ravi was far more relaxed, as though a great weight had lifted from her shoulders. On the other hand, Marin had only seen her when they had both been imprisoned in Idramar, and when on the road to find Tyrun, which had not been a stress-free journey. It was perhaps not surprising if she seemed more at ease now.

"The journey would be quicker if we were with the army," Alazar pointed out. "The Godsworn aren't all soldiers, used to marching." Marin's husband nudged him in the ribs. "Or camp followers, used to keeping up."

The Godsworn: that was what Tyrun's followers had taken to calling themselves. They were a varied bunch of young and old alike, with most of their number unsurprisingly made up of the lowborn, but there were a few sars and even a couple of former thanes with the party. Marin had been surprised at that, given Tyrun's stated intention to abolish the hierarchy, but perhaps he had been overly harsh on Narida's ruling class. They allegedly held their station by the will of the Divine One, as enacted by generations of God-Kings: perhaps there really were a few who respected that will so much that they would give up their rank when it was demanded of them.

It probably helped that they were in the West, which had always cleaved a little closer to worship of the original Nari, rather than His descendants on their throne far to the east. They still venerated the sitting God-Kings here, of course, but it was in the West where Nari and the Seven Companions had finally brought down and cast out the Unmaker and her most wicked servants, within the caves of Godspire itself. That kind of thing left its mark on an area.

Of course, it was not universal. Laz was from White Hill, a small town not far from the Torgallen Pass, but he was rather more reserved in his devotion to Tyrun than the others in their small group. On the other hand, given Laz's history with God-Kings, Marin could hardly blame his husband for retaining a certain amount of scepticism.

"Speaking of the army," Aranel said, "s'man heard that Marshal Torgallen is mustering the Western Army." The old soldier prodded the fire with a stick, prompting a tongue of flame to curl upwards.

"To what purpose?" Marin asked.

"And where'd you hear that?" Gershan demanded. "We're nowhere near Torgallen!"

"We're not moving that fast, though," his brother Kenan pointed out. "There's still people joining the Godsworn; could've brought news from the south with them."

"And that must've been it," Aranel said, nodding at Kenan. "As to what purpose, those joining us don't seem to be in the High Marshal's close confidence," he added, prompting a snort of amusement from Ravi, "but rumour is he's planning to recognise Tyrun as the Divine One."

Marin raised his eyebrows. "That'd be a bold statement. Not to mention a recipe for war."

"War was inevitable," Laz said. "Look at the Splintering. The kingdom nearly tore itself apart over who was the true heir to the God-King's line. How much worse is it going to be when there's someone claiming to be Nari Himself setting up in opposition to the undisputed heir? Short of Natan stepping down voluntarily, this is going to end in blood."

"Well, that's why it's so important to get the blessing of the monks," Marin said. "Once they make their proclamation, the country will fall into line. With that and the Western Army, the God-King might be left with no choice."

"There are still three other great armies, if the marshals assemble them," Channa the Nose pointed out. "Who knows which way they'll lean?"

"This is going to end in blood," Laz repeated, staring into the fire, and he said little for the rest of that evening.

*

It took them a further week to reach Godspire, by which point the Greenwater had split and split again. The tributary they now followed was no larger or more impressive than a hundred others Marin had seen in his travels, and the valleys through which it flowed grew higher and more steeply sided. Now the river thundered and roared through gorges that dwarfed it, and yet the occasional huge boulders in its bed were silent testament to the power it possessed when swollen from storms or meltwater.

It was past midday, and Marin was being reminded once more why he disliked mountains. Quite apart from the sheer effort it took to climb through even the lower slopes, it was virtually impossible to remain a comfortable temperature. When the sun beat down, as it was doing now in the early Naridan summer, he sweated constantly: when it was hidden behind cloud, or they walked in the shadow cast by one of Godspire's lowlier neighbours, he felt the chill seeping into his bones. Coupled with a mischievous wind that seemed to delight in finding any gaps in his clothing, it was enough to make him uncomfortable without being bad enough to justify complaining: quite the worst of both worlds, to his mind.

He was pondering on the injustice of it, and wondering whether they were going to be able to find somewhere reasonably sheltered to make camp that night, when a shout went up from ahead.

"Are we there?" Bones asked eagerly. The weeks of travelling since leaving Northbank had gone a long way to toughen the young city boy up into something approaching a wilderness traveller, but there was little doubt in Marin's mind that Bones was just as excited by the prospect of not having to walk any farther as Marin was at the thought of finally seeing the sacred monastery.

"How should we know? None of us have made this trip

before," Channa said shortly. She had cut herself a walking staff from a branch, lower down the slopes when the path had run through thick woodland rather than mainly being composed of grey rock with the occasional stunted tree too stubborn to realise that it was out of its element, and was leaning on it now while she caught her breath.

"Only one way to find out," Laz said, forging ahead.

"Slow down, will you?" Marin complained, hurrying after his husband as best he could. "Your legs are longer!"

"They're not *that* much longer, Mar."

"Your husband doesn't think you realise how much difference it makes over this sort of ground!" Marin puffed, using his hands to lever himself up onto a rock. Laz had managed to step up onto it, but it was just that bit too high for Marin to manage the same.

"You're not getting old, are you?"

"Your husband would like to remind you that you have seen one more summer than he has, thank you very much!"

"Why are you complaining, then? It should be your husband's joints giving out, not yours!" Laz said without turning, and certainly without slowing.

"Because your husband is *shorter*, he has to take *more steps* to keep up with you," Marin grumbled. "He'd have thought that would be obvious, even to someone more familiar with a blade than with—" He stopped, as he scrambled up another slight rise in the ground, and the monastery came into view.

Marin was not really sure what he had been expecting: certainly something larger than the shrines to Nari that were in every village, which could be little more than an alcove with a carved figurine and whatever offerings the local people had made. Towns and cities had temples, in which priests would lead services on holidays, and perform marriage rituals and funeral rites, but Marin had not thought to see anything of that size this far up into the mountains. And in one respect, he was correct.

The monastery was far larger than any temple he had seen before; even the Grand Temple of Idramar.

It was almost a village in its own right, with fields of tilled earth in which crops were growing – and how painstaking a job that must be, given the thin mountain soil! – and outbuildings that were clearly barns for storing food, or sheltering animals. However, the main structure was a two-storey affair of wood, decorated with carvings and paintings, that sprawled across an area of mostly flat ground. Above it rose the flanks of Godspire itself – for here was one of the points where the King of Mountains clearly diverged from its neighbours – and behind it, Marin could just see the edges of the yawning cave into which Nari and the Seven Companions had ventured, all those centuries ago.

"How did they build that?" he asked, his mind returning to the practicalities of what he was looking at. "How did they get all that wood up here?" Unless of course the reason they had passed so few trees in the last few days was because they had all been felled to make the monastery and its attendant structures . . .

"Your husband supposes they didn't build it all at once," Laz suggested, which was a valid point.

"By the Mountain!" Aranel said, arriving at Marin's shoulder. "That's a fair sight, and no mistake."

"Come on," Marin said, pointing ahead to where the front-most members of the Godsworn were already making their way along the wide path that ran between the outer fields, and up to the monastery's main doors. "S'man wants to be there for this."

Distant figures of monks were coming to meet the new arrivals, some holding tools of labour and others empty-handed.

Marin could see Mordokel's bald head, and the white robes of Tyrun and his guards were easy to pick out in the crowd: young and healthy as He was, the Divine One and his escort had been at the forefront of every day's travel.

They hurried forward, even feet weary from weeks of walking suddenly more eager to move now they were on the verge not just of the end of their journey, but also a moment that would pass into legend. Marin could feel excitement bubbling up within him like a pot of water over a flame. This was what he had dreamed of when he had spoken to his fellow Cupbearers back in Idramar: no, this was more than he had dreamed of! The idea that he was going to be present when his reborn god was confirmed and acclaimed by the monks of Godspire! Marin could almost feel the curve of history stretching out in front of him, waiting to be shaped by events that would take place here . . . and also waiting to be recorded, to be set down for posterity by a man of learning who witnessed them firsthand.

Quite apart from anything else – quite apart from the joy of having been allowed into the presence of the Divine One, of hearing His voice and seeing His face, and playing some small part in His rise to His rightful position, all of which were things that Marin considered as proof that his life had been well spent – Marin was looking forward to returning to the University of Idramar and presenting them with his accounts of the days in the immediate aftermath of the Divine One announcing Himself. Why, they would practically *beg* him to return, *and* take up a position, and any lingering unpleasantness about thefts when he had been a student would undoubtedly be disregarded . . .

He was mulling such things over in his mind and wondering if the salary of such a position would be able to support both him and Laz – and what a relief it would be, not only to be the one providing the bulk of their income for once, but also to make sure that his husband no longer had to risk his life to earn a living! – by the time they caught up. Tyrun was proceeding at a measured, dignified pace, as befitted a deity approaching the place of His confirmation, and the monks bowed their heads in greeting as He passed. They did not drop to their knees, but Marin supposed that was understandable: these were the keepers of the most sacred place in Narida, after all, and even if Tyrun's divinity was obvious to anyone who stood in His presence, it had not yet been officially decreed. Acknowledging Tyrun as Nari reborn before that judgement had been passed would probably be seen as premature.

"Mordokel doesn't look happy," Laz murmured to him. Sure enough, Marin could see enough of the priest's face in profile to make out the disapproving scowl he cast at the monks they were passing.

"He rarely does," Marin replied. He saw some frowns among the faces greeting them, and added, "although a couple of the monks don't look happy with him, either."

"Maybe it's the sword," Laz suggested. "Your husband doesn't know too much about the practices of priests, but he's never seen one wearing a sword before, let alone a longblade." He paused. "What's the difference between a priest and a monk, anyway?"

"You spent all that time around the Divine Family, and never found out?" Marin asked, then hurried on before his husband could take offence at his teasing. "Priests bring the word of Nari to the world; monks shut themselves away from the world to consider it for themselves." He waggled a hand in the air. "There's more to it than that, but that's the basics."

"Your husband doesn't see how anyone can spend that long considering *anything*," Laz said.

"Well, you are a man of action, dear," Marin pointed out, and leaned up to kiss Laz on his bearded cheek.

Up close, the monastery was even more impressive, an impression heightened by the simplicity of the monks' robes and the rustic surroundings of the fields. Every beam and joint had been lovingly carved to an exact fit, and the plaster of its walls was a riot of frescos. Marin could see many themes he was familiar with, such as dragons and drakes, and the crowned sunburst of the God-King, but there were other depictions as well. The most prominent was easy to understand: seven figures surrounded by radiances, cunningly distinguished by subtle differences in the lines and widths thereof, next to a larger figure of even greater magnificence, bearing arms and armour that looked outdated even to Marin's inexpert eye for such things. Opposing them were dark, almost featureless figures, their proportions stretched and distorted as would be a shadow cast on a cave floor, and behind them loomed a massive feminine shape from which tendrils of darkness snaked out in all directions.

"The Unmaker," Marin muttered, instinctively making the sign of the Mountain over his breast. It was generally considered an ill omen to portray the Queen of Demons in such a detailed manner – most depictions simply used a blank mask, to represent her ability to take on whatever shape she chose, or even possess another and make them do her bidding – but perhaps the monks of Godspire had little reason to fear such omens, here on the site of her final defeat? He looked around, and noticed Ravi was staring up at the mural with an expression on her face that was not far short of fear. He did not ask why; trying to get anything more from her than she offered openly had not previously gone well.

More interestingly, Marin noticed that Tyrun was staring up at the paintings as well, as He came to a halt at the foot of the steps leading to its main doors. Was He trying to remember the nature of that battle? Attempting to recall the faces of His companions on that fateful day?

"State your business!" one of the monks stationed halfway up the steps cried. Tyrun did not immediately move or reply, and after a moment Mordokel stepped forward.

"Tyrun, the Divine One and Nari reborn, has come to receive the confirmation of the monks of Godspire," the priest said. His voice was loud and confident, and had Marin been him, he might have put just a little more humility into his tone. The monks did not seem to take any great offence, however.

"So be it," said the one who had previously spoken. "The judgement of Godspire will be passed. Let he who claims divinity come to us."

"Does 'judgement' have a slightly different sound to you than 'confirmation'?" Laz whispered. Marin nudged him in the ribs to quiet him, but he had also noted the discrepancy in language. So had Mordokel, if the set of the priest's shoulders was anything to go by.

Now Tyrun moved. He patted Mordokel on the shoulder as He passed him, then ascended the stairs to where the two monks waited. They bowed their heads to Him, and the one who had spoken raised his head again to address the Godsworn.

"The supplicant will present himself to the Council of Godspire," the monk proclaimed. "They will consider his words, and will pray to the spirit of Nari for guidance. A decision will not be reached in haste; lodging and food will be provided for as many of you as possible in the meantime."

"Food was getting short on the way up here," Channa muttered. "S'woman hopes they've got some spare in those barns."

Tyrun did not look back at His Godsworn. Marin watched Him ascend the rest of the way to the monastery's great doors, which opened for Him, admitted Him, and then shut behind Him, leaving the rest of them on the mountainside.

Stonejaw

The dragons came, soon enough.

Even battered by the sea as it had been, it was always too much to hope that the great Flatlander city would be unable to mount any defence. At first the broken clans were just chasing the locals through the streets — ruddy-faced folk, who fled before them like shore crabs skipping away from inrushing waves — but then horns began to sound. These were not the throaty throbs of shell horns, that called warriors to their chief or bid them charge, but brazen, metallic notes, echoing through the streets. Zheldu Stonejaw had heard them before, and she knew what they heralded.

"Dragons!" she bellowed to her crew, as though any could have forgotten what that sound meant. The fear she had thought was under control welled up and spilled out. Where were the monsters coming from? Where should she run? These damned Flatlander buildings were so *tall*, not like Tjakorshi longhouses which were half-sunk into the ground: she had no idea where she was in relation to anything else, including the sea. The only near-constant was the occasional sighting she got of the massive stone fortress on its hill, but even that was of limited use. She might be a mediocre sailor, but give her a featureless sea, a prevailing wind, and a feel for the currents, and she would still be far more at home than in this warren of stone.

"What's the problem?" someone jeered, and she turned to see a different band of Tjakorshi hurrying past. She recognised none of them, but one, a woman with a thick grey streak in her dark hair, was laughing at her and her crew as they stood frozen in the street. "What're you scared of?"

"You'll find out!" Stonejaw spat. There was an alley a short way up the gentle hill on which they were standing, and she pointed her crew towards it. "In there! That's too narrow for a dragon!"

She received no arguments. No one who had been a part of Rikkut Fireheart's war fleet wanted to come face to face with those monsters again, and thirty-odd Tjakorshi warriors packed themselves between close-set stone walls, heedless of the jeers of those left in the open. Stonejaw listened to the Flatlander horns coming closer, and waited.

Then the horns were replaced by screams.

There were only two warriors between Stonejaw and her end of the alley, and neither were as tall as her, so there was nothing blocking her view when the first panicking Tjakorshi fled past in complete disarray. Three had the presence of mind to duck into the alley, coming to a startled halt when they found her and her warriors just inside. One of them was the woman with the streak of grey in her hair.

"What are you—?" one of the newcomers began, and then the dragons thundered past.

Stonejaw only got a glimpse, due to the narrowness of the alley mouth and the speed at which the monsters were travelling, but that glimpse was a nightmare of horns, feathers and blood. One of the fleeing warriors was ridden down, crushed into the dirt almost within arm's reach of the entrance. Stonejaw saw the light leave his eyes a moment before a massive, blunt-clawed foot smashed his head into a pulpy mess. Then the dragons were past, leaving nothing but broken bodies in their wake.

"What the *fuck* are those?!" the grey-haired woman shrieked, backing as far as she could into the alley, until she was pressed up against the shields of Stonejaw's warriors.

"Dragons," Stonejaw told her shortly. She shouldered her way past and poked her head out. There were half-a-dozen dragons and their riders farther down the hill, driving the last few Tjakorshi before them, and for a moment she considered leading her warriors out: terrifying though the things were, they were obviously heavy and cumbersome creatures. The incline of the street was fairly slight, but still noticeable. Surely they could not charge as well up a hill as they could down it? Perhaps gaining the upper hand over them was simply a matter of positioning . . .

Then she looked uphill and saw the ranks of Flatlander warriors advancing in the dragons' wake, pausing to slit the throat of any Tjakorshi that had made it through the dragons' charge wounded but alive. There were at least as many as in her crew, and while she might have fancied their chances in a straight fight, she was not going to lead her warriors into combat with the dragons loose at their rear.

"That way!" she bellowed, ducking back into the shelter of the alley and pointing over heads towards the far end.

"What if there are dragons that way too?" someone shouted.

"Then we're no worse off!" Stonejaw replied. "Get moving!"

There were no further objections, and her crew began to head in the direction she indicated. The grey-streaked woman fell in beside Stonejaw, her face still pale from fear.

"You've fought those things before?"

"No," Stonejaw said. "I've run away from them before, and that's what I intend to keep doing for so long as I've got a choice in the matter."

The other woman exchanged a glance with her two remaining companions. "Reckon we'll stick with you, then. I'm

Ari Tumeszhastutar, this is Okoza Kyraszhin and Kuadan Gaptooth." The two men with her nodded in greeting.

"Zheldu Stonejaw."

"Stonejaw?" the man identified as Gaptooth repeated, who was the taller and broader of the two. "Didn't you go west with Rikkut Fireheart?" He was missing one of his incisors, which at least explained his name.

"Yeah, and what a fucking disaster *that* was," Stonejaw muttered. She caught their expressions. "Look, where do you think we ran into these things before? Fireheart got his head taken off by some girl of the Brown Eagle clan, and the dragons ran us down. We were lucky to get away."

"The Golden didn't say anything about there being monsters here," Ari complained.

"Oh, and you'd have refused to come if it had?" Okoza retorted, in a surprisingly deep voice for someone of his sparse build. Ari was saved from the need to reply by shouts from ahead.

"Sounds like we've found a new fight," Stonejaw said, gripping the handle of her axe. Now she just had to hope she had not sent her crew into a situation as bad as, or worse than, the one they had left behind.

The other end of the alley disgorged them into an open space floored with cobbles, one of the largest Stonejaw had yet seen between these Flatlander buildings. The streets on one side had been blocked off with barricades behind which lurked armed Flatlanders, but these were not the uniformed warriors from which Stonejaw had instructed her crew to retreat; they looked like the regular people of this place, who had taken up weapons. Also, although the barricades had obviously been set up to prevent a Tjakorshi advance, and in one place was doing just that, Stonejaw's crew had come out behind them: the three Flatlanders set to watch the alley mouth had clearly not expected this many Tjakorshi to emerge from it so quickly, judging by the fact they were already down on the ground bleeding out from high tide wounds inflicted by the first few of her warriors.

This was a fight that looked like it might be worth taking on.

"Into them!" she roared, waving her axe for emphasis, and her crew charged forwards with the sort of unified resolve found in warriors eager to prove they had not been craven mere moments ago, simply sensible. The Flatlanders had only just realised that they were outflanked, and the shocked faces turned towards Stonejaw's crew reflected both fear, and indecision about whether to fight or run.

At least, until one of the Flatlander women shouted something in their tongue and waved a large metal knife in Stonejaw's general direction. That hardened their resolve, and the defenders began to coalesce into something more organised.

It did not help them. They only had a few seconds before the Tjakorshi charge hit home, and it was always going to be a poor shieldwall with virtually nothing in it to serve as a shield. Stonejaw picked her target – a large man with a metal-headed axe – and headed straight for him. He raised his weapon to swing at her, but his timing was off, and she slammed into him before he had finished his downswing. The weapon's haft struck the rim of her shield and was jarred out of his hands to clatter to the ground somewhere behind her, and the force of her impact bowled him over. She had time to lash out to her right and lay open the back of another Flatlander, ripping through fabric and flesh to let the red blood flow, then stabbed downwards at the first man's throat. He raised his hands to try to catch her weapon or ward the blow off, but only succeeded in shredding his hands on the blackstone teeth: then her axe punched into his throat, and he was as good as dead.

Another man came at her, his dark hair shot with grey but

his limbs clearly still strong, wielding a metal sword with the air of one who had at least some idea of how to use it. Stonejaw had no room to move backwards now she was in the crush of the fight with the bodies of her warriors pressed up around her, so she raised her shield and took the hit on it. He was strong, but his blow did not trouble her; he managed to parry her return axe-swing, but her shield was as much a weapon as it was anything else, and she punched the edge of it into his face before he could strike at her again. He staggered back, off-balance, and this time her axe blow came down on his wrist. The blackstone's wicked edge sheared through flesh and bone to take off his sword hand, and then her return swing took his head most of the way off before he had even registered enough pain to start screaming.

Something flashed towards her, and she managed to get her shield up in time on pure reflex. There was a *thunk* of impact, and Stonejaw lowered it again to see the woman who had shouted the defenders into some sort of order glowering at her, and a metal dagger embedded in her shield. By the Dark Father, the woman could *throw* weapons with that sort of accuracy?

"That's the chief!" Stonejaw yelled, pointing with her axe, and was rewarded with an expression of fear on the woman's face as she was singled out. She looked unremarkable — dark-haired, like so many of these Flatlanders, and dressed no differently to many of their women — but something about her commanded respect and obedience from those around. If Stonejaw had learned anything from Rikkut Fireheart, it was that getting your axe to a chief's throat could end a fight much more quickly than otherwise.

Ari Tumeszhastutar was on Stonejaw's left and Zhazhken Aralaszhin on her right. The three of them pushed forwards out of the press of bodies, shields held high. The Flatlander chief whipped her hand downwards in their direction, and

Zhazhken cried out and fell as a dagger buried itself into the meat of his left thigh, but the defenders were in disarray now, and no one lunged in to attack Stonejaw from her unshielded side as she charged on. The chief backed away, and seemed to be about to turn and run, then realised that she had left it too late. Stonejaw recognised the screwed-up eyes and bared teeth before the woman had even swung her knife.

It was a slow and clumsy blow, and Stonejaw batted it out of the way with her shield while she brought her other arm around. She did not bother with her axe; she simply hammered her elbow into the Flatlander's jaw and knocked her sprawling. The knife tumbled from the chief's hand, and Stonejaw seized her by her hair to drag her back to her feet, then whirled around to show the other Flatlanders how the teeth of her axe were now pricking their chief's neck.

Stonejaw lacked the words to shout for them to yield, of course, but they got the idea. All around the square, Flatlanders caught sight of what had happened and paused in shock; the Tjakorshi, unwilling to perform the craven's act of striking down a foe who had yielded, held their blows. Slowly, peace of a sort descended, broken only by the moans of the injured.

"So now what?" Ari asked Stonejaw quietly. "They've stopped fighting. What do we do with them? Do you know how to talk to these people?"

"No," Stonejaw admitted. "The only man I know who does is with The Golden. But this woman seems important to them, so I guess we take her to the draug anyway."

"This place is huge," Ari countered. "How are you going to find it?"

Stonejaw snorted, and tugged on her captive's hair to turn her on the spot until they were both facing the huge building that overlooked the city.

"Oh, there's only going to be one place The Golden is going."

Daimon

They were just setting out from Black Keep, over two hundred people who were still relatively hale by the standards of those who had survived the full fury of the ravening sea, when a familiar sight caught Daimon's eye.

"Is that . . . ?" Saana asked from beside him. They were at the head of the column, as befitted their rank and so, as Saana put it, they could find the really slippery bits of ground and fall on their arses, so others did not have to.

"It is!" The dull, deadening weight of worry and responsibility did not lift from Daimon's chest, but it shifted a bit. "Our dragons!"

Four of them, trudging across the waterlogged fields back towards the only home they had ever known, and Daimon's own mount Silverthorn was in the lead. Daimon hurried ahead, heedless of the mud, until he was approaching them with one hand outstretched. To his utter delight, Silverthorn gave out the breathy huff that signified a greeting, and allowed Daimon to rub his nose and scratch the spot between his eyes, where his feathers were particularly small and fine.

"This man has no treats for you, he is afraid," Daimon told his mount ruefully, "but he is *very* glad to see you, you old lump." Rattler hissed dubiously around his ankles, but the huge dragons paid the little rattletail no mind at all.

"You speak to that animal as an equal?" Saana asked from behind him. Daimon laughed.

"There is no point calling oneself a lord of dragons. It would be a folly and a conceit, and easily disproved."

"Hmm." Saana did not seem entirely convinced, but Daimon could not fathom why. "What will we do with them? Send them back to the stables?"

Daimon reached over to rub Quill's nose: another reminder of Darel's absence, for Quill had been his brother's mount since they had both been children. "There seems little point, given their fodder was soaked and scattered. They would be better coming with us, where they can find their own grazing as we travel."

"And a mounted lord will be more impressive to Darkspur than one walking on his own feet?" Saana suggested.

"There is also that to consider," Daimon conceded. "We shall have to go back for saddles and harness, but given we now have draft animals to pull the wagons, with any luck our people will not resent the delay."

They did not, since although the party's provisions and supplies had been limited, transporting them was still a daunting prospect for anyone so tasked. With the other dragons yoked up, and Daimon and Saana mounted on Silverthorn's back, the people of Black Keep advanced into the Downwoods on the North Road.

The journey was not an easy one, especially at first. Many trees had stood firm against the flood, but many others had not. Some had come down across the road and needed a dragon or two to be unhitched from a wagon to drag them out of the way. The road itself, never well-maintained this far south, was still waterlogged and muddy, and in some cases dipped through places where stinking, brackish water lurked in pools. However, the damage became less severe as they pressed on north and west, and moved farther from the coastline, until all that remained was the lingering smell of salt on the air.

"We are lucky, your wife supposes," Saana said as they lay down next to their fire on the third night, and looked up at the shadowy, underlit canopy of green above them.

"Lucky? How do you conclude that?" Daimon asked. Beside him, Rattler shifted slightly against his ribs, and made the hissing noise of a young rattletail dreaming of whatever rattletails dreamed of.

"We are alive," Saana said simply. "The wave did not take us, as it took the men of Darkspur. And it is summer, so we can sleep out under the sky with less fear of cold."

"The wave did not take us, because you remembered the lore of your homeland from a children's rhyme," Daimon replied. "That is . . . " He paused. "Very well, your husband supposes that might be lucky, actually. But it is also because you were clever, and thought quickly, and trusted your own instincts."

"And you believed your wife, and our people believed her," Saana said. "And she will admit, that is not luck, but trust."

"It is strange to say, with our home flooded and damaged, and our people on the road to another thanedom where we hope to either threaten or persuade them into helping us," Daimon mused, "but yes, we are lucky, in that sense. It could have been far worse."

"Your wife has had more than enough of leaving her homes behind her," Saana said. "She hopes this time will not last for long."

"It will not," Daimon said firmly. "Unless the sea comes back and claims Black Keep for good, we will return there." He squinted up at what he could see of the darkened sky above them. "However, as to the weather, your husband can make no such guarantees. Summer it might be, but if we have no rain between here and Darkspur then your husband will concede that we truly are lucky."

That did not prove to be the case.

Dawn the next morning was a muted affair, at least in terms of the amount of light it brought with it. Daimon was woken by uneasy ripples running through the camp, and he knew from the moment his eyes could focus properly that something was amiss: the fact that it took him a while longer than usual to be certain his eyes *were* focusing properly was one of his main reasons for concern.

"Is this normal for Narida?" Saana asked, staring up at the sky.

"No," Daimon said, his throat tight with unease. "No, it is not."

The sun had been swallowed. Not by cloud, or at least not by any cloud Daimon had seen before. Instead of the fluffy whites, stern greys or angry purple-blacks he knew, the sky between the tree branches above him was a hazy gloom, through which the sun glowered like an angry orange eye. It cast a distorted, eerily shadowless light, which under the canopy of the Downwoods was little better than murk.

"You have no children's rhymes about this?" Daimon asked Saana, who shook her head.

"No. Does Narida?"

"No children's rhymes of which your husband is aware," Daimon said, "but the Foretellings of Tolkar make mention of the sun going out, or being dimmed . . . Your husband does not remember the detail, in truth. Darel would know." He sighed regretfully. While it was true that Darel would not have been able to do anything about the strange sky, Daimon sorely wished his brother was with him, and not just for his learning and calm-headedness. Quite simply, Daimon missed him bitterly, and would have welcomed any news from Idramar.

"Your wife has heard that mentioned before," Saana said. "She wonders why so many bad things have to happen before your god is reborn."

"It is not your husband's habit to question either gods or sorcerers," Daimon told her. He got to his feet and stretched, easing out a kink in his back. "We should move on quickly, before people have too much time to dwell on this."

The haze remained in the air, drenching everything in strange colours, but the rain Daimon had predicted came on the day before they reached Darkspur, as clouds caught up with them from the south in the afternoon. Even the rain itself seemed dirty, more like very wet mud, and soon Silverthorn's feathers were not just sodden, but filthy. The camp that night was a thoroughly miserable one, with few fires possible, and everyone shivering up against one another.

So it was that when Daimon and Saana led their people out of the Downwoods the next morning, and along the North Road up to the gates of Darkspur, no one was in the best of tempers.

The sky was more natural, at least. The rain, which was now letting up, had washed some of the haze away, but it just left the light feeling strange once more, after the dullness of the previous three days. Colours were watery and muddy to Daimon's eyes, and Darkspur squatted like a coiled viper beneath the great lump of rock from which it took its name.

"They do not seem happy to see us," Saana observed from behind him. The gates were closed, and Daimon could hear the bells of their shrine ringing in the same sort of alarm as Black Keep's had on the morning of the flood, or indeed when Darkspur's army had arrived outside the walls. For a moment he experienced a fierce surge of delight at the thought of the fear that might be running through the bodies on the other side of that wall; fear that all too recently had been inflicted on his people.

He fought it down. He doubted many within the walls had

come to Black Keep with violence in mind and made it back again. There were eight men of Darkspur he knew to have survived, and all were in the column behind him, having sworn a variety of oaths not to take up arms against Black Keep again, and to generally behave themselves. He was here to make an offer of peace, not to start a new fight.

"Wonder how these bastards like it," Nalon mused, from where he was walking level with Silverthorn's hind legs. For once, Daimon did not find his manner objectionable.

He halted them just out of bowshot of the walls, then went on with Saana, two of her Scarred, and Ita and Sagel, two of his original household guards. All of them wore armour of one sort of another, and so might have some chance of making it back to safety if the reception they received involved arrows. Most of his people had no such protection, and Daimon would not risk their lives to no purpose.

"Now we see if she was really a friend," Saana murmured to him as they rode forward on Silverthorn.

"More likely, we find out how bold Odem's castellan is," Daimon replied, not taking his eyes off the figures atop the Darkspur walls. "Remember, Sar Lahel told us that Sar Asad was left in command of the town, rather than Yarmina. Your husband does not know the man, but the description did not paint him as one likely to be a friend to us."

They were some thirty paces from the gates when the cry came to them: "Who comes?"

Daimon had been considering how he would respond the challenge, but now the time came he found himself in no mood for fine words, or even much diplomacy. Darel would have been better at that; he had always loved words more, and found them easier to work with.

"This lord will give you three guesses!" he shouted back sourly, to the hastily subdued amusement of Ita and Sagel.

The guards atop the gate did not seem to know how to respond to that. There could be no actual question who Daimon was: having come from the south with a small army at his back, and wearing the crest of Black Keep on his breast, there was at most a choice of two possible names. However, one was not supposed to respond to a guard's challenge with sarcasm, and the break in routine had thrown them. Daimon wondered if being around the Tjakorshi was rubbing off on him.

A few seconds passed in awkward silence before one of the guards tried again.

"What is your business at Darkspur?"

"We come to inform the Lady Yarmina of the death of her father Thane Odem, and the failure of his attempted siege of Black Keep," Daimon called, as loudly and clearly as he could. Let everyone hear him, and his words. They would bring grief to many, but how many of those would have shed tears at his death, or those of his town? Very few, he suspected. "This lord would speak with her."

His words had the expected effect. Shouts and cries went up, not just from the gate guards, but from those members of the town who had made it up onto the wall to see what was occurring. They were keeping away from the gate itself, in case arrows began to fly, but some were still close enough to hear him.

"You will do no such thing!" a new voice declared, and Daimon squinted upwards to try to make out who had spoken. There was a sar up there, although he had been standing behind guards until now. "This sar is Asad, castellan of Darkspur, and you may address him!"

"You were appointed castellan by Thane Odem?" Daimon called.

"Indeed."

"Then since Thane Odem is dead, your appointment is no longer valid, and this lord will not waste his time with you!" Daimon said. "Bring the Lady Yarmina forth. She and this lord parted on good terms mere weeks ago, and he does not hold her responsible for her father's actions."

"Your claims are ridiculous!" Asad shouted down. "What evidence do you have for them?"

"You mean besides the fact that we are here, despite Thane Odem marching to besiege us?" Daimon exclaimed incredulously. "What do you suppose happened, goodsar? Odem got lost and never reached us, and Black Keep decided to take a walk to come and tell you lies? That we agreed to exchange castles? *That* is ridiculous!" He took a breath, and got some control on his temper, which had nothing at all to do with Saana nudging him in the ribs. "Very well, you may speak to one of your own."

He raised his hand and waved it, and Sar Lahel came forward from where he had been lurking within the ranks of the column. He looked dejected and downcast, as well he might: he had surrendered his coat-of-nails, and was dressed in borrowed clothes. He reached Daimon's side and looked up wearily, then made a slight bow in the direction of the gate.

"Asad."

"Lahel?" Asad's voice was incredulous. "What is the meaning of this?"

"Lord Daimon speaks the truth," Lahel said, his voice flat and brittle. "A great wave swept up from the ocean and drowned nearly all of us, while the folk of Black Keep predicted its arrival and fled to higher ground to avoid it. This sar has seen Thane Odem's body. He is dead."

Asad did not respond, but neither did he move, nor give any orders. Daimon could almost see his mind whirling as he tried to work out how to respond to this situation.

"Did you not hear this sar, Asad?" Lahel called. "Our thane is dead! Lady Yarmina must be informed!"

"Whose interests do you serve, Lahel?" Asad demanded.

"The Darkspur family's!" Lahel retorted immediately. "As should you! This sar dislikes these facts as much as you, but our thane is dead, which means the Lady Yarmina now rules!"

Daimon was impressed, despite himself. Lahel was behaving exactly as Daimon would have wanted him to, without any instruction. Daimon would never have attempted to pressure the sar into saying anything other than the truth, but clearly Lahel had no wish to linger outside the gates of his home, while Asad appeared to be minded to ensure that happened.

There was unrest on the walls, as well. Asad's position as castellan gave him authority concerning the defence of the town, but not to prevent news from reaching his lady. Daimon saw Asad turn and begin to speak to the guard next to him in a voice far too low for Daimon to hear what was being said, but then a new figure emerged above the line of the parapet.

"This lady came as quickly as she could," Yarmina Darkspur declared, shading her eyes as she looked down at them. "Lord Daimon? Lady Saana? What is going on?"

"Finally, someone notices your wife," Saana muttered, from behind Daimon.

"Here we go," Daimon said quietly. He and Saana slid off Silverthorn's back, although Saana hissed in quiet pain as she landed on the leg that Rikkut Fireheart had cut open, and which still gave her pain. Then he, Saana, and their four guards – even the Tjakorshi – all bowed in Yarmina's direction.

Daimon had planned this for as soon as Yarmina appeared, assuming that she did so. It was in Black Keep's interests to make it very clear to everyone that so far as they were concerned, Yarmina was the authority in Darkspur. If the potentially hostile force on your doorstep was only inclined to listen to one person, it made sense for the people behind the walls to also listen to that person.

"Lady Yarmina," Daimon called when he straightened up again. "This lord comes with grave tidings regarding your father, and the siege on Black Keep."

"Given your presence," Yarmina replied, her voice wobbling a little, "this lady can guess what has occurred."

"The broad details, perhaps," Daimon said, "but your father did not die at the hand of any warrior of Black Keep. The sea rose and drowned many, your father included, as Sar Lahel here just confirmed. The people of Black Keep were forewarned by the knowledge of Lady Saana."

Daimon could just make out Yarmina's head nodding slightly, as she digested his words. "And do you bring war to us, as this lady's father sought to bring to you?"

Even in the circumstances, Daimon recognised the connotations of that statement. Not "Darkspur", not "we", but "this lady's father". Yarmina had just hastily distanced herself and everyone standing behind her from the attack, but also from Thane Odem. Which was only sensible, given what she was looking down at; and who could watch their father the thane head off to war without considering what might happen should he fail and fall there? All the same, it was calculating, bordering on cold.

Careful, Daimon. Yarmina is not to be underestimated.

"No, lady," Daimon said. "Black Keep comes with a proposition. We have lost many of our fields to the great wave, and you have lost many of your farmers. The harvest and winter could be a harsh time for both of us, but we will work with you on your land in exchange for a share of the produce. Times may still be lean, but better for both of us than otherwise."

Especially since, as it stands, we are out here where your crops are, and you are in there. He did not add that sentence, in the interests of diplomacy, but it would be in everyone's minds anyway.

"Open the gates," Yarmina called. "Lord Daimon and Lady Saana may enter, along with any companions they may choose. Clearly we have much to discuss." She turned away and disappeared immediately, leaving Sar Asad with no chance to object even if he had been intending to. It took several seconds, but then the noise of bars being withdrawn reached Daimon's ears, and Darkspur's gates were pulled open.

"And now we go in?" Saana asked him.

"Yes," Daimon replied. "And *now* we find out if she was really a friend."

Marin

The Godsworn had descended on the monastery, and the valley had become one giant camp. However, what had been appropriate shelter for the river valleys was not going to be sufficient for the lower slopes of Godspire, and the few tents brought along by former thanes and sars were in high demand. The monks' haylofts were quickly filled, and then overcrowded as it became clear that the monastery itself, with its sturdy walls and well-fitted shutters, was not going to be opened up. Even sheltered spots out of the wind became worth fighting for, and Tyrun's guards, as well as anyone else suitably large or threatening that Mordokel could rope in, had to make sure that the weak were not left out to suffer. The few stunted trees nearby were quickly scavenged for fuel, although the whipping wind meant that keeping night fires lit was hard enough, even without the additional problem of sparks being suddenly blown up into the faces of those sitting around them.

Quite apart from the cold and the wind, however, one of the worst things about mountains, in Marin's opinion, was that there was nothing to *do*.

At first, he hoped to be admitted to the monastery to study whatever texts or relics they possessed, but quickly realised that this was not going to be possible. The monks were polite, but quite adamant: the monastery's interior was no more open to travelling scholars than it was to shivering pilgrims, especially under circumstances when the divinity of a supplicant was being deliberated. Marin's connections in Idramar or his identity as a Cupbearer meant nothing to them, and he was left to idly wander the outside of the building, examining the murals and trying to ignore the way the wind whipped at his clothes.

Another source of frustration was that so few of his current companions knew anything about Nari's history. Oh, every member of the Godsworn had heard of the Seven Companions, and the Unmaker, and so on, but few seemed to grasp the *detail* of the legends. None had heard of the binding oath recited by Nari and His followers before they plunged into the depths of the cave to vanquish the evil within; few had any idea of the Foretellings of Tolkar beyond the most basic, well-known parts, and even those were sometimes misquoted.

So it was that in the late afternoon of the third day, when Laz had taken up his blades and headed off with a sigh to help maintain order and ensure a fair and just allocation of sleeping places in accordance with need, Marin went in search of the Pool of Tears alone.

The weather was bright and sunny, which at least meant his fingers did not get chilled as he clambered up the narrow defile to the north of the main valley. One of the monks, an agreeable fellow named Danaran, had pointed Marin in this general direction, but it was still going to be a case of trial and error. He had already promised himself that he would turn back before it got too late, since the last thing he wanted was to be stumbling around in the dark, and perhaps twisting an ankle. Ravi had been busy enough dealing with the various complaints prevalent in a camp of this size, and was hardly going to take kindly to Marin injuring himself, no matter how holy the location in which he had done it.

As was so often the case in the mountains, it was not

immediately obvious what was a path, such as might be used by the monks, and what was an occasional water course. Marin followed what seemed like the best route until he reached the top of a rise, whereupon he found himself looking down into a small depression – at least in the scale of the mountains – in which lay a pool of water. The pool itself was perhaps a stone's throw across, and a large boulder that was the height of at least two men, and the width of five with their arms outstretched, rested at the end nearest to him.

This was it. Despite never having been here before, Marin recognised it from the descriptions given in the writings of Gemar Far Garadh. This was where Nari bathed the bodies of those He lost in the fight against the Unmaker, weeping over them as He did so. That boulder was the Stone of Sorrow, upon which the first God-King stood to address his followers in the aftermath of that conflict, and finally accepted His divinity. Marin picked his way down the slope, being careful not to dislodge stones and risk slipping, despite his eagerness to get to the bottom. Once there, he advanced cautiously. It almost felt as though this place would somehow disappear from his view, like a mirage receding before a traveller in the hot, arid lands of the north.

The pool was a deep blue, reflecting the near-cloudless sky above him. Despite being nothing more than water collected in a hollow in the ground, it was one of the most beautiful things Marin had ever seen. Perhaps it was simply because he knew what it was, and what it represented: a glance back into history, a place where his god had walked. Perhaps it was that, well-travelled although he was, and despite growing up with the ocean on his doorstep, Marin was still a city-dweller at heart. He would not have wanted to spend the night here in this lonely place, but the ability to be here now and still go back to join Laz in a comparatively warm hayloft – since his husband's usefulness had once more afforded them better lodgings than some – gave it a greater aesthetic appeal.

He reached the bank, knelt down, and scooped some water up in the palm of his hand. It had been a stiff climb in the sun, and he was a little thirsty.

The surface of the pool erupted upwards as something surfaced in front of him.

"*Shit!*"

Marin tried to scramble away, but his weight was leaning out over the water and although his legs propelled him upwards well enough, they failed to manage moving him backwards. He windmilled his arms frantically, overbalanced, and fell headlong into the water.

What had been refreshingly cool in his hand was oppressively cold as soon as it engulfed him, and his panicked yelp as he went under served no purpose other than to give him an unexpected and unwelcome mouthful of water. He tried to cough, and choked on more water, but his legs had apparently retained their senses in a way that his mouth had not, since they got themselves under him and found purchase on the pool's bottom, which was not that far away. Marin lurched upright again, and this time his footing was steady enough that although he staggered once his head and upper body breached the surface, he did not fall. Instead he bent nearly double, wracked with coughs as water streamed out of his nose and mouth and, in the form of tears, from his eyes.

"What the *fuck* do you think you're doing?!"

The shriek came from his right and he whirled, his vision still blurred by water and the refractions of the afternoon sun that were glistening through it. His fingers found the hilt of his dagger.

"Marin?!"

The voice was familiar, both in its tone and timbre, and the note of disbelieving scorn it held. Marin shook his head and swiped his hand across his face to clear his eyes somewhat, and was rewarded with a clear view of what it was that had breached the surface of the water and startled him into falling in the first place.

Ravi.

She, like him, was standing up in the pool with water streaming down from her hair. However, unlike him, who had fallen in with all his clothes on, Ravi was naked: at least from what Marin could see of her, which was the belly button upwards. It had been many years since Marin had seen a woman without her clothes on; he had not been particularly interested in the prospect then and had not developed any greater interest in the meantime, so it was not the shape of her breasts or the curve of her belly that made him stare like a fool. Nor was it the desperate, burning embarrassment that swept across him at the thought she might think he had sneaked up on her with the intention of seeing her undressed, when in fact he had no idea she would be here.

Ravi seemed to realise what he was looking at just as he opened his mouth, because she let out a yelp of alarm and ducked down so only her head remained above the water. She was too late, however.

"Your tattoos!" Marin blurted out, pointing at her. He had only seen the very tops of them before; a thick, dark mark that had crept above the neckline of her dress when they had been in neighbouring cells in the Idramar jail. Now, however, he had seen how they stretched and flowed all the way across her body, down her chest and across her stomach, down her upper arms to her elbows, and down to her hips and beyond, below the surface of the water.

"Marin," Ravi said, warningly. The tone of her voice was so sharp it could have cut the breeze, but Marin paid it no heed.

"S'man *knows* those marks," he stammered, uttering the words without thinking of the danger. He should have apologised, turned around, and left. He should have kept his understanding of what he had seen to himself, at least until he was well away from Ravi and surrounded by others.

Suddenly, a lot of things made a lot of sense.

"You don't know what you're talking about," Ravi said. "You said yourself, in that tavern in Northbank: lots of people have tattoos."

Her words came too quickly, and her eyes were too wide. Even Marin, his mind still racing from what he had seen, recognised the fear in her. He reacted by giving voice to his own.

"*Witch*."

"*No!*" Ravi screamed, bursting out of the water again and wading towards him. Marin tried to turn and make for the dry ground behind him, but his feet slipped in the mud and he went over again. He managed to reach out and grab the bank with one hand to prevent himself from taking another complete ducking, but he could feel the waves of water as Ravi closed on him, ready to drag him under and drown him now her secret had been revealed . . .

"S'woman is not a witch!" Ravi yelled at him, as her hands closed on his shoulders. "She's *not*! She can't be! The Divine One welcomed her! He said her heart is pure enough, just as much as yours is! You were there; you heard Him!" She spun him around to face her, the desperate panic in her voice reflected on her face. Tears were welling at the corners of her eyes, distinct from the droplets of water that still clung to her from where she had been submerged.

"Then why do you have the marks on your body?" Marin demanded, too terrified of what was happening to do anything except scream back at her. He had read widely within the library of Idramar's university when he had still been welcome on its campus, and he could still remember the nature of the runes that were supposed to have meaning to those who worshipped the Unmaker. Many were inscribed on Ravi's body in dark ink, connected to each other with sweeping lines that formed a web. In any other context, it would have been beautiful.

"Look at them, Marin!" Ravi shouted. She backed off a step, releasing him and spreading her arms. "Look at them! Do they look new to you?"

It took a moment for the meaning of her words to filter through Marin's fear, and another few moments after that for his eyes to catch up and register what he was looking at, but his mind was still capable of piecing things together even when he was scared.

"No," he admitted cautiously. Ravi was right; her tattoos did not have the fresh darkness of new ink. They were faded, as though they had been done many years before. But Ravi herself was not old; if he had to guess, Marin would have put her at younger than thirty summers, perhaps by several years. What was more, they looked warped and stretched, as though . . .

"Nari's blood!" he swore, as realisation somewhat belatedly dawned. "They were done when you were a *child*?"

"S'woman's family worshipped . . . " Ravi paused, her mouth twisting in distaste. "*Her.* The old faith of the witches, preserved in secret under the nose of the priests and the thanes. S'woman's parents swore their daughter to Her when she was young; wrote Her symbols into s'woman's flesh to mark her, and bind her soul."

Marin pushed himself upright until the bank was against the back of his legs. Ravi no longer seemed overtly threatening, but she had just confessed to having her soul bound to the Unmaker! How could she not be dangerous?

"What happened?" he asked, stalling for time as much as anything else, while his mind raced through possibilities. Should he draw his knife? But were witches not meant to be immune to steel, which was why Nari had decreed fire as their punishment? Had Ravi immersed herself to be more difficult to burn? No, that made no sense; she could hardly traipse around dripping wet all the time, and in any case, why should she fear discovery now, when she had managed to conceal her true nature from the rest of the Godsworn for so long?

"S'woman's aunt got her out," Ravi said, dropping her hands to her sides and letting them splash into the water. "Stole her away from her parents. We both escaped, and s'woman's aunt taught her the arts of healing. S'woman doesn't even know what happened to the rest of her family; they could be alive still, or discovered and burned. She doesn't know and doesn't care."

Marin bit his lip. "And your aunt?"

"Do you remember when we spoke in the jail, Marin of Idramar?" Ravi asked softly. "When s'woman asked you if you'd ever seen what they do to witches, out in the country?"

Marin nodded. He remembered.

"S'woman's aunt was burned by people she was trying to help," Ravi said bitterly. "'Witch', they called an innocent healer, not knowing what s'woman was. That would have been ten winters ago, now. They never knew s'woman was with her, but s'woman had to watch the burning lest she be marked out as different, and she could not afford that."

Marin swallowed. "So when you asked s'man if he'd ever been scared of something his whole life, and then found out that he'd not needed to be . . . "

Ravi nodded, but her expression was bitter. "All s'woman's life, she's feared that her soul's lost. That her heart's damned, and already sworn to . . . *Her*. And then the Divine One says

that's not the case. That s'woman's heart is pure. That *this* . . . "
She gestured at the lines on her flesh. " . . . achieved nothing.
They got it wrong, or, or the years broke its power, or . . . "

"And you decided to bathe in the Pool of Tears . . . Why?"
Marin asked. "For good measure?"

Ravi shook her head wearily, and shrugged. "Something like
that. The legends say Nari washed the bodies of His followers
here to free their spirits of any taint left by Her after the battle.
Perhaps it's just another mark of s'woman's unworthiness that
she struggled to believe in herself, even when the Divine One
said it. She thought perhaps bathing here would help further,
somehow." She laughed bitterly. "Instead it's merely revealed
her secret. Because Marin of fucking Idramar decided to take
a walk at the wrong fucking time."

"Marin of fucking Idramar is cold," Marin told her,
honestly. His legs were bleeding warmth into the water, and
the wind was cutting through the wet garments on his top half
like a knife. "All he wants to do is get out of this pool and find
some way to get dry before he catches his death."

"And then what?" Ravi asked suspiciously. She was shivering too, Marin could see, which surprised him not at all. Still,
at least she presumably had dry clothes near to hand; probably tucked under the Stone of Sorrow, away from the eyes of
anyone approaching the way he had come.

"And then find some supper," Marin said. He spread his
hands in what he hoped was an appeasing manner. "You've
treated any number of people, including patching s'man's
hand up when he cut it open, so if you've bad intentions, you
hide them well. And the Divine One said your heart is at least
as pure as s'man's, which might not be much of a claim," he
added, "but it means s'man can hardly judge you. This stays
between us. It certainly doesn't need someone like Mordokel
finding out about it."

Ravi's expression clearly suggested that she did not believe him; perhaps she did not think she could afford to. Marin sighed and levered himself up onto the bank as best he could, given that all of his limbs were beginning to have other ideas about responding as he wanted them to.

"Come on. Let's go back. Or you can go back in your own time if you want, but s'man's going now, before he freezes to death." He looked up at the sun, which was dipping very close to the horizon, high as that was up here with the mightiest peaks of the Catseyes crowding in around him. It was warm at the moment, but he had a bad feeling about the shadows he would encounter on the way down.

"Wait," Ravi said, wading towards the Stone of Sorrow. "Let s'woman dry herself, and she'll walk back with you. You'll probably only fall over and hurt yourself otherwise."

Darel

Darel had never felt the same level of sick anxiety and fear as when hurrying through the Sun Palace trying to organise the God-King's departure. Even when he had been watching the pirates approach from the deck of the *Silver Tide*, he could at least see what was going on, and had some idea of when pursuit was going to turn into combat. Within the walls of the palace he could see nothing, and knew nothing of whether the Tjakorshi ships had made landfall, of whether their warriors were being held back or were rampaging through the city, or even if they were in a position to threaten the palace itself.

They did not wait for the other members of the Inner Council. Darel shouted warnings to everyone they encountered as he and Natan descended from Eight Winds Tower, and servants ran off to find and inform who they would. Adan Greenbrook was Eastern Marshal, and so had overall command of all of Narida's armies, including the garrison stationed within the Sun Palace. He could oversee the city's defence himself, or flee and delegate it to a lesser officer. Darel had no intention of delaying to find out, and nor did Natan.

"Is there danger of pursuit on the road?" the God-King asked as they reached the level of the palace in which his chambers sat.

"Your servant doubts it," Darel said. "The Tjakorshi do not have any mounts of which he is aware, and fear dragons until they come to know them. The danger will be if their ships push upriver and can cut us off, but they are more likely to concentrate on the city, as the largest potential site for plunder."

"Tell this king truly, Darel," Natan said, taking hold of his sleeve. "You know these savages best. Do you think they come in this number simply to plunder and depart once more?"

Darel shook his head helplessly. "Your servant cannot say, Your Majesty, but he fears otherwise."

Natan nodded, as though he had expected as much. "Get whatever you need, and meet this king at the stables as soon as you may," he instructed, then ran off towards his chambers as fast as his robes would allow him.

Darel had been moved to more spacious and luxurious chambers since his advancement to the rank of Southern Marshal, which were also considerably closer to those of the Divine Family. They contained a number of items that had previously belonged to, or at least been used by, his predecessor Kaldur Brightwater: more importantly, at least to Darel, he found when he arrived that they also contained Hiran Threestone.

"Darel!" Hiran exclaimed, getting up from the chair in which he had been sitting. "Pardon the intrusion, but your friend heard the commotion and—"

"You have no need to seek you friend's pardon, and we have no time," Darel cut him off, hastily kissing him on the cheek to take any sting out of the words. "The Tjakorshi are here, Hiran: not the Brown Eagle clan, but others, many of them. We must flee the city now, before they overrun it. His Divine Majesty is meeting us at the stables."

"'Us'?" Hiran echoed.

"You may stay, of course," Darel conceded, unbuckling his

sword belt and slipping out of his robe to reach for his armour on its stand, "but your friend had intended to find you and beg you to come with him."

Hiran hesitated, and for an awful moment Darel feared he was going to declare that his duty was to stay and defend the city. It was a nonsense, of course: Hiran was no warrior, and was well aware of that fact, but the possibility tore at Darel's heart until Hiran nodded.

"Of course! But your friend cannot leave Yae behind. Let him find his sister?"

"Please do," Darel said, sliding his right arm into his coat-of-nails. He liked Yae Threestone, in any case, and she and Hiran were close. "But be quick! Your friend will try to hold them for you, but if the God-King commands us to leave, he will not be able to prevent it."

"We will meet you at the stables," Hiran said, and planted his own kiss on Darel's cheek before bolting for the door. Darel hastily fastened his armour up the front and rebuckled his sword belt, then donned his helmet. He felt like a fool, dressing for war in the middle of the Sun Palace, but it was better to feel a fool than feel a blade. If they were attacked as soon as they made it out of the gate, the Tjakorshi were hardly going to wait for him to be appropriately attired.

He reached for his gauntlets, then paused. Even though he was a sar, a thane, and now a marshal, Darel was at heart just as much a scholar as Hiran, and he could not bear the thought of more knowledge being lost in the wake of the destruction of much of the university. He had no time to pack a trunk, nor any servants near at hand to carry such a thing for him, but he had two large satchels which he hastily filled with his recently discarded robe and another spare, and then the most treasured of the books and scrolls he had brought with him, or obtained since arriving in Idramar. Finally, he folded up the large map of

Narida that had been laid out on his desk and added that, then pulled on his cumbersome gauntlets and headed for the stables.

Darel had worried, in a corner of his mind he tried to ignore, whether Natan might dawdle: if the God-King might underestimate the danger once Darel was no longer there to prompt him, or fuss over having exactly what he wanted brought with him. Instead Darel found to his delight that Natan was at the stables before him, with two servants and a guard of eight soldiers, and the little he had brought in the way of possessions already being loaded into the luggage compartment of the royal coach. Four imposing spirehorn dragons had been harnessed to the front of it and were hooting gently at the hubbub going on around them. Behind them, two other coaches were being hastily prepared.

"Word has been sent to Marshal Greenbrook?" the God-King was demanding of a terrified-looking servant standing nearby.

"Yes, Your Majesty!" the servant assured him, bowing low. "This servant does not know where he is, but—"

"Greenbrook's safety is quite literally his own concern." Natan cut him off with a wave of his hand. "Now stay or flee, whichever you think better. Darel!" he added, turning, while the servant bowed again to his back, then bolted away. "You have everything you need?"

"Everything your servant felt it wise to bring," Darel confirmed. He handed his satchels to one of the remaining servants, who added it to the luggage compartment, and with that action done Darel felt anxiety spread through him again, like insects swarming across his skin. The sensation had been lessened when he had been doing something – going to his chambers, packing, hurrying to the stables – because those were necessary tasks he had been completing as fast as he could. Now he had nothing to do except wait and worry.

Hiran and Yae arrived next, with Yae's maidservant in tow;

a stout woman named Elva, with forearms the size of Darel's biceps. Finally, Hada Narida the Queen Mother arrived, grey-haired and beautiful, and also out of breath and panicking.

"Natan!" she gasped as she was ushered out of the stairwell by a sar whom Darel did not recognise. "What is happening?"

"Raiders, Mother," the God-King said, as calmly as though an invading war fleet was an everyday occurrence. "A lot of them. We are leaving the city for now, until we can be sure it is safe."

"Raiders?!" Queen Hada gasped, looking around desperately, and giving Darel the momentary impression that she thought they were going to be set upon at any moment. "Tila! Where is Tila?"

Natan grimaced, and stepped in close to his mother to speak quietly into her ear. Hada pulled back, her expression one of shock.

"You cannot mean—"

"Yes, Mother," Natan said quickly, cutting her off. "Now please get into the coach, else your son will have to command Sar Ravel to force you."

Queen Hada's eyes widened further, but she clearly saw no sign of either jest or insincerity in her son's face, because she turned and climbed into the coach beside her without any other argument: which was just as well, since judging by what Darel could see of Sar Ravel's alarmed expression above his war mask, he was in no hurry to obey any such order.

"You four, and you, ride with the Queen Mother and Sar Ravel, and ensure she comes to no harm," Natan instructed half of his guards and one of his two servants, who bowed and rushed to obey. "Driver! If we are attacked upon the road, your king commands you to get his mother to safety without concern for him. Is that clear?"

"Yes, Your Majesty," the driver of Queen Hada's coach

replied, with a startled bow from the waist where he sat at the reins.

"Good," Natan said briskly, turning back to his own coach and stopping in surprise. "By the Mountain, what are you all standing there for? Get in!"

"We are to ride with you, Your Majesty?" Hiran asked, astounded.

"Unless you wish to walk," Natan snapped. He had his father's longblade on his belt again, Darel noticed, and although he had no real idea whether the God-King knew how to use the blade, its very presence gave him a more commanding air: an air which Darel and the Threestones obeyed, scrambling into the coach before Natan followed them.

The interior was richly upholstered in red velvet and polished dark wood, and Darel got the sudden impression that this one carriage might be considered as valuable as all of his family's possessions within their castle. The recurring worry of the great wave stabbed at him then, and he wondered anew whether his home still stood and his town had survived, but then he was moving over to make room for Natan, and the dangers of his current situation reasserted themselves in his mind. Daimon and Saana between them would have as good a hope as anyone of ensuring Black Keep's safety. Darel's responsibility now was to do the same for his monarch.

"Drive on the West Road until you are told otherwise!" Natan shouted up at the driver as he climbed in, followed by Elva and the other servant. There was a whistle and a crack of reins from outside, and the carriage lurched into motion as the spirehorns were goaded forwards.

"What is our destination, Your Majesty?" Hiran asked anxiously.

"Your king honestly had not got that far," Natan admitted, settling back into the seat beside Darel. On his other side, the servant — a young man with a spot-flecked complexion, and hair that compared unfavourably to a haystack in terms of general tidiness — shrank against the carriage wall in an attempt to make himself as unobtrusive as possible, and not to touch his king in any way. "Marshal Blackcreek was so eager to get away from Idramar that a destination seemed a secondary consideration."

Darel tried to calm his thoughts as they rattled over the flagstones of the Sun Palace's courtyard. He could hear shouts through the carriage windows and caught glimpses of liveried soldiers rushing back and forth: clearly someone had issued orders concerning the defence of the city, judging by the hastily assembling ranks.

"The Raiders may not stop here," he said, working it through in his head as he spoke. "When they attacked our coasts in the South they always struck and withdrew quickly, before any meaningful forces could be brought to bear. However, there were so many ships approaching here, and we have been so damaged by the wave . . . If they choose to stay and fortify, or even push on inland, it may be some time before we can bring a force of any meaningful size against them."

"They will find little enough food in Idramar, too," Hiran pointed out. "If they do not wish to starve, they may be forced to take more territory."

"So Your Majesty should withdraw to a secure location, far enough from Idramar not to be in immediate danger of further attacks," Darel said to Natan, fighting down the momentary dizziness brought on by giving strategy advice to the God-King, when a few months ago he had been merely the oldest son of a minor southern thane. "You will need somewhere close to major routes, so you can send and receive news, and inland far enough that its lands were not themselves damaged by the wave. Perhaps we could head north . . . "

"No." Natan shook his head. "We must go west in any case, but to go north and west puts us closer to the lands of Einan Coldbeck. He has not yet been apprehended, and that mess at Northbank was not well-handed by Lord Goldtree. We should cross the Idra, when possible to do so, and head south instead."

"Then this woman knows where Your Majesty should go," Yae spoke up. Hiran turned to his sister with a grimace.

"Yae, no, that is not—"

"It is a large castle, sufficient for his majesty's needs, and well-fortified." Yae cut her brother off crisply. "It stands on the Great South Road less than a week's ride away, and word can easily be sent on farther south and west. Its lands remain undamaged, and its lord is loyal to King Natan, not any other pretender. It is the obvious choice."

"Lady Yae?" Natan's voice indicated that he suspected there was something that was not being said. "Of where do you speak?"

"Threestones Castle, Your Majesty," Yae said, and had Darel not come to know her a little, and had not known the bad blood that existed between both siblings and their father, he might well have missed the slight shake in her breath, or the tightness at the corner of her eyes. "Our home."

PART TWO

Jeya

W hat's the difference between a city and a fight? Ngaiyu had
asked Jeya once. *Three missed meals and an insult.* Jeya,
who had missed more than hér share of three meals in a row
during hér life, had not really given the saying much thought
since, but shé thought shé now understood what Ngaiyu had
been getting at. Individuals went hungry in cities all the time:
that was nothing new or remarkable. What Ngaiyu had meant
was when the *city itself* went hungry; and in the aftermath of
the great wave, East Harbour began to experience hunger pangs.

Jeya knew, in a hazy, roundabout way, that farmers grew
food farther inland, although shé'd never been there to see.
Shé had lived all hér life in East Harbour, and had never considered leaving it. Why would shé? Shé didn't know anyone
outside its boundaries: fewer people meant less opportunity
for the sort of hand-to-mouth thievery that had kept hér
alive for so long, and there were many alarming stories of the
things country folk did to people from the cities: ranging from
robbery – less of a direct concern, since Jeya had little worth
stealing, although they would not know that before they tried
it – to cooking and eating them, which seemed unlikely, but
probably not worth the risk.

In the days immediately after the great flood, though, Jeya
quickly came to realise how much of the food on which East

Harbour depended arrived by sea. Shé heard stories of ships in the channels between the islands being swamped as the unnatural swell was forced between comparatively narrow gaps; of ports less well-protected than East Harbour's being devastated by waves that smashed everything in their path; of lives, and even entire towns lost. Many of the ships that had been sailing for East Harbour, or the City of Islands in general, were never going to arrive. Those that did found their cargos were in very high demand.

Three days after the flood had come and gone, Jeya and Bulang were on the waterfront. The Narrows had been ruined by the wave, and the remnants of its buildings — and, more grimly, its occupants — were still washing up. Those bodies that made it to shore needed to be dealt with, and both of them had seen enough death by now that the recovery work was little more than unpleasant, like having one's heart permanently immersed in a flow of greasy water.

Jeya was reaching out with a hookpole when shé noticed the huge ship crossing the harbour towards hér. It was one of the first shé'd seen since the disaster, and certainly the largest: an ocean-going trader, which had presumably been far enough from land that the great wave had not greatly troubled it. Cheers rang out as it glided in towards the quay, thrusting aside the detritus that bobbed on the harbour waves.

The cheers faded, however, as the ship approached. Jeya looked around, ignoring the sad shape still just beyond the reach of hér hook, and saw a double line of the Watch approaching along the waterfront.

"What do they want?" Bulang asked, distrustfully. Skhetul had survived the inundation, but hìs rooms had been flooded and hìs stocks of parchment and ink destroyed, which meant ruin for a scribe, so Bulang was helping Jeya for the promise of a few coins from the harbourmasters for their part in cleaning up.

"At a guess?" Jeya replied. "The cargo." The dock boss was clearly having the same conversation with the Watch sergeant, and was just as obviously not happy with the outcome, but stood aside as the double line of armed people trooped past to where the ship was now tying up.

Jeya exchanged a glance with Bulang, and they began to wander casually towards the ship. The dead of the bay were not going anywhere.

Dock workers made fast the ropes that were tossed ashore, and a gangplank was lowered, but the sailors seemed quite perturbed when the Watch went up it without waiting for an invitation. The unloading began shortly afterwards, and cask after cask was removed down to the quay under the Watch's supervision.

Jeya had never worked on the docks, but shé was friends with Nabanda for long enough to know this was not how things normally went. The Watch did not get involved unless violence broke out, or they suspected smuggling. This was weird, and felt ... wrong.

It was not until the dock workers began to move the cargo back towards the main waterfront that Jeya realised quite how many other people had gathered. Nor, until they stepped out in front of the rest, had shé realised who else was in the crowd.

"What's going on here?" Kurumaya demanded. The Narrows might have been ripped down and washed into the bay, but the Shark had escaped that fate. They were small, and apparently unthreatening, but the collection of dangerous-looking folk lurking behind them did more than enough to offset that impression. Jeya still experienced an equal mix of fear and cold hatred in hér gut every time shé laid eyes on them, thanks to Kurumaya's involvement in so many deaths of people close to hér and Bulang, but there was nothing to be done about it.

"None of your business," the Watch sergeant snapped. "Out of the way."

"That's food," Kurumaya said. They planted their feet and squared their shoulders, their dark hair falling to the small of their back. "That's food, and you're taking it away from those that need it."

"This cargo is going to be redistributed fairly," the sergeant began, but Kurumaya cut them off with a mocking laugh.

"Redistributed *fairly*? My *arse*, it will be redistributed fairly! That's going to the Hierarchs and their friends, living up high enough that they never even got a toe wet or lost so much as a bean to the flood, and don't think we don't know that!"

The sergeant's eyes narrowed, and Jeya could practically see them doing the numbers in their head: how many of the Watch there were; how many were on the dock and in their way; how many of those would actually do something . . .

"I'm not here to bandy words with you," the sergeant declared. "This cargo is coming off the dock, and if you don't like it then you can take it up with the Hierarchs."

"Fuck the Hierarchs!" Kurumaya shouted furiously, and pointed one small finger past the sergeant at the dock workers. "Listen to me! I am Kurumaya, and I am telling every one of you that if that food moves off this dock, there will be more bodies going in that water!"

It was unheard of. To stand there in the open, threatening to murder anyone who obeyed the Watch's orders? Jeya had never dreamed of seeing such a thing. And yet enough of the dock workers clearly had enough of an idea who Kurumaya was to take their words seriously, because cask after cask hit the stone, and labourer after labourer stepped away from their load with their heads down and their hands clasped in front of them, or behind their backs.

The Watch sergeant gaped, but there was nothing they

could do, short of ordering their own to pick the casks up and move them: and Jeya had a suspicion that if that happened, Kurumaya's threatened violence would simply find a new target.

"Now run back to the Hierarchs and tell them that what comes to the waterfront stays on the waterfront," Kurumaya ordered, their voice sharp as a knife. "If they want a share of what we get, they can walk down here themselves and ask us for it. They don't get to bleed this city more than they already have."

The Watch sergeant did another calculation as a path opened in front of them through the crowd, and came to the conclusion that anything other than concession was not going to end well for them. They barked an order, and the Watch filed away, deliberately looking neither right nor left as they passed through the throng. It was just as well. Jeya could practically feel the tension vibrating through the bodies of those around her: the fear of the Watch, the fear of Kurumaya, the hunger they were all experiencing, and the anger at the thought of the Hierarchs taking the goods for themselves. It would take only the smallest nudge to set everything loose.

That nudge came less than a quarter of an hour later, when everyone had cheered Kurumaya, the casks had been broken open, arrangements were being made to parcel the food out, and others were arriving to claim their share of the unexpected windfall. Jeya and Bulang crowded in and managed to snag some handfuls of what was on offer: salted meat, and plump fruits the size of Jeya's fist with a bitter skin but soft, sweet flesh beneath. Jeya was just starting to examine whether shé still hated Kurumaya quite so much, given the Shark was the source of the first sizeable meal they'd had in a day or so, when panicked shouts went up.

The Watch had returned, and in greater numbers.

Jeya's natural instinct was to flee from the Watch. They were only to be trusted in the most extreme circumstances . . . Well, they were never to be *trusted*, but they could sometimes be *approached*. Every now and then you found one you could rely on personally, like Matahir, whose word had cleared Jeya of any suspicion in Ngaiyu's death, and who had given their own life fighting Nabanda's thugs. As a rule, though, Jeya would avoid them. They worked to enforce the Hierarchs' laws, which Jeya often broke, and even at the best of times they would be largely indifferent to hér. Shé was neither rich nor powerful, and so no one important cared whether or not they protected hér.

Few of those around hér would have greatly different experiences. Kurumaya and their people were, of course, opposed to the Watch by the sheer nature of their criminal enterprises. The dock crews viewed the Watch as chancers who looked for bribes, and stuck their noses in where they were not welcome. None of the rest here were rich or influential, and all were eagerly taking the food that the Watch had now come to reclaim.

It was that which swung it. Whereas the crowd would normally have hastily dispersed, now it crowded together protectively, like golden-maned monkeys around a fallen tamar fruit. The Watch advanced slowly, giving their quarry time to scatter and avoid a confrontation, but that did not happen. There must have been fifty Watch, but there were probably twice that number facing them down.

"That cargo is the property of the city!" the sergeant shouted, when only one or two people had slunk away.

"And it's in possession of the city!" Kurumaya called back. They spread their arms. "Who do you think we are?"

"I think you're someone with blood on your hands!" the sergeant shouted angrily. "You say you're Kurumaya? We know that name." They began to move closer again, and the rest of the Watch shadowed them. "Everyone else here, this is your last chance: you can go, if you leave the goods, but *you* . . . " They pointed at Kurumaya. "You don't get to walk away."

Jeya would have taken that offer: get away with at least a half-full belly and leave Kurumaya to the Watch. Bulang might get out from under their influence, then.

Shé never got the opportunity. Someone threw a loose cobble; the first Watch member in its path ducked, but it struck the one behind them full in the face. They fell backwards with a shout of pain, and the Watch reacted as it always did when one of its own was attacked.

They closed ranks and charged.

Normally that would scatter the offenders, but normally the offenders were not gathered where a quay joined the waterfront, hemmed in by the ocean on two sides and with only a limited distance to retreat backwards. Jeya felt a momentary flash of panic as the sensation of being trapped washed over hér, but it was rapidly swept away by fury. All shé'd wanted was a meal, and now shé was being attacked? Shé gripped hér hookpole firmly in both hands, and as the people around hér surged forwards, shé went with them.

The Watch carried spears, but the last few days of scarcity had encouraged the people of East Harbour to take their own weapons with them as they walked the streets, and Jeya saw staves, cudgels, knives and even a butcher's cleaver brandished desperately in the moments before the two lines collided. The stevedore in front of hér swayed aside from a Watch spearpoint at the last moment and grabbed the weapon's haft, and before Jeya had really thought about it, shé swung hér hookpole.

The Watch wore open-faced helms, but the hook point lodged in the watchperson's cheek and pulled them off-balance, straight into a knife thrust from someone else at Jeya's right shoulder. Shé nearly dropped hér weapon in shock, but then another watchperson raised their spear and aimed it at hér.

Bulang's hookpole punched out past hér, and the blunt tip of it smashed into the watchperson's face, sending them staggering backwards. The stevedore wrested the first watchperson's spear completely from their grasp and turned it around, then stabbed out with it. The blade took the second one in the right shoulder and bore them back down to the ground with a shriek, but then the stevedore themselves crumpled with a cry, and Jeya found hérself faced with the Watch sergeant and their bloodied sword.

Shé got hér hookpole up to block the sergeant's first downward swing, and the impact of the blow nearly shuddered the pole out of hér grip. Shé tried to lash out with the butt end to knock the sergeant back, and hopefully make them someone else's problem, but the blow was weak and badly aimed, and the sergeant grabbed hér pole with their free hand and stabbed for hér chest.

The sword's point never landed; it was knocked harmlessly upwards by the thick blade of a falchion. The sergeant tried to recover themselves, but by that point the falchion's blade had flashed out once more to bury itself in their neck. Blood spurted and the sergeant went down, and Jeya's rescuer turned to hér.

"Watch yourself, little one," Kurumaya said, a fey light in their eyes. The Shark was no taller or more heavily built than Jeya, but in that moment something larger than they were seemed to be shadowing their every move. Jeya had seen people in the grips of the gods before – shé had experienced it hérself, when worshipping Jakahama – but it never failed to prickle hér skin, and that same chill ran through hér bones now. Jeya did not know what gods Kurumaya might worship, but unless shé missed hér guess one of them had extended a sliver of their will to lend their strength to the Shark, for reasons of their own.

Kurumaya turned away from Jeya with a shrill cry which was echoed by those around them, and the assembled people of East Harbour surged again. There were a few more moments of desperate struggle, when Jeya brought hér hookpole down on a watchperson's helmet hard enough to stagger them and Bulang pulled hér out of the way of a blade intended for hér neck, but then some intangible tipping point was reached. The Watch stopped pressing forwards with angry shouts and began to back off, trying to get enough separation to break away and run. A couple more of their number were brought down, but those remaining turned and fled away from the waterfront, pursued by ragged cheers. Jeya found hér voice among the chorus, hér fear and anger washed away by fierce joy at running off those who had tried to take what now belonged to hér, and people shé did not know were slapping hér on the back as they congratulated each other.

"This doesn't end here!" Kurumaya bawled. A space cleared around the Shark as people pulled back from them, to give them room to speak uncrowded. "We just showed the Hierarchs whose city this really is! They won't like it, but they don't call the shots here any longer! We know these streets! We walk them every day!"

Kurumaya brandished their falchion, pointing its bloodied tip towards the slopes overlooking East Harbour, where the rich lived.

"The waterfront is ours! Anything that comes into this city comes through us! We decide who gets what, and if our so-called overlords want any of it then they're going to have to bargain for it!"

"But what about the Watch?" someone shouted.

"What about them?" someone else replied, to general

laughter, but the laughter was nervous. There were dead bodies on the ground, pierced by Watch spears, and no one imagined that they would be the last. There were dead Watch too, and when the Watch was bled, they came back looking for blood. Kurumaya and their thugs might not blink at a few lives lost, but that was not the world in which most of this crowd lived.

"The Watch live in this city," Kurumaya said, and they smiled a smile that was all teeth and no mirth. "And so do their parents, and their children, and their loved ones. The same goes for anyone who takes their coin direct from the Hierarchs. They're all going to have a choice to make about where their loyalties lie. Everyone is." They looked around, and several of the crowd stepped back a pace as Kurumaya's eyes fell on them, so fierce was their gaze.

"You're saying you'll go after their families?" someone asked, uncertainly.

"You think they wouldn't do the same?" Kurumaya demanded. "You *know* how this goes. Those of you who have a house that didn't get washed away can go back to it and hope no one remembers your face, while you sit there and wait for the Hierarchs to come around and hand you the food they're trying to confiscate. Or you can stand up for yourselves, and for everyone else who needs it, and we can make sure people get what they need."

Jeya realised that Bulang was moving a moment before thëy pushed into the ragged circle that had cleared around Kurumaya, and a moment too late to grab thëir sleeve to stop thëm. Kurumaya turned towards thëm, and Jeya saw the Shark's eyes narrow in recognition.

"I was hungry today," Bulang said, and thëir words were not addressed to Kurumaya, but the group as a whole. "I was pulling dead bodies out of the water in the hope I could get a few coins and find someone with spare food to sell it to me, and then hope again that I could afford their price. I'm not hungry any more today, and that's thanks to Kurumaya."

Jeya bit down on hér tongue to prevent hérself from speaking. Supporting Kurumaya was certainly a better idea than shouting them down, but what was Bulang playing at? The fact that Kurumaya's eyes found hér in the crowd for a moment before darting back to Bulang suggested that the Shark was having the same thoughts.

"If it's a choice between Kurumaya and the Hierarchs, I'm standing with the one that gets me fed," Bulang concluded, to a growing consensus of nods and muttering, and other voices starting to speak up in support. Bulang's last sentiment, at least, was hard to argue with, but Jeya still could not bring hérself to believe that Kurumaya was doing any of this out of the goodness of their heart.

But then again ... did that matter? If Kurumaya wanted to bring down the Hierarchs, and thought the best way to do it was to make sure they were the one who organised the regular folk in East Harbour getting food, that was still good, wasn't it? Jeya was no stranger to stealing to feed hérself, which a lot of the gods and every single stall-owner seemed to think was wrong. Kurumaya was just stealing what the Hierarchs had declared was theirs, and then giving it out to other people as well.

Kurumaya seemed to have decided that enough of the crowd was with them now, because they began issuing instructions: to take the wounded to healers and find priests for the bodies; to go and act as lookouts in case the Watch meant to come back in even greater numbers; to spread the word to the other quays and make sure that the waterfront was united. Jeya saw a few of the toughs who had been shadowing the Shark disappear off as well, undoubtedly to rustle up more strength of arms in case of opposition, whether that be from the Hierarchs, or from regular East Harbour folk who had reservations about the way the tide was flowing now. Shé took the opportunity to pull Bulang aside.

"What are yöu doing?" shé asked quietly.

"Kurumaya has us under their control anyway," Bulang replied, thëir voice just as low. "They're holding a threat over us, and they have to think that we're not all right with it. Making them think we're with them can't hurt us."

"Í know what you mean," Jeya said cautiously, "but it is *never* a good idea to draw the attention of important people. The best thing to do is just stay out of the way and try not to be noticed."

"Mÿ family tried that," Bulang said bleakly. "It didn't work. Kurumaya already knows who Ï am, and when they think the time is right, they're going to use më, just like the Hierarchs wanted to use më. Once they don't need më any longer, they'll probably try to get rid of më, unless Ï'm useful enough to keep around."

Thëy looked into hér eyes, and Jeya realised that there was nothing but determination there.

"Jeya, if Kurumaya wants to take over the city to take down the Hierarchs, let them. We know Kurumaya freed the fighting pit slaves a few years ago. Now they want to free the rest, and feed the people. Is that such a bad thing? We don't have a good choice, but this might be the better one. Ï'm not saying Ï'd save Kurumaya if they fell into the harbour, but Ï'd rather do something Ï think is right than just wait for mÿ use to be over."

Jeya bit hér lip. Bulang's words made sense, to an extent, but still . . .

"Í have a bad feeling about this," shé said quietly. But bad feelings never made for better options.

Tila

They never really stood a chance, Tila realised.

She had been thinking in terms of a determined defence of the city, of the Sun Palace's garrison being sent out to drive the invaders back. In that situation, an organised resistance by Idramar's citizens would have been invaluable: slowing the attackers down, holding key streets, allowing the soldiers the time to get to where their strength was required. It might have worked, but clearly someone in authority had other ideas. She and her ragtag militia had seen half a dozen dragon-mounted sars and their accompanying footmen in the distance, and had cheered them as horns sounded and they advanced into what sounded like battle. When the Raiders came, however, there was no assistance to be found.

These were not children; these were adult warriors, battle-hardened and determined. Tila's defenders were overwhelmed, and their hastily constructed choke point fell. Then there was a blackstone axe at her throat, and her people were reluctantly throwing down their weapons.

She had not expected that. Not from people who did not know who she was. It was not until she was being marched through the city by the massive woman who had a fistful of her hair that Tila realised the people of Idramar *did* know who she was; it was just that they knew Livnya the Knife, and somehow Livnya was worth something to them.

Tila never intended for that to happen. She created Livnya on the spur of the moment, when she was a grief-stricken young woman who wandered into the city in stolen servant's clothing in the immediate aftermath of her father's death, and had considered throwing herself in the harbour. For some reason, she instead walked into the Blue Shark tavern on the waterfront and came to the attention of a man named Yakov after a game of flights had made it clear she had a natural affinity for throwing sharp objects with surprising accuracy. Yakov had recruited her into his criminal empire, and Tila, recognising a chance to have an eye and an ear in the enterprises that caused her father so much grief, began her strange double life.

She had also never originally intended to supplant Yakov, but he had given her little choice in the end. After all, once it had come down to her or him, there was little sense in allowing someone else to take his place.

Tila had no idea who the Raider woman thought she was, but it seemed she had guessed something that even Tila herself had not realised: that a threat to her life was enough to quell resistance in the lowborn around her. Now, as she stumbled along with a Raider axe never that far from her throat, Tila became aware exactly how isolated that resistance had been.

Marshal Greenbrook – or whoever had taken charge of the city's defence, and Tila dearly hoped it was not her brother – had not committed to it. The initial sally by the defenders had thrown the Raiders back, judging by the bloodied and trampled fur-clad bodies she passed, but there had been no overall strategy. The thundershock charge of mounted sars would shake and scatter any enemy, but they could not work in isolation. All too soon, Tila saw Naridan casualties: sars ambushed in close quarters and pulled from their dragons, and footmen cut down by blackstone axes, pierced by javelins, or with their skulls crushed by slingstones. The horn calls she could hear now were sounding the retreat, not the attack.

The Sun Palace was intending to sit behind its thick stone walls and leave the rest of Idramar to the mercy of a people not famed for showing any. Tila could have spat in impotent fury. These were Naridans out here, who had been condemned to death by the nobility's cowardice! Good people – and yes, bad people, which probably included most of the ones she knew, herself included – who had prayed at shrines, paid their taxes – sometimes – and toasted the health of the Divine Family on feast days. Tila was unsure what angered her more: the fact that whoever was in command had abandoned his own people, or that everyone out here would assume that she, Tila Narida, was safe and sound in the Sun Palace and looking out at them with the same callous detachment.

The problem with a double life was that it sometimes gave you an insight into who each half of you was, and the picture was not always a flattering one.

More and more Raiders were gathering around her now; a tide of fur-clad, salt-stinking humanity converging on the Sun Palace, most of them pale-skinned, and with their faces marked by the dark lines and whorls of tattoos. Tila tried to make some sense of what she could see, searching for anything that could be of some use to her, but the meanings eluded her. She could see motifs repeated across different faces, here and there, but they did not appear to have any relevance to who associated with whom, or who was giving orders.

A Raider barged into their path: a man, his dark beard plaited to halfway down his chest, and with an axe of steel rather than the wood-and-blackstone weapons like the one still hovering alarmingly near Tila's throat. The newcomer's eyes fixed her with a desultory stare, and he said something that sounded unfriendly.

The woman holding Tila's hair replied, just as hostile. Tila stiffened. Twenty years of playing politics with nobles and criminals had given her excellent instincts for when two people were clashing, and every sense she had was screaming that these two loathed each other. *When two cannot agree, a third profits*, was an old saying from Narida's south, and Tila had made the most of it wherever she could. She was not quite sure how she could take advantage of friction between two warriors whose language she could not understand, but it was something worth knowing. It was probably foolish for her to have thought of the Raiders as some unified group, completely free from infighting and jealousy, but it was good to see that this was not the case.

What was *not* good were the sounds coming from ahead.

The hand in Tila's hair tightened, and she bit down on a cry of pain as the warrior holding her pressed forwards once more, towards the noise of battle and the eerie throbbing made by the huge shells that the Raiders used as horns. She snatched a glance up at the Sun Palace to make sure she was orienting herself correctly, but it did nothing to reassure her: they were heading towards the main gates. If a battle was occurring there, it meant that either a siege had begun, or the bulk of the defending forces sent out into the city had been brought to bay in front of the gates as they attempted to retreat.

Something grabbed at her attention, and she twisted her head around to take another look up at her home, heedless of the pain it caused in her scalp. The woman holding her spat something that sounded like a swear word and hauled her back so she was once more walking along looking down at her feet, but Tila had seen what she needed to see.

One of the flagpoles was empty. One servant or other, loyal to their role even in the midst of chaos, had lowered the banner which signified that the God-King was in residence. Natan was no longer in the Sun Palace.

Tila briefly considered the possibility that it had been done to fool the enemy, but there was no chance of the invaders knowing what any individual flag meant. In any case, they were surely after plunder and slaughter. If they were going to try to take the Sun Palace, the presence or absence of Natan Narida was hardly going to factor into their decision-making.

It had to be genuine. Her brother had fled the capital, which was, she had to admit, another indication that he had started making sensible decisions. She would not be surprised if the young Blackcreek boy had been involved, either. He, probably more than anyone else in Idramar, would have been able to recognise the nature of the threat as soon as he saw it. If so, Tila hoped he had left as well: he seemed loyal, and genuine, and a rather more pleasant person than those she usually found herself associating with, whether in the city or the palace.

The fingers in her hair tightened, and she was forced into a trot to keep up with the woman holding her. Now they were approaching the Sun Palace's gates, and Tila fought her head upright so she could try to make out what was going on.

What she saw sent a shock of cold fury through her.

The gates were still partly open, even as battle raged in front of them. There was no sign of a sortie from inside to push back the attackers, merely the desperate struggle of beleaguered men who knew that salvation – temporary salvation, at least – lay behind them, but turning to run for it would quickly see them dead. It was foolishness. Tila knew that immediately: there was no question of a fighting retreat that could get the rest of the men back inside without simultaneously endangering the entire palace. The only thing to do was to close the gates and leave everyone outside to die. It was cold-blooded, but if the decision had been taken to abandon the city in order to save the palace then the palace had to be saved, or the sacrifice would lose what little value it had.

Had the commander not realised this? Had the men not obeyed orders? Had they refused to condemn their fellows to die, or had they delayed shutting the gates until it was too late, and they were simply blocked by retreating bodies? It did not matter. Unless the situation changed quickly, Tila's home was going to be overrun.

It was then that her eye was drawn to a glint of gold, as the last rays of the setting sun reflected off something metallic. For a moment she thought she was looking at the face of a demon, and then things swam into focus: it was a face mask, although unlike the war mask of a sar, which covered everything below the nose, this concealed all but the mouth and chin. It looked to be made of steel inlaid with gold, and it rested on the face of the man Tila immediately recognised was in command.

Tila had lived around power all her life. She herself wielded it in at least two different forms and contexts. She had watched Einan Coldbeck inhabit the office of Eastern Marshal until it fitted him like a second skin, and it was barely possible to think of it as something separate to him. She had watched her father command his kingdom as a child, and had marvelled at his poise and wisdom. Even her brother, poor monarch though he had been for most of his reign, had always exuded the confidence of a man who knew that whatever orders he bothered to give would be obeyed without argument or question. Tila knew power when she saw it, and she was looking at it now.

It was the lack of fear, she decided. Whoever this man was, he moved as though nothing could pose any threat to him, as though he was one of the pit fighters she had seen in East Harbour, basking in the cheers of the crowd while they stared down their opponent, seeking a psychological advantage for the clash to come. Defenders on the walls were firing arrows down into the attackers – and taking slingstones right back – but the gold-masked one paid the missiles no mind as he bellowed orders, rallying those falling back and ordering new arrivals into the fight with sweeps of his sword.

Tila frowned. That was a longblade! Had he killed a sar and taken his weapon, or was this some other plunder? Either way, he held the blade as though he knew how to use it.

She stole a glance up at the face of the woman holding her and saw anxiety writ large there. Either the Raiders' expressions were very different to Naridan ones, or Tila's captor – who seemed to have at least some authority of her own – was scared of the man in the gold mask. Again, this was potentially useful to know, although Tila could not see a direct application for it right now. Hopefully it would never matter: an arrow would find the Raiders' leader and he would fall, the Sun Palace's gates would shut, and the horde would be left outside. They might wreak havoc upon the city, but better that than the city *and* the palace . . .

Then the gold-masked man turned with a roar, raised the longblade in his hand, and plunged into the fray directly towards the gates. A new surge of Raiders followed in his wake, howling war cries, and a fresh barrage of slingstones rattled up against the wall's parapets. The archers ducked or fell, their shafts stopped coming, and the charge hit home.

Tila could get only the loosest sense of what was happening from where she was, since she could not see over the heads of all those in front of her, but she could hear the renewed clash of weapons and screams of pain. She could practically feel the balance of the struggle teetering: either the Raiders would push home their charge, or the Naridan troops would repel their attack and, perhaps, buy themselves enough space to finally pull back and get the palace gates shut.

Tila reached cautiously into her left sleeve. The Raiders had not searched her, and she still had three knives left. Drawing one with a blackstone axe at her throat would likely achieve nothing except getting her throat cut, but if there was the possibility of achieving something worthwhile then it might be a risk worth taking. If she had been thinking more quickly, she might have tried to break away and take a throw at the masked warrior, but she had barely registered his importance before he led his charge. Hopefully a Naridan blade somewhere would prevent her from regretting her slow reactions ...

A great shout went up, and it went up from Raider throats. The bodies in front of Tila began to press forwards again: the balance had tilted too far, and not in the favour of the Sun Palace's defenders. Tila did her best to fight down a wave of nausea, but she could just see the waving shapes of blackstone axes passing through the gateway, and figures starting to climb up onto the walls to drive the archers back, and her gorge was rising.

Her home was taken: the grandest structure in all of Narida, raised by the joint artifice and genius of Tolkar the Last Sorcerer and Nari Himself, and the symbol of Narida's power. It had stood for centuries, but its gates had been breached on the first occasion it had actually been threatened by a hostile force.

In the end, even the mightiest creation could fall if it was failed by the people to whom it had been entrusted.

She was dragged forwards again, and although she wanted to dig her heels in and refuse to see what was happening, there was nothing she could do to prevent it short of drawing a knife and stabbing at the arm of the woman who held her. That might mean she did not have to see her home being overrun, but only by virtue of taking an axe to the throat. When it came down to it, Tila Narida had not been the type of person to end her own life twenty years ago when she had looked down at the dark, dirty waters of the Idramar docks, and she was no more inclined to do so now, unless she could see a gain from it.

She tried to force her thoughts into order. There was more than one line of defence in the Sun Palace: the Sun Gardens were not just ornamental, but also a place in which to hold attackers in front of the secondary walls. Natan was gone, and presumably safe, at least for now. There was also no way her brother would have left without taking their mother with him . . .

Although he left without you, a treacherous voice in the back of her mind pointed out.

He knew this princess was not in the palace, Tila told herself firmly. *Waiting would have endangered both himself and mother. Natan would trust that this princess would be able to look after herself.*

And what a wonderful job you've done of that so far, her inner voice said snidely. Tila bit her lip. She had three knives, and the ability to use them should the opportunity present itself. That was all she would concentrate on for the moment.

Then she saw him in front of her. The gold-masked warrior, still just outside the gates of the Sun Palace, standing among the corpses of his own warriors and those who wore the crowned sunburst of Narida. Others were flooding past him, but he hung back and barked instructions. Tila's captor was dragging her right towards him, as though intending to present her as a prize. Perhaps that was the intention, but Tila had no intention of letting it happen. She had missed her chance before: she would not again.

She waited until the woman holding her hair had called out in her own language, and the masked warrior was beginning to turn towards them. They were perhaps fifteen paces away when Tila drew her knife.

She stabbed upwards, jabbing blindly behind her head. The

point of the blade struck an arm hard enough to cause Tila's captor to release her hold with a cry of pain, and Tila threw herself forwards into a roll to evade the anticipated axe swing intended to take her head off. She came up to one knee still undecapitated, drew back her arm, and flung her blade with all her might.

It struck home. The masked warrior fell backwards and Tila was suffused by a moment of pure, fierce joy before something crashed into her back, bore her downwards to the flagstones and held her there. She tensed, expecting the momentary sharp pain that would signal the detaching of her head, but with the knowledge that at least she had laid low the Raiders' leader.

A shout rang out, and the pressure on her back relaxed slightly. Confused, Tila looked up.

The masked warrior was back on his feet.

She had a single moment of absolute, abject fear, until she realised he was rubbing at a dint on his mask, and then her fear was replaced by self-loathing. She had gone too high: instead of taking him in the neck, her knife had simply glanced off his mask. Her one chance gone, and for nothing.

The masked warrior barked something else, and a new man came forward. It was hard for Tila to tell from her position on the ground, held in place by a wooden shield weighed down by a Raider's body, but this man looked different to the others. His clothes seemed odd, more familiar somehow . . .

She just had time to recognise them as the sort of clothes that were worn in the City of Islands before she was hauled back to her feet, with the blade of a blackstone axe now very definitely held against her throat.

The Raider in front of her looked almost shamefaced, which was confusing in and of itself, but at the moment Tila was still alive when she expected to be dead, so that was something that she could pay more attention to at another time.

"Do you have any idea what you just did?" the Raider asked her, and Tila gaped at him in shock when she realised he was speaking Naridan. It was accented Naridan, to be sure, but it was definitely Naridan.

"This lady . . . " She only narrowly avoided saying "princess" due to her surprise, which would not have done her any favours. " . . . threw a knife at the man leading the attack on her city. And how do you speak her language?" she added, since anything she could learn might be of value, assuming she was not about to be killed.

"This man speaks your language because he learned it on the docks of East Harbour, where he lived before he was forced to join in this . . . whatever this is," the Raider said. His eyes were nervous, and Tila knew immediately that he had no wish to be here. An interpreter, held against his will? Also interesting. "And you did not throw your knife at a man."

"What is he, then?" Tila demanded. Did the Raiders hold to the same notions of gender as the Alabans? Was this simply a case of translation issues?

Then she saw the naked fear in the translator's eyes, and understood that it was not.

"It is a draug," the Raider said, and the way his mouth twisted around the foreign word communicated the fear it held for him in a way that language had no need to. "It is The Golden."

The Golden stared at Tila for a few seconds, the sun's rays picking out its unblinking eyes of pale green through the holes in its mask. Then it turned its back on her and walked through the gates of her home, longblade drawn. Tall. Proud. Unhurried.

A conqueror.

Marin

Marin was still damp, although drier than he had been, thanks to the warmth of the fire. No one blinked at the story of how he had fallen in a pond, other than to laugh at him for it, or thought to ask why Ravi's hair was damp as well, yet her clothes were dry. Only Laz cocked an eyebrow, but he did not enquire further. Marin knew his husband guessed there was something else to the tale, but that he would hear it in good time. Marin would tell him the broad details later, when he was certain they would not be overheard. And certainly, Marin had told Ravi that things would stay between them, but he was hardly going to keep secrets from his husband, was he? Laz would not denounce Ravi as a witch, and honesty had been the cornerstone of Marin's relationship for all of its fifteen or so years.

They were roasting some tubers — half-withered things from the monks' stores, cut up and held into the flames on sticks: hardly a meal but the best they had to work with — when the gongs sounded, and everyone's heads came up at once.

"They've never rung that this late before," Channa said.

"Do you suppose . . . ?" Aranel began, looking over at the monastery. The merest hint of light escaped around the very edges of its shutters, giving it a ghostly, barely-there presence in the darkness of the Catseyes' night.

"They've made their decision!" Kenan said, scrambling up to his feet. Others had come to similar conclusions, judging by the general stirring and murmurs of increasing excitement across the camp.

"Bones, watch the fire," Gershan said, joining his brother.

"Go kiss the mountain," Bones retorted. "S'man's not staying here and missing the proclamation!"

"The *mountain* is right there," Gershan said, pointing at Godspire. "We're practically *on* it; s'man could go kiss it and come back, and you'd still have to watch the fire."

"S'man's not watching the fucking fire!" Bones got up. "Channa—"

"Don't even think about it," Channa the Nose said warningly. "S'woman came all the way across the country just like the rest of you, she's not staying here now."

"The fire will be fine for a short while; just don't leave anything too close to it," Marin said soothingly. He was certainly not going to volunteer. This was not just a once-in-a-lifetime moment; it was a once-in-*history* moment.

Ravi was already gathering up her things, since she never let her satchels of healing supplies out of her sight, so there was no chance of her staying behind either. Marin was not surprised, given what they had discussed at the Pool of Tears. If he had lived his life thinking his soul was already bound to the Unmaker, he would have a special interest in seeing the Divine Nari's rebirth be proclaimed, too.

They did not start out as hurrying — it seemed somehow improper — but as it became clear how many others were also moving to congregate in front of the monastery, their group picked up their pace through unspoken agreement. They all knew they wanted to be there, and if not at the front then certainly *near* the front, and so strides lengthened a little, and steps came slightly more quickly, until what they were doing could only still be called a walk by the loosest of definitions.

All around them, shapes were moving in the darkness as the Godsworn converged. Some carried burning sticks taken from fires to light their way, but most seemed content to trust in the fitful illumination from the half-full short moon above them, despite the clouds scudding across its face. Marin followed behind Laz, stepping more or less where he stepped, and if Marin was pretty much moving at a jog now, well, he could hardly be blamed for the fact that his husband's legs were longer.

They all converged at the bottom of the steps leading up to the monastery's main door. Mordokel was at the front, his shaved head gleaming in the flickering light of someone's firebrand, and certainly no one was disputing his right to be there. Everyone else tried to push and nudge into a good position without being obvious about it, since maintaining some level of decorum seemed appropriate under the circumstances. Marin's group were perhaps three rows of heads back, but he found a gap where no one in front was that much taller than him; besides which, the steps ran upwards to the height of at least two tall men, so his view was not impaired.

It seemed the monks had a sense of the dramatic, or at least no intention of repeating themselves. It was a few minutes after the gongs had sounded that the monastery's door finally opened, and four figures emerged. A ripple of anticipation ran through the crowd as Tyrun appeared, backlit as though the light was gathering around Him and clinging to Him in a halo.

Tyrun and the three monks began to descend. Two of the monks carried carved staffs, which looked to be badges or marks of office of some sort. The third wore more elaborate robes, and as they approached the lights carried by the Godsworn, Marin saw that he was older; most of his hair was grey, and a long, thin beard dangled from the point of his chin. He looked tired: perhaps the order had been debating the issue of Tyrun's divinity nearly non-stop. Or perhaps he simply had not slept well the previous night for some reason, and was now feeling the effects. It was easy to read meaning into ambiguous signs, Marin reminded himself, and a man of learning should always be aware of that.

Tyrun Himself looked tired too, Marin realised, which was the first time He had seemed anything less than fresh and serene. However, despite the slight bags under His eyes and the faint droop of His shoulders, His expression was one of calm elation, and His eyes were bright. Marin felt better simply for laying eyes on Him.

At some prompt or signal that Marin did not catch, the two flanking monks struck their staffs on the stone steps three times, which served well enough to attract everyone's attention and quiet the excited mutterings. The older monk raised his hands palms outwards, as though granting a benediction.

"The monastery of Godspire was called to proclaim on the divinity of the one known as Tyrun, who presented to us claiming to be the Divine Nari reborn into a new body, as foretold," the monk said. His voice was breathy, but had an iron core to it that carried easily through the night air, despite the wind that licked around Godspire's lower slopes. "We have spoken to the supplicant at great length, and debated his claim. We now give our judgement on this matter, the first time it has been voiced to anyone outside of our order."

Marin focused on Tyrun's face. Calm, smiling, expectant. Radiant. The very image of his god reborn.

"The monastery finds the youth Tyrun lacking," the monk stated baldly. "He is not divine, and has no claim to the throne of—"

"What?!" Marin shouted, outraged, and he was not alone.

The monastery's spokesman never finished his sentence; or if he did, no one heard his words. The Godsworn erupted into shouts of derision and anger that drowned anything else out. The old monk, who had recoiled slightly in the face of the initial reaction, raised his hands once more and tried to make himself heard again, to no avail. Those flanking him were suddenly holding their staffs in both hands across their chest, as though they thought they needed to defend themselves.

Amid the anger that had gripped him, Marin's eyes flashed to Tyrun again. His expression was one of utter shock, incomprehension, and even loss; His eyes moved back and forth, focusing on nothing, as though desperately seeking some sense. He did not look around at the monks.

Instead, when He did look at someone, His eyes bored into Mordokel with an intensity Marin had not seen on His face before.

"Oh shit," Marin heard Laz mutter, and then the Godsworn began to move.

Marin could not say who took the first step. There was no order given, no one person who advanced ahead of the others. Tyrun spoke no words. Nonetheless, the mass of people packed around the base of the steps surged forward like water released from behind a dam and, unlike water, moved *upwards*.

Marin staggered as people barged into him from behind, and would have fallen had Laz not reached out and caught him. One of the staff-armed monks raised his weapon to strike at the onrushing pilgrims, but was engulfed before his blow could land. The other turned to run, but was caught and dragged off his feet moments after the older monk, who still seemed to think he could calm the crowd with words, was likewise clubbed down. Marin heard his scream rise above the hubbub for a moment, and saw a blade raised that looked rather like the one Mordokel carried.

Marin's anger dissolved into sick fear as the rest of the Godsworn piled towards the monastery. The monks were wrong, surely they had been wrong, but *this* . . .

"This can't be right," he managed to say.

"What's not right?" Ravi demanded, her face hollow with alarm. "The fact they didn't proclaim Him, or the fact they're being fucking *murdered* for it?!"

"Both!" Marin spat. "The monastery will proclaim the Divine Nari's rebirth; that's what the Foretellings of Tolkar say! They have to change their mind, be persuaded somehow, not *killed*!" He looked around, but the others — the former soldiers, who had been with them since Northbank — had disappeared. Of the people he knew, only Laz and Ravi were still visible.

"People have been sat out here for days with little food, little warmth, and little shelter," Laz said grimly. He had one hand on the hilt of his longblade and the other gripping its blackened scabbard, but he had not yet drawn it. "Ask people to endure hardship in the name of their god and they'll do it; ask them to do it and then tell them that their god is not their god . . ."

Tyrun was standing exactly where He had been, as unmoved by the swell of people that had swarmed by on either side of Him as a rock would be by a river's flow. He had turned, though, and was now facing back up towards the monastery as the first of the Godsworn reached the doors. Those inside had witnessed what was occurring and tried to shut them again, but to no avail; they might have been able to hold them against five people, or ten, but more and more Godsworn were lending their weight to the attack now. Others spread out, heading for the lowest windows and clawing at the shutters, or beating on them to knock them inwards.

The main door gave way, and a great roar went up from the Godsworn. The crack of light widened, and body after body forced its way inside, like rats fleeing into their nest away from a predator. There would be no refuge inside for those who had denied Tyrun's divinity.

The crush at the bottom of the steps began to dissipate, as the last of those who had surged forward in anger moved onwards and away. There were many people still standing around Marin and his companions, and voices were raised in angry jubilation as their fellows forced their way into the monastery to exact vengeance. Others were already slinking away; either to depart entirely, or to help themselves to anything left behind while others were occupied, by Marin's guess, although he would not want to be the person caught stealing while the Godsworn were in this bloodthirsty mood.

Tyrun turned again, putting his back to the besieged monastery, and descended to the level of His remaining followers. Many of the burning torches had gone with the attackers, but there remained enough light that the young god's face was visible. His visage was stern and unyielding, and Marin's bladder nearly betrayed him when Tyrun changed direction slightly and began walking towards him.

"Divine One," Marin said breathlessly, dropping to his knees along with Laz and Ravi as Tyrun reached him.

"The monastery was your idea, Marin of Idramar," Tyrun said. His voice was flat and featureless, as though his words had been considered and put together by a spirit free of emotion. "You said the Foretellings declared that this god would be proclaimed by them, and so all the lands of Narida would accept His rule."

"So your servant believed, Divine One," Marin said, not looking up, and trying not to think about what would happen if Tyrun denounced him as a traitor or unbeliever. Those around would converge to tear him apart; Laz might take a few of them down with his longblade, but this was not the fighting pits of Kiburu ce Alaba, and the odds would be far worse than three-on-one.

Tyrun sighed. "This god wants you to understand, Marin, that this is not what He wanted to happen."

That, at least, was not an immediate death sentence. Marin risked glancing up, and found Tyrun looking down at him with a melancholy expression.

"Divine One?" he said, since something seemed to be expected of him, but he had no idea what to say.

"This god would have far preferred this to have play out as you imagined it would," Tyrun said, as calmly as though people were not being murdered behind Him. "But perhaps it had to be this way. This god has always said He has no patience with the existing order of this world. Who declared these monks the sole arbiters of who is divine, and who is not? In the end, the only authority in this land lies with this god, and what can He do with those who refuse to recognise Him? They were derelict in their duties, that much is clear." He nodded, as though this was only now occurring to Him. "Yes. If they ever had the knowledge the Foretellings ascribe to them, they have clearly lost it at some point. Perhaps they were simply ignorant, or corrupted by an agenda seeking to delay this god's claim. The system was as flawed as that of sars and thanes and lowborn, and so it too shall be swept away."

Marin did not say anything, but Tyrun's gaze focused back on him in any case.

"But you are a learned man, Marin, and this god still lacks some insight into how Narida works — or fails to. Do you think that without such a proclamation, there will still be resistance to His rule?"

Marin swallowed. "Your servant would not wish to speculate on such matters, Divine One."

"Marin," Tyrun said with a slight smile. "Your god is *asking* you to speculate. You risked your life to save Him from a knife intended for His heart, and you cannot be blamed for repeating what you knew of the Foretellings in an effort to ease His ascension to His throne. It is the monks of Godspire who are at fault, not you. Your counsel is still valued."

His smile widened, and a shiver of relief ran through Marin: relief not only that he was not to be denounced and killed, but that Tyrun still trusted him. All the same . . .

"Divine One, your servant truly does not know," he said honestly. "He cannot understand how someone could stand before you and not appreciate your true nature; and yet either these monks did not, or as you say, they were corrupted in some way." He shook his head. "Your servant feels that any who seek to bar your path might point at the lack of a proclamation as reason to dispute your rule, but as men of learning know, absence of evidence is not evidence of absence."

Tyrun nodded slowly and stroked His chin thoughtfully. "The most senior of the monks carries the title of Abbot of Godspire. He is a pleasant man, and this god . . . " He looked over His shoulder at the monastery, and Marin saw a flash of sadness and regret cross his god's face. "Well. The monks withheld their food and their shelter from this god's followers. Perhaps this is justice, after all. Perhaps there should be a new abbot, one who knows the truth about this god, and is prepared to make such a proclamation. And who else could have the authority to make such an appointment, if not the god to whom this monastery is devoted?" Tyrun looked back down at Marin. "Would you do such a thing for your god, Marin?"

Marin's throat dried, and his mind blanked. He hesitated, completely unable to form words, but Tyrun's calm smile did not falter, and His eyes did not waver. After a few agonisingly long moments, Marin managed to get his voice to respond once more and, more importantly, conjured up some words for it to utter.

"Your servant would be beyond grateful for such an honour," he said carefully, "but he doesn't feel like a holy man in his heart. If he might be so bold as to make a suggestion: what of Mordokel? He is a priest, not a monk, but if anyone should have this position, perhaps it should be him?"

"Mordokel?" Tyrun's smile widened slightly. "He has responsibilities enough, surely? But perhaps your suggestion has merit, Marin. Mordokel has a certainty to him that others find inspiring. He will be a good candidate for such a role when we return to the lowlands." He nodded again. "Yes. This god was wise to value your counsel still. Be at peace, Marin of Idramar, and Alazar of White Hill, and Ravi. This is a sad night in many ways, but a necessary one. Go back to your fire, and sleep. Tomorrow brings a new dawn, and the beginning of our next march."

"Where will we be marching?" Marin asked, before he could stop himself, but Tyrun did not seem to mind the question.

"Why, Idramar, of course," He said. "The West might consider itself the heart of Narida, but the throne lies in the East, and that is where this god must make His claim heard. And there may be new allies to encounter on the way," He added, looking away into the night as though searching for something only He could see. "This is only the beginning."

So saying, He walked away, and was instantly surrounded by other Godsworn who fell to their knees and reached out for His blessing now He was no longer engaged in conversation. Marin, Laz and Ravi cautiously rose, but it seemed that the punishment Marin had feared was not going to materialise after all.

"What do we do now?" Ravi asked weakly.

"We do as He said," Laz said firmly. "We go back to our

fire, and we sleep. We're heading back down this mountain tomorrow, by the sounds of it, and this sar wants to be awake enough not to trip over his own feet and fall on his face."

"But . . ." Marin could not tear his eyes away from the monastery, from which noises of violence were still spilling. "What about *that*?"

"If your husband was the sort to be kept awake by dead men, he would have lost his mind before we'd even met," Laz said with a shrug. He put his arm around Marin's shoulders and squeezed him, and the warmth and pressure immediately provided some small comfort. "You didn't make them make that choice, Mar, and you didn't take your knife to any of them. You didn't call for it to happen. Nor did Tyrun. If you'd tried to stop it then you'd be dead now, and your husband with you, and you'd have saved no one."

"Listen to him," Ravi said quietly. Her face was almost entirely hidden in shadow, but some spark of light caught in her eyes, and Marin could see their level gaze. "He's right. This wasn't our doing."

"Maybe not, but . . ." Marin allowed himself to be guided back towards where their fire was still sputtering, and their possessions were, so far as he could tell, unmolested by any of those who had disappeared earlier.

"But?" Laz prompted.

"This isn't how this was supposed to go," Marin said weakly. "It's not how *any* of it was supposed to go."

Darel

"When your friend was a boy," Darel said to Hiran, looking out of the coach's window, "that is what he thought a castle looked like."

Threestones Castle sat on a slight rise in the ground overlooking a bend of the River Yora, which flowed northwards to finally join with the Idra some way east of the city of Northbank. The castle was huge; not as large as the Sun Palace, but a much more overtly military structure. The residence of the God-King sat atop its sandstone bluff as though it were a natural extension of the rock that had merely been given shape by the hands of architects: Threestones Castle squatted in place and gave the impression of clinging to the ground and daring anyone to try to move it.

"Were you not raised in a castle?" Hiran asked.

"Your friend was," Darel agreed. "But when he learned to read the histories and legends of Narida, he realised that the Black Keep is but a shadow of structures such as this." By Darel's estimation, the boundary wall of Threestones was nearly as high as the Black Keep itself, and the white-tiled roofs he could see within rose higher still. He counted eight guard towers on the external wall, the largest of which was the gatehouse towards which they were now riding.

It had been a draining journey. They fled west along the

river road, searching for a way across, but the Idra was far too wide to bridge this close to the ocean, and many of the ferries had been wrecked in the great wave. It took a week before they found a crossing, and even that had not been without fearful glances to the east in case the sails of the Tjakorshi appeared on the river, bearing down on them while they were in mid-current.

They had ridden south since, following the crown road that wound down through the country, and which would eventually pass Darkspur to terminate, in somewhat less well-maintained form, at Black Keep. Darel felt the pull of it; the temptation to just keep going back to his home, and be reunited with his brother and all the people he knew well. However, although the Thane of Blackcreek might have business in the south, the Southern Marshal, somewhat perversely, did not.

"How bad is this likely to be for you?" Darel asked Hiran quietly, as the gatehouse loomed larger and larger. He could just see it, by resting his head against the coach door and looking ahead. Hiran, sitting opposite him, had steadfastly avoided looking at his home at all.

"Not as bad as it will be for Yae," Hiran replied. "If she can face our father, then your friend certainly can." Yae herself was not in their carriage: she had taken to riding with the Queen Mother, a decision which Darel both understood and regretted, since he enjoyed her wit. On the other hand, he was not surprised that she might not wish to spend her days cooped up in a carriage with a group of men, even if one of them was her brother with whom she got on very well.

"Your sister need not fear," Natan said firmly. "Thane Mattit will need the very best of reasons to speak ill of his own daughter in front of his king, when she is known to this king as a loyal and worthy subject."

Darel glanced at Hiran, but his friend did not look

particularly comforted. Darel could understand it, to an extent. His own father had not needed words to communicate displeasure, and the protection of another was always a fleeting thing where family was concerned. Natan's presence might still Thane Mattit's tongue, but Yae would not always be by the God-King's side, and there would be many chances for father and daughter to meet.

They had sent a rider on ahead, and the message had the desired effect: the gates of Threestones Castle did not close, and their procession passed through unchallenged into the first yard. A Threestones servant was ready to open the door almost as soon as the carriage came to a halt, and Darel stepped out first.

Technically speaking, they should have disembarked in reverse order of rank: Hiran first, Darel second, and Natan third. However, Darel had no intention of letting his friend be first out under his father's gaze, and the Unmaker take propriety.

The first yard of any castle was a utilitarian affair, a place of hustle and bustle where goods were delivered and unloaded, and Threestones was no exception. There were no cherry trees or carvings; no brightly coloured frescos on walls, or gardens of quiet solitude. There was mud, and the smell of bread from the bakery, and the household of the Thane of Threestones drawn up ready to welcome their monarch.

The thane himself was easy for Darel to pick out, for he stood front and centre in robes with the double-pleated sleeves of the nobility, and Hiran's features were obvious in his face. His chin was starting to sag into jowliness, his ears had smaller lobes, and his hairline was starting to recede, but no one could look at Mattit Threestone and his son without realising that they were related.

Hiran will retain his looks later in life, if his father is anything to go by, Darel reflected. He quickly glanced along the line of faces, picking out other notables: that had to be Hiran's elder brother Natan – named in honour of the God-King, which was not going to get at all confusing – and that woman would be his mother Lady Nadah, judging by her position next to Thane Mattit and, yes, her ears. There were two sars, one older and one younger – also father and son? – a plump man wearing robes that made Darel think he might be the steward, and a rail-thin one who was definitely a priest.

Thane Mattit's expression upon seeing Darel was one of uncertainty: he clearly had no idea who this newcomer was, which did not surprise Darel. His robes were travel-stained, and the sigil of Blackcreek was not likely to be known this far north, besides which Threestones was technically in the East. Although Thane Mattit owed Darel fealty as a Hand of Heaven – and *that* was a concept to which Darel was still adjusting – his liege lord was Adan Greenbrook.

Assuming Adan Greenbrook still lived.

Mattit's expression shifted as Hiran dismounted from the coach. It was not overt hostility, but the tightening of his eyes and mouth was not missed by Darel. Nor was it by Hiran, judging by his expression when Darel glanced sideways at him. His friend's jaw was set, and he looked, if anything, ready for a fight.

Then the God-King dismounted, and the entire household of Threestones dropped to their knees.

"Rise!" Natan called immediately. "No purpose is served by you muddying your robes in your own home, Thane Mattit!" He stepped forward, and Darel was struck by the change in his monarch. Natan's voice was more forceful, and his back straighter. Granted, there had been little use for either while they had been sitting together in the coach, but when Darel compared this to the relaxed, almost casual Natan Narida speaking to him atop Eight Winds Tower before they sighted the Tjakorshi fleet, or the somewhat snappy one presiding over meetings of the Inner Council, it had the air of a performance.

The idea that the God-King felt the need to play a role to impress his subjects was one that Darel had not previously considered, and it was oddly jarring. Thane Mattit did not seem to recognise it, though, or else hid his surprise.

"Your Divine Majesty honours us with your presence," he replied, rising from his knees. "Your messenger gave little information other than we were to expect you: how might we be of service?"

"First, this king asks that you extend your welcome to him and all those in his party as your guests," Natan said. Darel blinked – the God-King had no need of such a request, since he could go where he pleased, and it would be the gravest breach of honour to refuse him – until he realised exactly what had just been said. Hiran and Yae were in the God-King's party: if Mattit did as Natan bade him, he would be committing to treat them as his guests as well. A guest was a very different proposition to a daughter or a son, in terms of what respect had to be shown, and what conduct was considered appropriate. They might not be asked to sit at the high table for a feast, since their individual rank did not warrant it if they were not considered members of the family, but neither could they be singled out for criticism or abuse without committing a gross breach of honour.

If Mattit Threestone recognised the true purpose behind his monarch's words, he gave no sign of it. "Of course, Divine Majesty," he said, bowing low. "You and all of your party are welcome at Threestones."

"Good," Natan said. "This king assumes you did not recognise the new Southern Marshal, Lord Darel Blackcreek?"

Thane Mattit's eyes widened as he looked at Darel, and he began to drop to his knees again.

"Please, that is not necessary," Darel said hastily, his words arresting the thane's downward momentum. Mattit returned to standing, but kept his eyes lowered.

"Your pardon, High Marshal. Your servant had heard the news, but he had no idea the thane of Blackcreek was . . . so young. Had he known your identity, he would have—"

"No harm was done, nor offence taken," Darel interrupted him. He was not sure which was the more alarming prospect: that he would feel this embarrassed for the rest of his life, or that he would get used to such subservience and even come to expect it as his due.

Natan turned to look back at the second carriage. "And are you familiar with Queen Hada, the Queen Mother?"

"Your Majesty," Thane Mattit said, with another bow, as Queen Hada stepped down. Ahead of her, and unremarked so far due to the focus on the God-King and Darel, were her maid and, hands behind her back and face lowered as though trying to hide her features, Yae Threestone. Darel glanced back at Mattit, and saw his expression tighten further as he recognised his daughter, but no harsh words escaped from his lips. Lady Nadah looked uncomfortable, as though waiting for her husband to say something, but Natan Threestone's expression was pleased. It seemed the eldest child had no quarrel with his younger siblings, no matter their father's opinions.

"We have much to discuss, Lord Threestone," the God-King said, drawing attention back to himself. "There are urgent matters to which we must attend in private."

"Of course, Your Majesty," Thane Mattit replied, although his expression made it clear that he had no idea what was going on, and was somewhat alarmed by this state of affairs. "Would you care to refresh yourself first after your journey?"

"Refreshment can come later," Natan said. "Some things cannot wait."

"As you command," Threestone said. "Please, follow your servant to his study."

"Darel, Hiran, accompany us," the God-King said. Then he turned to his left. "Lady Yae, you too."

Yae's eyes widened and her mouth opened, but one did not contradict the God-King. Unless, of course, one happened to be the Queen Mother.

"The Lady Yae is assisting your mother," Queen Hada said gently. "We have only one maid with us, and in such circumstances, ladies must help each other."

"Threestones will have maids who can attend to your needs," Natan said firmly. "This king has come to value Lady Yae's mind since we left Idramar, and he would have her with us for this. After all, it was she who suggested Threestones as a suitable location, and her father as an appropriate ally in which to place our trust."

If Queen Hada had been of a mind to contradict her son further, she chose not to. Instead she nodded serenely and touched Yae on the shoulder, whispering something in her ear. Yae nodded, although she swallowed visibly before she made her way to the God-King's side.

"Lead on, Lord Threestone," Natan Narida said, and Thane Mattit had no choice but to comply.

"Idramar has fallen?" Mattit Threestone said in shock. He, the God-King, Darel, and the Threestone siblings were seated in the thane's study around the map Darel had brought from the Sun Palace, with cups of steaming yeng. Darel wondered briefly whether Hiran had got his taste for the drink from his father, or whether they had come to like it independently.

"We do not know," Natan Narida said. "It is possible the attackers were repelled, but the outcome was uncertain enough for us to flee, and we have outrun news of events since then.

One of our first priorities must be to ascertain what has actually taken place."

"Your Majesty was wise to come here," Mattit Threestone said. "We can send messages upriver to Brightwater, and—" He cut himself off, with a glance at Darel. "Although of course, that is no longer the seat of the Southern Marshal."

"The messages should still be sent," Darel said. "Brightwater remains the largest city in the South, and sits at a conjunction of routes, as does Waymeet. River or road, whichever is quicker for the messengers to get there: from those places, we can reach all of the south."

"To what purpose?" Yae asked.

"Raising levies, of course!" Mattit snapped, without looking at her. "With most of the Eastern Army's strength in the west, His Divine Majesty must call on the Southern Army, at least until Lord Goldtree can be reached to send men downriver."

"Goldtree's men are likely spread out all across the land, searching for the man claiming to be the Divine Nari reborn," the God-King said, his tone precise and clipped. "He may not be able to muster them back in anything approaching good time. The core of the Western Army may be more cohesive, but will be even farther away, and the Torgallen Pass must not be left completely undefended. The Northern Army is, of course, an unknown: we cannot count on word reaching Marshal Highbridge in time for him to supply meaningful aid if Idramar has fallen."

"But, Your Majesty, *has* Idramar fallen?" Yae interjected, with a nervous glance at her father, who still refused to look at her. "Should we not determine that before we act?" Her makeup was almost caked on, Darel suddenly realised; certainly far thicker than he had seen it applied at the Sun Palace. Perhaps it was due to the privation of living on the road for days on end: his own jaw was stubbled, where he had had less opportunity to keep his beard in check, so it was little wonder that a lady's make-up might be less refined than usual.

"Yae has a point, Father," Natan Threestone spoke up. "The Southern Army is one thing, but if the thanes are asked to raise levies then we would be pulling men away from the land as harvest approaches."

"We must of course find out what has happened in Idramar," the God-King said, "but if we wait for that information before we act then it could be too late. The Raiders have never struck in anything near to these numbers, nor this far north. We cannot assume that they will simply sack the city and leave, as they may have done in the past. We must be ready to throw them back into the sea."

Throw them back into the sea. That phrase struck a chord in Darel's memory: his father had used it, or one very similar to it, when they had been conversing with Saana Sattistutar on the salt marsh in front of Black Keep's walls.

"Throwing the Tjakorshi back into the sea when they do not want to go is not an easy task," he said. "However, even if they have sacked Idramar and moved on, they may then raid up and down the coast, and we should reinforce the towns to oppose them."

"They will find little enough on the coast," Mattit Threestone snorted. "The great wave struck in all the places we have heard from, to greater or lesser effect. Anywhere low-lying has suffered badly."

"So if they mean to stay, they must come inland to find whatever plunder they might be after, even if that is merely food," the God-King said. He tapped the map. "They have swift ships; they will surely come up the Idra. It is the lands surrounding the river that will be in the gravest danger."

"Your servant struggles to see how we could bring them to battle," Darel said. "Even if our troops line the shore, boats on the river would be far swifter. They could outpace us and strike where they choose, and would have no problem in remaining out of longbow range in the middle of the channel, given the river's width."

"Boats of our own, then?" Hiran asked.

"You would not say that if you had seen Tjakorshi ships in action," Darel told him grimly. "They outstrip our Black Keep fishing skiffs by some measure, and in the summer months they have been the most feared pirates along the southern coast for generations. Our troops would not only be outmanoeuvred; they might find themselves boarded in a river battle. Our one great advantage is dragons, but they would be useless there."

"These are conversations for when we know what our enemy's movements are, if indeed they are still plaguing us," Natan Narida said firmly. "For now, we must send out messengers to muster the Southern Army. Lord Threestone, your king presumes you will see to this."

"Of course, Your Majesty," Thane Mattit said, bowing his head.

"However, this king understands the concerns of Lady Yae and young Lord Natan," the God-King continued. "The harvest is always crucial, but even more so when the coastal lands have suffered such devastation. We will ask the thanes to send any men they can spare, but it will not be a royal command. Both the army and the country still need to eat." He cast a look at Darel, and Darel remembered the conversation in the Inner Council meeting, about sending aid eastwards across Narida. Those orders were unlikely to have gone out, unless Idramar had fared rather better against its attackers than anticipated.

"In the meantime," Natan continued, "this king intends to take residence in Threestones until we are able to get word of the situation in Idramar."

"You honour us with your presence, Divine One," Thane

Mattit said immediately, and Darel could detect no sense of resentment or reluctance at having such an imposition dropped into his lap. It seemed Yae had been correct: whatever the issue was within the family, Mattit Threestone was a loyal servant of the Sun Throne, and its current occupant. Besides, playing host to the God-King *was* a great honour, and would theoretically provide Thane Mattit with a chance for advancement in the hierarchy of Narida, if he was interested in such things.

"Then all that remains for now is to gather what forces you can command yourself," Natan said. "The sooner we begin preparations, the sooner we can move if we need to."

"Your servant will begin the muster immediately," Thane Mattit replied, getting to his feet, but Natan raised his hand.

"One moment. If young Lord Natan would see to it? And perhaps he would like the chance to properly greet his siblings; this king realises that he brought you all in here with great haste."

The meaning was clear: the Threestone children departed from their father's study, leaving Thane Mattit, Natan Narida, and Darel behind.

"Lord Threestone, your king will be blunt," Natan began. "Your daughter suggested your home as a place for your king to muster his forces. You have been most welcoming and gracious, but your king has still noticed tension between you and your two younger children. Both have proven to be quick-thinking and loyal, including taking up arms to defend him during the attempt on his life by the former Southern Marshal."

Mattit Threestone, who had been staring stonily into his yeng cup since he realised where Natan was going, looked up in surprise at that.

"Your king wishes to hear why it is that your family is at odds," Natan said. "We came here in urgent need, but if it is not suitable for Lady Yae and Lord Hiran to be here, he would know about it."

Mattit Threestone took a deep breath and set down his cup. "Your servant will obey, Your Majesty, if this is your express command."

"It is," Natan confirmed, his expression unchanged. Darel cringed internally, but he had not been excused, and although it felt like a breach of his friendship to listen to what was said, it would be a far greater breach of honour for him to leave the presence of his monarch without being instructed to do so.

"Very well." Thane Mattit exhaled again. "Your servant's oldest child, named in your honour, did not from a young age display the kind of martial manner we looked for in a son. Threestones is a mighty fortress and has an important role in safeguarding both river and road: it needs a thane who can command men in the field. Hiran, when he followed, was of a similar disposition, and so we adopted a child who seemed suitable."

"You adopted a daughter?" Natan asked, with a surprise that Darel echoed. Female children could technically inherit, but their claim would always be weaker, and prone to imposition. He had previously wondered why Yae's father had adopted her, but doubly so now he knew the professed reasoning behind it.

"No, Your Majesty," Thane Mattit replied. "We adopted a third son, between Natan and Hiran in age. Or so we thought."

Suddenly, a few things that Darel had paid little mind to at the time slotted into place.

"As Yae grew older, our misunderstanding became clearer," Threestone continued. He spread his hands. "So now we are left in this situation, with two sons who have shown little inclination towards the mindset of a lord, and a daughter who by her nature would leave our lands weak should she inherit. Not only is your servant's bloodline lacking, but apparently his judgement is as well. He will not disown his daughter, nor adopt again, for the sake of his sons' sensibilities, but neither will he pretend that he is not disappointed in them. At least Natan had the courage to stay and try to learn," he added bitterly.

There was silence for a few moments. Then Natan Narida spoke.

"If there is one thing that this king has learned in the last few months," he said, "it is that a martial mindset does not automatically make for a trustworthy individual. Two of this king's High Marshals attempted to take his throne from him, one through deception and one through force of arms. Marshal Blackcreek is a scholar as much as he is a warrior, but your king would trust him, and your two younger children, with his life. In fact, he has already done so. You might wish to think on that, Lord Threestone."

Natan rose to his feet. Darel, who had no intention of remaining behind whether or not he was bidden to follow, did the same. The last thing he saw before he turned to leave was Mattit Threestone staring down into his yeng cup once more.

Saana

Saana was still undecided on whether to trust Yarmina Darkspur. The girl had taken the news of her father's death very stoically, although part of that could be put down to the Naridan disdain for showing emotion, which seemed particularly prevalent in their nobility. Still, with the strange Naridan method of passing authority from parent to child, rather than having their leader selected by witches, Yarmina had undeniably gained from Thane Odem's drowning. Had she wanted her father to come back from his war? Had she encouraged him to go, having sent her letter to warn Daimon of it, in the hope that he would die? Saana could not say, but she was prepared to entertain the possibility that Yarmina had viewed her father's attempt to conquer Black Keep as something that would only benefit her in one way or another.

On the other hand, Saana most definitely did *not* trust Sar Asad. He walked with a pronounced limp, which explained why he had been left in charge of the town's defences instead of riding with his thane to attack Black Keep, but Saana could practically smell the ambition coming off him. Asad was the only remaining Darkspur sar who was neither dead nor sworn into the service of Black Keep, and Saana remembered how Yarmina's marriage had been dangled in front of Daimon by Thane Odem, courtesy of his cousin. What better way for a sar whose best fighting days were behind him to improve his station in life than by marrying Yarmina? Darkspur's nobility clearly held the girl's own wishes on such things in low regard.

All these things were running through her head as she, Daimon, and their four guards entered the town. She was anticipating them being taken up to the great fist of rock where the stronghold of the Darkspur family stood, but instead they were ushered into a building within sight of the gate. The sour smell of Naridan ale met her nose as they walked inside.

"A tavern?" Daimon asked in surprise.

"This lady has given instructions for the town's gates to remain open," Yarmina said, from the table where she was already sat, "at least so long as your troops do not try to enter. However, they can see the door through which you have just come, and so can be assured that you are not being ambushed or taken hostage."

"Very sensible," Daimon agreed. He cast a glance at Sar Asad, who stood stiffly beside Yarmina's chair. "May we sit?"

"By all means," Yarmina replied, extending a hand. Daimon pulled a chair up for Saana, who stifled a smile at the gesture. They both knew she was perfectly capable of finding herself somewhere to sit, but it was something deeply ingrained within his character. At least she had got used to using chairs regularly: they were normally only used in Tjakorsha when a chief was passing judgement, and her old chieftain's chair − a massive, carved thing that she always thought was ugly − was one of the few things Saana did not regret leaving behind in Koszal when her clan fled across the ocean.

"Let us get to the point," Yarmina said, as soon as they were seated. "Were your words outside of mutual aid genuine, Lord Daimon, or did they mask some other purpose for coming here with an army at your back?"

"What other purpose could there be?" Daimon demanded.

"Both of us will struggle this winter without the other's assistance; surely you can recognise that?"

"This woman had no part in her father's decision to march upon you, but you cannot know that," Yarmina said levelly. "Some men would seek revenge."

Of course, Saana realised. *She doesn't want Asad to know about the letter she sent to warn us. She needs him to think we have no reason to like her, in case she gets suspected of being in league with us.* She paused, as another thought occurred to her. *Unless they had a plan between them. Do away with the father, the sar marries the daughter* . . . She eyed the Darkspur pair. Asad was older than Yarmina, but was the age difference between them that much greater than between her and Daimon? Would they put aside such thoughts, in the interests of each getting power that neither of them could have hoped to hold with Thane Odem still alive? *And then there's nothing to say that one or both of them wouldn't be thinking about disposing of the other afterwards, to take all the power for themselves* . . . *by the Dark Father, Naridans make things so confusing!*

"Some men would have sought to die in accordance with the Code of Honour instead of allowing the Tjakorshi to settle in Black Keep, even though that was the path that clearly offered the least death and suffering all round," Daimon was saying levelly. "This man would hope his previous actions go some way towards assuring you of his intentions."

"We can have no assurances from a man who consorts with witches!" Sar Asad snapped.

"So what do you want to do?" Saana asked him, not bothering to hide her smile when he jumped at being addressed in Naridan by her. "If you will not trust us, you would prefer that we attack? Or that we wait until you have your harvest, then come and take it from you?" She folded her arms. "This man's people stopped raiding these shores once she became chief, but they still remember how to steal from Naridans."

"Saana," Daimon said warningly, but she brushed him off.

"What? You suggest we help each other, he says he cannot trust you, so what is his suggestion instead? That we go back to Black Keep and starve in the winter? Your wife will not do that."

"Chief Saana is blunt, but she raises a good point," Yarmina said, looking at Asad. "We *have* lost a lot of men who would have helped with the harvest. Lord Daimon has suggested a solution. If you think it is not a good solution, Sar Asad, it surely behoves you to provide a better one."

The castellan hesitated, but set his jaw. "Sometimes there are no good options, Lady Yarmina, but it is better for us to forge our own path than to ally with those who allow witches in their midst."

"A witch was found in Black Keep," Daimon said loudly. "One witch, who fled before we could execute him. It is a matter of great regret that we did not know of his nature sooner. However, in investigating his deviancy, we discovered many of the marks and signs that witches use. Would you like us to look through your town, Sar Asad, to ensure that you have none here?"

"That will not be necessary," Yarmina said firmly and quickly. "Darkspur does not tolerate witches. But it is worth noting, Sar Asad, that if the people of Black Keep truly allow witches to live among them, it was strange that they should choose to announce the fact when this lady and her escort were present. It certainly seemed to her that the Black Keep reeve was bringing the urgent matter to his lord's attention as soon as it was discovered, with no attempt made to hide it from outsiders."

Sar Asad scowled. "It sounds as though you wish to accede to Lord Blackcreek's . . . *suggestion*."

"There seems little reason to refuse," Yarmina said, with a glance at Saana. "Peace with our neighbours is desirable, as is eating. Lord Daimon has taken this lady at her word that she had no part in her father's decision to march on Black Keep, and so she will take him at his that he has no motive other than mutual benefit."

It all seemed to be going very well. Saana could tell that Asad was quietly furious about it, but he appeared to have accepted that he was not going to get to make the decision.

"With that agreement made in principle, we must turn to details," Yarmina said, steepling her fingers and looking over them at Daimon. "To whit, how many workers Black Keep will provide and on what land they will work, and how much of the harvest they would get in exchange."

Saana would not have noticed the slight shift in Daimon's features had she not got to know him well, but it was there. It was the expression of a man who had come prepared for one contest, and having succeeded unexpectedly easily in it now found that another he had not anticipated lay beyond it.

"Furthermore," Yarmina was continuing, "since this wave struck Black Keep, this lady imagines that much of Lord Daimon's supplies to last until harvest have been destroyed. If his people will need feeding until the work is done, we must discuss how much can be spared, and at what cost."

Saana did not even have to look at Daimon to know that he was wishing his brother was there, or the steward Osred. However, Darel Blackcreek was in Idramar with the Naridan God-King, and Osred was probably halfway there too by now, bearing news of treachery and an attack that had not, in the end, come to pass.

"This man will need to take an accounting of those who came with him," Daimon said, trying not to appear flustered. Saana was not sure how he came across to Yarmina and Asad, but she at least could tell that he was suddenly uncomfortable.

"By all means," Yarmina replied gravely. "Once you have the information, we can begin discussions about accommodation, provisions, and so forth."

Daimon got to his feet. "Then this man sees no point in lingering. He is glad that we have come to an agreement that will benefit us both, once the details are confirmed."

"This woman is also glad," Yarmina replied with a smile, which she turned towards Saana. "Lady Saana."

"Lady Yarmina," Saana replied. She flashed a smile of her own, and was perversely amused to see the girl jump just a little. Back in Black Keep, Saana made an offhand remark about punching her: or, more accurately, about how Saana had decided that she did *not* need to punch her. Either way, perhaps it had stuck in Yarmina's mind. She got up and followed Daimon out of the door and towards Darkspur's gate, with their guards falling in around them.

"Nari's teeth, did Odem raise a lady or a merchant?" Daimon muttered to her as they walked. "We came offering help in good faith, and now she seeks advantage!"

"Those things would need to be decided," Saana pointed out. "Also, she cannot look weak, or Asad will try to take power from her."

Daimon frowned. "You think so?"

"Given your people's attitudes to women?" Saana snorted. "Yes. So if we want the deal to continue, we must let her look a bit strong."

Daimon sighed. "It is at times like this that your husband can almost see the appeal of solving a problem by hitting it with a sword until it goes away. Almost."

"That just makes more problems, in the end," Saana said.

"So you make more swords." Daimon laughed humourlessly.

"Your husband thinks we might have just found a way to shorten the Code of Honour by about a third, while still preserving the essential meaning." They passed through the gate, and were walking back towards the expectant folk of Black Keep when Daimon sucked his teeth in annoyance. "But of course, we brought no parchment from Black Keep, if there was even any left dry in the first place."

"Yarmina would have some," Saana offered, but Daimon shook his head.

"No. Your husband has no wish to look foolish in front of her again." He looked down and kicked the dirt under his feet. "We will need a sharp stick, that is all."

"You are going to count people by scratching on the ground?" Saana asked dubiously.

"Yes," Daimon said stoutly. "Counting is simple. What could go wrong?"

Tila

Parts of Idramar were aflame. Tila could smell the smoke.

She had retained her head after her failed attempt to kill The Golden, but not the use of her arms. Her wrists were bound behind her back with leather cord, and only her long familiarity with the footing of the Sun Palace prevented her from falling on her face half a dozen times as she was prodded this way and that. She had fantasised about a rescue; maybe a small, determined group of sars sortieing out of one of the palace's innumerable doorways and cutting down the Raiders with her, severing her bonds with a longblade's edge, and then making a break for the main gate on dragonback. She would have welcomed the appearance of Adan Greenbrook. She would even have been grateful to see the face of someone like Sar Ravel, the man who had been instructed to lose on her behalf in an honour duel, until she had put paid to that plan with the unscheduled appearance of Alazar of White Hill.

However, her fantasies remained just that. The defence of the Sun Palace, so far as Tila could put it together afterwards, was a tale of multiple acts of individual heroism, but little co-ordination. Some Naridans met the attackers head on and sold their lives dearly, their blades cutting down attackers until they were overwhelmed. Others held fast in strong positions, only to find themselves attacked from behind as those seeking a glorious death were overrun, or comrades with less courage simply capitulated in the hope of saving their own skin. By the time the crescent of the short moon had reached its apex in the night sky, there was no more defiance to be had within the palace's walls.

It was then that Tila found herself brought into the Hall of Heaven, the place where she had watched her father and her brother rule over their nation, and where she had cast her defiance in the teeth of Einan Coldbeck's attempted coup. Now, though, the torches on the walls were unlit. Instead, two piles of wood were blazing in the middle of the flagstone floor. Barbarians' fires in the heart of civilisation, no more than Tila would have expected from Raiders.

What she had not expected, however, was the absence of guards. The mighty chamber seemed empty apart from the interpreter, hunched and miserable-looking, and The Golden.

The Golden was not sitting on the Sun Throne, which was another surprise. Tila wondered if it simply did not understand the concept of thrones, and what they represented. Perhaps The Golden saw the throne as nothing more than a large chair made of the same metal with which it had decorated its war gear. Either way, The Golden was standing in front of it as she was ushered forwards, bathed in the light from the two fires.

Now she had a proper chance to study it, and she took it. Tall, but not overly so: strong-looking, but not hugely stout or broad. Red-gold hair and beard, both cut short, unlike most of the other Raiders. Most striking, though, was the scar around its neck. Tila had seen enough people go to the rope over the years to recognise a hanging mark when she saw one, and yet The Golden was standing here in front of her.

Many years had passed since Tila had last been scared of a person. Wary, yes; alarmed at what their actions could potentially mean for her, or her country, or her criminal empire, certainly. But scared of an individual, to the point that being in their presence made the hair stand up on her arms, her breath come a little quicker, and her heartbeat thud with slightly more force in her chest? That had not happened since her youth, back when she did Yakov's bidding, and risked his dry, emotionless displeasure if she failed him.

She was experiencing it now.

"This man is Tajen," the interpreter said. "He speaks for The Golden."

"And who is The Golden?" Tila demanded. This was a very simple form of political bargaining, but it was one she was used to, and settled into automatically. There were few better ways to get concessions than if the other party was desperate, or in a hurry, and Tajen was obviously just as scared of The Golden as she was, if not more so. If he was anxious not to displease his master, Tila would get what she could from him first.

"This man told you—" Tajen began, then broke off. "Do you know what a draug is?"

"No," Tila said simply, and folded her arms.

"A draug is . . . It's a . . . " Tajen trailed off again, and actually growled in frustration. "Mushuru's ashes, this would be easier if you could speak Alaban," he added in that language.

"I can," Tila replied. "Sort of, anyway."

Tajen's visible shock rapidly morphed into something approaching relief. "*Right*. Fine. Well, a draug is a spirit that takes over the body of a dead or sick person. The Golden is a draug. It broke the clans of Tjakorsha by killing all the chiefs or making them swear loyalty to it, and apparently the witches say it cannot itself be killed. You are I are both dead unless we can tell it what it wants to know."

The naked fear in Tajen's voice filled in the gaps left by Tila's imperfect understanding of his words. Even more strangely, he used the word "it" despite speaking in Alaban, which had the gender-neutral "they". *The Golden is . . . a demon of some sort? It sounds like a children's tale, but . . .* She looked over at The Golden, and found it staring back at her, motionless and unblinking.

"And what does it want to know?" she asked, aware that her voice was not as steady as she might have wished.

The Golden stepped forwards, the firelight throwing strange, shifting shadows over it as it moved.

"I want to know where your god is."

It, too, was speaking Alaban. Tajen whirled around as though he had been stung. Tila, for her part, probably reacted with little more poise, although part of her mind registered the fact that The Golden was even using the formal neutral gender for them both, as most Alabans would with anyone whom they did not know well. So it did not speak Naridan, but it *did* speak Alaban, and its own interpreter had not known this. That was interesting.

It also ruined the idea of bartering information back and forth with Tajen. Tila silently cursed even as the draug stepped past the translator, who looked like he was about to throw up. It was only then that she registered what The Golden had actually said.

"You want to know *what*?" she repeated, her mind racing. What did it mean? Surely it could not be talking about Natan: how would a Raider know about him?

"The person who brought you to me told me of rumours they had heard," The Golden said, locking eyes with her. They were pale green, and their stare was one of the most unnerving things Tila had ever encountered. "Rumours that your god was ill."

Natan's "illness". Damn it. "The God-King was ill," she said cautiously. "Hè recovered."

The Golden's lip curled. "No matter. I still wish to find hìm."

Tila did her best to straighten her spine and keep her voice level. "Why?"

"I broke the clans of Tjakorsha, as my interpreter said," The Golden replied. "I set them free and brought them over the sea away from our land, before it died. Now I will break your god, set you free from hìm, and the Tjakorshi will live here."

Tila would have tried once more to put a knife into The Golden's throat had her wrists not been bound behind her, but as it was, the worst she could have done was kick it in the shin. She tried to fight down her reaction, but something in the draug's eyes told her that it had noted it nonetheless. She just had to hope it would take it as piety, instead of sisterly affection.

"You want to live here?" she managed.

"Fàther Krayk prepared you for our coming," The Golden said calmly. "Why should we not?"

The wave? Was it talking about the great wave? Tila remembered Darel Blackcreek mentioning Father Krayk, the sea god of his new allies in the south. She hardly wanted to believe that the god of these savages could wreak such destruction, but it was not as though anyone had come up with a better explanation for why so much of their coastline had been destroyed.

"Hè also ruined most of the food anywhere nearby," Tila said defiantly, "so Ī hope you aren't hungry after your voyage."

"Then we will move farther inland," The Golden said, as though this was a minor concern. "But yõu have not yet told me where I can find yõur God-King. Do yõu refuse to do so?"

Tila hesitated. She had no idea where Natan was now, which almost made this more difficult. If she answered, but accidentally sent the Raiders after him . . .

The Golden did not give her time to make up her mind.

It moved so swiftly that she barely saw it, and then there was a new grip on her hair and she was being propelled across the floor towards one of the fires. She struggled, but the draug was immensely strong, and with her hands tied behind her back she had no way of fighting. She could not even try to kick without losing her balance, which happened anyway when a blow struck the back of her legs and dropped her to her knees. They struck the hard flagstones of the floor with a loud crack, and a spike of pain that made her whimper and her eyes water.

The Golden pushed her head towards the fire, and heat bloomed across her face. For a moment it was simply the warm kiss of a midsummer's day, but within another heartbeat she could feel her skin starting to tighten, and the dampness in her eyes beginning to dry, and she was not yet very near the flames themselves. She tried not to think of her hair catching alight and burning down to her head.

"I will ask one more time," The Golden said, and now its voice held a whiplike tone of command. "Where is yōur God-King? Stonejaw said yōu were a chief of some sort, that others held yōu in high regard, which is why yōu have this opportunity to be useful to me. If yōu do not answer me, I will show yōur charred body to those who follow yōu in the hope that one of them may have more wisdom!"

"West!" Tila shouted desperately. "Hè's in the west!"

The hand on the back of her head pushed her a little closer to the fire. "Do better."

Inspiration struck.

"Hè's in the mountains!" Tila said. "The God-King has been reborn! Nari's true heir is in the mountains, gathering hìs followers!"

The pressure eased slightly. "What do yōu mean by 'true heir'?"

Tila tried to get some moisture into a mouth that already felt parched by the fire. "The real God-King, not the man who sat on this throne! People say Hìs time has come, and Hè's returned to us!" She racked her brain for all the addle-brained nonsense she had heard prated about. "They say Hè heals the sick, and Hè will bring down the laws of this land and raise new ones in their place, and the loyal will be rewarded! Hè'll be at Godspire, the greatest mountain in the world; if Hè has not already left there, in which case Hè will be coming here to take the throne!"

There was silence for a moment.

"If you don't believe Ī'm telling the truth, have your interpreter ask others," Tila added. "Some will say that the old God-King is the true one, but others will tell you that the one in the mountains is the Divine One reborn."

"Even supposing that they do," The Golden said softly. "Why would yōu tell me where yōur god can be found?"

Tila smiled the sort of smile she had seen on the face of Taladhar Torgallen when the uncomfortably pious Western Marshal had been looking at her or her brother. "If Hè is truly divine, Hè will triumph no matter what you send against Hìm. If not, Hè is only a pretender."

The Golden gave a snort of what might have been amusement, and then finally, blessedly, released its grip on her head. Tila shuffled backwards without any grace at all, and was so glad to be away from the choking heat that she did not at all mind when she toppled over onto her side. She rested her cheek against a cool flagstone, and took a deep breath of relatively pleasant air.

She was still alive.

What was more, she had just set a foreign demon towards the throat of an upstart god. One of them might win, but that would still be one less enemy than her family currently faced.

Natan, wherever you are, your sister hopes you make the most of whatever opportunity she manages to carve out for you.

Alazar

M arin was not sleeping, and Alazar was worried about him.

That was not entirely true, of course: Marin *was* sleeping, but only in the exhausted slump that came when even his frantically whirling mind could no longer keep him awake. He never seemed rested when Alazar woke him up in the mornings, and although he settled down readily enough with his arm across Alazar's chest at night, there was no sign that their closeness gave him the same sense of peace and reassurance that Alazar himself got from it.

Alazar knew what was bothering his husband, but that did not mean he could do anything about it. Still, he tried.

"It's not your fault," he told Marin in a low voice, murmuring into his ear.

"It was your husband's idea," Marin replied bleakly. He was stumbling along, one foot in front of the other, but the motion seemed more born of reflex than anything conscious. "He quoted the prophecy. He told the Divine One to go to Godspire."

"And you weren't the only one," Alazar pointed out. "Mordokel had the same idea, and there must have been others. One way or the other, He had to go there in the end."

But the reassurances meant nothing to Marin, no matter

how they were worded, or how often they were repeated. Alazar could understand why. He could still see the burning monastery, and hear the shrieks of the murdered monks as the Godsworn rejected their pronouncement and visited vengeance upon them. He had seen worse, during his time as a mercenary. He might have done worse, too, but being a blacksword did not mean he lost all of his morals along with his honour. His sword had been bought many times in the past, but not his soul. Some things were not worth the money you were offered.

The disturbing thing, the thing that still nagged at him as badly as it did at Marin, was that Tyrun had just watched it happen.

Alazar had tried to justify it. The Divine Nari of old had been a warrior king. He had forged Narida into one nation through bloody conquest, as He tore through the petty kings and burned through the witches to drive the evil, corrupted minions of the Unmaker from the land. Nari had not flinched from dealing death; He had excelled at it. There was no reason his successor should be any different.

The difference was, Marin pointed out, that the monks of Godspire were not Tyrun's enemies. They were devoted to the service of Nari, and the Prophecies of Tolkar said that they would proclaim His return.

"They didn't though, did they?" Ravi said, when Marin voiced this. "Perhaps the order was flawed. They're just men, after all, and it's been centuries."

"Or perhaps 'proclaim' means something different in this context," Alazar suggested. He was thinking out loud more than anything else, but Marin looked at him sideways as they trudged along. They were some way behind the main body of the Godsworn now, as they continued their descent from Godspire along the banks of what would become the River Greenwater, mainly because Marin was struggling to keep up.

"What do you mean?" his husband asked.

"If you kill a bunch of monks, that's another way of proclaiming yourself," Alazar said. He shrugged uncomfortably. He did not particularly like the notion, but he knew what it meant to make a statement. "Do the Prophecies say specifically how the monks are involved?"

Marin looked back down at his feet. He had fallen over them enough times already that keeping an eye on them was probably not a bad idea. "Your husband can't remember the exact wording offhand. But the meaning seems fairly clear."

"Mar, if there's one thing your husband learned as a sar, it's that what everyone thinks something *means* and what it actually *says* can be two different things," Alazar said, chuckling. Marin was a scholar, and Alazar was not going to argue with his husband if he said he was sure of something, but no one was immune from assumptions. "He won the honour duel for the Divine Princess because he paid attention to what the rules were, rather than what his opponent thought they were."

An exhausted smile crossed Marin's face, which made Alazar's heart glad. "And because you fought dirty, as your husband heard it."

"You think it was dirty? You go and ask the lad whether he preferred having his nose broken to his throat opened," Laz said with a snort. His opponent in the Sun Gardens had possessed all the confidence and vigour of a young man who had never been beaten bloody, and Laz was fairly sure he could have bested him even without his trick. There were some things you only learned once they had been done to you, and you just had to hope the lesson was painful rather than deadly. "Although your husband will admit, a few years in the Alaban fighting pits did broaden his skills a little."

The moment of levity passed, and Laz could almost see the hollowness settling into Marin's chest again. None of them spoke much until later in the day, by which time they had finally left behind the stunted conifers of the higher ground and were surrounded by the beginnings of the Greenwater valley's rich woodland.

"Are we not worthy, then?" Marin asked, as the sun began to dip towards the peaks behind them. "S'man isn't comfortable with what happened on Godspire, and he's worried that so many of the Godsworn are."

"The Divine One said you were welcome," Ravi said. Alazar was honestly not sure why she was hanging back with him and Marin, given how they had all met, but he had no objection to her presence. He quite liked her, she gave the two of them enough space for privacy when they wanted it, and she had caught Marin when he stumbled once without even complaining about it.

"S'man *was* welcome," Marin agreed dully. "But what about now? Was the monastery his test? Does the fact he can't accept it mean he is not a true follower of the Divine One after all?"

"In which case, your husband's not either," Alazar said. He was unsure how he felt about that. There was certainly something to Tyrun. He had a sense of peace and power that Alazar had never felt around either God-King he had met; or Tila, for that matter. The blood might have been divine, but even when he had been in love with Natan, Alazar would have been hard-pressed to say that he felt any sort of devotion that did not come from his own heart. Tyrun, though . . . Alazar did not know for sure what a holy being felt like, but Tyrun definitely came the closest of anyone he had met. When he looked into the Divine One's eyes, it felt like Tyrun had read his soul. More notably, he felt like Tyrun had accepted what he saw, even though Alazar himself had strong questions at times about what was buried in there.

Marin looked uncomfortable, and Alazar realised his

husband was feeling guilty at the thought that he had made someone else question themselves in the same way as he was. He changed tack. "It does seem kind of strange, when you think about it, that a bunch of men who've lived most of their lives on a mountainside get to say who is and isn't divine. Maybe it was never right in the first place. *We* didn't need their say-so to accept Him."

"But you could get rid of a monastery without killing everyone in it," Ravi said shortly. She was not looking at either of them, but down the thickly wooded slope towards where the river roared below, mainly obscured by tree trunks. "S'woman knows they didn't do what they were supposed to, but Marin's got a point. It still doesn't feel right, no matter what she tells herself." She tugged absent-mindedly at the collar of her dress, although Laz thought he knew what she was subconsciously trying to hide. Marin had told him about Ravi's tattoos, and the conversation they had at the Pool of Tears. It certainly made her furious reaction to being called a witch by the self-proclaimed physician in Northbank a bit more understandable; although to be fair, no one was going to take such an accusation well.

Alazar thought about it for a few seconds. "This sar doesn't reckon you could, actually."

"Could what?"

"Get rid of the monastery without killing them. They've been there for *centuries*, and the return of the Divine One was their whole purpose," Alazar pointed out. "If that's what you've devoted your life to, what do you do once it's happened?"

"You follow the Divine One once He has revealed Himself!" Ravi protested. "Obviously!"

Alazar chuckled. "You've never been around people in power, have you? They don't like giving it up." He sighed. "They also don't like letting anyone else have it, and proclaiming someone to be the Divine One would mean they gave up all the control they had. But whatever the reason, once they decided not to proclaim Tyrun, they had no reason to listen to Him. If He left them alive, they could proclaim against him. This sar's not saying that killing them was right," he added hastily, when Ravi looked at him in horror. "It's just . . . that's how people think. For that matter, this sar doesn't care what the Divine One has said, most of the thanes aren't going to go along with anything that brings them down to the level of the lowborn. One or two of the most pious ones might, but not the rest."

"How can you know that?" Ravi demanded.

"This sar's seen it happen with the Divine Family," Alazar told her. "All the nobles love the Divine Family so long as they think they can get something from them, and they'll all profess obedience and devotion to the God-King. Once they end up on the wrong side of a decision or a judgement, though, piety takes a hike."

"You sound awfully confident of that for a blacksword," Ravi said. Her tone was light, but Alazar noticed the glance she gave his scabbard, and something ugly twisted in his gut.

"How do you think this sar became a blacksword?" he demanded. "You have to start somewhere to be cast out from it." He shrugged his shoulders and grimaced. "It turns out that when you see Nari's descendant running away from a battle in fear, and then die sobbing of arrow wounds, you begin to have doubts about exactly how much divinity is left in the bloodline."

"You were there when the old King Natan died?!"

"And took the blame for it," Alazar muttered. He did not look at Marin, but suddenly regretted mentioning the whole thing. It seemed bizarre to consider the current God-King of Narida as a rival in love, but it was fair to say that Marin had done so for many years. Natan III was not completely out of Alazar's mind, and he had never pretended otherwise. Natan still dwelled there in a bitter corner, and Laz knew Marin had never been completely comfortable about it, no matter how many times Alazar had assured his husband that there was absolutely no possibility of any form of romantic reconciliation between them. Their conversation after the honour duel had not changed that, although it had at least brought Alazar some form of closure. He and Natan had not exactly parted on good terms, but perhaps more mature ones.

On the other hand, Alazar was at least able to tell his husband that he was *better* than the God-King, and not many men could say that from direct comparison.

They found a spot to sleep that night under the spreading branches of a huge whiteleaf oak, with Marin and Alazar next to each other, and Ravi on the other side of their little fire, as was usual. Alazar kissed Marin goodnight as they settled down to try to get to sleep, but his husband's finger was still tracing absent-minded circles on Alazar's chest by the time he dropped off.

Two days later, as they trailed along in the wake of the main body of the Godsworn, the morning rain striking down through the trees overhead parted for a moment to reveal the hooded shape of someone coming the other way up the muddy, rutted track they were following.

Mordokel.

Alazar immediately became a little more alert. He had met many dangerous people during his life, and to his mind the priest ranked among them. It was not just that he obviously knew how to use the blade on his hip; it was the air he gave off which indicated that he would do so without hesitation. *Two things can make a man deadly*, came back the words of

Sar Banan, the warrior who had raised Alazar to the ranks of Narida's sars, *the skill to do harm, and the will to do harm. Either should make you wary; both together should be treated with the greatest caution.*

Alazar had, perhaps, fallen down on the "greatest caution" front in the past, else he would not have shown off before the honour duel began. Had he been facing Mordokel in that situation, he would not have engaged in any such behaviour. He would still have used every dirty trick he knew, however, since he had absolutely no doubt that the priest would be doing the same.

"There you are," Mordokel said, when he was a few paces away. "For a moment, this priest wondered whether you had deserted us."

There was already danger lurking beneath his words. "Deserted" was never a good phrase to hear used in reference to yourself, as Alazar knew from bitter experience, and Mordokel clearly intended to put them on the defensive. The only question was whether that was deliberate, or simply his hard-edged nature.

"This sar's husband has not been well," Alazar said, deciding it was best if Mordokel focused on him for now. Given how Ravi had edged slightly behind him, it seemed she had no objections about this.

"This priest is sorry to hear that," Mordokel said smoothly. "It would not do for one of the Divine One's advisors to fall ill."

"Advisor?" Marin repeated, somewhat hesitantly.

"Indeed!" Mordokel said. He threw back his hood, allowing the water to run off his bald head, and fixed Marin with his disturbingly sharp eyes. "After all, was it not your advice that persuaded the Divine One to seek the proclamation of Godspire? Your name is celebrated among the Godsworn, Marin of Idramar, and the Divine One has missed your counsel."

Alazar did not need to look at his husband's face to know how Marin was likely to take that, and felt his own body stiffening reflexively. However, Mordokel hopefully did not know about Marin's doubts, and could not be allowed to find out. Alazar could vividly remember kneeling by his husband's side in the flickering light cast by the burning monastery, wondering if they were about to be set upon by those of the Godsworn not already engaged in butchery. He had no illusions about how Mordokel would react if he felt their faith was in question.

Thankfully, Marin was just as good at spotting danger, and he managed a smile. "S'man is honoured to hear it. What brings you back to find us?"

The faintest hint of a smile twitched at one corner of Mordokel's mouth. "An unexpected new development. Follow this priest, and he will show you."

"An unwelcome development?" Alazar asked, as Mordokel put his hood back up.

"That remains to be seen," the priest replied, over his shoulder. He paused, then added, "Although your blade would be welcome too, goodsar."

"That doesn't sound good," Ravi muttered from behind them, and Alazar was inclined to agree with her.

It took most of an hour to catch up with the main body of the group, so Mordokel must have begun tracking back to find them not long after the Godsworn had got moving that morning. Their numbers had grown, by Alazar's loose estimate: perhaps they had found more people on the road, either those heading to Godspire in the hope of finding the Divine One, or simply travellers who had been swept up along the way. The atmosphere was tense, and various weapons were on show. The Godsworn were not an army – they lacked the organisation, or the officers – but most of the able-bodied had something that could be used in a fight, at least in a pinch. As the monks of Godspire had found out to their cost, of course.

"This sar would really appreciate knowing what this is all about," Alazar ventured to Mordokel, but the priest flapped a hand dismissively.

"You can see for yourself shortly. We are nearly there."

That did little to reassure Alazar, and he kept both hands on his longblade as they moved through the crowd, which parted in front of Mordokel with little hesitation. It was only when the press of people began to thin that Alazar realised they were nearly back at the camp where they had first met Tyrun.

"Word of the Divine One's presence has clearly spread," Mordokel said, and his voice held a certain tension that Alazar had not heard in it before. If anything, he would say that the priest was a little bit unsure of himself, which was not something Alazar would have ever associated with him.

When Mordokel stopped at the edge of a rise in the ground and gestured forward, Alazar understood why.

The road swept on downwards, out of the woodland and onto the open land on which Tyrun had been camped. A new camp was there now, and it was both far larger and far more organised than that of the Godsworn had been. Alazar took in the rows and rows of tents, the pickets of the war dragons, the latrine ditch, and the grand pavilion at the centre of it all. The pennant from its spire hung limply in the rain, but he could still make out the white triangle topped with a golden sunburst.

"Fuck," he said flatly. "That's the Western Army."

"We assumed as much," Mordokel said. "You are sure?"

"That's Marshal Torgallen's personal banner," Laz said, pointing to the central pavilion. "Godspire surmounted by the sunburst. It has to be." He whistled. "The old man's not been idle after all. There are thousands of them down there."

"More than we have here," Mordokel acknowledged, "and a lot will be trained soldiers."

"They must have seen us, mustn't they?" Marin asked, weakly hopeful. "If they haven't attacked . . ."

"Oh, they've seen us," Alazar said. There were ranks of men drawn up and waiting in the rain. "But Torgallen's cautious. He won't push his men uphill into a force of unknown strength, not immediately. If we want to keep going this way, we have to go through them. Whatever we do will tell him about our intentions."

"You speak as if you know the man personally," Mordokel observed.

"This sar has met him a time or two, although not for many years," Alazar said, keeping his voice neutral, as he told himself that there was nothing wrong in trying to conceal his old relationship with Natan from both Tyrun and Mordokel. "This sar is from White Hill, which is between here and the Torgallen Pass."

"Well, it is good you are both here," Mordokel said with a smile, looking between Alazar and Marin. "The Divine One intends to go down and speak with the leader of that force." His smile widened. "And this priest thinks it would be an *excellent* idea for you both to accompany us, Marin of Idramar and Alazar of White Hill."

Otim

It had been a strange voyage. They stopped in at the port town called Tainmar, where Osred the steward was to send a message upriver to the local chief, who would hopefully go to Black Keep's aid. Otim expected trouble as soon as his taugh was sighted, but it seemed the piece of cloth bearing the Blackcreek symbol that Osred had insisted be tied to the mast helped convince the locals that they were not there to raid. The older Blackcreek boy had come this way as well, and brought news as he went of how the Brown Eagle clan had settled peaceably. Otim and his crew did not go ashore, and received their fair share of dirty looks from the Flatlanders, but no one actually drew a weapon.

"Good?" Otim asked, when Osred returned.

The steward waved a hand in a gesture Otim interpreted as meaning uncertainty. "Not *bad*. The sar will send a messenger, but neither he nor this man can say how Thane Gilan will respond."

Otim shrugged. He understood that Flatlander thanes were not exactly like Tjakorshi chiefs, but it was the closest likeness he had. One clan might raid another's land or sea, back on Tjakorsha, but all-out war between them was rare. A clan that was called on to aid another in that scenario would only do so if there was something in it for them, or some great debt that needed clearing. Otim had no idea how likely it was that this thane would side with one of his neighbours over another. He just hoped that if it happened, it was Black Keep that got the aid, and not Darkspur.

Then they headed northwards again, running before the wind. The sea was a wild place ruled by Father Krayk, whose moods were as powerful and changeable as a hooked spikefish, but Otim Ambaszhin had been sailing it for thirty years, and he was wise to its tricks. The *Longpride* was a good distance from the coast when the two great swells came tearing out of the east, and it rode them with nothing more than a few jarring bumps. Osred fell over, of course, but he was safely inside the deckhouse, and so at no risk of going over the side. He even managed a cheerful smile when Otim had poked his head in to see how the old man was.

Otim rather liked Osred, who was as stiff and upright as any Flatlander, and more so than most, but quite determined not to let it get in the way of the peace between their peoples. He did not help much on the *Longpride*, since he lacked the vigour or knowledge to haul on lines, manage the sails, or wield a paddle, but he made no complaint at what had to be a very strange existence for him, given he had lived most of his life in the Blackcreek family's big stone house. He stayed out of the way, ate Tjakorshi sea rations without turning his nose up at them, and was even picking up some words of the language. The same went for the other two Naridans on the crew: Elio, the fisherman whose father's actions had apparently set this entire chain of events into motion; and a girl named Ezi, whose brother Ravel had gone off into the mountains with Zhanna Longblade, and who had already shown Otim that not all Naridans lacked an instinct for the sea. They were good people.

It made it all the harder to bear their utter devastation when the *Longpride*'s crew saw the damage the great swells had done. Otim was shocked himself. He thought he knew what the ocean could do when it raged, but he had been mistaken. Whole swathes of trees were flattened and uprooted, leaving a tangle of flotsam near the coast through which no ship could sail. Great chunks of the shoreline had been carved away, leaving new sides of fresh, dark earth exposed to the air, and the entire place stank of rotting vegetation, as that which had been thrown on the shore began to decompose alongside the newly killed foliage on land.

That was terrifying enough, but what set the Naridans to tears was when they passed what had once been a village. It was right on the waterline, so close that it had probably been in danger from the high tides of a double moon, if coupled with an onshore wind. Only a few timbers and stones remained, so little that they nearly missed them among the general damage, but once seen it was obvious what had happened. The entire place had been swept away, and if anyone living there had survived then so far as Otim was concerned, they could claim to be kin with Lodzuuk Waveborn himself.

"We have to go back!" Osred said furiously, as they began to register exactly how wide-ranging the damage was. "We must return to Black Keep!"

Otim just shook his head. "No. Chiefs said go. We go."

In desperation, Osred dipped into the little Tjakorshi he had learned. "Otim, *please*!"

Otim sighed and held out one hand to represent the shore, then pointed to the very edge of his hand, and then at the ruins of the village now falling behind them. He looked at Osred to make sure the steward understood, then moved his finger to the middle of his hand. "Black Keep."

"Yes, it's farther inland," Osred said unhappily, "but do you really think that will make a difference?" He waved a bony hand at the damage, which had only spared the hills. "Look at this!"

Otim sighed, and gestured to his hand again. "Where Darkspur?" He had no real idea of the location of the enemy clan, but he did not think they were on the coast. That was borne out when Osred reluctantly pointed to somewhere far beyond the other side of his hand.

"Darkspur good?" Otim said. "Still come?"

Osred nodded gloomily.

"So we go," Otim said with finality. He was as worried about the people he had left behind at Black Keep as Osred was, but his chief had given him a task. If the sea had not taken care of Darkspur, then its thane might still be sending warriors to attack Black Keep. That meant it was still important for the *Longpride* to reach the Flatlanders' biggest city and find the Southern Marshal, the man who had helped fight off Rikkut Fireheart and his raiding party. Saana seemed convinced he was a big enough chief that he could tell the Darkspur thane to stop, and it would happen. It sounded wonderful, and Otim hoped it would work, but he had his doubts about what it said for the land in general. If Flatlanders would do whatever their chiefs told them, what happened when that chief decided he did not agree with you? You always had to hope they were on your side, which did not seem a good way to live. Otim was doing this because Saana had asked him to, and because he thought it might work, not because she could order him about no matter his own opinions.

Osred had not been the only one wanting to turn back, of course: Ezi had swallowed and looked very afraid when she realised what had happened to her home, and both Koren and Zalika had spoken up, saying that their first duty was to the clan. There was no real danger of a mutiny, but Otim still had to convince them that pressing on was the best course of action.

"Let's say we turn back," he said to them. "What are we

going to do to help? Are we shipwrights, to work wood and repair the Flatlander houses we were living in? We'll just be a dozen more bodies that need feeding and housing. And if we get back and then the Darkspur Flatlanders arrive, do you want to tell Saana that we didn't get the help we were meant to, and ruined her plan? Do you want to tell Daimon we never brought his brother back? *This* is our duty to the clan!"

They agreed with him readily enough in the end, but when the sun was swallowed by the west and the *Longpride* was steering by the light of the moons, and he was at the bow listening out for any sound of waves that might signify a danger to avoid, Otim still wondered whether he was right. Then he wondered whether Saana felt like this *all the time*, and decided he was glad the witches had never suggested that he should be chief when Black Kal died. Finding the right fishing grounds and navigating whatever Father Krayk could throw at his boat was enough of a challenge for him, and could still lead to the deaths of everyone on board it if he made the wrong call.

Osred had brought a map, which Otim found an amusing distraction, but ultimately useless when it came to navigating. He could not get his head around working out where he was from those marks, not when the wind and the waves told him about his surroundings. He did not need Osred's map to tell him when the large piece of land known to Flatlanders as Crown Island was to their west: he knew it from the change in the swell, and the distant pattern of clouds. Besides, he had been this way once before, which was more than any of the Naridans could say.

Many years ago, Otim had sailed with Iro Greybeard, and Tsolga Hornsounder, and his sister Avlja, among others. The Greybeard had his heart set on a summer of raiding, and they pillaged their way up the coast farther north than any of them had ever been before: possibly farther than any Tjakorshi had, or at least any of the Brown Eagles. They eventually reached what Otim realised must have been Idramar; or at least, if the Flatlanders had an even larger city on the coast somewhere, he struggled to imagine what that might look like. The Hornsounder had speculated that there might have been as many people in it as on all of Tjakorsha, and Otim was not certain that the old woman had been wrong. They picked Nalon up just north of there, when the Greybeard had run down the ship the iron-witch had been travelling on. Otim had no idea when he laid eyes on the squat, ugly little man that his sister was going to take a fancy to him, but life was always handing you surprises.

It did that again, when they were well north of Crown Island. Otim thought they should be getting close to their destination, and the summer sun was as fierce as he had ever felt it, even back in Tjakorsha during Long Day, when it never set at all. They had seen Flatlander ships, of course, and had easily steered well clear of them, so the shout announcing a new sail was nothing remarkable until he wandered up to the bow to take a look for himself.

"That doesn't look like a Flatlander sail," he remarked, peering northwards, and squinting against the reflections sparking off the wave crests. It was midday, so the sun was to the north as well, but it was higher than it ever got in Tjakorsha, and he was able to look directly ahead without blinding himself.

"It looks Tjakorshi," Zalika said uncertainly. "You don't suppose any of Fireheart's bastards could still be around, do you?"

Otim scratched at his moustaches. "I mean, it's possible. They could have been raiding all this time, I suppose. What's their heading?"

"Coming towards us," Zalika replied, then squinted herself. "Looks like they'll pass shorewards of us, if they don't alter course."

Otim bit his lip. A Tjakorshi ship far from home might cleave towards a familiar-looking sail just to exchange news, but raiders were usually just as happy to take prizes from rival clans as they were from whoever those rivals had first got them from. The *Longpride* only had a couple of actual warriors on board; most of those who had experience with a blackstone axe had been left behind to help defend Black Keep if it came to it. They were not in a great position to put up a fight against a raiding party, even if the numbers were equal. Judging by what scale Otim had to work with, the size of the vessel suggested that the *Longpride* would be at a disadvantage in that respect as well.

"We'll head east for now, and give them plenty of room," he said, signalling for the benefit of Koren on the steering paddle. "But we'll keep an eye on them, to make sure."

"What if they come for us?" Zalika asked.

"Run," Otim replied. "As best we can."

Larger ships tended to move faster than smaller ones, and the *Longpride* was a sturdy fishing vessel that was never going to have won a torc for its speed at clanmoot. If the other ship had a full crew and a competent captain, there would be little Otim could do, save ensure he had the biggest head start possible.

"Aren't you curious who they are, and what they're doing here?" Zalika asked.

"Oh yes," Otim replied. "Very. But not badly enough that I want to ask them face-to-face."

They steered north-east until the coast was the merest dark smudge on the horizon to the west, giving the other ship a wide berth, then came around to head back towards the shore once more. Otim began to breathe a little more easily and laughed out loud when he saw a distinctively shaped headland up ahead. It had been years since he had last seen it, but he remembered the huge pillar of rock standing just off it, which had apparently survived even the impact of the waves that had brought ruin to the shoreline even this far north.

"We're nearly there!" he cried in delight. "Once we round that, we should see the city." He was not entirely sure what state the city would be in, since he remembered it being close to the water's edge, but some parts of it had been on a hillside, so he had to hope that their voyage had not been in vain. His shout brought Osred out of the deck house, looking around curiously, and Otim beckoned the steward over. He was still trying to work out how to communicate his meaning in his very limited grasp of Naridan when another shout went up.

"New sail! New sail!"

Otim turned, his joy suddenly quenched by anxiety, and with good reason. The sail that had emerged from behind the headland was another Tjakorshi one, and far closer than the other had been.

"Shit!" Otim spat. They were so close to their destination! But there was nothing for it; he could not just steer past this vessel with a friendly wave and assume they meant no harm. Were these really the remnants of Fireheart's raiders? If so, they had picked the most populated area of the coast to harass. Surely they could not have made landfall at the city? They would have been overwhelmed!

"Come about, and be ready to run!" he bellowed, striding back down the length of the *Longpride* and peering to the south. "Where's the—"

He broke off, as his own question was answered by the speck of a sail to the south-east. It was the one from before, he had no doubt: they had sailed past, then turned back on themselves to trap him. Now he could run north into the new arrivals, break east and be converged on from both sides, or head south and be trapped against the shore.

"Who was watching for those goat-fuckers?" he bellowed, pointing at the sail. "Never mind! Arm yourselves! We don't know who this is, but I'd bet steel to straw that they're not friendly!"

Weapons were passed out from the deckhouse, and Otim belted on the steel sword Avlja had gained from a raid many years ago, and given to him as a very generous handfasting gift. He was far from skilled with it, but it had an edge and a point, and so long as he didn't drop it, there was no way for anyone facing him to *know* that his abilities were limited.

"What's our heading?" Koren asked nervously.

"Steer past them as though they're no threat," Otim replied, gesturing to the ship in front of them. "We can't avoid them, so let's pretend we're not trying."

It was a slim hope, and it predictably came to nothing. The other ship was a yolgu that must have been half as large again as the *Longpride*, and it changed course lazily to cut across their bow and come within hailing range. Otim's heart was pounding furiously, but he stepped up between the paddlers' places to face across the water, half-expecting to catch a sling-stone between his eyebrows at any moment.

He did not recognise any faces, but that had always been an outside chance; the Brown Eagles had been the most westward clan in all Tjakorsha, so their neighbours were comparatively few. None of the expressions on the other ship looked friendly, however. Amused, yes; friendly, no.

"Who might you be, then?" one of them bellowed. He was a man Otim's age or thereabouts, with a steel-headed axe thrust through his belt. In fact, now that Otim looked closer, he could see a *lot* of steel on the other ship.

"Otim Ambaszhin of the Brown Eagles," he called back. He had no idea what lie might buy them safe passage, if indeed any would, so he stuck with the truth. At least if he did not recognise anyone, there was a chance that they were not from a clan that bore a grudge.

The raucous laughter that went up did nothing to prevent his stomach from sinking down into his boots. "And you?" he shouted, unsure of what answer he was going to get, but certain by this point that it was not going to be a good one.

"Kullojan Sakteszhin, clanless and sworn to The Golden!" the first speaker replied jovially, and Otim's stomach dropped right through his boots and into the water beneath. "You've not got Saana Sattistutar on board that tsek, have you?"

Otim ignored the insult to the size of his ship: that was the least of his concerns at this point. "Why? Has The Golden got you out looking for her instead of doing the work itself?"

That stopped them from laughing, although judging by the ugly mutters it did not improve their opinion of him. Sakteszhin hawked and spat a gobbet of phlegm into the water between them.

"That's for your chief, Brown Eagle. The Golden stopped being concerned with her a while back, but it would amuse me to present her to the draug if she was with you. I don't imagine she is, though: even a chief as pathetic as her wouldn't be seen on a ship like yours."

"So what's your heading, then?" Otim demanded. How could the man be so casual, so close to Idramar? His vessel had to have been seen. Flatlander ships might be slow, but Otim knew from previous experience that they would put to sea in great numbers to chase off a lone yolgu. "Are you just going to insult my chief and my ship? Because if so, we'll be on our way."

"Oh, I'll insult your chief and your ship, but that's not all I'll be doing," Sakteszhin called back. "You've got a choice to make, Brown Eagle. We can board you, cut your throats, and send you down to see the Dark Father without so much as corpse paint and a song; or you can set your sails to follow us back to The Golden."

Otim swallowed. "That sounds like a long voyage to little reward."

Sakteszhin laughed. "Long? You'll be meeting the draug before the sun's dipped a handsbreadth in the sky!" He spread his hands. "So what'll it be?"

"Shit shit *shit*!" Otim turned away from the gloating captain for a moment and looked at the Flatlanders. They had clearly worked out that something was wrong, from the presence of unfamiliar Tjakorshi if nothing else, but Otim did not currently have the words to explain the full gravity of the situation to them.

"We can't run, can we?" someone asked.

"No hope of that," Otim replied, shaking his head. He exhaled. There was no way that he wanted to be anywhere near The Golden, but neither did he want to be killed here and now, which was what was going to happen unless he and his crew went along with Sakteszhin's demands. Where could The Golden *be*, anyway? There were no sails in sight farther out from the shore, so unless it was lurking somewhere over the horizon . . .

The explanation settled into his mind like an anchor stone into silt.

"The Golden's taken Idramar," he said dully. "It must have." He saw the horror and despair creep over his crew's faces as they understood what that meant. To have come so close, only to find the very thing their clan had fled from at the start of the year waiting for them? It was enough to make you weep.

Otim had no time to weep. He had a decision to make, but he could only see one option.

"We agree!" he shouted, turning around and blinking tears of frustration from his eyes. "Take us where you will!"

"Wise choice, Brown Eagle!" Sakteszhin shouted. "Maybe, anyway! Follow us in. If you try to escape, you'll be shown no mercy!"

"Do as he says!" Otim snapped, and the *Longpride* began to pick up pace again as the sails were brought back into line and the crew returned to their positions. He began to form the words to explain to the Naridans, then decided against it and beckoned them to the bow with him.

It did not take long. When they rounded the headland they found themselves in the wide estuary mouth of the great river, on the north bank of which stood Idramar. As they approached the city, the nature of things became clear.

A haze hung over the city: the lingering smoke of fires that had burned through much of the areas of higher ground. The parts closer to the water had clearly suffered from the impact of the great waves, judging by the damage. It was a wreck, a ruin; a place in which people might take shelter, but hardly where they might be expected to actually *live*.

And hauled up all along the shore was yolgu after yolgu.

"It's brought them all," Otim said to himself in horror. "All the clanless. It's brought them all across the ocean."

The question of how The Golden had taken Idramar was emphatically answered: it had fallen on an already half-ruined city with every warrior from every island. Otim could not even begin to guess how many Tjakorshi that amounted to.

The Brown Eagle clan followed Saana across the ocean out of belief in her wisdom; and, in some cases, no small amount of fear of the rising threat of The Golden, as the draug had broken clan after clan to the east, and then to the north and south as well. The Golden itself had brought all its followers here through ... what? Fear? Yes, undoubtedly, but Otim realised that there had to be belief underpinning it. An entire people, united – more or less – under one terrifying being, and *believing* that it knew best.

That was not a concept on which he wanted to dwell.

Osred was weeping, tears running down the lines of his aged face. Elio and Ezi were just staring in shock.

"We're going to die, aren't we?" Ezi stammered.

Otim understood enough of her language to know what she was asking, and he was hard-pressed to disagree. The Golden's warriors had not come in peace, as his clan had done. He and his crew would probably join the Naridans in death. What use would the draug have for three Flatlanders, and a small crew of Tjakorshi that had fled from it in the first place?

Then Otim realised that the fact he could understand what Ezi had said at all might just have given him an answer to that question.

"Sman speak you," he said quickly. "You speak sman. *They*," he pointed towards the approaching shore, "not speak you. We help. Live."

Elio blinked at him for a couple of moments before understanding dawned. "We should . . . *translate* for them? But we only know a few words!"

"It's more than anyone here will know," Ezi said. "He's got a point."

"We are not here to help these monsters," Osred growled. "We came here to help Black Keep! And now . . . "

Otim took him by the shoulder and looked into the old steward's tear-filled eyes. "Can't help Black Keep if dead. Live?"

Osred took a shuddering breath, and let it out again. Then he nodded slowly.

"Live."

Jeya

E ast Harbour was at war.
   The Sharks were traditionally rivals who accorded each
other a fair amount of respect, so long as one did not tread too
heavily into another's turf. The only time that changed was if
one stuck their neck out too far, or became obviously exposed
or weakened. Then their fellows would start to circle like the
predators after which they were named, sniffing for blood in the
water and ready to take a chunk of flesh once certain the victim
was in no state to fight them off. A shadowy, miniature empire
of streets and docks and contacts would be carved up and
swallowed down, and then the waters would settle once more.

Kurumaya should have been the same. Their stance of open
resistance against the Hierarchs should have marked them out
as exposed and vulnerable, easy to take down by someone
looking to gain favour with East Harbour's rulers, or worried
about the prospect of indiscriminate reprisals. Even Jeya knew
that, and shé was a long way from the top of the food chain.

It hadn't happened.

Maybe it was the wave; maybe it was the hunger that followed it, and the sight of the Watch taking supplies out of the
hands of the poorest. Whatever the reason, Kurumaya was
not found with their throat cut. Instead, their influence — or
that of other Sharks who aligned with them — spread until the

waterfront was under their control. Within two days, all goods that came ashore were distributed only by the Sharks' decree.

The Hierarchs did not take kindly to that, of course. The Watch was turned out, but many in the Watch decided that perhaps it was not the career for them any longer, when their partners or children or parents begged them to stay home for fear of what might happen: the Sharks knew the effectiveness of threats. All the same, there were enough who believed in the Hierarchs, or loved their coin, or feared them more than the Sharks, or hated a Shark more, and so the city became loosely divided. The waterfront belonged to Kurumaya and their allies, farther inland belonged to the Hierarchs, and between the two was a ragged, loosely defined area where the weapon-carrying gangs of each side would sometimes meet and clash. That line pushed forward and back, depending on how bold anyone was feeling at any given time.

Kurumaya had one rule: any slaves on their side of the line, whether they made it there themselves or belonged to a house or building that now fell inside it, were freed. The slave-owners objected, but not for long, since Kurumaya gave them a choice of keeping the lives of others or keeping their own. Most offered up weak smiles and the keys to chains; a few assumed the Shark was bluffing, and died choking on their own blood.

"Did yöu ever have slaves?" Jeya asked Bulang quietly, as they sat together in their house. It was within the boundaries of Kurumaya's territory, more by default than anything else: the Hierarchs had little interest in fighting over these poor streets. The big room was full of young people getting their heads down for the night, each with a bowl of stew inside them from the pot that hung over the still-glowing embers of the fire. In that, at least, Jeya could find some sort of comfort and continuity with what had come before.

"No," Bulang replied. They were together in the small room, for some privacy, and pressed up close together, from which Jeya still got a thrill and a sensation of contented warmth that had nothing to do with body heat. "We had servants. Real Naridans don't keep slaves."

"Why not?" Jeya asked, curious. It seemed like a rich person thing, although apart from Bulang shé had never spent any time around rich people for longer than it took to lift a purse.

"Ï . . . don't know, really," Bulang admitted. "Ï never really asked. It was just one of the things we knew. Naridans don't keep slaves. Ï don't think mÿ parents thought it was honourable. They certainly didn't think it was a sign of wealth, or importance. Ï think they thought that if you had slaves, it just meant you couldn't afford to pay servants."

Jeya thought about that. It seemed like a very arrogant reason not to have slaves, but shé supposed that doing the right thing for the wrong reason was better than doing the wrong thing for the wrong reason, or even the wrong thing for a right reason.

"So yöu think Kurumaya is right about it?" shé asked.

Bulang sighed. "Ï think Kurumaya is right about *that*. And they're probably right about the food. Ï used to spend some time with the Hierarchs: there's no way they would let themselves, or their friends, or their families go hungry to make sure other people were fed." Thëy fell silent, until Jeya thought thëy had stopped speaking completely, but then thëy started again.

"Kurumaya came to speak to më earlier."

Jeya sat bolt upright. "What? What about?"

"What they want më to do," Bulang said.

"When were yöu going to tell mé?" Jeya demanded, hér throat tight with worry. What did the Shark have in mind?

Why had Bulang not told hér this sooner? Had thëy decided to do something thëy thought shé wouldn't like?

"Ï'm telling yóu now!" Bulang protested, casting a glance at the door through to the big room. "When everyone else is asleep!"

Jeya's anxiety subsided a little, but only a little. "Fine. So what do they want?"

Bulang blinked at hér. "Jeya, are yóu *angry*?"

"Ï'm *worried*!" Jeya whispered back, furiously. "Kurumaya doesn't care about yöu except what yöu can do for them, and they don't care about *mé* at all!"

"Do yóu think Ï don't know that?" Bulang demanded. "But they're smart enough to realise that Ï'm not going to help them if they let anything happen to yóu, and so long as Ï'm useful to them, they won't let anything happen to më, either." Thëy sighed in frustration. "Ï grew up as the Hierarchs' pet; Ï know this game."

Jeya swallowed hér next words. "Just tell mé what they said."

"Kurumaya wants to arrange a meeting with the Hierarchs," Bulang said, although the look on thëir face suggested thëy still did not fully believe that Jeya was only worried. "They want to talk about the city and how it should be governed. They want më there, so they can show the Hierarchs they know their new Splinter King is an imposter. Mÿ family's presence was still a big status symbol for Grand Mahewa: the Hierarchs won't want their lies exposed."

Jeya gaped at thëm. "That's ridiculous! They'll just call yöu a liar!"

"But Ï know them, Jeya!" Bulang protested. "Ï know them, and Ï know things about the rituals, the festival days, all those sorts of things, that only the Splinter Prince would know."

Jeya tried to get a grip on hér frustration. "Bulang, these are *rich people*! Yöu can't just *embarrass* rich people into doing the right thing, or admitting that they're wrong! Otherwise they wouldn't be rich in the first place!"

Bulang's face twisted, as though thëy'd just tasted something unpleasant. "Ï don't know if that's—"

"Yöu could have had mé killed," Jeya told thëm flatly. "If yöu'd sent mé to the magistrates when yöur guard caught mé pickpocketing yöu, they might have hanged mé. It's happened to people Í've known! That's not right; that's just a way to make sure that poor people are too scared to take money from rich people, even though the rich people could afford it! But it suits the rich people who make the laws that the magistrates follow, so they don't do anything about it."

"So what do yóu want më to do?" Bulang said crossly. "Refuse Kurumaya? Yóu said yóurself, ï'm only valuable to them so long as Ï can do something for them. If Ï refuse them, we're both dead!"

Thëy were right, at least about that, but Jeya could not make hérself let it go. "Why do Í feel that yöu are not just doing this to keep us safe?"

Bulang threw thëir head back until it hit the wall and thëy were staring up at the ceiling. "Jeya, Ï spent mÿ whole life being told that Ï was special. Ï was the exiled ruler of a far-off land, the descendant of a god. Even though there was no sign we would ever go back to Narida, Ï was raised to believe that Ï should be ready to rule it. Ï had to think about what was best for mÿ people."

"But we don't even know if that was true!" Jeya protested. "We don't know if yöur family was who yöu thought they were, or if it was a Hierarch lie!"

"Ï *know* that!" Bulang snapped, jerking away from Jeya and turning to face hér properly.

Jeya's cheeks heated. "Well, of course—"

"But it doesn't make any difference!" Bulang continued fiercely. "Why should it? Even if mÿ family were just raised up to suit the Hierarchs, does that mean Ï shouldn't try to do the right thing? If Narida isn't mÿ place, if they're not mÿ people in any sense other than mÿ family came from there at some point, doesn't that make East Harbour mÿ home, and its people mÿ people? Shouldn't Ï try to do the right thing for *them*?"

"What about the right thing for *yöu*?" Jeya demanded. *Or us*, shé added in the privacy of hér own head.

"And what if doing the right thing for më means doing the right thing for them?" Bulang said softly. "Ï didn't ask to be the Splinter Prince! Ï didn't ask for mÿ family to be murdered because of it! And after that happened Ï would have liked nothing better than to live with yóu here and try to have a new life, but Ï can't get away from mÿ family's history. Shouldn't Ï use it to try to do something good? To try to help?"

"Yes, but . . ." Jeya trailed off, uncertain of how to put things into words. This felt like doing the wrong thing for the right reasons, but why? The Hierarchs were not great people; they had just always been so far out of Jeya's reckoning that shé had never really considered them. Shé had no loyalty to them, and had no idea how their removal might affect hér.

It was not the potential downfall of the Hierarchs that bothered hér, shé realised. It was who might be raised up in their stead.

"But it's *Kurumaya*," shé said, trying to get Bulang to understand. "They're a Shark, and if you swim with Sharks, you become bait. To help them because yöu have no choice is one thing, but if yöu think yöu have some sort of duty to do it then they've got their claws into yöu. Yöu might never get away, even if yöu get the chance!"

"But they're helping people who need it," Bulang began.

"At the moment, but it probably won't stay that way!" Jeya

said. "Feeding people and freeing slaves are good things, but Sharks don't get to be Sharks by being nice people! Kurumaya will be after power, and if yöu're standing any closer to them than yöu have to be then yöu're going to be in even more danger than yöu already are!"

Bulang's face fell, dropping into a stubborn expression Jeya had rarely seen before. "Ï'm used to being in danger, Jeya. Mÿ family got killed, remember? We nearly got killed."

"Yes, by Kurumaya!"

"No," Bulang said, shaking thëir head. "By Nabanda."

Jeya's mouth clamped shut. It felt like she had been punched in the chest. Bulang was right, in that it had been Nabanda's crew who killed Bulang's family, and who had been trying to kill them both in the Narrows. But Nabanda had been working for Kurumaya, even though Kurumaya had not known exactly who Bulang was, or anything about Jeya, and . . .

And Jeya had not realised until it had nearly been too late. It had taken Damau's death, on top of Ngaiyu's and several others, before shë'd tumbled to the truth. Kurumaya was a Shark who dealt in death, so the casual exchange of money for a life was not surprising: Nabanda had been Jeya's *friend*.

Or so shé had thought. But how good a friend could hê have ever been, if hîs response to finding out that hîs quarry was the friend of hîs friend had not been to talk to Jeya, but to keep trying to kill Bulang, even if Jeya got hurt in the process? If shé had only realised sooner then Lihambo, and Damau, and Ngaiyu might all still be alive.

How bad *was* hér judgement? How could shé actually know what the right thing was?

Shé scrambled up to hér feet, hér eyes blurry with sudden tears.

"Jeya?" Bulang said. "What are—?"

"Ï'm going out for a walk," Jeya said thickly, stepping over thëir legs and heading for the doorway. Shé was through it before Bulang could say anything else, quickly wended hér way through the sleepers on the floor of the big room, and then pushed open the house's main door. Thé two thugs Kurumaya had stationed outside looked up in surprise as shé clattered out and down the steps into the moonlight, but shé was already past them and onto the dirt of the street. Shé put hér head down and started walking, hér mind a furious whirl.

"Hey, shouldn't we——?" one of the thugs began.

"Nah, leave 'em. It's the other one the boss cares about."

The words, tossed so casually into the night air, buried themselves into Jeya's back. Shé hunched hér shoulders against them and kept walking, paying little mind to where hér feet took hér. Shé knew enough of the city to not get lost, which was almost a curse in and of itself. It was hard to walk down a street without it reminding hér of Ngaiyu, or Nabanda, or Damau, or even Bulang. Right at that moment, shé would have welcomed a fresh sight: something that held no connection to any of the things that had caused hér so much grief so recently.

Shé wiped hér eyes angrily and looked up at the dark bulk of Grand Mahewa's highlands, rising in the west to block out the stars, and bathed in just enough silvery light from the moons to emphasise the depth of shadows there. Even that had painful memories attached to it: the sun had been setting behind those slopes when shé and hér ragtag band of allies had confronted Nabanda and hîs crew. Shé could still remember what hê looked like as hê came towards hér, pretending friendship: a hulking shape, hîs arms stretched wide in false greeting. Hê had been a rock in Jeya's life for so long, the one shé could turn to for help and companionship, but it turned out that rock had been rolling on its own path, and would crush hér if shé got in its way.

Jeya closed hér eyes and let the tears come.

The angry, tearing screech of an alarmed golden-maned monkey split the air. Jeya's eyes jerked open again, but hér vision was still blurry. Shé wiped at them with one hand while the other instinctively fumbled for the small knife on hér belt, but shé only had time to register dark shapes around hér before her wrist was seized. Shé opened hér mouth to yell for help — whatever help might turn out to be, on these streets — but a gag was pulled between hér teeth instead, and then everything went properly dark as a bag went over hér head.

Saana

Saana thought that she might have quite liked Darkspur, had it not been so far from the sea.

It was a strange sensation, to be away from the coast for so long. She had lived within a literal stone's throw of the ocean all her life back at Koszal, and even at Black Keep she had been able to see it from the town walls, and smell it when the breeze was onshore, or when the tide flooded up the Blackcreek and turned its waters brackish. Now she had come days inland, far away from the salt and the spray, where even the gulls were far fewer, and it felt like something fundamental was missing from the world.

The tension around them was, if anything, more familiar. It was only a few months before when Tjakorshi and Naridans in Black Keep had eyed each other with the same suspicion and wariness as that which was now playing out in Darkspur, only this time the lines were not so clearly drawn between peoples. Darkspur and Black Keep had followed their previous thanes into general distrust and dislike over the last ten or so years, and the attempted siege had hardly helped matters, especially since many of Darkspur's able-bodied men had not returned, and there was now a sizeable group of outsiders present. Saana could see the same nervousness on the faces of the remaining population of Darkspur as had been present on those of Black Keep when her clan had first been walking the streets.

"Perhaps we should challenge them to the Great Game," Daimon suggested dryly one day, when they were looking down from the walls of the stronghouse at the town below, and picking out groups of Black Keep and Darkspur by the gaps each left between them.

"And have someone get stabbed again?" Saana asked, the vivid memory of a knife coming for her flashing into her mind.

"You were not actually stabbed," Daimon said, a little defensively.

"Only because Tavi stopped him!" Saana replied, and they both fell silent. Saana was not sure whether Daimon felt any guilt over the death of the former stable master, who had been dragged from the back of the great war-dragon Bastion and killed while defending Black Keep, but she had some tangled emotions about the man. She had liked Tavi's directness and sense of humour, and the way he treated her not as a Raider, but simply as a person. She had also found him attractive; at least attractive enough to take his clothes off and fuck him in the stables when she had been a little drunk, and more than a little resentful of everyone else having a good time. She was fairly sure Daimon did not know about that, and Saana had no plans to tell him. It had happened before he had proposed marriage to her – only the night before, but that was a minor detail – so really it was none of his business in any case, but it still seemed simplest to let sleeping krayks lie.

At least the negotiations with Yarmina Darkspur – now with her cheeks streaked with ash to signify mourning for her father – had turned out to be fairly simple, in the end. She proved just as shrewd as Daimon had suspected, but thankfully seemed minded to come up with the best solution for all, and the division of both labour and harvest was soon agreed to everyone's satisfaction. Sar Asad was present at their meetings, but as the days passed Yarmina paid less and less attention to him. Her intention was obvious: she believed that if Asad had intended to stake his own claim to authority then he should have done so at once, and the more time passed without him having done so, the more accepted she became.

Saana hoped that was true, but she was not so sure. Mannerisms might change between peoples, but she was quite good at reading Naridans now, and she thought she could see some hesitancy even among the Darkspur servants. They listened to and obeyed Yarmina, but they often looked to Sar Asad as though for confirmation, or to check whether he disagreed or disapproved. If servants were still unsure, Saana was willing to bet that the town was not fully convinced either. It all came back to the Naridan disregard for women.

"Your wife is not certain she should have come with you," she said quietly to Daimon as they sat together at the table that evening in Darkspur's great hall. Daimon was at Yarmina's left hand and Saana was to his left, while on the other side of the Lady of Darkspur was Sar Asad. Beyond him was Sar Lahel, whom Saana had released from his thrall vows as a gesture of good faith, when it became clear that Black Keep and Darkspur would not be fighting again. Yarmina was leaning the other way and talking with Sar Lahel, which meant Saana felt safe to voice her thoughts.

"What do you mean?" Daimon asked, keeping his voice equally low.

"Your wife is a Raider chief, a woman with power," Saana said around a mouthful of food. "What if Darkspur people think she is a bad influence on Yarmina?"

Daimon snorted. "Your husband thinks Darkspur knows Yarmina well enough not to think that anyone could influence her much."

"That is not a good thing for a chief," Saana said. "A chief should listen to their people."

"Well, she is not a chief," Daimon pointed out. "She is . . . not a thane either, but she is a lady."

"What are you two whispering about?" Yarmina said from Daimon's other side, and Saana saw her husband's face go into the flat mask he adopted so well when he did not want his feelings known.

"This lord was just discussing the nature of your title with his wife," Daimon said, turning in his seat to face their host. "How you are a lady both in honorific and in title."

"And not thane," Yarmina said. She stabbed a piece of meat with her knife and popped it into her mouth, then began to chew. "A foolish practice."

"What does your ladyship mean by that?" inquired Sar Asad, and Saana was sure she was not the only one who noticed the dangerous tone of his voice.

"This lady is a lady whether she marries or not, whether she commands these lands or not," Yarmina continued. "Lord Daimon, on the other hand, is lord instead of thane because his elder brother holds that title, since it is Darel who rules there. It feels as though this lady's title is merely a statement that she is not fit to rule in her own right."

"Well, you know the saying, your ladyship," Sar Lahel said with forced jollity, "'A lady is by nature in need of a lord'!"

"This lady needs a lord like a dragon needs a fishing boat," Yarmina said tartly, and Saana tried to disguise her snort of laughter, then had to try even harder not to choke on her food. However, Yarmina was not finished.

"Lord Daimon," she said. "If this lady was to say that she was no longer content to provide assistance to Black Keep unless you were to address her as a thane, what would your response be?"

"'Thane' is a man's title, Lady Yarmina," Daimon replied carefully. Saana kept her eyes on her food, doing her best to portray the image of a Raider chief uninterested in the delicate posturings of power going on to her right. It was not a bad option to have, now and then.

"But Lord Daimon, that does not precisely answer the question," Yarmina said, her voice silken and polite.

"It is foolishness!" Sar Asad barked. "You should not try to——"

While skewering another piece of boiled root, Saana nudged Daimon in the ribs. She could see no reason why it mattered what title the girl gave herself, and Daimon agreeing with Yarmina would make Yarmina look stronger at no cost to them, which meant it would be harder for Asad to undo any of the agreements she had made.

"To answer your question, this lord would conclude that this hall and these lands are yours, and so you may be addressed as you see fit," Daimon said levelly, "so long as it does not call shame upon the Divine Family."

"This thane thanks you for your answer, Lord Daimon," Yarmina said with a smile that held more than a hint of smugness.

"This is ridiculous!" Asad said, and thumped the table so hard that the heads of the others dining in the hall turned towards them all. "You are not a *thane*! What would your father have said?"

"We shall never know, shall we?" Yarmina snapped rounding on him. "Since he rode off to war and did not return! You dare to speak to this thane of her father, goodsar, when his bones lie in the earth of Blackcreek?"

"We can arrange for Thane Odem's body to be returned——" Daimon began, at the same time as Sar Lahel took hold of Sar Asad's arm.

"Asad, perhaps this is not the time—"

Saana looked up at the sound of running feet across the floor, and saw a servant hurrying towards the high table. She swallowed her mouthful, and waited. The evening was already a livelier one than any since they had arrived in Darkspur, and it looked like it might get more interesting yet.

The servant made his way to Yarmina's right shoulder, and she broke off her staring match with Asad to glance at him in acknowledgement. Saana did not hear what the servant murmured, but Yarmina gave a curt nod and he hurried off again. Yarmina and Asad then both looked away from each other and towards the hall's main doors, very much in the manner of combatants disengaging.

The doors creaked open to their full width, and the servant's voice rang out.

"Sar Benarin of Ironhead, vassal of Blackcreek, and his companions!"

Saana sat bolt upright, and felt Daimon do the same beside her. She did not know the bulky man with the sigil of crossed pickaxes on his coat-of-nails, but he must have been the sar mentioned: nor did she know the band of travel-stained men with him. However, she had heard the name of Ironhead before, and behind Sar Benarin and his men walked more familiar figures, including a flame-haired warrior with a longblade on her belt and the lean shapes of two adolescent rattletails padding alongside her.

"Zhanna!" Saana shouted, getting to her feet, and the wave that had nearly destroyed her new home did not seem as powerful as the one of joy and relief that washed over her in that moment. Her daughter's face lit up; grimy and weary, but also beautiful and delighted.

"Mama!"

Saana shoved her seat aside and made straight for Zhanna,

ignoring the startled looks from the Naridans in the hall. She tried to take their sensibilities into account most of the time, but nothing was going to stop her from greeting her daughter as soon as she possibly could. She barely even noticed the others with Zhanna before she had collided with her daughter and wrapped her arms around her; and, for a wonder, Zhanna hugged her back just as hard, instead of pulling away.

"I'm so glad you're alive!" Saana said, aware she was almost babbling in relief. "I knew you were in good hands, but the mountains can't be safe, and—" She pulled back, looking her daughter over, as a horrible thought reared back up into her mind. "What did you find? Were they—?"

"Darkspur had men there," Zhanna said, her voice low and her eyes furious. "They had the people in *chains*, Mama! We had to help them, and they're free now, but we lost . . . " She swallowed, and when she continued her voice began to break. "We lost Menaken, and Ingorzhak never even got there; a kingdrake took him in the mountains on the way up—"

"Chief Saana!" Yarmina called from behind her. "What is the meaning of this? You know these people?"

Saana opened her mouth to answer – and the conversation about putting the Smoking Valley people in chains was going to be a fun one – but she was beaten to it by the big sar.

"This sar is Benarin of Ironhead," he said loudly. "He was called to Black Keep to help defend it from Darkspur, but on our journey we learned of the great wave, and that Lord Daimon was marching here instead. We came to lend our efforts, and were joined by these travellers from Black Keep who caught up with us. They had journeyed into the Catseye Mountains to visit the people of the Smoking Valley."

Saana realised what Benarin was about to say next, but she was too late to grab him, or do anything else to arrest his attention.

"Lord Daimon," the sar said grimly. "Were you aware that Darkspur sent men into the mountains to enslave our allies and steal their gold?"

Naridans and their ridiculous Code of Honour which makes them say the right thing at the wrong time, Saana thought ferociously as the Darkspur great hall erupted into angry shouts from all those around her. *I'll make this one eat it, if I get the chance!*

She glanced at the two sars to Yarmina's right. Lahel looked unwell; Asad just looked furious.

"What are these lies?" Asad demanded. "How dare you, goodsar?!"

"Lies?" Zhanna shouted back. She reached into a pack and pulled something out, which she held up for all to see. "We don't lie!"

It was part of the uniform of a Darkspur soldier, with the Darkspur sigil clearly visible on the breast. The shouting in the hall died down abruptly.

"You could have got that from any of our dead men at Black Keep!" Asad declared. "That is not proof!"

"It came from the mountains," Zhanna said firmly. "This warrior brought it here!"

Sar Asad opened his mouth again, then glanced at Saana, and back at Zhanna, and down to the longblade on her belt.

Go on, Saana thought at him. *Call my daughter a liar. Naridan honour means she could challenge you to a fight for it, and I don't think you want to take her on with your weak leg, any more than I would want to with mine.*

"Sar Asad, Sar Lahel," Yarmina said into the uncomfortable pause. "This thane's father said nothing to her of sending men into the mountains. What do either of you know of this?"

Saana suppressed a smile. Yarmina had learned of it by overhearing Sar Lahel talking about it with his companions, so she was telling the truth in a very Naridan way, and one of the problems with the Naridan Code of Honour was how utterly trapped those who tried to follow it looked when they really wanted to lie. Like Sar Lahel now, for example.

"The Raider girl speaks the truth," Lahel said, while Asad was still reinflating himself, then raised his hand as his fellow sar turned towards him. "Peace, Asad! You know it too!"

"Sar Asad, is this thane to understand that you knew her father had sent men to attack and enslave Blackcreek's allies in the mountains, which in itself could lead Blackcreek to attack us, and you said nothing throughout our discussions with them?" Yarmina demanded. "You did not even speak to her in private, to warn her of what might occur if they learned of our actions?"

Now Saana did smile. Yarmina had waited until she had proof from another source, proof enough to make Lahel confess, then used that to shame Asad. The expression on his face made it clear he knew he was caught, and his lack of an immediate and vehement denial was as good as an admission.

This girl was definitely not one to underestimate.

"You may remove yourself from this table," Yarmina said sternly. "And you are relieved of your duties as castellan of Darkspur."

Asad, to his credit, did not argue or rant. He simply thrust his chair back, rose with all the dignity a man could under such circumstances, and made his way to one of the lesser tables.

"Are there people of the Smoking Valley in your group, Sar Benarin, who can understand our speech?" Yarmina asked. The sar did not answer, but instead stood aside as a woman Saana recognised from Black Keep stepped forwards.

"This woman is Amonhuhe of the Mountains," she said, and her voice was just as stern as Yarmina's had been. "She was born in the Smoking Valley and now lives in Black Keep. She is the voice here for the people of her birth." She gestured at some of those with her whom Saana did not recognise: mainly thin-faced, and dressed in furs and beads.

Yarmina rose and bowed, rather lower than Saana would have expected. "Amonhuhe, you may be aware that this thane's father died attempting to attack Black Keep. He never told his daughter of his actions, and she deeply regrets the damage caused. She hopes we may be able to right some of these wrongs."

Amonhuhe spoke to the Smoking Valley people in a language that sounded half-familiar to Saana's ears, almost like Naridan, but not quite. Then she turned back to Yarmina.

"Those are fine words. We hope your actions will match them."

Those were *not* fine words, especially not from a lowborn to a noble, and there were more than a few mutters in the hall. However, Yarmina smiled.

"Fine words are worthless without actions. This thane is content to be judged in such a manner." She clapped her hands. "Places for our new guests! Sar Benarin, and Lady Saana's daughter, whose name this thane is afraid she does not know: you are welcome at this table. May the rest sit where they will."

"I thought women couldn't be chiefs here?" Zhanna said quietly to Saana.

"She seems to have other ideas," Saana said. She squeezed her daughter's shoulder. "Be careful of her, Zhanna. She's nicer than her father, but she's not our friend. Not yet, anyway." She put her arm around her daughter's shoulders and hugged her again. "Now, come with me, have some food, and tell me *everything*."

Marin

"Are we *sure* this is safe?" Marin asked, as they walked down the hill in the rain, towards the ranks of spears that awaited them. They were a small party of half-a-dozen: Tyrun, Mordokel, Alazar, Marin, and two more: Sar Disman, a sardonic man who had apparently joined Tyrun after his thane had tried to stand against the Godsworn and had been killed; and Barstan Broadfield, a barrel-chested former thane in his forties who had pledged himself to Tyrun despite therefore losing the rank he had only recently gained due to his father's death. Approaching a camp of several thousand soldiers sworn to the service of the Sun Throne with these few companions, one of whom was a being technically opposed to their monarch, certainly did not feel very safe to Marin.

"Safety is an illusion," Mordokel said calmly. "There is only service."

"Thank you," Marin muttered. "That makes s'man feel so much better."

"Marin," Tyrun said, and Marin looked past Mordokel at the Divine One, and into those eyes that seemed young, and yet contained depths that spoke of something ancient. "Do not fear. Everything is as it should be."

And damn it all, even after the monastery, even after Tyrun had watched His followers butcher those who refused to acknowledge His divinity, there was still something about His presence that inspired calm and confidence. Marin found his breaths coming a little slower, and the anxious knot in the pit of his stomach loosening slightly. The men they were approaching were *only* men, whereas Tyrun was something more: and through his presence at the Divine One's side, Marin was something more as well.

The men they were approaching were also wet men, and men who had seen people lurking in the trees and were uncertain of exactly what was going on, or whether they would be called to fight today. Spears were levelled at Tyrun's party, hard points of dripping steel behind which were eyes that looked barely any softer.

"State your business!" someone shouted. Mordokel threw back his hood once more, and stared the spears down with the expression of someone vexed by a toddler's tantrum.

"The Divine One, Nari Reborn, wishes an audience with High Marshal Torgallen!"

Marin had expected laughter or derision. Tyrun Himself was still robed and hooded, and not at the front of their party, but it seemed word or rumour had run ahead of them. Instead of devolving into crude humour, the expressions he could see looked slightly more apprehensive, not less.

"Do you claim to be the Divine One?" the same voice called. Marin could not quite make out who was speaking, lurking as they were behind the row of spears.

"This priest does not!" Mordokel replied, sounding mortally offended. "He stands behind this priest, eager to converse with your marshal! Send word at once!"

There was a muttering, and then Marin caught sight of someone running away through the mud towards the middle of the camp, where Marshal Torgallen's banner hung from the central pavilion. A short, broad man, darker-skinned than many in Narida's west, with a scar down one cheek and the first hints of grey in his hair, shouldered a pair of spearmen aside and stepped forward into view.

"Word's been sent, stranger," he said, eyeing Mordokel warily. "This captain is Toren of the third regiment. Do you have a name?"

"Mordokel."

"Mordokel," Toren repeated. "Well, Mordokel, this captain will be honest with you: the High Marshal is a powerfully pious man. If he accepts your claims, you'll have an influential ally. If he doesn't, we'll all be having cold meals tonight, because the firewood we've got under shelter from this rain will be hauled out and lit to burn you all alive." He sucked his teeth. "So unless you're prepared to stake your life on what you're saying, you might want to consider saving yourself from death, and this captain from cold beans, by turning around and disappearing."

Mordokel laughed with genuine amusement. "Captain, this priest appreciates your candour, and your generosity of spirit, but he has already staked more than his life on this. We will wait for the High Marshal."

Marin swallowed. It was not that he had any doubts about Tyrun, but how could he not have doubts about this Marshal Torgallen, a man he had never met, yet who would decide whether Marin would see another morning? Marin's life was quite precious to him, and it seemed unfair to place responsibility for it in the hands of someone who had no real appreciation of its value.

They stood under the leaden skies and waited. It seemed to Marin that the rain was entirely inappropriate for this moment, when the Divine One would reveal Himself to the Western Army. It should have been bright, glorious sunshine, or perhaps an actual storm with great gusts of wind, and thunder and lightning. This steady rain was heavy enough to be unpleasant and inconvenient, but was not in any way monumental or noteworthy. It was as though the weather was totally disinterested, and had no sense of narrative.

Marin was not sure how long they waited, only that his feet were starting to settle into the mud beneath them, and Toren had long ago ordered his spearmen back into rest positions given that Mordokel showed no indication of drawing his blade and rushing them. Marin was also getting decidedly cold, since warm though the summer weather was in a river valley, the rain was doing its best to leach that from him. He shifted in place and hunched his shoulders a little as though that would somehow turn into a revolutionary new method for keeping the rain off. The endless patter and spatter of falling water off his own hood, the armour of the soldiers facing them, and the mud all around was almost soothing; so much so that he actually jumped when Toren spoke again.

"The High Marshal will see you now."

The spearmen parted in front of them, and Mordokel strode forwards with the expression of a man who had expected nothing less. Toren and ten of his spearmen formed an escort, five on each side, with the captain leading the way. Marin hurried to keep up through the squelching mud, and tried not to look around too much in case anyone decided he was trying to scout the camp out for a potential attack.

In truth, there was not much to scout out: one Naridan army camp was much like another, and Marin had seen enough of them over the years. He supposed there was some sort of accepted protocol in terms of how one was organised, although he had only spent much time with Laz in the Brotherhood's Quarter, with the professional mercenaries. The Brotherhood was always a more mixed bag than the army, varying from rich bands of notorious warriors with banner-bedecked tents containing luxurious furnishings to rival that of any Naridan general, to hard-faced killers or desperate men trying to carve out a life on the edge of their blade, who had nothing more than a cloak to wrap themselves in at night. The Naridan army proper might sleep ten men to a small, cramped tent, but at least they all actually had tents.

Marshal Torgallen's pavilion was huge, and must have required a cart all of its own when it was packed down for transport. It, and the guards outside, were vaguely reminiscent of the tent in which Marin had first met Tyrun, which had surely not been far from this very spot. However, Torgallen's was far more ostentatiously decorated, and the guards were if anything less trusting than Tyrun's had been, given they demanded the new arrivals disarm before they entered.

"Peace, friend," Tyrun said gently, laying a hand on Mordokel's arm when the priest opened his mouth to argue. "There is no danger here. We intend no harm, and the Marshal cannot threaten this god."

That statement placated Mordokel, who unbelted his long-blade and handed it over with nothing more than a direful stare, but it did little to comfort Marin, who felt that he was very capable of being threatened. All the same, he surrendered his dagger, and when the others had similarly disarmed, he followed them inside.

Pious or not, Marshal Torgallen travelled in style. An actual wooden-framed bed with mattress was just visible behind decorative screens, and a red-upholstered couch sat near a brazier in which flickered flames for light, and which gave off the thin, pale smoke of dry wood. A large table, richly carved despite its obviously collapsible nature, took up the middle of the tent. It was covered by a map, and poring over that were three men.

Marin took them in at a glance. The one on the left was obviously Brotherhood, judging by clothes that would not have looked out of place on an Idramese merchant-lord. He could not wear the double-pleated sleeves of the nobility, but his robes were a riot of colour, and the helmet under his arm was inlaid with gold. Standard practice was for the mercenaries to be represented by the leader of the largest or richest contingent among them, unless there was an obvious discrepancy in experience.

The man opposite him wore the uniform of a high-ranking Naridan officer, but lacked a sar's braids: he had presumably risen through the ranks, rather than being appointed straight into command. Marin knew enough about Narida's standing armies to know that there was often tension between sars and the sons of thanes, and lowborn officers; "birth versus worth", as Laz had termed it. This officer had clearly had some time to work his way up, since he was older than the mercenary facing him, although not as old as the man standing between them.

Taladhar Torgallen was easily old enough to be Marin's father. His hair had mostly gone to silver, with only a few dark threads hanging grimly on. The bones of his face jutted out above his sagging cheeks, and the lines on his skin looked like a map of river systems, but the dark eyes that flicked up to play over the new arrivals were still sharp, and unclouded by age.

"You are in the presence of a Hand of Heaven," he said, straightening up with only the slightest wince. Marin's knees twitched reflexively, for he who did not pay proper respect to a High Marshal usually found himself shorter by a head, but he found himself glancing sideways at Tyrun. After all, the Divine One *had* said that he was removing the old order of things.

"Make your obeisances, friends," Tyrun said calmly. "Do not risk the High Marshal's displeasure on this god's account."

Marin knelt gratefully, along with Laz, Sar Disman, and Broadfield. Mordokel hesitated for a second, and when he did lower himself it was clearly due to his master's instruction rather than any desire to do so. Taladhar Torgallen paid the bald priest little mind, however.

"You name yourself as a god?" he demanded of Tyrun. "You claim to be Nari, reborn to us in accordance with the prophecies?"

"This god is who He is, regardless of prophecies," Tyrun replied. He lowered His hood, and Marin felt again a brief flash of the wonder that had suffused him when he had first laid eyes on the Divine One: a sense that all might not be right with the world, but that it would be; a warmth that went beyond purely physical temperature; and the feeling that the being in front of him was far, far older than He looked.

"Come, approach Him," Tyrun said, beckoning to the Western Army's commanders. "See for yourselves."

The mercenary, Marin noted, had placed his hand on his sword hilt, and did not remove it. Marshal Torgallen, by contrast, picked his way past the Brotherhood man and walked towards Tyrun with the expression of a man caught halfway between hope and dread.

"You have made the pilgrimage to Godspire?" Torgallen asked. Tyrun nodded.

"Indeed."

"And the monks proclaimed you as the Divine One?" Torgallen demanded. His eyes bored into Tyrun's face. "The truth! This marshal will have the truth from you."

Tyrun smiled. "Mordokel?"

"Tyrun presented Himself to the sacred monastery at Godspire," Mordokel said, from his position on his knees. "His claim was considered, and we found it to be true. He is the Divine One, the true heir of Nari, reborn to reunite this land. The order has now been disbanded, our purpose fulfilled."

For a moment, just a moment, Marin thought he saw

uncertainty in Torgallen's face. Then the old man saw something that gave him the answers for which he was looking, for his features were suffused with a smile that was the mirror of Tyrun's, and his eyes filled with joy.

"Blessed is the day!" he breathed. "He has returned to us! Divine One, we are your servants, and this marshal's army is yours to command." He began to lower himself somewhat slowly to his own knees, but Tyrun reached out and caught him beneath the arms. The army officer half-drew his blade at the sight of someone touching the High Marshal, but paused in confusion before the sword cleared its scabbard.

"Do not trouble yourself to kneel, friend," Tyrun said gently to Torgallen. "That is, if this god's friends may rise?"

"Of course, of course!" the Western Marshal said hurriedly, straightening again. "Please, all of you, stand! We are all as one before the Divine One."

Marin got back to his feet, but did not miss the glance that passed between the army officer and the mercenary captain.

"All as one, indeed," Tyrun said, still smiling. "The old order of Narida based on accident of birth is outdated, and must be replaced. However, an army is not a country, and for it to be more than a simple band of armed men, there must be a chain of command. Only a fool would hamstring an army by declaring that its officers now held the same rank as every other soldier. If you pledge yourselves to this god's service, He begs that you retain your command, for He will have need of your experience and wisdom."

That drew a glance between the army officer and the mercenary captain as well: a more considered and less nervous one. Army and Brotherhood often regarded each other with some dubiousness, if not outright contempt, but Marin could quite imagine that each had been apprehensive about what the High Marshal's words would mean in practice. If anything would have been likely to prompt resistance from them, it would be the prospect of losing their command.

The army officer slid his sword fully back into its sheath, and returned his hand to his side.

"Divine One, these are this marshal's highest-ranking officers," Torgallen said, turning to gesture at the two men standing at his table. "First Captain Benel of the Army, and Captain Reden of the Brotherhood. Benel has been with this marshal for many years and is a fine man of unquestionable loyalty. Captain Reden commands the famous Greenrun Razorclaws, a mercenary company known for their efficiency and tenacity."

Tyrun smiled at them both, and Marin saw the same thing that had happened with Torgallen; as the Divine One turned His attention to them, they too relaxed, and acceptance and peace crept across their faces.

"This god's companions are Mordokel; Barstan son of Barlan, formerly thane of Broadfield; Sar Disman, formerly of Rumedell; Sar Alazar of White Hill; and his husband Marin of Idramar, a scholar who risked his own life to intercept a knife meant for this god."

Marshal Torgallen's expression changed to one of utter shock. "Who would do such a thing?!"

"A knifeman, sent west among the ranks of the Eastern Army," Tyrun said, and the hint of displeasure that crept into His tone seemed to throw back a little of the brazier's warmth.

"The Eastern Army?" Torgallen glanced at Benel, who looked grim. "We have heard of its mobilisation, of course, but the word was that its purpose was to find you and escort you to Godspire, Divine One, not to take your life!"

"Perhaps those were the instructions given to its leaders," Tyrun said. "However, there are clearly those in Idramar who had their own agendas, and with the ability to insert men to see those agendas carried out."

"If the Eastern Army is compromised, that places us in a difficult situation," Benel said, in a voice that was deep and resonant. "We had prayed that the rumours of your return were true, Divine One; if they were, we hoped to spread the news to Lord Goldtree, who is acting as the Eastern's general. If we cannot trust him, or cannot trust his men to follow his lead . . . "

"Word also says that Goldtree is spread thin, still scouring the countryside for you," Reden said, planting his hand on the map. His voice was hoarse and raspy, in contrast to the First Captain's, and his teeth were stained from brownleaf. "What are your wishes, Divine One? What would you have us do?"

Tyrun stepped forward to look down at the map. Marin went with him, partly out of the sheer novelty of being allowed to move around a High Marshal's tent unchallenged. The map was beautiful, but also highly detailed: it was clearly a tool that had been made to look good, rather than a decorative fancy that bore some passing resemblance to reality. The scholar in him wished for a few hours to study it closely, but he knew without asking that Taladhar Torgallen's indulgence would not stretch that far.

"The Sun Throne is in Idramar," Tyrun said, tapping the capital. "This god understands that Narida has come to view it, along with the Sun Palace and other associated baubles, as being nearly as key to the mantle of God-King as the man who carries the title. This is unfortunate, but undeniable, and it leaves only one clear course of action. This god must make haste to Idramar and let the people see Him take His place at the heart of where they think the power lies in this country."

Marin expected opposition, but instead the commanders of the Western Army just nodded soberly.

"And if God-King Natan does not relinquish the throne?" Marshal Torgallen asked.

Tyrun spread his hands. "Friends, there is no reason why

that should happen. Reason may prevail upon even the most entrenched. And do the people not wish for this god's return? Surely the man who claims to be of this god's bloodline will realise that his time as ruler has come to an end." He sighed. "However, should his mind have been poisoned by his lust for power, or by other, darker things, and should a significant number stand with him ... Then, friends, this god will have need of you."

A new Splintering. Tyrun was talking about a new Splintering, a war where Naridan turned upon Naridan. Marin desperately hoped that such a thing would not come to pass — after all, who could look upon Tyrun, speak to Him, without realising His divinity? — but he could imagine it all too easily. There was nothing to say that a lord or general would not send an army against Tyrun before they had seen him: might do so, in fact, specifically to avoid it, and the dilemma it might bring them.

"Marin," Tyrun said, and Marin's throat tightened as every face turned to him. "You are a common man of Idramar; low-born, as the nobility would class it. Is there an appetite for this god's return in that city? Do the people still honour him, or has their loyalty transferred solely to this man Natan?"

Marin swallowed. "Your servant begs you to understand, Divine One, that he was absent from Idramar for many years before he returned there recently, so his opinion may not be—"

"Spit it out, man," Benel interrupted testily. "You will know the city's mood better than we, no matter how you prevaricate."

"Well." Marin tried not to glower at the First Captain, although the temptation was great. Typical Westerner, thinking himself better simply because he was born nearer to Godspire! Well, Marin could tell him a story about a certain monastery that would make him—

No. No he would not.

"People in Idramar hope for your return, Divine One, but few expect to see it," he said, addressing Tyrun. "If they are confronted with it then some may deny it out of fear, some may panic at what this means for the world, while others will be joyous. Your servant would humbly suggest that you should make all effort to announce your coming far in advance, so the people have time to get used to the idea."

"An army does not typically announce its movements to those that might prove to be its enemies," Benel said disapprovingly.

"An army is not typically accompanied by the Divine Nari reborn," Reden replied dryly. "The Easterner is right, Benel. If we are with the Divine One, we can only expect attention. With luck, that will work for us, and Narida will rally behind Him."

"What of the Eastern Army?" Barstan Broadfield asked. "The fastest route to Idramar is surely downriver from here to the Idra, and then to follow its course east to the sea. That will take us past Northbank."

"They are spread thin, as this captain said," Reden repeated. "We also believe that we outnumber them, even were they at full strength." He caught the look he was getting from Benel, and shrugged. "If we have to fight those who won't acknowledge the Divine One, this captain would prefer we did it sooner rather than later. If half the Eastern Army has either been broken or has joined us, the remnants in the east will be that much less of a threat."

"It is not a prospect that this marshal relishes, by any means," Taladhar Torgallen said gravely. "However, if there is to be strife in this land, we must make it as brief as possible. Lord Goldtree will be given every opportunity to join us, but if he or his men refuse to acknowledge the Divine One then we will have no choice. The road to righteousness is rarely paved with easy decisions. The Divine One is correct: He must get to Idramar and take the Sun Throne, so the entire land understands that His rule is unchallenged. We cannot have King Natan in Idramar and the Divine One in the west. That way lies war for certain. We must move swiftly and with strength."

Tyrun nodded. "Then you will give the orders?"

"Your servant will," Torgallen replied, with a low bow. "We will strike camp at first light and make for the Idra. In the meantime, your servant's tent is yours."

"That will not be necessary," Tyrun said, with a wave of His hand. "This god has become used to more modest conditions. However, He has a great many followers, the Godsworn, who are waiting for him in the woodland to the north. They will need to march with us."

Marshal Torgallen nodded. "Of course, Divine One. First Captain, see to it."

Benel's mouth twisted, but he bowed in turn. "Yes, High Marshal. Captain Toren!"

The tent flap opened, and Toren entered with the expression of a man who might have been listening from outside, and already knew that he was being handed a difficult job that was unlikely to lead to any thanks from anyone.

Marin nudged Laz. "How likely do you think it is that the Eastern Army are going to be fine with this?" he asked his husband quietly.

Laz's cheek twitched. "Goldtree's stubborn. Loyal, but stubborn."

Marin thought on that for a moment. "Loyal to who?"

Laz let out a sigh. "Your husband guesses we're going to find out."

Tila

Tila was starting to get a picture of what had happened, and it was both better and worse than she had feared.

The city of Idramar had been ransacked and damaged, but not destroyed. The Raiders had killed and plundered, but they had not slaughtered wholesale: those who did not resist were now left largely unmolested, unless they had something the Raiders wanted. Unfortunately, the little food that remained available was the first thing the invaders laid claim to. Those who could leave, did. On one occasion when she was walking the palace walls, Tila saw a stream of ragged refugees heading west from the city.

"Why do you let them go?" she asked The Golden, her amazement overcoming her caution.

"Why should I not?" the draug replied. "Let them go and die elsewhere, instead of here where their bodies will rot and bring sickness. They will not fight us in the future; we have killed the warriors."

That was not entirely true, although it was close enough. Some Naridans had thrown down their weapons and surrendered when it became clear that the alternative was death, and to Tila's surprise the Raiders had not executed them as she would have expected. She was brought before a group of them that had been assembled on their knees in the trampled, mangled remnants of the Sun Gardens: a couple of dozen Eastern Army soldiers who had been part of the palace guard; perhaps the same number of townsfolk who had fought to defend their homes and not been quick enough to melt away into obscurity when they were overwhelmed; and even a shame-faced sar over whom the Code of Honour had obviously not held a strong enough sway for him to either die fighting or on his own blade.

More worryingly from Tila's point of view was the presence of Morel of Godspire and Sebiah Wousewold. Adan Greenbrook had died with longblade in hand; as, perversely, had Meshul Whittingmoor, although Tila could not imagine that the old Law Lord had managed much more than a sharp insult before he had been brought down. Master Temach of the university was missing, and she had not seen his face among the dead. Nor, crucially, had there been any sign of her brother or mother; or indeed Darel Blackcreek.

The two living members of the Inner Council, however, could prove problematic. Tila was not so concerned at this moment about the ramifications of anyone piecing together the disparate identities of Livnya the Knife and the Divine Princess, but she most certainly did not want The Golden to learn she was related to the God-King. For one thing, that might see it try to use her as leverage; for another, such a revelation would surely throw into doubt her entire plan to redirect it away from her brother and towards the nebulous threat of the allegedly reborn Nari.

"Tell them what I told you," The Golden instructed her. Its mask was glinting in the morning sun, and it was stripped to the waist. Tila was not sure whether it was simply warm – many Raiders seemed to have taken a dislike to the weather of the Naridan summer – or whether it wanted to show off its impressive collection of scars. Certainly, Tajen's claim that the draug could not be killed had gained more weight when Tila laid eyes on evidence of all the times that people had apparently tried and failed.

Tila cast a glance sideways at Tajen, who stood dispiritedly on The Golden's other side. The Golden had decided that Tila, as a "chief", would disseminate its instructions, but Tajen was here to make sure her translation into Naridan did not contain any subversive elements. Tila had been half-tempted to try to find common cause with the Raider — although she supposed that he was technically an Alaban — given he was obviously thoroughly miserable with the entire situation, but she doubted he had the backbone for it.

"Some of you may know this lady," she began, and saw heads come up, including those of Morel and Wousewold. "She is Livnya, known to some as Livnya the Knife." She was not going to start using "woman", even though Livnya should by rights have knelt before the Master of Scribes. Livnya the Knife had always used "lady" to mark herself out from the ruffians over whom she had control, and Tila was not going to abandon that now.

"We've been captured by The Golden, a demon of the Raiders," she continued. She was not going to go into the specifics of what a *draug* was, especially given she barely understood it herself. "*You* have surrendered in combat, which means that by their code you owe them service for a year and a day, during which time you can't raise a weapon against them."

She had to remember to speak in Livnya's more common tones, despite the familiar surroundings of the Sun Palace, and avoid the eyes of Sebiah Wousewold. The veil she had worn for all those years as Tila might have prevented lowborn who had seen the Divine Princess from afar from recognising her as Livnya, but she was rather less convinced of how well it would have hidden her features from those within the palace.

"However, The Golden doesn't believe we understand this properly, which is why it's told me to explain this to you," Tila continued. *Because after this princess was taken prisoner, she got free and threw a knife at it. Sorry.* "So you've all got a choice: to accept what the Raiders think you were asking for in the first place, and serve; or be killed. If one of you chooses to serve and then betrays them . . . " She could not help but glance at the draug's impassive metal mask, which was still somehow more expressive than its pale green eyes. "They will kill all of you, and any of your families they can find."

"That's barbaric!" someone shouted.

"They're Raiders," Tila said with a shrug. "To be honest, this lady is surprised any of us are still alive."

"And why are you speaking for this demon?" Sebiah Wousewold spoke up from the back, fixing her with a steady stare.

"This lady was captured while fighting in the streets. The Raiders saw other people obeying her, and assumed she had authority," Tila said, addressing them all rather than meet Wousewold's eyes. "Also, she knows some of the Alaban tongue, which the demon speaks."

"Yōu expect mè to believe that this demon speaks Alaban?" Wousewold called in that language. Why had Tila never known that he spoke Alaban? It would make sense, though, given his propensity for gathering information.

"Yòu would be wise to heed yòur chief," The Golden replied in the same tongue, and Tila got a momentary flash of pleasure as Wousewold's mouth snapped shut in astonishment. The draug flicked its fingers at her to continue, and the pleasure instantly soured. She was the Divine Princess, damn it, not some servant for this creature to treat so dismissively . . . Except that she was not the Divine Princess any longer: she could not afford to be, not here, and not now. She could only be

Livnya, and hope that she could make Livnya valuable enough to keep her alive.

The sar, whose name Tila did not know, chose death. She was not sure what he had hoped for in the first place, but it seemed the prospect of serving Raiders was one he could not countenance. The Golden began moving as soon as she translated his words, drew the longblade it carried at its side, and struck off his head with a casual strength that, at the very least, meant the man's suffering would have been minimal.

Everyone else chose to serve.

There were, it turned out, several Raiders who could speak some Alaban, although far more could not. Similarly, there were a few Naridans who could do the same, Tila and Sebiah Wousewold among them. The Golden might have been a possibly immortal demon, but Tila had to admit that it knew what it was about when it came to conquering. It had gone for the enemy's strongest bastion and taken it, and now it was using every tool at its disposal to ensure that those it had conquered understood its wishes. It had no compunctions about killing her countryfolk, but it wanted to be sure that anyone executed for disobeying it was doing so deliberately, and not out of ignorance.

That meant Tila was constantly being dragged out around the semi-ruined streets of Idramar to translate instructions and orders to the scared, frightened Naridans who remained. Whether by accident or design, she ended up being assigned to the same group of Raiders who had caught her in the first place: the towering woman known as Stonejaw and her cronies. The translator on the Raider side was a woman named Korsada, who carried a thin steel sword, and was far darker in complexion than most of her fellows.

According to The Golden, Stonejaw had been the one who

had suggested coming to Narida, and for that alone Tila would quite happily have put a knife into the woman's eye. However, in the days that followed she quickly got the impression that Stonejaw and her followers were no happier to be in Narida than Tajen was. They spent a lot of time in the city, but generally just mooched about without doing a great deal. It was almost as though the goal was simply to be away from The Golden. On the one hand, Tila welcomed that, because the draug did not get any less unnerving the more time she spent around it. On the other, the longer she was away, the less idea she had of what it might be doing. Her mind also conjured up worrying images of Sebiah Wousewold approaching The Golden, speaking to it in Alaban, trying to gain influence, and perhaps even speculating about Tila's true identity.

Tila knew that she should be trying to find some way to converse with the former Master of Scribes, to coordinate their efforts to do . . . something. The simple fact was that she could not risk it. The longer she spent in close proximity to the man, the more likely it was that he would become an even greater risk to her than Kaled Greenbrook had been, and Tila no longer had her knives.

They were down at the water's edge — they spent a lot of time there, almost as though Stonejaw was sizing up how possible it would be to take a ship and leave — when they were hailed raucously. Tila noticed chins raising and hands checking the position of weapons on belts, and she felt the absence of her own blades anew when she saw who had shouted.

Another, larger group of Raiders were approaching, and at their head was a man who looked vaguely familiar. Tila recognised him as the one Stonejaw had exchanged unfriendly words with on the day Idramar had fallen, when she was being marched through the streets towards the Sun Palace with Stonejaw's fingers in her hair.

"Is this going to be trouble?" she hissed at Korsada.

"That's Kullojan Sakteszhin," Korsada replied. "They're so sour a shark would spit them out, but they're no threat to yōu."

It was strange to hear the Alaban formal neutral coming out of the mouth of a Raider: Tila had not seen any sign they had the same strange attitudes towards gender as the Alabans, but perhaps it was just how Korsada had learned the language. "Why not?"

"Because yōu're a thrall," Korsada replied, with a frown that suggested she thought Tila was somewhat slow on the uptake. "So long as yōu behave yōurself, and don't touch a weapon, no one will hurt yōu."

Tila blinked in surprise. That seemed remarkably civilised. However, she pushed that thought to the back of her mind when something odd about the approaching group occurred to her. The Raiders that made it up seemed to be escorting another group of Raiders, who looked rather more downcast, and among them ... Yes! There was definitely a Naridan face, or more than one.

The leader of the newcomers shouted something at Stonejaw, and Tila did not have to speak their language to hear the swagger in his tone.

"Sakteszhin's captured ... " Korsada began, then trailed off and spat something in her own language that sounded like a curse. "Oh, no. What are *they* doing here?"

"What is who doing here?" Tila asked as Stonejaw shouted something back. She did not know how long Korsada was going to be absent-mindedly translating for, and wanted as much information as she could get.

"It's the Brown Eagle clan," Korsada said miserably. "The ones we chased ... Well, yōu wouldn't know about that."

"The Brown Eagle clan?" Tila repeated incredulously. "The ones who settled at Black Keep?"

Korsada whirled around to look at her. "How *do* yōu know about that?!"

"Word travels," Tila said. "What are they doing here?"

"I asked that! If yōu'd shut up for a moment ..." Korsada muttered. Tila obediently clamped her mouth closed, but her mind would not stop racing. Word could not have reached that far south about Darel Blackcreek's ascension to the rank of Southern Marshal, and in any case, why would this crew of mainly Tjakorshi have been sent north? It must have been for some other reason than to honour their thane. To request aid in the aftermath of the great wave? Had it truly had so great a reach? But even though the Raider ships were famously swift, Tila still struggled to believe that one could have got to Idramar so soon.

"Sakteszhin doesn't know, and doesn't care," Korsada said in disgust, as the other party swaggered past. "Apparently the Brown Eagle clan and yōur folk each know a bit of each other's language, so Sakteszhin just wants to improve their standing with The Golden by finding more interpreters."

Tila digested that for a moment, then took a calculated risk. It all depended on what "behaving herself" meant, but nothing ventured, nothing gained.

"Black Keep!" she shouted, squeezing between a couple of Stonejaw's warriors. "Why are you so far north?"

One face snapped around. It belonged to an older Naridan man, thin-cheeked and grey of hair, and Tila caught a glimpse of his clothing: not that of a noble, but still fine as those things would be judged in the far south, and with the emblem of Blackcreek on his breast. A steward? Blackcreek's steward, come north on a Tjakorshi ship? What was going on here?

"Darkspur marches to war with us," the old man said dejectedly. "We came to seek the judgement of the Southern Marshal."

"Were there any other ships with you?" Tila called, as the steward was shoved on by one of Sakteszhin's warriors. "Did any get away to carry word of Idramar's fate?"

"No others," the steward managed to answer before he was hustled on, and Tila's hopes went with him.

"Well?" Korsada asked, appearing at Tila's side. "Come on, fair's fair. I told yōu what Sakteszhin was saying."

"There's war in the south," Tila said dully. "They came to get help."

"There's war everywhere these days," Korsada said. "And that's not going to change any time soon."

Tila eyed her, a new tension creeping into her gut which partially displaced the despair that had settled there, after her brief flare of hope had died. "What do yōu mean?"

"Yōur city doesn't have enough food," Korsada said. "The Golden's taking us all farther inland. It also seems to think that there's a god waiting for it there. Tajen said yōu might have something to do with that."

Tila swallowed. She had dangled that prospect in front of The Golden in order to distract it from her brother, but there was an awful lot of her country between the draug and its quarry.

Well, that just meant more thanes and sars to rally against the invaders and push them back. That had to be a good thing.

"It's true," she said. There was no point telling Korsada anything different: the Raider might be acting as though they were in this together, but Tila suspected she would go running to The Golden the moment she learned anything she could use to her advantage. "When are yōu leaving?"

"When are *we* leaving?" Korsada snorted a laugh. "Guess again, Livnya. Yōu're coming too: yōu and everyone else who can speak a useful language. As for yōur people here, The Golden will be giving them a choice: join the Clanless and come to find food with us, or stay and starve."

Tila gaped at her. "Yōu'd ask these people to turn on their own country?"

"What, are you all one big clan or something?" Korsada screwed up her face. "You Naridans are so strange. I know languages are a bit different, but it's just a piece of land, isn't it?" She shrugged. "We're going to be taking the food anyway. We're leaving tomorrow, and yōu'll get the job of telling everyone that they can either join us and be near the food, or not. It's a simple choice."

It was indeed a simple choice. And, Tila realised, in a city where hunger had already set in, she thought she knew what the answer would be.

Bulang

Bulang did not go after Jeya, partly out of stubbornness and partly out of wisdom. If Jeya wanted to be somewhere else for the moment, Bulang was not going to chase hér down and crowd hér. Shé had spent most of her life alone, at least in comparison to living in a house with family and servants, so it was only to be expected that shé might want solitude now and then. Bulang had certainly wished for it often enough, even with the luxury of thëir own room, in a house surrounded by a large garden and high walls.

Thëy had never wanted it to come like this, though. Bulang had always honoured Nari as an ancestor, rather than praying to any of the various gods of Alaba, but perhaps some had heard thëir wish and decided to grant it in their own way. Some gods were supposed to be fickle, others cruel, and some merely struggled to understand the ways of people.

No, that was not the truth of it; it could not be. Bulang's family was dead because Narida had wanted them dead, as they had for centuries. Even if Bulang was not who thëy had always thought thëy were, it was still the Naridans who had caused this: the Naridans and potentially the Hierarchs, who perhaps at some point in the past had taken a family and raised them up to be their puppets, casually wiping away the blood-stained bodies of whoever had died before them. And as for Kurumaya . . .

Bulang hated them, but whatever Kurumaya had done was not *personal*. The Shark was vicious, and ruthless, but they had not travelled for weeks by sea simply to organise the deaths of Bulang's family. It had been business, and Bulang had learned enough about the political history of the Naridan Divine Court to understand people acting in their own interests. At the moment, thëy were more valuable to Kurumaya alive than dead, and that state of affairs was contingent on thëm playing along with the Shark's schemes. That was what was keeping both thëm and Jeya from dying, and it was frustrating that Jeya . . . Well, shé *did* realise it, but not in a way that changed hér opinions of what Bulang should be doing.

Bulang loved Jeya. If keeping hér alive meant letting thëmself be used as leverage by Kurumaya, then so be it. At least this time thëy were making thëir own decisions, instead of being born into a situation about which thëy had little awareness. Being caught between a Shark and the Hierarchs was an awful position to be in, but it was relatively simple to understand. If only—

A faint sound carried in on the night air from outside caused thëm to jerk thëir head up. It sounded like a monkey's alarm chatter in the distance, like the one that had yelled at Jeya and thëm just before they had discovered Ngaiyu's body. Jeya paid a lot of attention to the monkeys of East Harbour; shé said that Sa, the god of thieves and tricksters (among other things) could take the form of one. But monkeys were not up and around at night; they went to sleep when the sun did.

Apart from once. Jeya said that a monkey had shown hér the way into the Old Palace when shé'd lost the gap in the wall, on the night that Bulang's family had died, and shé was convinced that it was Sa. And if the god of thieves and tricksters (among other things) would be watching out for anyone in this city, surely it would be someone who had been stealing to live since shé was a child?

Bulang scrambled up and out through the main room, without heeding who might be disturbed by thëir passing, then through the front door. One of Kurumaya's thugs made a hurried grab for thëm as thëy dashed past, but Bulang twisted away from them.

"Which way did Jeya go?" thëy barked, backpedalling into the street.

"Hey now!" one of them replied. "You're not supposed to—"

"Which way!" Bulang demanded. "You can come with me, just tell me!"

"Fine, that way," the other thug said, hopping down off the step on which they had been sat and pointing away from the harbour, "but— Jakahama's paddle, will you slow down?"

Bulang ran in the direction indicated, calling Jeya's name, leaving the pair of them to follow as well as they could. There was no one up and around at this hour, only the faint yellow light of night fires or candles slipping out through shutters and outlining windows against the dark shape of houses. If shé had been outside, and anywhere nearby, Jeya should have heard thëm without too much trouble, so why did shé not reply? Was shé truly that angry or upset about what thëy had said? Or was there some other reason? Had that monkey's alarm call been the work of one of the gods that Jeya held dearest, trying to alert hér to danger?

Thëy cut left and right through the streets that ran between East Harbour's houses, calling in vain, and the worry settled more and more heavily on thëir chest as each repetition of Jeya's name left their lips without response. There had to be something wrong: shé could not have gone out of earshot already, and there was no way Jeya would refuse to reply if shé heard thëm shouting so desperately.

"Hey! Will you get back here?!"

Kurumaya's thugs were still on Bulang's tail, but their feet had not been lent wings of desperation. Bulang hesitated for a moment, caught on the precipice of indecision. Kurumaya had resources, and knew the city. They would be a powerful ally in finding Jeya, but only if they decided that they wanted to help, and that was by no means certain. If Kurumaya thought Bulang was distracted by Jeya going missing, might they not decide to shut thëm away somewhere for safe-keeping? Jeya meant nothing to the Shark, except possibly as leverage over Bulang.

Leverage.

Bulang was guarded by Kurumaya's thugs: Jeya was not. If the Hierarchs had got wind of Kurumaya's plans – might there be spies within the loose leadership circle of the waterfront? – then Jeya would be the obvious way to get to Bulang. Because no matter what happened, no matter how many people had already died, anyone near Bulang was always in danger.

Thëy could not go back. If Kurumaya thought there was a risk of thëm trying to get away, thëy would never be allowed to go anywhere alone again. Bulang knew in thëir heart that *something* had happened to Jeya, thëy just did not know what.

But thëy were going to find out. Jeya had helped Bulang hide from the people trying to kill thëm, had been at thëir side when thëy had tried to approach the Hierarchs, and had come up with the plan to get rid of Nabanda. Bulang was not going to sit around and wait to see if shé turned up of hér own accord.

Thëy made thëir decision, and darted away from the following thugs, who gave chase. Bulang was quicker, though, and managed to get enough of a lead to round a corner and scramble up the trunk of a paddleleaf that stood by the side of the street.

The action triggered a shockingly intense memory of

climbing in and out of thëir garden on the Second Level, and thëy fought back tears at the resurgent pangs of loss. Thëy swallowed hard and silently as the pair pursuing thëm came puffing past beneath, swearing in frustration and exclaiming about what punishments Kurumaya would inflict if they did not find thëm.

Bulang waited until the sound of their complaining had faded, then lowered thëmself back to the ground again, and headed off in a different direction. Climbing trees was noticeably easier now thëy were no longer binding thëir chest, and that thought just made thëm even more determined to find Jeya. Shé had been the first person to truly accept Bulang for who thëy were, without demanding something else from thëm. Not even Bulang's parents had been able to do that.

Everyone back at the house would have to look after themselves: Bulang had something more important to do.

"This is a curious fruit to find under my stall."

Bulang jerked awake, and wondered for a moment where thëy were, and why thëir bed was so lumpy and uncomfortable. Then memory reasserted itself, along with the thin light of the pre-dawn.

Thëy had searched for Jeya, but found nothing. When tiredness overwhelmed even thëir tightly wound anxiety, thëy had located what shelter thëy could for the rest of the night.

"And a pretty fruit, too," M'bana continued, squatting down to peer at Bulang. "But not one I'd expect to see here. What's the problem, that you're not sleeping in Ngaiyu's old place?"

Bulang tried to speak, coughed, then had another go. "Jeya's gone."

"Gone?" M'bana sat back on their haunches, their face a picture of concern. "Explain."

"They went out last night to take a walk," Bulang said. "We had . . . We hadn't had a *fight*, but we were talking about something important, and I think they wanted to clear their head. And then . . ." It sounded foolish now thëy came to describe it to someone else. "I heard a noise. It was a golden-maned monkey, screeching like they do when they're angry or afraid."

"Monkeys don't come out at night," M'bana said. "Unless someone disturbed one while it was sleeping—"

"Jeya worships Sa," Bulang interrupted, "and there's been a couple of times where monkeys have seemed to warn them of danger, or shown them something, or . . ."

M'bana's face did not show immediate understanding, but neither did they look like they thought they were dealing with someone who was delusional. "Very well. A monkey called. What happened?"

"I ran out to try to find them, but couldn't. I was shouting their name and running all over. I looked for half the night, in the end, but they never answered me. They would have answered if they could, I *know* they would." Bulang sat up and hugged thëir knees into thëir chest. "I think someone's taken them."

M'bana pursed their lips and frowned. "Any idea who would do that?"

Bulang frowned back. "You don't seem surprised."

"It's a strange city at the moment," M'bana said. "I come here to set up the stall every day, but it's not like we're getting much produce in, and a lot of what does arrive is taken by Kurumaya for distribution. It means everyone gets fed, but I don't know whether it can continue, or how long the Hierarchs will put up with it, *or* what they'll decide to do. I've seen families turn on each other over whether they should back the Hierarchs or the Sharks. Kind of makes me glad I don't have a family, myself," they added.

They grinned. Bulang did not return it.

"Well, anyway," M'bana continued after a moment, skating past the sudden awkward silence, "someone being snatched off the street is far from the oddest thing that could happen. I've heard of freed slaves being grabbed and carted off up into the hills, so the Hundred alone knows what else might be going on. This city feels like it's on the edge of the storm to end all storms, and every day that passes without it breaking just builds it up that much more." They raised their eyebrows. "Did you pick my stall at random?"

"I remembered where it was, and that you know Jeya," Bulang said dully. "I need help, and I need to stay out of sight as much as possible."

"Out of sight of who?" M'bana asked. "This is East Harbour: you can't hide from everyone."

Bulang hesitated, but thëy had few other options except to trust M'bana, even though thëy did not know them well. M'bana had been willing to put their life on the line against Nabanda's crew, and that had to mean something.

"Kurumaya," thëy admitted, prompting a low whistle of surprise.

"That's a tall order, right here and now," M'bana pointed out. "Is this just a case of keeping a low profile, or are they actually going to be looking for you?"

"They're going to be looking for me," Bulang said. "I don't think they're going to want me dead, but they're going to want to know where I am."

M'bana pinched the bridge of their nose. "I get up early to show willing and come and set the stall up, and this is what I get. The Hundred do like their little jokes."

"This isn't a joke!" Bulang snapped. "I need your help! *Jeya* needs your help!"

"And you'll both get it," M'bana said soothingly. "It was

Jeya who realised what that guttershit Nabanda was doing; they deserve anything I can do, just for keeping any more of us from getting knifed. But I tend to talk while I'm thinking, so you're going to have to get used to that." They tutted through their teeth. "You're from West Harbour, Jeya said? You don't know many people here?"

"Just the ones Jeya introduced me to," Bulang said, choosing to avoid the West Harbour story completely.

"Well, then," M'bana said. "I've been around these parts long enough to know a few people who have eyes and ears in useful places, so I'll start asking about the pair of you. If neither of you are where you should be, it'll draw attention if I'm only asking about one, won't it?" They smiled, which lit their whole face up. Bulang did thëir best to smile back this time, but thëir heart was not really in it. Thëy were desperately tired, thëy were still worried, and thëy could not bring themself to truly trust anyone, no matter what circumstances dictated. A lifetime of looking over their shoulders for assassins and being wary of letting anyone get too close had not been enough for thëir family, and things had only gotten worse since then.

"In the meantime, I've probably *just* got time to run you over to mine and still get back here before anyone else arrives," M'bana added, with a quick glance at the lightening sky. "Maybe you can get some proper sleep, since you've been up most of the night, and then we can talk again this evening. How about it?"

Bulang nodded wearily. Thëir head felt like it weighed three times as much as normal, and the prospect of more sleep was a truly enticing one. Thëy were not going to be any help to Jeya if thëy fell over thëir own feet through tiredness, or stumbled around and got noticed by one of Kurumaya's people.

"Come on, then," M'bana said, offering their hand. "Let's get going."

Bulang let thëmself be pulled to thëir feet, and hurried after M'bana through East Harbour's streets as dawn broke over the city once more.

Marin

"Why do they flee before this god?!"

Tyrun was angry, and Marin was terrified.

The Divine One was not supposed to get angry; although, Marin realised, he was not sure *why* that was the case. Certainly, Nari of old had waxed fearsome in His wrath at times, or so the texts said. He had been a mighty and imposing God-King, whose righteous anger at the suffering inflicted by witches and wicked men had been the burning force behind His desire to drive them from the land and make it a better place for His followers. With that in mind, was it any surprise that Tyrun, the Divine One reborn, might not grow angry when His designs were thwarted?

It made sense, but Marin was still terrified when his god raged and His noble features were suffused with vitriol.

"They flee before you because they are unworthy of you, Divine One," Mordokel said, bowing low. "Their minds are still ensnared in service to the pretender currently occupying the throne in Idramar. But they are fools, and their numbers are dwindling," he added. "After all, have the noble family of Greenbrook not sworn themselves to your cause?"

Marin looked over to where the Greenbrooks clustered in one corner of the hall that had once been theirs, looking ready to drop to their knees at a moment's notice. He had not caught all of their names, but even Marin knew that they were hardly the finest representatives of Naridan nobility. The old thane was in his bedchamber, and by all accounts now struggled to remember who his family were, let alone comprehend that his god was reborn and in his home. His son Adan was on Natan III's Inner Council in Idramar, his wife was three years dead, and the affairs of his household were apparently split between his eldest daughter, a nervous-looking woman with streaks of grey in her hair, and his steward, who reminded Marin of what might happen if a skinny man's face was replaced with one of last year's dried-up apples.

"This family are not the Eastern Army!" Tyrun snapped at His high priest. "The soldiers garrisoned here did not come to this god and welcome Him as their ruler; they fled before us."

"But this city has welcomed you, Divine One," Marshal Torgallen pointed out. "Greenbrook is one of the great cities of the West, and stands at the confluence of the Greenwater and the Idra. From here we can follow the Idra eastwards to Northbank."

"Which is where those traitors will have fled to," Tyrun said. "Is that not true?"

"It is most likely, Divine One," Torgallen agreed. "If Lord Goldtree is still using the city as his base camp, the Eastern Army will have its strongest presence there."

"And they will seek to deny us the city?" Tyrun asked. He looked up from the map laid out on the table around which they were stood, and fixed Torgallen with a piercing stare. The old marshal met it respectfully.

"It may be that Goldtree will accept your divinity. If so, his men are likely to follow his example. If he does not, then we will indeed find the city held against us." He pursed his lips. "Northbank is not a fortified city as such, but it has defensive walls, and Goldtree is a stubborn man. Your servant does not doubt that he would give his life for whoever he considers his rightful ruler."

Marin bit his lip. Would *he*? He certainly did not think he would have done so for Natan III, for all that he had theoretically acknowledged the man as God-King for the last twenty years. So far as Marin was concerned, the fates of God-Kings were great affairs that were rather out of his hands, and it was unfair for anyone to consider that he should have any input one way or the other. God-Kings ruled, and Marin lived his life as best he could, and it was probably easiest for everyone if their paths never crossed.

Except now their paths *had* crossed, because Marin had come west to seek out the Divine Nari reborn. He had walked into Tyrun's presence and accepted Him as his god, and had thrown himself at Elifel to prevent the man from burying his knife in Tyrun's chest, but now? Tyrun had all these soldiers around him now, great warriors like Taladhar Torgallen. Surely Marin would never *need* to give his life? If it ever got to the point when that would be necessary, things would almost certainly be so bad that one life more or less would make little difference.

"Marin."

Tyrun was looking at him, with those ageless eyes in His young face, and Marin covered his sudden apprehension with a bow. "Yes, Divine One?"

"You spent some time in Northbank before you met Mordokel, is that true?"

"It is indeed, Divine One," Marin acknowledged, straightening up again. "We came west with the Eastern Army, and stayed there for a short while before we deserted." He felt no shame at saying that, even in the presence of a High Marshal. After all, they had done it in order to find Tyrun.

"What was your opinion of the city, while you were in it?"

Tyrun asked. "Its mood, the opinion of the populace with regard to Idramar, and so forth?"

Marin scratched his chin. "The mood was poor, Divine One. Lord Goldtree brought news of Marshal Coldbeck's treachery and used that as an excuse to take Coldbeck Tower as his own. The populace didn't much take to his manner, and a fight broke out between soldiers and city folk at the inn where we were staying, to which other soldiers responded rather more violently than was needed." He neglected to mention that Ravi and Laz had a large part in starting the fight in question, since that seemed entirely beside the point. "The city as a whole may or may not be minded to accept you as their ruler, but this servant would be surprised if they think favourably of Lord Goldtree and his troops, or of King Natan who sent them there."

Tyrun nodded, and some of the residual anger drained from His expression. "Perhaps that is the best that we can hope for, for the moment. A city may welcome this god as an alternative to the pretender, and come to realise His divinity after that. In such small ways may we retake this land."

"If this marshal might make a suggestion?" Torgallen spoke up, and Tyrun signalled for him to continue speaking. "We would be well advised to test the mood of the city before we advance on it. Lord Goldtree may suspect we have a numerical advantage, and not seek to meet us in the open field. Nor can we afford to leave Northbank untaken, if it stands against us: it would mean leaving a powerful force at our rear, and the numbers required to contain it in any meaningful siege would greatly weaken us. It must be dealt with one way or the other, but if the populace is minded to side with you, Divine One, they could rise up and overthrow Goldtree's garrison, and he must know that. Knowing their minds could be crucial in determining the approach most likely to grant us success, whatever that might look like when all is said and done."

"Wise words, marshal," Tyrun said. "Do you have any men who hail from Northbank?"

"This marshal does not know, Divine One," Torgallen admitted. "The city stands on the border between East and West, but given Einan Coldbeck's long tenure as Eastern Marshal, most Northbankers seeking a career in the army probably went to serve under their thane, rather than coming west. There may be some, though."

"Put word out and find them, if they exist," Tyrun said. "We should send them to Northbank to do as you say, to test the mood. They may have friends or family there, and they will be able to avoid attention."

"An excellent idea, Divine One," Mordokel said. "However, those men might not have been to the city in years. Would it perhaps make sense to also send someone who has been there more recently? There could be some within the Godsworn who came from Northbank originally, or . . . " The priest's eyes slid sideways to light on Marin.

Oh no, don't you dare, Marin thought viciously, but to no avail.

"Marin, for example?" Mordokel continued. "He would be able to tell us how the general mood of the place compares to when he left it."

"Divine One," Marin said, ignoring Mordokel to make his appeal direct to Tyrun. "Your servant only wishes to be of use, but he's not certain he'll be able to assist you in this matter. His husband, as a blacksword sar and a member of the Brotherhood, was distinctive within the ranks of the Eastern Army. If we should return to Northbank, there's a good chance of us being seized as deserters. If so," he continued, warming to his excuse, "that could cause suspicion to fall on other recent arrivals, and anyone else you send might find themselves unable to return to you with any information. They could even be compelled to speak about your numbers and whereabouts!"

"Marin," Mordokel said softly. "This priest made no mention of sending your husband with you."

"How did it go today?" Laz asked, when Marin opened the door of their room. They had once more managed to get lodging at an inn, although this time no one had started any fights with the locals. However, Marin was surprised to see that Ravi was present once more; in this case, sitting opposite his husband and playing dice with him.

"S'woman can't believe you're actually one of the Divine One's advisors," Ravi said, looking at him with an expression hovering somewhere between awe, envy, and disgust. "All those marshals and captains and thanes – well, former thanes – and He also wants the thoughts of a thief from Idramar?"

"What is she doing here?" Marin demanded, ignoring Ravi and speaking to Laz. He had no objection to the healer, in truth, but right now he was angry and scared. Laz's eyes flickered to Ravi, and back to him again.

"We were just playing a game to pass the time. Your husband takes it that it didn't go well?"

"Your husband has been commanded to go to Northbank to determine the mood of the city," Marin said, ignoring Ravi's glare, which now shifted into an expression of uncertainty. "Mordokel's idea."

Laz's lip twitched. "That priest needs to stop sticking his nose in where it doesn't belong, or someone's going to cut it off."

"The Divine One agreed, Laz!" Marin practically shouted at him. "It's *His* will! Your husband has to go to Northbank!"

"Fine, fine," Laz said, raising his hands calmingly. "It's no big deal. It's, what, a week's travel? We'll head in, get an idea of what's going on, and—"

"You're not coming," Marin said bitterly. "That's the Divine One's will as well. Your husband pointed out that you would be easily noticed by our former cohorts in the Eastern Army, so Mordokel concluded that you shouldn't come. But don't worry," he added, with insincere cheerfulness, "your husband won't be unprotected! Mordokel will be travelling with him!"

Laz's eyes went flat. "He'll be *what*?"

"Mordokel is coming to Northbank as well," Marin said dejectedly, slumping down into an old wooden chair with little consideration as to whether it would take his sudden weight. "He's promised to protect your husband from any dangers we may face either on the way, or within the city. What more could your husband ask for than the close proximity of the Divine One's high priest?"

"He used to be a sar," Ravi said. "Surely he knows how to use that blade?"

"This sar does not doubt that he does," Laz said grimly. "That's not the point. The point is that Mordokel is a fanatic, and this sar does not trust him as far as he could throw him. Mordokel sometimes seems to like Mar, and sometimes appears to think that Mar is a danger to his position, and you can never be certain which way he's going to be thinking on any given day. Besides, what happens if they go into Northbank and find some folk mouthing off about Tyrun? Do you honestly think Mordokel will be able to restrain himself from drawing his blade on them, blowing everyone's cover, and putting Mar in danger?"

"Should the high priest of the Divine One *not* be a fanatic?" Ravi demanded, and Marin saw tears sparkling at the corners of her eyes. "Who should be a 'fanatic', if not Mordokel? What does that word even mean? The Divine One is here! We've met Him! How can it be fanatical to obey the God-King? To love Him?"

It was not hard to understand why Ravi's response was so emotional, given the conversation she and Marin had at the Pool of Tears. Nonetheless, Laz was not backing down.

"There's obedience, and there's fanaticism," Marin's husband growled. "Obedience is doing what's commanded of you. Fanaticism is where you decide that you can do no wrong, because anything you want to do has been commanded of you: when someone tells themselves that they're always acting in the *spirit* of what's been said, even if it was never said outright. This sar has seen that play out more than a few times in the years he's been wandering the world, and he's rarely seen it end well."

"The Divine One trusts Mordokel and made him His high priest!" Ravi argued. "How can His decision have been wrong?"

"This sar isn't saying the Divine One is wrong," Laz said stubbornly. "Maybe Mordokel is the best high priest for Him. That doesn't mean Mordokel's got Mar's best interests at heart, or that he won't get this sar's husband killed by taking offence at something when he's trying to play spy!"

"Don't you have faith in the Divine One?" Ravi demanded. "He is here to save us! Here to save all of us!"

"Like he saved the monks?" Laz snarled, and Ravi actually recoiled from him. "If the affairs of gods and kings were easily resolved by rightfulness, there'd be no need for men like this sar! *People are going to die*, and this sar doesn't want his husband to be one of them."

Ravi stood slowly. "So if you could only meet the needs of one, you would choose your husband over your god?"

Laz shrugged. "This sar already chose his husband over his god once, a long time ago. He sees no reason to alter that decision now, just because the god's changed."

Ravi blinked a couple of times, her eyelashes scattering the traces of tears that still lurked at the corners of her eyes, then departed. She did not exactly slam the door behind her, but it was not far off.

Marin reached out and squeezed Laz's hand, in an attempt to communicate something of the warmth that was currently flooding his chest. "Your husband loves you."

"He knows," Laz smiled. "And he loves you as well."

"It might not be the best idea to speak like that, though," Marin continued miserably. "You're right; Mordokel is a fanatic. Your husband doesn't want to give him any reason to harm either of us."

"Ravi won't say anything," Laz said with a certainty that Marin did not completely share.

"She's got her own reasons to be invested in the Divine One, beyond anything we might have," he reminded his husband. "Her loyalty to us basically consists of the fact that you got her out of the jail cell your husband got her put into in the first place. If she decides to go talking . . ."

"She's a good girl, with a good heart," Laz said. "She'd not put us at risk like that. Now, when is it that you're supposed to be leaving?"

"Tomorrow morning," Marin said miserably. Laz sighed.

"Then we'd best make the most of the night, hadn't we? Come here."

He reached out to cup Marin's face tenderly in his hand, and leaned in towards him.

Zhanna

"What do you think of Darkspur?" Thane Yarmina asked, as they walked around the town walls together. They were given a wide berth by others, although Zhanna was not sure whether that was because of respect for Yarmina, or wariness of Talon and Thorn who were trotting at her heels.

"It is not quite what this warrior was expecting," Zhanna replied.

Yarmina quirked an eyebrow. "Why so?"

"There is less fighting," Zhanna said honestly.

Yarmina laughed. "How much were you expecting?"

Zhanna paused, uncertain how to answer. She and her party had caught up with Sar Benarin and his men down the course of the Blackcreek, and made plans to push on and try to help break the siege they assumed would be happening at Black Keep. When they reached a village and heard tell of the great wave, and how most of Black Keep was now marching on Darkspur, they changed direction and thought they would find another siege underway, just with the roles reversed. Instead, they found a cautious alliance.

"Perhaps that was this warrior's mistake," Zhanna said. "Neither her mother nor Daimon fight without good reason."

"For which this thane is very grateful," Yarmina said with

feeling. "Her father gave them reason enough, had they chosen to pursue it. She is glad they do not wish to take his mistakes out on her people."

"You should be grateful," Zhanna said. "Daimon is a very good fighter, and he has strong Naridan honour. He challenged one of Mama's Scarred, one of our best warriors, because the man had killed one of Daimon's town ten years ago."

"What happened?" Yarmina asked, pausing to look out over the fields to the north.

"Daimon killed him," Zhanna said. "Rist was Mama's friend. That nearly ruined everything."

"Your mother agreed to marry Lord Daimon even after he had killed her friend?" Yarmina asked, incredulous.

Yes, although he's too young for her. Zhanna loved her mother, and knew exactly why the two of them had married, but it still rankled. Zhanna was reckoned a great warrior now, having helped to free a captured people and fought one of the giant dragons known as a thundertooth, but that praise was not enough to wash away resentment.

"They both have strong honour," she said, leaning her elbows on the parapet. "It needed to be done."

"Well, at least they seem to be getting some joy from each other," Yarmina said lightly. "This thane thinks there is some genuine affection there."

Zhanna gritted her teeth and said nothing, but Yarmina was not the sort of person around whom that worked.

"*Oh,*" the other woman said after a couple of moments. Zhanna did her best not to glare.

"*What?*"

"Nothing, nothing." Yarmina held up a hand. "Just . . . Well, this thane thought *her* family situation was awkward."

"It's not *awkward*!" Zhanna protested. "They just . . . This warrior does not want to talk about it," she finished gruffly, folding her arms and giving Yarmina a stare that any of her crew would have backed down from. The Naridan just smiled.

"What is your family, then?" Zhanna said, trying to shift the conversation's focus.

"This thane's father was Naridan; her mother is Morlithian, from beyond the mountains," Yarmina said. "Morlithians are not well-liked in Narida, especially when this thane was younger. Her mother got tired of how she was being treated, and went back to her home." She seemed surprised by Zhanna's lack of response, and added, "That does not normally happen in Narida. Does it with your people?"

"Why would it not?" Zhanna jerked a thumb over her shoulder at the town behind them. "This warrior's father is down there, somewhere. He is nice enough, most of the time, but Mama never married him. He can be an arse," she added, which Yarmina laughed at prettily.

"Some of your Tjakorshi ways sound a lot better than what we have here," she said. Zhanna held her tongue, because she knew full well that *some* of their ways were not so readily accepted by Naridans. On the other hand, Mama had sworn as a marriage vow that she would prevent the clan from acting against men who loved men, or women who loved women, and she had held to it. That did not mean that all the clan were fine with it, by any means, but they had been told in no uncertain terms that what did not involve them did not concern them. And who would have thought it? It turned out that it was not just Kerrti the witch who had feelings in that direction. Zhanna had noticed at least a couple of pairs of "good friends" had taken to acting a bit differently in the time she had been away.

"You are a thane," she said instead, and this time Yarmina's laugh was more scornful than pretty.

"Hah! This thane is doing her best, but she knows she would never get away with it if we were not so remote." Yarmina sighed. "*If* no one like a High Marshal or the God-King look in this direction, and *if* she can avoid some sort of forced marriage from another thane or his son, and *if* she remains vigilant at all times against ambition or disloyalty from within her own lands, she might be able to keep the title she has claimed for herself instead of being compelled to become someone's *lady*." Zhanna saw Yarmina's fingers curl into fists on the parapet top. "Things are not like this in Morlith. They have an empress there, can you imagine? Unquestioned and supreme."

Zhanna had her doubts about whether anyone would truly be unquestioned, but she decided not to voice them. "What will you do about the mountains?" she asked, changing the subject.

"This thane will send messengers to the mountain folk," Yarmina said wearily. "They attack our farms; we hunt them down. It cannot continue. Or at least, it *should* not continue. If Naridans can find common cause with your people from across the ocean, we must be able to do the same with those who have lived near us for so long. Perhaps this thane should talk with Sar Benarin, since his town sits on the edge of the mountains, with little trouble between different peoples. If he will even accept her as a thane, and not as a girl," she added bitterly.

"He accepted this warrior as a warrior," Zhanna said encouragingly.

"You *are* a warrior!" Yarmina laughed. "Your mother told this thane how you slew the Raider chief in defence of Black Keep and saved her life, and this thane has also heard how you got that." She reached out and touched the huge, carved tooth that hung around Zhanna's neck. "We must find an artist to decorate your scabbard with your deeds, but the fact it is still bare does not mean they did not happen. Benarin will respect your ability with a blade, if nothing else, but that is not the sort of thing a good Naridan noble daughter learns."

Zhanna frowned. "Why not?"

"For the same reason we struggle to inherit power!" Yarmina exclaimed. "Because women *cannot be trusted*, and the people who make the laws are men, who have no interest in changing them."

"You are taking power," Zhanna said. "Why not learn blade too?" Yarmina looked at her, and she shrugged. "If ship is going over anyway, better to jump into sea than fall."

"Who would teach this thane?" Yarmina asked the sky, spreading her hands. "She has pushed Sar Asad away because he was too ambitious; Lahel would bleat about decency and propriety and never agree, no matter how much this thane cajoled or ordered him. All the rest are drowned."

Zhanna did not yet have her mother's grasp of Naridan, but translating back and forth on the journey to the mountains and back had made her a lot better than she was, and she thought she knew an unspoken question when she heard one. "This warrior could."

Yarmina turned towards her, eyes wide and eager. "You could? You *would*?"

Zhanna shrugged. "Why not?" The obvious answer to that question was that her mother had told her to be careful of Yarmina, but Zhanna could see no harm in this. If anything, she would be doing Black Keep a favour by giving the new ruler of Darkspur another reason to be indebted to them. "When would you like to start?"

Yarmina bit her lip. "Tonight?"

"Why not today?" Zhanna asked. "Better light."

"This thane would rather no one saw her trying to learn," Yarmina said hastily. "It will be hard enough to make people accept her doing it as it is, let alone if she goes dropping her sword all over the place. But if you come to her chambers after the meal this evening, you can show her how to begin."

Zhanna thought it over for a moment. She did not see any

shame in being bad at something at first – how else were you supposed to learn? – but perhaps it was different for a Naridan learning to do something that her people did not think she was supposed to.

"Daimon might teach you," she suggested. Would Yarmina feel more comfortable learning from another Naridan? "He knows more of the longblade than this warrior; he taught her."

"This thane is *not* inviting Lord Daimon to her chambers after the evening meal!" Yarmina said with a slightly desperate finality. "It would not be right! People would notice!"

Zhanna raised her eyebrows. "This warrior is Tjakorshi. People might notice that too."

"We are two young women only a couple of years apart in age," Yarmina said. "Why should we not be friends? That was why this thane asked you to walk the walls with her today. You are a great warrior, you know our speech well enough that this thane can learn about your people from you, and you are clearly noble and honourable . . . Of all the Tjakorshi she could befriend, you would cause the least comment. And you seem nice," she added after a moment, "and this thane has not had many friends in her life."

Zhanna knew when she was being flattered, but Yarmina seemed genuine underneath it. And besides, what could be the harm? Yarmina was likely to be more a danger to herself with a blade than to Zhanna.

"Very well," she said. "This warrior will come to your chambers after the evening meal."

"Wonderful," Yarmina said, her eyes lighting up. "This is going to be so much fun!"

Zhanna had been given her own room to use in Darkspur's castle, which was not – to her mild relief – near the one being used by Daimon and her mother. As a result, she ran little risk of bumping into them when she left her rooms and made her way through the passages to Yarmina's chambers.

Darkspur's new thane had wasted no time in moving her possessions into the master suite of rooms, most likely to reinforce her status in the minds of those who served her. It was an imposing door, and Zhanna thought she probably bruised her knuckles by knocking on it loud enough to be heard. It was jerked open almost before she had finished, and Yarmina stood there with a slightly nervous smile on her face.

"Come in! Come in!" She stepped back and allowed Zhanna to enter, then hurriedly closed the door again.

"You changed your clothes," Zhanna observed.

"Well, yes," Yarmina admitted. "Everyone expects this thane to wear her dresses, but they did not seem suitable for this, so . . ." She gestured vaguely at herself. She was wearing dark-coloured, tight-fitting leather trousers and vest over a soft, pale shirt. "She decided to wear her hunting clothes."

"You should wear them more often," Zhanna said approvingly, and the smile that got from Yarmina was wider and happier than any Zhanna had seen from her before. "Maybe make them thane clothes?"

"One thing at a time, perhaps," Yarmina said, with a chuckle. "It will be hard enough getting anyone to take this thane seriously as a woman, let alone if she looks like a huntsman." She took a deep breath, and let it out. "But that is an issue for another day. If you are still willing to show this thane how to handle a sword, she would be grateful."

"That is why this warrior came," Zhanna said. "Do you have one?"

"This thane took two practice blades from the armoury earlier," Yarmina said with a grin. "Here!" She picked up a pair of blunt-edged swords from where they leaned against her bed and tossed one to Zhanna, who caught it by the grip.

"Daimon said you Naridans have lots of strange ideas about swords," Zhanna began.

"Daimon said that?" Yarmina queried, raising an eyebrow.

"No," Zhanna admitted. "He tried to tell this warrior about some of them, and she thinks they are strange. You have lots of different ways of using swords, and this warrior does not know any of them, or the names they have, so she cannot teach you that. But she can tell you how *she* uses the sword."

"That will be fine," Yarmina said with a smile. "Where do we begin?"

"Standing," Zhanna said. "Must be balanced and ready to move. What is best way to not be hit?"

"Parrying?" Yarmina suggested, moving her blade up as if to block an incoming strike.

"No," Zhanna told her firmly. "Not being there. If enemy can't reach you, enemy can't hit you. If can be hit, use shield. If you don't have shield, use sword to knock sword aside, that is parry." She twitched her own blade to demonstrate. "If you can't knock sword aside, *then* block." She raised her sword as Yarmina had done, crossways to the imagined incoming strike. "But that can damage sword, and will tire your arms, and you will probably be smaller than most people you ever fight, so will tire fast if you do that."

Yarmina nodded. "So what is the best way to not be there?"

"Be ready to move," Zhanna said. "Daimon said he knows when he can take one step and hit enemy, but . . ." She shrugged. "Enemy will not be standing still. So you must move. Hold sword and stand."

Yarmina did so. Zhanna reached out and pushed her shoulder, and she took a startled step backwards.

"Not stable," Zhanna said to Yarmina's reproachful expression. Was she even supposed to put her hand on a lady, or a thane, or whatever Yarmina was? Well, they were here to do things with swords, so surely Yarmina had imagined that they might have to touch at some point? "Which is strong hand?"

Yarmina held up her right one.

"That leg forward," Zhanna said, pointing at Yarmina's right leg. "Other back. Be steady front, back, and sides, so can be ready to move anywhere." Yarmina adjusted her stance, and Zhanna nodded. Having any sort of proper set to your feet was a luxury in an actual fight outdoors, where stones, animal burrows or tree roots had their own ideas, not to mention your enemies, but it was best to know what you were trying to achieve.

"Now, holding it," Zhanna said. She weighed Yarmina with her eyes for a moment. She usually used her longblade one-handed, to allow for a shield in the other hand, but Yarmina was smaller and slighter. "Two-handed, for you."

Yarmina obediently held her sword out, with the point levelled in Zhanna's direction. Zhanna shook her head.

"You will tire your arms. Look." She tilted the blade upwards until it was at an angle halfway between horizontal and vertical. "Hands are good, though. Just move this one down a bit." She took hold of Yarmina's left hand, and was struck by how soft it was; which probably made sense, if she had never needed to cut wood, or haul on a fishing net. Zhanna shifted it slightly farther down the grip and squeezed it into place, then straightened up again, but Yarmina's arms were still a bit too rigid.

"Can be looser," Zhanna said. "If too tight, cannot move fast." She stepped up beside Yarmina and reached out to put one hand on Yarmina's far shoulder to steady her. She placed the other in the crook of Yarmina's elbow to bend her arms a little and bring her elbow down closer to her waist. Yarmina shifted her weight slightly in response, and suddenly her hip was pressing against Zhanna, and her hair, which smelled of something pleasant and flowery, was brushing against Zhanna's nose.

Zhanna abruptly became aware, *properly* aware, that she was in the private rooms of a girl a couple of years older than her, who was now pressed up against her for reasons that were entirely explainable, but which she had expressly requested. Also, Zhanna's heart was beating rather faster than might be expected, given she had not been doing anything strenuous. She also found herself wondering how many more minor corrections to Yarmina's posture she could find excuses to make, given that Yarmina did not seem in any hurry to move away, *and* exactly what Zhanna's mother would say if she could see her at this moment.

But may all the heroes help her, this felt ... nice? And she did not want to offend Yarmina by acting like a typical Tjakorshi and recoiling. That would only serve to reinforce negative impressions about her people, after all.

Yarmina turned her head to look at Zhanna, so their faces were separated by a mere handspan, and her lips parted to say something.

There was a knocking at the door.

Zhanna jumped, and had taken a step away from Yarmina and had her hand on the sheathed longblade at her side before she realised exactly what she was doing. Yarmina herself seemed barely more composed, but she swallowed hurriedly and answered.

"Who is there?"

"*Sar Asad, Lady.*"

Zhanna looked from Yarmina to the door, and back again. Yarmina bit her lip.

"It is late, goodsar. What is so urgent?"

"*A matter of the town's safety, lady, and your own. This sar may no longer be your castellan, but he cannot ignore such matters.*"

Yarmina grimaced. "Very well. This thane will be with you in a moment." She hurriedly beckoned Zhanna over to her, then handed her the other practice blade and pointed to the curtain. "Get behind there," she whispered. "This thane will get rid of him as soon as possible, but it may be important."

Zhanna nodded, and pulled the curtain across to hide herself as Yarmina hurriedly picked up a robe and threw it over her hunting clothes, then belted it shut. She heard Yarmina cross to the door and open it, and the scuff of Sar Asad's feet as he entered.

"Well?" Yarmina demanded. "What is so urgent that it could not wait?"

"The Raiders, lady," Asad said. Zhanna heard the soft thump as he closed the thick door behind him. "They have attacked."

Zhanna blinked in shock and horror. What had happened? Had there been some squabble that had degenerated into a fight?

"Attacked?" Yarmina demanded. "Attacked who?"

"You."

"What do— Asad? *Help!*"

Zhanna threw the curtain aside just in time to see Yarmina scrambling backwards out of the way as Asad swung for her with, of all things, a blackstone axe. The blow barely missed, and Yarmina was backing towards the corner of the room. Asad would have her in moments.

Zhanna threw the practice blades at his back with a yell, and drew her sword. The sar whirled around with a blind swing of the axe at whatever had struck him, and Zhanna pulled up short rather than run into its edge. Asad smiled at her.

"And here is the culprit," he sneered. "What a shame this sar was too late to stop you."

He threw the axe at her head. Zhanna ducked, and by the time she had recovered herself he had drawn his own longblade and was moving to the attack.

Zhanna had sparred with Daimon a few times, and had fought against Rikkut Fireheart's raiders in Black Keep and Darkspur men in the mountains, but this was the first time an actual sar with a longblade had come at her with the intention of killing. There was no time to think, only to react, as his blade came flashing for her again and again. She had a slightly longer reach, but Asad was more experienced, and hemmed in as she was by the bed and the walls she could not circle to see if she could take advantage of his bad leg.

On the other hand, she was younger, and stronger. If she could just hold him off long enough for him to begin to tire . . .

Their blades tangled once more, and Asad drove his upwards, seeking to force the tip of her blade aside so he could cut at her face. Zhanna's lessons with Daimon leaped into her mind, and she took a step towards the wall and jammed her left hand against the flat of the blade to press Asad's sword away.

The resistance she had expected was no longer there. Asad dipped his blade under hers and cut diagonally upwards into her left wrist.

Zhanna felt a momentary sharp coldness, more of a sting than anything else, and it was not until she tried to make a counter-cut that she realised she only had one hand on her longblade. Warmth dripped down her forearm.

Zhanna screamed.

She parried his next two strikes one-handed and on instinct, but she was backing away from him now, backing away from *her own hand* that now lay limp and motionless on the floor. Tears of shock and rage threatened to blur her vision, but she gritted her teeth and fought on, desperately meeting Asad's two-handed swings, aware that her right arm was tiring and that blood was dripping out of the wrist she now had tucked in at her waist.

There was a scream that was not hers, and Asad staggered forwards as Yarmina brought one of the practice blades down on his skull from behind. Blunt or not, the impact was enough to buckle his legs.

Zhanna drove her knee up to meet his jaw as he began to fall, and he slumped sideways into the wall with eyes glazed. This time he made no defence when she slashed at his throat, and her longblade opened a high tide wound that sent his blood sheeting down over his chest.

"This thane is sorry!" Yarmina babbled. "She couldn't get to the swords until he moved forward, they were under his feet—" She broke off and began ripping at the sleeve of her gown, pulling it off with a strength born of desperation, and reaching out for Zhanna's wrist. "We must bind it, we must get you to the apothecary! Help! *Someone help!*"

She began to tie the sleeve around Zhanna's wrist, and the sudden jolt of pressure seemed to knock the world sideways.

Zhanna staggered, tried to grab at Yarmina with a hand that was no longer there, and fell.

PART THREE

Tila

The Raiders went west, and some of Idramar came with them.

Tila did not know whether it was out of fear that the Raiders would kill anyone who did not join them, simple hunger, or some other rationale she could not fathom. Perhaps it was a mix. Whatever the reason, a good few hundred Idramese boarded the Tjakorshi ships, with their heads down and expressions grim.

The Raiders left the rest of the city alive, of course – The Golden had neither the patience nor even the inclination for such savagery – but they left it starving and leaderless. Some supplies had arrived by sea, but the Raiders seized it all, and any captain arriving now would find only hungry faces, and no coin to be offered for whatever their ship carried. They would likely seek port and customers elsewhere, and so Idramar would continue to starve. Perhaps travelling with the Raiders for their scraps really was the best way to find food.

Tila herself had nothing to worry about on that front. The Raiders considered her to be a chief of her people, and recognised her value as an interpreter, and so she was fed. It was not the quality of food she was used to, either as Tila Narida or as Livnya, but the quantity was enough that her stomach did not growl at her at night.

By the Mountain, all the spirits, and her divine ancestor Himself, she hated these Raiders. And yet, for all that they were violent savages, she found herself envying them as well.

They had no king, divine or otherwise. Women fought as warriors, and led as captains, and no one thought this at all strange. The Golden ruled them, but that seemed to have nothing to do with the fact that Tila would have classed its body as belonging to a man. Korsada and Tajen had both been very clear that The Golden was a draug, a malicious spirit, and as such it had no gender. It could have taken a woman's body, and there would have been no difference.

What was important was that all the Raiders were terrified of it, yet also viewed it with an awe that verged on religious. It had apparently predicted the death of their homeland – Korsada had speculated to Tila that the great wave was caused by their sea god swallowing the lands on which they once lived – and led them across the ocean to safety.

Tila had her own ideas about exactly how safe Narida would prove for them, which involved a lot of mounted sars, an open plain, and a quite staggering amount of bloodshed, but she recognised power when she saw it. She had wielded it often enough, in different guises. In the way the Golden barked orders and was instantly obeyed, she saw hulking palace guards ducking their heads meekly when she passed, or her collection of criminals around a table in a yeng house taking a verbal lashing from her without raising their voices in response, let alone threatening her physically. The Golden was a fearsome warrior, but no matter how fell it was in battle, it could not hope to prevail against all of its followers should they turn against it. Even if the Nari-damned thing could not die, it could surely be overpowered and bound?

But no one would risk it. Even Tila's brother, weak and ineffectual a ruler though he had been for much of his reign, had been protected by the trappings of power. Anyone who stepped up to challenge the way things were risked being pulled down by their peers in the hope of reward, or out of fear that change would make things worse for them rather than better. Tila could see that fear in the eyes of the captains who obeyed The Golden. They at least had some authority as things stood, but would that continue if one of the other captains managed to depose The Golden and take power? No; in their minds, if anyone should take power from the draug, it should be them. However, each was too scared to act alone, and so the thing wearing the masked, scarred body of a man continued to give them orders, and they continued to obey.

They swept down on Idraby before nightfall of their first day on the river. Tila had envisaged that everyone for miles around would have fled from the horror inflicted on the capital, but she had reckoned without people's reluctance to leave their homes. Perhaps she should not have been surprised: Raiders struck and disappeared, after all, so why should a town a few miles upriver be concerned if Idramar had been sacked a few days before?

By the time the people of Idraby realised the answer to that question, it was too late. The town's walls were old and in poor repair, a vestige from the days of Nari, when rival warlords had been at each other's throats across the land. Somewhere this close to the God-King's seat had not seen such trouble in centuries, and the half-fallen piles of mouldering stone offered no resistance worth the name to The Golden's horde. Tila watched from the river as they swarmed through the houses, killing any who tried to stand against them. Stores were ransacked, the steel weapons of dead defenders were claimed by their killers, and food was parcelled out.

When the battle was done, and she was allowed on land, Tila got half a loaf of bread, some bean curd, and two apples taken from the orchard; small and too early, and very nearly too tart to stomach, but just about edible. She ate it without considering that her people had died trying to protect this food. She could not bring them back to life by refusing it.

Other Naridans were doing the same; people from Idramar eagerly taking the offered food, as their conquerors made good on their promise. It was not much, but it was more than they could have reasonably expected had they stayed. Tila saw hatred and resentment, but the first glimmerings of gratitude, as well. All had come of their own will, and all knew that the Raiders had no need to keep them alive.

She saw Sebiah Wousewold giving a group of Idraby survivors the same message as had been given to Idramar: stay and starve, or follow and feed. Most stayed. Some, with dead eyes and dragging steps, ignored the heartbroken and angry cries from their fellows and families, and moved towards the option that might see them eat in the foreseeable future. And so The Golden's numbers and power grew slightly, as it pulled in people who viewed following in its wake and being fed morsels as the least worst of the options with which they were presented.

Tila almost admired it. Impose suffering on people, take them with you, then point them at those who had what they now lacked. The harvest was a couple of months away at least, and most fields of these riverside towns had been swamped in any case. Where else would food come from, for these people, except by taking it? And who commanded the force that had the ability to take it? Oh, you could try to take revenge on those who had wronged you, even though they had you greatly outnumbered, but even if you managed it, you would remain hungry. Or you could do as they wanted, and remain alive.

However, Tila had not pulled her strings across Idramar, Narida, and beyond, to simply smile and take her food from a

Raider's hand. She had tried to put a knife into The Golden and had failed: that just meant she needed to find another method.

She found the Blackcreek party sitting listlessly near a fire made from the wood of a cart that an enterprising Raider had hacked up. Those who had refused The Golden not only got no food, they got no fire either, while their possessions were burned by their conquerors. However, those in the draug's service – even involuntarily – received their rewards.

"You're the Blackcreek steward," she said, walking up to them and sitting without being invited. She had no time or inclination to pay attention to proper manners, given their circumstances.

"You are correct," the old man said, with a weary nod. "You are another of the interpreters, are you not?"

"Livnya of Idramar," Tila replied. Neither the steward nor the other two Naridans with him gave any indication that they recognised the name, which was potentially both useful and hindering. On the one hand, Tila wanted them to trust her, which might not be the case if they thought of her as a notorious crime lord; on the other, it left her utterly without any form of authority or intimidation, unless anyone from Idramar was still willing to do her bidding.

"Osred," the steward replied. "This is Elio, and Ezi, of this steward's town," he continued, gesturing to a middle-aged man and a girl somewhere in her teens, who both gave Livnya the sort of half-hearted neck-bow that was used when someone did not want to be overtly rude, but really had no interest in putting themselves out. Or perhaps southern lowborn were just that uneducated. Tila could not be sure: Darel Blackcreek had been a stickler for propriety, but he was a thane's bloodson, and a scholar to boot.

She expected Osred to stop there, but the man continued to speak, gesturing at the Tjakorshi with him: "This is Otim, whose sister married a Naridan many years ago; Nasjuk, and Andal Clubfoot, his sons; Koren; Zalika; Enga Stormshoulders; Ikzhan; Kyzhan; Jandut the Tall; and Kora Crow-nose."

He rattled off the names without pausing, and Tila saw the pale faces of those to whom the names belonged nod or smile slightly as he did so. They were glad to be introduced, she realised, rather than just left in the background while the Naridans talked. She did her best to memorise them, which would have been a lot harder without practice at a variety of courtly functions throughout her life. The translated descriptors that some of the Tjakorshi bore were handy, at least: Jandut was indeed tall, even sitting down; Enga looked like she could lift a spirehorn by herself; and if Kora's nose was not quite as sharp and prominent as a crow's beak, it was not far off. Andal's feet were not obvious from where she was, but both he and the young man next to him had their father's nose and eyebrows.

"Pleased to meet you all," she said politely. "You speak each other's tongues?"

"A few words," Osred said. "Enough to be of use, and we are learning more every day. But please, tell us," he said, and his thin face took on an expression of desperate hunger that had nothing to do with appetite, "what happened? What of the God-King, and the Divine Family, and our dear Thane Darel?"

"The Raiders swept down on the city while we were still recovering from the great wave," Tila said. "The garrison was unable to stand against them, although their commander was as much to do with that as the numbers involved." She pushed down her disdain for Adan Greenbrook's blundering of the city's defence, in the face of Osred's shocked expression. Besides, despite the ordering of his questions, she knew which answer was of most importance to him. "So far as this lady knows, Lord Blackcreek and the Divine Family escaped the city prior to the attack."

"He lives?" Osred's face lit up in joy, and Tila realised that this man must have watched over Darel since he was a baby. "Nari be praised! And the Southern Marshal?"

Tila barked a laugh that clearly shocked him. "Ah yes, you would not have heard! Your Lord Darel *is* the Southern Marshal now; he saved the God-King's life from an attempt on it by Kaldur Brightwater and was rewarded for his loyalty and bravery with the rank of the man he slew."

Osred's eyes grew as wide as moons. "Darel is ... That is, *Marshal*?" He licked his lips. "Well. That is ... quite remarkable."

Tila could not help but smile at the man's understatement. "It was a surprising appointment, to be certain, but the God-King knew his own mind." *A shame he did not do so more often, prior to Coldbeck imprisoning him*, she added in the privacy of her own head, *but better late than never*.

"You said you came north to seek aid," she said, and Osred nodded, his delight and relief fading.

"Yes. Lord Daimon received word that the thane of Darkspur intended to march on our town and destroy it, as he wished to before the Southern Marsh— ah, that is, Marshal Brightwater, declared that the Tjakorshi should live among us."

Tila frowned. "Why would Odem go against his liege-lord's orders like that? It makes no sense."

"We do not know for sure," Osred said glumly. "We had sent a party to determine the well-being of our neighbours in the Catseye Mountains, and it seems Darkspur may have been involved with whatever misfortune they have suffered. Perhaps Thane Odem feared we would learn the truth and take up arms against him, and wished to strike first."

Tila could not help but laugh. "Black Keep would take up arms against another Naridan thane over his treatment of the mountain people?" She thought for a moment of Darel

Blackcreek's earnest, honest young face, and how both he and his brother had ended up turning on their father in the interests of what they believed was right. "Actually, that does not perhaps sound so far-fetched."

"Forgive this steward," Osred said cautiously, eyeing her clothes. "But you referred to yourself as a lady, and you knew Thane Odem's name. The far south is a long way from Idramar, and it is surprising to hear that you know so much about us. Are you a member of the Divine Court?"

Shit. Tila had forgotten that, now she was no longer in the familiar surroundings of either the Sun Palace or the streets of Idramar, her idiosyncrasies would draw attention. Besides which, even the well-connected criminals of Narida's capital were unlikely to know the names of minor thanes from the far-flung corners of the kingdom.

She smiled Livnya's smile at Osred and watched him withdraw slightly. Power was as much about personal confidence as it was the obvious ability to impose one's will.

"Perhaps personal stories can wait for another day," she said politely. "Besides which, although she does not begrudge you it, this lady did not come simply to give you news. Your . . . friends." She nodded in the general direction of the Tjakorshi. "Is this lady to understand that they do not follow The Golden out of choice?"

Kora Crow-nose caught Tila's eye, then held her gaze while she hawked and spat on the floor.

"That about covers it," the man called Elio said with a chuckle.

"They fled across the ocean from it," Osred told Tila. "They fought with us to defend Black Keep from its raiders. We serve it now only because Otim pointed out that we have more hope of helping our kin at some point in the future if we remain alive than if we resist and are killed."

"True words for all of us," Tila said, giving Otim an acknowledging nod. She wondered about demanding more proof of the Tjakorshi's allegiance, but what could she ask for? The disgust and contempt in Kora's gesture was clear enough. "As it happens, this lady has an idea on that front."

Osred frowned. "In what manner?"

"You have seen that The Golden is gathering Naridans to it," Tila said. "This lady has no doubt that it intends to turn us against our own country, so that we will be both weapon against our kinfolk and a lure to them to join it. This cannot be allowed to happen, but desperate and hungry people may follow any chance of salvation, even if it is the one that caused their misery in the first place. We must resist, subtly."

"There are an awful lot of axes around us," Osred said bluntly.

"This lady said 'subtly', steward," Tila said. "We must be seen to play along, but be ready to act when the opportunity presents itself. What is more," she added, remembering Stonejaw's wistful looks towards beached ships and the open sea, "this lady does not think that all of the Raiders here like being ruled by The Golden, not by any means. They are just too fearful to do anything about it."

"You are suggesting that we foment a rebellion?" Osred asked, raising his eyebrows. "That sounds like a short road to a slit throat. And while this steward is certain that our Brown Eagle neighbours would love to see such a thing come to pass, neither of us have a sufficient grasp of each other's language to coordinate anything with any delicacy. They could speak to The Golden's warriors, it is true, but we cannot tell them what we would like them to say, or even that we want them to do it."

Tila smiled. "There is one person who can help us, who speaks both our language and theirs to the degree that we need. He would not be enough for our purposes on his own, and he strikes this lady as a coward to boot, but we may be able to get him to translate between you and your neighbours."

"How're you going to do that?" the girl called Ezi asked, looking confused. "Why would he go against The Golden if he's a coward?"

Tila smiled Livnya's smile again. "If there is one thing this lady has learned about cowards, it is that they live very much in the moment. What *might* threaten them in the future is rarely as scary as what *is* threatening them in the here and now."

Osred was studying her again. "You are no lady, are you?"

"No," Tila admitted, which was true enough, although in the opposite direction to what he was supposing. "But she has the beginnings of a plan to do more than just sit around while this demon and its followers destroy our country. Does her rank matter so much to you?"

"Lord Daimon married Saana Sattistutar, who is the chief of the Brown Eagle clan, and was appointed to that post by her own people's council," Osred said levelly. "She is a remarkable woman in many ways, and this steward considers her good sense and wisdom to be a valuable asset to Black Keep, despite the fact that she is still somewhat odd. Lord Daimon was adopted from a lowborn family. This steward has learned not to dismiss someone out of hand, regardless of their status or gender, the circumstances of their birth, or even from where they hail."

Tila smiled at him genuinely, without any of Livnya's habitual edge. It was generally assumed within Idramar that the yokels of the deep countryside were far more backwards than the capital, and yet Osred was ignoring the prejudices that had plagued her at court for her entire adult life.

"But this steward is no fool," Osred continued, his voice hardening. "You are clearly someone accustomed to violence, and he does not think you feel any kinship with the Brown

Eagle clan, who have risked their lives for us. If your schemes involve them taking risks so you do not have to, you will learn how much we prize loyalty in the South."

Tila paused. Osred himself would likely pose her little direct threat – he was old and spare, and did not look to be in the best of health – but she did not have her knives, and it would only take a couple of the man's companions to cause her trouble that she could not endure. In this scenario, it was the old steward who had the power. And yes, she might be able to find people from Idramar who still respected or even feared Livnya the Knife, but she was not interested in trying to intimidate these folk of Black Keep.

"Your concern is understood," she said, keeping her expression calm. She would neither laugh at his threat, nor show fear, and so he would not know how far he could push her. "There is one enemy here, and it is not sitting around this fire."

Osred nodded cautiously. "Then perhaps we can help each other."

"This lady certainly hopes so." Tila got to her feet. "She will find you again when her plan has developed further." She gave them all a slight bow, which most of them returned – even the Tjakorshi, for a wonder – and walked off.

She had lost her home, she had lost most of her influence, and she had no idea where her family was, but Tila Narida had only ever needed two things in her life: her wits, and someone who underestimated her. She still had the first. Now she had to get a handle on the second, and then the game would begin anew.

It might be a different setting, and for different stakes, but it was always the same game.

Marin

Travelling with Mordokel was both better and worse than Marin had imagined it would be.

It was better in that the sar-turned-priest did not, as Marin had feared he would, spend the entire journey along the river road proclaiming the glory of Tyrun the Divine One. Marin had visions of Mordokel attempting to convert any and all they might come across, and so blowing their cover before they were five miles from Greenbrook; either that, or talking about the Divine One so continuously that Marin's head would slowly overflow and perhaps topple off his shoulders with the sheer amount of words that had been poured into it. Nor were they walking, since Mordokel had procured a cart from somewhere, along with an old and somewhat surly frillneck to pull it. He even knew how to handle the beast – which was unsurprising, since most sars would have at least some knowledge of dragon care – and so their journey did not have the same foot-punishing nature as the one to Tyrun's camp after they first met.

On the other hand, Marin was a man who enjoyed conversation, and although Mordokel was not constantly babbling about his devotion, he barely said a word on any other subject either. He would give a terse instruction here or there, if he needed Marin to aid him in some small way with getting the dragon into its harness or similar, but otherwise he remained largely close-mouthed. Marin tried making observations about the lands through which they were passing, or the weather, and got little more than a grunt. He even, out of desperation, asked about Mordokel's previous life, before he had found Tyrun and become the Divine One's high priest. He got nothing more than a silent, steady glare for his pains on that front, and quickly abandoned his attempts.

So it was that when they reached Northbank at around noon on the fourth day after they left Greenbrook, Marin had probably exchanged fewer words with another person than he had over any four-day period in all of his adult life, including when he had been in Idramar's jail. He was almost looking forward to being challenged by the gate guards, just for the chance to say something and receive a reply, but he changed his mind as they got closer.

"Goldtree's making his position clear," he said, staring up at the banners flying above the city's west gate. The general's own sigil – a five-pointed golden leaf on a black background – flew alongside the crowned sunburst of Idramar, but there was no sign of the city's own symbol, nor that of the Coldbecks who had ruled these lands until recently. Marin did not know who, if anyone, had been granted the thanedom in the former marshal's absence, and wondered if Goldtree might be trying to claim it in addition to his own by simple right of occupation until everyone just got used to the idea.

"This priest does not see the Eastern Army's camp," Mordokel replied.

"It was mainly around the northern gate," Marin replied. "But you're right: s'man's fairly sure we'd have been able to see some of it from the road in, but there was nothing there. He supposes they've either dispersed across the countryside, or Goldtree's found room for them inside the walls."

"Either of which could be disadvantageous for us," Mordokel said. "This just shows how important such scouting is. We need to learn not just the mood of the city, but the disposition of the troops Goldtree has under his command."

"Unfriendly, by the looks of it," Marin punned, although his observation was a genuine one. They were drawing closer to the city gate, and the backed-up line of wagons waiting to enter spoke to the checks being made. "Those are soldiers of the Eastern Army on the gates, not Northbank's own guards."

"So the army rules here in truth," Mordokel said, nodding. "Interesting."

"You'd best hope they don't find your sword," Marin muttered. "That will cause all manner of trouble."

"Fear not, Marin," Mordokel said. "We cannot be stopped. We are on a mission from the Divine One."

Marin debated replying, but held his tongue. He had the distinct feeling that anything other than unconditional agreement on his part would not be welcomed, and Marin had rarely unconditionally agreed with anything in his life. He slouched down next to Mordokel on the driver's bench instead, and tried to look bored instead of nervous.

The line crawled on, with wagons and carts being investigated, and those on foot cursorily inspected to ensure they were not smuggling weapons in under their clothing. Marin hardly thought someone would be concealing a polearm beneath their cloak, but one man turned out to have a sword belted around his waist that was of sufficiently fine quality for the guards to become suspicious of his motives. His protests only served to get him clubbed to the ground by spear hafts, and he was dragged away for, Marin supposed, further questioning.

"They seem to think people might be sneaking into the city with bad intentions," he commented to Mordokel.

"Don't worry yourself, Marin," the priest replied.

"S'man's just saying, that's exactly what we're doing—"

"What would you suggest, turn the cart around and go back?" Mordokel snapped, his calm manner evaporating. "That will surely draw attention! Settle yourself down and *stay calm*."

Mordokel had a point: Marin was not sure whether the gate guards would actually chase after them if they left the line now, but it could only look suspicious. On the other hand, going through the gates with Mordokel's longblade strapped to the underside of the board on which they sat seemed like a more and more tenuous proposition the closer they got.

"What've we got here, then?" one of the guards said, as the wagon in front of them was waved through and the trio of men who inspected it turned their attention to Mordokel's cart. "Hay, hey?"

His two companions gave him the sort of long-suffering looks which suggested to Marin that they had heard that joke from him several times already, and it got progressively less funny each time.

"Is he always this sharp?" Marin asked one of the others, and received a sly smirk in response. Humour was often good for deflecting attention, and annoying one of them might be outbalanced by fostering some good feeling from the other two.

"A jester, eh?" the punster snorted. He raised his spear and, without warning, shoved it violently into the hay several times.

"Is it dead?" one of the other guards asked jovially.

"Well, there's no one hiding in there," the first guard said. He eyed Marin, then sniffed. "Might be other things hiding though. Weapons, perhaps?"

"Why would we have weapons in our hay?" Marin asked him. He adopted an expression of alarm as the man clambered onto the back of the cart and began kicking the hay around. "Hoy, what're you doing?"

"Lord Goldtree's orders," one of the others said. "It seems this city doesn't like the rule of Idramar too well, and some of those who've taken issue with the army have done so with good steel; better than you'd normally find in the hands of a city lowborn." He leaned casually on their frillneck and fixed Marin with an appraising stare. "So we need to check that no one who comes in has got anything on them that might end up in the hands of those it shouldn't. If so . . . " He drew one finger across his throat with a comedically exaggerated expression of wide eyes and protruding tongue. It was classic guard behaviour of trying to intimidate someone into giving themselves away, and Marin was having none of it.

"Are you finished back there?" he demanded of the first guard, who was deliberately spilling some of their hay over the side of the cart and onto the mud of the road. "Look at the mess you're making!"

"Got to be sure," the man said with a wide smile, but even his most energetic efforts failed to find anything suspicious, and he hopped down again with the expression of a man who was disappointed at having no grounds to take further action, but satisfied that he had thrown his weight around nevertheless.

"What about this fellow?" the third guard asked, peering at Mordokel. "Doesn't he speak?"

"He prefers to avoid antagonising men holding spears," Mordokel replied levelly, casting Marin a glance that could have killed. The guard laughed.

"A wise man, this." He looked at the line behind them, and let out the sigh of someone who could see the rest of his day, and knew it was going to consist of minor variations on a theme of which he was already thoroughly bored. "On your way, then."

Mordokel slapped the reins, and their frillneck began to plod forwards again. Marin waited until he heard the guards behind them begin speaking to the next driver, then smiled.

"That went better than it could have."

"Why did you provoke him?" Mordokel snapped. "We should have kept our mouths shut and been on our way!"

"If you wanted a travelling companion who was going to do an impression of a wooden carving in front of guards, you should have said so before we left Greenbrook," Marin replied with a sniff. "S'man could have told you to find someone else. That fool kicking the hay never got around to prodding about anywhere else; and anyway, s'man thought you said we couldn't be stopped because we're on a mission from the Divine One?"

"Even the Divine One's favour may not prevail against your foolishness," Mordokel muttered.

They found an inn – Marin made sure it was in a different area of the city to the *Jolly Riverman*, where the ill-fated brawl had started – where he bargained with the ostler for the hay they carried. He probably got a poor price, but not so poor that it was obvious he cared little for the outcome of the deal, and he and Mordokel retired to the taproom to see what news they could gather.

It was not what he had expected.

"Excuse s'man, friend," he said, catching the sleeve of a neighbouring drinker. "He's new in the city today. What this 'wave' people are talking of?"

"Word from the east," the man said, with the self-importance of someone getting to break momentous news to ears that had yet to hear it. "A great wave raged up out of the ocean and struck the coast. They say half of Idramar's been swept away!"

Marin gaped at him, all thoughts of God-Kings forgotten as an image of the capital being swallowed by a raging torrent of saltwater flashed up in his mind. His home . . . his friends . . . the university . . . what family he still had there . . . Even his cousin Sarvon did not deserve such a fate. He sat back aghast, leaving the man who had spoken to blink uncertainly, having clearly not expected such a stunned reaction.

"What of the God-King?" Mordokel leaned forward to ask from beside Marin, his voice tense and his expression focused. "What of the Divine Family?"

"Sat up on their rock, weren't they?" the man replied. "All fine, not like the poor folk down on the water's edge. Nari be praised," he added after a moment, just in case such an intense interlocuter might somehow take his words as a criticism of the God-King's circumstances.

"Hnh." Mordokel sat back on his stool again, his face giving nothing away.

"Was it . . . Was it just Idramar?" Marin stammered.

"All the coast, so far as s'man's heard tell so far," came the reply. "There's not been word from the north or the south, but water's water, ain't it? S'man can't see the ocean rising up to swallow Idramar, but leaving Bowmar be."

Something about the man's words snagged Marin's attention, and one glance at Mordokel's face told him that the priest had heard it too.

"The Prophecies," Mordokel murmured.

"Aye, well, that's another matter," the man said, his mood subsiding a little. Clearly, news of disaster in the east was of rather less concern to him than events closer at hand. "S'man can't say as he has much knowledge of that, but word is this fellow who calls himself Nari Reborn has reached Greenbrook, would you believe?"

"He has," Mordokel replied, "and he has the bulk of the

Western Army with him. Marshal Torgallen has pledged his sword to the cause."

Marin nudged him. There was a difference between spreading gossip to see what sort of reaction it got and openly declaring one's allegiance to a pretender to the throne in the middle of a taproom where the opinions of the others around them were far from clear. Right at that moment he was not sure that Mordokel was going to stop on the safe side of that line.

Heads turned and drinks were replaced on tables as Mordokel's words grabbed the attention of those gathered there.

"The Western Army?" someone repeated.

"Old Torgallen's with him?" someone else asked.

"Marshal Torgallen would bow to a tree if you nailed a crowned sunburst to it—" a third voice began.

"You're talking about a Hand of Heaven, you little—"

"None of that!" a stern voice barked, and Marin looked up to see a middle-aged woman get to her feet, stave in hand. The assembled drinkers quietened down with surprising alacrity, and Marin was just about to take a swig of his ale in relief at not going two for two in terms of fights started to inns visited in Northbank, when she crooked her finger at Mordokel and him. "You. Outside."

Marin looked at her in surprise, his ale still halfway to his mouth. Mordokel made no move to obey her, although his body language suggested that this was more due to disdain than anything else.

"Well?" the woman demanded, tapping a small metal shield set into her stave. "S'woman's waiting."

"She's a constable," Marin muttered to Mordokel. "We'd best do as she says, unless we want a lot of attention." He drained his ale, since he was far from sure if he would get a chance to come back for it, and he was blowed if he was going to waste any of the meagre money he had made from the sale of the hay. Then he got to his feet, with a subtle hand under Mordokel's arm to bring the priest up with him. Mordokel did follow, although he looked decidedly reluctant about it.

"That's more like it," the constable said with a nod, and jerked her head towards the inn's door. To Marin's surprise she led the way, so it seemed that they were not simply being instructed to leave. Once outside, and standing underneath a window a few steps away from the entrance, she turned to face them.

"You sound like you know what you're talking about with regard to this Nari Reborn," she said without preamble. "You've come from Greenbrook way, then?"

Marin saw no point in denying it. "Aye, arrived today."

"Is the Divine One coming here?" the constable asked, and her face lit up. "Is he coming to Northbank?"

"S'man can't say as he knows for sure," Marin hedged, glancing at Mordokel and wondering exactly how he was supposed to be playing this, but quite certain that he did not trust the priest not to give them away entirely. "It doesn't look like Lord Goldtree is minded to acknowledge any God-King that's not from Idramar."

"Goldtree's shitting his robes, and his army's not much better," the constable said with a low laugh. "Bastards, the lot of them, and they're already seeing enemies everywhere. You're asking for a beating if you so much as look twice at anyone in an Eastern Army uniform, and that's if you're lucky. Forty-three years s'woman's lived here, and she's been a constable for twenty of 'em: kept the peace, and aye, broke a few heads along the way, but nothing like what they're doing now." She sighed, and spat. "A few fools decided to make an issue of it, and got themselves and a bunch of innocents strung up as a 'lesson to us all'. All this Nari Reborn has to do is not hang anyone, and that itself would be better than the rule we're receiving from Idramar."

"It sounds like Lord Goldtree's concerned with imposing his will," Marin ventured, not wanting to get drawn into saying something that would condemn him, should this be a particularly elaborate trap.

"The God-King needs to keep his animal on a shorter leash," the constable declared with finality. "Either he's told Goldtree to treat us harshly, or he doesn't care, or he can't control his own general. Whichever it is, it's done nothing to make us think kindly of Idramar." She looked at Marin, her eyes searching his face. "This new God-King; he must be going to Idramar, right? He must be heading east along the river? He'll have to come past Northbank if that's the case. S'woman would dearly love to lay eyes on Him," she added. "She's never seen a single member of the Divine Family, and nor did her parents before her. Have you seen Nari Reborn?"

"We have," Mordokel replied, before Marin had decided what the best answer was to give.

"What does He look like?" the constable asked, her face filling with wonder.

Mordokel smiled his smile that never truly reached his eyes. "He looks like glory."

"Please, tell us true," Marin said, breaking in before Mordokel could get too weird. "A fight's no place for us, and any time two armies meet, there's a chance of that happening. You know this city; if the Western Army appears championing Nari Reborn, and Lord Goldtree holds to King Natan, which way will Northbank lean?"

"When Marshal Coldbeck was still Eastern Marshal, s'woman would have said we'd have followed his lead," the constable said with a shrug. "But now he's a traitor, according to the declarations, and no one knows where he is. So she'd say that Northbank would probably take whatever side Goldtree doesn't, to tell the truth."

Marin snorted. In that case, the city had better hope that Lord Goldtree decided to oppose Tyrun, because otherwise it would be faced with at least a quarter of Narida's entire standing armies allied against it, and he could not see Tyrun and Mordokel being even as merciful towards resistance as Lord Goldtree had been.

And is that not a problem? his mind nagged at him. He tried to push the thought away, but the memory of Tyrun's rage in the great hall of Greenbrook Castle would not be banished. That had been aimed at absent soldiers who had retreated instead of pledging themselves to Him: what would His mood be like if a city at his mercy decided to resist His rule? *But He is the Divine One*, Marin told himself, *and His will is just. What would have happened if Nari had been merciful to the witches and petty kings who opposed Him when He was founding Narida?*

"Are there even enough soldiers here to defend the place, if Lord Goldtree decides to make a fight of it?" Marin asked, trying to look like a man who would much rather be heading in the opposite direction rather than getting involved on one side or the other: which was not, in fairness, very far from the truth. He had not been joking when he said that a fight was no place for him. "S'man had heard that they were spreading out and looking for Nari Reborn."

"S'woman doesn't know numbers, but there are enough of the bastards still around," the constable said sourly. "Goldtree garrisoned a whole load in Coldbeck Tower, once he'd finished throwing the family out, and more than a few inns have very conveniently been declared as 'disloyal', the owners cleared out, and soldiers moved in."

"Sounds like this might not be the place to be in the

near future," Marin said, with a pointed look at Mordokel. "S'man's not eager to get caught up in it." So far as Marin was concerned, getting outside of Northbank's walls and back to Greenbrook as soon as possible was the best option, and not just because that would mean he could see his husband again. He was used to trying to avoid the attention of guards, and guards were not that much different to soldiers in the contexts he usually encountered them, but it was one thing to be a thief and quite another to be considered a traitor.

"Thank you for your counsel, constable," Mordokel said, inclining his head to the woman. "We hope you get the chance to see the Divine One for yourself."

"Nari be willing," the constable replied, then smiled. "And perhaps He will. Good journey to you both." She nodded to them both and walked off, her stave thumping the ground in time with every other step.

Marin leaned closer to Mordokel. "We should leave, and report back."

"On the basis of one woman's opinion?" the priest replied with a snort. "That is hardly sufficient information with which to return to the Divine One."

"The city is jumpy," Marin argued. "That much is clear. S'man doesn't feel like waiting around for someone to notice your sword doesn't match your outfit. We should leave by the north gate, so the guards we came in past don't get suspicious, then cut across to the river road."

"You are a coward," Mordokel said, his eyes flashing. "The Divine One tasked us with this, and we shall not fail Him!"

"We'll fail Him if we get hanged!" Marin hissed, but Mordokel brushed his words aside.

"Such are the risks of serving our god. Now, come: we should try another inn and see what the mood there might be."

He walked off, leaving Marin staring after him. "So are

we definitely not going to fail Him, or are we at risk of being hanged?" he muttered, quietly enough that neither Mordokel nor any passers-by could hear. "It surely can't be both!" He debated abandoning the priest and just leaving the city, but something told him that there was no scenario in which returning to Greenbrook without Mordokel would work out well for him, especially if Mordokel turned up later, so he cursed and hurried after him.

It was not until much later, when the sun was dipping in the sky and the shadows were lengthening, that Mordokel finally consented to head towards the north gate. The news they had heard had been split between the great wave and the imminent arrival of Nari Reborn, and details about both were so divergent that any listener could be sure of only the very simplest facts in either case. Marin had heard that the Divine One was approaching alone, with the Western Army, or at the head of a force of Morlithians who had crossed through the Torgallen Pass after He had converted them from their sun-worshipping when He had travelled in their land. Bearing that in mind, he decided he could not trust news of Idramar any further than to acknowledge that clearly *something* had happened involving the sea.

Marin was probably going there anyway, one way or another, and there would be nothing he could do for anyone he cared about by the time he arrived, even if he got on a boat and sailed straight downriver. One thing that did seem certain was that, regardless of what form Tyrun's approach to Northbank apparently took, the people of this city were broadly in favour of His arrival: certainly when compared to the prospect of ongoing existence under the heel, as they perceived it, of Lord Goldtree. All in all, there seemed nothing for it other than for Marin to head back to Tyrun and the Western Army with the news, hope Northbank was either subdued or capitulated in short order, and that the journey eastwards to Idramar thereafter encountered no other major obstacles.

He was still musing on this, and trying not to think about what parts of Idramar might now be nothing more than wave-washed wreckage, when he walked into Mordokel's back.

"What is it?" he asked, rebounding.

"The gates are shut," Mordokel said grimly. Marin peered past him, trying to see through the crowd of people, carts, and wagons that clogged the street ahead of them. Sure enough, the big gates through which he, Laz, Ravi, and the rest had run as they fled from the brawl outside the *Jolly Riverman* were indeed closed. Marin looked up at the sky, but the sun was still up: and besides, the gates of a city the size of Northbank stayed open well past sundown, even in the summer.

They barged, dodged, and excused their way to near the front of the congestion, past sour-faced people coming the other way, to find a line of Eastern Army soldiers standing in front of the closed gates. One of them was repeating the same thing over and over in a voice that was already showing signs of strain.

"Orders of Lord Goldtree!" the man declared, to the sound of general mutterings that stopped just short of something for which the mutterer could be pulled out of the crowd and beaten for disrespect towards the general. "Henceforth, no one is permitted to enter or leave the city without a permit granted by either him or one of his staff!"

"Why?" someone shouted.

"You want to ask Lord Goldtree that?" the soldier said, scanning the row of faces to see who had spoken. "We can take you to him, no problem. Just step forward!"

No one moved.

"Do you think they're worried about spies?" Marin whispered to Mordokel.

"Shut up, Marin."

"Do you think we should have left earlier, when s'man suggested it?"

"Shut *up*, Marin."

"What are we going to do now?" Marin demanded. Mordokel turned his head and glared at him, and Marin waited for the priest's acidic, possibly fanatical response.

But it never came. Mordokel's lip twitched, then he turned and pushed past Marin back into the city, and away from the line of soldiers who barred their way.

Bulang

Bulang had not been able to sleep at first, partly because daylight bled through the shutters in the loft room that M'bana called home, and partly because the couple of hours of sleep thëy had managed to snatch under the market stall had left thëir mind just rested enough for worry and anxiety to resurface and begin gnawing at it again. However, sleep managed to worm its way into thëir head at some point before the noon bells rang, and thëy woke again, disoriented and thirsty, in the warm, sticky fug of the late afternoon.

Thëy rolled off the old blanket on which M'bana had directed thëm to lie and cautiously investigated a brown earthenware pitcher, which proved to contain water that did not smell stale. Thëy took a few grateful mouthfuls. Fresh water was, at least, a resource in plentiful supply in East Harbour, given how often it was drenched by rainstorms. Even during drier times, the many streams that ran down from Grand Mahewa's heights still provided the city with drinking water, although in the lower areas they also carried waste from higher up. That was another reason why the wealthier families liked to live on the hillsides.

M'bana returned not long after Bulang had woken, their expression grim.

"What is it?" Bulang asked, thëir stomach tightening in a way that had nothing to do with hunger. "Did you find them?"

"Perhaps," M'bana said, closing the door behind them and squatting down. They pulled a pangpang fruit from their pocket and tossed it to Bulang, who bit into it eagerly. "I asked around, and no one's seen Jeya as such, but Pamaru from the docks saw someone being hauled down a jetty late last night. They didn't get a good look, and there was a sack over the person's head, but it could have been Jeya."

Bulang swallowed. "Did they see where this person was being taken?"

"Yes," M'bana said. "A ship moored at the far end. The problem is, Pamaru might not have known the person with the bag over their head, but they recognised the people hauling them around: a couple of toughs who work for Kurumaya's people."

"Kurumaya?" Bulang repeated. "That doesn't make any sense."

"You said Kurumaya might be looking for you," M'bana said. "Maybe they'd already found you."

"No, that's ..." Bulang trailed off, uncertain how to explain that Kurumaya had been guarding them. Why would Kurumaya have people lurking around to snatch Jeya when shé left the house, when the Shark had two of their thugs just outside the door? Did they think Jeya might be trying to persuade Bulang not to go along with Kurumaya's schemes? Did they want hér out of the way, but not want Bulang to think that they were responsible for it? Might they have even tried to blame the Hierarchs for it, had Bulang stayed around for them to talk to?

None of that mattered. What was important was that the best lead Bulang had right now suggested Jeya was being held on a ship in the harbour.

"Do you know which ship?" thëy asked M'bana. "Do you know if it's going to sail, or when?"

"I know which pier," M'bana said, "because Pamaru told

me. I don't know anything about the ship. The dock bosses might have a good idea about if one is going to sail, but they all answer to Kurumaya now, if they didn't already. If the Shark's people took Jeya, then anyone asking questions about that particular ship might draw a lot of attention of the sort that could get very nasty, very quickly."

"We've got to do *something*!" Bulang hissed in frustration, then raised a hand in acknowledgement and apology. "That is, *I* have to do something. You've helped me already."

"Jeya is my friend," M'bana said steadily, "and like I said before, they helped all of us. Kurumaya's done some good things since the flood, but they're still a Shark: they've hurt a lot of people, and I don't want them to hurt Jeya. If Kurumaya's people stashed Jeya on a ship then they've got to have some use for Jeya alive, which is good, but as to how we're going to get them out of there ... "

Bulang sat back, thëir mind whirling. The whole point of Kurumaya's toughs was that they were, well, tough. They were fighters and bruisers, people used to violence and intimidating others in the name of their boss. M'bana and the others had managed to take down the three other members of Nabanda's crew, in that desperate fight which led to Nabanda tumbling into the waters of the Narrows, but only through greater numbers. Trying to rush the narrow gangplank of a ship moored in the harbour would surely be doomed to failure, especially if they could be seen coming down the length of the pier.

There has to be something we can do, were the words that came to thëir lips, but did there? Bulang could do nothing to save thëir family when Nabanda came for them. Jeya had been unable to help Ngaiyu or Damau when they had been killed. Wanting something to be true did not change the facts, no matter how desperate the want.

But sometimes, the facts did not change the need to act, no matter how dire the situation.

"I have to try to get Jeya out of there," Bulang said. Thëy heard thëir own voice shaking with fear, and did thëir best to ignore it. "Even if it's hopeless. I'd be dead without them. Can you think of anyone, or anything, that might be able to help? Maybe a rival Shark that would want to ruin Kurumaya's plans, or . . . ?" Thëy trailed off, still painfully aware of how little thëy really knew about the society in which thëy now moved.

"All the Sharks seem to have fallen into line," M'bana replied, shaking their head. "They must have seen Kurumaya taking on the Hierarchs as the road to more power, and decided to jump on the boat. Besides, you can't trust a one of them; if you swim with Sharks, you end up as bait."

They paused.

"What?" Bulang said, leaning forward again. "You look like you've thought of something."

M'bana sighed. "This is a bad idea, but Hundred help me, I don't have any others. We might have to run with it and see what happens."

"A bad idea is one more idea than I have, short of walking up to the ship in the open," Bulang said. "I'm listening."

"Right," M'bana said, cracking open a shutter and glancing out at the sky. "We'll wait for sunset, then head out to see the Morlithians."

"The Temple of the Rays?" Bulang asked, confused. "That closes at sunset, doesn't it?" Thëy had eaten there several times, thanks to Jeya knowing about the temple's charity, and one of its volunteers had been among those who had fought against Nabanda. However, it did not seem like an obvious recruitment point for a force to take a ship held by thugs in the pay of a Shark.

"Not the priests," M'bana said. They ran their tongue around the inside of their mouth, as though encountering an unpleasant taste. "A magician."

"There are actually Morlithian magicians?" Bulang asked, as thëy followed M'bana through East Harbour's darkening streets. The afternoon's humidity had given way to a gentle drizzle, which at least meant no one looked twice at the wide-brimmed rain hat on thëir head, the better to hide thëir face from any of Kurumaya's people. "I always thought that was just a rumour."

"Well, they don't talk about it much," M'bana said. "You won't find them on a stall in the market like you might a fortune teller. Hundred, I don't know if it's all just some big trick, but I *have* heard that there's one in the Morlithian Quarter."

"Why hide themselves away, if that's who they are?" Bulang asked. M'bana sighed.

"My guess? Between the Hierarchs and the Sharks, they've got more sense than to let themselves come to the attention of anyone who might try to lean on them. It doesn't matter who knows about me, I just sell fruit with a smile. You think that if someone like Kurumaya found out about a magician, they wouldn't try to get their claws into them? No, I can't blame them for keeping within their own community."

"So how come you know about them?" Bulang asked. M'bana sounded more like a name from Adrania than Morlith, even though M'bana didn't paint their cheeks with bright powders or wear bells in their hair. Thëy glanced down an alley as thëy spoke, when thëy heard a noise from it, and hurriedly looked away again when thëy realised it had come from two people getting rather friendlier with each other than was generally done in anything approaching a public place.

"Not everyone keeps things to themselves," M'bana said, a

little uneasily. "I knew someone who might've had some business with this magician once. They didn't talk much about it, but I think I know where we might need to go, and who we might need to talk to."

"And what will this magician be able to do?" Bulang asked. Thëy would do anything thëy needed to that might help Jeya, but this was sounding more and more like one of the bedtime tales told to thëm by thëir fàther when thëy were a child. Bulang knew about witches, of course, the evildoers that had been driven out of Narida by thëir ancestor Nari – assuming thëy were actually related to Him, of course, which was no longer certain – but living in Kiburu ce Alaba meant thëy had grown up around many things that Narida would have considered strange or wrong. All the same, a magician did not sound like the sort of person to approach lightly.

"I don't know!" M'bana snapped. "Like I said, this was a bad idea! It's just the only one I have!"

They pressed on, until the buildings began to change a little. They were still Alaban – the flat roofs of dry Morlith would never have shed Grand Mahewa's rains – but there were little flourishes here and there hinting that some of these structures had been created by people trying to bring a bit of their old home with them. Bulang saw a lot of sun motifs carved into stone or wood, and places with written signs sported the script of Morlith. Bulang had learned it as a child, but it was always very different to see it being used in an everyday setting, as opposed to the clean, pale pages of the texts in thëir fàther's study. A little farther down the street, banners bearing letters in a more stylised form hung across from one side to the other. Bulang squinted at it, instinctively trying to make out what it said, as though thëir tutor might test thëm on it at any moment.

Then movement beneath the banner caught thëir eye, and thëy grabbed at M'bana's sleeve.

"What?"

"In here," Bulang said quietly, tugging M'bana into another alley opening as casually as thëy could. One of the things Jeya had passed on was the importance of looking natural if you wanted to avoid notice. People's eyes were attracted to guilty, jerky movements: anything sudden or occurring at speed would attract glances. Slow, smooth, and confident was the key.

"What are you—"

"There are two people coming the other way who I know work for Kurumaya," Bulang said quickly, "and they seem to be looking for someone."

"As in, you?" M'bana asked.

Bulang shrugged uncomfortably. "It could be. I'd rather not take the risk."

M'bana looked past thëm down the alley, to where a pile of rubbish sat against a wall. "This is a dead end!"

Bulang looked up and around, but there were no obvious ways up the walls. Besides, thëy weren't Jeya: shé might have been able to clamber up something and get over and away, but shé had spent much of her life navigating walls and rooftops. Bulang had some experience at climbing trees, but these were very different surroundings.

"Come on, we might still be able to sneak the other way," M'bana said, starting towards the alley mouth. Bulang grabbed their arm again as an idea struck thëm.

"Wait. Pretend you're kissing me."

M'bana turned back, and the shock on their face was visible even in the darkness of the alley. "*What* did you say?"

"They'll be too close by now, but no one trying to hide from them would be kissing in an alley," Bulang said desperately, feeling thëir cheeks heat. "Hopefully, they'll ignore us."

"*Hopefully?*" M'bana repeated. They glanced over their

shoulder again, but the alley mouth was a dangerous bet. "I want your promise that you won't let Jeya knife me."

"Cross my heart," Bulang replied, doing thëir best to ignore the fact that thëir heart was jumping all over the place. It was not a suggestion thëy were comfortable with making, but thëy thought it might work. If anything, it was made more difficult by the fact that M'bana was quite good-looking and had seemed to be trying their charms on Bulang when they first met, at least until Bulang had made it very clear that thëy were in love with Jeya.

"Fine," M'bana said. "Just let me know when they're past. Or if I'm about to get stabbed in the back." They stepped in, and brought their face close, pushing Bulang's rain hat slightly up and back on thëir head as they did so. Bulang felt M'bana's breath on thëir lips as M'bana's arms wrapped around thëir shoulders. Thëy placed one hand in the small of M'bana's back, and felt the warmth of their skin through the thin, damp fabric of their maijhi.

M'bana swallowed, the muscles in their throat moving visibly. "So," they whispered hoarsely, their breath warm on Bulang's lips, "are we—"

Two shapes hove into Bulang's view at the alley mouth: the same thugs who had been stationed on the door of the house when Bulang had run off in search of Jeya. Even the dim light did not disguise the cuts and swellings on their faces. It seemed Kurumaya had indeed been displeased that they had let Bulang out of their sight, and Bulang had a sudden vision of what fate might befall thëm if thëy were found. As one of the thugs looked towards thëm, thëy panicked and pressed thëir lips to M'bana's.

M'bana did not jerk in surprise, or pull back. They leaned into the kiss, and Bulang felt fingers creeping up the back of thëir neck to twine through thëir hair where it met thëir scalp. Bulang's fingers gripped tighter as well, not to dig into M'bana and tell them to stop, but enough to feel the muscles of their back. Their lips remained together for several long, warm, spine-tingling moments, then parted, then sought each other out again, and again. When M'bana finally pulled back slightly and let go of the back of Bulang's head, Bulang's heart was hammering so hard in thëir ears that thëy did not at first hear what M'bana said.

"Hmm?"

"Are we good?" M'bana repeated, not taking their eyes off Bulang's. Bulang looked down the alley, which was empty apart from the two of them.

"Yes. Yes, we're good."

"You weren't even watching?" M'bana demanded, and for a moment Bulang saw genuine anger on their face, until one side of their mouth quirked up into a smile. "Î guess Î'll take that as a compliment," they said, using the low masculine tone.

It seemed only reasonable to gender yourself to someone you had just kissed, even if the circumstances were unusual. "Ï was trying to make it look genuine," Bulang muttered. "Sorry." It was a poor excuse, and at least half a lie, and thëir cheeks felt hot enough that the moisture from the drizzle should have just been flashing off into steam. That sensation was not helped when M'bana reached up and stroked thëir face gently with a forefinger.

"Given that neither of us got stabbed, Î'll forgive yöu."

"Thank yôu." Bulang stepped back, releasing thëir hold on M'bana, who did the same. "We should . . . probably be getting on."

M'bana looked like hê was about to say something else for moment, but then nodded. "Yes. It's not far now. Follow mê."

Stonejaw

Zheldu Stonejaw had wondered how long it would be before the Flatlanders actually tried to mount some sort of proper resistance to The Golden's arrival, and she got her answer the day after they sacked the first town since leaving the coast. The wind had dropped, but the smooth surface of the river was so much more welcoming to paddling than the waves of the ocean that the fact the current was against them barely mattered. Their ships forged upstream, powered in part by Naridan muscles. Those Flatlanders who had decided to throw in their lot with The Golden were hardly familiar with the techniques of yolgu paddling, but they wanted to keep getting fed, and so they obediently began to imitate the crews.

Naridan ships on the river were clearly not expecting the invasion, and Zheldu saw three overhauled and boarded before the sun was a handsbreadth above the horizon. However, it was close to noon when she spied movement on the river's northern bank.

"Dragons," Korsada the Dry said, shielding her eyes against the sun. "Dragons with riders."

Zheldu squinted towards the shore. They had left the estuary behind, but the river was still wide enough that the main body of their fleet could be out of arrow range from either bank, so it was hard to make out any details. All the same, dragons were large creatures, and there were several of them. They had seen a small wild herd shortly after dawn, which had prompted a false alarm, but this time the sun was glinting off metal.

"Scouts?" she asked the air in general. She looked farther to the west, but a bend in the river, and the road that ran alongside it, meant she could not tell if there were more Flatlanders coming.

"They seem agitated enough," Korsada commented, then chuckled. "Look, there they go!" The dragons had turned, and were hastening away in a rolling gait that looked almost comical from distance. Zheldu, who had seen the damned things close up, knew exactly how fast they could cover ground, and how hard they hit when they reached you.

"Scouts," she said, her suspicions confirmed. The *Storm's Breath* was one of the frontrunners in The Golden's fleet, and she could not be sure that anyone else was paying attention, so she snapped her fingers at Kuadan Gaptooth. "Pass the word back: there could be enemies on the northern bank before long."

Gaptooth nodded, and picked up the signal sticks that allowed Tjakorshi ships to communicate back and forth without relying on shouting: invaluable when the noise of wind and waves could render your voice inaudible even to someone on the other side of your own vessel. Others picked up the message, and word began to spread throughout the fleet. Zheldu saw the Flatlander Livnya look up from her paddling and watch Kuadan curiously, and stepped into the woman's line of view.

"Looking at something?" Stonejaw demanded, and even though Livnya could not understand her — unless she had rapidly added Tjakorshi to the languages she spoke — the woman turned her attention back to the water, and put her head down once more.

"You're not worried about her, are you?" Korsada said with a laugh. "What's she going to do, learn the signals and use them against us?"

"I'm not *worried* about her," Zheldu snapped back, then lowered her voice. "Look, you've heard the rumours. The Golden is taking us upriver based off something *she* said to it?"

"I heard you were there when it happened," Korsada replied.

"Apparently, but I couldn't understand what in the depths they were saying," Stonejaw said. "They were speaking the island tongue, from what I can gather." She waved the detail away. "My point is, that one has the potential to be trouble, and I don't like the idea of her learning anything more about us than she needs to."

"She's a chief, or something like it," Korsada said. "She's going to be smart, but that means she's smart enough to know the situation she's in here. What's she going to do?"

Stonejaw stared at her for a couple of moments. "By the Dark Father, you actually like her, don't you?"

Korsada shrugged, as though the matter was of no great import. "She's not exactly friendly, but I like her better than some of our own. She's got a vicious sense of humour."

Stonejaw grunted. To be honest, *she* preferred Livnya to some of those who had come across the ocean, since that category included Kullojan Sakteszhin and his cronies. She could see the *Firelight* now, running closer to the northern shore, and a little way astern of the *Storm's Breath*. He had insinuated loudly and often that Zheldu and her crew were little better than traitors, but never quite plainly enough that it was worth risking The Golden's displeasure by starting a fight with him over it.

Besides which, it was arguably true. Stonejaw was not running at the head of the fleet out of eagerness, but to keep the draug convinced that she would not rather be turning around and putting all the water she could between it and her.

The riverbanks rolled on, propelled past them by the rhythmic grunts of paddlers, both Tjakorshi and Naridan. When they rounded the great bend, Zheldu finally saw what she had been half-expecting to see ever since they had left the coast.

Flatlander warriors. Not one or two, or scattered piecemeal through a city's streets, but a great chunk of them on the shore.

"Well, here we go," Ari Tumeszhastutar said, brushing her grey-streaked hair back from her face. "Looks like they decided to put up a fight."

Stonejaw was already breathing a little more easily. For one thing, the Flatlanders were on the shore, which meant the fleet did not have to engage unless they chose to. For another, although there might have been a full clan's worth of Flatlanders there, their numbers still paled into insignificance compared to The Golden's fleet, which contained virtually all the clans of Tjakorsha.

"That won't be a fight," Korsada said flatly. "That'll be a massacre."

Stonejaw squinted, and tried to guess at what the Flatlanders had rounded up. There were a few hundred warriors there, perhaps twenty of the sars on their dragons, and a line of wheeled wagons which Zheldu suspected would contain their food and other supplies. It was hard to tell from a distance, but there seemed to be a lot of commotion going on that looked very much like panic.

"Do you think they expected us to be on the river?" Ari asked.

"No, I don't think they did," Stonejaw said, amused despite herself. The fleet might not have much wind to work with, but even when relying on paddles, they could still outpace warriors on foot. If The Golden chose to, the Tjakorshi could go right by the Flatlander force and leave them stranded.

However, this was not like sailing across an ocean, where

you had no option at night other than to keep going and try to keep the yolgu level, but were unlikely to run into anything solid if you had any sort of wavesense. Rivers meandered and bent, and threw up unexpected barriers like reed beds and sandbanks. The best place to be after dark was either on the shore or moored to it, so leaving an armed force loose to fall upon you was not a sensible course of action. Far better to engage them at a time of your choosing.

As new instructions were passed forward via signal sticks, it became clear that the time of The Golden's choosing was now.

Slingers stung the Flatlanders as the fleet closed on the shore, raking their ranks with a hail of rocks. Arrows came back in return, but in numbers too few to make any real impact compared to the dark rain that pounded the riverbank. The Flatlanders were forced back as they tried to escape the punishment, abandoning the road in favour of the fields beyond it, and so allowing the Tjakorshi to come ashore unopposed. A smaller knot of resistance lurked stubbornly in the lee of the wagons, marshalled by a handful of sars who knew the importance of not letting their supplies be taken, but when the first yolgu touched the shore and the first Tjakorshi feet stormed up the bank, those defenders fell back as well.

The Flatlanders had a choice: to stand and die, or turn and run. To Zheldu's astonishment, they set up for a fight. The Tjakorshi spread out, beginning to encircle the beleaguered Flatlanders prior to closing in on them and swamping them.

It was then that the sars charged.

A brassy wail split the air, and the dragons that had been milling back and forth lumbered towards the Tjakorshi lines, the heavy-bladed spears of the riders levelled and the metal-tipped horns of the steeds flashing in the sunlight.

"Shield wall!" Stonejaw yelled, for all the good that would do. The monsters would go straight through any resistance offered. She would live or die in this moment not down to any skill of her own, but simply through whether a sar happened to aim his dragon at her.

She had been in shield walls many times, and you could get a feel for the mood of one. This one was scared, and getting twitchy. Normally that would spell disaster, but Zheldu did not think it would actually matter here. In most cases, if the warrior next to you turned and ran, they would die and you would die. Here, both of you could stand your ground and still get trampled flat by a creature that weighed as much as a yolgu's entire crew.

Bearing that in mind, it greatly increased the temptation to run for it herself, but Zheldu held her ground. Running from dragons and staying alive would not help her if The Golden decided to set her alight for cowardice, so she planted her feet, readied her axe, and waited for the sound of Father Krayk calling her name.

The sars . . .

. . . veered.

They changed direction almost as one, something Zheldu would never have thought possible given the size and momentum of their mounts. All at once, the horns coming for her swung to her left, and aimed away from the main mass of Tjakorshi, towards the thinner, encircling arm to the west. The warriors there, who had been jogging forwards with the intention of falling on the sars from the side and rear as soon as they got bogged down in the main body, panicked. A couple of captains called for a shield wall, and had they been facing enemies on foot, they might have managed it.

They were not, and they did not.

The sars smashed into them, broke them apart, and rode straight through them. They barely even slowed. Warriors frantically scrambled to get out of the way: Zheldu even saw one or two cutting down their own fellows from behind, so desperate they were to have a clear path to something that might approach safety. Then the sars were through and past.

They had punched a hole in the Tjakorshi line, and Zheldu waited for them to circle around and come back. She had no idea how many times the dragons could charge before they got tired, but it was obvious that the sars could not win this battle on their own, twenty against thousands. The question was how much damage they could do before they died, not just in terms of lives lost for The Golden, but to the draug's aura of invincibility. It had led Tjakorsha across the ocean to escape disaster, and it had led them almost effortlessly to victory in Idramar. Getting badly blooded here by such a small force might finally make those who followed it reconsider how sensible a course of action it was to follow the draug on its quest inland to break a god.

But the sars did not wheel around. They kept going, riding hard for the west. A few desultory slingstones chased them on their way, but none fell from their saddle as a result. If anything, Zheldu suspected that those who had loosed did not actually want to cause any damage, lest the fleeing dragon riders decided they wanted another go after all.

The ranks of the Tjakorshi closed up once more, and attention returned to the remaining Flatlander soldiers, all of them on foot. Zheldu thought they looked like a reasonably equal split between archers and spears. If they did not manage to get away, there was no hope for them. The sars had been their only hope, slim though that had been, and that had evaporated.

The throbbing call of a shell-horn rang out, but it was not the call to charge. Instead, it was the order to halt.

Stonejaw obeyed, somewhat confused, along with all the warriors around her. What was The Golden doing? Then someone stepped out of the massed ranks near where the draug was surrounded by its Scarred, and began to walk across the field towards the Flatlanders.

It was Livnya.

"Who the shit let her over there?" Zheldu demanded desperately, looking around at her crew. "Who was watching her?"

Her crew avoided her eyes sheepishly, and no one replied. Zheldu looked back at the Flatlander, and saw her spread her arms wide and begin to speak.

Marin

The walls of Northbank were now off-limits to the people of the city, and were patrolled by soldiers of the Eastern Army. However, news of what was going on outside still filtered back to those inside. Lord Goldtree had not prevented all traffic in and out, merely that for which he saw no need. It was the fishers, still working the waters of the Idra, that first brought back word of the approaching force.

The Western Army had arrived.

"They were supposed to wait for our report!" Marin hissed at Mordokel, within the confines of the small room they shared. Mordokel had found lodging at a temple sympathetic to the idea that Nari had been reborn, and which accepted his priesthood: Marin suspected he was allowed in as well simply because Mordokel did not trust him to be left alone. "Why have they come so soon?"

"The Divine One waits for no man," Mordokel replied serenely, "and it is not our place to question Him. We could not return to His side, due to the restrictions placed on the city, so the Divine One has taken the necessary steps."

"And do our necessary steps involve getting out of this place before it's attacked?" Marin demanded. "S'man doesn't know about you, but he does not like the idea of being in a city under siege!"

"The guards are vigilant and numerous," Mordokel said. "Those people who have tried to sneak out have been killed outright; or caught, and an example made of them. Lord Goldtree seeks to subdue the city through fear, while also relying on fear of the army outside the walls being even greater. It is a delicate balancing act, and not one this priest believes Goldtree has the finesse for."

Tensions were certainly running high within Northbank's walls, and food was, in contrast, already running low. There was still plenty for the soldiers and nobles, of course, and Marin noticed that the priesthood were not suffering any hardship, but the market stalls were more and more bare, and the quality was poorer. The best produce that came in through the gates had been diverted to the stores of the Eastern Army, and now the Western Army was here and surrounding the city, even that traffic was going to stop.

Marin had heard the tales of cities under siege, and how the desperate inhabitants resorted to eating first the dragons, and then the rats, and then – depending on the nature of the tale, and exactly how horrific it was intended to be – sometimes each other. It sounded like nothing a sensible man should be involved in.

"What happens if Lord Goldtree doesn't join his cause to the Divine One, and the Western Army attacks, and we're still here?" he asked.

"Then we shall play our parts within these walls," Mordokel told him. The priest lay down on the blankets that served him as a bed and closed his eyes, then opened one of them to look at Marin again. "The road to the Divine One's glory will not be an easy one, Marin of Idramar, and not all of us will see the end of it. This priest accepts that. Do you?"

"Accepting it and being fine with the idea are not necessarily the same thing," Marin muttered, but he too lay down to try to get some sleep. By Nari, but he missed Laz! It was so very strange, not to mention unpleasant, to lie down only an arm's length or so away from another man – the room the temple had granted them was far from large – when it was not his husband, but this hard-eyed fanatic. Marin had almost preferred his time in the Idramar jail, when at least there had been bars between him and the other inmates. This felt too intimate, and significantly less safe.

By the next morning, the whispers running through the city had become shouts, and the initial attempts made by the Eastern Army to quell the rumours were abandoned. Hearsay solidified into fact, and everyone within Northbank's walls with the capacity to know their own name also knew that there was a new military force in the area. What was not clear, however, was the true nature of the force, or its leadership.

"S'man's heard that it's the Morlithians," said an old man with a nose like a withered potato, taking a pull of his ale. "They've smashed through the Torgallen Pass, and they're heading east to finish what they started when they killed the old God-King!"

"It's not the Morlithians, they'd not dare set foot past the mountains," someone else opined. "It's a bandit army, taking advantage of all this confusion."

"If it was just bandits, Lord Goldtree would ride out and scatter them," said a man whose bulky shoulders and burn-scarred skin suggested he might be a blacksmith. "There's enough soldiers in these walls to make short work of any outlaws."

"Not if he's scared of what might happen inside the city with his soldiers gone," the second speaker countered.

"It's the Morlithians, s'man's telling you," the old man muttered. "Enough of 'em that His Lordship don't dare ride out and face them."

"This man had heard that it's the Western Army," Mordokel put in. "That's what those coming from Greenbrook said."

"Aye, but who can trust their eyes on anything?" the old man snorted. "Bloody westerners!"

Marin, for whom anything more than a few days' ride in this direction from Idramar was "the West", sipped at his ale and said nothing, then made a face at the taste. It was weaker than he was used to: clearly this tavern had decided to stretch out its business for as long as possible by diluting the wares.

"This man has seen them with his own eyes," Mordokel said smoothly, fixing the old man with what was, for him, a fairly neutral look, but from most other people would suggest imminent violence. Mordokel was not the sort of person who was easily able to blend into the background.

"You have?" the blacksmith asked, eyeing Mordokel with interest. "Made it up on to the walls, did you? S'man thought Goldtree's lot had it locked down tight."

"It's the Western Army, and they fly the banner of Taladhar Torgallen," Mordokel said, to various intakes of breath. "What is more, they fly the banner of the God-King."

"The God-King's in Idramar!" someone protested. "We'd have heard if he'd come west!"

"That rather depends," Mordokel replied, taking a sip of his own drink, "on who you think the God-King is. It seems Marshal Torgallen has come to his own conclusions."

Mutters of "the pretender!" and "Nari reborn!" ran though the taproom. Marin watched Mordokel's eyes flicker around, marking out who seemed delighted and who seemed angry, and sighed to himself. He gripped Mordokel's shoulder and leaned forward to whisper into the priest's ear.

"Do you even understand the *concept* of subtlety?" he demanded.

"There is an army outside the gates," Mordokel murmured back. "Subtlety, like time, is a luxury we no longer have."

"*Walking around* and *breathing* are going to be luxuries we'll no longer have, if Goldtree's men get wind of what you're stirring up!" Marin snapped. "How are we supposed to serve the Divine One if we're dead?"

"Perhaps our service will already have been sufficient," Mordokel said, with infuriating calmness. "Besides," he added, "they have more pressing concerns. Goldtree cannot just let an army appear outside the gates without doing something. Courtesy and honour would demand that he greets Marshal Torgallen in some form, even if he chooses to stand against him. This priest suspects that a lot of the soldiers are waiting to hear if they are going to be ordered to fight against their comrades."

Marin had been wondering about that. If faced with closed gates and defiant walls, would Taladhar Torgallen *really* command an assault? It was one thing to fight for your life against someone trying to kill you, no matter who they might be: it was surely quite another to attack a city filled with your own people when they were just sitting there, waiting for you to go on your way. What if the army refused? What if *some* of the army refused? Marin had an ugly image of the Western Army fracturing outside Northbank's walls, of detachments turning on each other, or even fighting among themselves. Laz would be with the Brotherhood, who of all the Western Army would be most likely to follow orders in this scenario – mercenaries might refuse to take a job in the first place, but having signed up they would usually see it through – but might that just leave them isolated against the city's forces, while their supposed allies disintegrated behind them? The Brotherhood detachment alone could not take Northbank, and an attempt to do so would surely see them killed.

Bells began to toll. The taproom looked at each other collectively for a few moments, then everyone drained their mugs and began to file out to see what was occurring. Marin suspected that he knew. Temple bells might warn of fire, or call people to a great celebration. Under the current circumstances, however, it seemed far more likely that an attack was coming. He wiped his hands on his robe, trying to dry his palms. What was he even supposed to do in this situation? He was no warrior! Trying to fight the soldiers of the Eastern Army would result in his death occurring very quickly, but he had no wish to experience what it was like to be in a besieged city newly breached by attackers, either. The Code of Honour was all very well, but a soldier with his blood up was likely to see enemies where none existed, let alone be able to tell who was secretly on his side.

The tide of people was moving to the nearest square, where a cart had been dragged into place. A dozen men in the livery of the Eastern Army stood in front of it, their spears grounded, but ready to be deployed if necessary. Another soldier, this one with the armband of a bannerman, was climbing onto the cart bed. A crowd was already gathering, and Marin was sure he was not imagining the tension within it. No one knew quite what was going on, but everyone was fairly sure that they were not going to like the answer, whatever it was. Marin and Mordokel squeezed in near the front, only a few people back from the line of spears.

The bannerman — broad-chested and possessed of a neck wider than his head — took a deep breath.

"People of Northbank! Traitors to the crown have marched upon this city! The force outside these walls consists of elements of the Western Army, in league with brigands and mercenaries! They have slain Marshal Taladhar Torgallen, and carry his banner before them in an attempt to trick us into opening our gates!"

Muttering of various flavours ran through the crowd. Some people seemed shocked and outraged, others highly dubious of what they were being told. Taken on its own merits, Marin thought the statement was fairly clever: it acknowledged the reality of what people would see if they managed to get a look at the besieging force, but weighted it to make them distrustful. After all, what were the odds of anyone inside seeing Marshal Torgallen's face? For that matter, how many would recognise him, even if they saw him? The notion of a rabble of renegades was probably a more comforting notion than the actual Western Army camping outside, and that made it a good choice for a lie.

However, it completely avoided the question of Tyrun, and *his* banner.

"What do they want?" Mordokel shouted from beside him, and Marin jumped. "What does the army want?"

His voice was loud and clear, and rang out above the murmurings that were running through the crowd. The bannerman squinted, looking for who had spoken.

"What was that?"

"You say the army wish us to open the gates," Mordokel shouted. "To what purpose?"

"To pillage the city!" the bannerman retorted.

"That's surely not what they said!" Mordokel replied, to a few scattered laughs. "You said they were trying to trick us! What is their attempted trickery?"

The bannerman's expression was quickly slipping into that of a man who had been ordered to carry out a task about which he had been given insufficient detail, and was now finding out the shortcomings of his superiors. He had no way of taking his frustrations out on them, however, and so he settled for the next best thing.

"Seize that troublemaker!" he ordered, pointing at

Mordokel. His men took up their spears, and the crowd began to shrink back a little: laughing at a soldier being made to look silly was one thing, but getting in the way of a business end of a spear was something for which a bit more preparation was needed. Marin glanced nervously at Mordokel, wondering what in Nari's name he was supposed to do now. Stand with the priest? Avoid capture? Of the two, avoiding capture seemed like the preferable alternative.

"*Stand down!*"

The bellow came from behind them both, and carried over the heads of the crowd with ease and clarity. Marin turned to see who had spoken, and could make out nothing for a few moments. Then people began to move aside, and an awed murmuring rippled through those assembled. However, it was not until Marin saw the face of the man who had spoken that he realised what was really going on.

It was Einan Coldbeck.

It had been many years since Marin had seen the former Eastern Marshal, and that had been at a distance, but he was dressed in the full finery of his former office, which helped with the recognition: he had presumably managed to smuggle at least one of his official robes out with him when he fled the capital. His longblade and shortblade rode on his hip, and he still carried the air of pure, unquestionable command that had been his defining feature for decades.

He made his way to the front of the crowd, staring down the astonished bannerman with an iron gaze, and, perhaps more pertinently, in the company of half a dozen fully armoured sars. Marin did not recognise all of the heraldry on show, but only two wore the sign of Coldbeck's own household. It seemed the former marshal had not lost all his allies since his fall from grace.

"High . . . " the bannerman began, then corrected himself

to "Lord . . .", then corrected himself again. "You have been declared a traitor, and you no longer have any rank! Your arrest has been warranted by the God-King himself!"

If the bannerman expected the crowd to act on his words, he was in for disappointment. His men did not move with any alacrity either, in all likelihood because of the hands placed on longblade hilts by the sars at Coldbeck's side. The sars might have been outnumbered two-to-one, but Marin's money would be on them if it came to a fight.

"The man you know as the God-King has proven himself to be nothing more than a spoiled brat, controlled by his sister, and unworthy of ruling!" Coldbeck thundered. Nari's teeth, but the man knew how to speak! Every word was as sharp and final as the click of a key in a lock. "This marshal no longer recognises the so-called Divine Family as heirs of Nari, when the true God-King, Nari Reborn, is with the army that stands outside the gates of this city! Marshal Torgallen is not dead!" he continued, raising his voice as the crowd began to shout. "He is with the Western Army, and they are not renegades, but true patriots! The real traitor is Lord Goldtree, who seeks to claim this marshal's ancestral lands as his own, and stands against the rightful God-King in the name of the whelp who cowers in the east!"

He drew his longblade, and pointed it at the bannerman atop his cart, and his wide-eyed men. "This marshal was your commanding officer since the moment you became soldiers! Every vow of service you made, every oath of loyalty you took, was ultimately to him! Will you honour those words now, or will you take sides with the faithless and risk dooming not only yourselves, but this entire nation as well?"

Einan Coldbeck knew his audience. This crowd were his people, who had grown up under his rule and been proud that their liege-lord was a Hand of Heaven, and the foremost among even that elite group. They rallied behind him, cheering and shouting, and more than a few weapons were drawn in the process. The soldiers, staring into the eyes of death and their former commanding officer, did not hesitate. The bannerman hopped down from his cart, and they all went down to one knee before any local hothead could decide that they were opposing Coldbeck's will. It was sensible, Marin knew: the crowd felt like a single hungry animal ready to spring, and it would only take one punch to be swung for it to converge on the perceived threat and destroy it.

"Good men!" Coldbeck said, loudly and clearly. He pushed his way past the few remaining bodies in front of him and pulled the bannerman to his feet. The man desperately cast his eyes downwards, but Coldbeck was smiling.

"Your adherence to orders does you credit, but so does your good sense, and your faith," he said. He was still speaking more loudly that was necessary, and Marin realised it was to ensure that none of the crowd felt the need to make a point of something at the soldiers' expense. "Now, we must move quickly."

"High Marshal!" Mordokel called, and raised his hands placatingly as two of Coldbeck's sars turned towards him. "This priest is Mordokel, and is honoured to be a close confidant of the Divine One!"

One of the sars laughed, but Coldbeck cocked his head and studied Mordokel for a moment, then grunted. "Yes, this marshal had heard that the Divine One's high priest was a bald man with a sar's blade under his cloak. Approach."

Mordokel grabbed Marin's sleeve, and tugged him forwards before he could react. The sars stood aside, and Einan Coldbeck's cool eyes flicked from one of them to the other.

"Why are you in Northbank, Priest Mordokel? And who is the man with you?"

This man is the husband of the sar whose victory in an honour duel saw your attempted coup fail, Marin thought hysterically. *Oh, this is going to get interesting, this is going to get* really *interesting, and by "interesting", this man means "dangerous"*.

"This is Marin of Idramar, a scholar," Mordokel said, and Marin dropped to one knee, on the basis that it was best to placate a man who considered himself to be a High Marshal, even if that status might be disputed. "We came to the city to determine its mood, and see whether the people were likely to accept the Divine Tyrun as their rightful ruler. However, Lord Goldtree's measures meant we were unable to leave again."

"Yes, we only just made it in before the gates were closed ourselves," Coldbeck said. "Luckily, it seems that the men on the Eastern Gate did not know this marshal's face, or did not think to look for him under the disguise he was wearing." He looked around, and his manner became one of ferocious focus. "But we can discuss matters further another time, High Priest. This marshal must rouse his city, and lead it against any of the Eastern Army who are foolish enough to stand in our way. The Divine One is the true ruler of Narida, and he must be welcomed: nor would this marshal see his own city come under attack from Torgallen and his men. For both those reasons, we must eliminate resistance and open the gates to welcome the Divine One within."

"Agreed, High Marshal," Mordokel said with a bow, his eyes flashing eagerly. "In this matter, this priest's sword is yours to command."

"And you, scholar?" Coldbeck asked, looking at Marin. "Do you fight?"

"This man's talents lie in other areas, High Marshal," Marin replied, rising to his feet again.

"Hnh." Coldbeck's grunt was dismissive, but his eyes

lingered on Marin for a moment. "Well, we must all serve the Divine One as we can."

Indeed we must, Marin thought, as Coldbeck began barking orders and mobilising the crowd to start to sweep through the city. *And this man does not forget that by his husband's account, your coup was not intended to place Tyrun on the throne, but yourself.*

This man will be watching you very carefully, High Marshal.

Daimon

Daimon had never considered Zhanna to look small, until now. She was of a height with her mother, which meant she was of a height with him, and probably weighed more than he did. She was outspoken and forthright, even by Tjakorshi standards, and her personality filled the room and drew even more attention than her size and flaming red hair already did.

The loss of her hand had changed that. Now Zhanna was laid in bed, her skin even paler than usual in the early morning light, and the vitality seemed to have leached from her. She smiled at Daimon wanly, but then returned to slow, weak exchanges with her mother in their own tongue.

"She lost a lot of blood," the Darkspur physician said. "Luckily, this man always has a stock of resin ready to seal wounds, and his fire was already high."

"What are her chances?" Daimon asked him quietly. The man shrugged.

"The cut was clean, and she was brought to this man quickly. He has some experience with longblade wounds. With a little luck, and Nari's blessing, the arm will not get infected, in which case there is no reason why she should not recover after sufficient rest." He looked over at the bed again and his expression faltered a little; perhaps at how likely it was that a Raider would attract Nari's blessing.

Daimon nodded. "Thank you for your assistance. Given the history between our lands, it would have been very easy for you to have let her bleed out, and blamed the wound."

"Lord Daimon," the physician said, looking aghast. "You are guests in this castle! This man did not study his art merely to let someone die when they could be saved! Besides which," he added, "the Lady Yar— That is, the new thane, was most insistent that this man should do everything within his power to aid the young ... lady," he finished, having apparently cast around for a term to describe Zhanna without finding any he considered an appropriate fit.

Daimon looked over the man's shoulder to where Yarmina Darkspur stood, on the far side of the room. She was still dressed in hunting leathers, and her eyelids were drooping, but she had refused to retire even though the sun now peeked over the eastern horizon. The front of her outfit was streaked with Zhanna's blood from where she had helped her in the immediate aftermath of the injury.

The injury inflicted by the sar that Yarmina had man-oeuvred out of his position of power, and publicly shamed in the Darkspur grand hall.

"Please excuse this lord for a moment," Daimon said to the physician, who bowed at the mere suggestion that his feelings were being taken into consideration, and headed back to the bedside. Daimon took the few steps over to Yarmina. "Might we have a few words, outside?"

Yarmina looked up at him wearily, past him at the bed on which Zhanna laid, then back at his face. "Of course."

Daimon led the way out of the room, and closed the door behind them. No one else was in the corridor, but he took a couple more steps away from Zhanna's room before he whirled around on Yarmina. She stopped, startled.

"This lord is going to ask you this once, and once only,"

Daimon said through gritted teeth. "Did you know of Asad's intention to come to your room?"

Yarmina's face registered only weary bewilderment. "What? No, why would you ask such a thing?"

"Because you are a very intelligent woman, Yarmina," Daimon said bluntly, "and you provoked a man you have known your entire life. Might you not have known how he would react? Might you then have thought to protect yourself, by finding a ruse to invite Zhanna into your *bedchamber*?" Yarmina's face twitched at that, and the smouldering anger that had been lurking in Daimon's belly, eager for fuel on which to feed, sprang into life. "She is big, and she is strong, but she is not a trained warrior, and you should not have drawn her into your schemes!"

He was not expecting the punch that flashed out of nowhere and caught him on the jaw. He stumbled sideways and caught himself on the wall, and his hands went instinctively to the longblade on his belt as he centred himself again.

"Draw on this thane, then!" Yarmina spat at him, her face contorted with anger and misery even as she shook out the hand with which she had struck him. "You can cut her down in a moment, but that will be the end of any peace between us! Your people might be out there, but you and Saana and Zhanna will not make it out alive, so if you wish to kill us all, then draw!"

Daimon glared at her, pain blossoming in his jaw, but she had the truth of it.

"How dare you suggest that this thane would stoop to such things?" Yarmina hissed, when Daimon did not draw his weapon. "If she had intended any such deceit on Sar Asad then she would have ordered her own guards to lie in wait, not risk the life of the daughter of an ally!"

"Then why the subterfuge of inviting her to your

chambers?" Daimon demanded. "Had you truly wished for instruction in the longblade, this lord would have obliged you! He tutored Zhanna in it; he would have done the same for you!"

"Are you really so obtuse that you think that is the only reason this thane might have to invite Zhanna to her chambers?" Yarmina asked incredulously.

It took Daimon a moment to apprehend her meaning.

"Oh, this thane had every intention of learning the longblade," Yarmina elaborated, his expression having apparently changed sufficiently for her to know that he had caught on, "but she will admit that was not her only motive, had Zhanna shown any similar interest!"

"The Tjakorshi do not approve of such things," Daimon said reflexively, but even as he said it, he knew that it was not entirely true. Most still held to their prejudices, even if they mainly refrained from voicing them, but their witch Kerrti had begun a romance with Henya, the daughter of Black Keep's apothecary.

"This thane considers Zhanna to be quite capable of voicing her own opinion on such matters," Yarmina said flatly. "She certainly is not shy on any other topics." She raised her chin defiantly. "Do you accept that this thane's actions were genuine? Or do you accuse her of deceit and double-dealing, and so doom our alliance, and condemn our peoples to bloodshed and likely starvation?"

Daimon slowly removed his hand from his longblade's hilt. Nari help him, but Yarmina's anger at his accusation seemed genuine, and it would explain why she flinched when he suggested a motive for bringing Zhanna to her chambers. It was simply a different motive to the one he had suspected, if her words were to be believed.

Also, although it burned him to think in such a manner, there was indeed the matter of their alliance to consider. Blackcreek and Darkspur were engaged in a joint venture to help feed everyone, with Black Keep folk now spread across Darkspur farmlands doing the work that they would have been doing in their own fields, had their crops not been destroyed by the ocean. A rift between thanes now would endanger everyone, and at least Asad was no longer around to stir discontent. Even if Daimon did not completely believe Yarmina's account, perhaps Zhanna's hand was not too high a cost when set against so many other lives? It galled him, but he could see no other truth.

"This lord accepts your word," he said gruffly, straightening up from the slight stoop he had habitually adopted when on the verge of drawing his sword. "You should perhaps consider that abrupt though he was, his actions were likely more mannered than Saana's would have been, should the thought have occurred to her."

Yarmina sniffed. "As Zhanna told it, Saana was able to overlook your slaying of her friend in order to maintain the peace between you. This thane does not doubt Chief Saana's love for her daughter, but she does not consider her likely to have been any less restrained than you under such circumstances: she seems to have an excellent grasp on what is necessary to avoid undesired bloodshed."

Daimon pursed his lips. Perhaps Yarmina was correct, but it barely mattered. "Should she raise the subject, this lord will inform her of our conversation, and hopefully she will be satisfied."

"Hopefully so." Yarmina swayed slightly, and caught herself. "Now, if you will excuse this thane, it is probably time that she returned to her chambers in the interest of getting some sleep. The blood should have been cleaned up by now," she added, a little weakly. "Lord Daimon. Please give this thane's regards once again to Chief Saana, and her thanks to Zhanna for saving her life."

"Thane Yarmina," Daimon replied levelly, with a bow. Yarmina set off past him with the determined air of someone remaining upright and walking more or less straight through willpower alone. Daimon watched her go. He still had fond memories of the girl who had once guided Darel and him around this castle, and had screamed in disgust at the bloody sockets of his missing teeth, but there was no sign of her now. In her place was a hard-edged young woman whom Daimon found hard to read even when she was confronted in bloodstained clothing, exhausted after a night of no sleep. Her apparent openness around him at Black Keep now seemed like another ploy, compared to her ruthless manipulation of her own people here. It was hard not to feel resentful, and distrustful of her.

Daimon sighed, and tried to calm himself. His own father had been stern and demanding, quick to criticise, and slow to praise, let alone show affection. Thanes were supposed to be just and unyielding, fearsome in war and respected in peace, but Lord Asrel had never once spoken to Daimon about love, or even friendship. Daimon had tried to model himself on his father, on what he thought a thane should be, and had found only emptiness as a result. He had come to love Saana: perhaps not in a way of which an epic ballad would be composed, one that spoke of a gaping hole in a lover's chest when their beloved was absent, but it was a love built on mutual trust and respect, and he felt it deserved the term. He loved Darel, too, and whereas their father had seemed to regard their filial affection as something that blinded them to each other's faults, Daimon felt it merely allowed them to better see each other's qualities.

How much worse must it have been for Yarmina? To not only have the hard, stern aspects of a thane as the model for her life, but to always be told that due to her gender she would never be able to truly emulate them, no matter how hard she tried? Could Daimon really blame her for her schemes, her changing faces depending on her company and situation, her lack of openness? He had thrown off his father's expectations to try to make his own path through the world; was Yarmina any different?

At least she had not killed her own father in order to do it.

Daimon sighed. Yarmina had warned him of Thane Odem's plans to attack Black Keep, and he could not believe that had come from anything but the goodness of her heart, and a wish to avoid a massacre. He had to believe that she bore him no ill-will, provided he did nothing to directly challenge her as ruler of Darkspur. He could never truly know another's mind, only the results of their actions. To date, Yarmina's had mainly benefited him, and those he cared about.

He stretched out his fingers, which felt cramped and tense in the aftermath of preparing to draw his blade, and went to check on his wife, and her daughter.

"Do we at least know where Asad got the weapon from?" Yarmina asked, later that afternoon in the study of the thane of Darkspur. She looked about as tired as Daimon felt, but had risen again, and set about trying to organise things in the aftermath of this new development. Sar Lahel was beside her, and now found himself granted the position of both castellan and steward, on the basis that he was the sole surviving sar of Darkspur's household. Daimon would have been uneasy at the concentration of power this gave him, but Lahel seemed withdrawn, and far from ambitious. He had, after all, seen his thane and most of his comrades-in-arms drown, so it was hardly surprising. Daimon wondered about talking to the man about it, of calling on the experience he had of mourning the deaths of his townsfolk in the aftermath of Rikkut Fireheart's attack, or even the death of his father, but he found himself without the words.

"One of the Tjakorshi, a man named Timmun," he replied to Yarmina. "It seems Asad approached him with a steel-headed axe and, through the use of signs and mummery, offered to swap weapons with him. Timmun thought it a good trade, so agreed. He had no idea what purpose Asad had for his axe."

Yarmina nodded wearily. "This thane hardly thought it likely that Asad would have found an ally among the Tjakorshi, but it is good that we know."

"Indeed," Daimon agreed, nodding. He had set Nalon to asking around about whether any of the clan were missing an axe, partly so he could persuade Saana to finally get some rest herself, and the answer had returned in fairly short order. Nalon had been scornful of Timmun's assumption that the offer was a genuine one, but Daimon could find no fault with the man's reasoning. Besides, Nalon had his own hang-ups about Naridan nobility, which undoubtedly influenced his opinion of what was and was not an innocent request.

"On the positive side," Yarmina said, very obviously trying to push the conversation aside, and give the impression of a thane rather than a nineteen year-old who had watched a man be killed in her bedchamber the previous evening, "the word from the farms is good. There have been no reports of problems between our peoples, whether Naridan or Tjakorshi. It appears everyone is working hard, and we have high hopes for a good harvest when the time comes, which may not have been possible otherwise."

Daimon smiled. "That is good to hear. 'Many hands make light work', as the lowborn's saying goes, and in times such as these the presence of the hands is probably of greater importance than who they belong to."

Yarmina winced, and Daimon recalled a moment later that

Zhanna now had one less hand than the day before. He was still wondering whether he should make clear that it had been an unfortunate choice of words, rather than an implied criticism, when a brisk knock sounded on the study door.

"Come," Yarmina said, looking somewhat grateful for the interruption, and the door cracked open to reveal the face of one of the castle servants.

"Begging your pardon, Lady, but a Crown Messenger has arrived."

The servant's voice betrayed her own excitement at the news she carried, and Daimon glanced at Yarmina only to find her looking back at him with a similar expression. Crown Messengers were the official heralds of the Sun Palace, under the control of the Lord of Scribes, and their relay network was used to carry official decrees and pronouncements across the land. Daimon could only remember a handful of occasions when one had made it as far as Black Keep.

"This thane's father always received Crown Messengers in the great hall," Yarmina said, slightly uncertainly. Daimon realised she was looking for guidance on the etiquette of the situation.

"This lord's father did likewise," he said. "If the message was a private matter for the ears of our family only then the messenger would advise us that the servants should be dismissed, but we always received them there."

"The position of Crown Messenger is one of the most revered that a lowborn man can rise to without gaining acceptance into the ranks of the nobility," Sar Lahel agreed. "Indeed, some messengers have received titles for delivering particularly important messages despite grave hardship. He should be received with due honour for his position as a messenger of the God-King, unless the urgency is such that no delay can be brooked."

Yarmina nodded, as though Daimon and Lahel had merely confirmed what she had already decided, and turned her attention back to the servant. "Has the messenger given any such indication?"

"No, Lady," the servant replied, shaking her head. "He said 'earliest convenience', but not that he needed immediate access to your person."

"Then we shall receive him in the Great Hall as soon as possible," Yarmina told her. "Make it ready."

The servant bowed and departed, closing the door behind her, and Yarmina got to her feet. "This is an unexpected development. Whatever could it be?"

Daimon rose as well, his mind racing as he tried to calculate times. Darel must have reached Idramar some time ago, unless disaster had struck at sea, which was a possibility Daimon was not prepared to contemplate. Would there have been time for his brother's petition to be heard, a decision made, and a decree sent out by Crown Messenger to have reached Darkspur? He did not know how long it would take the relay service to reach them, but he thought it highly likely. Could this man be carrying the God-King's judgement on the future of Black Keep?

"This lord does not wish to delay you," he said, "but with your permission, he would like to go and wake his wife. The news may concern her people, and their status at Black Keep. She is not likely to take long to be ready," he added. Saana could, after all, throw on her entire usual attire in the time Daimon imagined it would take a Naridan noblewoman to have properly arranged one sleeve of her gown.

Yarmina nodded. "Of course, but please make haste. We shall await you in the great hall."

Daimon hurried from the study, his stomach churning with uncertainty. Black Keep had been in a state of uncertainty since Darel had departed with Marshal Brightwater, its

Tjakorshi members granted permission to live there for the moment, but with a future and final judgement still to come. Daimon desperately wanted closure on that and an end to the waiting, of course . . . but only if the result was the correct one.

It had to be the correct one. Darel was intelligent and erudite, and Marshal Brightwater was a Hand of Heaven with the ear of the God-King, who had seen first-hand how valiantly the Brown Eagle clan had fought in defence of their new home. It was inconceivable that the God-King might not see the righteousness and worthiness of their arguments.

And yet . . .

Daimon tried to push his doubts aside. He would find out the truth in short order. Until then, there was nothing to be done.

They sat on the dais, as they might do for a grand dinner: Yarmina in the thane's chair, Sar Lahel at her right hand, and Daimon and Saana on her left. The window shutters were thrown wide to allow the remaining afternoon sun in, and shafts of golden light slanted across the interior as the great doors opened.

"Crown Messenger Kanam," a guard shouted, and the man himself entered the hall. He was whip-thin and weather-beaten, but the red sash across his chest marked his profession out, as did the knot of gold braid on each side of the collar of his travel-stained green robe. He walked briskly down the hall and paused exactly the correct distance from the dais, before making a bow of the precise depth and duration appropriate for a thane. Clearly, Daimon realised, practice made perfect.

"Greetings, Thane Yarmina of Darkspur," Kanam said smoothly, as he rose. Daimon glanced down the hall at the guards, and wondered if someone had had a quiet word with Kanam before he entered, advising the man of how Yarmina wished to be addressed. Perhaps Kanam had decided that making an issue of a noblewoman's fancy was far more trouble than he felt like embroiling himself in.

Kanam's eyes moved to Daimon, and the man's eyebrows rose as he saw the Blackcreek sigil on the front of Daimon's robe. "And Lord Daimon of Blackcreek? Apologies: this man had not expected to see you here."

Daimon waved the apology away, and Yarmina spoke. "Greetings to you, honoured messenger. What word do you bring from the Sun Palace?"

"This man has several pieces of news of import," Kanam said, glancing back at Daimon, "some of which is of particular relevance to the present company. He shall begin:

"Firstly, Einan Coldbeck, previously the Eastern Marshal of Narida, is declared a traitor. He is stripped of his rank, and his lands are forfeit to the crown."

Daimon felt his mouth drop open in shock. Of all the things he had imagined, expected, or braced himself for, this was not one of them.

"Honoured messenger, this thane does not wish to suggest that you are at fault," Yarmina said slowly, "but can this truly be the case?"

"Your reaction is no different to this man's own when this message was passed to him," Kanam replied with a rueful smile. "However, unless there has been a catastrophic fault with the entire messenger system, there is no mistake. Einan Coldbeck raised his hand against the God-King, then fled Idramar when his scheme failed. He is a traitor, and the rank of Eastern Marshal has gone to Adan Greenbrook, formerly Lord Treasurer."

Yarmina sat back on her chair, her expression studiously blank. On her far side, Sar Lahel looked like he had been poleaxed.

"Secondly," Kanam continued, with another glance at

Daimon, and at Saana, "his Divine Majesty Natan III recognises that the Raiders known as the Brown Eagle clan have settled on the lands of the thanedom of Blackcreek, and have pledged themselves to the good of Narida. His Divine Majesty instructs all his subjects to treat these Raiders as they would any other Naridan, and none should raise their hand against them except in the situations already covered by Naridan law."

Daimon let out the breath he had been holding, and his shoulders slumped as tension drained from. Nari bless him, but Darel had done it! Until this moment, Daimon had not admitted to himself exactly how afraid he had been that his brother's arguments would go unheeded. He reached for Saana's hand and squeezed her fingers in celebration, and she squeezed back just as hard. He could tell that she wanted to jump up and shout for joy, but was restraining herself out of respect for the sensibilities of Naridan nobles. Daimon himself was having a hard time retaining the sort of composure his rank called for in such a situation, and he briefly wondered why being a noble meant you should not show genuine joy when you had reason to. What purpose did it serve?

"Thirdly," Kanam said, "Kaldur Brightwater, formerly Southern Marshal, has been declared traitor, stripped of his rank and his lands—"

"Honoured messenger, now you truly do stretch this thane's credulity!" Yarmina burst out, voicing Daimon's own reaction to the messenger's words. "How can this be?"

"This messenger merely passes on what he has been instructed to," Kanam said forcefully, looking Yarmina in the eye. "If the thane of Darkspur distrusts the veracity of his statements then he can only suggest that she travels to Idramar to demand confirmation from Lord Wousewold of what he ordered be proclaimed throughout the kingdom!"

Yarmina's eyes flashed at being addressed in such a manner, but a crown messenger was officially a member of the God-King's household. As such, Kanam had rather greater leeway in terms of proper conduct when addressing members of the nobility; or at the least, could expect that few nobles would dare punish him for such a minor infraction.

"Please, continue," she said after a moment.

"Kaldur Brightwater, formerly Southern Marshal, has been declared traitor, stripped of his rank and his lands declared forfeit to the crown," Kanam said, as though the interruption had never occurred. "The rank of Southern Marshal has been granted to . . . "

He glanced at Daimon, his expression unreadable.

" . . . Lord Darel Blackcreek."

"*What?*" Daimon demanded, standing up. This had to be a mistake, or a trick of some kind, although to what end he could not guess. "Say that again, man!"

"The rank of Southern Marshal has been granted to Lord Darel Blackcreek," Kanam repeated. "He saved the life of His Divine Majesty, and slew the traitor Kaldur Brightwater in the process."

Daimon sank slowly back into his seat, still unable to truly comprehend what he had just heard. The messenger's news had already fulfilled his greatest hopes and left him weak with relief after months of underlying tension. This new development was a concept so outlandish he could not get his head around it. Darel? Southern Marshal? Daimon's brother *a Hand of Heaven*? It was an impossibility, as though a third moon had suddenly appeared in the sky and everyone else maintained that it had always been there.

"This is truly a momentous day," Yarmina said weakly. "Do you have any other news for us, messenger?"

"What of the wave?" Saana asked, and Daimon jerked as

he realised that should have been his first question. "Did the wave hit Idramar?"

Kanam looked uncertain for the first time. "This man does not know; judging by what others have said, he believes these messages left Idramar before the wave struck anywhere on the coast. However, if it is the safety of the Divine Court and Marshal Blackcreek that concerns you, this man has seen the Sun Palace many times, and the rock it stands on rises high above the city. The wave would have had to be terrifying indeed to come anywhere near even the palace's foundations, so he believes that anyone inside it at the time would have been safe."

Daimon nodded with relief, even while he noted how strange it was to hear his brother referred to as "Marshal Blackcreek". That was going to take some getting used to.

"In response to the thane's question," Kanam continued, "there is indeed more news, although this is not an official proclamation from the Sun Palace. The rumours of a pretender to the God-King's throne in the west have gained strength, and His Divine Majesty has dispatched a portion of the Eastern Army under Lord Goldtree to find him and accompany him to Godspire so the monks may make their judgement."

"Oh, so just a small detail then!" Sar Lahel exclaimed. "Just the minor matter of the Divine Nari perhaps being reborn!"

"A crown messenger must always deliver the pronouncements of the Sun Palace first, goodsar!" Kanam objected. "This man would be derelict in his duty had he not done so."

"Was the treachery of Coldbeck and Brightwater related to these rumours?" Daimon asked. "Did they seek to depose the God-King in favour of this newcomer?"

Kanam shrugged. "This man is only the most recent carrier of these messages, Lord Daimon, so he cannot say for sure, and gossip is discouraged among messengers."

Yarmina laughed. "A likely story."

Kanam gave her a look Daimon could only describe as long-suffering. Clearly the man was used to having such assertions challenged. "*However*, what this man has heard would suggest that Lord Daimon's guess is correct." He bowed. "Does this man have the thane's permission to make his pronouncements to the town?"

"You do," Yarmina replied. A crown messenger would deliver messages to the thane first, Daimon knew, and then ask for permission to tell the lowborn such information as the Sun Palace decreed they should know, but it would be a foolhardy thane who refused that permission when it was requested. Indeed, such a thane might at a later date find themselves answering uncomfortable questions about why they sought to block the God-King's pronouncements to his kingdom.

Kanam withdrew, and once the main door had been closed behind him, Yarmina turned to Daimon with a self-mocking smile. "So, Lord Daimon: are you *certain* your newly elevated brother would not be interested in a proposal of marriage?"

Alazar

"The party from Northbank approaches, Divine One!"

The shout came from outside the tent in which the commanders of the Western Army had gathered. Alazar was no such thing, but Captain Reden had requested his presence, and so he stood with the Brotherhood's leader, along with two others: Mera the Tall, a Naridan woman who could look Alazar level in the eyes and was followed by fifty archers; and Hoko, who claimed to be an exiled prince of the mountain people from somewhere to the north of Godspire. Alazar had no idea whether that was true or not, but the man carried a battle-axe and shield like someone who knew how to use them. Still, with one of his companions a woman and the other a mountain man, it was perhaps no surprise that Reden wanted a sar in his party, even a blacksword.

The Godsworn were represented by Barstan Broadfield and Sar Disman, and the Western Army itself by Taladhar Torgallen, with First Captain Benel and Captain Toren flanking him. Despite the politeness between them, Alazar could not help but mark the contrast between the smart army officers and the three with whom he stood, who looked like nothing more than successful ruffians. Which was, he conceded, basically what they were.

In the middle of them all stood Tyrun, serene in His plain

white robe, and crowned with a simple circlet of gold. It was a far cry from the ornate robes and heavy crown of the God-King in Idramar, and Alazar approved – not that he had been consulted, of course. Natan had never looked comfortable when dressed for state occasions, and the clothes were cumbersome on him. His father had worn it better, so far as Alazar remembered, but there was still always the feeling that the monarch was trying to make up for in sartorial magnificence what he lacked in natural regality. Tyrun had no need to rely on such things: He looked more like a ruler in his simple clothes than anyone else in the tent, even Marshal Torgallen.

"Who comes?" Torgallen asked. "Has Lord Goldtree answered the summons?"

"We shall see momentarily," Tyrun said calmly. "If he has not, that in itself tells much."

Alazar shifted his weight. He was not looking forward to the spectacle of Lord Goldtree coming face to face with the Divine One, mainly because he had grave doubts about exactly how flexible Goldtree would be. With luck, he would recognise Tyrun's divinity and swear allegiance to him. If he decided to be stubborn, however, things would get very uncomfortable, very fast.

The tent flap opened, and four men entered. Alazar recognised one of them as Sar Morel, of Goldtree's household, and another he thought was the son of the Thane of Bowbridge, although he could not remember the man's name offhand. The other two were also sars, but not ones he recognised. Sar Morel's eyes skated past Alazar as he looked around the tent, then came back to him and widened in surprised recognition.

Alazar waited for Lord Goldtree himself to enter, following his retinue as would be appropriate, but no one else came through the tent flaps.

"So the general of the Eastern Army elects to remain behind his walls," Tyrun said, and His voice was stern.

"This lord is Okadin Bowbridge," the thane's son announced himself. He and his men bowed, but not in the manner they should have. By rights, they should have been on one knee simply for the presence of the Western Marshal, let alone the Divine One. "Lord Goldtree sends his regrets that he cannot be here in person."

"Does Tarel Goldtree truly place so little faith in our good intent that he will not come and speak to the Divine One himself?" Taladhar Torgallen demanded, shocked and outraged. "To send the son of a thane as his representative is an insult!"

"This lord has been instructed to bear a message to the leaders of the Western Army," Okadin Bowbridge said, eyeing Torgallen. "Specifically to the man claiming to be Nari reborn."

Alazar's jaw tightened in anger, and his was not the only one: angry words began to fill the tent as the assembled commanders were unable to keep their fury at this disrespect from overflowing. However, they quietened when Tyrun raised His hand and stepped forward.

"This god *claims* nothing," He said, His voice flat with anger. "Do you stand before Him, and dispute His divinity?"

For a wonder, Bowbridge held Tyrun's gaze. "This lord was not tasked by his general with making any such judgement. He simply bears a message."

"Then this god shall have it from you," Tyrun demanded, holding out his hand.

"It is not written," Bowbridge replied with a shake of his head. He straightened his spine and squared his shoulders. "Lord Tarel Goldtree, General of the Eastern Army in the field, sends his greetings to the man who claims to be Nari reborn. The general recognises no ruler other than the God-King Natan Narida, the third of his name, and he will surrender neither the city of Northbank, nor command of the Eastern Army to any other, without being instructed so to do by King Natan. Unless," Bowbridge added, cutting off the new angry intakes of breath, "the man claiming to be Nari reborn can justify his rightful claim to these things by defeating Lord Goldtree in single combat."

Alazar bit his lip. Let no one say that Tarel Goldtree lacked bravado. A general, offering single combat to a rival, with his army as the stake? And by the Mountain, Goldtree was not challenging a rival, he was challenging his *god*. The man's arrogance bordered on the unbelievable!

And yet . . .

Goldtree would have trained with the longblade since he was a child. Tyrun might be the spirit of Nari reborn into a new body, but that body had not been the child of a noble family: Tyrun, like Nari Himself, had risen from obscurity to shake the world. Did He know how to use a sword? Alazar had never seen him with a weapon. Nari had been a warrior king, but even He had needed to learn the ways of war. There were whole stories about Nari's training, and although He had come to surpass his teachers, He had to work in order to do it. Nari had been a man who became a god, as His spirit grew and filled Him with purpose.

Did Tyrun possess the skills of His former self?

Sar Morel's eyes found Alazar again, and he did not look comfortable. Alazar let his right hand drift down to the front of his belt, ready to grip and draw his longblade should he need to. He did not know Morel well, but a sar being jumpy was never a good sign.

"This is an outrageous suggestion!" Taladhar Torgallen declares. "On what grounds does Lord Goldtree presume to challenge the Divine One?!"

"On the grounds, High Marshal, that he is in possession of

both an army and a city that you wish to take!" Bowbridge snapped. "He is willing to cede command of both, should he be bested in combat by the man who claims that authority. And no other!" he added, and Sar Morel looked at Alazar again, which was not that surprising: Alazar had spent much of the journey upriver to Northbank from Idramar trying to avoid talking about the honour duel he had won for Tila, but the stories and rumours had gone through the army, even if not everyone knew that he was the man involved.

Tyrun breathed in, and the entire tent waited.

"This god will have no part of such a display," Tyrun declared coldly. "Lord Goldtree is to surrender the city of Northbank and command of the Eastern Army to this god. If he does so promptly, he will be allowed to continue to serve as an officer within it. If he refuses, the force you see here will be sent against Northbank's walls, and there shall be no mercy for those that resist us."

"This lord can already tell you what Lord Goldtree's response will be to such a threat," Bowbridge replied. The faint quiver in His voice suggested to Alazar that said response would not be favourable for the messenger who delivered it to him, either.

"This god is not the slightest bit concerned," Tyrun said. He raised His eyebrows when none of the emissaries moved. "You have a message to deliver."

"As you wish," Okadin Bowbridge said.

His hand flashed to his longblade, and he performed a draw-cut.

Alazar had his own blade out in a draw-cut of his own before anyone else in the tent reacted. He slashed the weapon up one-handed across Sar Morel's chest to clear him out of the way – a debilitating wound, but not an immediately fatal one – then took the grip in two hands and hacked into Okadin

Bowbridge's left shoulder. The thane's son cried out in pain, and his second blow aimed at Tyrun flew wide. The Divine One staggered back behind Marshal Torgallen and First Captain Benel, who were also drawing their blades, and Bowbridge whirled around to face Alazar. His wild slash was the attack of a man inexperienced in combat, for whom pain and panic were new experiences. Alazar leaned back from it, then lunged to drive the tip of his blade into Bowbridge's throat before he could recover his balance or his guard. Bowbridge staggered, blood gouting from his neck, and then things ended as abruptly as they had begun: the rest of the tent's occupants fell upon the party from Northbank, who were bludgeoned to the ground and butchered in short order.

But did any of that matter now?

"Divine One!" Alazar shouted, extricating himself from the mess of rising and falling weapons and hastening to the side of Taladhar Torgallen. The Western Marshal still had his longblade drawn, but was also supporting Tyrun, who had one hand clasped to his own chest. He pulled it away as though to check it, and Alazar saw red dripping through the God-King's fingers. His own heart seemed to stop in horror.

"Surgeon!" Torgallen bellowed, his old lungs still up to the task. "Get a surgeon in here immediately!"

"It's not deep," Tyrun declared, pulling his slashed robe gingerly away to look at the wound inflicted on His flesh, and Alazar breathed again with a sigh of relief. "The wretch's blade barely reached," Tyrun continued. It is— *Gah!*" He winced in pain, then shoved Torgallen away from him. "*Fuck!*" He turned around and kicked over the war table, scattering maps and markers. "*Fuck!*" He bellowed again, and when He turned back to face the rest of them, His expression could have cut through steel.

"Order the attack!" Tyrun bawled. "Now! Northbank is

to be taken, Goldtree's guts are to be torn out, and his head brought to this god on a spear! *Now!"* He repeated, when no one moved immediately.

"Divine One," Marshal Torgallen said, dropping to one knee. "What of our men who are inside the city? What of Mordokel?"

"What of them?" Tyrun demanded. He reached down and grabbed Torgallen by the front of his robe, hauling the marshal up to his feet with no apparent care for the new wave of blood that the exertion loosed from His injured chest, or the red smears his fingers left on Torgallen's clothing. "What of *him*? Mordokel is a man, nothing more, and he has pledged his life to serve this god! None of them matter, High Marshal! Only this god matters, and you should not forget that! The spirits of any who die doing His bidding shall be honoured, but that city *will* be taken! Now see to it!"

He released His hold on Torgallen's robe, and the marshal bowed again before turning away and heading for the tent's entrance, ushering his fellow commanders before him. Alazar caught a glimpse of Torgallen's expression as he passed. It was one of furious contemplation.

"And get these cowards out of here!" Tyrun shouted, pointing at the still-bleeding bodies of Tarel Goldtree's would-be assassins. Alazar made a hasty bow, took hold of Sar Morel's wrists — the man himself was now missing half of his face, courtesy of Hoko's axe — and dragged the body outside. He kept his face calm and lowered to the ground, but a thought was circling inside his head.

Tyrun was the Divine One, and He was Nari reborn, but He had said that none of the men He had sent inside Northbank mattered. Alazar had come west to find the Divine One because he believed in Him, and he no longer believed in the so-called Divine Family in Idramar, but he could not accept this. Marin mattered to him: Marin mattered to him more than anything else in the entire world. If Tyrun had turned to Alazar and told him that he had to choose between Marin and his legs, Alazar would have asked which one the axeman should take first.

"Laz! What's going on?"

It was Ravi. The healer had her satchel under her arm, and she recoiled in shock and horror from the mangled corpse of Sar Morel. "Nari's teeth! What happened!"

"Northbank's party tried to kill the Divine One," Alazar told her. "He's wounded."

"He's wounded?" Ravi gasped, her mouth falling open. "How can that—"

"He says it's not bad," Alazar said, trying to cut her off before she began panicking. "It didn't look bad: He was able to kick over a table. He'll need stitches, though." He held out an arm to block her way for a moment, as she turned to hurry inside. "And . . . be careful. He's not in a good mood."

"He's the Divine One," Ravi said, as though explaining something to a child. Alazar was not sure what she meant by it – that Tyrun could not be a bad mood? That it made no difference if he was? – but he withdrew his arm and let her duck through the entrance to do her work. All the same, the memory of the rage on Tyrun's face held him where he was for a moment, until he was sure he was not going to hear the sound of Ravi being struck.

And what would he have done if he had? Drawn his sword and gone in to her rescue?

Alazar Blade was a pragmatic man. The incident at the monastery was unpleasant, but there had been nothing he could do about it. The monks had denied Tyrun's divinity, and neither Marin nor he had been under threat. Things were different now. Tyrun had said that He did not value Marin, that He did not care about Marin. Few people in Narida knew as much about the fallibility of the divine as Alazar, and he realised he had come to a decision.

He would go back to the Brotherhood. He would take part in the attack on Northbank. And then, once inside the walls, he would find his husband, and they would leave. Tyrun's feet had been set on the course that would lead him to the Sun Throne: that did not mean that Alazar and Marin had to stick around and see it through.

The choice between his god or his husband's welfare was, for Alazar, no choice at all.

Tila

T he sars had fled, saving their own lives in order to carry word back west about the size of the force that was coming. Tila could understand the logic of that, despite the fact that each one should probably blacken his scabbard. The honourable thing would have been for one or two to punch out and take the message, while the rest sold their lives as dearly as possible. However, it seemed the sort of heroic last stands that made for epic poems were less appealing in person.

What was more, the sars had left a few hundred Naridans behind them to die. These were not the stunned survivors of a sacked town, however, but armsmen. Tila could not stand by and let their lives go to waste.

She had already slipped away from Stonejaw's crew and nudged, squeezed, and slipped her way through the press of Raiders towards The Golden. Such ill-discipline would be stopped in short order in a Naridan army, but the Raiders were not an army: they were a very large collection of fighters, and even Tila knew that there was a subtle difference. By the time the mass cowardice of the sars had become clear, Tila was close enough.

"Let mē talk to them!" she shouted in Alaban, and was rewarded with The Golden's metal-masked face snapping around to face in her direction. Nari's blood, but the draug was unnerving! She took a breath and fought down her unease. "Let mē talk to them! They might join you!"

The Golden did not move, as seemed to be its way when it was considering something. For a moment it resembled nothing more than a particularly lifelike painted statue. Then it raised its arm to point at her.

"Come forward, then," it called, and even though most could probably not understand the words, the Raiders between it and Tila melted aside from its gesture. She pressed forwards through the suddenly cleared space, and came to its side.

"Yōu think yōu can turn their hearts?" The Golden asked. Tila thought she could hear icy amusement in its voice, but she could not be sure.

"Ī'd rather try than let them all die," Tila said honestly. "They might see reason. There's no hope for them if they oppose you."

The Golden's ice-green eyes studied her. "That is true. Very well. Speak to them. If they pledge themselves to me, they shall keep their lives. As shall yōu."

Tila swallowed. "And if they don't?"

The Golden's mouth moved into a very slight smile. "Then yōu will learn why it's unwise to make me a promise yōu cannot keep."

Tila opened her mouth to point out that she had made no such promise, but realised before she said a word that such a protest would get her nowhere. Such was the cost of drawing attention to herself in these uncertain surroundings. She nodded instead.

"So be it."

The Golden said something to a warrior at its side, who raised an enormous shell to his lips and puffed out his cheeks. The deep, throbbing sound rang out, and Tila felt some of the tension around her die away. She had her opportunity.

Now she just had to make the most of it.

She strode forwards through the ranks of warriors in front of The Golden, considering how she wanted to present herself to these soldiers. The manner of Princess Tila would not do in this situation: she had no wish for anyone to start questioning exactly who she was. On the other hand, why would a large group of armed, undoubtedly scared Naridan men listen to a lone woman talking to them unless she claimed authority somehow?

She decided to fall back on Livnya once again. The crime lord's air of confidence had only ever partly been due to the unpleasant retribution she could wreak on those who displeased her. Come at someone with enough confidence that they would respect you, and they would often be halfway there before they realised what was happening.

In fact, she realised, she had been in situations like this before. This was little different to confronting a group of toughs who had run up against Livnya's shadowy empire and needed encouragement to throw their lot in with her for mutual benefit, instead of forcing her to have them disposed of. The fact that she as well as them would die if she failed was a situation she had not been in since she deposed Yakov to take control of Idramar's underworld, but the stirrings of fear in her stomach had always been good motivation.

She spread her arms as she approached them, and gave them Livnya's smile. "It looks like you lads are in a bit of a situation!"

"Who the fuck are you?" shouted one of the bannermen. He was a tall man with a decidedly lopsided jaw, and the strained expression of someone who was desperately hoping for a way out, but did not dare let himself believe that such a thing might come to pass.

"This lady is the way you might live to see the sundown," Tila replied. "It all depends on how sensible you're feeling."

"You mean you're a traitor?" someone shouted. "Following this filth around?"

"This lady is a survivor!" Tila snapped at the unseen voice. "Look around you, men of Narida! Do any of you think you can win this fight? Do any of you think you can escape, even if you turn and run?"

There was an uncomfortable shuffling of feet, and eyes that left her face to glance fearfully sideways at the ranks of Raider shields that faced them on three sides.

"We should die fighting!" the first bannerman declared, although the tremble in his voice gave the lie to his determined words. "That's the honourable thing!"

"Honourable?" Tila repeated, and laughed. She was exaggerating things, but she was dead if these men did not follow her lead, so this was no time for half measures. She pointed in the general direction that the sars had fled. "What about the nobles? Do they live with honour? They broke out and left you to die! And this lady is sure that when they get back to a castle they will all be very sober and solemn about how necessary it was that they all lived to fight another day, and carried word of the size of the Raider army, and how noble your sacrifice was. That doesn't change the fact that *they* will be alive, and *you* will be dead!"

One or two expressions wavered. Tila could tell that some wanted to shout her down, but were being held back by their own fear. They desperately wanted her to be able to convince them to stay alive, even if they could not consciously accept that.

They had to live in order for her to live. She fought down any remnants of Princess Tila's beliefs, and addressed them as Livnya: powerful within certain circles, but still a lowborn who had worked her way up through subtle influence, and the occasional well-placed knife.

"Why do the sars get the best armour and the best weapons?" she shouted. "Why do they get dragons to ride, so they have a chance of getting out of a situation like this, while you're left here to die? Are you any less Naridan than them? Or is it just that the nobility always looks after its own?"

That hit a nerve. Several of the soldiers spat.

"What're you saying?" someone asked. "That we should join the fucking Raiders?"

Tila threw her hands up. "What options have you got? Really? You wouldn't be the first. The Raiders see to it that we're fed. They don't have nobles; they have captains, and so far as this lady can tell, anyone can become a captain so long as enough other people are willing to serve under them. No one rules anyone else because they were born in a castle!"

"They're attacking Narida!" the first bannerman said. "How can we join ourselves to that?"

Tila shrugged. "The same way as this lady is right now. She's trying to prevent you from dying. The Raiders aren't killing those that join them. If you want to save lives, come with us. The more Naridan voices we have, the more likely it is we can convince others like you."

She was dancing on ice now, trying to keep her balance while spinning up rationales to counter any objection raised, but Tila had been playing this game in Idramese back streets and the Inner Council chamber since her father had died. She could do it with her eyes closed.

"You'll never convince the sars, or the thanes," someone said.

Tila raised her eyebrows. "Then fuck 'em. They die, you get their stuff. There aren't *that* many of them."

She saw glances being exchanged. She was appealing to greed now, not just the base instincts of survival. Which lowborn had not looked at a noble and coveted their wealth, their clothes, their possessions? Such things were out of reach for the poor, unless they took to a life of banditry and got lucky. It was the same logic as the power that allowed The Golden to keep its control over the Raiders, or Livnya to maintain her influence: the fear that you could not achieve anything alone, and that others would turn on you in order to save or improve their own position.

Now, however, there were thousands upon thousands of Raiders to factor into the equation. Tila could almost see the thoughts churning around in the soldiers' heads. The Raiders were going to be pushing farther into Narida anyway; they would face and fight other Naridan forces, including sars, and undoubtedly kill them unless they yielded. Would a few hundred Naridan bodies make much difference in those fights? Perhaps not. In which case, what was the harm in saving their own lives? If one could not influence an outcome, was it so wrong to tag along and see what you could gain? Being surrounded and vastly outnumbered by armed savages was bad enough: how could things realistically get worse?

"What about Nari? What about the God-King?" someone shouted, and Tila cursed silently.

"Do you see the God-King anywhere?" she asked. "He left Idramar the moment the Raiders arrived! He didn't stay to fight and die! Why should you? As for Nari . . . " She took in the banners they carried. "You're Eastern Army? You were sent west to look for the man claiming that he's Nari Reborn?"

"First off, yes, but our detachment got retasked with finding Marshal Coldbeck," the bannerman said. He shook his head. "But then Lord Tunstone heard of the Raiders attacking Idramar, and led us back east."

"Well, the leader of the Raiders is heading west to find this Nari Reborn," Tila told them. "So that's another reason to come with us." Several voices demanded to know why the Raiders' leader would be doing any such thing, and Tila spread her hands. "This lady hardly knows for sure. But if you want to be there when it happens, and see whether he really is the Divine One returned to us, you should listen to this lady's offer."

"But what about—"

"Here's the deal!" Tila shouted, interrupting yet another objection. She was tired of these men's stubborn insistence that she should not save their lives, and her own into the bargain. "Any man who wishes to die today, step forward now and make yourself known! Because you can twist it any way you want, but those are your options: you can live, or you can die! If you want to die, then let's get this over with! If you want to live, then stay where you are."

Her words were no accident. Breaking ranks would be hard to do, no matter what criteria she lay down for it. Few men would want to be the first to set themselves apart from their fellows in order to save their own life; even fewer would want to do so in order to confirm their own deaths. Her best chance of survival rested with tipping the hand in her favour.

There was a long, sullen, and uncomfortable silence. Then one man stepped out, his face shining with sweat and his eyes wide but determined.

"S'man's not afraid of the Raiders," he said, which had to be one of the biggest lies of his life. "He'll die like a Naridan man, and face Nari with pride!"

Well, the part about you dying will be true, at any rate, Tila thought. She looked over the rest of them. "Anyone else?" She had no idea how many would have to join The Golden for it to consider her successful, but she was fairly sure that just one would not count against her.

Another man stepped forward, one whose time with the army must have been drawing to a close in any case, judging by the thick patches of grey in his hair. Then another, his eyes closed and his mouth already whispering a prayer. Tila's stomach clenched, and she waited for the floodgates to open and most of the detachment to step forward with bold cries of how they would sell their lives dearly rather than let the savages continue unopposed.

It did not happen. The first man looked back over his shoulder, and many would not meet his eyes, but the shame any of them felt was clearly not sufficient to move their legs. A fair few stood tall and uncaring; probably the ones who had heard what Tila had said about taking things from sars and nobles, and decided that this was a chance they were going to seize with both hands.

"Very well," Tila said, addressing the three men who had stepped out. "All you have to do is take your weapons and charge any of them." She gestured at the Raiders. "They'll take care of the issue quickly."

That was one ask too far. Faces grimaced and eyes glowered at her, but one by one, all three stepped back into the ranks of their fellows. Tila breathed a sigh of relief.

"Good choices, everyone. Now, follow this lady and don't point anything sharp at anyone, and you'll all get a meal at sundown after all."

She turned her back on them, and began to walk back across the field towards where The Golden was waiting. Part of her wondered for a moment about pointing it out to these soldiers and seeing if she could coordinate a charge into the Raiders' ranks that might actually be able to reach the draug to bring it down, but she dismissed the notion out of hand. The Golden was no fool, and would surely be on the lookout for treachery; especially from a woman who had already tried to end its life once with a knife, and was now in the company of soldiers of her own land. It would have predicted such an obvious ploy.

No, Tila was going to have to be smarter if she wanted to pose any threat to The Golden. However, the more Naridans she had in the ranks, the better her chances would be when the time was right to make her move.

She returned her confident smile to her face, held her head high and proud, and led her reluctant recruits back towards a demon wearing the body of a man.

Marin

O ne of the things that Marin had very definitely wanted
to avoid in his life was being inside a city that was under
attack, and yet here he was.

Apparently, all notion of Tyrun waiting for reports on the
mood of the city had been forgotten: either that, or some of the
other spies He sent had better luck getting out of the gates or
over the walls than Marin and Mordokel, because the Western
Army attacked at about the same time as Einan Coldbeck led
his newly recruited militia in an assault on the Eastern Army's
positions from inside the walls. Marin was startled at how
rapidly Coldbeck's numbers swelled, but it seemed the sight of
their former thane and his sigil was the only thing required to
tip many of Northbank's citizens over the edge from unhappy
and resentful into openly rebellious. Lord Goldtree's soldiers,
concentrating on the very large, loud, and obvious threat outside, did not look behind behind them until it was too late.

At least one gate had fallen, thanks to the determined efforts
of the militia, and now soldiers wearing the emblem of the
Western Army were inside the walls. The Eastern Army still
had far greater numbers within Northbank, so far as Marin
could tell, but confusion reigned: some of Goldtree's soldiers
wanted to throw their lot in with Tyrun and their former
commander, others pretended to do so in order to gain an

advantage, and confrontations between groups of armed men
stalled, as officers yelled at each in increasingly angry tones
to stand down and submit to the will of whichever God-King
they themselves obeyed. It seemed very few people actually
wanted to fight those who were nominally their allies, but there
was usually someone without such compunctions, or more
devout in one direction or another, or simply scared or angry
enough to loose an arrow, throw a spear, or lead a charge.
Then, inevitably, fear took over, and blood was shed.

Marin stayed near Coldbeck, Mordokel, and the others long
enough that his commitment to the cause was unlikely to be
doubted, then slipped away as best he could. As one small and
unthreatening man, without obvious weapons or badges of
allegiance, he was beneath the notice of any of the groups of
soldiers cutting back and forth through the city in search of
enemies. What he really needed was somewhere he could lay
low until everything was over, then resurface safe and sound
with a story about getting "separated" from his erstwhile
allies, after which he could get back to Laz and steer well clear
of any other such dangerous situations.

He rounded a corner and came to an abrupt stop. A group
of six or seven men – civilians, judging by the lack of uniform – were battering on the door of a silversmith's. The door
in question began to give with the cracking noise of wood
stressed beyond endurance, and one of the looters looked
around in guilty reflex. His eyes locked with Marin's, and
narrowed as he realised that someone was watching them.

Marin did not wait to see whether they decided he needed
to be silenced: he turned and fled, down a street that ran at
cross-angles. It seemed some of Northbank's inhabitants were
more interested in turning a profit from the chaos, when
everyone in authority was distracted. It was possibly not a
bad idea, and Marin's fingers itched at the idea of forgotten

valuables laying around in the houses of rich merchants who had hurriedly disappeared before the conflict arrived at their doors, but without knowing the city . . .

He was crossing one on Northbank's major thoroughfares when the tramp of many feet grabbed his attention, and he looked to his left to see a large contingent of the Eastern Army making its way towards him. Marin fought down the instant and instinctive moment of panic he always experienced in such situations, but shrank back against a nearby wall nonetheless, and tried to get his bearings. They were heading away from the walls and towards Coldbeck Tower, the castle that until recently had been the ancestral home of the former Eastern Marshal.

And *that*, unless Marin was very much mistaken, was the personal banner of Lord Goldtree himself, in among the mass of soldiery. Was he abandoning the walls, and heading for the castle in an attempt to hold out there? If so, the struggle for the city was practically over! If Marin headed for the West Gate, he might even run into his husband.

He cut back on himself, making sure to skirt the place where the looters had been, and broke into a run. He still did not know Northbank properly, but he had enough of a head for directions to make sure he was heading broadly the right way. The walls were not tall enough to be seen from very far off – Northbank was not a fortified city, like some towns in the far north, with their walls built to the height of six men – but he could orient himself on Coldbeck Tower, and the roof of the temple, and—

He rounded another corner and nearly ran on to multiple spearpoints, which were levelled at him with angry shouts. He had only gone and blundered into another knot of soldiers!

"Whom do you serve?" someone shouted at him.

"The God-King!" Marin replied immediately, on the grounds that the ambiguity over which one he meant might at least buy him some time. It took an effort of will to look past the spearpoints and at the tabards of the men brandishing them, but he saw the emblem of the Western Army and breathed a sigh of relief. At least he would not have to lie when asked for clarification.

"Marin?"

Mordokel stepped through the bristling spears, his longblade unsheathed and bloody, and his expression stern. "Where in the name of the Mountain did you disappear to?" the priest demanded, and Marin's planned explanation of getting separated from them suddenly did not sound particularly convincing, even in his own head.

"Lord Goldtree!" he panted instead, pointing behind him. "He's left the walls, he's heading for the castle with an escort!"

Mordokel's expression sharpened. "You saw him yourself?"

"S'man wouldn't know his face, but his banner was there," Marin said. "We saw that on the march west."

Mordokel's eyes searched Marin's face for the space of a couple of heartbeats, but the priest seemed satisfied with what he found there, because he turned and raised his voice. "To the castle! We will cut the traitor off from his retreat!"

The mass of bodies – a mix of soldiers and armed citizens, Marin realised – began to press forward in a jog, and he scrambled to one side of the street so as not to be either trampled beneath their feet, or driven before them. Any hopes he had of sending them off on their way and being about his business vanished, however, when Mordokel emerged from the press.

"You had best come with us," the priest said. "The streets are still not safe."

"Are they going to be safer where you're going?" Marin asked. Mordokel's brows lowered.

"Do not give this priest reason to doubt your dedication to the Divine One's cause, Marin of Idramar."

"S'man doesn't even have a weapon!" Marin protested, gesturing to the knife on his belt. "Not a proper one!"

"Hmm." Mordokel stepped back into the flow of bodies, nimbly dodging around the swaying horns of a sar's mount, and reappeared a few seconds later with a halberd. Marin was not certain whether the priest had recovered it from a corpse underfoot, or simply snatched it off someone else, but he had no option other than to take it. It was taller than him, and felt decidedly unwieldy, but it certainly had more reach than a belt knife.

"Now come on," Mordokel told him, in a tone that brooked no argument, and Marin reluctantly fell into step. It was just his luck to end up in the one place he had spent much of the day trying *not* to be; armed with an unfamiliar weapon, and heading for a fight against people who had much more experience in this sort of thing. He half felt like silently asking Nari what it was he had done to draw such misfortune down on himself, but reconsidered when he thought about Tyrun. If Marin prayed to Nari now, would Tyrun hear it? Would He know Marin's thoughts? He had seen into Elifel's soul, and recognised the treachery there, but did He have to be near someone in order to do such a thing? Did Nari's rebirth into Tyrun's body mean the original God-King's spirit was now more limited than it had been?

These were all questions that Marin's scholarly mind refused to let go of, as he tried to keep pace with those around him through the streets and avoid tripping over the haft of his halberd, but also ones he knew he would never dare ask the only being capable of answering them. The other cupbearers might call him a coward for not pursuing knowledge, but they had not been in Tyrun's presence, and experienced the power of His spirit. It made Marin feel at peace, of course, but also tiny and insignificant in comparison, as though he were alone and exposed on a gigantic, bleak mountainside.

The other cupbearers had also not seen Tyrun's calm expression fail to falter as His followers had stormed the sacred monastery and slaughtered its inhabitants, all because they had made a mistake. That kind of thing made a man think twice about offering up an impertinent inquiry.

Part of the Idra was diverted through the city to make a moat for Coldbeck Tower, with the castle's southern side fronting onto the river itself. The only crossing of the moat was a single bridge, and it was just north of this that Mordokel's hodgepodge of troops made contact with the enemy.

Marin was some way back in the column, by design as much as by accident, and he heard the screaming, shouting, and clatter of weapons from ahead before he could see what was going on. It was not a sound that engendered a great deal of confidence in someone unused to battle, and his hands felt slick and sweaty on his halberd.

"That way!" someone shouted at him. It was an army officer, gesturing desperately to another street off to the left, trying to change the direction of at least some of the column. "Go that way! Flank them!"

Attacking from the side seemed like a much better idea than standing directly between a lot of soldiers and their intended destination, so Marin was among those who cut left with alacrity, while others carried on to reinforce those already engaged. He looked around for Mordokel, but the priest had disappeared. Nonetheless, Marin did not fancy chancing his luck with desertion, given all those around him who might take exception to such things. With any luck he could stay well back from the fighting and look as though he had played his part, while avoiding anything resembling actual risk.

"Move! Move!"

Marin darted aside as two mounted sars thundered forward from behind him. More men desperately scattered out of the way before the sars turned to the right and disappeared down a street beside an inn: moments later, Marin heard the bellowing of their war-dragons as they encountered enemies, and a new chorus of screams and shouts split the air. That sounded rather too much like a real fight, so Marin hurried on past the inn and kept going north.

Or at least, he did until a hand caught at his sleeve.

"We're supposed to flank 'em!" a man shouted at him. He was a Western soldier, his square jaw shaded by dark stubble.

"They'll break out from farther back!" Marin replied, thinking quickly. "We need to surround them, or they'll take us in the side too!" He gestured to the north, as though that made what he was saying make sense.

Astonishingly, it seemed to work: the soldier considered for a moment, then nodded and swept an arm forward. "This way, lads! Let the sars have their fun here!"

A chunk of men listened, and broke off from the press. Marin turned and hurried onwards, hoping that action would fill in for competence until he could let someone else take over, since the last thing he wanted was to actually end up leading soldiers into combat: that could surely only end badly for everyone involved, except perhaps the opposite side.

The next street that cut off to the east did not appear to have any enemies at the far end of it, but Marin stopped to direct his new followers down it, just to make sure they were between him and any potential danger. "This way!" he shouted. "We'll get behind them, and box them in!" So far as Marin knew, Goldtree and his men would actually be able to break away farther to the east, but that did not sound so impressive. Regardless, his encouragement worked: the soldiers hurried in the direction of his urging. There were perhaps thirty, all told, and Marin fell in with the last few. With any luck, they would come out some distance behind the enemy's rear, and not need to do anything except watch everyone else deal with them.

It turned out, when he emerged onto the main thoroughfare, that luck was still refusing to look in his direction today.

The street was utter chaos: a tightly packed mess of men and blood and weapons, as two sizeable forces clashed without any room to manoeuvre. Marin saw a sar's charge falter after a few yards due to the simple resistance of the bodies all around him, and the warrior himself get hauled from the saddle moments later by the companions of the men he had just ridden down. Some soldiers were breaking into buildings simply to get out of the crush and find a more defensible position. Marin was no military tactician, but he thought he knew how that was likely to end: some bright spark would try to burn them out the moment they could lay their hands on some lamp oil, and then half the city would go up.

Of more pressing concern, however, was the knot of men heading straight for him.

"Ready!" someone bellowed, and the men with him lowered or raised their weapons, as appropriate. Marin did the same, desperately trying to ignore the fact his halberd suddenly felt like it weighed as much as a full-grown man, and had a mind of its own. There were enough men with him to cut off the street, but only in a single line, and although they outnumbered the enemy breaking towards them, it was not by much.

What was more, several of those approaching wore the armour of sars.

There were five sars, Marin's eyes told him; two holding the big, thick-bladed spears that sars used from dragonback, and the others with longblades drawn. He could immediately see how trying to get back through such a crush of your own men while mounted on a dragon would be doomed to failure: they would have had to dismount and push their way through on foot, but what sar would abandon their dragon like that? Laz had no dragon, partly because he could not afford one, and partly because their itinerant lifestyle meant that it simply was not practical. These were not blackswords, however: these were fully honoured sars of the Eastern Army, or a thane's household, and it would take an extreme circumstance indeed for them to—

One of them was Lord Goldtree.

He was no longer accompanied by his banner, but the sumptuously worked gold thread design on his coat-of-nails shouted his identity. The sars with him bore a smaller version of the same device on their chests, but the trunk and great, spreading branches of a golden oak took up the entire front of Tarel Goldtree's armour. The general of the Eastern Army had abandoned his attempt to return to Coldbeck Tower and was making a break for it, leaving his dragon to get away from the battle that had bogged down his escort, and he was heading straight towards Marin.

Goldtree and his men only appeared to notice Marin's blockade, or at least register that they were not allies, as weapons were readied in their direction. There was no hesitation from the soldiers of the Eastern Army before they charged, and Marin lost all semblance of wider awareness as his vision narrowed down to include only the man sprinting towards him.

Marin was vaguely aware that there was an art to fighting with a halberd, something involving hooking and pulling, but so far as he was concerned he had a long stick with a spike on the end of it, and an axe blade slightly below that, and the most important thing was to make sure that no one got closer to him than the other end of the spike. A sar was coming at him, bellowing a war cry and with longblade raised, his face hidden behind a snarling war mask that made him look even more terrifying. Marin screamed and lunged, shoving the halberd's spike directly at the centre of his enemy's chest.

The sar tried to twist aside, but did not fully manage it. The halberd's point ripped into the fabric of his armour and lodged beneath his right breastplate, and the shock of the impact nearly jolted the weapon from Marin's grasp. He gasped and held on grimly as the sar staggered to the side, trying to get himself free: Marin pivoted with him, and the sar realised too late that he had stumbled into range of one of Marin's companions: a simple straight sword cut into the unarmoured back of the sar's thigh, and Marin pushed forward with a desperate cry to dump him on his back, then withdrew his halberd to let someone else deal with the business of butchering the lamed warrior.

The man on Marin's left fell with a scream, red blood and white bone showing through his tunic as a longblade sent a fine mist of red into the air. Marin whirled, his heart hammering, but the killer did not come for him next. He was breaking through and away. Marin, his blood up and his mind in the grip of unfamiliar battle rage, let out another scream, and swung the axe of the halberd as hard as he could at the back of the sar's helmet.

The axe blade struck home with an impact that jarred Marin's arms, but which had a considerably greater impact on the fleeing sar, who stumbled sideways and fell on his face like a man trying to walk on the deck of a wave-tossed ship for the first time. Marin checked over his shoulder to make sure no one was about to run him through from behind and advanced on his fallen adversary. The sar was trying to push himself back up, but Marin kicked his longblade out of his grip, knocking that arm from under him in the process. The sar groaned and rolled onto his back, and Marin aimed the halberd's point down at his face.

And stopped, as his eye was caught by the sigil of Lord Tarel Goldtree, General of the Eastern Army.

"S'man's got him!" he shouted, halfway between elated and terrified. "He's got Lord Goldtree!"

He lowered the spike until it rested under the dazed Goldtree's jaw, below the protection of his war mask but above the collar of his coat-of-nails, and looked around. The clash had been short, but brutal: all but three of Goldtree's escort were dying or down, and over half of Marin's group were in a similarly bad situation. Even as Marin watched, the last sar fell, pierced by two spears. The other two men broke and ran back the way they had come: a blade found the back of one, but the other managed to get to the dubious safety of the main body of Eastern Army soldiery, still locked in sprawling combat with the forces under Mordokel's command.

At any moment, Marin realised, the rear of Goldtree's forces could turn and come for them, and they would not last more than a few seconds.

"Help s'man get him up!" he shouted at those left with him. "He's the key to this!"

Three men came to help hoist the wobbly general to his feet, while others grabbed fallen weapons if they were better than the ones they already carried. One of Marin's companions took up Goldtree's longblade and held it towards his throat, but Marin slapped it away.

"No!" he snapped. "He'll open his own throat on it, that's the Code of Honour!" The others looked at him blankly, and Marin sighed. "Look, s'man's married to a sar, he knows what he's talking about. Don't let Lord Goldtree get near a blade: just bring him, before the rest notice us!"

Northbank fell in under a day, which would have been a stain on the honour of any city, had it not been partially taken by its own populace, and had some of its defenders not turned their coats. The cost in lives would have been far higher had that not been the case, but even so, many soldiers died. Still, in the aftermath of the battle, when the remainder of the Eastern Army garrisoned at Northbank had surrendered themselves and realised that not only were their erstwhile enemies commanded by the Divine One and Taladhar Torgallen, but they had now been joined by Einan Coldbeck, the vast majority elected to join Tyrun's cause. The resulting boost in numbers swelled the Western Army – or the Divine Army, as it was now being called – to even larger than before the conflict had occurred.

"Two long-serving High Marshals on the same side?" Laz muttered, as he and Marin stood next to each other and waited for the Divine One to arrive. Laz had been among the Brotherhood warriors first through the Western Gate, but had come out of the fighting without so much as a scratch, which was something for which Marin had no problem offering up a prayer of thanks to either Nari or Tyrun, whichever was appropriate. "With Highbridge still in the north, and Brightwater dead? It's going to be a rare soldier who turns his back on this force, whatever Natan might have decreed."

"Do you reckon it'll be enough?" Marin murmured back. "The South and the North could still rally behind the Sun Throne, especially if the new Southern Marshal is just the puppet people think he was appointed to be."

Laz shrugged. "Who can say?"

"It seems to this woman," Ravi said, from Laz's other side, "that it shouldn't come down to the size of the army. Surely it's about who is *right*?"

There was a yearning in her voice, and in her face, that had not been there since they had found Tyrun. Ever since that day, Ravi had seemed . . . settled. At peace. Now there was an edge to her once more. Marin wondered what had happened while he was in Northbank, but he had no time to ponder how to phrase that question, let alone the time in which to ask it, because the trumpets were sounding.

All those gathered in Northbank's main square – the officers of the army, high-ranking citizens of Northbank, and certain favoured members of the Godsworn – dropped to their knees as the Divine One appeared. Tyrun walked up onto the wooden platform erected at one side of it, followed by Mordokel, and Marshals Torgallen and Coldbeck. The platform was used for public addresses, and for public executions.

It seemed that it would see both, this evening.

"People of Northbank!" Tyrun said, raising His arms with a smile. "Rise."

They all did so, Marin not without a wince at a twinge in his back. Swinging a halberd could have unexpected consequences for those unused to such exertions.

"This god is so pleased to be within your walls," Tyrun continued. "He thanks all of you for your contributions: those who worked from within, those who were with Him without, and those who have turned from the pretender on the Sun Throne to join the true ruler of Narida."

A general swell of approval and gratitude travelled through the assembly, mixed with occasional cheers, but Tyrun raised His hands again, and the noise died down once more.

"Sadly," the Divine One continued, "there were some who did not heed this god's words. Some refused to accept His claim to the throne, and could not be allowed to join those that still wait to the east. We must mourn their foolishness."

Marin swallowed uncomfortably. The execution of those soldiers who would not swear allegiance to Tyrun had been carried out in a grimy corner of Northbank, but word had still got out of the blood running in the street.

"However, there is one death left to tally," Tyrun announced. "When this god was camped outside Northbank, His camp was approached by men carrying a message on behalf of Lord Tarel Goldtree. The message was one of insolence, and when they were rebuffed, they tried to kill this god."

Marin gaped in disbelief, and turned to look at Laz. "You didn't mention that!"

"Your husband was going to tell you about it later," Laz muttered, looking uncomfortable.

"These actions were carried out on the instruction of their commander," Tyrun said, and now His voice sounded like the tolling of a bell ringing out someone's doom. The crowd began to shout angrily: a message carried between commanders was one thing, but to send an assassin's blade along with it? Even in open warfare, that was not something to which anyone should countenance stooping. "Therefore, their commander will pay the price for his treachery. He was captured alive, by one of this god's most devoted servants."

Marin nearly swallowed his tongue as Tyrun's eyes found him unerringly in the crowd, despite how many people were standing between them. The gaze of the Divine One did not carry peace at the moment, however: merely a hard and furious vengeance. A few others followed their god's gaze, despite not knowing for whom they were looking, and various faces turned in Marin's direction. One caught his eye as being vaguely familiar, and he tried to get a better look, but someone else stepped between them.

For a moment, he could have sworn that had been the strange old man who had briefly confronted him when they first arrived at Tyrun's camp on the shores of the Greenbrook. The one who, when Marin had asked if he knew him, had laughed and replied, "Not yet".

"Bring forth the prisoner!" Tyrun declared, and Marin's attention refocused as Tarel Goldtree was dragged into view.

The former general of the Eastern Army was bound in

chains, hands behind his back and ankles shackled together. Marin had only really seen his eyes before, given that most of his face had been obscured by his war mask. Now he was bareheaded and dressed in nothing except the undergarments he would have worn beneath his armour, he was revealed as a man whose warrior braids were greying, but who had an athletic build. One of the men hauling him along – a member of the Godsworn, Marin noted, not a soldier – kicked him in the back of the leg and dropped him to his knees.

"In the aftermath of the attempt on this god's life, He called for Lord Goldtree's head to be brought to Him on a pike, and his entrails removed," Tyrun said, his words rolling out hard and clear across the square. "Now justice shall be performed."

He held out his hand, and Mordokel placed his own longblade into it. Tyrun did not hesitate; did not offer Lord Goldtree an opportunity to repent, or to take his own life. Instead he lashed out.

Not at the neck, in a decapitating strike, but across the belly. A bright red line began spreading outwards across Goldtree's front, and he would have slumped forward, but was held in place by the men with his chains in their hands.

Tyrun handed Mordokel's longblade back to him. Then, His expression grim, He rolled up the sleeves of his simple robes and reached out—

Marin looked away before he could see his god's justice. He turned his head and buried it into Laz's chest, instinctively seeking comfort from his husband. Laz's arm came up around his shoulders, pulling him in.

"By the Mountain," Marin heard Ravi say, in a small voice. All around them, however, cheering broke out. It was neither quite loud enough, nor at the right pitch, to fully drown out Lord Goldtree's screaming.

Tarel Goldtree had said little after he recovered his wits, but

Marin got no indication that he was a particularly evil man. He seemed a man caught in war, doing his best to discharge what he believed to be his duty. Misguided, perhaps. Arrogant, certainly, but that came with the territory of being a nobleman and a general. But did misguided arrogance deserve this death? Marin could not bring himself to believe that it did. Just like at the monastery, the reason this death was occurring in this manner, at this time, was down to the choices Marin had made; and once more, the red-hot blade of his piety was plunged into the quenching barrel of his guilt.

"This sar thinks," Laz said in a voice so low that only Marin and Ravi would be able to hear it, "that this is no longer a place in which he wishes to be."

Marin looked up at his husband's grim face, then sideways at Ravi. The healer's eyes were wide and terrified, and Marin saw her reach up to tug the neckline of her dress upwards in an unconscious movement before she nodded in agreement.

Marin swallowed. Tyrun was the Divine One. He was Nari reborn. He was the rightful God-King of Narida.

And He was terrifying.

He could be all of those things, without needing Marin of Idramar anywhere near Him.

"Agreed," he said softly. "First light?"

Laz nodded. "First light."

Bulang

M'bana led Bulang to what looked like an apothecary's shop, judging by the bunches of dried herbs that hung over the door under the shelter of the overhanging porch. A lantern still burned in one small window, throwing glimmers of light out over the darkened street. M'bana did not approach the front door, but cut down the side of the building instead. Bulang thought it risky to potentially intrude on someone who had anything to do with magic, but thëy were doing this for Jeya. M'bana did not seem to have any doubts, so thëy followed hîm to the rear of the building in time to see hîm knock on another door.

There was no answer.

Bulang looked expectantly at M'bana, but M'bana was looking nowhere except at the door, as though hê could make it be answered through sheer force of will. The nervous hope that had been collecting in Bulang's stomach began to sour.

"Ï thought yôu said—"

"Î know what Î said!" M'bana snapped, still not looking at thëm. "Î also said this was a bad idea!" Hê knocked again, louder and longer.

This time the door did jerk open, and both of them took half a step back in alarm.

For a moment Bulang thought they had somehow awakened

a spirit of the wood from which the door was made; one of the sprites rumoured to lurk in the high forests, which would take revenge on a person who cut down their tree. Then things flashed into focus in thëir mind, and thëy realised thëy were looking at someone wearing a wooden mask. A carved sunburst was visible on the brow, and beautifully detailed workings of leafy vines climbed up from the jaw and across the cheeks to terminate in flowers at the temple. There were two eyeholes, a few slits in front of the mouth, and a slight protrusion for the nose, but otherwise the face beneath was essentially invisible.

"What do you want?" the masked figure demanded. Their head tilted slightly. "I don't know you yet."

"Yet?" Bulang managed to squeak.

"You're at my door," the figure replied. "I know you now, hee? How well I shall know you remains to be seen. What do you want?"

Bulang looked at M'bana, who glanced back at thëm nervously. Now it came to it, it sounded like a ridiculous thing to say, but what option did they have? What option did Jeya have?

"A friend of ours has been kidnapped," Bulang said. "We need help to free them."

The mask did not move, but even though thëy could not see anything in the dim light, Bulang got the distinct impression that the figure's eyes were now studying thëm.

"And what makes you think I can assist?"

Bulang looked at M'bana again, really not sure what to say to this. M'bana swallowed.

"I was told there was a magician here. Who ... helped people sometimes."

"That's a tall tale you've been told, and I would like to know who told it to you," the masked figure replied.

"A friend of mine called Damau," M'bana said.

"An easy tactic, to blame one who is no longer with us," the masked figure said. "However, that name is known to me. You claim to be friends of Damau?"

"I'm not," Bulang said immediately, not wanting to be caught in a lie, even by omission. "I never knew them."

"Let me see your face," the masked figure said, beckoning to M'bana, who took an uncertain step forward. The figure reached out a hand and cupped hîs face, turning it this way and that, although Bulang could not understand what they hoped to make out, given the gloom in which they were all standing.

"Hmm," was all the figure said, when they lowered their hand again.

"Please," Bulang said. "Our friend who's been kidnapped was the one who came up with the plan to stop Damau's murderer. If you knew Damau, and valued them at all, can you help us?"

The mask did turn towards Bulang now. Then it grunted.

"You can come in. You," the figure pointed at M'bana, "stay out here."

M'bana raised hîs hands in appeasement. "No problem."

It's a problem for më, Bulang wanted to say, but there was nothing for it. The masked figure stood back from the doorway, and Bulang stepped across the threshold after them. The door swung shut, and the latch clicked into place with an awful finality.

"There was love in your voice," the masked figure said, laying a hand on Bulang's shoulder. It felt surprisingly hot and heavy. "With love, we can maybe do something. Let us see." They moved ahead of Bulang, a patch of slightly more solid darkness within the deep shadows of the hallway, then pushed open a door. The room beyond was lit: not brightly, but it seemed so in comparison. The magician – for so they had to be – was silhouetted against the light, and beckoned Bulang after them without turning. "Come."

Bulang found thëmself in what thëy would have once considered a small room, but perhaps not so much by the standards of most of East Harbour. It was certainly made to feel smaller by the amount of things crowded around the edges. All manner of strange items and devices were stacked on shelves or piled in corners. Some were easy to explain, like the jars and sacks that likely contained the ingredients an apothecary would use in their remedies. Others were more esoteric, such as the glass jars in which unfamiliar objects lurked, half-obscured by cloudy fluids; the small dragon skeleton bound into a life-like position by wire and glue that reared up on one shelf; or what looked like some sort of flute carved from crystal, hanging by a leather cord from the ceiling.

"Sit," the magician instructed, pointing to a cushion beneath where the dragon reared. Bulang lowered themself down cautiously, but nothing sprang up from the shadows to attack or devour them.

"Now then," the magician said, doing the same, and placing their hands on their knees. Bulang noticed that their knuckles were swollen, and their skin deeply lined. "Tell me who your friend is."

"Their name is Jeya," Bulang began. "They're an orphan, they—"

"Ah," the magician tutted, holding up one hand. "I do not need to know their *name*. I need to know who they *are*. Any two people can share a name. What is it that makes them special to you?"

Bulang paused. It felt strange to voice it, especially to another person. However, the magician was clearly waiting.

"They're beautiful," thëy began. "Both on the surface, and

deeper. They are brave, and kind, and generous. And mischievous," thëy added honestly. "They saved my life. They want the best for everyone."

"Hmm." The magician rubbed their fingers together. "Do you know where they are, or is this something else you require help with?"

"We think they're on a ship in the harbour, but I don't know which one," Bulang admitted. "M'bana does. That's the person with me," thëy added.

"The harbour," the magician murmured, then chuckled dustily. "That does not narrow it down all that much, hee? No matter."

"I can go and get M'bana," Bulang suggested. "They could—"

"Sit where you are," the magician replied, before thëy had even begun to shift thëir weight. "That detail is not so important as the love in you, we can proceed without it." They rubbed their fingers together again. "You have desperation, too; that can assist, although it must be harnessed carefully. But there will be a cost. Do you have any understanding how magic works, child?"

"No," Bulang answered, looking at the magician warily, and suddenly aware that thëy should have perhaps thought on this more before venturing so gladly into this parlour. What would be needed? Blood? Bone? All the gruesome childhood stories of witches floated up into thëir mind again, clamouring for attention with snippets of grisly detail.

"Of course you do not," the magician said, with another chuckle. "Were that so, you might not need my assistance. I cannot overpower your love's captors, nor give you the strength to do so. However, I may be able to even the odds a little, if you are prepared to take action yourself."

"I am," Bulang said instantly. "I think M'bana will too, maybe some others. We just need a *chance*."

"That is the desperation I spoke of," the magician said, although their voice sounded approving. "But you must understand, power can be moved and redirected, but it cannot simply be brought forth. A connection must be found. What gods do you worship, child?"

"I . . ." Bulang hesitated. "I don't know, I thought I . . . I was raised to believe in Nari," thëy said, deciding that was the safest wording which was still reasonably honest. "However, I'm not sure any longer."

"The Naridan màn-god?" The magician's voice sounded as though it was touching the words with tongs to avoid coming into contact with them. "Hè hoards his power jealously, and will be of little use to us. There is a reason Naridan witches make their bargains with spirits."

Bulang swallowed, feeling like thëy should defend thëir heritage and bloodline, but equally certain that this was neither the time nor the place for words that might have been misguided in any case. Besides, if thëy truly were the heir of Nari, would thëy need a magician's help to save the person thëy loved?

Caution made them guard thëir tongue, as well. This magician who hid their face behind a mask of wood was a questionable ally borne of desperation, and their allegiance was by no means certain should they learn Bulang's true identity.

"What about your friend?" the magician asked. "What powers might care for them?"

"I know they honour Jakahama, and Mushuru, and Sa," Bulang said. "They thought . . . That is, they said Sa appeared to them once. And the night they were taken, I heard a golden-maned monkey calling in alarm."

The magician leaned forward, and Bulang did not think thëy were imagining the intense scrutiny coming from behind the mask's eyeholes. "Mushuru is a dead god, whose influence in the world is weak. One cannot burn to ashes and still hold power, hee?" They chuckled. "Jakahama comes and goes, but shē would be better invoked if your friend were near death. The monkey god, though, the god of thieves and tricksters, among other things? If your friend has a connection to Sa, that is a god who might delight in blinding the eyes and binding the hands of those who consider themselves powerful. Sa could be the ally your friend needs, although the monkey god is no god of mine."

Bulang swallowed, caution warring with eagerness. "You said there would be a cost."

"There is," the magician replied. "But not, perhaps, in the sense that you are thinking. This is not a service that can be paid for with copper or silver."

"I suspected as much," Bulang said grimly. "What do you require from me?"

The magician sat back and said nothing for a few moments, the wooden mask giving no clue as to their expression. Then they spoke again:

"I need you to bring me a golden-maned monkey."

Bulang screwed thëir face up in consternation. "You need me to bring you *what*?"

"The power must be moved, child," the magician said flatly. "Sa is no god of mine, you recall? Nor are they yours. I must have a connection to them, and for that I need a vessel with which they are associated. An adult monkey will do."

Bulang peered at them distrustfully. "That's it? You simply need a monkey, nothing more?"

"There are so many gods here," the magician observed lazily. "I have not yet had the opportunity to make a connection with Sa, and this will be a valuable opportunity to do so." Their head tilted to one side. "Perhaps you would prefer a more tangible cost, like one of your own hands?"

"No!" Bulang said instantly, trying not to yelp. "No, that's fine. I'll get you the monkey."

"Very well," the magician said, with a nod. "You understand that I cannot do what must be done until I have the vessel? It will take some time, thereafter. Not too long," they added, as Bulang's face fell, "but I cannot present you with your assistance as soon as you return."

"But I don't know how much time Jeya has!" Bulang said desperately. "We don't even know what they're planning for her!"

"Then I suggest you move as quickly as you may," the magician replied. "I have agreed to help, if you can provide me with what I need. I have no more control over another's timing or intentions than I do over the sun or the moons. I can offer nothing else to you."

"Then I'll get you the monkey," Bulang said, getting to thëir feet, even though thëy were wrestling with the urge to denounce the entire thing as a waste of time, march to the harbour, and try to free Jeya there and then. However, if that had been a viable plan, thëy would have already tried it. There simply was not an obvious way onto a ship crewed by Kurumaya's thugs that did not involve invoking some form of help, and it seemed the magician was, unfortunately, the only even vaguely realistic source of that.

The magician's offer might not be much, but it was something.

M'bana was still waiting outside, and hîs head jerked up nervously as the door opened. Relief flooded across hîs face as Bulang stepped out, and began to recede again as the door shut behind thëm.

"What happened?" M'bana asked anxiously. "What did they say? Did they help?"

"They say they will," Bulang told hîm, "but we're going to need a few things first."

M'bana looked at thëm quizzically. "What sort of things?"

Bulang bit thëir lip thoughtfully. "Fruit, and a basket."

"Î've got both of those," M'bana said slowly. "But why?"

"And a net," Bulang added, running things through thëir head. "Something like a fishing net, but not a huge one."

M'bana's eyes narrowed. "This is getting stranger. What does a magician need with these things?"

"It's not the magician that needs them, it's us," Bulang said. "Come on. If we can pick the fruit and the basket up, maybe we can find a net on the docks, if we're careful not to be seen."

"But *why* do we need them?" M'bana protested, as Bulang headed back towards the street. Bulang hesitated, but this was going to sound just as odd no matter when thëy said it, so thëy might as well get it out of the way now.

"We need to catch a monkey."

Marin

Northbank was in that special sort of chaos that occurred in the aftermath of a major shift of power, when all the same things still needed to be done, but were now being done by different people, or by the same people under different instructions. The guards on the North Gate did not seem particularly sure whether they were meant to be stopping anyone from entering or leaving, or if so, who, so it was a simple matter for Marin, Laz, and Ravi to wander out by dint of looking unthreatening and unimportant.

Then they were back on the Crown Road again, heading north into a new day. The weather was not as appropriate as Marin might have wished, given that instead of a bright dawn and clear skies to mark this new chapter of his life, a featureless, low bank of dull grey cloud had rolled in to smother the entire sky. However, the most important thing was that he was heading away from Northbank, a city he had now visited twice, and of which he had almost entirely unpleasant memories.

"So what happened to you?" he asked Ravi, once they had put a bend and a bank of trees between them and Northbank's walls. It was not as though being in sight of the city meant there was risk of being overheard, but Marin still felt more comfortable once he could no longer imagine curious eyes watching his back as he walked away.

"What do you mean?" Ravi said, frowning at him.

"Last time s'man saw you, you were pretty adamant that Tyrun could do no wrong," Marin said. "But now you're tagging along with us again."

Ravi pulled her cloak slightly tighter around her shoulders. "Even Crown Roads aren't always safe places. It makes sense to travel with a talented warrior when you can."

"S'man's not disputing that," Marin said with a laugh. "He's just wondering why you decided to leave the Divine One's side."

He was sure he did not imagine the slight shudder that ran through Ravi. "S'woman went to the Divine One's side when He was injured by the attackers. She cleaned the wound and stitched it. And . . . " She trailed off.

"You didn't think He could be injured?" Marin said. He was not entirely sure that he had, either. Oh, he had tackled Elifel to the ground when the man had drawn his knife, but that had been a reflex. Marin had desperately wanted to ensure that no harm came to Tyrun, even if part of him did not consider that it was particularly likely, or even possible.

"It wasn't that," Ravi said, shaking her head. "Divine One or not, He . . . He is made the same as us, flesh and blood. Nari was a man: that's why He was such a great warrior, because He *could* have fallen in battle at any time, but He always won."

Marin opened his mouth to point out that actually, some scholars differed on that point, but Laz nudged him, and he shut his mouth again.

"It was just that . . . He was so *angry*," Ravi continued, looking down at her feet as they walked. "S'woman remembers how He was when we first met Him. He was calm and peaceful, even when Elifel had tried to stab Him. This was different. You remember how He would thank you?"

Marin nodded. He did.

"There was nothing of that about Him," Ravi said sadly. "He snapped and shouted, as though He thought the wound in His chest was s'woman's fault because she was not able to do her work quicker, or painlessly. S'woman did her best!" she blurted out suddenly. "She'd be surprised if anyone in the camp could have done better! And then, with that . . . *display* yesterday . . ." She shuddered. "S'woman will be honest, she dared not stay. What if she was called to attend the Divine One again for some reason, and she displeased Him further? What if He takes issue with her stitching, or the way His wound heals?"

Marin nodded again, gloomily. "Perhaps it is the way of gods to be disappointed in their followers." *But s'man never thought he would be disappointed in his god, and yet here he is, walking away from Him.*

They had no real destination in mind, other than putting the Divine Army and all the risks associated with it behind them, so they headed north on the basis that the Crown Road towards Wousewold Haste made for the easiest going. They could have stopped in the small town of Dayrun for the third evening, but travellers from the south would almost certainly be asked for news, and they had no wish to discuss their business with inquisitive locals. This was still Coldbeck land, after all, and news that the former Eastern Marshal was not only alive and well, but now at the Divine One's side, would probably be the source of great rejoicing: or possibly great tension, depending on whether or not the locals supported King Natan. Either way, they would draw attention, and none of them wanted to answer questions about why they were trying to get away from such momentous events.

So it was that instead of an inn's beds, or even a comfortable hayloft, the three of them did their best to bed down in a dell just off the road and to the north of Dayrun. It had a small stream at the bottom, flanked by silverbarks, and was quite a beautiful place: or, Marin considered, would have been in bright sunlight. Instead, the cloud that had found them on the day they left Northbank not only rendered the dell into a dull, oddly shadowless world, but had also chosen today to begin gifting them with a steady drizzle. It was not quite rain, but heavier and more persistent than mist, and somehow seemed more pervasive than either.

"S'woman's beginning to think that inquisitive locals might be preferable to this," Ravi complained. She had her hood over her head and her cloak drawn around her as much as possible, and resembled nothing so much as a particularly sulky package as she sat on the ground and watched Marin trying unsuccessfully to coax some twigs into catching light.

"One night out in the rain won't kill you," Laz said. He was standing farther up the slope of the dell, one hand on the hilt of his longblade, looking out into the rapidly encroaching gloom. Sunset was impossible to make out, thanks to the grey blanket of the sky, but the light was definitely going.

"S'woman's been on the road before, you know," Ravi commented sourly. "With you, you might recall. She's not bothered by rain so much as she is by the wild dragons that might come upon us in the night, should we not have a fire to ward them off."

"Dayrun's not large, but this sar doubts any predators will come this close to it," Laz said. "We're not out in the wilds yet."

"You're volunteering to take first watch, then?" Ravi asked.

"If you're the one worried about dragons, perhaps you should," Marin said, prodding his kindling and striking a spark from his flint and steel for the fifth time, which still refused to catch. "S'man wouldn't trust his husband to stay awake."

"That's hardly fair," Laz said mildly, looking around.

"Your husband loves you, Laz," Marin told him, resisting the impulse to swear at kindling, "but it's true. The ability of a warrior to sleep in virtually any situation is a well-known quality, which you have elevated to an art form. It just also happens even when you don't intend it to."

"You're just envious," Laz said, looking away again.

"Of course your husband's envious!" Marin said, sitting back on his haunches and scowling at the fire, or more accurately, the complete lack of fire. "He would *love* to be able to get to sleep as quickly as you do! But no, *he* has to lay awake listening to you just . . . breathing." He snorted. "It would be infuriating, if it wasn't so endearing."

Laz chuckled. "That's the price you pay for having such an active mind, dear. You might know the names of the stars, and the beasts, and what a God-King two centuries ago had to break his fast, but all that knowledge doesn't go away when you want it to. Your husband's sure all the thoughts just chase each other around inside your skull and make it so you can't sleep."

"The pair of you are sickening," Ravi put in. "Even your *arguments* are sickening." She huddled even further into her cloak, arms crossed atop her knees so that only her eyes and the top of her nose were visible beneath her hood. "Why can't you argue like normal people, and actually insult each other?"

"This man hates to break it to you," Marin told her, "but insulting your husband is hardly the best way to maintain a marriage."

"Besides which, we both already know our faults," Laz added. "There seems little point drawing further attention to them." He turned around again, and took a step further into the dell. "Do you want your husband to have a go, Mar?"

"Are you suggesting your husband doesn't know how to light a fire?" Marin protested.

"Not at all," Laz replied. "Your husband's seen you do it countless times, but if it doesn't catch and we spend the night without one, we're both going to wonder whether someone else could have managed it, so we might as well find out."

"Fine," Marin said. In all honesty, the notion of actually having a fire far outweighed the embarrassment he would feel if it turned out Laz could light it. "Just don't gloat."

"When has your husband ever gloated?" Laz protested as he approached. Marin opened his mouth, and Laz raised a hand to stall him. "Relating to you, that is. Other people don't count."

Marin threw the flint and steel to him. "Here. Knock yourself out."

Laz caught them, and crouched down to take a look. Marin had placed the fuel as much under the shelter of a tree's branches as he could, but it was still getting damper and damper. "Let's see what—"

"We're not alone," Ravi interrupted him, standing up and turning to face the lip of the dell. Marin stood too, and unsheathed his belt knife. Laz followed suit a moment later, his longblade slipping out of its blackened sheath without so much as a whisper.

"Who's there?" Laz shouted. Marin knew that the question would have sounded tremulous and scared coming from his mouth, but his husband's voice made it into a threat.

"Is that you down there, Sar Alazar?" someone called. Marin peered up at the shapes that were just visible in the burgeoning darkness. He could barely make out the outlines of people at this distance, but the voice sounded familiar. In fact, he could place it.

"Bones?" he asked, surprised. Laz grunted, but did not lower his sword. Nor would Marin have wanted him to.

"Evening to you too, Marin," the voice called back, and the shapes came closer. Three of them, slightly darker than the sky beyond, blending down into the ground once they began to dip below the skyline as they descended. The one in the lead threw back his hood, and the remnants of the day's light revealed a face dominated by the strongly sculpted cheekbones that had given Adal his nickname.

"Who're your friends?" Ravi demanded. The other two newcomers revealed themselves as well, and Marin's stomach tightened slightly as he saw Gershan and Aranel's features. That made three of the six Eastern Army soldiers who had come with them the first time they had fled Northbank. Elifel had been killed when he tried to stab Tyrun, of course, but . . .

"Where are Kenan and Channa?" Marin asked. "If the three of you are here, s'man's surprised not to see them."

Gershan swallowed audibly, and his voice was bleak when he answered. "S'man's brother didn't survive Northbank."

"Channa did, but she took a spear in the leg," Aranel said. "Even assuming she keeps the limb, she won't be walking anywhere for a while."

"Sorry to hear that," Marin said automatically. "Both of them."

"This sar's more concerned about why you're here," Laz said cautiously. "Mighty strange that you should be coming this way, seeing as how the Divine Army was heading east, let alone that you should chance upon us."

"There's no chance involved," Bones said simply. "Just the Divine One's will. Your absence was noticed, and He's disappointed. As your former companions, we've been sent to find you, and bring you back."

Shit. Marin glanced to the sides, but could not see anything to suggest anyone else was sneaking up on them. "And the Divine One thought you'd be able to persuade us?"

"You all remember about that honour duel back in Idramar, right?" Laz asked. "You know this sar was Princess Tila's champion? So you can maybe understand that he doesn't want to hang around, now Einan Coldbeck is back in the picture? Coldbeck strikes this sar as a man who might hold a grudge."

"The Eastern Marshal's opinion doesn't matter," Bones said with a chuckle. "Only the Divine One's does. If He doesn't want you harmed, you won't be harmed." He smiled. "Come on, Sar Alazar. We went in search of the Divine One together! Can't you trust s'man?"

"You were planning to stick a knife in the Divine One all that time, so no, this sar doesn't trust you as far as he can throw you," Laz said flatly. "Stop where you are, all of you."

Their three former companions stopped walking, a few paces away, but Marin could practically taste the tension in the air.

"Let's say you try to convince us to go back to the Divine Army," he said carefully, "and we refuse. What happens then?"

"Marin!" Aranel said, shocked. "The Divine One wants you back at his side! *You!* We're only here because Mordokel remembered us, and came to find us to perform this task: the Divine One knows your name, and wants your counsel! Why would you refuse that? S'man would give his right arm for that honour!"

"You're wasting your breath," Gershan said in a low, bitter voice. "He's asking the question because he's already decided. They're not faithful anymore."

"It might just be that s'man doesn't believe you," Marin countered. He was fairly sure he could see where this was going to end, but he was going to try to avoid that outcome if possible.

"The fact you left without telling anyone makes you look guilty," Bones said. "The Divine One's willing to give you a chance to go back to Him, Marin, but you've got to take it gladly, with both hands!"

"S'woman will go back," Ravi announced, stepping forward.

Marin gaped at her. "What are you—"

"A few days on the road with you two has reminded s'woman that tents and roofs are *greatly* preferable to trees and roots," Ravi said dryly. "This was a mistake. Besides, it sounds like Channa needs someone competent to take a look at her leg. There may still be time to deal with it." She walked between Gershan and Bones, and came to a halt behind them. "Come on, blacksword. You know how this is going to go."

Marin looked at his husband, but Laz did not so much as twitch a lip at the jibe. "That rather depends on our friends here. They can accept our answer and turn around, and we can all go our own way."

"The Divine One wants to you return," Bones said, and he took a step forward, mirrored a moment later by the other two. "If you don't do that, you don't get to go your own way."

"This sar kind of likes all of you," Laz said. "Or he did, anyway. Are you sure you want to do this?"

"You're outnumbered three to one, Alazar," Aranel said gruffly. "We all know Marin doesn't fight."

"Hey!" Marin protested. "S'man captured Lord Goldtree!"

Laz rolled his shoulders. "He did, you know. Besides, this sar has faced worse odds." He drew his shortblade, then passed it back to Marin. "Take this."

Marin took hold of the hilt gingerly, the weight of it unfamiliar in his hand. He had not spent much time with Laz's weapons: husbands or no, a sar's blades were still very much their individual property, and Marin had never been able to pick up much from the times Laz had tried to give him pointers on the use of a sword. All the same, the shortblade was longer and keener than his belt knife, so it was a good thing to have to hand in the current circumstances.

The three soldiers drew their respective swords. They were

simple straight swords, nothing like as well-made as a sar's long-blade, but perfectly sufficient to end a life with violence. Bones had only joined the Eastern Army just before it had left Idramar, but Livnya the Knife had intended him to kill Tyrun, so he presumably had some skill with weapons. Gershan and Aranel were old hands, and had probably trained with their blades to some extent. Marin did not fancy his chances against either of them.

The three men took another step closer, and then another. Laz did not move. Marin knew his husband was an excellent judge of exactly how close someone could get to him before he could cut them, but this was not like that time in the Alaban fighting pit, when he was up against three amateurs. These three were probably going to work as a unit, or near enough, and even Laz would be hard-pressed to take all of them down . . .

Ravi reached around from behind Bones and grabbed his wrist, pressing into it with her thumbs. The young man dropped his sword, shrieking in pain that Marin remembered well, from when Ravi had done the same thing to him through the bars of their neighbouring cells in the Idramar jail. Gershan and Aranel both started in surprise, and looked instinctively towards their suddenly stricken companion.

Laz moved.

He flowed towards Gershan, who was on the side of Bones's sword arm. The soldier dragged his attention back to Laz, but the momentary distraction had cost him. He retreated desperately, trying to block Laz's cuts.

Marin screamed, and rushed at Aranel, but he was neither as quick nor as close as his husband had been to Gershan, nor nearly as intimidating. Aranel snarled and swung his sword, and Marin only just managed to kill his own momentum in time for the point to skim past his ribs. He stabbed out with Laz's shortblade in a clumsy feint that was well short of landing: the old veteran completely ignored it, and made a lunge that Marin had to skip back from hurriedly.

"Captured Lord Goldtree, s'man's arse!" Aranel spat.

"Did so!" Marin retorted breathlessly. He had two weapons to Aranel's one, which should surely give him some sort of advantage, but he could not for the life of him figure out how he was supposed to reach the man with either without getting spitted on Aranel's sword in the process.

Someone screamed, off to his left, the sort of sound that implied the person who made it would not be alive for much longer to make many more. Marin did not dare look to see who it was: he simply backed away another step, praying he would not trip over anything.

Of course, those prayers might no longer be going to someone with any interest in heeding him.

"C'mere!" Aranel spat, making another lunge towards the left side of Marin's chest. Marin backpedalled to his right, something caught at his ankle, and he fell backwards into the mess of sticks he had been attempting to set light to before everything started to go wrong. Panic grabbed him, and he tried to scrabble back up to his feet and slash with the short-blade to ward Aranel off at the same time, with a significant lack of success at either. He heard the veteran cough a laugh and saw his sword draw back . . .

. . . and then Aranel coughed again, weaker and pained this time, as something bulged outwards from his chest. Marin could only stare in confusion for a moment, wondering if one of the man's ribs had somehow snapped outwards, or something equally bizarre. Then Aranel's knees crumpled, and he collapsed unsteadily to slide forwards off what proved to be Bones's blade, wielded by Ravi.

Marin managed to get up to his feet this time, and looked around. The relief he had felt at Aranel's fall redoubled as he saw Laz walking towards him, away from the dark, crumpled shape that had to be Gershan, and past the body of Bones.

"Give s'woman that," Ravi said, holding her hand out towards the shortblade.

"What?" Marin stared at her. "Why? And, er, thanks, by the way."

"He's not dead yet, and we should kill him quickly," Ravi said shortly, as Aranel stirred, and Marin jumped. He handed her the blade, and she bent down to swiftly open the soldier's throat. Aranel gurgled, but even though Marin could barely see it, the speed at which the blood leaked out suggested he would not be suffering for long.

"Are you hurt?" Laz asked. "Either of you?"

"Fine," Marin said quickly. Hopefully, Laz would not have noticed that he fell over the fire.

"Fine," Ravi confirmed, although her voice did not sound certain.

"Was this your first time killing someone?" Laz asked, sympathetically.

"S'woman's seen worse," Ravi answered shortly, which was not precisely an answer. Marin had an involuntary image of a memory that was not his, but been described to him: Ravi watching her aunt burning alive, and being unable to do anything about it unless she wanted to share the same fate.

Laz sighed. "We can either cart the bodies somewhere else, or we can take our stuff and find somewhere different to camp. Fire or not, this sar doesn't want to spend the night this close to them: they *will* draw predators in."

"Let's just move on," Marin suggested. "There's probably too much blood here anyway."

"Agreed," Ravi said. She handed Laz's shortblade back to him, then looked at Marin. "You didn't think s'woman was actually going to go with them, did you?"

Marin hunched his shoulder defensively. "It seemed odd, but . . . Well, you're a convincing actress, and that's all s'man has to say on it."

"S'woman left her satchel behind," Ravi said testily, picking up the item in question from where it still sat on the ground. "She thought you would've realised she wouldn't have done that."

"It's fair to say s'man's thoughts were elsewhere," Marin muttered. He scooped up the driest of the kindling, and as many of the sticks he had already gathered as he could carry. "Come on, then. Let's try this again."

Ravi, it seemed, had no intention of leaving Bones's sword behind. Marin took Aranel's, at Laz's urging: he found the notion uncomfortable, but the world was getting more and more dangerous, and perhaps an obvious weapon might deter trouble before it even looked his way. The three of them found their way back to the road and walked on for a while longer until a bank rose on their left, crowned with pines. It was well and truly dark now, but there was little wind to make them regret taking a higher campsite, and with any luck it would be drier than next to a stream. Marin gathered a handful of resinous pine needles, and what sticks he could find, and began to work on the fire again. Laz sat against a tree trunk and pretended he was not dozing off, and Ravi did something which involved rummaging in her satchel and muttering. If anyone had asked Marin's opinion, he would have conjectured that she was still working through the shock of killing two men, but no one did, and so he said nothing.

At least, until he was bent over with his arse in the air, the third time he managed to get some sort of flame to briefly catch in his kindling, and the light it cast revealed a pair of boots standing a few paces away from him.

"Well, Marin," a voice said. "You've well and truly fucked *everything*, haven't you?"

Marin gasped in shock, and wrenched his new sword from its scabbard to point it at the newcomer. "Who are you?!"

His companions were up within a moment, but Marin already knew the answer to his own question, at least in part. In the heartbeat or so before his miserable attempt at a fire died yet again, it faintly illuminated the face of the old man from Tyrun's camp on the Greenbrook; the old man whom Marin thought he had seen once more in the square, just prior to Lord Goldtree's execution.

"This man's had many names, over the years," came the reply from the newly returned darkness. "But you're most likely to know him by the first one he ever carried.

"Tolkar."

Alazar

Alazar stared at the dark shape that had, for a moment, been illuminated as an old man, and kept a firm grip on his longblade. "That's a big claim, not to mention a ridiculous one."

"'Ridiculous' is very much a matter of perspective," came back the voice. "You were prepared to believe Tyrun's claim; what's so different about this one?"

"We stood in the Divine One's presence and felt the power of His spirit!" Ravi snapped. The old man sighed.

"You need a demonstration? Very well. You seem to have had some trouble with your fire. That's understandable, in this rain. Perhaps this man can help you with that." The shape shifted and shrank, in a way that suggested squatting down. Alazar squinted, trying to make out what the man was doing, but it seemed to be nothing more than passing his hands above the wood. Then the old man grunted, there was a spark, and—

Whoomph

—the fire caught.

However, instead of the small, flickering tongues of a new fire, this set most of the sticks Marin had gathered alight at once, and these flames were tinged with purple. Alazar shielded his eyes from the new light with one hand, but kept his longblade pointing at the old man, who was now shuffling backwards with a wide smile on his face.

"Hah!" the man who called himself Tolkar barked in delight, shaking out one hand. "That never gets old."

"That's witchcraft!" Ravi hissed. The healer had her sword drawn as well, and she looked like she was about to fly at the old man and attack him, unnatural fire or no.

"It's *sorcery*, Ravi," Tolkar said witheringly, gesturing with a hand at the fire. "You're welcome."

"Tolkar's dead," Marin said shakily. "He's been dead for centuries. S'man doesn't know who you are, but you can't be Tolkar!"

"Interestingly, Tolkar's death was never recorded," Tolkar replied, sitting down cross-legged, laying his staff across his knees, and his swollen-knuckled hands atop that. "He left Idramar shortly after Nari died, of course, but unlike the other notable figures of that era, nothing is known of his end." He looked at them all, and cocked an eyebrow. "Doesn't that strike you as odd?"

"Not everyone's death is recorded," Alazar pointed out. "Some people die out in the wild, without anyone else knowing," he added, pointedly.

"Is that supposed to be a threat, Sar Alazar?" Tolkar asked. "This man presumes you killed those three that Mordokel sent after you. Mordokel," he added, and spat. "That's a man far too full of himself."

"Knowing our names isn't impressive," Marin said warningly. "S'man saw you in the Divine One's camp, you could have easily learned them there."

"This man isn't trying to *impress* you, he's trying to make you listen," Tolkar said wearily. "Will you sit down? You're more likely to listen when you're sitting down and comfortable, and you're making this man's legs ache, just standing there. The fire is warm, and it won't hurt you unless you do something foolish, like put your hand into it."

The flames were losing their unnatural hue. Alazar looked at Marin, and then at Ravi. The old man did not seem to be a threat, other than his apparent ability to summon purple fire: which was certainly a concern, but would how close he was make any difference to that?

Alazar had seen many strange things in the years he had travelled around the world. Purple flames were a new one, but he was a practical man at heart. Tolkar had lit their fire, and now they had light and warmth. That was not something to be disregarded.

"Fine," he said, stepping closer to the flames — which did indeed give off warmth, so they were no illusion — and sinking down to the ground. "Speak your piece."

He kept his longblade drawn and held across his lap in the same manner as the old man had his staff. He saw Tolkar's eyes stray to the sword, but the supposed sorcerer said nothing.

Marin and Ravi followed suit a couple of heartbeats later, although neither looked happy at the idea. Tolkar, however, clapped his hands and smiled as though they were old friends reuniting for the first time in many years.

"That's better, isn't it?" he said happily. "Now then—"

"First things first," Marin interrupted. "If you're claiming to be Tolkar, you're going to have to tell us how that's possible. Tolkar got older at the same rate as everyone else: he was a young man when Nari first appeared, and was starting to go grey by the time Nari died: contemporary sources agree on that."

"Huh, listen to the university scholar," Tolkar said, pulling a face. "So convinced that men have learned all there is to know!" He sighed. "If you want the very, very simple version: flesh ages, but the spirit is eternal. This is not the body that this man was born into. All one has to do is . . . find a new vessel."

Alazar tightened his grip on his longblade's hilt. "That *is* witchcraft."

"That's what the Unmaker did!" Ravi said, her eyes wide. "She stole bodies!"

"The Unmaker had the way of it, that's true," Tolkar said calmly, as though he had not just confessed to a practice from the darkest corner of myth and rumour. "It's a handy practice though, when the need calls for it. This man can't remember all the people whose bodies he's been through, now, but they're all in here somewhere." He tapped the side of his head. "He can hear them talking, if he concentrates. In fact, most of the time, the trick is to *not* listen to them. By the way, don't call the Unmaker 'she', for pity's sake," he added. "It's a demon, not a woman."

Alazar frowned. "A she-demon, though."

Tolkar groaned, and rubbed his forehead. "Fucking Gemar. A brilliant general, but quite the most unpleasant person this man's ever met, and given how long this man's been walking the world, that should tell you something. Gemar got it into his head that there are such things as 'she-demons', because he hated women, for some reason that this man never bothered to investigate further. And look where that's left us."

"All the records of the time—" Marin began, outraged.

"*Gemar burned everything he didn't agree with!*" Tolkar shouted. "The man was an arsehole, but he wasn't a fool! He knew he had one shot at remoulding into his own image what Nari built, and he wasn't going to let anyone contradict him. That's why this man disappeared when he did," he added, prodding at the dirt with the forefinger of one hand, and not looking at any of them. "He'd have probably ended up like Nari, otherwise."

". . . What do you mean, 'ended up like Nari'?" Alazar demanded.

Tolkar did not look up. "Nari's deathbed wasn't a deathbed until Gemar Far Garadh entered that room, that's all this man is saying."

Alazar controlled his anger, with some effort. "General Gemar is the father of the Code of Honour! He set down the framework for every thane, every sar in this land!"

"He was all those things, and a vicious, disloyal bastard to boot," Tolkar said dismissively. "Truly honourable people don't go writing things called a 'Code of Honour', because truly honourable people expect others to do the right thing without needing to be told! Gemar wrote those rules because he was scared of other people betraying *him*. Those that write the rules rarely intend to follow them."

"This is ridiculous," Marin said flatly. "Not only do you expect us to believe that you're Tolkar the Last Sorcerer, you want us to believe General Gemar killed the God-King? Why not murder Nari's son as well, in that case?"

"Too obvious," Tolkar said, as though the question was ridiculous. "And unnecessary. The boy was a child, and Gemar claimed that Nari – on his deathbed, mind you – had created the post of Eastern Marshal, and granted it to Gemar. Gemar got to solidify his power, control a puppet ruler, and shape the kingdom as he saw fit. He was God-King in all but name! No wonder you fucked everything up," he added under his breath. Marin bristled, but it was Ravi who spoke next.

"And what did you do?" she demanded. "You're saying that you just hid for centuries? You didn't do anything to try to stop him?"

"Gemar was always better-liked than this man," Tolkar said, eyeing her. "You'd have thought that going into the caves of Spirithome with Nari and helping defeat the Unmaker might have made people see that this man was not one of the demon's witches, but no such luck. He was never properly trusted by anyone except Nari, so he didn't have much basis on which to challenge Gemar. Besides, the Morlithians started stealing all the magic," he added.

Alazar blinked. "What? Stealing magic?"

"*Yes*," Tolkar said impatiently. "They've been at it for lifetimes. They're stealing all the magic. They've got a hollow mountain, or something, where they store it. This man couldn't get near it, but it's definitely there, he could feel it. Nice people, the Morlithians, apart from that," he said, "so long as you don't feed them cheese. Most of them get unnaturally grouchy if you feed them cheese."

Alazar decided to ignore that last part, in the hopes of corralling what the old man was saying into some sort of sense. "This," he said, pointing at the fire, "was magic, yes? You said it was sorcery."

"Well, lighting a fire doesn't take much, but *obviously* there's a bit more magic coming back into the world *now*," Tolkar said impatiently. "There was bound to be, once the Unmaker returned."

"The Unmaker's *returned*?" Marin demanded. Alazar looked at Ravi, who had frozen in terror.

Tolkar sighed. "Dear, sweet fools. You didn't actually still think that Tyrun was *Nari reborn*, did you?"

They stared at him.

The Last Sorcerer rubbed his forehead again. "Oh, we're fucked. For ten lifetimes of men has this man wandered the world, and now when it actually *matters*, he's sitting across a fire from three slack-jawed dolts so naïve you could sell them a stone and tell them it was a dragon's egg."

"S'man has *stood in His presence*," Marin said harshly. "He's felt the power of the Divine One's spirit!"

"And how do you think the Unmaker got its followers?" Tolkar snapped. "A particularly appealing ale recipe? You felt the power of Tyrun's spirit, sure enough, but it wasn't what you thought!"

"He's healed people!" Ravi burst out. "There are stories of—"

"Nari never healed anyone!" Tolkar shouted. "You tell this man of a story, a single story, where Nari used magic! He never did! *This man* did the magic! Gemar did the tactics! Nari had the vision, and the charisma, and could actually make people . . . come together, and think they would be better off if they did so." He sighed again, and his eyes seemed to be looking at something far away. "We conquered the land, sure enough, but we couldn't have done it all with swords. Nari had a way of talking to people's hearts. He could really make them *believe* in something." He shook his head, and Alazar realised there were tears sparkling at the corners of his eyes. "He was a good man."

"He was a god," Alazar said, softly.

"No, he wasn't," Tolkar said, just as quietly. "He was a great man, and a great friend, and this man curses the day he left Nari alone with that bastard Gemar, but we'd argued, and . . . Well, that doesn't matter now. But he wasn't a god. That was Gemar's idea: he picked it up from the Morlithians, they were just getting their empire going with that sun god of theirs. Gemar thought we could unify people better if something was raised above them all, but we wanted a concept of our own. Gemar suggested Nari."

"Nari proclaimed His divinity after defeating the Unmaker!" Marin snapped.

"He *accepted* it," Tolkar corrected. "Even the histories acknowledge we'd been claiming it before then. Nari didn't like the idea at first, but once we'd been under Spirithome, and saw what was in the caverns there . . . " Tolkar shuddered.

"Nari realised we needed something people could hold on to, something to make them cast the Unmaker aside. So he agreed."

"What's in the caverns?" Ravi asked, her voice tight with fear.

"This man won't say," Tolkar replied flatly. "He was terrified people would open them up again when the monastery got destroyed, but thankfully that's about the only part of that day that *didn't* end in disaster." He looked at Marin, who stared belligerently back at him.

"You're a foolish old man, who can't even keep his story straight!" Marin hissed. "If you are who you say you are, *you* wrote the Foretellings claiming Nari would return! Why would you do that, if you did not believe in His divinity?"

"Two reasons," Tolkar said. "First, this man was drunk, and upset. Secondly, to piss Gemar off. This man wanted the memory of his friend hanging around that bastard's shoulders for all of his waking moments, and there was no better way to do that than to write a prophecy which said that whatever Gemar did, whatever name he made for himself, Nari would return one day, and take his kingdom back."

Marin was shaking his head. "Do you have any idea how many scholars have examined that document over the years? How every line has been examined for meaning and context? And you're suggesting they were all wrong?"

Tolkar shrugged. "Serves them right for paying too much attention to poetry."

Alazar coughed into his hand. "This sar does not know much about prophecies and documents. What he wants to know is why you're here. Let's say all your stories are true: you're Tolkar, Tyrun is the Unmaker in a new body, everything. What do you want from us?"

"Well, this man had hoped that Marin would see through

the Unmaker's deception, and denounce Tyrun as a fraud," Tolkar said bitterly. "Master Temach thought him quite intelligent. Don't look at this man like that, boy," he added, to Marin's shocked expression, "Temach does not know this man as Tolkar, and we've exchanged letters from time to time. However, since that didn't happen, and Tyrun has accumulated more and more power, someone needs to kill the vessel in which the Unmaker resides. And that task, of course," he said, looking at Alazar, "would fall to you, goodsar."

"You want *this sar* to kill Tyrun?" Alazar asked, incredulously. The heat from the flames seemed to disappear, and the leather cord which wrapped the handle of his longblade suddenly felt particularly rough under his fingers. "Divine One or Unmaker, that's a tall order! Besides, this sar would be executed for deserting as soon as he entered the camp."

"If it was easy, anyone could do it," Tolkar said. "This man certainly can't: the Unmaker could overwhelm any magic this man could bring to bear, not to mention detect him as soon as he got close. There's a reason this man has been keeping his distance. You, though." Tolkar raised his eyebrows. "You seem to be living a charmed life, blacksword. A great warrior, who always avoids injury? That's the sort of man who can slay a demon."

"There's nothing special about that," Alazar argued. "It's just hard work and luck. This man's lost count of the times he could have died."

"And yet you never did," Tolkar said. "You've seen what Tyrun is becoming: the Unmaker is getting bolder, and putting more of itself forth. First it was all friendliness and peace, then it let its followers run amok at the monastery instead of reining them in, after Marin had the *wonderful* idea of taking it there—"

"If you want this sar's help, repeatedly insulting his husband is not going to endear you to him," Alazar said hotly.

"—and now it's moved on to pulling out the entrails of those who stand against it," the Last Sorcerer finished, without acknowledging his words. "Where do you think this is going to end, Sar Alazar? Another glorious reign of peace and prosperity for Narida, under the true heir of Nari? Or a return to the misery and senseless slaughter we got from the petty kings and demon-worshippers?"

Alazar hesitated. He had seen the reign of two God-Kings, and while both Natan and his father definitely had their flaws, neither had ever shown the sheer *ferocity* of Tyrun executing Lord Goldtree. And if two God-Kings, unchallenged in their rule and at the centre of their power, were less capricious than a newcomer halfway across the country, whose claim to power lay in the army He had gathered and the fact that no monks remained to contradict stories of how He had been proclaimed as Nari reborn . . . .

"Goldtree sent assassins to kill Tyrun," Alazar said, dubiously. "Of course He was going to be angry about that."

Tolkar sighed, and threw up his hands. "It's *the Unmaker*. It delights in suffering! There will be more excuses made and more reasons given for why it acts in the way it does, but all it comes down to is that a good ruler should restrain those impulses, and the Unmaker will indulge them. Unless someone stops it." He stared hard at Alazar, as though in challenge, but Alazar had met the eyes of fearless killers over the years, and had no problem in staring right back.

"This man doesn't understand why we're still listening to this fool," Marin said angrily.

"If you're so comfortable with Tyrun being the Divine One, why aren't you still with him?" Tolkar protested, jabbing a finger in Marin's direction. "You all know there's something wrong, you were just so set on something being true that you can't accept other explanations!"

"Men can't understand the minds of gods," Marin said. "The fact that we're not worthy to—"

"Oh, forget it," Tolkar said crossly. He set his staff down on the ground and lay down, knees curled up into his stomach and his head pillowed on his hands.

"What are you doing?" Alazar asked, wary of some new trick.

"This man is going to sleep, of course."

"Not there, you're not!" Marin said. "This is our fire!"

"This man started it, so an argument could be made that it's his fire," Tolkar replied, closing his eyes. "Besides which, you can banish him into the night and then spend until morning keeping an eye out in case he returns to get his revenge, or you can leave him here where you can easily keep an eye on him."

"Or we could cut your throat," Ravi said viciously.

"You could try," Tolkar said, without opening his eyes. "If you like the idea of being on fire."

"Let's not cut any more throats tonight," Alazar suggested. Ravi glared at him, then got up and walked away, and he silently cursed his own tongue. He looked at Marin, and nodded at Tolkar. "Watch him?"

"Certainly," Marin replied. His eyes were fixed on the Last Sorcerer so intently that Alazar was unsure how likely his husband was to blink.

He got to his feet and headed after Ravi. She was standing next to the trunk of a tree, staring out into the blackness in the opposite direction to the fire.

"Sorry," Alazar said, as he came alongside her. "What you did earlier was merciful and necessary, this sar didn't mean—"

"He said that s'woman was welcome," Ravi said over him. "He said her heart was pure. Pure enough."

Alazar did not have to ask who she was talking about.

"What if it's all a lie?" Ravi said, in a small voice. "What if Tyrun never was the Divine One? What if we all got deceived by a demon?"

"He's just a strange old man," Alazar said, looking over his shoulder at where Tolkar was laying, although he could not make the words sound quite as comforting or genuine as he intended.

"He started the fire with magic," Ravi said. "S'woman's never seen that before."

"Nor has this sar," Alazar admitted. "But even if he can do magic, that doesn't mean everything he says is true. Jumping his spirit from one body to another? Nari not being a god? Tyrun being the Unmaker? Why should any of those things be true?"

"Why should Tyrun be the Divine One?" Ravi asked, looking up at him. The firelight glistened in dampness at the corner of her eyes. "Why is that more likely? Even if he *is* the Divine One, after what we've seen, does that mean anything? Does *any* of it mean anything?" she added angrily, rubbing her arms through the sleeves of her dress. Alazar saw the end of one sleeve hike up slightly, and got a glimpse of the thick, dark line of a tattoo for a moment, just above her wrist.

"Maybe. Maybe not." He sighed. "This sar used to be in love with the God-King. When you're that close to something that important, you sort of see things in a different way. It's like you can see inside the light to what's making it, and it's not always as beautiful as it should be." He put one hand on her shoulder. "Nothing we say or do tonight will change anything. This sar's certainly not rushing to head back and take on an entire camp to try to cut someone's head off. Let's sleep."

Ravi nodded wearily, but when they got back to the fire, she sat down. "You two sleep. S'woman's not going to be able to for

a while, in any case. She'll take first watch and make sure *he* –"
She glowered at Tolkar, who was so unresponsive that he might
have already dozed off. "– doesn't try anything . . . strange."

Alazar was going to ask if she was sure, but the set of her
jaw answered that for him. Besides, he was not going to object
to finally getting some proper sleep. "Thank you. Wake this
sar up whenever you need to."

Ravi nodded, and Alazar lay down close enough to the fire
to get some of its warmth, but not so close that he was likely
to catch alight if he rolled towards it. Marin settled down next
to him, and put his head close.

"Do you trust him?" he asked, so faintly that Alazar could
barely make out the words.

"No," Alazar whispered back. "But enough of what he says
makes a sort of sense that we probably shouldn't just ignore it."

"Your husband was worried you were going to say
that," Marin sighed. "Fine. We'll interrogate him again in
the morning."

"Agreed." Alazar draped his arm across his husband's side.
"Sleep well, Mar."

"Sleep well, Laz."

Alazar woke up to bird calls, grey light, the gentle sighing of
soft rain on pine needles, and a coldness that spoke of a fire
which had long since died. He jerked upright with a sudden-
ness that prompted a squawk of alarm from Marin, who had
been gently snoring.

The fire was dark and cold. Tolkar still lay on the other side
of it, but of Ravi there was no sign.

She never woke him.

"Where is she?" he bellowed, stamping around the fire
and kicking Tolkar in the ribs. The sorcerer jerked awake
and grabbed his staff, which he pointed at Alazar as though

to ward him off, but Alazar was angry enough that threats of purple fire no longer held any weight.

"Ravi!" he shouted, drawing his longblade. "Where is she?"

Tolkar looked over the fire's ashes to where Ravi had been before they had all gone to sleep, then back up at him. "No idea! Didn't she wake you up?"

"No," Alazar bit out, "she didn't." He eyed Tolkar distrustfully, but the sorcerer – or alleged sorcerer – did not look deceitful. For what that was worth.

"Her satchel's gone," Marin reported. "And the sword she had. Nothing of ours is missing."

Alazar closed his eyes. "So if someone or something took her, they managed to do it without waking any of us, and were considerate enough to take her medicines with them." He opened them again, and looked at his husband.

"She left of her own accord," Marin concluded grimly, getting to his feet. "Leaving us asleep next to *him*!" he added furiously, pointing at Tolkar. "Why? Why would she leave in the night?"

Alazar swore. There was only one explanation that made sense. "She's going to try to kill Tyrun."

"*What?*" Marin looked like someone had hit him in the face with a skillet. "*Why?*"

"Think about it, Mar," Alazar said softly, walking back to his husband's side and lowering his voice so Tolkar could not overhear. "You told me what she said at that pool. She thinks she's been freed of those marks her parents put on her, and then she hears that the Divine One might actually be the being she's beholden to? *And* she hears that a sharp sword in the right place might be all it takes to solve the problem?" He shook his head sadly. "She's going to try to kill him, your husband knows it."

"That's ridiculous," Marin said flatly. "She's going to die."

Alazar sighed, and Marin's eyes widened. "Laz, tell your husband you're not thinking of going after her!"

"She can't have got that far," Alazar said wretchedly. "Your husband doesn't want to go back to Northbank either, but we should be able to catch her long before that! She's tired, she's upset, she'd just killed two men last night: she's not thinking straight. We'll find her, talk it over, explain why it's an awful idea. We've dragged her into some bad things, between us," he added. "We should probably try to keep her out of this one."

Marin exhaled through his nose. "You are entirely too moral for a mercenary, you know that?"

Alazar smiled at him. "I've been told that. Once or twice. Although literally only once or twice," he added.

"But you're a good man," Marin said, not without some resignation. "Which might be why your husband loves you. Fine. We go after her, we try to talk her out of it, but if we can't, we let her make her own decisions, yes? Your husband doesn't want *her* dragging *us* into something bad."

Alazar nodded. "Deal. And thank you."

Marin shook his head. "The world must be in a bad state if a thief and sellsword have to . . . " He trailed off, eyes widening. "Hey, where's the old man?"

Alazar turned around, but the piece of ground that had recently contained the form of Tolkar was decidedly empty. "Tolkar? Tolkar!"

There was no answer. Alazar peered around through the trees, but there was no sign of any cloaked shape hurrying away. There was no one on the road, either, although it curved to both north and south quickly enough that someone moving fast might just have got out of sight before he and Marin noticed they had gone. Maybe.

"If this is the sort of thing we can expect now magic is

coming back into the world," Marin commented sourly, "then your husband can live without it."

"Likewise," Alazar muttered. He sheathed his longblade, and reached for his pack. "Come on. We've got a healer to catch."

Darel

Waymeet would have impressed Darel greatly, had he never been to Idramar.

It was a trading town, where the Yora River that flowed from the hills of the south was swelled by the Greenrun, coming down from the Catseye Mountains in the west. The South Road ran through the city as well, and branched off into smaller routes connecting the towns of the eastern woodlands and the western grasslands to each other.

"Behold your domain!" Hiran said, as they stood on the New Bridge, which spanned the Yora over the course of three massive stone arches. "Everything south of the Greenrun is the South, and the South is yours."

"This is all still so strange," Darel admitted. "Not least because when you are from Blackcreek, everything is the North. We must be a month's travel from home, yet this is still considered the South?" He gestured around them. "They do not even build their houses the same! Have these people ever seen snow?"

Hiran laughed. "The middlelands get snow, from time to time! Your friend must have seen snow in Threestones at least four times in his life."

Darel looked at him to see if he was joking, but despite being jovial, Hiran seemed serious. "Four *times*? Hiran, in

Blackcreek the snow is on the ground for something like four *months*, give or take."

Hiran shrugged. "Then you will seem hardy and impressive to your new vassals."

"Stop mocking," Darel muttered. "No one who looks at your friend will mistake him for hardy, let alone impressive."

"Your friend was not mocking," Hiran assured him. "At the very least, the South cannot complain that they have had an outsider set over them. You are the southernmost thane of all! And you saved the God-King's life. And before you say that anyone would have done the same," he added, as Darel opened his mouth, "remember that Kaldur Brightwater and his men were *not* doing the same, and that is why your intervention was required at all."

Darel huffed a laugh. "If only everyone over whom your friend has authority will be as accepting of it as you! Not that he has authority over you," he added hastily.

"You are a Hand of Heaven," Hiran pointed out. "So, you do."

Darel folded his hands into his sleeves and looked southwards once more, uncomfortable with how the conversation was going.

"Besides," Hiran said. "There are more ties between us than just those of duty. Or so your friend would like to think."

Darel felt his cheeks heat from twin sources of embarrassment: both hearing someone expressing affection towards him, and the thought that he might not have been clear enough with his own thoughts. "You know that is true! Your friend——" He stopped, and corrected himself deliberately, albeit with a fast-beating heart. "Your *lover* wants you to know how much you mean to him, Hiran."

Now it was Hiran's turn to look embarrassed. "Darel, that was not meant to—— You did not need to——"

"Your lover has said what he has said," Darel said, as firmly as he could manage while his stomach turned backflips. He and Hiran had been intimate, it was true, but no one would be surprised if they drifted apart after some time spent in each other's company. That was not what Darel wanted; he just had to hope Hiran felt the same way.

"Your lover thanks you," Hiran said, with a bashful smile, and threaded his fingers through Darel's in a manner that somehow felt more meaningful than it had done before. Darel smiled back. His cheeks were hot enough already, but it felt like a new warmth was spreading up his arm from the hand placed in his; a warmth that had nothing to do with the sun.

"Your lover would like nothing better than to stand here with you all day and watch the river," he said honestly. "However, for now, he has matters that require his attention."

"The kingdom must come first, of course," Hiran agreed with a smile. "But know that your lover is with you, in everything."

Darel smiled back and kissed him on the cheek, and they turned together.

Strongway Point sat in the wedge of land between the southern bank of the Greenrun and the western bank of the Yora, and overlooked the main bridge of each river. Thane Kyrel Strongway was an old man, somewhere near his seventieth year, but although his vision and hearing were going, he remained sound of mind and relatively sturdy in body. Darel got the distinct impression that Kyrel Strongway had seen a few different Hands of Heaven in his time, and if he ever had been overawed by them, he certainly was not now: however, his courtesies to Darel since his arrival had been, if not an iota more than propriety demanded, certainly not less.

The same could not be said of the officers of the Southern Army, or such of them as messengers from Threestones had been able to gather, who now met with Darel in Strongway Point's hall.

"The coastal thanes won't do anything to aid the kingdom," Captain Tenan of Stoneside said flatly. "They claim their lands have been so damaged by the wave that they need all their people to rebuild. High Marshal, this is the greater threat we face, not outlandish rumours of Raiders at Idramar."

"They are not rumours, Captain," Darel said, as sternly as he dared, "nor are they outlandish. This marshal saw their sails himself; as did the God-King."

"But we don't know their numbers, nor their intention, nor their current location!" Tenan said. He was a large man, broad as well as tall, which was why he had received the somewhat unimaginative nickname of "Big Tenan". He bore it without comment or complaint, mainly due to the presence of his namesake.

"Big's correct," Captain "Little" Tenan of Brightwater said, with an acknowledging glance at the man who was a foot taller, perhaps twice as heavy, and possibly ten years younger than him. "Our duty is to protect the kingdom, High Marshal, and we can't do that if the thanes are allowed to defy the crown with no consequence. We'd be marching to fight an enemy that may no longer even be there, while the fabric of the kingdom crumbles behind us."

"The fabric of the kingdom is the people who make it up," Darel argued. "They will crumble – they will *starve* – if we strip the thanedoms bare. Besides which, this is not a divine order: the God-King made a request for bodies that could be spared, not an order to send levies." He sighed. "Captains, your logic confuses this marshal. You play down the threat of the Tjakorshi, yet you call for action against the coastal thanes because they will not send men to help us meet that threat?"

"We can only deal with one problem at a time, High

Marshal," Little Tenan said. "We know where this problem is, and the nature of it."

"And it means bullying farmers instead of facing warriors," Captain Yamrel of Lenby put in dryly, cleaning under his nails with his dagger. "Don't forget that, Little."

The other two captains glared at their companion. "This man doesn't like your tone, Yamrel," Big said, ominously.

"And this man couldn't give two shits about that," Yamrel replied, looking up. He affected a pair of long moustaches, but was otherwise clean-shaven. "Bloody northerners, the pair of you. The High Marshal is from the real south, and the coast, like this man. Nari save us from mountainsiders and lakemen who've never seen a Raider in their life!"

Both Tenans bristled, and Big's hand strayed towards the hilt of his sword.

"Gentlemen!" Darel said forcefully. "This is unseemly!"

"You're not better than us simply because you come from some salt-stained shithole on the coast!" Little snapped at Yamrel, ignoring Darel. "This is about the kingdom's welfare, Yamrel, not avenging something that might have happened in your town when you were a child!"

Darel gritted his teeth in frustration. Was he supposed to shout at these men to get them to pay attention to him? How would that show authority? Even worse, what if they still ignored him?

He glanced over at Hiran, who was lurking unobtrusively on the other side of the hall in his official capacity as Darel's aide. It was an appropriate position for him given their respective ranks, and meant Darel was able to have at least one friendly face near him in this mission to muster the Southern Army's forces. Hiran nodded encouragingly, and Darel felt somewhat heartened. He knew the God-King had faith in him to be Southern Marshal, but the God-King was a week's travel to the north in Threestones: and besides, Natan III did not hold quite the same aura of wonder since Darel had actually met his ruler. He was still loyal, of course, but the golden image of serene perfection he had envisaged before arriving in Idramar had been replaced by something rather more down-to-earth. Hiran was not only here, but held a very special place in Darel's heart, and the knowledge that Hiran believed in him was fortifying.

"This is about obeying the God-King," he said flatly, into the burgeoning argument. "Captains, we have our orders, and they are clear. Regardless of whether or not we receive any additional forces from any of the thanes, coastal or otherwise, we are to gather all available soldiers and return north. To do otherwise is to go against the wishes of the God-King himself," he added, "and that is not something that this marshal will countenance. Any officer who feels unable to comply with these instructions is welcome to hand in his commission, lest it be removed from him."

The Tenans exchanged a glance, and Little tried a different tack. "High Marshal, how much combat have you seen?"

"Skirmishes only," Darel acknowledged. He had been ready for this question. "This marshal fought against a Tjakorshi champion when the Brown Eagle clan first came to Black Keep, against another raiding force some weeks later, against pirates on the deck of the *Silver Tide*, and against Kaldur Brightwater and his traitorous sars in the God-King's chambers at the Sun Palace."

"So you've not commanded men in battle," Big said. It was not a question.

"No," Darel said. "This marshal has studied the works of noted commanders from the past, as befits the son of a thane, but he has not had the chance to put those lessons into practice. He will be relying on the counsel of his captains to ensure success in the field," he added pointedly. "He must be sure of those who advise him: those who do so well, without giving thought to their own position, will find themselves spoken of highly to the God-King."

The three men glanced surreptitiously at each other. Big and Little might agree when it came to pushing the coastal thanes around rather than heading north to challenge the Raiders, but Darel did not think they were longstanding friends. Both of them, and Yamrel as well, would have an interest in their own advancement.

"We do not know of the whereabouts or well-being of Marshal Greenbrook," Darel said, after a moment. "It is possible that his Divine Majesty may require another Hand of Heaven. A great opportunity, for men who prove themselves in times of great need."

"High Marshal," Little said, putting a little more respect and thought into the title than he had done so far. "You're saying that you . . . do not intend to wield overall command?"

"This marshal has been given the authority, and so he must take the responsibility," Darel said. "The command will be his, but that does not mean he will be so foolish as to ignore more experienced voices. You all have different perspectives. This marshal will direct you as to which enemy we shall fight, in line with the commands of the God-King: he will expect you to give your opinions on how this can best be achieved with the resources at our disposal. Once he has those opinions, this marshal will make his decisions on our course of action."

Big, Little, and Yamrel all nodded in slow unison, and Darel tried not to let his relief show. All these men were older and more experienced than him, and he had still not mastered the effortless air of command that Kaldur Brightwater had projected. "There will be no more discussions of the coastal thanes, unless any of them should actively take up arms against the crown," he said. "Now, this marshal would like your best estimates on what further reinforcements we are likely to receive in the next two days, and then your suggested march plan for us to return to Threestones with all reasonable speed. You will all be more experienced than this marshal in the practical matters of moving a large body of armed men cohesively over distance."

In the end, they were army officers. They might question authority, especially if the basis for that authority seemed uncertain, but they would stop short of open disobedience except in the gravest circumstances. The prospect of future influence and advancement – and the reassurance that Darel did not intend to pursue his own inexperienced agenda in defiance of their advice – brought them back together to discuss what other help they might expect, and the likely schedule of marches to get them to Threestones most efficiently. Some dirty looks were still cast between the Tenans and Yamrel, but openly hostile words were kept behind teeth.

Darel risked another glance over at Hiran, received a smile in return, and felt a new flush of warmth that bordered on pride. He hardly thought that Hiran's good opinion of him rested on how well he wrangled recalcitrant army officers, but it was nice to get approval nonetheless.

Father, if you were here now, even you might approve of your son. Did you ever think he could be Southern Marshal?

Darel paused for a moment, as the last memory of his father flashed up in his mind: Thane Asrel, falling forward on to his own shortblade and spitting his hatred of his two sons, one by blood and one by law, and the choices they had made.

But now it comes to it, do not stir your spirit from wherever it rests. Your son no longer either needs nor desires your approval.

Tila

Tila was rarely wrong about people. Tajen was far from home, alone, and miserable: even more so than Tila herself, who was at least in her own country, for all that she was surrounded by invaders. The Alaban had no spirit to resist being threatened, and he translated back and forth to the members of the Brown Eagle clan with little objection other than whining about it.

"But will he tell others what you made him do?" Osred asked, after the deed was done. Otim and the others had agreed that overtly opposing The Golden would be foolish, but that trying to sow seeds of dissension within the Tjakorshi ranks was far more viable. The draug might be untouchable, but it would be far less efficient if its own captains were at each other's throats.

"No," Tila said, with some certainty. "He's a coward. He'll be too worried about the consequences for what he's done to risk turning us in. He'll simply keep his head down, and hope nothing can be traced back to him."

"You are very confident of this," Osred noted, and Tila shrugged.

"This lady has spent her life reading people, steward. It's an ability she sometimes wishes she never needed, but she doesn't deny that it's come in useful."

"Well, we shall see what fruit this brings," Osred said. "This steward hopes it is not too sour."

Their Naridan ranks had been swelled once more, to the point where The Golden's forces could no longer all fit on the ships, and their progress west along the Idra had slowed dramatically as a result. Raiding parties were venturing out to towns and villages northwards, in search of supplies to keep everyone fed now they could not move fast enough to rely on plunder from the riverside alone: each time, a few Naridans went out in the company of greater numbers of Raiders, and each time, a few new Naridans came back. Sometime their expressions were downcast and miserable as they wrestled with their own consciences in the pursuit of staying fed, but equally often they were hard-faced and eager at the thought of taking what they wanted from the nobility.

Tila had expected that. It was a necessary side effect of the story she had spun to bring the armsmen onside, when her own life had been on the line. That message had reverberated through the lowborn, and gained more traction that she anticipated, but it was still a variable over which she felt she had some control. She – or at least, Livnya – was recognised by many of her countryfolk, who seemed to have some idea that she was genuinely agitating for change. Some even apparently thought that she was in league with The Golden, or had been working with it from the beginning, which was a notion she had to force herself not to laugh at.

She had no trouble in preventing herself from laughing when she came across Morel of Godspire preaching, however.

She was not sure how the priest had survived this long, given his utter and obvious dedication to Nari. She would have expected him to fall foul of a blackstone axe for pointless resistance, or frantic haranguing of a Raider best left alone. It was not until she stumbled across the back of a crowd and heard him speaking that she understood what had actually happened.

"—prophecies speak of many things, many portents," Morel was saying, his voice raised so that all could hear him. "The heavens spoke with nary a cloud to mar their face! The ocean rose and swallowed cities! The signs cannot be ignored: the Divine One has been reborn!"

Tila sighed. So much for Morel waiting until the monks of Godspire had their say before he accepted the upstart in the west as Nari's heir. This was why she pointed The Golden in this direction, and away from her brother, but the aim had been for them to annihilate each other. If Morel got this crowd too worked up, the rebellion from within might start before she was ready for it.

"But Narida has grown too complacent!" Morel continued. "The rich gorge themselves, while the poor labour for crusts! We have abandoned the vision the Divine Nari had for our land!"

"And what do you know of that?" Tila muttered under her breath. "Were you there?"

"He has not returned to us in a guise of friendship, but of conquest!" Morel shouted. "He is the warrior king, returned to take this land back for those who will give themselves to Him, and follow without question! As Nari Himself was an outsider to many of the lands He subdued, so He is now an outsider once again. He will throw down the systems that have governed our people, and break the chains that have bound us!"

Tila frowned. What did Morel know about the pretender to paint him as an outsider? That seemed an odd—

"The Golden is masked in glory, as foretold in the prophecies, and He will lead us to glory, for He is Nari returned to us!" Morel declared, and Tila froze in horror. *What* had he said?

She was not the only one dubious about the priest's

assertion. Shouts of outrage sounded among the crowd . . . but not as many as Tila would have expected. The Golden was a Nari-damned demon, by the Mountain and all the spirits, wearing the shell of a man like Tila would wear a winter cloak! How could anyone take such foolishness seriously?

But, she realised, most people did not know that. She was one of very few Naridans who had been in close proximity to The Golden, let alone had been able to exchange words with it, or learn its true nature. To the uneducated lowborn, those who did not even know that Morel's line about being "masked in glory" was so great a mangling of the Prophecies that it basically counted as being plucked from his own imagination, The Golden was simply an imposing warrior masked in gold.

"He is not Nari reborn!" someone near the front shouted angrily: a large man, possibly one of the men-at-arms she had recruited.

"Then how did He conquer Idramar so swiftly?" Morel shot back, all fire and passion. "The jewel of Narida, the seat of power in this country, taken in a day by forces from across the ocean! This priest was there, he saw it happen! Our defences were no match against His will, and our men were overwhelmed by His warriors! He came to take back His land, and He started where the rot was greatest: from where the so-called Divine Family had been leading us astray!"

Oh, you treacherous little bastard, Tila thought viciously. *It's like that, is it?*

"It seems your narrative has found a receptive audience," a voice said from beside her. Tila jumped slightly, and turned to find Sebiah Wousewold at her side. The former Lord of Scribes looked a little thinner in the face than he had when still enjoying the kitchens of the Sun Palace, and his robes were not only stained, but the lower hem had been raised and his sleeves turned back to allow for greater freedom of movement.

He no longer looked like a lord of the Inner Council, but he had always struck Tila as somewhat more adaptable than most of the nobles she had encountered over the years.

"What?" she demanded. She would not waste fine words on Wousewold: she had no wish to be identified by him, for one thing.

"The woman known as Livnya has been talking of how this is a marvellous opportunity for the lowborn to rise up and seize riches from their lords," Wousewold said. His tone was conversational, but his dark eyes did not leave her face as he spoke. "It appears the high priest agrees."

"What's he playing at?" Tila muttered, casting a glance in the direction of Morel, who was still pontificating. "The Golden as Nari's heir? It's ludicrous."

"Perhaps," Wousewold conceded, looking around them. "But not unpopular. It must be easier for men like Morel to accept such great changes overtaking the land if they can attribute it to a divine cause. Otherwise he would have to accept that the God-King was sent fleeing by mere savages, and the divinely appointed Hand of Heaven's failure to protect Idramar was down to incompetence. This lord sat on many council sessions with Morel, and he does not think that those are conclusions the former high priest would readily come to of his own accord."

Tila paused for a moment to consider Wousewold's words; which she always tried to do, for she had long suspected that a very shrewd mind lurked behind his unmemorable face. Most importantly, judging by his comments about being on the council with Morel, he did not seem to have realised her true identity.

Unless, of course, he was intending his words to startle her, and help him confirm his suspicions.

"Does a grand lord such as yourself regularly talk about

such things with common women?" she asked, testing him for a response.

Wousewold chuckled. "More frequently now than before the sacking of Idramar, it must be said. But this lord does not think you are that common a woman, Livnya. That name is well-known in Idramar's streets, and carries a taint of fear with it."

"You spent time in Idramar's streets, did you?" Tila scoffed. She looked him up and down, putting some mockery into it.

"Not often," Wousewold admitted, "but this lord knows people who did. He always did his best to keep a finger on the pulse, as it were."

This princess knew *you knew more than you let on*, Tila thought. "And what did that pulse tell you?" she asked out loud.

"That Livnya the Knife was not to be underestimated," Wousewold said, looking away from her and towards Morel. "That only the brave or the foolish criminal risked going against her. That she had built, or at least expanded upon, a web of crime and corruption which went well beyond the city boundaries." He snorted in amusement. "This is almost an honour."

"This lady has no time for your highborn games," Tila said flatly. "What do you want?"

"A bargain," Wousewold said softly, and Tila had to work to hide her surprise. A high lord of the Inner Council, offering a bargain to someone he considered a lowborn criminal? This was unheard of.

"Go on."

"The future is unclear," Wousewold said, still keeping his voice so low that Tila leaned toward him slightly to hear him properly. "The response of the God-King to the threat of The Golden is as yet unknown; similarly, the true strength of the man claiming to be Nari reborn in the West was a mystery even before this lord lost access to his network of informants. Any one of the three might triumph."

And only one can possibly be a good outcome, Tila added to herself. "And?"

"You have some influence with The Golden," Wousewold said. "This lord's attempts to ingratiate himself have been less successful. Should The Golden win out, you do what you can to ensure this lord's well-being."

Tila raised her eyebrows. "And in return?"

"Livnya the Knife was a person whose name was known by many, but whose face was known by few," Wousewold said. "That is no longer the case. However, should the God-King triumph, this lord will use whatever influence he retains to see that any associations of you with the crimes you may have committed are ignored or forgotten. There may even be scope for you to join the ranks of the nobility."

"Despite having called for their overthrow?" Tila asked, suspicious of a trap.

Wousewold shrugged. "If the God-King wins, it was clearly unsuccessful. And probably merely a ruse to flush out the disloyal."

"Some might say that even planning for The Golden's victory is treasonous," Tila suggested.

"They might," Wousewold agreed, still not looking at her. "But they are not here, are they?"

Tila considered. "This doesn't leave either of us much scope for success should the pretender come to power."

"Then we shall just have to hope that does not happen," Wousewold said, his tone neutral. Now he did glance sideways at her, and Tila did her best to hide a smirk. It seemed she might not be the only one who considered that throwing The Golden against the pretender was the best outcome.

"What about Morel?" she asked, lowering her voice further.

Wousewold frowned. "What about him? He does not seem to have the sort of . . . *pragmatism* that we share."

"Oh no, this lady wasn't suggesting we should recruit him," Tila clarified. "Is he dangerous? Should he be allowed to continue with his heresy?"

"You are considering sticking a knife into the high priest?" Wousewold said, sounding amused. Tila did not reply, and his eyes widened in surprise. "You are."

"It's not a perfect solution to every problem," Tila admitted, "but it is a simple one."

Sebiah Wousewold tapped the tips of his index fingers together in front of his chest while he considered. "No. Not at the moment. We might need to harness whatever following he gathers, and that will be easier if he is around to receive suggestions."

"Good thinking." Tila extended her hand. "A deal then, Your Lordship."

"A deal, Lady Livnya," Wousewold said, clasping her hand in his. "And may it benefit us both."

Bulang

"This," M'bana said quietly, "has got to be the strangest thing Î've done to help a friend."

"Quiet," Bulang hushed hîm. "Just be ready with the net."

"Let's say we catch one," M'bana persisted. "What are we going to do with it then? Carry it back across the city in the net?"

"That's what the basket is for," Bulang said absently.

"Yöu're not going to keep a monkey in a basket!" M'bana protested. "Unless yöu're planning on killing it first. Are yöu?" hê added.

"The magician didn't say whether they wanted the monkey alive or not," Bulang admitted. *And Î didn't ask*. "So we're going to bring it to them alive, and then they can . . . do whatever it is they're going to do with it. So we keep the monkey in the net, and put the *net* in the basket."

"And what about the noise?" M'bana said. "If yöu're trying to avoid notice, carrying a screaming monkey halfway across East Harbour isn't going to——"

"*Î don't have any choice!*" Bulang hissed in frustration, rounding on hîm. "Unless yôu have an idea for how to shut a monkey up when it's wrapped in a net, then shut up yôurself and help më do this!"

M'bana did not reply, and even in the darkness Bulang

could see that hîs expression was not a happy one, but thëy were starting to lose patience, and the need to hurry was clawing at thëm. The two of them had pilfered a small fishing net from the docks – it had a few rips, but nothing through which anything decent-sized would be able to escape – and located a pangpang tree in which a group of monkeys were sleeping. It was in the grounds of the Old Palace, of which Bulang had no fear after having spent several nights sheltering there with Jeya, although M'bana was somewhat jumpy. Unfortunately, the animals were high above the ground, and Bulang considered that trying to climb that high with the net in thëir hands was a recipe for disaster.

"Are yöu going to try the fruit?" M'bana asked.

"No," Bulang said, shaking thëir head. "Monkeys don't come down looking for food in at night, do they? So there's no reason why they'd come down just because we're here. Ï'll go up and chase them down, yôu be ready to net one."

M'bana tilted hîs head back to look up at the shadowy branches. "Really? Yöu're going to go up there?"

Bulang tried to sound confident. "Ï'm good at climbing trees. It'll be fine." Thëy reached up and ran thëir hands over the bark, which was rough and full of crevices, but without much in the way of knots or other sizeable features that might give thëm decent purchase. The branches that spread outwards and upwards did not begin until some distance above thëir head.

Thëy turned to M'bana, and tried not to sound as embarrassed as thëy felt. "Can yôu give më a boost?"

M'bana sighed, but cupped hîs hands and went down to one knee. Bulang stepped up onto hîm, balancing thëmself as much as possible on the tree's trunk and trying to think light thoughts. "Ready."

"Not sure Î am," M'bana muttered, but hê began to

straighten up again. Bulang wobbled as thëy rose into the air, but steadied thëmself and reached upwards.

"Just a little more . . ."

"Î don't think Î can get yöu much higher," M'bana said, the strain evident in hîs voice.

"Just a bit, Ï only need a bit," Bulang urged. Thëir fingers were scraping one of the branches, but thëy could not quite get enough grip to pull thëmself up.

"Then yöu'd best grab on well, because Î'm not going to be able to hold yöu up there, and Î'm probably going to drop yöu straight afterwards . . ."

"That's fine!" Bulang said. "Just get më up higher, then be ready with the net!"

"On three, then. One, two, *three!*"

M'bana grunted with effort. Bulang stretched up as far as thëy could, and *just* managed to get a proper hold of the branch thëy were aiming for. With that done, thëy pulled thëmself up into the fork where the trunk began to split, which took only a few moments of straining and grunting. Thëy heard a rustle above thëm, and a faint chatter and hooting. The golden-maned monkeys had realised something was coming into their tree, and they did not sound happy about it.

Well, that was the general idea. Bulang had entertained notions of luring monkeys to thëm using fruit, or appealing to Sa in the hope that one would simply walk up and present itself, but thëy had no time to indulge such fancies. Thëy could not hope to catch a monkey in the tree, but with any luck thëy could chase one out of it. After that, it was up to M'bana.

Bulang peered upwards. Smaller branches and leaves got in the way, but the second branch to thëir right seemed to have the highest concentration of monkeys perched in its upper reaches, so that was where thëy would start. This branch was narrow enough to embrace easily, and sloped outwards at a more forgiving angle than the vertical trunk, so thëy began to shuffle up it. Branches the thickness of thëir wrist or thinner jutted out at inconvenient angles, and when thëy tried to get round one, they lost thëir grip, and nearly fell sideways. Only a last-moment grab at the offending branch prevented thëm from toppling headfirst out of the tree and back down to the ground.

"Are yöu all right up there?" M'bana whispered hoarsely up from the ground. Quite apart from the risk of ghosts, they could not be sure who else might be haunting the Old Palace grounds on any given night, so they were trying not to draw attention to themselves.

"Ï'm fine," Bulang replied through gritted teeth, wrenching thëmself back into a more stable position. The monkeys above seemed anything but fine, however, since Bulang's sudden shift of weight had set the branch swaying a little, and they were all now widc awake and agitated. Bulang set off upwards again, not making any attempt at stealth. The idea was to flush the monkeys out of the tree altogether and on to the ground, after all.

Harsh chattering met thëm as thëy kept climbing, as the monkeys got more and more alarmed. The branch was starting to bounce more as it got thinner, as well, and it was getting harder for Bulang to navigate thëir limbs past the increasing number of thinner offshoots. Thëy stretched out, reaching upwards with one hand and trying to appear as threatening as possible in the dark. The shapes of the monkeys backed off even farther, clustering back on the narrower reaches and bunching up together, the faint moonlight reflecting dimly off bared fangs as the bigger animals snarled. Bulang shuffled forwards another handsbreadth, balancing thëmself as they went . . .

A monkey fell, knocked from its precarious perch by another one backing into it. There was an alarmed squeal, and a small, dark shape plummeted downwards. As if that was the signal they had all been waiting for, or dreading, the rest sprang into motion. There were suddenly monkey bodies everywhere, bounding shadows that sprang through the night with terrified calls as this strange predator continued its inexorable advance towards them. Most jumped to neighbouring branches, but some came straight for Bulang, apparently deciding that getting past thëm in a rush was safer than taking a jump in the dark to a landing point they could not see. Bulang made a grab at one furred shape, but thëir fingers closed on nothing except empty air, and then thëy had to throw thëir head sideways as another animal nearly trod on thëir face in its panic. Within a matter of moments the branch was bare, and a chorus of angry alarm raged around Bulang's ears.

Thëy slithered backwards along the branch as fast as thëy could, seeking to keep up the pressure on the animals. Some were still clinging to the highest parts of other branches, but others . . .

Bulang looked over thëir shoulder and saw flashes of pale fur as monkeys darted out of sight, down the trunk towards the ground. "M'bana!"

"Î see them!" M'bana called back. There was a grunt, followed by the faint patter of the net hitting the ground after it was thrown. "Shit!"

Bulang ground thëir teeth in frustration. All that, and they had still failed? The branch beneath thëm was wide enough to get thëir feet under thëm once more, and thëy got up into a crouch and turned around.

There was a monkey, perhaps two arms lengths away in the fork where the branches met to become the main trunk, watching Bulang warily. It was one of the larger ones, with the ruff of longer, thicker fur around its neck. Bulang shifted thëir feet to balance themselves. "M'bana, did yôu get anything?"

"No, Î missed all of the little shits," M'bana replied harshly.

"There's one more up here," Bulang said, trying to keep thëir voice level so the monkey was not startled before thëy were ready. "Ï'm going to try to send it towards yôu. Are yôu ready?"

"Probably not," M'bana's voice came back dejectedly, "but give it a go."

Bulang lunged. Or at least, thëy tried to.

It was a foolish thing to do, when close to twice thëir own height off the ground in a tree. Thëy envisaged a graceful leap that would end with the monkey either fleeing towards the ground and the waiting M'bana, or seized in Bulang's grasp as thëy landed between the branches. However, thëir body had clearly worked out that going ribs-first into solid wood was a bad idea, even without the risk of falling out of the tree and landing on thëir head. As a result, what actually happened was that Bulang jerked forward a few inches, panicked, stiffened up, and slewed sideways. Thëy desperately grabbed at a thinner branch to try to keep thëmself upright, and swung down to an undignified and somewhat precarious rest, heart pounding, with thëir chest and shoulders resting over one limb, and thëir feet still on the one where thëy had started.

However, the monkey had gone, and from the ground came an angry, tearing screaming.

"Ï've got it!" M'bana called up, their voice hitting the strained pitch of someone trying not to shout, but also attempting to make hîmself heard over the noise of a screaming monkey. "Get down here and give mê a hand!"

Bulang shifted thëir weight around, and shuffled thëir feet off the branch to drop downwards. Thëy hung from the tree by thëir hands for a moment, wishing that the ground beneath thëm was better lit, then let go and fell into the risk of an unstable landing and a broken ankle. A twinge of pain shot through thëir left leg as thëy hit the grass, but it receded in a moment, and thëy were able to limp around the tree to where M'bana was wrestling with a thrashing, screaming net.

"Why did yöu have to scare down one of the big ones?!" M'bana demanded, jerking hîs hand away from the bulge in the net as it snarled and snapped at hîm.

"Because yôu missed all the smaller ones!" Bulang replied testily. "Yôu could have gone up the tree if yôu'd wanted!" Thëy fumbled about on the ground, finding the edges of the net. The monkey was flailing around, but at least did not seem to have any idea of how best to get free, and was simply entangling itself even further. "Get the basket."

"Î really don't think this is going to work," M'bana said dubiously, but backed away from the monkey gladly enough.

"We won't find out if we don't try," Bulang said, "and Ï'd rather get it to the magician in a basket than just hanging down mÿ back." The monkey rolled again, barking in distress, and Bulang managed to grab the far side of the net from under it. Now thëy could bring all the edges together in thëir hands, and unless the monkey managed to chew a hole in the mesh large enough to get its body out, it was going nowhere.

"Ready?" M'bana asked, approaching tentatively. Hê had one of the baskets hê used to carry fruit to and from the market stall: a sturdy wicker thing, and deep enough to hold a monkey so long as it could not move very much. Bulang got the best grip thëy could, and hoisted thëir struggling captive off the ground.

The monkey weighed more than Bulang had expected, and its thrashing did not make it any easier tø manoeuvre, but thëy managed to lift it high enough for M'bana to get the basket underneath it. Bulang lowered it in with relief, then dumped the surplus net on top to foil any attempt it might make to get free.

"We're going to need something else," M'bana said, as the monkey set the basket rocking in hîs hands. "If we have to keep pushing it down to keep it in there then we're going to lose fingers!"

Bulang looked around for inspiration, and found it in the shape of the pangpang's leaves. They were large and thick enough that thëy only needed to pluck a few from the end of spindly, low-hanging twigs to have a reasonable makeshift covering for the basket, so at least they would not have to keep pressure on the monkey with nothing but the question-able protection of a net between its teeth and their flesh. The monkey screeched some more as Bulang layered the leaves on top of it, but it could not thrash or kick enough to actually dislodge them.

"What now?" M'bana asked, shifting the basket in hîs arms. "We just go back to the Morlithian Quarter and hope no one wonders why we're carrying a basket that's screaming?"

"Pretty much, yes," Bulang said. Thëir hands were sore from climbing, thëy had what felt like several small cuts, and thëy still had no idea what the magician was going to be able to do to help, but at least thëy were one step closer. "Come on. We can take turns carrying it if yôu want, but we need to get back as soon as possible."

"Oh, we'll be taking turns," M'bana muttered, as they headed for the hole in the wall through which Bulang had first come with Jeya, what now seemed like a lifetime ago. "Don't yöu go thinking that yöu're getting out of that."

The monkey did not exactly get resigned to its fate, but it did at least seem to wear itself out with its struggles. They switched the basket back and forth between them twice before they got back to the Morlithian Quarter, and the thrashing had stopped and the desperate screaming gradually morphed into unhappy whimpering from under M'bana's left arm by the time they reached the apothecary's shop. They received a couple of curious glances from some of the other folk out and about at this late hour, but no one stopped or challenged them. Perhaps, Bulang thought, everyone else had better things to do than investigate exactly why a basket carried by two shadowy figures was screaming.

Thëy knocked on the magician's door before thëy really thought about it. It was late, and most people would be in bed: was it rude to come back now? Would the door be answered at all? On the other hand, who knew what hours a magician kept? Bulang did not even know if the magician ran the apothecary store, was in any way associated with it, or simply lived in the back of the same building. Did you come to the apothecary during the day, and the magician at night?

The moments dragged out without a reply, and Bulang was just starting to wonder if thëy should knock again, or if the door not being answered was a message that should not be ignored if thëy and M'bana did not want a magician angry with them, when the sound of a bolt being drawn back reached their ears. The door opened, and warm candlelight illuminated the shape of the magician, their face once more obscured by the carved wooden mask.

"Back so soon?" the magician said, without any comment on the lateness of the hour. "Did you find what I require?"

"Yes," Bulang said with relief, gesturing M'bana forwards. Hê proffered the basket with both hands, which swayed slightly and chattered angrily.

"Come now child, that looks heavy," the magician tutted. "I can hardly manage that and my candle. You'll have to bring it inside for me."

M'bana looked at the magician for a second, then nudged Bulang with hîs shoulder. "Go on. I've had this for long enough, it's your turn."

Bulang exhaled in frustration. "Fine, give it here." Thëy were not, thëy realised, anywhere near as sanguine about entering the magician's chambers for a second time. Thëy were not quite sure why that was, but perhaps the possibility of imminent magic involving the monkey played a part. Even though it was why thëy were there, and it was the only option thëy had which might possibly help Jeya, it was still a possibility that made thëir skin crawl. Nonetheless, thëy forced down their unease, took the basket from M'bana, and followed the magician as they backed away down the entrance passage.

"That's right child, come this way," the magician said encouragingly. "Mind your step: we don't want it getting loose, hee?" They nudged open the door behind them, and held it open for Bulang to bring the monkey into the same room in which they had sat before.

Things had moved. There was now a large piece of slate lying flat in the middle of the floor, perhaps a handwidth thick, but half as long as Bulang on each jagged side, and covered with chalk markings. Bulang glanced at the magician, then back at the slate: if they could move that into place, they would have been able to handle the monkey's basket with ease.

"Just put it down on that," the magician said, gesturing at the slate. "Don't worry about getting it out, I can do that part myself."

Bulang set thëir burden down, and looked back up at the magician. Thëy did not want to wait around, but would it be rude to simply leave again? The tales of witches from thëir childhood meant thëy had no wish to be near whatever was about to happen, but everything relied on the magician's good nature, and them honouring the deal that had been struck.

"Let's have a look at you, then," the magician said, pulling the leaves aside and throwing them over their shoulder. The monkey screeched anew as its covering disappeared, and the magician tutted. "No need for those sort of dramatics. Now, let us see . . . " Their fingers abruptly held a long pin, which Bulang could have sworn had not been anywhere visible a moment before. They reached into the basket with both hands, and the netted monkey screeched: then the magician withdrew the pin again, the very end now smeared with red.

"Just a small discomfort, dear, so we can see what we are working with," they murmured, raising the pin to their face and sniffing. Bulang thought thëy saw the mouth behind the slits move into a smile, and the voice that emanated a moment later certainly sounded satisfied. "Yes, this should do. It is a strong creature, of the type the god favours. We may yet be able to find some assistance for your friend, if they are indeed beloved of Sa."

"How long will it take?" Bulang forced thëmselves to ask.

"A couple of hours, no more," the magician said with some satisfaction. "You can wait outside, so long as you do not disturb me."

"Right, right," Bulang said, as the potent mixture of sudden hope and desperate fear set thëir stomach churning. "And, uh, what is it that you're actually going to *do*? The result of the magic, I mean," thëy hastily added, as the mask's eyes snapped towards thëm, and thëy realised it might have sounded like thëy were trying to pry into mystical secrets. "How will it help us?"

"That remains to be seen," the magician said briskly. "There is power here that I can potentially use, yes, but the nature of it will depend on the god, and that I have not yet investigated. We can only ever make the best of what the gods hand us, child: in this case, we can perhaps push their hand a little, but that does not mean we can predict the outcome, hee?" They flapped their fingers. "Leave me to work, and wait outside. I will find you when I am done."

Bulang backed away, thëir eagerness to be elsewhere over-taking thëir desire to press for more definite answers, which did not seem likely to be forthcoming in any case. Thëy had never had much cause for faith, seeing as how thëy had been raised to believe that thëy were the divine descendant of a god, but perhaps now was the time to embrace it.

Either this would help thëm rescue Jeya, or it would not. What Bulang knew for sure was that thëy were going to make the effort regardless.

M'bana was eager to hear the news that the magic was prob-ably going to work, and was just as eager to get away from the magician before it occurred. Hê disappeared, promising to rouse anyone and everyone hê could think of who might have reason to help Jeya, and that Bulang should come and find hîm at the market stall. Bulang settled down to wait, thëir back propped against the building's wall, grateful that the night was a clear and dry one.

Thëy must have dozed off, despite thëir anxiety, because the next thing thëy knew thëy were jerking awake with a foot prodding them in the ribs, and staring up into a terrifying, shadowy visage.

"You are still alive?"

Bulang got a grip on thëir hammering heart as the face swam into focus as the magician's wooden mask, which was still not the most settling sight in the world, but better than what thëir newly awakened mind had conjured it into. Thëy swallowed and found thëir voice at the second try.

"Y-yes."

"Good. It would be a shame to have done this for no pur-pose." The magician tutted. "Are you getting up?"

Bulang scrambled to thëir feet, then nearly screamed in fright as the magician's shoulder swelled and shifted, and it took thëm a moment to realise that it was actually the monkey climbing into view from behind the magician's back. The creature crouched there as though it had known the magician all its life, and stared at Bulang with eyes that seemed to hold judgement for indignities such as fishing nets and baskets.

The magician's head tilted slightly. "Is there a problem, child?"

Bulang swallowed again, and shook thëir head. "Uh, no. No. Did it work?" Thëy had not known for what use the magician had intended to put the monkey, and had tried not to think about it too hard. Thëir mind had conjured up images of being handed something bloody and slippery and told that the magic lay within it. It now seemed that was not likely, but the relief of that was possibly outweighed by the sheer uncanniness of a creature that had been screaming and thrashing a couple of hours before now sitting on the magician, calm as an old person on a porch watching their grandchildren at play.

"Did it work?" the magician repeated. "Only you can answer that now. Hold out your hand."

Bulang did so, still somewhat hesitantly, and the magician placed something warm and moist and greasy into it. Bulang tried not to flinch, and forced thëmself to look at it.

It was a cake of soap, similar to what thëy washed thëmself with in the days when thëy lived on Second Level. Thëy looked back up at the magician, uncertain what was going on.

"Take it to the harbour before the short moon sets, and dissolve it in the water," the magician said. "Then be ready to do whatever it is that you intend to do."

"What will happen?" Bulang demanded. The magician shrugged with the shoulder that did not have a golden-maned monkey resting on it.

"I am a magician, not a fortune-teller. It seems Sa holds your friend in some regard, but I cannot predict what form the favour of a god will take." They paused, then sniffed. "But for what it's worth, I wish you luck, hee? You seem a good-hearted person, and the world could use more of those. Normally I would wish for God to light your way, but," their mask tilted back as they looked up at the sky, "I get the feeling that God's light will not be helpful to you. So find the best course you can." They clapped Bulang on the shoulder in a half-absent manner, then turned and headed back inside the building. The door closed behind them, and Bulang heard the bolt slide across.

Thëy looked down at thëir hand again, and tried not to imagine what M'bana – let alone any of the help hê had rounded up – would say when Bulang turned up with a bar of allegedly magic soap. Even though it had been M'bana's idea to come here in the first place.

Bulang sighed. This had always been a desperate hope. Perhaps it would come to nothing after all. In a sense, it did not matter. One way or the other, thëy were going to try to save Jeya before dawn. If any gods wanted to help, so much the better.

If not, Bulang would have to trust that whatever divinity thëy might or might not possess would be enough.

PART FOUR

Darel

"Our scouts report that the Raider force is advancing up the Idra, but mainly on the north shore," Big Tenan said, jabbing a thick finger at the map. "They have their ships in the channel, but no real strength of arms to the south."

"So we must cross the river to bring them to battle," Mattit Threestone said, scratching at his jaw. "Not an easy endeavour, even with the ferries."

"We have our own ships," Little Tenan said. "And we can commandeer those in the town in the God-King's name."

"Our own ships are already laden with supplies," Captain Yamrel pointed out. The Southern Army had marched down the Crown Road from Threestones with ships and boats doing the haulage work that would normally be undertaken by wagons, and the backs of the men. Darel had slightly in excess of six thousand of those men under his command: five thousand or so from the Southern Army, along with three hundred of the Brotherhood, eight hundred men mustered from levies in the middlelands, and nearly fifty sars. It was a formidable force, and one that had come together in very good time, but he still harboured doubts.

"Are there sufficient ships in the town to make the crossing in a timely manner?" he asked. Yoraby sat on the Idra's south bank, just to the east of where the Yora flowed into the Idra, and was a hub for river traffic to and from the south. However, news of the approaching threat from the east had clearly spooked the locals. The docks lacked the same bustle that Darel had briefly seen when he had travelled through with Natan, Hiran, and the others as they fled from Idramar, and even the streets of the town felt half-deserted. It seemed most people with the ability to go elsewhere had gone, even if that meant leaving their homes behind, and many had gone by water.

"There will have to be," Little replied.

"That is not a sufficiently detailed answer," Darel said, but the captain simply shrugged.

"We must get across the river, High Marshal. One way or another, we will have to make it work, unless we wish to fail the God-King."

Darel suppressed a sigh. His blunt statements to the captains had brought them into line in one respect, it was true, but now he found it working against him whenever they wished to pressure him into a course of action.

"None of us wish to fail the God-King, of course," he said, with carefully managed patience. "However, we need to know how many vessels are available to make the crossing before we begin, otherwise we will not know how best to organise it. This marshal is also wary of leaving our force split, and exposed on either shore," he added.

"All the more reason to start as soon as possible," Little said, as though stating the obvious. "High Marshal, we should begin at once. We know the Raiders have their forces concentrated on the northern shore, so we should get as many of our men across the water as fast as we may. Stragglers left on the southern bank will be at less risk in any case."

Darel drummed his fingers on the table. They had convened in a tavern, for ease, rather than go through the time-consuming motions of hospitality at the castle. The army captains were used to such simple lodgings, and Thane Mattit had raised no objection either: Yoraby was the thanedom directly to the north of his own, and Darel got the impression that relationships between the Threestones and the Yorabys were roughly as convivial as those between Blackcreek and Darkspur. The local thane had sent a message of welcome, and the promise of his own armsmen to join their numbers, and they had left it at that.

"There is one other factor we must consider," Darel said, placing his finger on the map at a point to the west. "These Godsworn, as they call themselves. We know they are there, somewhere, but we do not know their precise numbers, whereabouts, or intentions. The rumours that they have been joined by some of the Western Army and Marshal Torgallen are concerning, to say the least."

The Southern captains looked at each other, and Darel could see the uncertainty on their faces. In truth, he did not know how he would react if he was confronted with a man many years his senior in terms of age and experience, and with an equal rank, proclaiming his support for a different God-King. What did one do in such a situation? Declare him a traitor, and order the attack?

"These two forces appear to be heading towards each other, each following the Idra," Darel said. He took a deep breath, then plunged on. "If there is one thing that the arrival of the Brown Eagle clan at Black Keep taught this marshal, it is that knowing how to fight is sometimes not as important as knowing *when* to fight. Should we even be crossing the river at this time?"

"You are suggesting we should let them meet each other head on?" Mattit Threestone asked, his eyes searching Darel's face.

"There is a saying in the south," Darel said, fighting against the feeling that he was exposing himself as a dishonourable coward. "'When two cannot agree, a third profits'. It seems very unlikely that the Tjakorshi will find common ground with the Godsworn. Should we not, essentially, leave them to it?"

He knew immediately that he had said the wrong thing. Subtle shifts in the postures and expressions of the men around the table communicated their feelings without the need for words.

"High Marshal," Captain Yamrel said, the tone of the title a touch more condescending in his mouth than at any point before. "We are not seeking to keep as many men of the Southern Army alive as possible. We are seeking to fulfil our duty."

"His Divine Majesty wants the Tjakorshi dealt with," Darel pointed out. "That is his primary concern. Now we have learned of the Godsworn, they are also a threat. Why should we not let our two problems cancel each other out? At the very least, it would decrease the numbers we would have to face in the field, should it come to it."

"If the two forces come together," Thane Mattit said, "and the Godsworn break the Raiders and this demonic despot they are rumoured to follow, while His Divine Majesty's army cools its heels on the southern bank of the Idra: how does this look to the rest of the country?"

Darel felt his cheeks heat, and not from anything like the reasons they did when he was around Mattit's younger son. "You suggest a convincing win in the field for this Tyrun could open his path to the Sun Throne."

"In more ways than one," Captain Yamrel said, tracing his finger along the Idra from their location to Idramar. "His Divine Majesty is still in Threestones, which is the safest place for him, this captain thinks we can all agree. But if the Godsworn smash through the Raiders, not only does Tyrun have a great victory against Narida's enemies to his name, he's got a clear run on to Idramar." He sucked his teeth. "Possession is nine-tenths, and all that. This captain doesn't fancy finding the city and palace held against us by the army which killed those that sacked it in the first place. Claims to the Sun Throne are the business of monks and high lords, but the hearts of the lowborn are more likely to be won by vengeance."

"If we cross the river immediately, we can bring the Raiders to battle soon," Little Tenan said. "High Marshal, you've said yourself how greatly they fear dragon-mounted sars. We can break them in the field, and slay this leader: at the worst, we end one threat to our nation, and deny Tyrun a victory on which he could build his claim. With good fortune, our victory will leach support from the pretender, as the Godsworn see that the followers of King Natan saved the land from the savages."

"Any battle against the Tjakorshi will see our numbers depleted," Darel said stubbornly. "They are fierce fighters, and they brought more ships than this marshal could count to Idramar. We have nowhere near enough sars to terrorise them all. Even if we triumph, if we then have to face the Godsworn in combat—"

"Then we may die," Big Tenan said with finality. "We didn't join the Southern Army for the guarantee of a long life, High Marshal. Duty comes first."

"The God-King will have more men at his disposal soon," Thane Mattit added. "Other Southern Army garrisons that did not join us in time, other levies. The Northern Army, perhaps. Any wounds we can inflict upon the Godsworn, should they oppose His Divine Majesty, can only benefit him in the long run."

Darel forced himself to appear calm and reasoned, despite the turmoil inside him. His gut was telling him that crossing the river and taking on the Tjakorshi would not go well, but how was he to balance his gut against the advice of three experienced captains, and an older thane? He could dig his heels in and lean upon his rank as Southern Marshal, and it was likely they would go along with him rather than openly rebel, but he knew in his heart that he would have lost them from then on. Hand of Heaven or not, no army could function if those immediately beneath its commander neither trusted nor respected his decisions.

Perhaps they were correct. Perhaps, grotesque although it seemed, this was indeed as much about when to fight as it was how to fight, just not in the manner he had thought. His duty was to his monarch, and if that duty involved winning a victory for the God-King that might leave the warriors under his command vulnerable to a second battle, perhaps that was just how it was. War was not a puzzle that could be solved neatly. It was the lack of an ability to solve things neatly that led to war.

"Very well," Darel said reluctantly. "Begin with all speed. This marshal leaves the decision of which forces should be prioritised for the crossing in your hands."

He tried hard to shake the feeling that he had just drawn his sword again, and was once more squaring up to the imposing shape of Ristjaan the Cleaver in a fight he could not win, while his father attacked Saana Sattistutar in a fight that no one needed.

"Make way! Make way for Lord Blackcreek!"

Darel looked around to see who was shouting. Two companies of the Southern Army were already on the far bank at North Ferry, which was little more than a village based around the crossing from the Crown Road that ran east-to-west from Idramar to Torgallen to the beginning of the South Road at Yoraby. The ferries themselves were hard at work, as was every other vessel they had been able to press into service, but Darel was still stood on Yoraby's docks, preparing to embark. He was not in need of anyone making way, other than possibly the fish in the river, and could not understand why someone would be shouting for this to happen. Besides which, they were not even getting it correct: he was *Marshal* Blackcreek now . . .

Then, as the ongoing commotion to his left took on a slightly new flavour, he realised the shouts had got it right after all.

A large longbrow was plodding along the wharf, with the unconcerned air of a dragon that could see flat ground along which it could walk, and so had little interest in whether or not any people were nominally in its way. Somewhat more unusual were its companions trotting at its side: three adolescent rattle-tails, close-on full-grown but lacking their adult plumage, from which sailors and soldiers alike recoiled in alarm.

Darel recognised the dragons. More importantly, he recognised the warrior sat on the longbrow's back.

"Daimon?" he called disbelievingly, then began to wave frantically, and the Unmaker take anyone who thought it was behaviour unbecoming of a Hand of Heaven. "*Daimon!*"

His law-brother's eyes turned towards him, and a wide smile split Daimon's features, a mirror of the one Darel could feel on his own face. Silverthorn huffed a breath and turned where he was directed, and within a few moments Daimon was slipping down from the saddle onto the stones of the Yoraby quay, whereupon Darel immediately engulfed him in a hug, which Daimon returned.

"Your brother was so worried about you!" he said immediately. "We did not know how badly the wave might have effected Black Keep, or—" He became aware of a persistent pressure at hip height, and backed out of the embrace slightly to find the somewhat disconcerting sight of a rattletail head pressing in between them.

"Don't mind Rattler," Daimon said with a laugh, reaching

down to stroke the dragon's head. "He gets jealous, is all." He gripped Darel's shoulder with his other hand, as though to reassure himself that their embrace had not been a figment of his imagination, and that Darel was in fact real. "It is so good to see you! Your brother hopes you will forgive him if he does not prostrate himself before you, Southern Marshal though you may be."

"Your brother thinks we can make an exception," Darel replied, grinning, then sobered. "But why are you here? What happened in the south? How is home?"

Daimon's face fell too. "Black Keep was struck by the wave, but Saana realised it was coming. Some old Tjakorshi children's rhyme saved us: nearly everyone made it out in time. Also, it took care of Odem Darkspur and his men, who were attempting to besiege us."

Darel reached up and grabbed his brother's arm in shock. "They were *what*?"

"It is a long story," Daimon said, glancing back over his shoulder. "Suffice to say that Thane Odem is dead, and we have forged an alliance with Darkspur, where we are sharing resources to best manage the harvest. Yarmina is styling herself as a thane rather than a lady, and while your brother might not fully trust her, he thinks we can rely on her for so long as our interests coincide. Besides," he added, with another smile, "your brother left Saana in Darkspur to keep an eye on her, and Yarmina still seems a little scared of her."

"So why are you—" Darel cut himself off as swearing in at least two languages erupted from the vicinity of Silverthorn, and there was the thud of boots hitting the ground. Daimon turned and reached out as though to assist, but his hands were swatted away.

"This warrior is fine," Zhanna Saanastutar snapped, fully disentangling herself from Silverthorn's rear saddle. The lines of her face had shifted slightly since Darel had last seen her – her cheekbones stood out a little more sharply now – but there were other, more obvious changes. The massive, carved tooth hanging around her neck was one, and it held his eye for long enough that he could not hide his obvious shock when he realised she was now missing her left hand.

"Nari's teeth!" he exclaimed. "What happened?"

"Zhanna lost her hand protecting Yarmina," Daimon said, and the tone of his voice suggested to Darel that there might be slightly more to the story than that.

"The sar lost his life," Zhanna replied, sticking her jaw out pugnaciously. "This warrior won."

"It is still not a trade you can afford to made again," Daimon told her sternly, then looked at Darel, slightly shamefaced. "Your brother did not want to bring her along, but—"

"But you are not this warrior's mother, and she is both mother and chief and she can *still* not stop this warrior from going where she wants," Zhanna interrupted him, folding her arms and doing her best to hide the wince that the action provoked.

"It was either bring her on Silverthorn, or have her make her own way, and probably get attacked on the road as soon as someone recognised her as a Raider," Daimon muttered. "The sigil of Blackcreek makes people offer far fewer objections than they might otherwise, these days." He raised his eyebrows. "And about that: the messengers said that you saved the God-King's life?"

Darel's cheeks flushed again. "Technically, yes. Or at least, your brother helped. But why are you here?" he continued. "Your brother is delighted to see you, but surely word of The Golden could have not even reached Darkspur in time for you to get here?"

"No," Daimon said, his expression souring at the mention

of the demon's name. "Once your brother was certain things were in hand in the south, and our peoples were as well as they could be, he decided to come north to plead for aid from his newly influential older brother. Then when we were on the road, we began to hear news: first that the great wave had struck at least as far up as Idramar as well, and then that The Golden had landed and taken the city." He spread his hands. "Your brother was not going to turn back at that point, and nor were his allies."

"Allies?" Darel took a couple of steps to the side to see around Silverthorn's neck plumes, and realised that Daimon and Zhanna were not alone. Two of the small procession of dragons drawn up along the dock were intimidating war beasts like Silverthorn, but the other half-dozen or so were less imposing creatures.

"Sar Natan and Sar Osrel are from Tainbridge," Daimon said. "Thane Gilan met us on the road shortly after we left Darkspur. He was also coming west to seek aid in the aftermath of the wave, and sent two of his sars with us to help ensure we got to Idramar."

The two Tainbridge sars slipped out of the saddles of their war mounts, and went down on one knee to Darel without any trace of hesitation or embarrassment. Darel waved them up, reflecting as he did so that what with yet another Natan around, it was a good thing that the God-King and Thane Mattit's oldest son had both remained at Threestones Castle. Natan II giving his heir his name had had predictable consequences on the naming patterns of the country, it seemed.

He recognised most of the others, some of whom were doubled up on dragonback: there was Ravel, son of Achin and Inba; Avisha, Osred's granddaughter, who had acquired a necklace of carved beads similar to the ones Amonhuhe of the Mountains wore; and Ita, the tall, thin guard from the castle.

Then there were some of the Brown Eagle clan: the big youth known as Tsennan Longjaw; another whose name Darel could not remember, but whom he recognised as one of the sons of Nalon the iron-witch, as the Tjakorshi called him; sharp-faced Inkeru, who had been a witness at Daimon's wedding that Darel and his father had interrupted; and the grey-haired, gap-toothed Tsolga Hornsounder. Finally, there were two people Darel did not know at all, but he recognised their clothing and beads.

"You have folk from the Smoking Valley with you?" he asked, astonished.

"Amonomin, brother to Amonhuhe," Daimon said, "and Nenatoyo. Zhanna led a party there to find out why they had not come to trade at the Festival of Life. It turned out that Darkspur had enslaved them, so Zhanna freed them."

"They freed themselves," Zhanna corrected. "We helped." She came to stand beside Darel as the rest of the party dismounted and approached. "Ravel, Avisha, Tsennan and Tamadh are this warrior's crew. Amonomin and Nenatoyo wanted to see more of Narida. The Hornsounder has seen Idramar from the sea, but now wants to see it from the land."

Darel nodded, then looked at the one person Zhanna had not named. "And . . . Inkeru?"

"She too much fight," Inkeru replied in heavily accented Naridan, pointing at Zhanna. Then she pointed at herself. "Captain. *Sensible.*"

Darel looked at Zhanna, waiting for a defiant outburst, but none came. It seemed that while her mother and chief might not be able to overawe her, Inkeru was another matter. Darel could understand it: he would not ever want to cross Saana, but she was reasonable. Even with her thumbs tucked into the belt from which her blackstone axe hung harmlessly, Inkeru still gave off the impression of someone whom you would only realise you had insulted when your nose parted company with your face.

Two sailors were openly staring at the Tjakorshi. Tsolga waggled her eyebrows at them and leered suggestively, and each one rapidly found somewhere else to direct their eyes.

"You are crossing the river?" Daimon asked, ignoring the Hornsounder's exploits.

Darel nodded, suddenly uncomfortable. "The Golden is coming, with most of its strength on the north shore. The Tjakorshi have not yet faced a large force of Naridan men, or a sizeable number of mounted sars. The captains believe we have a good chance of breaking them."

"The captains?" Daimon looked around, then lowered his voice. "What do *you* believe? You are the Southern Marshal!"

"Your brother lacks their experience," Darel muttered. "He is not so proud as to place his misgivings above their knowledge."

"How many warriors does The Golden have?" Daimon asked, his face a picture of concern.

"We are not certain," Darel admitted. "Scouts have not been able to get close enough to get a good idea. There were many ships bearing down on Idramar when we left, but as to how that translates to fighters, and how many of those died in the taking of the capital ... " He threw up his hands. "We are working with guesses. The only certainty we have is that the demon must be stopped."

Daimon sucked his teeth, prompting a vivid memory for Darel of their father slapping him, but it seemed Daimon no longer cared if his habits were thought to be common. "And what of the other news we heard, of this mass called the Godsworn coming from the west?"

Darel sighed. "They are a problem for a different day. Your brother knows that this is not what you came north to find," he said, laying his hand on Daimon's arm, "and he is sorry. He would like nothing more than to order help for Blackcreek, and Tainbridge, and any other parts of the south that need it, but for now his duty lies in combat. We must ensure the nation survives, and your brother's new rank requires him to take the lead in this."

Daimon nodded. "Does the Southern Marshal have his own guards?"

Darel shook his head. "Normally that role would be fulfilled by sars of the marshal's household, but the marshals are usually powerful thanes even before they assume that rank. It has been a long time since anyone of our humble status has held such a position."

"Then it is fortuitous that we arrived when we did," Daimon said. "We may be an ill-matched group, but there are some fierce fighters here nonetheless."

It took a moment for Darel to grasp his meaning. Then he coughed, to try to cover his surprise. "Daimon, you cannot . . ." He leaned closer. "Avisha is—"

"Do not let Naridan thinking rule your head, brother," Daimon said softly, cutting him off. "Avisha is a young woman now, and the Tjakorshi have no issue with women fighting. Under the terms of your brother's marriage vows, neither should we. Besides," he added, "she went into the mountains with Zhanna, fought the men of Darkspur, and made it back again. She is not to be underestimated."

Darel looked at the group again. His brother; two Naridan sars; three Naridan . . . well, he would use the term "warriors", since "armsmen" was not entirely accurate; four Tjakorshi; and two people of the Smoking Valley. A group strange enough that it could have come out of an old tale, but perhaps appropriate nonetheless.

"Your brother would feel safer with you by his side," he admitted. "You always were better with a blade."

"Your brother remembers how he used to want to fight for the God-King, and you wanted to broker the peace afterwards," Daimon said. "He feels he should keep you safe, so you can get the opportunity to do that."

Darel smiled gratefully at him, but his stomach had knotted again. He had accepted his own duty as Southern Marshal to face The Golden's force, whatever might come of it, but was somewhat less sanguine now his brother, and the people of Black Keep and its neighbours, were risking their lives as well.

Then again, was that not the point? Darel was willing to risk his life for them, and was willing to risk the lives of the Southern Army for them, so he should not balk at the people from his own land risking their lives as well. It was either a risk he was prepared to take, or it was not: a Southern Marshal should not place higher value on the life of a Naridan from one place than on that of one from another. If these people wanted to fight, that was their choice.

"What?" Inkeru asked, spreading her hands to indicate that she had not followed their conversation. To Darel's surprise, rather than waiting for Zhanna to translate, Daimon answered her with a few words of what had to be Tjakorshi, pointing east down the Idra, then at them, and then at the opposite bank.

"Huh," Inkeru grunted. She unslung her blackstone axe and spat on the wharf. "'Sensible'."

Zhanna

Zhanna was not unhappy about saying goodbye to riding on Silverthorn's back. She was grateful to him, since the big dragon's mighty strides had carried them near-tirelessly, and faster than they could have gone on foot: his walking pace was the speed of a swift jog for her, as she had found out when trying to keep up to stretch her legs out. However, the rocking, swaying motion of riding a dragon did something to her spine. When she first dismounted after a day in the saddle her legs gave way beneath her, and she collapsed, to much amusement from the Naridans. She had got more used to it since, but it still felt like her legs belonged to someone else after a long time on dragonback.

Now she was on a boat, which felt far more natural, even if it was a Naridan ship instead of a yolgu, and they were traversing an enormous river rather than the salt water of the ocean.

"I honestly didn't know rivers *got* this big," she said to Inkeru. Even the Blackcreek was huge compared to the streams of Kainkoruuk, and the Idra dwarfed the Blackcreek, yet was supposed to be even wider by the time it reached the coast.

"Everything is big here," Inkeru said, leaning on the rail. "The rivers, the mountains, the animals . . ."

"The fights," Tsolga Hornsounder put in. The old woman

was staring downriver to the east, with an uncharacteristically thoughtful expression on her face.

"There are certainly a lot of warriors here," Zhanna agreed. It was easy to see, now, why her mother had been so determined to make peace when they landed at Black Keep, quite apart from simply not wanting to fight and kill for a place to live. They would not have stood a chance once the Naridans had organised themselves.

"But enough?" Tsolga said. "How many did The Golden bring with it?" She sighed. "This is going to make the battles of song look like fist fights over a spilled drink. That river is going to run red with blood."

"You're feeling cheerful today, then," Inkeru commented.

"I'm feeling *old* today," Tsolga replied, sourly. "I thought I'd come and see this land, have an adventure that didn't involve the risk of drowning, then maybe go back to Black Keep and shout at my children and grandchildren to do things for me until Father Krayk lays his eye on me. But no, it's not bad enough that I think my spine is half the length it used to be after riding a dragon for so long, that bloody draug has ruined everything *again*."

Zhanna glanced at Inkeru, whose brother Koren had gone up the coast with Otim on his taugh, to seek help from Idramar against the threat of Darkspur. Even if they had survived the great wave, who knew if they were still alive if Idramar had been in the hands of The Golden by the time they arrived? Judging by the way Inkeru was eyeing the east, and fingering the handle of her axe, the same thoughts were playing through her mind.

"How many do you suppose The Golden has with it?" Zhanna asked, more to make conversation than anything else. She was still getting used to having the older women treat her as an adult, but her station in the clan was in no doubt now she had returned from the mountains. Inkeru's daughter Olagora had wanted to come to Idramar as well, insisting that she was still part of Zhanna's crew, but Inkeru had overruled her.

"Who can say?" Inkeru replied. "It had united or broken most of the clans before we left: it's probably got them all now, those it hasn't killed. Maybe it brought all the warriors with it. That might make sense, since it seems to want to push inland."

"But why would it do that?" Zhanna asked, but Inkeru simply shrugged her shoulders wearily.

"Why did it decide to conquer the clans? Who knows the mind of a draug? Maybe it just wants—"

Zhanna looked up at her as Inkeru stopped talking, then followed the captain's gaze to the east. Pale specks had just rounded the nearest bend in the Idra.

"Oh shit," she said with feeling, as more hove into view, and the bottom of her stomach dropped into her feet. "Are those—"

"Sails," Inkeru said tightly. "Tjakorshi sails."

"Sails!" Zhanna shouted, turning around, then realised she was using the wrong language. "Sails!" she tried again, in Naridan. "Raiders! *Raiders!*"

That got the sailors' attention, and head after head snapped up and around at her shout. Their ship was nearly at the northern shore, where perhaps half of the fighters under Darel's command were already assembled, but there were many more vessels still strung out across the river channel, and a lot of men remained on the south bank. War dragons severely limited the ability of the army to cross swiftly, since a single longbrow could weigh as much as a hundred men or more. The ferries that plied the crossing were reinforced to carry such loads, but every dragon and sar taken meant a huge number of men who had to wait.

They might have waited too long.

"They'll be cut to pieces on the river," Inkeru said grimly.

"And we'll be cut to pieces on the land!" Tsolga spat. "Look what's coming!" She pointed to the bank, where a dark mass had emerged from the trees to the east. While the river looped around, the Crown Road ran straighter, only meeting the river at certain points. One of those points was the village that Daimon had told Zhanna was called North Ferry, which was their destination but, it seemed, also the destination of The Golden's warriors who were on foot.

"That's a lot of people," Zhanna said, her mouth dry. There were not yet enough to match the numbers Darel had, but they were still coming, and then there would be the crews of all the ships . . .

"My da used to tell me," Inkeru said, "that if you want to win a fight you have to be in the right place at the right time, but if you want to survive it, you have to *not* be in the wrong place at the wrong time. And so far as I can see, everywhere near here just became the wrong place."

"Looks like my children are going to get off easy after all," Tsolga said with a sigh. "I got through fifty summers of raiding without dying, but the Dark Father does like the last laugh. I'll tell you one thing," she added. "If those bastards leave me without painting my corpse, I'm coming back to haunt the lot of them."

Tila

Oh, brother, why did you send so few?

The Golden's ships had swept up the river and caught the Naridan army in mid-crossing. Some turned back for Yoraby – although that would not be a safe haven for long – while some pushed on to make the landing at North Ferry, and others simply turned tail and fled upstream. Fights raged, as ferries of Southern Army troops were boarded by multiple ships of Raiders. The invaders had greater experience of fighting on the water, of that Tila had no doubt, but when it came down to it, the business of killing was still the business of killing. Naridan troops had weapons, and a fervent desire to see another sunrise, so the Raiders did not have it all their own way.

Nonetheless, it was not looking good for her countrymen. Had the Southern Army managed to get all its men across the Idra and drawn up into a battle line, they might have been sufficient to give The Golden pause. At the very least, they could have bloodied its nose. As it was, the two thousand or so soldiers that was Tila's rough estimate of the force on the Idra's northern shore would be overwhelmed in short order. She took in the banners as she approached, matching them to her knowledge of heraldry: Threestone, Strongway, Yoraside, Scartop, and Coldford had all sent men. The bulk of the soldiers were Southern Army, though, and most importantly, there was no sign of the God-King's personal banner. She hardly expected Natan would have taken it with him when he fled Idramar, but nor did she imagine that any of those lords would have ridden to battle with their monarch without having their people make a replacement up for him.

Then a new banner was raised, and pushed to the fore. This one did have the slightly haphazard appearance of one that had been created hurriedly, but it was not the crowned sunburst of the God-King.

It was the green and black of Blackcreek.

Shit.

The last thing Tila needed was to come face to face with Darel Blackcreek. Sebiah Wousewold might not have recognised her, but Sebiah Wousewold, for all his intelligence, had never seen her unveiled, whereas Darel Blackcreek had. Only for a moment, and in her brother's dimly lit chambers at the Sun Palace, in the aftermath of having just killed Káldur Brightwater. Blackcreek's attention had mainly been on Natan, but it was still a risk.

On the other hand, Tila was currently walking side-by-side with The Golden. If anything should draw eyes away from her, it was the demon that had sacked Idramar.

A small handful of The Golden's captains were with it, as was Tajen: presumably to make sure Tila translated the draug's words correctly. Tajen avoided looking at her, or anyone. He was probably still fearful of his small part in her attempted mutiny being found out.

A party set forth from the Naridan lines to meet them. Tila eyed them as they approached, and nearly stumbled in surprise at what she saw. There was Darel Blackcreek, sure enough, along with a couple of men wearing the insignia of army captains, a thane that had to be Mattit Threestone, and another sar in Blackcreek colours and carrying the Blackcreek banner – where had Darel found him? – but it was the others that drew her eye. There were three Raider women with them, as plain as day with their milk-pale skin and barbaric weapons ... except that one of them, a big girl with her left hand missing, had a sar's longblade tucked through her belt! And then, strangest of all, were a man and a woman Tila could not place at all, bedecked with carved wooden beads.

"It seems we have a few more lost Brown Eagles to contend with," The Golden said in Alaban, sounding amused. Tila supposed that it must be correct, but how had Darel got reinforcements from the south so quickly, and why so few? She shook the thought out of her head as the two groups approached to a distance where they could easily be heard.

"Speak," The Golden instructed, extending its hand. Tila took a deep breath, deliberately did not look at Darel Blackcreek, and began.

"You're all going to die," she said flatly, leaning as far into Livnya's manner of speech as she could without sounding like a parody of an Idramese criminal. "The Golden has killed everyone between here and Idramar that hasn't joined it, so that's your choice. Join it, and live, or resist it, and die." She sighed. "Seriously, look around you. You're not getting any more help from Yoraby, and the Raiders behind us could eat you for lunch."

Darel Blackcreek's eyes found her, and narrowed. Tila tried to hide her discomfort at the scrutiny, although anyone standing next to a demon and opposite an army of her own countrymen on what was about to become a battlefield was probably allowed to be uncomfortable.

"What made you abandon the God-King?" Darel asked, and to Tila's astonishment there was sorrow in his voice, not judgement.

"He abandoned *us*!" she snapped back, without thinking. "*You* abandoned us! As soon as Idramar was threatened, you hopped into a carriage and ran away!" She bit down on her lip to prevent herself from saying more, but she was astonished at how natural the venom felt on her tongue. Looking at him, this young man that Natan had promoted to glory, stirred a fire inside her that had long been banked, but which still glowed fiercely. Darel Blackcreek could not be much older than Barach had been: why was it fair that the son of a thane lived, but her bodyguard had died? Why was it fair that Blackcreek had worked so hard to get Natan to safety, but neither of them had tried to reach her? Oh, she had been in the city, but what if Natan had been taking a tour of the merchant's district, or the docks? Would Blackcreek have abandoned him to his fate?

No. No, he would not. He would have charged out of the Sun Palace with as many soldiers behind him as he could muster, and would not have rested until either Natan was safe, or he had died in the attempt. Tila was only the Divine Princess, and she was disposable.

Even Tila's damned *mother* had left her behind. Hada Narida had always known her daughter did not matter. She tried to tell Tila that, when Tila was at odds with Einan Coldbeck, but Tila refused to listen. She continued playing the game, but even though she won that round, she could never *win*.

Tila was abruptly, violently sick of it all. No one cared what gender you were in Kiburu ce Alaba; they literally had five variations, and never told anyone what they were unless they were friends. The Morlithians had an empress. The Raiders would follow anyone who could show they were worth following. Why was she putting so much effort into trying to keep her brother on the throne, when he would die without issue in thirty or forty years, at best, and end their line anyway?

Why was she so invested in helping a country that simply did not *care* whether she lived or died?

This army was useless to her. It was not large enough to defeat The Golden. It was not even large enough to provide the sort of challenge that might cause disquiet among the less fanatical captains, and give her leverage to chip away at the draug's power base.

Blackcreek opened his mouth to begin speaking again, but Tila cut him off.

"There is nothing more to say," she snapped. "Join The Golden and renounce the titles that you only have because of who your parents were, and you'll live. If you have any decency at all, you'll take that offer back to the lowborn you've brought here to die for you and give them the same choice. But none of you will," she added, contemptuously. "You'd rather they died for what you believe in than risk them making their own minds up."

"We will not surrender to this demon," Darel Blackcreek said, his voice tight with anger. "We are all Naridan here, whether we were born in Narida itself, in Tjakorsha, or in the Catseye Mountains, and we say that The Golden will advance no farther into our land without paying in blood."

Tila looked along the line. The line about the Catseye Mountains explained who the people with the carved beads were, at any rate, but she had neither the time nor the inclination to find out why and how Blackcreek had dragged a couple of them here.

"They'll fight you," she told The Golden in Alaban.

"My fires told me as much," the draug replied calmly. "I will wet my blade with blood today."

Tila frowned. She hoped it was not simply going to draw its sword and begin laying into those drawn up against them. Their parties were roughly equal in number, but that was not good odds when The Golden could just walk back to the rest of its warriors and let them do the work. On the other hand, who could say exactly how much attention the draug paid to odds? The Raider witches had said it could not fall in battle, if Korsada the Dry was to be believed, and whether or not that was true, The Golden certainly seemed to *believe* it was true.

"Wait."

The sar with the banner of Blackcreek stepped forward. Darel Blackcreek put out his hand to grab at his man's shoulder, but the sar shook it off, and in that moment Tila knew who he must be.

"This lord is Daimon Blackcreek, brother of the Southern Marshal," he declared. "When the Brown Eagle clan came to Black Keep, this lord defeated their champion in single combat." He raised his hand to point at The Golden.

"And now he challenges you."

Tila looked at The Golden in shock, but the draug was as still as it always was when not doing anything in particular. However, the mouth of the body it wore was quirked into a slight smile, and its ice-green eyes were calm.

"Hè challenges you," Tila said.

"I know," The Golden replied. "What do they seek to gain from it?"

Tila shook her head, and turned back to the younger Blackcreek. "Why? What's the point? The Golden has a massive numerical advantage: you can't possibly think that the Raiders are just going to give up and turn around, even if you win."

"This lord is aware of that," Daimon said. "However—"

"Daimon—" Darel Blackcreek tried to cut in.

"Shut up, Darel!" Daimon Blackcreek barked, and the tone of his voice startled even Tila. "Let your brother do this!" He strode forward until he was a mere yard or two from The

Golden, and stared at it. "This lord wants your head, you bastard. Fight him, or run away behind your shields and show yourself as a coward. Let your warriors come at us afterwards, if they still wish to."

Tila opened her mouth to translate, but Tajen beat her to it. However, he did not speak in Alaban, but in Tjakorshi. What was more, he spoke loudly enough that not only did all the captains with them hear it, but when he had finished, the oldest of the three Raider women with the Naridan party whooped, and made an obscene gesture.

Tajen was doing his job, but in a way that left The Golden no room to hide. All its captains now knew what had been said. The Golden could fight Daimon Blackcreek, or it could turn around and be labelled a coward. That might not be enough to topple it, but Tila would be amazed if it did not leave some sort of cracks in its authority.

The Golden did not seem perturbed. It simply nodded, and drew its longblade.

Daimon

"**D**aimon!" Darel said, grabbing his shoulder. "What are you doing? Your brother— *This marshal* forbids this!"

"The challenge has been issued," Daimon replied calmly. Oddly enough, he felt calm as well. "To withdraw now would bring great shame not only upon your brother, but upon the house of Blackcreek. You cannot command this."

"The Unmaker take shame, and our house!" Darel hissed, pulling Daimon around so he had no choice but to look at his brother's face. Darel's eyes were wide and fearful. "Daimon, this serves no purpose! This isn't the Lay of the Golden Sword, where single combat decides an entire war! They will attack us whatever the outcome!"

"Probably," Daimon agreed. He took his brother's hands in his own. "But think about it, Darel. They follow the demon: from what the other Tjakorshi have told us, it destroyed their entire way of life, and rebuilt it around itself. What will it do to the morale of their army if they see it cut down? They will be in a foreign land, deprived of the leadership that brought them here. There will be doubt, there will be infighting ... they'll undergo their own Splintering, right here." He smiled. "It might not end the war, but it could deliver them a blow from which they do not recover. Against that, the life of a thane's younger brother is as nothing."

"Your life is *not* as nothing!" Darel said, his voice shaking. "Daimon, your brother loves you. You are the most important person in his world, and he cannot let you do this!"

"High Marshal," said the man whom Darel had introduced to Daimon as Thane Mattit Threestone, and the father of someone called Hiran with whom, Darel had whispered hurriedly to Daimon, he was now engaged in a romance. "Your brother speaks truly. To issue a challenge and then revoke it is a violation of the Code of Honour."

"This marshal has it on the highest authority that the Code of Honour does not apply when dealing with 'savages'," Darel muttered. That was a story Daimon had not heard from him, but it would have to wait.

"Lord Daimon makes a good point, High Marshal," one of the army captains chimed in. "If we cut the head of the dragon off, the body might not have much stomach for a fight. And this so-called demon doesn't look much more than a man, in any case."

The other two captains nodded, and made noises of agreement. Darel gritted his teeth, and looked up at Daimon.

"Damn you," was all he said, softly, and those two words cut Daimon to the bone. Then Darel embraced him, briefly and fiercely, but pulled away before Daimon could properly return it. The rest of the party began to back away, but as Daimon turned back to face The Golden, he realised Zhanna was standing next to him.

"Mama is going to kill you," she said, her tone flat. Daimon realised that her lip was trembling, and her eyes were glistening. He was touched: he had never been quite sure exactly how Zhanna felt about him, and it was not a conversation that would have come easily, even had they both been natural speakers of the same language. It seemed that she had enough affection or respect for him to be scared for him, even though she was projecting it onto her mother.

And it was true. Saana *would* be furious with him. But, Daimon hoped, she would understand how the potential gain outweighed the possible loss.

"Then let us hope she gets the chance to do so," he told Zhanna. "Please keep hold of Rattler's collar; your friend would not want him to get involved, and get hurt." He hesitated, as emotion tugged at his gut. His instinct was to shove it down, but his instinct was borne of the long years growing up under his father's tuition, and he was learning to ignore it. "If The Golden should triumph, take care of your mother and Darel. And yourself," he added. "Will you do that for your friend?"

Zhanna's mouth screwed up, and for a moment Daimon thought she was about to cry, but she simply sniffed once, sharply, and nodded. "Your friend will."

"Thank you," Daimon said, honestly. Zhanna backed away to join the others, and Daimon turned to face his opponent.

The rest of the Raiders, along with the Naridan woman who had been translating for them, had retreated a little way as well. The Golden stood alone, with its longblade unsheathed and held lightly in one hand.

Daimon studied it as he drew his own blade. The demon, if that was truly what it was, stood a couple of finger-widths taller than him, and had a rangy build that hinted at a combination of speed and strength. Besides the metal mask that obscured much of its face, it wore a long leather jerkin as armour. Leather in itself would not stand up to a longblade's edge, even when treated, but virtually none of the bare leather was visible, since it was covered in metal discs. They looked oddly familiar, and it took Daimon a moment to realise that they were similar to those that decorated Saana's belt. The Golden must have taken the belts of defeated chiefs and used them to make its armour, like a prizefighter displaying trophies. It struck Daimon as a strange mix of disrespect, and continuation of tradition.

He felt the silence stretching out in front of him, but there was not just nothing to say, there was nothing he *could* say that this thing with a man's body would understand. The challenge had been issued, and accepted. Now there were simply two warriors, waiting to play their part in what was to come.

He met The Golden's eyes, and did his best to suppress the shiver that ran through him as he did so. Daimon had seen corpses, but he could not remember seeing eyes that looked quite so *dead* as those staring back at him. Perhaps it was something to do with how pale they were, as though they had partially frozen over. Still, he was a sar of Narida, and both the brother of a thane, and the son of one. He would not show fear, or even discomfort, in the face of an adversary.

He raised his blade in both hands, and began to advance, measuring the distance between them with his eyes. The ground underfoot was short-cropped grass, where the people of North Ferry grazed their animals, and although a little slippery from recent rain, should be free of unexpected hazards like tree roots. It would all come down to speed, and technique. How experienced was The Golden with the longblade that it held?

The Golden had not moved. Daimon was only a pace away from being able to lunge and reach The Golden with his blade. He lifted his foot—

Now The Golden moved, flowing into action just as Daimon shifted his weight. It took two quick steps forward and darted to the side around his blade, lashing out towards Daimon's eyes with its own weapon as it did so. Daimon flinched backwards and sideways, avoiding the strike, but his counter-cut was nowhere near making contact. He regained his balance and footing, but now that The Golden had started to move, it did not seem inclined to stop. It came at him again, quick and light on its feet, with its blade held in a guard position that was unfamiliar to him, yet seemed as natural as his own. Daimon retreated two steps to be sure of his measure and timing, then engaged.

He feinted a lunge, seeking to off-balance The Golden with its own momentum, but the demon moved seamlessly to its left to avoid where his thrust would have landed, and was quick enough to knock Daimon's sword down with its own as he attempted a backhanded cut towards where he had anticipated it would be. Daimon brought his blade back up in time to turn The Golden's next strike, and circled to his left as he did so, but The Golden stepped backwards to evade the thrust he aimed at the right side of its chest. Then, even before Daimon had returned to his guard position, the demon was coming for him once more.

This time, Daimon's feinted thrust did not garner a response: The Golden shifted its weight only slightly, and it was inside Daimon's guard and driving the tip of its sword into his ribs. The maille of his coat-of-nails held up under the blow, but it still felt like he had been struck with a hammer. He disengaged with a hasty sidestep, and a clatter of swords as he clumsily knocked The Golden's weapon away before it could strike him again.

Daimon took an experimental deep breath, and tried not to wince. He did not think anything was broken or cracked, but he was not going to have full freedom of movement. The Golden was a mere three paces away, watching him with those dead, dispassionate eyes, but when Daimon showed no sign of keeling over it raised its sword again.

It was fast, and it was skilled. Daimon had no idea where the demon had learned how to fight, if indeed they were the abilities of the body rather than the intelligence driving it, but it was clearly deadly. It seemed very direct, however, with little use of feints or fakes. Every motion was an attack, and although The Golden's speed meant those motions were still a threat, perhaps Daimon did not need to read anything more into them than what was there. The thing was simply trying to kill him as swiftly and efficiently as possible, every action an attempt to lay its blade on his flesh, and that was an end to it.

It was an alarming concept in many ways, and – his ribs reminded him – a painful one, but Daimon still felt a momentary sensation of satisfaction, as he might when solving a puzzle. He had been mistaken to approach this fight as though it was against another sar, or even against a champion like Ristjaan the Cleaver. The Golden was a killer, not a duellist.

Now it just remained to be seen whether Daimon had the ability to turn that realisation into victory.

He took up his guard stance again, and stepped forward. This time when The Golden moved, Daimon tried not to second-guess his enemy, or himself. The Golden lunged for him, another serpent-swift move with no disguise except its own speed, and Daimon brought his blade up to turn the strike harmlessly past his left shoulder, then stabbed for the demon's throat. The Golden twisted away from the full force of the impact, and the tip of Daimon's blade skittered off one of the metal discs over The Golden's collarbone rather than punching into its throat, but Daimon allowed himself a small smile as he stepped away again out of blade range. He had landed a strike on the demon; let it think on that.

It did not think for long.

The Golden gave no cry of rage, but it moved back into the attack with the swiftness of one for whom combat was second nature. Its blade leaped out, questing towards Daimon's face, and he gave ground, tangling its sword with his. Demon or not, unfamiliar fighting style or not, there were only so many ways that the body it was using could move, and Daimon was familiar with them from the countless hours of blade practice he had engaged in since childhood. He wrenched upwards to throw the demon's guard high for a moment, then ceased his retreat and stepped forward and past it to its right, slamming his sword into its belly with a squeal of metal on metal.

The Golden's return strike landed diagonally between Daimon's shoulders, but although he staggered an extra step before spinning to raise his blade again, his maille turned it. Now it was The Golden's turn to breathe in deeply and straighten its spine, for although Daimon's blade had not found a gap between the discs of its armour, the impact of his strike had surely winded it a little. So be it: combat between armoured sars was often less about whose blade made a telling strike during such passes, and more about who tired sooner, and allowed their opponent an opening. Daimon rolled his shoulders, and satisfied himself that The Golden's blow had done nothing except give him what would undoubtedly be a long line of a bruise by the morning.

Assuming he survived this fight, of course, and whatever came after it.

He pressed forward, keen to put The Golden on the back foot, but caution did not appear to be in the demon's nature. It swung double-handed for his legs, and Daimon was so surprised that he awkwardly changed his own motion halfway through, bringing his sword down to block the strike even while trying to step back from it.

It was a feint.

The Golden's sword had no sooner twitched towards Daimon's legs than it twitched back again, and came up to land a full-blooded strike on the left side of his helmet. Daimon, already off-balance thanks to his hasty attempt at a defence, staggered to his right as the world exploded in his left ear. Everything wobbled, but it was far from the first time that Daimon had taken a blow to the head, and his instincts cut in. For a moment he was back outside the walls of the Black Keep itself, drilling with his blade under his father's instruction and obeying Lord Asrel's shouts to return to guard position, even though there were now two Darels in front of him, asking nervously if he was hurt.

He was not facing Darel now, though. The Golden came at him again, a blurry mess of shining metal on dark leather, and Daimon raised his blade once more. Evade if you can, parry if you cannot, block if you must: that was the lesson that had been ground into him by his father's punishing tutelage, and with his legs unsteady and his eyesight fuzzy, he had no time for finesse. He swung his sword at the dark line of The Golden's blade as it swept towards his head, and battered it aside a moment before it landed another punishing strike on his helmet.

He did not, however, see the kick that tripped him as he took an instinctive step backwards. He left leg tangled on something, what little balance he had left deserted him, the world moved unexpectedly, and something enormous hit him from behind hard enough to drive the air from his lungs and slam his helmet into the back of his head. His vision clouded over for a moment.

It was the ground. Nothing had hit him: he had hit the ground. He had fallen on his back and was now looking up at the sky. Why was he on the ground? Everything seemed distant. Someone was calling his name. Was it Darel? Why was Darel calling him? He sounded scared. Was something wrong? Daimon should go to him. Darel was Daimon's brother, and Daimon would always keep him safe.

A dark shape appeared in his vision, outlined against the sky. Daimon just had time to realise that it was not Darel, because Darel did not have a metal face, when something long and thin flashed towards—

Zhanna

"*No!*" Zhanna shrieked, as The Golden buried its sword in Daimon's skull, and he went limp. Her shout did nothing: the draug did not even look up at her. It simply withdrew its blade and stepped back, then turned and began to walk towards its cheering captains. Zhanna had the sudden urge to chase after it, to draw the longblade that had belonged to Daimon's father and strike it down from behind, but she would never have reached it before it got to its lackeys.

She was not the only one with that impulse, however. Darel started forward with his own cry of grief and loss, and two of the men with him had to wrestle him backwards.

"He's dead, High Marshal!" one of them shouted.

"Then we must get his body!" Darel cried, struggling to free himself.

"There's no time!"

The Golden had reached its captains. They began to walk back towards the waiting lines of their warriors, who were waving their weapons and shouting in celebration of the draug's triumph. Zhanna got a quick glimpse of the Naridan woman who had been translating, looking back at Daimon's body with what seemed like regret, but then she disappeared behind someone else.

One of the Tjakorshi captains raised a shell horn. The deep, throbbing call to war sounded, and The Golden's battleline began to thunder forward. It was a slow trot at the moment, but it would accelerate into a whooping charge by the time it hit the soldiers defending North Ferry.

"Shit!" Inkeru spat. She looked around at Zhanna, as the Naridans with them began to retreat back towards their own men. "We can't leave him there!"

Zhanna took a moment to weigh up the distances involved, then nodded. "Let's go."

She started running, the three rattletails with her, and was relieved to find Inkeru beside her without another word being exchanged. Tsolga was shouting something from behind them, but Zhanna ignored her.

"Take one arm each!" she called to Inkeru, as they reached Daimon. "You'll have to get his sword!"

The weapon had fallen from Daimon's right hand. Inkeru snatched it up from the ground and shoved it through her belt. "Ready?"

Zhanna tugged the heavy gauntlet off Daimon's right hand, and seized his arm by the wrist. She very deliberately did not look at his face, nor at Rattler sniffing at it with what seemed like concern. "Ready."

Daimon's flesh was still warm, of course, which was probably more disconcerting than if it had not been. As Zhanna turned and hauled, dragging him across the ground after her like a sledge, it could have almost felt like she was bringing him back to get an injury treated. However, his fingers dangled limply, and there was no fluttering pulse for her to feel in his wrist.

She looked up. The Naridan soldiers, their expressions halfway between resignation and despair, were readying spears and shields. Someone shouted, and bowstrings thrummed: arrows arced out from behind the Naridan line, sailing over

Zhanna's head towards the Tjakorshi warriors approaching from behind her. She desperately called on Father Krayk to turn his eyes on his own children, and call many of them back to the depths today, even though she knew the sea god was not swayed by entreaties. There was nothing to say he would even consider her one of his own any longer: was she not about to fight against her own people, in defence of a foreign land?

Well, so far as Zhanna was concerned, this land was her land now, and her people were whoever she wanted her people to be. If the Dark Father disliked that, she would deal with the consequences.

The rain of arrows brought a chorus of screams and cries of pain from behind her, but also an answering round of grunts. Zhanna hunched her shoulders instinctively, knowing what was coming: a moment later, a hail of slingstones clattered against Naridan shields. One caught her between the shoulders with an impact that made her panic for a moment that some adventurous warrior had run ahead of the rest and plunged his weapon into her, but her sea leather held, and she did nothing more than stagger a step and cough out a startled gasp. Inkeru yelped, and her steps faltered as well.

"My fucking leg!" the captain snarled, when Zhanna looked around at her. A sharp-edged stone had torn a gash in her woollen leggings, and Zhanna could already see blood welling up underneath. Inkeru resumed pulling, but she had to use one leg more than the other, and the strain was showing on her face.

"Nearly there!" Zhanna said encouragingly. The closest few soldiers began to shuffle apart, creating a gap in their line for Inkeru and her to get through with their burden, not to mention the rattletails. Zhanna gritted her teeth and tried to speed up: these people were giving her an opportunity to get to safety out of respect for her efforts to retrieve the body of one of their own, so the least she could do was make sure they had the chance to reform and meet the oncoming charge.

"Come on!" she shouted at the world in general, and with one last stumbling rush, they were past the first line of spearmen, which began to reform behind them. That did not mean they could stop, of course: they were still in danger, and in the way. Zhanna hauled with all her might, dragging Daimon's body past ranks of worried faces. She did not even truly know why she had risked so much to retrieve him, given she was likely about to die in any case, but perhaps that was the point.

Perhaps, what mattered most was what you did when nothing was going to matter at all.

Clanks and thuds filled the air, and someone an arm's length to her right toppled backwards with a gurgle of agony as something arced down and skewered him through the shoulder. Zhanna glanced sideways: it was a javelin, and if they were close enough for javelins—

The rising tide of noise behind her became a roar, as The Golden's warriors sought to drown out their own fears through speed and volume, and then they hit the Naridan line with a crunch so loud that Zhanna thought for a moment that she had gone deaf. Everyone around her staggered back a step or two, as the sheer force of impact rocked the defenders back on their heels. Thorn, Talon, and Rattler hissed in alarm, and shook their tails.

"Where in the Dark Father's name are the others?" Inkeru yelled over the noise. Someone pushed in behind Zhanna, into the gap where she had just been, and she became abruptly aware that she was a Tjakorshi warrior in the midst of Naridans being attacked by Tjakorshi warriors. There was no red or green cloth here, to tie around her arm like Darel had had her folk do when Rikkut Fireheart had attacked Black Keep. They would just have to hope that anyone who saw them knew that there were three Tjakorshi with Daimon Blackcreek, and that the ones hauling his body around were two of those three.

"Probably with Darel!" she shouted back, straightening up as best she could to see over the rows of helmets and spears. She caught sight of the big Blackcreek banner, and pointed. "That way!"

"We're never going to be able to drag him there," Inkeru said helplessly, gesturing at all the frantically milling soldiery. Zhanna nodded.

"Help me get him up."

"What are you— Oh." Inkeru hoisted Daimon's body off the ground enough for Zhanna to take him over her shoulders, right arm around his neck, and left arm behind his knees. She reflexively tried to grip his legs with her left hand for a moment, until the dull bump of her wrist against fabric reminded her once more that this was no longer an option she had.

Fine. Well, she had two legs, that would have to do.

Daimon was tall for a Naridan, but fairly lean. His armour, however, added considerable weight to his frame, and Zhanna's thighs felt like they were about to burst into flame as she forced her way upwards with a strangled shout of effort. She wobbled for a moment, but Inkeru steadied her, and together they hurried as best they could towards where the Blackcreek banner was flying and, as it turned out, an argument was raging.

"—marshal will not have his first command end in his cowardice!" Darel was shouting at one of the captains. He had the reins of his dragon in one hand, and was jabbing at the man's chest with the first two fingers of his other.

"This'll be your last command if you stay!" the man protested. He was significantly taller than Darel, with bulk that spoke of muscle. "We misjudged the Raiders' progress, and we'll pay the price: your presence or absence can't change that, but—" He broke off as Zhanna staggered up to them with

Daimon over her shoulders, and his eyebrows rose in shock. "You . . . went back for him."

"He was this warrior's friend," Zhanna said thickly, the words sticking in her throat. She avoided dwelling on the other thoughts and wishes she had had about Daimon, at various times. She had never told him; and more importantly, it seemed her mother never had either. That was just as well, since Zhanna could not imagine anything more mortifying.

She might have been imagining it, but the other Naridan men with Darel looked ashamed as she spoke. Darel did not: he bowed to her, to the shock of the men with him, and his face showed nothing but naked relief as he straightened up again.

"Thank you," he said quietly. He turned back to the big man. "Captain Tenan—"

"You made it, then," Tsolga Hornsounder said. The old woman had her blackstone axe in her hand, incongruous though it looked at the end of an arm which was more skin and bone than anything else these days.

"No thanks to you," Inkeru replied, but Tsolga just spat on the ground.

"I'm not carrying bodies around at my age, girl! I'd have fallen over before I got halfway to him. Not like our Zhanna there; strong as any dragon, she is." Tsolga grinned, showing her few remaining teeth. "Although that's probably not how you wished for him on top of you, hey?"

"Tsolga!" Inkeru barked, and actually squared up to the Hornsounder as Zhanna's cheeks heated ferociously. She crouched down and let Daimon's body slip off her shoulders as respectfully as possible, leaving Rattler to nudge at it with his snout, then got back to her feet and swiped at her traitorous, watering eyes. Tsolga had crossed a line, and there was a limit to how much respect Zhanna was prepared to show her.

"What?" Tsolga was protesting to Inkeru. "We're all about

to die, I can't make a joke just before the Dark Father takes me home? The problem with young folk today is that you take everything so—"

Zhanna shouldered Inkeru aside, and Tsolga's indignant tirade stuttered to a halt as Zhanna grabbed her shirt.

"He. Was. My. *Friend*," she bit out, finding a moment of vicious pleasure in the sudden look of fear in the Hornsounder's eyes. "You can make your horrible jokes about me, but not him, when he's just been *killed*!"

She finished with a shout that was only half-intentional, and which was echoed by snarls from her rattletails. Tsolga jerked her head back. The Hornsounder's authority in the Brown Eagle clan came from a mixture of age, experience, and the sheer size of her family, but right now Zhanna was angry enough to have none of it, and it seemed her dragons had picked up on her mood.

"Sorry, Zhanna," Tsolga said, which might have been the first genuine-sounding apology Zhanna had ever heard the old woman give anyone. "I didn't mean—"

"Enemies!" someone shouted in Naridan, and Zhanna glanced up to see Amonomin fitting an arrow to his bow. The Valleyman was looking to the north, and sure enough, shapes bearing roundshields and blackstone axes were engaging the Naridan soldiers there.

"They've flanked us already!" Inkeru groaned. She drew Daimon's longsword, cut it back and forth through the air experimentally, then grimaced and stuck it back through her belt in favour of her axe.

"Darel!" Zhanna shouted.

"This marshal sees them," Darel said, his voice tight. "Captain—"

"High Marshal!" someone shouted. "The rearguard has been engaged! Raiders have landed in the village!"

Everything was going to the depths. "Get my shield!" Zhanna told Tsolga, and for a wonder the old woman did as she was bid, grabbing it from the pile of possessions they had left behind when going to meet The Golden for the ill-fated parley.

"You sure this is going to work?" the Hornsounder asked, holding it out for Zhanna to slip her handless arm into. Without a hand, Zhanna was going to have to rely on buckles alone to keep the shield on her arm, but it was probably better than going into battle without one at all.

"No," Zhanna replied, grabbing the rim to hold it in place, "but I don't have many options. Come on, tighten it up!"

"These fingers don't work as well as they used to," Tsolga snapped, struggling with the buckles. "Why do you think I'm on the lookout for another husband?"

Zhanna groaned. "You're disgusting," she told Tsolga, as the straps were finally tightened enough.

"There's nothing disgusting about a woman's pleasure," Tsolga replied haughtily, slipping her own shield on to her arm.

"Oh, you can make *anything* disgusting," Zhanna told her. Most of The Golden's warriors were being held back, but a small group had broken through. Instead of turning to help their allies, they forged on, coming straight for where the standard of Blackcreek flew. It seemed they had learned to tell where a Naridan commander was, and each one wanted the glory of bringing Darel down.

Zhanna's throat was dry, her hand was shaking, and her bowels were water. She was scared when she led the Unblooded against Rikkut Fireheart's raiders, and she was scared when leading the rescue attempt in the Smoking Valley, or fighting off the thundertooth that had tried to eat them, but something was different now. Now, she had been hurt, and that injury was why her shield was strapped so tightly to her arm. Zhanna had heard older raiders talking about how young people thought they were invincible, and had laughed at it then, but now she knew what they had meant. This time, when battle called, she felt no excited anxiety, merely a cold dread. She had no wish to prove herself: she simply wanted to run.

But she would not.

Zhanna had not been able to save Daimon, but before he died he asked her to look after her mother and his brother. Nothing short of death was going to prevent her from doing just that.

"Here they come!" she shouted in Naridan. She heard long-brows snorting behind her, but she did not look around to see what was going on. There was no way that she, Inkeru and the Hornsounder could make a shield wall with just three of them, and the enemy were not charging as a unified battleline, so this was going to come down to individual combat.

Zhanna waited until she could see the whites of the eyes of the warrior charging her; a wiry man with the scarred cheeks of one who had been marked as an elite, loyal warrior by his chief, or perhaps The Golden itself. Then, instead of setting herself to meet his rush, she ran at him instead, screaming loud enough to terrify both him and her own fear.

Her enemy was caught off guard by her aggression, and did not have his axe quite ready to strike. Zhanna smashed into him with her shield before he could lash out at her, and dumped him off to one side. He clattered to the ground with a great *whoomph* of expelled breath, and she stabbed downwards. His groin was the most immediate target, so she buried her longblade in that. He howled in agony, and she ripped it out to turn and meet her the next warrior trying to kill her, while Thorn and Talon piled on to deal with her fallen enemy using claws and teeth.

She caught a flash of red hair, nearly the same shade as her own, and instinctively caught one, two, three strikes of a blackstone axe on her shield, backpedalling as she did so. One of the dark shards of stone stuck in the unrimmed edge on the third strike, and Zhanna wrenched the weapon aside to slash down at the arm wielding it. Cloth and flesh parted, and the other warrior fell back, abandoning their axe as blood began leaking from their forearm. Zhanna pursued, feinting high with her sword and then cutting low into her enemy's left calf as they raised their shield to protect their head. She was rewarded with a scream, and her opponent's leg giving out. A fire-haired woman was revealed as she instinctively flung out her shield arm to catch herself, and Zhanna drove her own shield into her enemy's face, sending her sprawling backwards in a spray of shattered teeth and blood.

Two down, at least for the moment, but more coming. Zhanna heard Inkeru's shrieking war cry, and someone else screaming immediately afterwards, so the Brown Eagle clan's most fearsome captain was clearly not dead yet. An arrow flashed past Zhanna and took one onrushing attacker in the throat, while another just missed: Amonomin and Nenatoyo were doing their part in this fight that they had landed themselves in by dint of following Zhanna to Darkspur and beyond. Zhanna wished ferociously that the two Valley people made it out alive and back to their kin somehow, rather than dying here in the north for a cause so remote from their own borders.

The man the arrow had missed bellowed in rage, and focused on her. He was big, and wielding a weapon that was more stone-tipped club than a true blackstone axe, all blunt brute force. He handled it easily enough, though: Zhanna just had time to step back before it whistled past her nose in a backhanded swipe, clipping the axe still stuck in her shield. The impact knocked the weapon loose and sent it spinning away, but it also tugged her off balance, and she could not avoid the forehand blow he transitioned seamlessly into directly afterwards. The force of the blow staggered her even through her shield, and the second one numbed her arm. She sidestepped and stabbed at his face with her longblade, but his downswing knocked the weapon from her hand, leaving her defenceless.

Thunder from behind her, and a momentary expression of alarm on her enemy's scarred face, were the only warnings she had before a mountain galloped past her and a broad-bladed spear buried its entire head in the big warrior's chest. He was punched off his feet and carried backwards by the impact, and landed with the spear's haft jutting straight up from his chest like a sapling.

Darel Blackcreek steered his war dragon to the right and rode clean through another warrior, who did not manage to avoid the monstrous longbrow that tossed him into the air with a flick of its metal-shod horns. Sar Natan and Sar Osrel followed to either side of Darel, riding down their own victims. The rest of the straggle of Tjakorshi warriors that had forced their way through the Naridan lines came apart as the sars plunged into them. It was as Zhanna's mother had told her on the *Krayk's Teeth*, when Zhanna was getting her first ever sight of the Black Coast: the place you did not want to be against dragon riders was on flat ground in the open. Then, you were dead.

There were nowhere near enough sars on this side of the river to turn the tide of the battle in general, though. There were about twenty drawn up as a reserve, but even if each one took down ten or more of The Golden's army, that would do little to dent the enemy's numbers. Zhanna picked up her sword from where it had fallen, and walked to the big man laying on his back with Darel's spear jutting out of his chest. He was still alive, gasping for air as blood ran into his lungs. Zhanna cut his throat with a slash of her longblade, more for mercy's sake than anything else.

"Zhanna!"

That was Inkeru: Zhanna looked around, then ran over to where the captain was kneeling. As she got closer she realised that Inkeru was not, as she had first thought, struggling with an enemy who refused to die. Instead, she was hunched over Tsolga Hornsounder.

"Tsolga!" Zhanna shouted, her earlier anger at the old woman forgotten. Tsolga was pale and sweat-soaked, and the reason was obvious: the gaping wound across her belly, where she had been caught by a blackstone axe's slash.

"Told you I was about to die," the Hornsounder muttered as Zhanna grabbed her hand. "I should have stuck to blowing my shell and— Gah!" She winced in pain. "And telling others where to fight. Too old to do it myself now."

Zhanna fought down tears; not because she was embarrassed by them, but because she was in the middle of a battle that might sweep her up again at any moment, and blurry vision could cost her life. Tsolga Hornsounder had been the mainmast of the Brown Eagle Clan for decades, and it was unthinkable to lose her. She was the one responsible for keeping the clan organised in battle, and letting everyone know when to charge and when to . . .

. . . retreat.

Zhanna looked up and around. The Naridan soldiers were holding for the moment, but they were already being ground down by weight of numbers and pressed backwards by sheer weight. The defence would break down before too long, and Zhanna knew well enough from tales told by older warriors of the carnage that occurred when a shield wall splintered.

"Tsolga," she said urgently. "Do you think you've got one more horn blast in you?"

"Of course she hasn't!" Inkeru said sharply, wiping away her own tears. "Her belly's cut open!"

"You don't blow from the belly, girl," Tsolga said through gritted teeth. She looked at Zhanna. "One more, yes, but why?"

"You need to sound the retreat," Zhanna told her.

"Retreat?" Tsolga winced in pain. "They can't retreat now, they'll just be slaughtered quicker! Besides, they wouldn't understand it!"

"Our side won't," Zhanna said. "But the other side would."

Tsolga blinked, and then the old woman managed to smile in understanding through her pain. "They'll think any shell horn they hear is their own."

"It won't be enough to turn this for us," Zhanna said, "but we might confuse them long enough to break out to the north."

"And then what?" Inkeru demanded. Zhanna shrugged.

"That's a problem for later. I promised Daimon I'd look after his brother and my mother, and I can't do that if we die here. His captains want him to run away and save his own life anyway."

Inkeru looked behind them, towards the assembled dragon riders, then nodded. "If the sars break out with us, they can turn into the battleline from the side, and start to roll it up. They won't win, but they'll do a hell of a lot of damage before they die."

"We'll get you out of here," Zhanna told Tsolga, smiling down at her, but the Hornsounder just spat.

"Pfah! The Dark Father's called my name, girl, and it doesn't matter to him where I die. Leave me here. If The Golden's people find me afterwards and assume I'm one of theirs, I might at least get my corpse painted and dumped into the river, and my soul might be carried downstream for Father Krayk to find, if he wishes."

Zhanna swallowed and nodded. "As you wish. And thank you."

*

Riding up the Crown Road of Narida behind Daimon had been a challenging experience for Zhanna, mainly due to being in close proximity to him for so long without any sort of recognition that he registered her presence as a woman rather than as a young warrior of her clan. And to be sure, she was grateful that he had respected her in that manner, when even some of her own clan still thought of her as a child, but even so . . .

What she was about to do was a challenge in an entirely different way, however, because not only was she attempting to control Silverthorn by herself, but she was not going to be on the well-maintained surface of a Naridan Crown Road. Instead, they would be riding over the ground of a battlefield.

Fast.

At enemies.

"Ready?" Darel shouted, raising a spear into the air, and the sars with them brandished their weapons and cheered in response. They knew they were riding to their deaths, but if there was one thing that Tjakorshi and Naridan could agree on, it was that it was better to face your death head on, and on your own terms.

Darel had Daimon's body slung over his saddlehorn, behind his dragon's neck. Zhanna had insisted on it, mainly because entrusting his brother's body to his care was the best way she could think of to make sure Darel did not break from the plan and veer off into the main battle with the rest of his sars. He had finally accepted the hurried arguments of his captains that he should save his own life, since he was the last High Marshal whom the God-King knew he could trust, and Zhanna's entreaties that no one wanted her mother to be left as the sole ruler of Blackcreek, least of all Saana herself. However, Zhanna thought it wise to make sure that Darel did not get overcome in the heat of the moment by the peculiarly Naridan self-destructiveness that called itself honour.

"*Charge!*" Darel bellowed, and their party lurched into motion, the sars of the Naridan army forming a protective ring around Darel, Zhanna, and the rest of their party. Zhanna clutched at the reins with one hand and wrapped them around the stump of her other wrist, and hoped the few weeks she had spent learning how to ride Silverthorn under Daimon's eye would at least keep her on the beast's back for long enough to get clear. She caught a glimpse of fighting through the bodies ahead of her. There were few Naridans left standing here, and they were being overwhelmed by Tjakorshi.

Tjakorshi who looked up in confusion as a sound they were not expecting split the air.

A shell horn rang out from behind Zhanna: loud and throbbing, and lifting the hair on the arms and the back of the neck. It was sounding the unmistakable call to retreat, but it was not just the tone and pitch that carried through the air and ran fingers of ice down the spine. Many fools could get a sound out of a shell horn, Tsolga had been fond of saying, but only the best could put their soul into it. Those who truly understood it could bolster the hearts of the fearful with a call to charge, or lend wings to the feet of the survivors with the order to retreat.

This sounding was being given life by Tsolga's dying breaths, and the old woman had put every bit of the pain and fear she was feeling into it. It was like nothing else Zhanna had ever heard, and like nothing she ever wanted to hear again.

Fear crept across Tjakorshi faces as the horn call washed over them. They could hear the desperation in it, and just as they were wondering what could have happened to cause such a drastic reversal of fortunes, dragon riders appeared. Zhanna heard screams as the leading sars smashed into their enemies, skewering them with spears, cutting them down with longblades, and trampling them beneath the enormous feet of their mounts. Then she was riding over bodies, those that had fallen victim to their charge and those who had died earlier alike, but it made little difference to the dragons: their great weight simply stamped everything flat beneath them.

Zhanna had learned that a war dragon, once it was up to speed, was virtually impossible to stop against its will. The charge of warriors on foot could get bogged down within a pace of their first contact with an enemy line, but dragons *just kept going*. Sars wheeled off to her right and left, slamming into the sides of the Tjakorshi tide that was battering at the rapidly weakening rock of the Naridan defenders. Ahead of her, Darel and the two Tainbridge sars kept going straight, and rode over the last few warriors between them and the distant treeline. Zhanna caught a glimpse of one brave or foolhardy Tjakorshi taking a running jump at her: she kicked out instinctively and was nearly jarred loose from her seat as her boot met his chest, but she managed to retain her balance, and she heard a *crunch* as one of the dragons behind her rode over the unlucky man.

Then they were through. Zhanna took one quick look away to her right, and saw the full mass of The Golden's force for the first time. The sars that had piled into it were leaving a trail of destruction, but two had already been brought down, and the others were sure to follow before long. It was brave, but ultimately futile.

Zhanna turned away, put her head down, and concentrated on not falling off. All she could do for the moment was stay alive, and try to keep as many as possible of those with her alive as well.

Darel

They burned Daimon in the third village they came to.

It was deserted, like the others before it: clearly, news of The Golden and its army had spread quickly enough for the locals to decide that this was no place for them. The inhabitants had taken most things that might be of use, but had left firewood enough for Darel's group to build a pyre in a blacksmith's yard. Darel set the flame himself, and made no effort to hide his tears as he did so. Let the Tainbridge sars judge him if they wished: he cared not. His brother's absence was a pain-filled void inside his chest, and although tears would not fill that void, they soothed the raw edges of it. Zhanna was weeping too, and while Naridans might consider women to be more prone to emotions, Darel knew the girl to be a fiercer warrior than he. If she wept openly, he felt no shame in doing so.

The fire burned into the evening. Darel sat and watched it while the rest of his small party searched the village for any food that might have been left behind. There was not much to be found, but it supplemented the rations their dragons were carrying. Darel ate mechanically, prompted not so much by hunger as by the stern look Inkeru gave him when he tried to refuse.

When the fire had burned low, Darel reached out, daubed his cheeks with his brother's ashes, and began to speak.

"Daimon Blackcreek was perhaps the best man this marshal ever knew," he began. "As children, he was not only this marshal's brother, but also his friend: a bond not always shared between siblings, or so it seems. As a man, it was his kindness, and his wisdom, that prevented war from engulfing our home when the Brown Eagle clan first arrived. He had the strength to see that he should do what he thought was right, not what was expected of him by others."

He paused, fighting with the ache at the base of his throat that threatened to strangle his words.

"It would be expected of this marshal to talk about how Daimon rose above the situation of his low birth by dint of our father adopting him, and how he lived up to and repaid that honour. However, this marshal feels that this would not be true. Daimon did *not* live up to that honour, as it would normally be understood, and it is that very fact which made him such a great man. Daimon received an *opportunity*, an opportunity that would likely have been denied to him had the plague not taken this marshal's mother before her time, and he used that opportunity to not only think for himself, but to influence the actions of others and make this world a little brighter, a little better, and a little more peaceful. His honour called on him to die: his courage required him to live."

Darel looked around: at Naridan, at Tjakorshi, and at the people of the Smoking Valley.

"Daimon's courage has helped us all, in one way or another. By preventing bloodshed at Black Keep, he kept some of us alive directly. By forging peace, he ensured that warriors of neighbouring lands had no need to ride to war against the Brown Eagle clan. Black Keep's survival meant it could send aid to our allies in the Smoking Valley, and work with Darkspur and Tainbridge for mutual benefit when disaster struck. Daimon was not solely responsible for those things," he added, glancing at Zhanna, not wanting her to think that he was discounting the role her mother had played in it all, "but this marshal thinks it is safe to say that they could not have occurred without him."

He swallowed.

"His brother misses him already, and will miss him every day. But he will not swear vengeance on his killer."

Sar Natan looked up at that, surprise in his eyes. Darel ignored him.

"This marshal's decision to cross the river led to our defeat. It led to the situation in which Daimon, and so many others, lost their lives. This marshal feared looking like a coward, and so he erred. He should have learned from Daimon's example on the salt marsh next to our home, and been more concerned with being brave than looking brave. He will not make that mistake again. We have seen how those we once thought of as enemies can become friends, even family, and we have seen how a boy born beneath the notice of nobility can help shape the lives of many, if he is only given an opportunity to do so.

"This marshal's concern is, and should have always been, to prevent the loss of life wherever he can do so. Sometimes that will not be possible, because sometimes protecting yourself or others requires fighting, but it should not be sought out. So, this marshal will not make vows of future bloodshed. Others have paid for his mistakes with their lives today: no amount of killing can bring them back, and no matter how great our victory, we would lose more lives in the process.

"The lesson Daimon taught his brother, if only his brother had the wit to learn it, was that knowing how to fight is not as important as knowing *when* to fight. That wisdom shall be the legacy of Daimon Blackcreek, who was a loving and wise brother, and the best of men."

Darel sat down again. The tears rolling down his cheeks

were smearing the ash, but that did not matter. He had paid tribute to his brother, even though his meagre words felt like a poor eulogy, but he had done his best. Darel had never been more conscious of his own limitations than he was at this moment, and bearing that in mind, knowing he had done his best was all he could ask for.

"This warrior will miss him," Zhanna said gruffly. For a moment Darel thought she was going to say something more, but she subsided again.

"Did you want to say something about your loss?" he asked, after a few heavy moments had passed. "Tsolga?"

Zhanna shook her head. "The Golden's people might send her soul to Father Krayk. If not, she will have to find her own way." She stared into the ashes of Daimon's pyre again, and Darel felt suddenly self-conscious about his speech. He had only intended to honour his brother's memory and verbalise how much Daimon had meant to him, but now he worried that he had seemed self-indulgent and maudlin in front of the Tjakorshi.

Well, if so, that was too bad. Darel had only just finished talking about how he intended to do what he thought was right, rather than worrying about what others expected of him.

"What are we to do now, High Marshal?" Sar Osrel asked respectfully, when no one else spoke. "Should we ride north in search of Marshal Highbridge and the Northern Army?"

Darel bit his lip, pondering. It was certainly tempting to flee from the horror of the slaughter at North Ferry and the army of The Golden, in the same way as it was tempting to go in search of someone who could make it right.

"No," he said slowly, examining his own thoughts and trying to make sure he was thinking clearly, and being true to himself. "We might hope that the Northern Army has begun to mobilise, but we do not know that it has: and if it has, it will not need our guidance to find The Golden. The God-King, however, must be informed of this marshal's failure. We will return across the Idra when we can, to see what has become of Yoraby, and the troops we left on the southern bank. With luck, the invaders will continue to press west, rather than turn south."

"If they do continue west," Ravel said hesitantly, "won't they meet the army we heard of? Led by the man claiming to be the Divine One?"

"That seems likely," Darel acknowledged. "And who knows how that will play out?"

"Lord Darel," Ravel said, then swallowed, and corrected himself quickly, "High Marshal. Shouldn't we find out? Will the God-King want to know what happens? We could shadow the army, learn if there's a battle, and if so, who won. Then, when we return to Threestones, His Majesty will have a better idea what enemies are left."

"Mind your tongue!" Sar Natan snapped at Ravel, clearly outraged at the idea of a lowborn youth – and with his face marked with a Raider tattoo, no less – questioning the decision of the Southern Marshal.

"Mind *yours*," Darel told him, and the sar's mouth snapped shut in shock. "Ravel raises a good point. Knowing not just what enemies are at large in Narida, but who they are, could be critical." He tapped his fingers on the hilt of his longblade, thinking. "Sar Osrel, Sar Natan: you will return to Threestones as this marshal first envisaged. You will carry a message to the God-King from this marshal, explaining the circumstances. As Naridan sars, you will be able to pass through the land unchallenged, and will be granted an audience: things which might not be true for all of our number," he added.

"High Marshal," Sar Natan said carefully. "We swore to protect your brother, and we failed in that: please, do not allow us to also fail in protecting you."

"You failed to protect Daimon because he challenged a demon to single combat," Darel said bluntly. "Even this marshal could not protect him from that decision. Should we be unfortunate enough to encounter The Golden's army again, your presence or absence will not make a difference to whether this marshal lives or dies, and he does not wish to waste the lives of two men sworn to Thane Gilan. All he asks is that you take with you any of the rest of us who do not wish to go with this marshal."

Ostel and Natan looked at each other, but their honour held them fast: if they were commanded to do something by the Southern Marshal, they were duty-bound to obey.

"Your servant will come with you," Ravel piped up. "If it pleases the High Marshal, that is."

"This warrior will, too," Avisha declared. Darel bit his lip again to hide his smile at how Osred's granddaughter now chose to refer to herself, and deliberately did not look at Zhanna.

"This warrior will obviously be going," Zhanna said. "And so will Inkeru. She does not have to ask Inkeru," she added. "She likes to say that she is sensible, but she will not go back to a castle if three young warriors like us are going somewhere more dangerous."

Inkeru did not look up from the food she was still busy demolishing, but said something in Tjakorshi which sounded sharp, and which Zhanna did not translate. If Inkeru had understood why her name was being mentioned, however, she did not raise an objection. Tsennan Longjaw and Tamadh Avljaszhin appeared to want more clarification, and began asking Zhanna questions in their own language.

"Zhanna goes; we go too," said Nenatoyo of the Smoking Valley. He was a younger man, and the hair on his chin was not yet thick enough for him to have threaded beads through it, as Amonomin had. Amonomin himself, who was somewhat older, glanced at his companion, then at Zhanna, and then at Darel with a wry smile and a shrug.

"Tamadh and the Longjaw are coming," Zhanna said, having concluded her discussion with them, and apparently oblivious to any suggestive movements of Amonomin's eyebrows. "When do we leave?"

"We will give The Golden's force time to move on," Darel said, swallowing the guilt that tugged at him, clamouring that it was his mistakes that had led to the invaders being delayed, and ineffectively at that. "We will leave here at noon tomorrow. In the meantime, we should set a lookout in case they, or any other force, should come this way. This marshal will take first watch."

He stood up and walked away, leaving the rest to organise themselves as they saw fit. He suddenly felt the need to take no decisions, and have no one asking him what to do. He would stand on watch in the summer evening for a few hours, and let his thoughts wander where they may.

Behind him, a low song started up in a language which sounded familiar, but which he could not place. It took him a moment to realise that it was the same song, or very similar, as the one he had heard Amonhune of the Mountains sing when someone in Black Keep had died. It seemed Amonomin and Nenatoyo were paying their respects to Daimon in the manner of their own people, despite only having known him for a few weeks.

Darel studiously dried his eyes again. He might not feel any shame about weeping for his brother, but tears would not serve a lookout.

Jeya

Jeya did hér best to fight, but shé was neither big nor strong, and hér kidnappers definitely were. Shé could do nothing against the arms that held hér, or the bonds that tied hér hands, and nor could shé shake loose the sack over hér head. The gag in hér mouth prevented hér from forming words, and hér desperate, muffled noises did not result in any help appearing. Shé was dragged away through the streets, and although hér captors did not injure hér, they were none too gentle with hér when shé struggled.

Jeya did not know who had grabbed hér, or why, but shé silently cursed Kurumaya's name as hér legs were forced to walk. East Harbour might now be partially under Kurumaya's control, with the resulting benefits that brought for slaves and former slaves, but the Shark's rule basically amounted to them and their people doing as they wished. There were no universal laws, and no Watch to call on, so people were more likely to turn away from things they saw just in case it was happening at Kurumaya's bidding. Someone being marched through East Harbour with a sack over their head? Well, maybe they had angered Kurumaya: best not to intervene, just in case you found yourself on the wrong end of the Shark's displeasure as well.

Despite the fear that pounded in hér chest, Jeya could tell

shé was mainly walking downhill. The sack smelled of something earthy, but it was not tight around her neck, so enough
air wafted up to catch a tang of salt, and the general stink of
the harbour. Shé could hear the lapping of waves, too. It did
not take a genius to work out that shé had been brought to the
docks: but why? Shé tried to work the gag loose with hér teeth
and tongue in an attempt to demand information, but it had
been tied securely, and shé was unable to do anything more
than bite angrily down on the increasingly spittle-soaked rag.

Still shé was marched forwards. The gentle sound of water
was on both sides of hér now, and the stones underfoot had
the flat, regular feel of the stone jetties, which were well
maintained to reduce the risk of porters slipping off them into
the harbour while carrying valuable cargo. Was shé going to
be taken to the end of one and pushed into the water? Jeya
tried not to think about it, but with hér hands tied behind
her shé would almost certainly drown in short order. Unless
Kurumaya had decided to get revenge for Nabanda after all,
and shé would be knifed first to ensure the sharks came for hér.

The hand on hér right arm tightened its grip, and brought
hér to a halt. A voice spoke, rough-voiced but quiet, close
to hér ear:

"You need to walk up a gangplank now, so let's hope your
sense of balance is good. Get on the ship and do as you're told,
and you might just come out of this in one piece. Mess about,
and odds are you'll end up in the harbour with your head
staved in. Nod if you understand."

There was nothing for it. Jeya nodded, and the sack slid
back and forth around hér ears.

"Right then," the same voice continued. "I'm going up first,
you're following me, and my friend here will be behind you.
Just walk straight in the direction we point you, and you
should be fine. Try anything funny, and you'll be lucky to still

be alive come sunup." Hér right arm was released, and Jeya heard the creak of wood beneath a heavy tread, moving away from hér. Shé swallowed anxiously.

The person that still had hold of hér left arm took hold of hér right as well, and turned hér around. "Just walk forwards until your feet reach the plank, then go up it," they murmured. "It's not a very steep incline. Move slowly. If I tap your right shoulder, move to your left. If I tap your left shoulder, move to your right."

Jeya could hear the waves below, and could not make hér feet move.

"If we wanted you dead, you'd be dead," the voice pointed out, in a reasonable tone of voice. "We were told not to take the sack off your head until you're on the ship, so this is how it is." Their voice hardened a little. "I'm not dealing with a struggling child: you can either walk up the plank yourself, or we hit you over the head first, and carry you. It's up to you how badly you want to avoid a headache."

Jeya had no desire to take a blow to the head, so shé took a deep breath and edged forward until hér toes found the bottom lip of the gangplank, then eased hérself up onto it. It felt wider than many a wall shé had walked along in hér life, but it was a very different proposition when shé could not see where shé was putting hér feet, or use hér arms to balance. Shé took a step forward, and then another, and felt the wood flex again as the person behind hér followed hér on.

"That's right, you're doing fine," they said encouragingly. Jeya took another step, and another, and another.

Then the plank tilted unexpectedly, and shé was falling to hér right.

"Shit!" Strong hands caught hér, but there was a terrifying moment when shé could *feel* hér weight tilted out over the side of the plank, and knew that the only things preventing hér from falling into the water shé could sense beneath were the sinews of hér captor. Shé waited for the moment when their grip would fail, or they would both overbalance and fall in together, or they would let her go in order to save themselves . . .

"Mushuru's ashes!" the other person growled, and Jeya felt hérself slowly being hauled back onto the level. "No, stay there!" the voice barked past hér ear. "I've got them! You'll only unbalance the plank again!" They patted hér on the shoulder. "Straight on. Three more steps and you're on the deck."

Jeya tried to calm hér heart's frantic beating, and did as shé had been instructed. Sure enough, her third step found no further rising plank, but set her down on a blessedly level and broad timber surface.

"Get them below," someone ordered, and a hand seized hér shoulder again to propel hér in a new direction. Now, however, another hand grabbed the sack over hér head, and pulled it away. The closing fingers snagged some of hér hair as well, and shé cried out in pain as hér vision returned.

"Oh, be quiet," muttered the first voice, that of the person who had gone up the gangplank ahead of hér. Fingers fiddled with hér bonds, and finally, finally hér hands were free once more. Jeya had no time to enjoy the sensation, although the tingling as full circulation returned to hér hands was not exactly enjoyable in any case: shé ducked instinctively as shé was pushed towards a doorway, even though the top of it was higher than hér head, then grabbed desperately at the edge as shé realised shé had been about to go headfirst down a drop, not having seen the ladder that awaited.

"Down," the same voice said, and Jeya turned around to find hérself faced by a broad-shouldered person in a sleeveless linen shirt that displayed muscular arms decorated with multiple, interlinked tattoos. They did not need the knife that was being waved under hér nose to threaten hér, but it certainly added to the general intimidation. Shé turned wordlessly, and made hér way down to the deck below. Broad Shoulders followed with enough alacrity to suggest that they knew their way around ships, or at least this ship, and took hér arm again. "This way."

Jeya was shoved through another door, this one leading not to a drop but to a tiny cabin. There was a porthole, which let in just enough light from outside to outline the shape of things: other than a cot which was small enough that even shé would have to curl up to sleep on it, there was only a jug of reasonably fresh water, and a wooden bucket, the purpose of which shé could guess at.

The door was closed behind hér, and a bolt slid across. Shé had no idea why shé had been brought here, or where the ship might be going, or indeed why shé was wanted at all. Worst of all, shé had no way of getting word to Bulang, to explain what had happened. What if this ship weighed anchor in the morning, and departed on the tide? Bulang would never know where shé had gone, or why: would thëy assume shé had run away and left thëm as a result of a . . . a *disagreement*? It was not even really worthy of the term "argument". Jeya had just wanted to get away and be with hér own thoughts for a while, and now shé might never see Bulang again.

Shé wanted to rage and beat at the door, but shé knew what was on the other side of it: a big person with a knife, and probably a crew of others with similar dispositions. Jeya had not lived as long as shé had on the streets by pointlessly antagonising and challenging those stronger than hér. Shé might yet get an opportunity to do something that mattered, but hér chances would be lessened if her captors thought of hér as likely to resist. That was a good way to have hér hands bound again.

Shé reached up and wrestled the gag loose, then folded the strip of damp cloth away into hér maijhi. Anything might come in handy at some point, particularly if hér captors had forgotten that shé had it.

With that done, Jeya sat down on the tiny cot, and let the tears come.

Stonejaw

It had been a good fight against the first real army the Flatlanders had raised to send against them, by which Zheldu meant that they had swept the enemy aside without too much trouble. There had been a few uncomfortable moments when the dragon-riders had broken out and caused chaos in the lines, but they were never going to be enough to turn the tide. The last mounted warrior had actually been brought down by Flatlander troops who had sworn themselves to The Golden, and the man who struck the killing blow claimed his victim's sword for himself. The Flatlanders in the city on the other side of the river decided not to stick around and wait for the draug to turn its attention to them, and by the time the Tjakorshi descended on it for plunder most of the occupants, and whatever fighting forces had been unable to cross the river in time to aid in the battle, had fled southwards.

Still, The Golden had not lingered. It directed the place be stripped bare of anything they could use and pushed its forces on westwards, chasing the setting sun, and rumours of a god and its army.

Two days later, they found that at least some of the rumours were true. Whether or not it was actually led by a god was something on which Zheldu was going to withhold judgement, but the army was unquestionable. There were thousands of them, and they had drawn themselves up with the river on their right flank, and their left protected by a hill which, although not unscalable, did not offer an easy route into battle.

"That banner is our target," The Golden said, pointing to where a giant piece of red and green cloth waved in the breeze. Even at this distance, Stonejaw could just see a design picked out on it in gold: a stylised sun, surmounted by some sort of many-pointed helmet. "Livnya tells me their god will be found beneath it."

"Forgive me, master," Kullojan Sakteszhin said, obsequious as ever. "How do we know we can trust the Flatlander? Could she be trying to deceive us?"

"She has turned her own people to join us," The Golden said. "She knows what she must do in order to continue being useful, and therefore to survive. Besides, that's the largest banner: given how these Naridans think, it makes sense their man-god would mark out his presence in such a way." Its bearded mouth quirked into a slight smile. "He brings his doom down upon him. I'll kill him myself."

Stonejaw cast a surreptitious glance at the other assembled captains, but no one else's face was showing the unease she felt. Any chief or captain would go into battle surrounded by their best warriors, and she failed to see why it would be any different for a god. This Flatlander force was close on as large as The Golden's, by her estimate, and had to contain more dragon riders. Some of "their" Naridans had claimed possession of the war mounts of fallen enemies, and were even able to ride them, but Zheldu knew the difference between a youth with a blackstone axe and a seasoned warrior. She was willing to bet that there was more to fighting from dragonback than simply pointing the beast's head at an enemy and shouting "Go!", in the same way that only a small part of foot combat was how hard you could swing an axe.

Any charge at the Flatlander god was bound to encounter experienced dragon riders coming the other way, and that was a situation that Zheldu Stonejaw wanted to be nowhere near. And yet, it seemed to be what the draug wished.

It did not look as though anyone else was going to say anything. Stonejaw took a breath, screwed up her courage, and opened her mouth.

"If we charge straight into them, we'll die," she said flatly. "Or at least, I know I will. The witches haven't declared any doom for me which states I can't be killed."

The Golden's ice-green eyes snapped to her, and Zheldu steeled herself for its hand to go to the longblade at its belt. If the cursed thing drew on her then she would fight it – what did she have to lose, at that point? – but she had no illusions she would win.

"I have no intention of 'charging straight into them'," The Golden said dismissively. "We'll draw them onto us. They have archers, whereas we mainly have slingers. Once they've shot their arrows, there will be none of ours loosed at them for them to pick up and reuse. We, on the other hand, have an entire riverbank of stones at our disposal." It pointed towards the enemy. "The shield wall will advance and protect the slingers. Their archers will loose, and they may even get the best of it at first, but the time will come when they have no more arrows. Then they will have three options: to stay still and continue to be injured by our missiles; to withdraw in defeat, which I do not think is in a god's nature; or to close with us."

Stonejaw nodded slowly. Breaking a shield wall was a far more daunting prospect than holding one, although it carried a great deal more glory with it as a result. Half of the art of battles between clans on land was trying to get the other side to charge you when it was not advantageous for them to do so, and most of the rest was realising when your own charge stood a chance of success.

It was easy to forget, when faced with its dead eyes and slightly wrong speech, that The Golden was not just a deathless spirit that had stolen a man's body. It had conquered Tjakorsha, breaking the clans one after another, and to do that it had needed an understanding of battle beyond that which merely related to its own weapons. By the time its forces had reached the Stone Eaters, Zheldu's clan had been greatly outnumbered. However, at the beginning of its rise to power, The Golden must have either faced situations where the odds had been against it, or had acted carefully to ensure that they never were.

Zheldu wondered if the god that commanding the army they now faced had gone through similar trials and tests.

As it turned out, the Flatlanders had no patience for the sort of protracted ranged duelling that The Golden had envisaged. Either their supplies of arrows were low indeed, or the god hungered for blood. The slingers and archers had only been in range for a matter of minutes when the Flatlander battle line began to lumber forwards, propelled by the brassy war cries of their horns.

"Looks like we'll be done early, at any rate," Korsada the Dry commented, drawing the long, thin steel blade that had belonged to her mother.

"Done *for* early, perhaps," Zhazhken Aralaszhin said grimly.

"None of that!" Stonejaw barked, eyeing the oncoming mass of warriors. She turned to face her own crew: those that had been with her since they fled Black Keep, and those who had joined her since. "We're a long way from the sea, and a long way from Father Krayk, but that doesn't make us any less his children! We've landed on the Flatlands and taken what we want from it, and we're not going to stop now!" She herself would like nothing better than to be back on the sea, and far from the draug and its strange obsession, but voicing that would not encourage her warriors for the fight to come.

Truth was a hindrance, at times like this. People needed something snappy and heartening, to get them to stick in the line alongside the warriors next to them, and believe not only that their side could win, but that they would be among the living when that occurred.

"The Golden wants to kill a god!" Stonejaw shouted. "Well, it's going to have to beat us there! So get your shields up, because I am *fucked* if I'm going to die with a Flatlander blade in me today! Are you ready?"

Her crew shouted wordless acknowledgement back at her, shields up and weapons raised. They had all done this before, and everyone knew how it worked: the captain or the chief shouted something generally encouraging, everyone cheered, and then they tried to kill the other side. Within those broad parameters, the specifics were of limited importance.

Stonejaw turned back to face the enemy: a tide of shouting faces and shields, so similar and yet so very different to those people alongside her. One last barrage of slingstones was launched with a mighty grunt, and a few more of the Flatlanders fell.

I honestly don't care about killing you, Stonejaw thought briefly, in their general direction. *But I'm here now, and it's you or us. So I'm going to make sure it's you.*

The Flatlander horns brayed again, and the massive shapes of dragon riders loomed up through the ranks of infantry, galloping through the channels that had been left for that very purpose. Zheldu's heart fluttered with relief when she realised that no such charge was coming directly at her.

The shell horns sounded, and The Golden's own cavalry surged forwards.

They were fewer in number, but they would still be effective. Three such beasts thundered past Stonejaw on her right, heading for the enemy lines with great whoops from the riders. Here and there, opposing dragon riders came together in combat, or simply collided. Then the Flatlander cavalry slammed into the Tjakorshi shield wall line with a sound like the mightiest hammer in the world striking a forest, and a moment later those of The Golden's riders who had not been intercepted hit back. A line of oncoming Naridans a dozen warriors wide, now a mere yolgu's-length away from where Stonejaw stood, disappeared beneath the mighty forms of three war dragons that ploughed into them as though they offered no more resistance than thick vegetation.

This was the time to charge.

Zheldu was moving before she even realised it, her instincts responding to an enemy's failed attack before her mind had properly caught up to what was going on. Other captains might have a better grasp of wind and wave and sail than her, but Zheldu Stonejaw was a raider and a warrior first and foremost, and she knew when to hold position in a shield wall, and when to move. Her crew came with her, and then their entire part of the battle front was surging forward to take advantage of the hole punched in the Naridan line. The surrounding elements of the Naridan infantry charge faltered as the dragon riders went clean over and through their friends, and now their momentum was lost.

Zheldu saw one man's eyes widen in fear as she closed on him, saw him struggling to deal with the twin terror of unexpected dragons, and now bellowing Raiders from across the ocean. He was torn between turning to flee, and getting his weapons up to defend himself, and was still in half-turned, paralysed indecisiveness when she swung her blackstone axe and took him in the neck. Blood gouted out in a high tide wound, and he dropped: the first to fall to her today, but by no means the last.

After the first few strides into the Naridan force, her own momentum was lost. Now it was a case of butchery, of heaving forwards and lashing out where she could, a combination of brute strength and opportunism. Kuadan Gaptooth lost a few more teeth as a sword blade punched into his mouth and up into his skull. He sagged and went limp, but did not immediately drop, as the pressure of bodies on all sides kept him upright. His killer, struggling to withdraw his blade, was cut down in turn by a grim-faced Ari Tumeszhastutar, the grey streaks in her hair already stained red by other people's blood.

"*Push!*" Stonejaw yelled, and the warriors around her slammed their weight against their shields anew, driving the Flatlanders back a step. They were a smaller people, in general: Zheldu had met few that could look her in the eye, and although she was a big woman, she was not the largest Tjakorshi warrior. In the ruck of a shield wall like this, where bulk could be the telling factor between holding your ground or being pushed back and off-balance, such a difference could be key.

"*Push!*" she bawled again, and her warriors responded. This time several of the Flatlanders stumbled. Zheldu hacked downwards at the one who fell at her feet before he could get his shield in the way, then caught a blow on her shield from the man who pushed forward to try to take his place, and landed a cut on his leg bad enough to send him tumbling as well. Zhazhken tripped forwards over another fallen Flatlander, and got stabbed in the back before he could recover himself, but his killer was cut down by Enga Zhargistutar.

They were winning. It was slow work, and brutal, but they were driving the Flatlanders back, and killing more than the losses they were taking in return. "*Push!*", she bellowed once more, and this time something seemed to break in the Flatlander ranks. A crucial tipping point had been reached: the pressure on her shield relaxed and was not renewed, and the weight of the enemy's bodies did not crush back in to hold her in place. The Flatlanders staggered backwards in disarray, and those at the rear began to back off, began to turn and run.

For the ones within reach of Tjakorshi weapons, there was no escape. Stonejaw's warriors surged forward and swamped them, like the tide claiming a child's sand fort on a beach, and left about as much standing in the aftermath. Then they were running, the headlong, whooping charge of warriors who were still alive and, counterintuitively, were searching for the next way to put that state of affairs to the test. For Stonejaw, it came down to the simple fact that she was going to end up in another fight somehow, and it was better if it was one she chose herself.

A shell-horn sounded to her left, and the glance she snatched in that direction revealed warriors she knew. There was Kullojan Sakteszhin, and there was Kulmar Ailikaszhin, another refugee from the attack on Black Keep who had been scooped up by The Golden's fleet at the same time as she had ... and there was The Golden itself, its mask flashing in the sun as it turned its head to roar at the fighters behind it, longblade in one hand and a blackstone axe in the other, both dripping red. It pointed the Flatlander sword it held, and Zheldu followed the gesture with her eyes.

The god's banner.

It looked ridiculously large, now she was closer, and her aching arms and shoulders winced in sympathy at the thought of the toll that holding it aloft would take on whatever luckless soul had that responsibility. She would certainly have placed a wager that the god would not be holding it himself. If there was one thing that Zheldu Stonejaw could say about The Golden, it was at least that the draug was not given over to that manner of superiority. Its focus was too narrow, too focused on the necessary to be concerned about the trappings of power that so many chiefs treasured. It would consider a warrior holding a banner to be a waste of a potential killer. The Golden cared nothing for who did a thing, so long as everything that it desired to be done, was done.

It also cared nothing for who had to die in order for a thing to be done, which was the other side of that particular blade.

"Are we racing The Golden to the Flatland god?" Ari Tumeszhastutar shouted in her ear, with the jubilant bravado of a warrior who knew how easily she could have died a few moments before, and Stonejaw silently cursed herself for her bold words in the shield wall. Still, there was nothing for it. They could pick an enemy and charge them, or stand around here for a few more breaths and wait for someone to pile into them instead.

"*For Tjakorsha!*" she bellowed, pointing her axe at the banner, which was a damned foolish thing for her to yell. Tjakorsha had never been one place: the inhabitants of the different islands had harboured contempt for those from other islands, and generally disliked even their own neighbours to one degree or another. They had the same god and the same heroes, and that was about an end to it.

Except here and now, across the ocean and up to the elbow in this strange, bleeding land, they *were* all one. The Golden had broken them first, it was true, and had forged them into something new, but then it had ripped them from their home and brought them here. Now they were Tjakorsha, simply because they very definitely were not anything else.

Her shout worked, again. The warriors around her broke into a run once more, their eyes set on the grim ranks of Flatlanders advancing on them beneath the monstrous, flapping banner that announced the presence of the being The

Golden had come here to kill. Zheldu had no idea how the rest of the battle was going: such wider scope was always lost in the press of combat. Her awareness extended little farther than the closest enemy, and she was almost on top of them now.

The Golden's warriors surged up alongside her own, and Zheldu felt the brief rush of jubilation that came from being one of many, all with the same purpose in mind. Then they smashed into the enemy, and jubilation was lost in the crush of battle.

Zheldu stumbled from the impact, but managed to keep her shield up, and her axe blow took some luckless Flatlander in the face. She caught a glimpse of red flesh and pale bone, and then someone else hacked the wounded man down. Those behind her crushed in, pressing her forwards, and she could do little except angle her shield to give herself as much protection as possible against the enemies she was being driven into, step by step. She ducked her head instinctively as a blade stabbed towards her, and it glanced off the metal helmet she had looted from a Flatlander corpse at North Ferry. She lashed out in return, and someone screamed.

Push. Hack. Push. Hack. It was hard to even think of it as battle any longer. It was simply work: unending work that you kept at even though your shoulders and arms were burning and your chest was heaving, because to stop or slow meant that you died. Zheldu found herself waiting for the moment when a group of fresh Flatlander troops would pile into them and overwhelm the warriors with her, not through greater strength or skill, but simply because their bodies obeyed them more readily. Even the greatest fighters tired.

Except, it seemed, for The Golden.

It was the draug that broke through and turned the hammer blow of two groups of warriors colliding with each other into a knife thrust to the enemy's heart. Zheldu saw The Golden's twin weapons rising and falling ahead of her, and to the left, and she felt the mass of Flatlanders begin to collapse as they became aware of the gold-masked predator slicing into their ranks like a shark into a school of fish. Warriors began to worry about their flanks, and moments of inattention were all it took for the rest of the Tjakorshi to press home their advantage.

Just as they had before, things changed swiftly. Within the space of a few laboured heartbeats, the Flatlanders broke, and grim resistance melted into panicked scrambling. Zheldu staggered forwards and took an exhausted swipe at someone's back as they turned to flee, but her blow fell short. The Golden's backhanded swing of its longblade did not, and a luckless enemy's legs gave out beneath him as the steel's edge sliced across his spine.

The banner still flew. The fleeing Flatlanders washed around it, and the small, white-clad group of barely a dozen warriors, all armed with spears, who encircled it. This was it. Zheldu had reached whatever passed for Scarred on this side of the ocean, and within their number would be the god that wore the body of a man.

Zheldu had perhaps half of her crew left, plus a few hangers on. The Golden had a similar amount. They surged forward one more time, their weariness forgotten, or at least capable of being ignored. Their goal, and all the glory that came with it, was within their reach.

A young-looking warrior whom Zheldu did not know managed to get ahead of The Golden, howling a war cry as though she thought she was Kydozhar Fell-Axe come again. A bald Flatlander wielding one of their longblades slipped out from between two of the spearmen and raised the sword, his eyes so hard they could have been weapons themselves. The warrior lunged for him with a massive overhead swing powerful enough to split his head clean down the middle.

The blow never landed. The bald man slid to one side, with the ease of someone for whom combat is second nature, and ripped his longblade across the warrior's midsection. She stumbled and collapsed, landing with a howl of agony at the feet of the spearmen.

The Golden . . .

. . . slowed.

Zheldu found her own pace dropping, but two more warriors raced past the draug to launch themselves at the bald warrior. He wore no armour, but he appeared to barely need it. The first man reached him slightly ahead of the other, but ran into a head-height sweep of the longblade which opened his throat in a high tide wound, and flowed straight into a guard position that deflected the blow of the second. The bald warrior's counterstroke ripped upwards from the crotch to the collarbone of his attacker, who fell backwards with a scream of agony.

Now The Golden arrived, just as the bald man stepped back behind the rank of spears, which lowered in the face of the massed Tjakorshi charge. The Golden sidestepped a point that jabbed for him, as easily and lazily as though it were a shark and its enemy's thrust was slowed by water, and lashed out with both weapons to kill the Naridans on either side of it. The Tjakorshi charge, which had faltered for a moment as the bald man had cut down its frontrunners, reignited. Zheldu raised her axe, raised her shield, bellowed—

And saw a god.

That was who it had to be. He stood tall, clad in simple white robes like the spearmen around him, but with a thin golden circlet on His brow. His hair was dark and His face was young, but His eyes were something else entirely. The brief glimpse Zheldu got of them showed her something ageless, and furious; something that met her gaze, and held it, and seemed to reach out across the space between them.

Zheldu staggered as her legs stopped obeying her, and the world began to tilt. It felt like a hand had closed inside her chest, and the air abruptly seemed thin, no matter how frantically she breathed in and out. The warriors around her surged past her to engage the spearmen, but it was all she could to do remain upright . . .

A dark blur flashed through the air, and resolved into a blackstone axe that buried itself into the meat of the god's chest. He howled in agony, and stumbled backwards, but whatever malign power it was that had hold of Zheldu Stonejaw did not release her. One of her own warriors buffeted her off balance in their eagerness to close with the enemy, and she fell into the mud, unable to remain upright. She got one more glimpse of the god, red blood now staining His white robes, being hauled away while the rest of His guard sold their lives as dearly as they could.

The mighty banner began to waver, then fell. The expanse of cloth enveloped a handful of warriors on Zheldu's left, hampering them for a few seconds until they managed to free themselves, but Zheldu herself could not escape what ailed her. Her vision was starting to go fuzzy.

"Stonejaw."

The voice seemed to come from a long distance off, or as though heard underwater. Zheldu blinked, trying to focus on it, focus on anything except the cold pain of the god's fingers in her chest, slowly squeezing their way outwards.

A dark shape bent over her. A stray ray of light glanced off its face and sparkled gold, so bright it nearly dazzled her.

"I have wounded a god," The Golden said. "Now I need a new axe, to help me finish it." It reached out, and Zheldu felt its fingers pluck her weapon from her hand. She tried to resist, but no part of her body was truly obeying her any longer.

"It seems you had one last use after all," The Golden said,

its voice echoing and becoming less distinct as it straightened up again, out of reach of her rapidly clouding vision.

Then there was nothing certain. Only muffled buzzing and thuds, vibrations beneath and around her, and an encroaching darkness that enveloped everything. The last thing Zheldu Stonejaw thought she might have seen, just as the icy fingers clawed their way up through her neck, was flashes in front of her eyes which could have been nothing, or which might have been the teeth of Father Krayk as he rose up to claim her.

Ravi

R avi had run from the campsite, and then run through the night, pressing on when she could, and snatching sleep when she could go no farther. All the time the old man's words ran through her head, circling it like a whirlwind, stripping everything else bare.

It made no sense, or at least, little sense. He was a liar, or delusional; he had to be. He claimed to be Tolkar, the Last Sorcerer, for Nari's sake! Yet he had coaxed the fire into life in a downpour with unnatural flames, and what he said hung together just well enough for her to be unable to ignore it.

Had she been deceived? After a whole life of running from the Unmaker, had she presented herself to it unknowingly? Had she felt the power of its presence, and mistakenly assumed it for the aura of her god? Had she been *welcomed* by it, and known peace for what might have been the first time in her life, on the basis of a lie?

She needed to see Tyrun one more time. She needed to look at Him, or it, or whatever He was, with fresh eyes. She needed to make the decision for herself as to what manner of thing she had pledged herself to.

If she was satisfied He was Nari Reborn, she would take whatever punishment He enacted on her as a deserter. If she had doubts . . .

Well. She had a sword on her belt. She only had the most basic of ideas of how to use it, and Tyrun's guards had defended Him against attacks from assailants far more dangerous than her, but she knew what she had to do. Every one of the cursed lines upon her body marked her soul as the property of the Unmaker: trying to kill the arch-demon's vessel with a sword would probably not be enough to break that unholy covenant, but it was the best idea she had.

Of course, first she had to find Tyrun. However, following an army was not hard.

The Divine Army had left Northbank, seeking to meet a force of Raiders — Raiders, of all things! — rumoured to be coming from the east. The army was marching steadily, not pressing ahead with full speed, and so Ravi gained on them enough to catch up, two days downstream. She slipped into the camp at dawn, one more unremarkable Naridan in a place that was preparing to face pale-skinned Raiders, and lurked with the baggage train as the Divine Army slowly began to crawl into motion once more.

It did not have to move far before the river road was blocked by the very adversary they had come east to seek.

The Divine Army drew itself up to meet the threat, resembling nothing more than a kicked beehive of hurried horn blasts and urgent shouts. Ravi placed herself with the other healers in the tents set aside for their use, showing her bag of remedies, bandages, and needle and thread to justify her presence, but she lingered by the entrance, and her eyes barely left the billowing banner of the God-King. She even saw a flash of white beneath it once, as men milled to and fro, but she was too far distant to be certain of who she saw, let alone make the judgement for which she had come.

She would have to get closer. Luckily, if that was the right word, a battle would provide an opportunity to do so.

Everyone would be so focused on the Raiders that no one would pay attention to a healer, even if they were near the fighting. Besides, Tyrun would not be leading any charges Himself, surely?

Horns blew, and banners began to advance. In the distance, Ravi heard a faint, sonorous answer to the Naridan horns.

"What's that?" someone asked, alarmed. It was an old man, his face wrinkled but his hands still steady as he prepared strips of cloth for the wounded who would soon be dragged to them.

"It could be the demons the Raiders worship," a woman replied, sounding even less happy than the man who had asked the question. "May Nari protect us all, and may the Divine One drive them out!"

Ravi bit her lip. Even if there were demons with the Raiders – which she was not prepared to rule out – and even Tyrun *could* drive them out, what would that mean? The Unmaker was the Queen of Demons, after all, and if the man claiming to be Tolkar had disputed some elements of that, he had not argued with the Unmaker's rank among such malicious spirits. Could it turn other demons to its will? Would anything that fled before Tyrun not be running from the power of a god, but simply from something like itself, but more powerful?

For a few weeks, Ravi had enjoyed a measure of peace and certainty for the first time in her life. That was gone now, and she was not going to regain it by standing around here.

"S'woman will be back shortly," she said, as casually as she could, and picked up her bag of remedies. She double-checked that she had not removed her sword – not that she could miss it, given how the damned thing bumped against her leg every time she moved – and stepped out of the tent.

And nearly walked into Alazar Blade.

"There you are!" the blacksword said, his eyes wide with

what Ravi at first took to be anger, but then realised to her shock was actually relief. He held out one finger towards her in an unspoken instruction not to move, then turned his head and shouted. "Mar! She's over here!"

"What are you *doing* here?" Ravi demanded, looking around in expectation of Tyrun's men descending on them at any moment. She was fairly unobtrusive, she thought, but the dark-bearded blacksword was anything but. He was surely about to draw down on her exactly the sort of attention she needed to avoid.

"Trying to stop you doing something foolish," Alazar replied, lowering his voice as he turned back to face her. His eyes were serious and sympathetic, but the set of his mouth was determined. She was not going to be able to reason with him. "Ravi, we need to go, *now*. Before anyone recognises us."

"You don't know why s'woman came back," Ravi told him stubbornly, but Alazar shook his head.

"This sar isn't a betting man, but he'd take that wager." His eyes glanced meaningfully towards where Ravi knew the Divine One's banner fluttered in the breeze, and her heart sank. She never should have told Marin the truth of her tattoos, but that was yet another mistake she could not take back . . .

"Oh, thank Nari," a voice puffed, and Marin hurried up. "Come on, we need to—"

"Goodsar!"

That was a new voice, shouting from Ravi's right. All three of them turned to see a man in an army uniform hurrying towards them. "Goodsar, should you not be in the battle line?"

"Fuck," Alazar muttered, and one hand began to stray towards the hilt of his longblade.

Ravi took her chance.

"*Raiders!*" she screamed, pointing towards the rear of the

camp, in the opposite direction to where the battle was taking place. Everyone's head whipped around to following her trembling finger, as they wondered what stealth or sorcery the enemy had employed to outflank them so comprehensively.

Which they had not done, of course. Ravi turned and fled as soon as Alazar and Marin were no longer looking at her, running past the startled army officer and directly towards the fighting.

Every instinct in her body screamed at her to turn back, to head for the relative safety of the camp, and then perhaps farther away in the company of two men who, frustrating though they might be at times, had come here at the risk of their own lives to try to keep her safe. What they did not understand was that Ravi was *not* safe, she could *never* be safe: not while any doubt remained as to the ultimate fate of her soul. Either she was pure of heart, or she had been lied to by the very being of which she had lived in fear ever since she had been old enough to understand what her parents had done to her.

She headed for Tyrun's banner. There was no longer any time for subtlety: Alazar and Marin's arrival had ruined that, since they would either be trying to drag her away, or would simply call enough attention for them all to be detained, or worse. Middle of the battle or not, this was something she had to do.

No one paid any attention to her. Everyone had too much to think about to be bothered with one woman probably carrying a message for one commander or another. Ravi could get little idea of how the battle was going, but Tyrun's banner still flew tall and proud.

Until it began to waver.

The fighting was closer, now: although there were still Naridan soldiers between Ravi and any sight of the Raiders, she could pick out the clash of weapons, and individual voices screaming or shouting, instead of a general, dull roar. However, she did not realise quite how close it was until Tyrun's standard fell, and two men appeared out of a press of bodies, dragging a third between them.

The third body was Tyrun Himself.

All was turning to chaos. Ravi could practically feel the wave of uncertainty that washed out through those blocks of the Divine Army that had yet to reach battle, as the Divine One's banner disappeared from sight. She stumbled to a halt, staring at the being she had thought was her god laid low, while those carrying Him bore down on her inexorably.

"You!" one of them barked, pointing at her. "Healer! Assist the Divine One!"

Ravi's mouth dried, and she could do nothing except nod. The world tightened, sound dropped away, and all other vision blurred into meaninglessness as they laid Tyrun at her feet. Had this been a normal patient she would have insisted that they withdraw farther, back towards the tents, but she had come here for this opportunity, and she would not squander it. She could be recognised at any moment, and—

"Well?" a sharp voice snapped, and Ravi's throat constricted in terror as she realised that one of the two men carrying Tyrun was Mordokel. The bald priest had his longblade out, wet with blood, and was looking back towards the Raider lines instead of at her. It would surely only be a moment before he realised to whom he was speaking.

She had to move fast.

She crouched down over Tyrun, her heart hammering with fear. Fear of the Raiders, fear of Mordokel, and most of all fear of the being that now lay bleeding beneath her. One way or another, her fate was tied to His.

There was a deep, irregular gash in the left side of His chest, not far from the wound inflicted by the would-be assassins in

His tent outside Northbank, and His white robe was stained red. It was not necessarily a deadly wound, but nor would Ravi have placed any wagers on a mortal man surviving it. The question was whether Tyrun was mortal at all, or at least whether His body was.

"Divine One," she murmured, bending low over him. "Can you hear s'woman?"

His eyes, which had been screwed shut in pain, opened and focused on her. She met His gaze, and the shock of that deep connection ran through her as she fell into the depths of his stare.

"Ravi," Tyrun whispered. His eyes and His voice, tight with pain although they were, still seemed in some way ageless, and at odds with His face, which was younger than her own. He reached up with His right hand, cupping her jaw. "You returned."

"Yes, Divine One," Ravi whispered. She did not look away from Him as her hands delved into her bag, able to navigate by touch and familiarity alone.

"Good," Tyrun breathed. "You must help this god, one more time."

His hand moved slightly so that He was no longer cupping her jaw. Instead, His thumb slid across her throat, and Ravi abruptly felt the pulse of her own heartbeat beneath His fingers. It seemed to echo in her head as His fingers tightened slightly, drowning out all other sounds.

The Unmaker could steal bodies, it was said, and Ravi realised she had no idea how that could happen.

"Divine One," she husked. "Is s'woman still pure of heart? Is she still welcome?"

"Of course," Tyrun replied, and He smiled.

But His smile was a reptilian thing, and the depths of His eyes held nothing but emptiness.

Ravi's fingers closed on a bottle, and she removed it from her bag and unstoppered it with hands that did not shake.

"This will purify the wound," she said, and upended it.

Tyrun grunted as the liquid touched his damaged flesh, and a twitch of pain broke the eye contact between them. Ravi replaced the bottle in her bag, and looked away from Him entirely as she delved for something else. She had nothing in mind, but she needed to look busy for a few moments. The elixir was fast-acting, and when administered directly to the bloodstream by means of an open wound, should take effect within seconds.

Certainly in the amount she had used.

For a few moments, nothing happened. Tyrun lay still, His breath coming fast and ragged. Then Ravi felt a twitch in the fingers at her throat, and she stiffened.

"What . . . ?" Tyrun murmured. Ravi did not look at Him, and kept her eyes fixed on the contents of her bag. His fingers twitched again, and the loose grip on her neck began to relax. Now she dared to look up, and met His eyes once more: eyes where the pupil had contracted down to a pinpoint, beneath lids that were fluttering treacherously.

Her heart was not pure, and Tyrun had not been able to read it. Otherwise, He would have known that what she had just applied to His wound was going to kill Him. One of the peculiar wisdoms of healers was the knowledge that what could help could often also kill, and the difference between the two was simply a matter of situation and dosage.

Ravi had never deliberately poisoned anyone before; but then again, she had never before been held by the throat by something claiming to be her god.

"You," she whispered hoarsely to whatever lived behind Tyrun's eyes, as His fingers fell from her neck and His eyes began to close, "are not welcome here."

She had one moment of terrified triumph before a hand seized her hair and dragged her upright.

"*What did you do?!*" Mordokel bawled in her face, spittle flying. The man with him fell to his knees and began to sob as he cradled Tyrun's increasingly limp body in his arms, but the priest's reaction was one of instant rage.

"His wound!" Ravi protested desperately, grabbing fruitlessly at the fingers that held her. "It was too deep, s'woman couldn't—"

"*Lies!*" Mordokel bellowed. Now he released her, but only to give himself the space to draw his longblade back for the blow that would end her life. Ravi staggered, off-balance, and unable to get her legs under her to run. The world slowed as Mordokel began to swing, his rage making the blow come sweeping and wide . . .

And something wrenched her out of the way, then dumped her on the ground next to Tyrun's body and the oblivious man in white, who was still clutching it and sobbing. Ravi looked up, and saw Alazar Blade turning back to face Mordokel, his own longblade drawn.

"Traitor!" Mordokel spat. "She poisoned the Divine One!"

"He can't have been that divine then, can He?" Alazar said, adopting a two-handed guard position. "You've got bigger things to worry about than one healer, Mordokel: the bloody Raiders, to start with."

"There is *nothing* else," Mordokel ground out between gritted teeth. "Stand aside, or die."

"Have it your way," Alazar said with a shrug, then raised his blade and attacked.

Their swords tangled, never striking edge-on-edge, each seeking to bat the other's guard aside and land a clean strike. Ravi had time for three hurried breaths before Mordokel let out a feral yell and swung at Alazar's neck with what would have been a killing stroke, had it connected.

However, Alazar ducked under it to one side, and landed a solid punch into Mordokel's groin.

The priest's scream of rage exploded into a gut-deep groan as he doubled over. Alazar straightened, took his blade in both hands, and hacked downwards to separate Mordokel's head from his shoulders. The priest's body fell like a puppet with the strings cut, and his bald head rolled a little way away before coming to rest face down in the mud.

Ravi stared at him. "Tolkar was right. Your life *is* charmed."

"Bollocks to that," Alazar replied, with feeling. "These bastards just never learn to fight dirty, is all. Come on, let's—"

"*Raiders!*" Ravi yelled, pointing past him, and this time she was not lying. A small knot of pale-skinned men and women were charging them, and the leading figure wore a gold-chased mask of steel. Alazar wheeled around, and she saw the panic on his face as he looked back towards her.

"Fuck. *Run!*"

"Come on!" Ravi screamed, grabbing her bag and backing away, but Alazar Blade looked down at Tyrun's dead body, then back at her, then at the onrushing Raiders, and set his jaw.

"No. Tell Marin his husband loves him. This sar will buy you both time." He drew the second, shorter blade from his belt, and turned away from her.

Ravi ran.

Alazar

A charmed life, indeed.

Alazar had travelled too far and seen too many strange things to completely disregard the notion that such a thing might be possible, but he was fairly sure that if it was, his own did not fit the criteria. To his mind, "charmed" suggested something other than heartbreak, shame, and having to spend your entire adult life moving from place to place and killing strangers, either to survive, or simply to make enough money to feed yourself.

Then again, he supposed there was nothing to suggest that "charmed" had to mean "good". That was language trickery, and Marin's area. Alazar just killed people.

He spread his arms, longblade in his right hand and short-blade in his left, and adopted the fiercest scowl he could muster, burying his fear deep down. Looking angry and unafraid was sometimes enough to make potential assailants look elsewhere for an easier or less obviously confident target, even if they were in a group. On the other hand, sometimes it simply invited challenge. Even so, perhaps he could hold them up long enough to prevent them breaking through to the back lines before Ravi and Marin could get away.

Besides, Alazar had a reputation of leaving one God-King to die already. Even though that was not true, and regardless of

Tyrun's divinity or otherwise, some perverse part of Alazar's soul dictated that he would not run again. He was no longer sure what he believed when it came to gods, but he *was* certain that these warriors did not belong in his country.

The gold-masked leader barked a word in the language of the Raiders, which Alazar had heard more than once during his time in the City of Islands, but had never learned. The other warriors slowed uncertainly, but the leader's mouth spread into a wide smile.

"You're Sar Blacksword, aren't you?"

Alazar stared, stunned. He understood those words well enough, because they were delivered in Alaban.

"How do you know mè?" he demanded in the same language, pointing his longblade at the leader. He had borne that name in the Alaban fighting pits, and acquired quite a reputation with it, but his fame could hardly have spread across the ocean to the Raiders' homeland.

"My fires show me many things," the leader replied, walking closer. Alazar could see pale green eyes within the shadows cast by the mask now; eyes that were unblinking, and unafraid. With a chill, Alazar realised that this must be The Golden itself. It was supposed to be some sort of Raider demon wearing a man's skin, and it did not move like a man: or at least, not like most men. Alazar had seen dancers at the Divine Court in his youth that moved like this being, all elegant grace and perfect balance, with no wasted motion. It picked its way towards him across the churned ground, a sar's longblade held in one hand and one of the vicious Raider blackstone axes in the other, with no more trouble than Alazar would have had crossing a stone-paved courtyard.

"I didn't know how Sar Blacksword would come to be here," The Golden continued, "but the fires never lie to me. And now yòu stand between me and my destiny, that fled from me after

I wounded it." It pointed towards Alazar's feet with its long-blade: or rather, he realised, at Tyrun's body.

"You're a bit late," Alazar said. If he stalled the thing for long enough, it was possible that help might arrive. Every troop in the Divine Army was committed to the fight now, but surely at some point someone would come?

The Golden's smile slipped. "Hè's already succumbed to the wound I dealt hìm?"

"The way Ì saw it, Hè was poisoned by a healer," Alazar said, trying to keep all of the Raiders in view at once, and not think too much about what he was saying. He had replied glibly enough to Mordokel, it was true, but the priest had only needed a nudge to fight with more fury than reason, allowing Alazar to solve that problem with the edge of his longblade, which was the way he solved most problems. He did not doubt Mordokel had been correct, though, and Ravi *had* poisoned Tyrun. Whatever Alazar's misgivings about Tyrun and His true nature, he was not sure he was ready to truly consider what that meant.

"Hìs death was mine," The Golden snarled. "It should have been *mine*!"

It leaped forward on the last word with its weapons raised, and all its rage focused on Alazar.

Alazar gave ground before it, because he had not lived this long by meeting an unknown opponent blade to blade until he had their measure. It was immediately obvious to him that despite its anger and frustration, The Golden was still fighting with more control than Mordokel. It was not overextending itself, nor was it putting more power into its blows than it needed to. It was a skilled and deadly fighter, equally comfort-able with either weapon and either hand, and its movements were fluid and practiced.

And familiar.

Alazar parried The Golden's longblade with his shortblade and its blackstone axe with his longblade, but the demon was not fighting like either a sar, or any of its Raider kin that Alazar had ever fought. Its style was more similar to the Alaban twin axe technique: modified for the weapons it carried, of course, but still recognisable. Alazar had fought and learned from warriors trained in that discipline, during his time in the City of Islands, and he knew enough to realise that this blow would be followed by that blow, and then *that* blow, and then that feint, which was actually a disguise for—

He leaned back, and the tip of the blackstone axe whistled past his face close enough that he felt the breeze of it.

For a moment after what would have been a killing blow had failed to connect, The Golden's balance was less than perfect, and its eyes widened in surprise.

"You're going to have to do better than that," Alazar Blade told it, and attacked.

He did not use either a sar's swordplay or Alaban axework, but a hybrid of both that would have seen a teacher of either discipline eject him from their presence in disgust. Alazar was not fighting for approval, however, or for show. He fought in the only way he had ever fought, which was to end the fight as quickly as possible, with him still on his feet.

The Golden's two weapons were more or less of a length, which gave it a reach advantage over Alazar's shortblade. Swift though the demon was, though, it still had to manoeuvre the two hafts around each other if it was to properly use the angles and feints on which its discipline relied, while Alazar's short-blade could slip past the length of his longblade with less risk of entangling his own weapons. A sar's bladework lacked the wrist techniques and flexibility of the Alaban style, but Alazar had learned and incorporated them, and he drew on all his knowledge now. It was the only thing that was going to save him.

He advanced with a whirling double guard, and cut, slashed, and thrusted, forcing The Golden to react defensively for the first time. The demon's reflexes were up to the task, and it slipped away from his blows or batted them aside enough for them to pass harmlessly by, but even its mask could not hide its ferocious concentration. He had the thing's respect, at least: its counter-cuts, when they came, were more cautious, and less threatening.

However, respect was not going to win Alazar this fight. The other Raiders had stood aside for the moment, treating this as whatever passed for honour combat in their society, but there was nothing to say that state of affairs would continue. Honour, as Alazar well knew, was often only heeded when it benefited the party with more power to do so. Besides, he had no idea if The Golden would tire, or was already tiring, but he could already feel a slight ache in his own arms. He could not keep up this pace for ever, so it was time to improvise.

In a move that would have caused his old blademaster at the Sun Palace to strike his knuckles with the flat of a blade and yell at him not to show off, he spun his longblade into an inverted grip and jabbed out with it in a surprise reverse thrust that split The Golden's guard and struck the demon in its stomach. The strike glanced off one of the metal plates serving the demon as armour, but it was the first solid connection of their fight, and The Golden took a step backwards with a huff of expelled air. Alazar grinned tightly, and advanced to press his advantage.

The demon threw itself forwards and downwards, pivoting on its left forearm and lashing out with a sweeping kick that took Alazar's legs from under him. He landed on his back with a startled curse, and felt the breath leave his own body to be replaced with an aching hollow in his chest. The

Golden swirled back up to its feet like a spider, then lunged for Alazar's face with the tip of its longblade.

Alazar could have tried to block, or parry. He could have rolled away from the blow. Instead, he rolled *towards* the demon, letting its blade pass over him and land in the mud where his head had been, and turned the motion into a stab of his own. He aimed for The Golden's midriff, at a point in the leather where the strange, engraved metals discs did not meet, but the clumsiness of his motion threw his aim off, and his blade sliced down the inside of The Golden's thigh instead.

The Golden let out a muffled grunt and stumbled backwards in surprise, and Alazar only just got his longblade back and up in time to ward off the demon's reaction strike with its blackstone axe, which nearly knocked the longblade from his grasp and buried itself in his head.

Nearly, but not quite. And now, as the inside of The Golden's left leg grew dark with blood, its balance was no longer anywhere near perfect.

"All right, you little fuck," Alazar spat, rising back to his feet. "Let's end this."

He pressed forwards, his blades questing out to test the demon's mobility. Now the mouth under the mask showed gritted teeth, and The Golden did not flow aside from his strikes as easily as it had. It moved its left leg little, pivoting around it rather than using it with confidence, and the stain of blood from the wound grew with each passing moment.

"The witches have said I cannot be defeated in battle," The Golden snarled, as though by speaking the words it could make them true. It lunged onto its right leg, and the twirl of its longblade nearly disarmed Alazar's shortblade. He backed up, inviting the demon to press its advantage, but it remained where it was and glared at him with those dead, ice-green eyes.

"I bet that scared a lot of folk who believe in your witches,"

Alazar replied, "but Ì don't. A sorcerer told mè Ì have a charmed life. Ì'm fairly sure he was lying, but Ì guess we'll see."

He rushed it.

Against a mobile opponent, it would have been a foolhardy strategy. It was risky even against a one-legged one, but Alazar had seen too many duellists stabbed in the back when it became clear that the observers' favoured fighter was going to lose. He had to win before the reality of the situation won out over whatever faith the other Raiders still had in their leader's invincibility, so he rushed the demon wearing a man's body, and hoped for the best.

The Golden reacted instinctively, but its left leg gave way beneath it. Alazar caught the desperate swing of its longblade on his shortblade, and then he collided with the golden-masked warrior, and sent it tumbling backwards into the mud. He lashed out with his longblade and caught it under the jaw – an ugly cut, not a clean decapitation of the sort that had ended Mordokel, but a fatal blow nonetheless – and hastily retreated out of range of a counterstrike.

The Golden tried to rise. It got to one knee, panting wetly, with blood pouring from its neck and still leaking from its thigh, before it keeled over onto its right side. This time, it did not move again.

Alazar glanced from side to side without moving his head. The Raiders that half-surrounded him were, as one, staring in horrified disbelief at what was rapidly becoming the corpse of the creature that had led them across the ocean to Narida. He was either about to die under a dozen blades – which would at least have the benefit of being rapid – or it was *just* possible that he might be able to back away and leave them to their grief, find his husband, and get as far away as they could from the utter chaos of this day.

One of the Raiders, the darkest-skinned one he had ever

seen, turned towards him with a scream of distraught rage, and raised the long, thin sword in her left hand.

And keeled over, as the side of her neck suddenly sprouted the hilt of a knife.

Alazar looked around in shock, as did the rest of the Raiders. More Raiders had arrived, but also some Naridans, standing shoulder-to-shoulder with them as though they were allies, and in the lead . . .

"Livnya?" Alazar blurted out, staring at the woman who had shared the voyage back from the City of Islands with Marin and him aboard the *Light of Fortune*. "What in the name of the Mountain are *you* doing here?!"

"Surviving," Livnya replied absently. The knife she drew from her belt was a dagger, rather than one of her balanced throwing blades, but the dead Raider was evidence that she was still lethal even with improvised projectiles. She was glaring at the Raiders who had been with The Golden as though daring any of them to make a move, and they seemed too startled to do so. "And looking for an opportunity."

"By walking into the middle of a *battle*?" Alazar demanded incredulously.

"The situation changed rapidly!" The crime lord of Idramar saw the body of The Golden, and her eyes widened. "Tolkar's arse, you killed the draug?"

"Killing things is what this sar does best," Alazar said wearily, eyeing the assembled Raiders. He was not sure whether they were going to attack each other, or him, or no one, and would feel a lot more comfortable if he had some clarification on that. "But right now, he's planning on getting out of here."

"No!"

The note of imperious command in Livnya's voice brought him up short, blinking in surprise.

"What do you mean, 'no'?" he demanded. "Sooner or later,

one side or the other is going to win, and no matter who that is, this sar does not intend to be found next to the bodies of The Golden *and* the Divine One!"

"*What?*" Livnya practically ran towards him, and actually grabbed his arm. "Tyrun is dead? Where? *Where?*"

"There," Alazar said, pointing at where Tyrun lay, not far from The Golden. "You see? We need to get out of here, before someone decides we're responsible!"

"Oh no," Livnya said, and her tone was not wracked with grief, but laced with delight. "Oh *no*. We are *exactly* where we need to be. This is better than this princ—"

She stopped talking, but not quickly enough, and Alazar's mouth went dry. While he might not have been as clever as his husband, he was not so oblivious as to ignore someone's true face when she let her mask slip.

"What," he said quietly, angling his shortblade so it touched her ribs, "did you just say?"

Several things added up at once. He had thought the Divine Princess seemed oddly familiar when they spoke in Idramar, but had put it down to a surprisingly good memory of his youth. Instead, now he looked at Livnya's face and compared it to the features of Tila Narida through the obscuring veil she always wore, and those of Natan, he saw what he should have seen when he had first encountered this woman in ... Kiburu ce Alaba? What had she been doing in the City of Islands, anyway?

Livnya – Tila – drew in a breath, then sighed and let it out again.

"Fuck," she said bitterly. "Twenty *fucking* years without a slip, but of course it had to be *you* that made this lady forget herself. Yes, 'lady'," she continued, when Alazar opened his mouth. "So far as anyone else knows, the other woman was lost when Idramar fell."

Alazar stared at her. Part of him felt that he should just drive his shortblade home and have done. The woman next to him was poisonous, deceitful, manipulative, deadly, and too many other pejoratives to list. He might be doing Narida a favour if he simply removed her and her meddling from the world.

On the other hand, Narida was already in flames, and Tila was something else besides all her negative characteristics: extremely capable. And while he would kill without compunction when necessary, Alazar tried to avoid doing it for spite.

"You sounded like you had a plan," he said, although he did not remove his shortblade. "This sar is listening."

"Both these armies are united by religious fervour, or the nearest thing to it," Tila said hurriedly, "and the individuals that were the focus of that fervour are both dead. We were following The Golden in the hope of bringing that about, but you saved us the job. If we can make that fact known, perhaps through the medium of two heads and a couple of long spears, that will leave a void; a space into which someone with the right abilities could step, and perhaps get everyone to stop killing each other!"

"Even supposing that works, what then?" Alazar demanded. "How are you going to persuade the Godsworn, and these Raiders and the Naridans who sided with them, to submit to the rule of your— Of the God-King?"

"Oh," Tila said, and her eyes bored into his. "This lady rather thinks that Narida has had enough of God-Kings, and thanes. There are two armies here, each bent on upsetting the order of the rich and powerful of Narida: they simply differed in why, and whose vision they were following. When they learn their leaders slew each other, which is obviously what actually happened . . . "

"There are some witnesses who might disagree," Alazar

pointed out, nodding in the direction of The Golden's retinue, but Tila simply snorted.

"This lady has come to know some of them. They're a long way from home, and now without their guiding light. They might have the sense to take their lead from her. And if not . . ." She shrugged. "There are always knives."

Alazar nodded slowly. "And in this new Narida, one where God-Kings and thanes no longer hold power . . . who would?"

"Well, to begin with," Tila said, looking up at him levelly, "whomever could persuade this army to do what she wanted. After that, we'd have to see."

She backed away from him, turned to those who had come with her, and began barking instructions involving heads, and spears. Alazar watched as they hurried to obey, watched as some of the Naridans spoke to Tila's Raiders, as he thought of them, then watched as those warriors began speaking urgently to the ones who had been with The Golden.

He could still get to her, of course. Knives or no knives, he reckoned he could reach her, and cut her down. Kill whatever plan she had for these armies, and for Narida. And then . . . What? Leave the slaughter to continue? Let the Divine Army rampage pointlessly eastwards if it was victorious, or splinter into bands of outlaws, raiding the countryside now their holy purpose was gone, until they were eventually hunted down? Wait for Einan Coldbeck to press his advantage and declare himself a new God-King, assuming Taladhar Torgallen did not try to knife him for his temerity? Or alternatively, if the Raiders won, let them pillage at random?

Or he could join her. He could sign up to Tila's vision for the future and bring about the change he had wanted to see ever since his scabbard had been blackened over his divine ruler's cowardice. He could help her bring down her brother's rule – Natan would undoubtedly survive, at least if Tila had any say in it, and would likely live out his days in a degree of comfort and lack of responsibility that would suit him down to the ground – and begin to replace the broken system of hereditary power with something more inclined to acknowledge individual ability. Tila was cold-hearted and amoral, but if she had truly managed to expand her influence over twenty years by living a double life as Idramar's notorious crime boss, there was absolutely no doubting her capabilities. If anyone could hit Narida until it broke, and then piece something functional back together out of the wreckage, it was her. Perhaps that would be a Narida where Marin's low birth – and admittedly poor adherence to the law – would be no barrier to achieving a position of note at the university, assuming anything of it had survived the great wave and the Raiders' invasion.

Or, Alazar could simply turn his back on the whole affair, and the person planning to take control of a lot of armed people, who had already spoken openly to him of killing anyone who did not keep their mouths shut about the truth of what had transpired today. This seemed like an especially notable risk to Alazar since he was, as he understood it, the only person anywhere in the vicinity who knew Tila's true identity.

"Yeah, fuck this," said Alazar Blade, and ran away while no one was looking at him.

Tila

There were apparently many methods by which an unmarried woman of good standing could attract the attention of men of influence, but Tila was willing to wager that none were so successful as mounting the heads of a god and a demon on spears.

It was a desperate gamble, but what wasn't, at this point? Everything she had done since taking command of an impromptu militia in the streets of Idramar had been one gamble after another, desperately trying to keep her balance as cracks ran through the world she knew and split it asunder beneath her feet. Tila had managed to stay one leap ahead of disaster so far, but sooner or later she was going to lose her balance and fall. It was time to find solid ground, or learn to fly, or whatever worked best for the analogy she was using with herself.

It was a shame that Alazar had disappeared, since having a fighter of his calibre by her side would have been reassuring, but perhaps it was for the best. He had done her – and Narida – an invaluable service by slaying The Golden: she could hardly begrudge him the urge to disappear and ensure his husband's safety, and she had a suspicion he knew better than to start any rumours about her true identity.

"Are you sure this is going to work?" Elio the fisherman

asked, as Tila's ragged band scrambled up on to the lower slopes of the hill and began to circumnavigate it, trying to keep well away from the fighting that was still taking place around the base. Luckily, everyone below was too busy with each other to worry about them, unless and until they actually joined in.

"That depends on your definition of 'work'," Tila replied absently. She was not used to explaining herself to fisherfolk, but she had to work with what she had: and what she had was the core of the Black Keep contingent – minus Osred, who was lurking somewhere in the rear of The Golden's force with the others too frail to fight – the remnants of Zheldu Stonejaw's crew, who had seen The Golden die and were still half-stunned by that fact, and a very reluctant Tajen, who had not exactly been dragged along in a headlock by Enga Stormshoulders, but near enough. None were ideal allies, but all were very interested in not dying, and Tila had quickly outlined a plan that might help with that.

Of course, it might not, but Tila had not spent twenty years living by her wits to stop now.

She took stock of where they were: far enough up to be easily visible, even over the heads of many others, but not so far away that what they carried could not be recognised. It would have to do.

"Now!" she ordered, and her grisly trophies were raised into the air.

On her right, the head of Tyrun, self-proclaimed Divine One and Nari reborn, leader of the Divine Army. His golden circlet still adorned His brow, but the rolled eyes and lolling tongue did little to lend Him an air of divinity in death. Elio the fisherman held that spear, his teeth gritted, and his entire posture screaming that he would rather be anywhere else.

On her left, the head of The Golden, draug and breaker of the clans of Tjakorsha, still wearing its gold-chased mask: since, so far as Tila was aware, no one would have recognised the face beneath in any case. That spear was held by Nasjuk, son of the fisherman Otim, whose fierce grin suggested that there was nowhere he would rather be. Tila had already worked out that Nasjuk and his younger brother Andal Clubfoot were somewhat less enthusiastic about Naridans than most of their clan, but the young man was hungry for glory. It seemed the opportunity to hold aloft the decapitated head of the thing that had driven his family from their home was sufficient incentive for him to do as she said, at least for now.

However, two heads on spears were not going to be enough: they needed something to attract attention, and they had it in the shape of one of the Raiders' enormous shell-horns, which Andal Clubfoot had looted from a dead body at some point. According to Elio, Andal's grandmother was the official hornsounder of their clan and had at some point shown the boy how best to do it, although Tila thought that "best" was an interesting description of the hollow, spine-chilling noise that emerged.

Ghastly though the sound was, it had the desired effect. All combatants beneath them who were not actively swinging a weapon at that very moment turned to look at Tila and her companions, expecting to see either enemies or allies who had unexpectedly appeared on their flank.

Instead, each side saw the rays of the summer sun gently caress the face of the man, or god, or demon in which they had placed their trust, removed from its body and still dripping gore.

Tila watched the impact spread out like ripples from a stone landing in a pond. It was astonishing how people were so keyed to the reactions of others: despite being in the midst of battle, a warrior might pick up that the person next to him had stopped fighting, or even that the enemy he was about to engage was distracted, and then *would take a moment to look around and find out what was going on*. People would fight like cornered animals in the heat of the moment, but give them the slightest suggestion that fighting was not the most important thing they should be doing and their minds would latch on to it.

Very few people, in Tila's experience, wanted to fight to the death. Sometimes they wanted to kill someone else, but that was a very different thing: the ability to kill other people without risking one's own life was why hired knives existed. The ability to put a knife into people at someone else's bidding had been what had given her a starting point in Idramar's criminal underworld, back when she took her first ever big gamble. In many ways, the ability to kill other people without risking one's own life was what, for rulers and warlords, led to the creation of armies at all. They just had to hope that the people who made up those armies did not at any point start asking themselves how what they were doing benefited *them*.

Show an army that their leader was gone, and you might be able to hasten that process along.

It helped that both The Golden and Tyrun had been held in such awe by their followers. The sight did not provoke grim determination to fight on in honour of a fallen comrade, but shock, horror, and dismay. Tila saw weapons fall from hands, warriors drop to their knees and howl with grief, or simply stand and stare in stunned disbelief. The realisation spread, as those too far away to see clearly for themselves caught a flash of the sun on a metal mask, or the glint of a golden circlet, and took that as evidence of what the whispers running through their fellows were already telling them. By the time the disturbance reached the river, Tila had no doubt that people were stopped in their tracks not by any ability to see for themselves what her companions bore, but by the simple fact that so many people who were close enough to see what was going on clearly believed the word that was spreading.

"Come on," she said, and began to descend towards the battlefield. She heard a hiss of alarm from Elio, but her mismatched band from Black Keep followed in her footsteps nonetheless, Naridans shoulder-to-shoulder with Tjakorshi. The warriors parted in front of her and shrank back in horror, as she had hoped, although the way was far from clear: she was picking her way over the bodies of the dead and dying, which was an element of battle that the songs and tales rarely covered in detail. On the other hand, the songs and tales were usually about sars, thanes, and other lords who would ride dragonback, in which case a body underfoot was nothing except ground that was slightly squishier.

Once more, initial reactions were mirrored by others. The nearest warriors drew back from the decapitated head of their leader, while the ones behind crowded forward to make sure their eyes had not deceived them, and so Tila and her procession made their way through a tight wall of horrified souls. No one seemed to want to approach too closely, in case maintaining some distance would allow it to become a dream or a vision rather than reality. In any case, no one appeared to have any idea of what to do, except weep or wail. What *was* there to do? Both heads were clearly dead, there was now a gap between them and their enemies once more, and it would be foolhardy in the extreme to be the first one across it to renew hostilities.

The confusion and hesitation lasted long enough for Tila to get some distance away from the hill, until a sour-faced Naridan with a freely bleeding scalp wound and in the uniform of a Western Army captain shouldered his way into her path. He was flanked by a shorter man with a similar uniform, but the features and colouring Tila would have normally associated with a Morlithian, and another whom she would have pegged as a mercenary commander even without the Brotherhood tattoo on the back of his hand.

"What's the meaning of this?" the bleeding man demanded, swiping angrily at his forehead as blood trickled down towards his right eye: a path which, judging by the pink smears, it had already attempted more than once. "Who're you?"

"Livnya of Idramar," Tila replied calmly. "And you?"

"You keep the company of Raiders?" the man demanded, and Tila saw his sword begin to rise.

"First Captain!" the Morlithian-featured man said, softly but urgently, taking hold of his superior's arm.

"We stand between two armies who've just stopped fighting," Tila said, looking the man addressed as First Captain in the eye. "It might be wise not to do anything that could spark that conflict into life once more, unless we're certain that's what we want."

The First Captain's lip twitched, but his glance at the Raiders standing only a few feet from him seemed to persuade him to caution. "Why do you carry . . . *that*?" he demanded instead, pointing at Tyrun's head.

"The man who claimed to be the Divine One is dead," Tila said, a little more loudly than was strictly necessary if she had only been addressing him. "As is The Golden, the demon who led the Raiders. We found their bodies lying next to each other." And that at least was true, or near enough. "Both were following their own prophecy; and both, it seems, failed to fulfil it. Which rather begs the question of why you're all killing each other."

"The only question is why we should be listening to you at all," the first captain retorted.

"Because this lady might just be the only person who can persuade the Raiders not to start fighting again either," Tila snapped. There was no place for false meekness here, no lessening herself to soothe the vanity of this officer. She had to show herself as strong, capable, and in command from the very beginning. "Everyone around us has been caught in the middle of a step, First Captain: if we're very careful, we can guide where their feet come down, and lead them away from another bloodthirsty charge to all of our deaths."

Perhaps her words would have been enough, and perhaps they would not: she did not get the chance to find out, because at that moment a white-haired old man and a considerably younger woman pushed their way out of the Raiders' lines, staring up at The Golden's head with expressions Tila found hard to read.

The First Captain shifted his feet in response. The captain by his side grabbed his arm again, and placed his own body between that of his superior and the newcomers, while the mercenary surreptitiously loosened his shoulders. The Raider woman – whom Tila recognised as one of The Golden's trusted captains, Kashallo or some similar name – turned towards the Naridans with a snarl. The old man, however, did not look away from The Golden's head.

Then he began to laugh.

It was a high-pitched wheeze that huffed out between what teeth he had left, but it was definitely a laugh. Kashallo looked around at him, her expression somewhere between shock and outrage, while the old man simply slapped his thigh and doubled over, laughing ever harder.

"What's he laughing at?" the first captain demanded. Tila looked helplessly at Tajen, and to her amazement the interpreter gave a quick half-bow to the startled Naridan officer, and replied.

"That's Ludir Snowhair, one of the last chiefs to pledge fealty to The Golden. It seems he still harbours some resentment."

"You speak Naridan?!" the mercenary captain asked, open-mouthed, and Tila saw the two army officers hastily sizing Tajen up as well.

"This man speaks many languages," Tajen replied, sounding slightly huffy about it.

Kashallo shoved Ludir Snowhair, but the old man was still steady enough on his feet to avoid landing on his arse, and instead shouted something in his own tongue at the assembled warriors.

"What did he just say?" Tila demanded of Tajen, worried that she was rapidly losing control of this situation.

"It probably best translates as 'Not so bloody smug now, is it?'" Tajen replied with a grimace, and the Naridan captain with the Morlithian features actually laughed.

"Right," Tila said in Alaban, and pushed Tajen in the direction of the people who were, ancestrally at least, his own. "You get them not to start a fight with each other; I'll handle the Naridans; we'll meet back in the middle assuming we're both still alive." She did not wait for his response, but turned back to the officers.

"First Captain . . . ?" she said in Naridan, leaving the pregnant pause after her words.

"Benel," the first captain replied, having apparently decided that Tila at least deserved to be given his name. "This captain's deputy, Captain Toren; and Captain Reden of the Greenrun Razorclaws."

Tila's eyebrows raised as she looked at Reden, and it was not an act. "The Greenrun Razorclaws? That's a regiment of note."

"You're familiar with Brotherhood companies?" Reden rasped, somewhat sceptically.

"More than you might expect," Tila said. "What about Marshal Torgallen, and the former marshal Einan Coldbeck?"

Benel's lip twitched again when she said "former", but he

did not chastise her, for reasons that became apparent when he replied. "Marshal Coldbeck lost his life to a slingstone that struck early in the battle. Marshal Torgallen is currently dying on his own shortblade," and here he jerked a thumb over his shoulder, "after he was overcome by grief upon seeing the head of the Divine One."

Oh, Taladar, Tila thought. *You always were too devout for your own good.* She nodded, desperately trying to keep a lid on the excitement that bubbled up within her at the first captain's words. "You're now the commanding officer of the Divine Army?"

Benel grimaced, but nodded. "This captain can't say for sure how many of the Godsworn will follow his orders, but the bulk of the Western Army may well, some of the Eastern Army which we assimilated into our number, and the Brotherhood . . . ?" Here he looked at Reden, who nodded in his turn.

"Insofar as this captain can speak for anyone under such circumstances, the Brotherhood are with you."

"But who *are* you?" Captain Toren demanded of Tila. "And how are you so familiar with the Raiders? You've not answered that!"

"This lady is Livnya of Idramar, as she's already said," Tila told him. "She had some influence in the city before it fell: in the time since, she survived by being useful enough to The Golden that it didn't suspect she was working against it."

"Well, whoever you are," Captain Benel said, "this captain doesn't think you truly grasp the situation here. He and Toren are lowborn, and we rose through the ranks of the Western Army by dint of hard work and the eye of the High Marshal for talent wherever it flowered. But we joined the High Marshal in rising up against King Natan and the hierarchy of Narida! We helped the Divine One throw down thanes: we fought against Lord Goldtree, and watched the Divine One execute him!" He waved a hand at the head, still held aloft on its spear by Elio. "What would you have us do now? Pledge our service to the God-King again? We'd be executed, without question!"

Tila took a deep breath. This was it.

"Let's remove the Divine One from the conversation for the moment. Regardless of the fact that He's no longer here to lead you, and take the throne should your rebellion succeed, do you believe in His aims? Do you think Narida should cast aside its traditions of hereditary rank passed down from father to son, with women and the lowborn too often passed over or ignored?"

"That," Toren said, waving a finger at her, "is a leading question."

"And one that will, hopefully, lead us to a solution," Tila said. "The Raiders' society works in that manner, and they follow whoever shows themselves worthy of leading. You must have seen the Naridan soldiers in their ranks: they might have turned their coats, but they did so because they were promised a similar future to what your Divine One was laying out for you!"

She did not explain that she was the one who had made those promises. It did not seem like the right time.

"The Raiders fled their homeland because The Golden told them that it was going to be destroyed, and whether or not that's true, most seem to believe it," she continued. "They don't believe they have a home to go back to, and attempting to force them to leave is unlikely to end well for anyone. But what if both of you carried on the dreams of those you once followed, together?"

Benel's eyes nearly popped out of his head. "Ally with *Raiders*?"

"The town of Black Keep's already done so!" Tila said hastily, pointing at the group of people behind her. "They found a way to coexist! Think of it, First Captain! You command much of the Western and Eastern Armies. The first muster of the Southern Army was shattered by this force of Raiders two days ago, and there's no sign that Marshal Highbridge has even heard word of what's going on here, let alone is mustering the Northern Army. By the time he gets anywhere near us, this force could have achieved its goal."

"Which would be?" Benel asked.

Tila forced herself to smile. "Persuading King Natan to abdicate the throne. Removing the burden of rule from a single bloodline, which can be vulnerable to tragedy or, as is the current situation, no heir. A second Splintering is coming on the day King Natan dies, and then Narida will tear itself apart as the lords and marshals fight and claw for a throne to which they can have no right other than that of a conqueror. We will be opened up to the possibility of Kiburu ce Alaba presenting their imposters to us and claiming legitimacy. All of that can be avoided, and greater justice ensured for all, if we take this opportunity to act *now*!" She took a much-needed breath, and tried to keep herself from shaking as the adrenaline coursed through her. "The Raiders will fight for a new homeland for themselves anyway, so why not ally them to our cause and promise them land, and our support, when we take power? That way we can direct where they settle, to minimise the conflict between them and our people who live in this land already."

Captain Toren folded his arms and stared at her. "How long have you been planning this, *Lady* Livnya?"

"This, exactly?" Tila shrugged. "Since we found both bodies. So, perhaps half an hour?"

"You developed a plan to overthrow the monarchy, and reshape the country to your liking, in *half an hour*?" Captain Benel repeated.

"More like ten minutes," Tila admitted. "But it took a little while to get ready, and attract everyone's attention." She smiled brightly at them. "What will it be? Skulking away to hide from your own names in a desperate attempt to avoid the consequences of your treason; further pointless bloodshed here and now; or a chance for the lowborn of the future to be recognised in accordance with their abilities, rather than relying on catching the eye of a genial High Marshal?"

"That," Toren said sternly, "is also a leading question." He sighed. "But Nari's teeth, this captain doesn't have a better idea."

Benel folded his arms. "You think you can persuade the Raiders to go along with this?"

"They're people," Tila said. "They're strange, and somewhat savage, and there will undoubtedly be arguments, but The Golden was the one most driven to conquest and bloodshed. If we offer them a chance not to have to fight to the death here and now, and the prospect of somewhere to live in the future, this lady thinks most of them will be interested."

"They've killed a lot of Naridans," Benel said uncertainly.

"Yes," Tila acknowledged, feeling an unfamiliar lump in her throat. "You may recall, this lady is from Idramar. The Raiders killed a man there whom she'd known since he was a boy. They killed many others. But as she understands it, the Divine Army has killed not a few Naridans itself." She spread her hands. "Do we say only death can pay for death? If so, this lady asks if you'll let her and her followers leave the battlefield before you charge. If not . . . sooner or later, common ground must be found."

Benel glanced sideways at Reden again, whose grin exposed teeth stained with brownleaf. "So long as we're getting paid."

The first captain looked back at Tila and, reluctantly, nodded. "Very well. If you can persuade the Raiders not to fall upon us the moment our backs are turned, this captain will try to turn the Divine Army towards this plan of yours. But he has one question," he added. "Who's going to rule in this new world of yours, where the God-King no longer sits on the throne?"

Tila smiled at him, attempting to keep calm despite the fact her stomach was turning backflips.

"Well. We have from now until we find King Natan to figure that out. Don't we?"

Bulang

M'bana had half a dozen people at the stall, which was more than Bulang had feared, but significantly fewer than thëy had hoped. Thëy hurried over, and some of the tension just visible on M'bana's face in the moonlight disappeared.

"Î was worried about yöu," hê said in a low voice, grabbing Bulang in a quick, one-armed hug. "The magician didn't do anything . . . too weird?"

Bulang thought about the strangely tame monkey, no longer interested in escape or biting fingers, but shook thëir head. "Î could stand not seeing them again, but it wasn't too bad."

"Did the magic work?" M'bana asked, releasing thëm and standing back. "What did they do?"

Bulang brought the soap bar out of thëir pocket and showed it. It seemed even more ridiculous now, as though they were in the children's tale where the farmer's child sold their prize dragon for a handful of supposedly magical beans and was scolded by their parents for their foolishness. On the other hand, the beans *had* turned out to be magical in that tale, so hopefully the analogy was not so far off the mark.

"I have to dissolve it in the harbour," thëy said, falling back into formal neutral tones now the rest of M'bana's companions could hear thëm. Thëy recognised a couple of faces, but others were unfamiliar.

"What will that do?" asked the largest one present, dubiously. They had been to the house once or twice, and Jeya had introduced them as Hanala.

Bulang shrugged. "Something magical that might help us, apparently. But I have to do it before the short moon sets."

"We'd best hurry, then," M'bana said, looking up at the sky. "It'll be below the horizon before long."

"Remind me why we're out of our beds for this, again?" yawned someone Bulang did not know.

"Because we all know Jeya," M'bana snapped. "They found out the truth about Nabanda, and helped stop hîm. More importantly, Jeya's one of ours. Hierarchs, Sharks, and the Watch be damned: the only ones we can trust to look after our own, is our own. You know Jeya would do something foolish to help save you, so we do the same for them."

"Fair enough," came the grudging reply, and Bulang let out a breath of gratitude.

"Thank you," thëy told them all. "You have no idea how much this means to me."

The race to the docks was an uneasy balancing act between speed and stealth, because so far as anyone knew, Kurumaya's thugs were still out looking for Bulang. Bulang stayed in the middle of the group with thëir rain hat pulled down, and they all did their best to look as though they were in a hurry on the Shark's behalf, without going too near anyone for whom that might actually be true.

One of the group – Pamaru, Bulang realised, the one whose keen eyes the previous night had given them this tip – took over the lead as they reached the docks, and led them over mooring lines and discarded fishing nets towards the sea front of the Naridan Quarter. When their group reached the end of a jetty that reached out into the waters of the harbour, Pamaru pointed to a ship at the far end.

"That one," they said. "That's the one I saw the person being taken onto."

"Time to see what that monkey bought us," M'bana said, looking at Bulang. Bulang's stomach turned over once again at the thought of actually doing magic, or releasing magic, or whatever this counted as, but there was nothing for it. This was why thëy had gone to the magician in the first place: the desperate hope of finding something, anything, that might help thëm get Jeya back from whoever had snatched hér away.

This was all assuming the person Pamaru had seen was actually Jeya, of course, but they had nothing else to go on. Waiting too long to be sure it was hér might mean they were too late. It was a miracle the ship had not already left.

Bulang lay on the edge of the jetty, and reached down. The tide was fairly high, so the water was within arm's reach.

"Tell me if anyone's coming," thëy muttered uncomfortably.

"Just hurry up, so we don't need to," Bulang murmured back.

The soap, if that was what it really was, was loose rather than dense and hard-packed, so it began to dissolve immediately. Bulang rubbed it vigorously to hasten the process, trying not to think of it slipping out of thëir grip and disappearing beneath the waves. The odds of it dissolving by itself in the timescale required were miniscule, and the chances of Bulang finding it again were probably even worse.

Thëy kept a firm hold on it, but not so firm that it squirmed away, and kept washing. The repetitive movements reminded thëm of cleaning themselves before meals in thëir house, and they swallowed back uncomfortable memories of thëir family. They were treasured recollections, to be sure, but nothing more than distractions here and now.

"How's it going?" someone asked quietly.

"It's going," Bulang said, honestly. The bar was significantly smaller, perhaps more than half gone. "Does anyone . . . notice anything?"

"Like what?" M'bana said.

"Like magic!" Bulang said urgently. "I don't know! Anything magical? At all?"

There was a general murmur in the negative. Bulang scrubbed harder. Perhaps all the bar had to be gone before the magic would work? Thëy hoped the splashing would not attract anything sharp-toothed and hungry that might view thëir hands as a snack: hopefully the cloud of whatever it was the bar had been made up of would put such predators off, but what if the scent of grease and fat actually attracted them?

It did not matter. This was what thëy had to do, so it was what thëy *would* do, no matter how thëir head was starting to throb from hanging down towards the water for so long.

Thëy washed and washed, until the last bit of mush dissolved into a slightly thicker pale cloud than that which was already colouring the water, and a few more passes removed the residue from thëir fingers. Then thëy levered themselves up, grateful to no longer have thëir blood running to thëir head, and checked the horizon to see if thëy had managed to obey the magician's instructions in time.

It took a moment to pick out the short moon, and Bulang blinked a few times to make sure thëir eyes had not stopped working. "Has it . . . got misty?"

"Yeah, it has a bit," M'bana said, after a moment. "I hadn't really noticed."

Bulang peered towards the far end of the jetty. The dark, indistinct bulk of the ship was now impossible to make out, and the jetty itself appeared to peter off into nothingness. Under the light of day the mist would probably not have been worthy of mention, but it added greater obscurity to the shroud of night.

"I think it's getting thicker," Pamaru ventured, looking around.

"Anyone notice anything magical?" M'bana asked. "No one's feeling any stronger or faster, suddenly?"

Heads shook.

"It's the fog," Bulang said, suddenly certain. "The magician said they would call on Sa. A god of thieves probably won't make us stronger or faster, but they might make it so guards have a harder time seeing us."

The group M'bana had gathered huddled a little closer together. The notion of magical fog was one that did not seem to greatly comfort them, and Bulang would certainly have preferred a glowing warrior to lead them and defeat their enemies, but if fog was what they were given, fog was what thëy were going to use.

"They only need to see us coming up the gangplank, and they'll still be able to do that," Hanala said dubiously. "We'll be able to get closer to the ship without being seen, so they might have less warning, but that's not going to help us. And that's if the gangplank's even down: it might not be."

Bulang bit thëir lip. "It'll be moored though, right? With a rope?"

"Yeah, but I don't fancy climbing up that, either!" Hanala said. "If they have anyone on watch at all, they'll see us coming!"

"That might depend," Bulang said. Thëy nodded down the jetty. The fog had thickened again, and now the next closest ship was no longer visible either, hidden behind a pale wall that merged with the darkness.

"This isn't natural," Pamaru said, nervously.

"It's just fog," M'bana replied, with what sounded like forced cheerfulness. "Magic or not, it's going to be helpful, right?"

Bulang thought for a moment. The gentle slap of waves on the quay seemed more muffled now, and the direction of it harder to make out. "The fog might help us approach from more than one direction. We need a boat. Some of us try to get on board from the jetty, some of us bring a boat alongside and try to get on board that way."

"Have you ever tried to climb up the side of a ship from a rowboat?" M'bana demanded.

"No," Bulang admitted. "How much harder can it be than climbing a tree?"

"Much," M'bana sighed. "And can you row?"

Bulang tried to look confident. "I know what you're supposed to do."

"That's a no." M'bana sighed, and scrubbed at hîs face with hîs hand. "Fine. You, me, and Pamaru will get that that boat from the next jetty over, and we'll try to get on board from the water. The rest of you—"

Someone hissed a warning, and M'bana fell silent immediately. Bulang's ears picked up the sound of approaching footsteps through the fog, and as one, their group shrank back from the jetty and scattered. The footsteps continued unabated, now accompanied by a low mutter of conversation, and Bulang got the faintest impression of two figures who turned off the quay and onto the jetty, whereupon they walked off and disappeared into the murk.

"The rest of you," M'bana continued, after a few more seconds had passed and no one else had followed the new arrivals, "give us a three-hundred count, then see what you can do from here. And remember," hê added, "these are Kurumaya's people. They won't go easy on us, so don't go easy on them."

Hê did not bother with any more words. Bulang and Pamaru followed hîm to where a rowboat was tied up, and M'bana and Pamaru took up the oars. Bulang was convinced that it did not *look* that difficult, as they pulled out into the harbour and began to swing around to approach the ship from open water, but the other two clearly did not want thëm to have a go.

The fog was truly thick now: so thick that steering was not reliable. It was not until Bulang saw a faint bloom of warm light spilling out diffusely through the fog that thëy knew they were heading in the right direction.

"Left a bit," thëy muttered, and the rowing changed slightly to bring the nose of the boat – the bow? – around. Then, so suddenly it made thëm jump, the blank dark wall of the fog dissolved into the darker, solid side of the ship on which Jeya was, if Pamaru was correct, being held. The glow was coming from a window – and it was large enough that Bulang was sure that it was a window, and not a porthole – halfway up the ship's side, towards its stern. One of its panes, a wooden frame in diamonds of glass sat in a lead lattice, was open.

Bulang tapped the other two on their shoulders. The fog was so dense that Bulang could not even see the ship's rail above thëm clearly, but thëy kept thëir voice down as they pointed to the window. "I want to take a look in there."

"We're here to get *onto* the ship, without being noticed," M'bana protested in a whisper. "Not climb into the one place we're fairly sure there will be people awake!" Hê stopped speaking as a voice came from the window. The words were not distinct enough to make out, and nor were they in the voice that replied, but Bulang knew the second voice well enough that the words were immaterial. It grabbed thëm by the heart with fingers of relief and new, tightly focused anxiety, all in one.

Jeya.

Darel

D arel had predicted that The Golden's army would be easy to find. What he had not expected was that the army would find them.

It was not difficult to work out which way they had gone. Sar Osrel and Sar Natan returned to North Ferry, to cross the Idra, but Darel had no wish to revisit the site of the massacre from which they had so narrowly escaped. He and his companions cut west instead, and picked up the crown road a few miles upriver. The passage of so many people left no trace on the stone with which the road was paved, but was obvious in the grass worn bare on either side, and the snapped-off twigs of bushes that brushed up against the road where it passed through woodland, not to mention the ashy remnants of countless fires.

They were passing through one of those places, where The Golden's forces had presumably spent a night, when Darel saw movement in the trees ahead.

"Who's there?" he shouted, drawing his longblade. His party were all mounted on dragons, so they were hardly the stealthiest of groups, and they could not have already caught up with the rear of The Golden's forces: the old fires looked like they had been burned out and cold for a day or more. Perhaps these were local people, who had withdrawn away from the river as the Tjakorshi passed, and had now returned to their own land . . .

Or, he conceded to himself as armed man after armed man emerged into view ahead of them, he could be completely and utterly wrong.

"Whom do you serve?" he called. They were Naridans wearing the uniform of the Eastern Army, but that could mean practically anything at this point. Several carried bows, but there were too few to pose a true threat.

"Well now, that's a question, isn't it?" one of the men called back. He and those with him began to amble a little closer, keeping their hands away from their weapons, and their bows still slung across their shoulders. "These are strange times." He squinted. "Are those Raiders with you?"

"Yes," Darel replied, warily. "But they are people of Black Keep, and have been declared as much by the God-King himself. Now, whom do you call master? The Golden, or the man known as Tyrun, or the God-King?"

A couple of the men laughed. "Well," said their spokesman, "two of those are dead, and we've seen neither hide nor hair of the third, so we're going to say none of them."

Darel gaped at him. "Dead? But who— The Golden? And Tyrun?"

"Aye. Killed each other, or so it's said," the man replied. "S'man didn't see it himself, but he saw their heads. Or at least, he saw the head of a man others said was Tyrun, and he saw a head wearing the mask of The Golden with no sign of the demon itself turning up to claim it back, so he supposes it's probably true."

"You knew The Golden?" Darel asked, his elation at the man's news rapidly overtaken by wariness. Were these Eastern Army deserters, who had fallen in with the Tjakorshi?

"What happened to their armies?" Zhanna demanded, from her mount next to him. "Did they kill each other as well?"

"Made a good go of it at first," the man acknowledged. "But once word got out of how The Golden and Tyrun were dead, things changed a bit. As to what happened to those armies . . . Well, you've just walked into it."

He put his fingers to his lips and let out a piercing whistle, causing the trees on either side and behind them to disgorge many more armed men, most with arrows notched to the strings of the bows they carried. Darel drew his longblade, already cursing his own inattention, but the man who had been speaking raised his hands.

"Easy there, goodsar, there's no need for this to get ugly. We'll just need you to come and have a talk with the Lady Livnya, that's all." Darel saw his eyes rove over their party once more. "S'man thinks she'll be very interested in your little group, given as how she's trying to do the same thing on a much larger scale right now."

Darel frowned at him, his guilt and dread subsiding slightly, as cautious curiosity forced its way to the fore once more. "How do you mean? Who is this Lady Livnya?"

"Like s'man said, these are strange times," their captor said with a shrug. "The Lady Livnya and her captains have big ideas, and one of them is that we shouldn't be killing each other."

Darel looked at him, then looked backwards. "And if we try to ride back the way we came?"

"Well," the man said, spreading his hands and grinning slyly, "it's an idea rather than a rule. So why don't you come with us, and you can talk to her about it yourself?"

If Darel had been amazed by the sight of the full body of Livnya's army, marching eastwards down the River Road with Tjakorshi ships shadowing them on the water, he was even more astonished when he met the Lady Livnya herself.

"You?" he exclaimed in disbelief, and no little anger, as he was ushered into a carriage, of all things, and found himself face to face with The Golden's translator.

"You?!" the woman called Livnya replied, apparently equally incredulous. "The runner said they'd found some sar with a few Raiders, not the damned Southern Marshal!" She sat back and curled her fingers up over the lower part of her face, while she studied him contemplatively.

"How have you managed this?" Darel demanded, gesturing around him.

"The carriage?" Livnya spoke through her fingers. "Tyrun apparently picked up a fancy to travel in style before He met His end, and it seems a minor noble of Northbank tried to buy His goodwill with a gift."

"Not the carriage," Darel said, with forced patience. "The *army.*"

"Quick thinking, considerable effort, and no small amount of natural intelligence," Livnya replied. "Much like your brother," she added, "may Nari rest his spirit."

"You should not speak about this marshal's brother!" Darel snarled at her. "Or must he remind you how and why Daimon died?"

"This lady tried to talk him out of it, you may recall," Livnya said wearily. "She tried to talk all of you out of fighting, but you didn't listen. She'd managed to gain some small influence with The Golden by that point, but nowhere near enough to prevent it from ordering the attack."

She still had not moved her hand: it was almost as though she was trying to hide her mouth, or her chin. Was she self-conscious about her teeth? Darel could not recall any such hesitancy on her part when she had been stood at The Golden's side outside North Ferry, but the main part of his attention had been on the demon and its army, not its mouthpiece. Besides, they had not been so close to each other then. He could remember Yarmina Darkspur's reticence about her teeth when they were children: perhaps it was a more common hang-up among women than he had thought.

"You did try," he acknowledged reluctantly. Should he have listened? He knew precious few others would have, but that did not prevent the question from nagging at him. "You succeeded with two entire armies?"

"The situation was a bit different," Livnya said. "There was an opportunity to offer them both something they might want, and a way out of their predicaments, without any obvious clashes. The Divine Army wanted to place Tyrun on the Sun Throne, which they couldn't do after he'd died. The Golden intended to kill a god to clear the way for its people to settle, but its death doesn't change the fact that the Raiders need a place to live now. Both forces offered their lowborn Naridan followers the chance to remove the nobility, and share out wealth and opportunity more fairly." She waved her free hand vaguely. "That seemed like the obvious place to start."

Darel gaped. "You want to *remove the nobility*? That goes against . . . everything! The Code of Honour, the laws dating back to General Garadh——"

"All of which are obviously outdated!" Livnya interrupted him. "Their purpose is not to make Narida strong or healthy, their purpose is simply to *keep things as they are*, and you of all people should realise how foolish that is! Didn't the God-King quote Garadh when he ordered your Raider friends to be driven into the sea, before you saved his life, and he changed his mind?"

"How do you know about that?" Darel demanded, eyeing her closely. Had he seen her in the Sun Palace? Her manner of speech sounded lowborn to his ears, but he had not spent enough time in Idramar to truly become used to their accent.

"You don't think everything said in the Hall of Heaven stayed there, do you?" Livnya replied, with a nasty laugh. "Servants talk, Lord Blackcreek. Or did, before the wave and the Raiders came." She sighed. "Look, this lady used to be a staunch supporter of the Divine Family, and she certainly never had any time for Tyrun and his cult, but she's come to realise that things have got to change. Things have already changed, for that matter; the country can't go back to how it was, it's not possible. We can keep clinging to the idea that a line of fathers and sons will somehow safeguard us against calamity, or we can open our eyes to the calamities that have already befallen us, and realise that *this isn't working.*"

Darel stared at her, trying to process her words. "You are suggesting, what? That we renounce Nari? We renounce his teachings?"

"No!" Livnya's eyebrows jumped. "Not at all! But perhaps it's time to accept that His descendants – if we can even be sure that they *are* His descendants, that was what the Splintering was about, after all – simply no longer have enough divine blood to be worthy of the name. There's nothing to say Nari won't still return to us in time, as prophesied, since Tyrun must have surely been a pretender. But perhaps rather than relying on one family to guide the country until then, the responsibility for it should be placed in hands chosen for their suitability, not because they happen to have been born male, and to the right parents."

She sat back. "This lady has spent some time with the Raiders, and that's how *they* seem to do things. You can't be that opposed to their ways, seeing as how you've welcomed them into your town."

Darel scoffed. "It is not that simple. None of the thanes will go along with it!"

Livnya regarded him steadily. "You could probably fit all

the thanes in Narida into the Hall of Heaven, if they stood shoulder to shoulder. You could fit all their families into the Sun Palace with room to spare, probably enough room for most of the sars as well. If enough of the lowborn decide this lady's suggestion works better for them, why should the thanes opinions hold any weight whatsoever?"

"But this is how the country *works*!" Darel protested.

"Do you tell your fishers how to fish, or your farmers how to farm?" Livnya asked. "Your herders how to herd, your miners how to mine, your woodcutters . . . You get the idea."

"Not the fine detail," Darel admitted. "But the thanes make the laws of their land, we dispense justice, we protect our people—"

"All of which are important!" Livnya agreed. "But there's no reason why it has to be hereditary! How does Black Keep appoint a reeve?"

"The thane appoints him," Darel said immediately. "Although the town as a whole makes the choice, the thane just . . ." He trailed off, eyeing Livnya suspiciously.

"Now you're getting the idea," she said, with a hint of mischief.

"But that is for one town," Darel protested. "You cannot expand that out to cover whole thanedoms, or whatever you would call them if there were no thanes; it simply would not . . ."

He paused. Would it not? What if each town or village made a choice of someone, like they did for a reeve, and then *those* men – or, yes, women – selected one of their own number – there would have to be a rule that you could not vote for yourself, perhaps – to take the higher office. And perhaps you could actually expand that system out further, right up to—

"It would need to be repeated semi-regularly, of course," Livnya said quietly, into his thoughts. "Anyone raised up must be capable of being removed again, or we'd have simply created a new nobility."

"This marshal never said—" Darel began, but Livnya cut him off.

"Lord Blackcreek, there are thousands upon thousands of lowborn soldiers around us who believe they should have their share of the nobility's wealth, and thousands more Raiders who want somewhere to live. None of them are going to get what they want under Narida's current ruling system, and that's going to mean bloodshed that will make what we've seen so far look like a fucking tavern scuffle, if you'll pardon this lady's Alaban."

She leaned forward. "You might not think this will have a chance of working, but you're an intelligent man, or so this lady's heard. Nothing's going to be perfect, and nothing's going to please everyone, but you've got the opportunity to help make whatever comes out of this as least shit as possible."

The infuriating thing, Darel realised, was Livnya had a point. If the forces held together, they easily had enough numbers to make *something* happen. Darel could not prevent that, but he might be able to guide it.

It came back, once again, to the salt marsh outside Black Keep. Daimon had seen the inevitability of what was coming, and had decided to make the best of it. Darel and his father had resisted, and had risked ruining it for everyone.

"The God-King and the nobles must not be harmed," he warned.

"This lady has no intention of harming anyone," Livnya said, with what appeared to be complete honesty. "Besides, if the lowborn view their nobles to be good and just, they might be able to keep their influence, let alone their lives." She shrugged. "This lady wouldn't put a wager on that being the case for all of them, mind. But they shouldn't be harmed, unless they take up arms against us," she clarified, seeing Darel's expression.

"You know that some of them will."

"This lady isn't their mother," Livnya said. "They'll make their own choices, and then they'll have to live with them. Or not, depending on how insistent they are about it."

Darel thought of Daimon, and of Saana; a lowborn man, and a woman, neither of whom would normally have risen to any sort of prominence in Narida, and both of whom had become respected not only in their own communities, but in each other's as well. Then he thought of himself, and although his rank as Southern Marshal had come as a result of his own actions, he had never been destined for anything less than ruling Blackcreek. Was he inherently *better* than Daimon, or Saana?

No. No, he was not. He had greater skills in certain areas than either of them, and lesser abilities in others. None of them were, or had been perfect, any more than Zhanna was perfect, or Gador the smith was perfect, or Hiran Threestone was perfect, or the woman sitting in front of Darel at this moment was perfect. Their strengths and weaknesses had little to do with their birth or gender, but the opportunities they received assuredly did.

"Very well," he said, praying that Nari would forgive him. "This marshal will not himself take up arms against the God-King, but he will help you make plans for what should happen, if you find yourself in a position to enact them."

"A fair deal," Livnya replied.

"But this marshal wishes to discuss this with others," Darel said. "Zhanna Saanastutar is the daughter of the chief of the Brown Eagle clan, and has a good command of Naridan: she can share insights on how the Tjakorshi think about things. There are also two men of the Smoking Valley with us, who may provide another useful perspective."

Livnya smiled through her fingers. "This lady has already been grateful for the counsel of Captains Benel and Toren, formerly of the Western Army. They're both lowborn men who were raised to command, and she suggests that they're included in our discussions."

"That is a good idea," Darel agreed, sitting back in his seat. Thoughts were already whirling through his head: of power structures, and responsibilities, and delegation, and timescales.

Daimon had always said that Darel was never happier than when he had a problem to solve. Now he faced the biggest problem of his life, and it was already calling to him. He might not have ever felt truly comfortable as a thane, and certainly not as Southern Marshal, but this . . .

This was what he was good at.

Tila

It had not been easy, of course.

Taladhar Torgallen was not the only member of the Divine Army to take his own life in despair at the sight of his god's decapitated head. Quite a few of the lowborn known as the Godsworn did the same, with much wailing and crying. Even some of the soldiers did, although far fewer by comparison. Tila was not surprised by that: soldiers tended to be pragmatists, and she was still unsure how many had followed Tyrun out of genuine belief, and how many because they did not get paid enough to question orders from their commander. Or indeed, in the case of the Eastern Army who joined after Northbank was taken, because they would have been put to death if they refused.

Deaths like that were unfortunate — or so Tila would maintain, although privately she considered that she was far better off without the fanatics — but provided few actual difficulties. More problematic were those who took exception to her mounting the so-called Divine One's head on a spear, and tried to start a fight over it. Thankfully, cooler heads like Benel and Toren's prevailed, and no one actually got close enough to stick a knife between Elio's ribs.

Some people split away of course, slipping off in ones and twos, or small groups, unable or unwilling to hold to a common purpose now their leader was dead. However, the majority of the Divine Army stayed together, either through the belief that Tyrun's divine purpose of overthrowing the monarchy and reordering Narida was going to continue after His death; or that divine or not, the idea sounded like a better deal for them, if they could make it work. Or, possibly, because they were not sure what else to do, but figured that they might still end up on the winning side, even if they were no longer quite sure what that side was.

The majority of the Naridans who had fallen in with The Golden were still with Tila. In fact, they constituted what she considered her own true following, given she had won many of them over. If any had taken Morel's proselytising about The Golden being Nari reborn to heart, they had discarded it just as quickly as it had taken root. It did not take long to bring them on board with the new direction, especially with Sebiah Wousewold's help. The former Lord of Scribes had stayed well back from the fighting, but any worries Tila harboured about his willingness to turn on Natan now both other contenders were out of the picture quickly vanished after she saw him encouraging his fellow countrymen that their promised future was still within their grasp, despite The Golden's death. Quite clearly, Sebiah Wousewold saw no chance of Natan's triumph against this horde, and every possibility of carving out a niche of his own in whatever came next.

There had, of course, been the Tjakorshi themselves to contend with.

Very few had the same sort of devotion to The Golden as some Naridans had for Tyrun: their loyalty was based far more on opportunism and fear, mixed with a healthy amount of respect for what the draug had actually achieved. Now the fear and respect were gone, and opportunism was a difficult mount for Tila to saddle and steer. Devoted or otherwise, many Tjakorshi had cleaved to the belief that The Golden could not truly fail, and so they had followed it with the certainty of travellers on a well-maintained road who might not know exactly where they were, but knew they had to be going *somewhere*. Now the road had disappeared and left them in treacherous, unfamiliar ground, and everyone and their mother thought they should be the one to find the way out.

Tajen proved invaluable. Tila suspected that some of his interpreting had been slightly more conciliatory than word-perfect, but she had no objections. Some of The Golden's followers had, of course, been determined that fighting, and possibly dying, was the only course left open to them. However, more rational captains and chiefs, or those who had once been chiefs, recognised the opportunity.

Which did not mean that they were entirely trusting about the whole affair.

"This chief has dealt with conquerors before," Ludir Snowhair had said to Tila and her officers, through Tajen. "The fact you offer instead of demand doesn't change things. If we join our axes to yours and bring down this other man-god for you, what's to stop you turning on us once you've achieved your purpose?"

"Firstly, that would still be a brutal fight that would kill a lot of us," Tila replied. "Secondly, we know your people and ours *can* live together." And she had called forward Otim, who explained to Ludir Snowhair, and the other chiefs and captains with him, how the Brown Eagle clan had settled at Black Keep.

In the end, the hotheads either calmed or, when they insisted on trying to solve things with their axes, were turned on sharply by their own fellows in the interests of keeping everyone else alive for a while longer. So it was that, by the end of the day in which the Divine Army and the forces of The Golden had clashed, a fragile peace built on self-interest had won out.

Then they headed east again, and Tila met Darel Blackcreek, which was both a blessing and a curse. A blessing, because the young man was undoubtedly intelligent, and far more suited to tasks of civil logistics than pretending to be a war leader. A curse, because she spent every moment in his presence worried he would recognise her as the Divine Princess, and then ... Well, she simply did not know what would happen. Theoretically, of course, her rabble-rousing speeches about opportunities for the lowborn, and for women, did not become any less true simply because she was of higher birth than everyone thought. In practice, she suspected no one would believe she was not leading them into a trap for the benefit of her brother.

She *was* being dishonest, in a sense. On the other hand, Livnya the Knife was as real a person as Tila Narida to many of those who had lived in Idramar: more real, in many ways, since much of what Tila Narida had done would have been impossible without Livnya. Tila felt like she was a butterfly, newly emerging from a chrysalis and leaving her old self behind for good.

Or nearly for good. There was still her brother to deal with, and there was no way she was going to be able to pretend to be Livnya with him. The question was whether he would call out her deception and, in so doing, potentially doom them both.

Tila desperately wanted to see her brother. She wanted to know that he was well, she wanted to hear him make a sarcastic joke. She would even have been happy to happen across him canoodling with a dragon groom, as though nothing had changed. However, everything had changed. She was at the head of an army intent on removing him from the throne, and she had no idea whether or not he would capitulate; or exactly what would happen if he did not.

Or even if he did.

*

"Are you surprised the God-King has agreed to this meeting?" Captain Benel asked, as they rode towards a manor house a day's travel north of Threestones.

"In some ways," Tila admitted. "In others, no. Meeting with us gives us legitimacy, it's true, but so does the size of our army. If he runs from us, it looks bad. If he ignores our messengers and stays behind the walls of Threestones, he's got no guarantee we'll still want to talk when we get there. This way he can hear our demands without having them shouted up to him in front of an entire castle."

"You sound like you've managed more than a few tricky negotiations like this," Captain Toren said. He was smiling, but his eyes were sharp.

"Not involving forces of this size, obviously," she said easily, "but this lady has some experience in these areas."

"So this captain has heard," Toren said, his smile still in place. "He's asked around about you. The word is that you were . . . somewhat notable, in Idramar."

Tila refused to give him even a moment's glimpse of uncertainty. "If we're choosing this moment to forgo the dance steps, then the words you're looking for are 'crime lord', captain. This lady managed her own little kingdom, and all the power plays and backstabbing that involved; and managed to do it while keeping clear of the keepers, to boot."

"Which this lord can testify was no mean feat," Sebiah Wousewold put in from beside her. Tila was still a little uncertain about his involvement, but his knowledge of the Crown Messengers would prove invaluable in coordinating the kingdom if they actually managed to pull this off.

Captain Benel shook his head and looked at his deputy, with an expression that was rueful, but lacked surprise. "You're right, Toren: it was the only explanation that made sense."

"Those days are in the past," Tila said stoutly. "You

gentlemen can see everything this lady's doing now, so she's no longer a criminal hiding from view. Either that, or we're all engaged in the greatest crime of all."

"Which is undoubtedly true," Toren replied. He shook his head. "Still, we've come too far to back out."

Tila, who had seen many people back out of agreements long after it was sensible to do so, held her tongue. If her officers ran out on her now, the consequences for everyone involved were going to go well beyond a few broken kneecaps or a burned-out shop.

Their destination was a country retreat for the thane of Threestones when he wished to spend some time away from his castle. It was reached by a long driveway which wound through stands of mature whitebeam, which had Toren looking out of the coach window and muttering about the potential for an ambush. No such thing occurred, however, and their party finally passed through the mighty stone gate pillars and onto the close-grazed land immediately in front of the house itself.

They were a strange group, Tila had to admit. Besides herself, Wousewold, and the two Western Army captains in her coach, they numbered Darel Blackcreek and Zhanna Saanastutar, both riding dragons; Barstan Broadfield, a former thane who had renounced his rank to join Tyrun, and was now acting as some sort of voice for the Godsworn, driving a wagon; and Tajen, Ludir Snowhair, Inkeru Kjanjastutar, Kashallo Merngustutar, and Naska Halfsmile, a portly middle-aged man who only spoke out of one side of his mouth, but was apparently considered worth heeding by his fellows. Those Tjakorshi all rode in the back of the wagon driven by Broadfield, and when Tila had asked why Inkeru was with the others instead of with her two Blackcreek compatriots, Darel and Zhanna had laughed.

"Inkeru has learned to ride a dragon, but prefers to avoid it," Darel had replied with a smile.

"Also, she does not trust them," Zhanna had added in a hoarse whisper.

"Dragons?" Tila had asked, and Zhanna had pulled a face.

"No. *Them*."

When Tila looked back, she had seen Inkeru sitting with her arms folded, apparently engaged in a staring match with Kashallo Merngustutar, and had suppressed an amused smile of her own. Her limited interactions with Inkeru Kjanjastutar had given Tila the impression that the other woman was a capable warrior and sailor who did not suffer fools gladly, which was something Tila could respect.

The day was warm and dry, and the sky was clear, which was presumably why the Divine Court — or whatever now served as it — had set up on the lawn instead of crowding into a house that, while large, would struggle to accommodate them all in the same place without everyone becoming very friendly with each other's elbows. Tila, looking out of the coach window as they approached, could see a large chair of carved wood, which would serve as her brother's makeshift throne, but of Natan himself there was currently no sign. She picked out a few of the southern nobles by their sigils, though: Strongway, Highpike, Stonefall, Threestone — presumably the eldest son, wearing a mourning veil for his father, who had died at North Ferry — and there was either Coldhearth or Wreckpoint, they looked very similar from a distance, and there too was Tainbridge, and . . . Darkspur? And that large, blonde, pale-skinned person towering over what looked like the young woman in Darkspur colours, surely that could not be—

Zhanna Saanastutar bellowed a word in her own tongue and put her heels to her dragon to goad it forward into a gallop, with her three pet rattletails skittering along behind her.

"Fucking Raiders!" Benel spat, his face a mask of anger and

fear as he lunged for the coach window to see what was happening. "Why is she attacking?!"

"She's not," Tila said, more calmly than she felt. "Unless this lady misses her guess, Zhanna's greeting her mother."

"Will the rest of them realise that?" Toren demanded, one hand on his sword.

"If what this lady has heard of Saana Sattistutar is correct, she'll straighten them out if they don't," Tila replied, but her heart was still hammering as she tried to see around the side of Benel's head. Youthful enthusiasm was all very well, but it would only take someone loosing an arrow at Saana's daughter for everything to go very wrong, very quickly.

Thankfully, it seemed that if any of the assembled nobility or their servants had a bow, no one decided to use it. Zhanna reined her dragon in before it was in serious danger of trampling anyone, and hopped down from the saddle to cross the remaining distance on foot, whereupon she threw herself into her mother's arms while the rattletails gambolled almost playfully around the pair of them.

"Those creatures still disturb this captain," Benel said. "Their good nature is unnatural."

"Try to consider them a lesson in what can be achieved if a different approach is taken," Tila suggested. In truth, she had also found the tame rattletails somewhat unnerving at first, but it was very difficult to spend any time speaking with Zhanna Saanastutar and come to the conclusion that there was anything sinister about her. Not that that had stopped both Naridans and Tjakorshi from giving her the nickname "the dragon girl" among themselves, apparently quite separately. Neither group was used to seeing a young, one-handed Tjakorshi woman wearing a sar's longblade and followed by three biddable rattletails. If Tila was any judge, Zhanna was already halfway to becoming a figure of legend.

Right now, though, the legend-in-the-making had been released from her mother's embrace, and was being held by her shoulders at arm's length while they talked earnestly. Tila hoped Saana Sattistutar had already been informed of her husband's death. Darel Blackcreek had instructed his two Tainbridge sars to carry word, but there was always the possibility they had not made it. She glanced out of the window and saw Blackcreek himself, still riding alongside her coach rather than racing ahead as Zhanna had done. Of course, not only did he have the death of his brother on his conscience, but that of Mattit Threestone, whose son he was about to come face to face with. Not to mention that regardless of refusing to bear arms against Natan, Darel would undoubtedly still be painted with the broad brush of treason.

The carriage came to a halt. Under normal circumstances, Tila would have waited for a servant to attend, but Livnya of Idramar would not have been used to such niceties. She opened the door herself and stepped out, smoothing down the skirts of her dress and doing her best to appear like someone unused to such methods of transportation. There was still no sign of Natan, and the tension was starting to fray her nerves. Was he even here? It surely could not be a trap: this many thanes would hardly have agreed to be bait. So where was he?

The two groups would have lined up in an uncomfortable standoff, had it not been for the Black Keep contingent. Zhanna was already by her mother's side, and when Darel dismounted, Saana Sattistutar wasted no time in walking to him and enveloping him in a hug that spoke of mutual loss; one which Blackcreek returned without reservation, somewhat to Tila's surprise. Then Inkeru arrived, and Saana broke off her hug with Darel to engage in a somewhat less tender embrace of mutual backslapping, and Yarmina Darkspur – for so it must surely be – moved forward and bowed solemnly to

Darel in a gesture which he returned. Then Zhanna decided to hug Yarmina, her cheeks flushing slightly as she did so, while Yarmina looked simultaneously mortified and happy.

"What an uncouth display," Sebiah Wousewold muttered, from beside Tila.

"This lady couldn't have asked for better if she'd planned it herself," Tila murmured back. "Look around! Everyone's watching them demonstrate how it's possible for us to coexist without killing each other."

"The nobles don't like it," Wousewold observed.

"They're not going to like a lot of things," Tila retorted. "They don't have to like this, just accept that it's possible. Then we can—"

"His Divine Majesty, the God-King Natan, third of his name!"

The door of the manor house had opened without Tila noticing, and now the herald stood aside.

And out swept Tila's brother.

He was dressed in the red, green, and gold of Narida, with the triple-pleated sleeves that denoted him as royalty. A servant walked behind him, holding the train of his robe off the ground, to avoid the dishonour of his clothes being sullied by dirt. He was not wearing the state crown of Narida, that ghastly half-helmet affair he always complained about, but a smaller, more reserved one: Tila wondered if he had picked up any of the crown jewels before he fled the palace, or whether some were even now in the possession of warriors that had followed The Golden.

What hit her in the stomach, however, was the black veil that draped down from under the crown to hide his face.

No. No. Not mother . . .

Damn it all, Blackcreek had been adamant that the Queen Mother was well when he left Threestones! Tila made sure she found that out when she, as Livnya, had asked him casually about who fled from Idramar with them. What could have happened in the weeks since? Sudden illnesses happened, yes, but Tila realised with a start that she had always thought of them happening to other people. Not the Divine Family.

Not *her* family.

"Your Majesty," Sebiah Wousewold said, his voice a little unsteady. "This lord expresses his sympathy for your loss."

"Be silent, traitor!" Kyrel Strongway snapped, but Natan waved his hand for silence as he took a seat on the carved chair, and the train of his robe was laid carefully across his lap.

"Peace, Strongway. Although this king is disappointed to see his former Lord of Scribes in such company, Lord Wousewold's words may well be genuine."

"How—" Tila's voice cracked, and she forced herself to gain control. Natan had not immediately denounced her, so she could not afford to give herself away. However, nor could she not ask. "How did the Queen Mother die?"

"The Queen Mother?" Natan's head cocked, and Tila could imagine the single raised eyebrow that always accompanied that tone of his voice, even though she could not make out his features. Damn that veil! Had hers been so infuriating for everyone else?

"The Queen Mother remains well," Natan continued, and Tila was suddenly able to breathe again, although confusion flooded in to take the place of grief.

"But—"

"This king mourns the death of his sister, the Divine Princess," Natan said, with the smallest hitch in his voice. "We were unable to find her in time to take her with us as we escaped Idramar, much as this king wished we could have done so. There has been no word of her presence since, so he must assume she perished there, alone and unidentified. It is a loss that hits this king hard, for she was more dear to him than most could ever know."

Tila swallowed, and tried to keep control of herself.

Oh Natan, you genius. You wonderful, beautiful genius. Probably.

The message requesting this meeting had borne the names of those who would be present, and given her prominence, there was no question of leaving Livnya's off. Tila had hoped Natan would realise that this Livnya was the one his sister became when she sneaked into the city, although she could not predict what his reaction to that realisation was going to be.

It seemed he had reacted by doing everything he could to prevent anyone from associating Livnya with Tila, right down to declaring her dead and veiling his own face to ensure no one could directly compare them. Surely that boded well?

Either that, she realised, or Natan intended to kill them all without being labelled a kinslayer. However, even leaving aside the fact that Saana Sattistutar would have no part of that, Tila simply could not imagine her brother doing something so cold-blooded. It was not in his nature.

It was conceivably in Tila's, though, and Natan knew it. Men could do things that were very out of character if they felt they had been backed into a corner.

"If this were taking place in a grand hall, there would be all manner of courtly rigmarole to negotiate," Natan declared, his voice clear and proud. "It is not, and so there is not. This king wishes to get to the point. You have assembled a large force of men — your pardon, of *warriors*," he corrected himself, "who until recently were part of two separate forces wreaking havoc across Narida. Now you have turned south and demanded an audience with this king. What are your intentions?"

Tajen was muttering a translation for the Tjakorshi, but no one was expecting them to speak for the group. Benel and

Toren looked overawed, as might be expected for lowborn military men who now found themselves in front of the divine monarch they had once sworn to serve. Wousewold showed no sign of putting himself in harm's way, and Tila did not trust Barstan Broadfield to speak without putting his foot well and truly in it. She opened her mouth, hoping she was about to gauge her voice and language well enough to sound natural, without also drawing attention to any similarity between her speech and her brother's.

Darel Blackcreek stepped forward from Saana's side, turned to face the throne, and bowed.

"Divine Majesty."

"Darel Blackcreek," Natan said, his tone studiously neutral. "You faced down four attackers to save this king's life, and pledged you would remain true to him. You appear to have an interesting definition of 'remaining true'."

"In fairness, Your Majesty, there were rather more than four this time," Blackcreek said, a witticism which provoked splutters of outrage from some of his fellow thanes. "However, your servant has not truly joined his cause to those you see before you. He was asked by the Lady Livnya to join her, and others, in solving a logic problem. Your servant believes we have a solution that is, while not perfect, as good as could reasonably be devised in the time available."

"What logic problem would that be?" Natan asked.

"The army to the north seeks to remove you from the throne, and the thanes – including this servant – from holding power by right of birth," Blackcreek began.

"Treason!" Thane Wreckpoint shouted.

"*Yes*, treason," Natan snapped, raising his hand. "We gathered that much when they brought an army! We are here to find out what they are proposing." He lowered his hand again. "Blackcreek, continue."

"Should they be successful, whether by persuasion or by force of arms," Blackcreek said, "a new regime would need to be installed, in order to ensure the wellbeing of this nation. This was the logic problem: what shape such a regime should take, to ensure a fairer, better life for all those under it."

"And you willingly took part in this, despite knowing it would remove your own power?" Natan asked.

"Divine Majesty, this logic problem was predicated on the success of the rebels," Darel replied. "If they did not succeed in removing you from power, the point was moot. If they did succeed, it behoved your servant, as Southern Marshal and therefore responsible for a quarter of the kingdom, to ensure that whatever came next was the best possible outcome. In this, your servant tried to learn from the lesson taught to him by his brother Daimon," he added, "who faced a similar dilemma when the Brown Eagle clan landed on our shores. Daimon had never envisaged or desired the Tjakorshi settling in our town, but he saw the reality of the situation, and worked with Chief Saana to everyone's advantage."

"Divine Majesty, surely you will not listen to this?" the thane of Stonefall protested, and Tila winced on the man's behalf. She had seen her brother in this sort of mood before — mainly since Einan Coldbeck had tried to depose him — and attempting to naysay him was unwise.

"We will all listen, Stonefall!" Natan said shortly, "and then we will consider. To reject their proposition outright dooms us to a bloody war. That may still be the course we have to choose," he added, "but there may be other options."

"Divine Majesty, you are of the line of Nari," the elder Threestone boy said. He had avoided looking directly at Darel, so Tila suspected that the death of his father while under Darel's command was going to be an issue there. "Your rule is not just righteous, it is required!"

"To keep the kingdom from harm?" Natan asked. "This king has heard that one many times. And yet harm has still come! His father's death was followed by a plague. The great wave savaged our shores, and then the Raiders we see before us landed, matched by the uprising in the west that turned a formerly loyal army against their king!" He sighed, and his veil fluttered slightly. When he spoke again, his voice was level once more. "This king cannot see evidence to suggest that his presence as ruler has warded off any great misfortune. That does not mean he will simply step aside for any ruffian at the head of an army, no matter how large, but nor will he send his country to its death for the sake of pride, and long-standing legends. After all, if this king is divine, whatever decision he makes must be correct. If he is not, he has no business holding on to the throne by right of blood alone."

He beckoned. "Blackcreek, this king knows you well enough to know that you will have written such things down, probably at great length. Bring them out, and we will discuss them. If they are not sound, you and your companions can expect nothing from this king except defiance and bloodshed."

His head turned slightly, until Tila was certain that he was looking at her, through his veil.

"If they *are* sound . . . we will see where we go from there."

Jeya

The rest of the night passed in misery. The day that followed was just as bad, if not worse, because with only a tiny porthole Jeya's cabin sweltered in the heat and humidity. Shé had little appetite for the crusts of bread shoved in through the door on a tray, but ate them with the reflexive action of someone for whom food of any sort had too often been a luxury. Jeya's childhood had taught hér to eat when the opportunity presented itself, and so shé chewed and swallowed mechanically, moistening hér mouth with sips of water as shé did so. Shé kept an eye at the porthole as well, but no one came down the jetty, and the noise of the docks would drown out any attempt shé made to shout for help: besides which, any such attempt would have been overheard by hér captors. And who would help? The harbour was under the control of Kurumaya, and no one would risk going against the Shark to help hér.

When it came down to it, shé was an orphan thief who had made it to adulthood through luck, and the kindness of one or two people like Ngaiyu. Shé was not important enough for anyone to pay any attention to: at least, no one who could do anything. It was not as though shé was Bulang, born into luxury, and heir to a bloodline on which great matters of state hinged. Not that it had worked out particularly well for thëm: thëir family was assassinated, and thëy ended up living with an orphan thief in an old house that had belonged to a murder victim.

Jeya believed Bulang loved hér, but as shé sat and sweated in the afternoon heat, shé wondered whether thëy would ever be truly happy in a life with hér. Thëy were raised to believe thëy were the rightful heir to a distant throne, even if the chances of claiming it seemed remote. How likely were thëy to settle for a hammock in a single room? Was that why thëy had been drawn to Kurumaya's plan? Cruel and manipulative though it was, it was still a link back to thëir old life, and thëir importance in the world.

Shé was desperately tired, but the stupefying temperature of hér tiny cabin prevented Jeya from achieving anything approaching real rest, especially curled up as shé was, with hér body pressed in on itself. It was late evening before the warmth began to leach out a little, and shé finally managed to slip into something like real sleep.

Shé was woken by the bolt scraping back and the door opening, to reveal the shape of a person holding a lantern from which emanated a chink of light. The world outside had changed from long shadows and the richly coloured skies of dusk to pitch blackness. Shé took a quick look out of the porthole and was surprised to see nothing: no moons, no stars, just an enclosing darkness. The ship was not moving any more than it had been before – merely the gentle bobbing of a vessel at anchor in a harbour – so presumably they were not underway.

"Come with me," ordered the person at the door: the same broad-shouldered one who had brought hér to the cabin in the first place. "You can walk, or you can be dragged. It's your choice."

"I'll walk," Jeya said, getting to hér feet, and wincing as

hér body protested at the cramped position in which shé had slept. Unlikely though escape seemed, shé would have a better chance of it if shé was on hér own feet, rather than in the grip of others. Shé grabbed the jug on hér way past, and swallowed the last mouthful of water from it. Drinking water was one thing shé had not lacked as a child, although somewhere to shelter from the plentiful rain had been, but who could say where shé might be incarcerated next? Best to make use of what shé had.

Shé had no idea what to expect, although hér mind quickly threw up colourful and painful scenarios. These ranged from being marched back off the ship into the city for some manner of showdown with Kurumaya for whatever unknown transgression had prompted hér kidnapping in the first place; to being transferred to another ship and borne away across the ocean to the gods alone knew what fate; to being pronounced unnecessary, hér throat cut, and hér body dumped over the side for the sharks to feed on. Instead, shé was directed through several claustrophobic walkways and doors until shé entered what had to be the captain's cabin.

It was probably a large space as ship cabins went, although Jeya had little experience of them. It took up the entire stern of the ship – Jeya could see windows on each side, and in the back wall – and boasted a bed, hooks from which a hammock could be slung when the seas were choppy, a desk, and things on the wall with which Jeya was unfamiliar but which she guessed to be charts, and other instruments concerned with navigation. Beside the desk stood a person whom Jeya would have assumed was the captain: they had the general look of a sailor, but their clothes were of a finer quality than many. Behind the desk, however, seated in the chair and looking at something written on paper, was someone very different.

They looked like a scar that had grown arms, and legs, and a head. Their hair was cut short into greying stubble, through which ran a shiny scar line in which nothing grew, their nose was no natural shape, and their knuckles were flat from being broken at some point in the past. However, their maijhi had long, wide sleeves, and was beautifully decorated: not at all the sort of practical clothing Jeya had seen sailors wearing, when they bothered wearing much at all. What was more, shé had seen this person before, and not anywhere near a ship.

They had been with Kurumaya, on the night the Shark had come to the house, and Bulang had disclosed thëir true identity.

"Honoured Turakandu," the broad-shouldered person said respectfully. "The captive, as ordered."

Turakandu. One of Kurumaya's deputies, or so Jeya had heard. Shé could put face and name together now, but shé was not certain that would help hér in any way. Why had the Shark ordered one of their underlings to kidnap hér?

"I hope yòu'll forgive the delay," Turakandu said, not looking up from the papers in front of them. Their surprisingly soft voice held an edge of amused malice, like a knife blade wrapped in flower petals, and Jeya got the impression they were enjoying themselves. "It's so very difficult for me to get away unnoticed these days, now Kurumaya has made their play for control of the city. But we shall have to see what we can do about that, won't we? Given the news of the God-King's sickness, I think there might be a lot of people in Narida willing to pay handsomely for the last scion of the Splinter King's line: either to set yòu up as their puppet, or just be sure that they're properly rid of yòu. So long as the money is good, I don't care which it is."

Now they looked lazily up at Jeya, a smug smile twitching at the corners of their mouth. A smile that disintegrated as soon as they laid eyes on hér face.

"Who the fuck is *this*?" Turakandu snapped, their humour disappearing like silverfish scattering from a sudden light. It was replaced by a tension so thick that Jeya could almost taste it. Turakandu was not only suddenly angry, but scared as well. The captain, standing beside them, was glancing from the Shark's deputy, to Jeya, to the thug by hér side, with the expression of someone who realised that things had taken an unexpected turn, and was relieved that they were not directly involved. Jeya felt the thug stiffen, through the hand that gripped hér arm, and knew that they *were* directly involved, and were not at all confident about the direction things had taken.

"This is the youth, the one you told us to take," the thug ventured, their voice suddenly sounding much less gruff and threatening than it had. "They came out of that house—"

"You utter, fish-brained *fool*!" Turakandu spat, rising to their feet like a battered thundercloud. "You were supposed to snatch the Naridan! *The Naridan!* Does this youth look Naridan to you?"

"They've got long hair, they lived in that house, they knew the guards on the door," the thug protested stolidly. "That was all we were told."

"*This* is not the Splinter Prince!" Turakandu said, rounding the desk. Their fingers flexed angrily as they spoke, as though they were envisaging wrapping them around the thug's throat and squeezing. "Look at them! We can't sell *them* to the Naridans!" A knife appeared in their hand, summoned from the sleeve of their maijhi. "This means the Splinter Prince is still somewhere in East Harbour, and Kurumaya could recover them at any moment!"

Jeya did hér best not to move or breathe, to minimise the

chances of Turakandu's wrath selecting hér as its target. So Kurumaya's deputy was betraying the Shark in the hope of profit? It was a bold move, and a risky one; but more risky than holding true to Kurumaya's side? The Hierarchs theoretically controlled all of Kiburu ce Alaba, after all, and there was no telling how long Kurumaya's rebellion would last if the other islands sent forces to retake East Harbour.

More importantly, these people wanted Bulang, but had ended up with hér instead. That did not just mean they did not get what they wanted, it almost certainly meant hér death. Shé was not important: just a mistake picked up by accident, and which would now be discarded to ensure shé could not interfere with their plans.

"You. You're the one called Jeya, yes?" Turakandu asked hér.

Jeya saw little point in denying it. "Yes."

"Do you know where the one called Bulang is?" Turakandu asked hér. They did not put the knife blade to hér skin, but they held it up so it drew hér eye. The lurking menace of what they *might* do with it was possibly more unsettling than an overt threat.

"No," Jeya answered honestly, although her stomach was tight with fear for Bulang as well as for hérself. Where were thëy? Were thëy not at the house?

"Child, I'll ask you one more time," Turakandu said, with no pretence at patience. "If you tell us where we might find Bulang, you can live. If not, you're no use to me."

"I don't know!" Jeya said fiercely. "Your people took me from our house! That was the only place I know where Bulang might have been! Maybe you shouldn't have sent fish-brained fools!" shé added, and felt the thug who had hold of hér stiffen once more, this time in anger.

"Gah!" Turakandu spat angrily, then addressed the thug. "We know Bulang has disappeared, and *I* thought that was because *we* had them, but apparently not! Go to the city, and *find them*. And remember, this time, that you are looking for the long-haired *Naridan*."

"What about Kurumaya's people?" the thug asked, and Turakandu sighed.

"I have no more patience for—" They cut off as a resounding thump came from above, and they looked questioningly up at the cabin ceiling. A moment later, Jeya jumped as shouting erupted. It was coming in through the windows, but as more thumping sounded it became clear that the disturbance was not on the jetty, but on the deck of the ship itself.

"Get up there and find out what's going on!" Turakandu snarled. "Both of you!" The thug and the captain obeyed without question, hurrying out of the cabin door. Turakandu lifted their knife and pressed it into the flesh under Jeya's chin, a cold sharpness matched by their eyes. "In the meantime, there's no reason why we should not have a more extended conversation about exactly where your friend—"

"Over here!"

It was Turakandu's turn to jump, and Jeya felt the point of the knife nick hér skin as they whirled around to face the voice that had called out, in a cabin that should have been empty except for the two of them. Jeya took a step back, and hér eyes confirmed what hér ears had already told hér.

It was Bulang. One leg through the cabin window, a knife in thëir right hand, and determination plastered across thëir face. Jeya's heart jumped with both relief and fear at the sight of thëm.

Turakandu lunged for Bulang, their fingers outstretched. Jeya kicked one of their legs into the other, and they tangled: Kurumaya's traitorous deputy fell on their face in a flail of embroidered sleeves, but began to push themselves back up immediately. Bulang struggled in through the window, pulling thëir other leg after them, only for Turakandu to lash out with one arm and sweep thëir legs from under thëm. Bulang tripped with a cry, and lost thëir grip on the knife: Turakandu lunged for thëm from their knees, blade in hand.

Jeya snatched the gag out of hér maijhi, wrapped it around Turakandu's neck from behind, and heaved them away from the person shé loved.

Turakandu let out a strangled cry of panic and clawed at their throat, but Jeya crossed the ends of the cord over to fully encircle their neck and pulled on each end with all hér strength, causing bulges of flesh on either side of where it dug in. Turakandu stabbed backwards blindly with their knife, but they were off-balance, and the blade missed Jeya's shoulder by a finger's width. Bulang scrambled up and threw themselves at Turakandu, grabbing the wrist of their knife hand and pulling it away from Jeya, and all of them tumbled sideways onto the floor.

"Get the knife!" Jeya hissed. "Get the knife!" Shé was pulling on the cord so hard it felt like hér shoulders were going to give out, but shé dared not let go. Bulang was practically laying on top of Turakandu's knife arm now, pinning it to the floor while thëy wrestled with the deputy's fingers. Turakandu was clawing desperately at the cord around their neck with their other hand, and trying to kick Bulang off them, but the angle meant they could not muster enough force into the blows, and Bulang gritted thëir teeth and held on.

Turakandu's thrashings became weaker until, with one final twitch, they went limp. Bulang snatched the knife from their nerveless fingers, but Jeya kept pulling even as she rolled the deputy off her, so they were limp and face down on the floor.

"Let's get out of here," Bulang said, wrapping an arm around hér. "Come on! M'bana's in a boat, outside the window!"

Jeya let go of the cord with something that was halfway between a sigh of relief and a sob, and stood up. Turakandu did not move as the cord slowly peeled away from their neck. Jeya was not sure if they were still alive. Nor, shé realised, did shé care.

"Go on," Bulang urgéd. "Yóu first." Thëy held Turakandu's knife ready and faced the door. Jeya peered out of the window and saw M'bana's anxious face looking up hér.

"What in all the hells is happening up there?" they demanded desperately. "Jeya, are you hurt?"

"No," Jeya replied, swinging hér legs over the window's sill, then hesitating. The drop to the rowboat was not a long one, had it been onto a decent surface, but shé had no intention of landing next to M'bana only to tip them all into the harbour. Shé twisted around and began to slide backwards out of the window, holding on as best shé could to prevent hérself from falling. Hér shoulders screamed at hér for this renewed effort, but the threat of a dunking in the water made hér bully them into cooperating long enough for hér to look around and see hér foot dangling just above the edge of the boat. Shé let go and tumbled into it, landing on hér backside: everything rocked precariously, but shé rolled to the middle so her weight was as centred as possible, and they did not capsize despite M'bana's alarmed squawk.

"Coming down!" Bulang whispered hoarsely from above, and Jeya looked up to see thëir legs dangling just like hérs must have. Shé crawled as far into the bow as shé could manage on such a small boat, and Bulang dropped with little more grace than hér, but roughly the same end result.

"Let's get out of here!" the person on the other oar said. Jeya peered at them, and just managed to make out Pamaru's features through the darkness, and ... was this *fog*? Where had that come from?

"M'bana?" a voice shouted from above, and Jeya looked up in shock, hér heart hammering again.

"Hanala?" M'bana answered, and Jeya breathed a little more easily once more. "We've got Jeya! What happened up there?"

"Damned strangest thing," Hanala said, their voice lower again now. "There wasn't many of them, and they didn't seem to notice us until we were right on top of them. The fog must have muffled any noise we were making, or something."

They did not sound very convinced by what they were saying, and Jeya noticed that M'bana looked uneasy as well. But it was good news, surely!

"Anyone hurt?" M'bana asked.

"Us? Not badly. This lot won't be getting up again, though."

"Great. Now make yourselves scarce, before anyone comes!" M'bana ordered, and the dim shape at the rail nodded and disappeared.

"How did you find me?" Jeya asked, as M'bana and Pamaru dipped their oars into the water. "And thank you! For finding me. And for coming after me," shé added, grabbing Bulang into a hug. Thëy melted against her, squeezing hér just as hard in return.

"I saw someone being taken there last night," Pamaru replied softly. "When M'bana started asking around, it seemed like it could have been you."

"I found M'bana," Bulang told hér, from somewhere near hér shoulder. "We owe them everything for this, Jeya."

"How did you know what had happened?" Jeya asked them. "I was worried you'd think I'd just . . . run away, or something."

Bulang's face came up, and Jeya caught a shift in shadows that hinted at a smile. "I think Sa warned me. I heard a monkey scream, and knew that something was wrong."

A shiver ran through Jeya that had nothing to do with the cool fingers of fog brushing against hér cheek. Shé looked out into the night and tried to frame the image of a golden-maned monkey in her thoughts. "Thank you."

"The most important thing now," M'bana said, from where they were pulling on an oar, "is what you're going to do next. If Kurumaya's people snatched you then you're not safe in East Harbour, and the sun will be up before long."

"They weren't Kurumaya's people," Jeya said. "Or, well, they sort of were. But they were trying to betray Kurumaya."

Pamaru made a choking noise. "*Betray* Kurumaya? Someone working for the Shark was going to turn on them? How foolish can you *get*?"

"But you're right," Jeya said, looking at M'bana. "We're not safe in East Harbour anymore. Or at least," shé added to Bulang, "you're not safe. They wanted you, they got me by accident. And I don't think the danger's gone just because they're not around anymore."

"If I'm not safe, then you're not safe either, for so long as you're with me," Bulang said miserably. They took a deep breath, and let it out slowly. "We need to leave."

Jeya bit hér lip. Leave East Harbour? It had been hér home for all of hér life. Everything shé knew was in this city: all the ways shé had to survive, all the people on whom shé could rely, all the places shé felt even remotely safe.

But how much of it was safe, now? How much of it would *ever* be safe?

It came down to one question: what was more important to her? The life shé had known so far, or the future shé dared to hope for with Bulang? For that matter, was Bulang suggesting they leave for hér sake, or for thëir own?

"Are you sure? I know you . . ." Shé hesitated, well aware of the other two in the boat with them. It was not that shé distrusted M'bana and Pamaru, given they had just risked their lives to save hér, but there was a difference between not distrusting someone, and disclosing Bulang's deepest secret to them. "I know you wanted to make a difference here."

"Ï don't think Ï can," Bulang said, so quietly that the other two would not be able to overhear. "Not më. Someone else might make a difference to something by *using* më, but it won't be mÿ choice, and it might not be the difference Ï'd want to make. Ï know that now, and Ï don't want that to hurt yóu, or . . . Or for it to come between us. *Yóu* are the most important thing to më, Jeya. Ï don't care what stories other people want to tell about where Ï might come from. Ï just want to have a future with yóu, and . . . " Thëy broke off as emotion choked thëir voice, then swallowed and continued. "And Ï don't think we can do that here. Too many people know about më, and would find us again."

Jeya nodded slowly. The Hierarchs, or Kurumaya, or someone else: there would always be people after Bulang, it seemed, for so long as thëy remained where someone knew who thëy were.

"Yöu are the most important thing to mé, too," shé said softly. "Yes. We'll leave." Shé thought about the house they had lived in for such a short time. There were things there shé would have liked to take – the piece of crystal, perhaps, as a memento of Ngaiyu – but it was far too risky to return. In the end, all shé really needed was in the boat with hér.

She raised hér head and looked up at M'bana and Pamaru. "We need to leave East Harbour."

"Well, I'm not rowing over to Lesser Mahewa in this thing," M'bana said with a snort. "Where were you thinking of going?"

Jeya shrugged. "I honestly have no idea."

"Perhaps you should take a ship," Pamaru suggested.

"I think I've had enough of ships for one night," Jeya said ruefully.

"We can't pay for passage," Bulang added. "We've got nothing."

Pamaru tutted at them both. "Not all ships in the harbour belong to Kurumaya or their people, silly, and ships are always taking on new crew members. You won't have a choice in where you go, but if the most important thing to you is getting away from here, that's not so much of an issue, is it?"

Jeya screwed hér face up. "I know *nothing* about being crew on a ship. And I doubt Bulang does either."

"Pamaru's got a point, though," M'bana said. "People run away to sea with no experience all the time. You won't get a first mate's cabin or anything, but if you really do want to leave, there might be one that would take you on. Then just make the best of it wherever you end up. I'll miss you," they added, "but given what's been happening recently, I can see why you'd want to get away."

"I'll miss you too," Jeya told them, honestly, and M'bana flashed hér a smile. Shé realised shé could see their face a little more clearly, and looked around. "The fog's lifting."

"Mmm. Can't say as I'm unhappy," M'bana said, with a glance at Bulang, but no further explanation. "Dawn's coming, too. Pamaru, any ideas?"

"There was a northern ship that came in a couple of days ago, so it might be set to leave soon," Pamaru said. "It moored near the Adranian quarter. The captain seemed rather put out by Kurumaya's people running the docks, so I don't think they're involved with the Sharks at all. Maybe they'd be interested in a couple of young hands willing to work for food and passage?"

Jeya looked at Bulang. "Are you sure about this?"

"No," Bulang admitted, "but I'm more sure about it than I am any other ideas."

"Good enough for me," Jeya said, hugging thëm a little tighter, and feeling a new knot of excitement and anxiety building in hér stomach. "Let's give it a try."

The ship was one of the largest in port, and was richly decorated with lusciously painted beasts along its sides. More unusually, Jeya noted, the figurehead that many ships had was absent, and instead what looked like a person's skeleton was affixed to the bow by a method shé could not make out: or rather, it would have been a person's skeleton, if people had two, many-pronged antlers rising out of their skull. The dawn light cast deep shadows within its bones, and Jeya could not shake the idea that its empty eye sockets were somehow looking at hér.

"Do we really want to try this ship?" Bulang asked quietly, looking at the skeleton with wide, nervous eyes.

"If the crew have horns, we turn around and leave, deal?" Jeya muttered, and squeezed thëir hand. Shé realised shé had no idea how one hailed a ship, let alone when you wanted to get work on one. "Um, hello?"

There was no response to the first time she shouted, or the second. The third time, however, a figure appeared at the rail, and Jeya nearly squeezed Bulang's hand right off in alarm.

It had horns!

Then, with a wave of relief that was so comprehensive it made her knees slightly weak, she realised that the horns were attached to a hat, which the figure removed from its head as it looked down at them.

"Who are you, bellowing up here like that?" a voice called down. Its accent was strange, but it spoke Alaban well enough.

"We want to sail," Jeya said, trying not to trip over hér own tongue, which felt thick and clumsy in hér mouth. "We've not sailed before, but we'll work, and all we're asking is food and a place to sleep."

"That's so, it is?" the voice said. "Well, the captain I am, so the right person you are talking to. Be holding your wind." They stepped back from the rail, and Jeya looked at Bulang.

"Any idea what that means?"

"I think we're supposed to wait?" Bulang ventured. A few shouts came from above them, and then two more people came into view with a gangplank, which was lowered onto the jetty. The captain, horned hat and all, walked down it and stood there for a moment, studying them, and Jeya took the opportunity to study them back.

They had long, red-brown hair, and a tanned face that struck Jeya as slightly mischievous, but not instantly untrustworthy. Their clothing was unfamiliar – a light shirt fastened with buttons of bone, a patterned wrap of thicker cloth around their waist and reaching down past their knees, and sturdy boots – and they sported silver rings all the way up the backs of both ears.

"Captain Jarka, I am," the captain said, after a few moments. "No experience, you said?"

"Not on ships," Jeya admitted.

"Well, a ship this is," Jarka declared, waving at the vessel. "The *Bone Daughter*, you would call her. So what can you be doing, not knowing ships?"

"I can climb well," Jeya said, looking up at the mast. "I've got good balance and I'm . . . I'm good with my hands."

Jarka's mouth slipped into a smile. "So a thief, you are." Jeya opened her mouth to protest, but Jarka raised a hand to forestall her, and laughed. "Thieves on ships must learn to change their ways, or the next shore they will never see. Know that, you must."

Jeya nodded.

"And you?" Jarka said, looking at Bulang. "Another thief?"

"I'm not so good at climbing," Bulang said. "But I . . . know a lot. I understand numbers, and I can read and write, and I speak Naridan, and some Adranian, and some Morlithian."

Jarka tilted their head. "The seas to Morlith are farther than we go, and I have some Naridan. How well is your Naridan speaking?"

Bulang smiled, and bowed, and rattled off a sentence so smoothly and rapidly that Jarka's eyebrows climbed involuntarily.

"That," they said, wagging a finger, "is well speaking. And you have letters and numbers, you say? Letters in Naridan?"

"Yes," Bulang said eagerly. "As good as my Alaban."

Jarka nodded thoughtfully, and looked at them both again. "Food and a place to sleep, you say?"

"For now," Jeya said. "Until we can prove how useful we can be."

Jarka smiled. "Sensible. Bargaining." They looked over hér shoulder towards East Harbour, and sighed. "A strange place, this has become. Better, and worse. Understandable why some might wish to leave."

Jeya held hér breath, and said nothing.

"Very well," Jarka said, stepping back. "Over the side you will go, if we find you have stolen anything. Otherwise, useful you may be. Come. Meet the crew, you should."

They turned, and walked back up the gangplank. Jeya kissed Bulang on the cheek in delight.

"Are yöu ready?"

Bulang smiled. It was a nervous smile, but in that sense it exactly matched what was going on inside Jeya's chest. Shé felt like an adventurer in a story, ready to see new lands and wonderful sights. It did not matter that other people would have already been there: the adventure was hérs, and no one else's.

Although there was one person in particular with whom shé intended to share it.

"Ï'm ready," Bulang replied, and kissed hér in return. "Let's go."

They walked up the ramp, out of the shadow of the ship, and into the young light of a new day.

Tila

They started discussing the proposals in the mid-morning, and noon came and went. The thanes with Natan were opposed to the idea, of course: even Yarmina Darkspur, despite her apparent affiliation with Blackcreek, although Tila got the impression this was because the girl had elected to call herself a thane and had no intention of relinquishing the title. Tila had not, of course, expected Narida's nobility to universally applaud her plans to strip them of their right to power, but she had hoped they might at least defend their positions by pointing out flaws, which could then be corrected. Instead, they were relying entirely on the fact that power had been granted to their ancestors by past God-Kings. That encouraged her that there were no gaping logistical flaws in what she and Blackcreek had come up with, but was of no use in terms of moving forwards.

Servants brought luncheon out in the early afternoon, and while the tense atmosphere was not exactly lessened by it, there were at least more reasons for people to avoid talking to each other while they ate. However, Tila had barely started her food when her brother rose from his throne and approached her.

"Lady Livnya," he said, his tone as formal as it had been throughout the proceedings. "Walk with your king."

Tila was suddenly unsure of how to respond. Had they been alone then she would have told him to piss off for addressing her in such a manner, but she always attempted to maintain some manner of respect in front of others. Besides, she was not the Divine Princess here: she was Livnya of Idramar, a lowborn woman clearly adopting a rank above her station, but who just as clearly had a certain amount of power to back that up. Should she bow? She was technically a treasonous rebel, but they were treasonous rebels who were trying politeness first . . .

She elected to make a bow, as a compromise between the kneeling that would normally be expected of a lowborn in front of the God-King, and the defiance of someone who would stare their ruler in the eye, then fell in beside him. Natan carried the train of his own robe draped over one arm, in a clear sign that he wanted no servants trailing behind him, but one of the thanes still felt the need to intervene.

"Your Divine Majesty," Natan Threestone said, in a tone of some concern, as he hastily rose from his seat and placed himself in front of them. Tila found herself in the unfamiliar position of being the only person out of three who was unveiled, as the husky young man made a fresh bow. "If this Livnya of Idramar is the one rumours speak of, she is a dangerous criminal. Your person might be at risk should you speak with her alone."

"This king thanks you for your concern, Threestone," Natan said, and Tila could hear the amusement in his voice as he spoke, "but he does not consider an attempt on his life to be likely in these circumstances. Please, return to your meal."

Veil or no veil, Tila could tell Natan Threestone was unhappy, but he equally could not disobey a direct order from his monarch. He bowed again, and moved aside, and the pair of them began to walk once more.

"What in the name of the Mountain are you doing?" Natan asked levelly, once they were far enough away from the others to avoid being overheard.

"Your sister is fine, thank you for asking," Tila replied, slightly stiffly. "Despite being left behind in Idramar."

"This king's sister is *dead*," Natan replied. "That is why he is wearing this veil. And while he regrets many things he allowed to occur under his rule, not hauling your arse out of the double life you chose to lead in his city, organising and encouraging others to break his laws, is not one of them. You were always very clear that you knew the risks: that included not being behind the walls of the Sun Palace when disaster struck. It was a mercy you were not out there when the great wave came, but you still went back." He paused for a moment. "This king is truly glad to see you alive and well, though. Even under circumstances such as these. But you did not answer this king's question. What *are* you doing?"

"Taking what you offered this lady last winter, and several times before that," Tila said. It seemed Natan was unwilling to acknowledge their relationship even when alone, and although it was probably safer, it still felt like a wall had been thrown up between them. "You offered her the crown, on the basis she would be a better ruler than you, and she refused because the thanes would never accept it. The obvious solution was to remove the thanes from the equation, but that was never feasible. Until now."

Natan laughed bitterly. "So the plans you had Blackcreek work so hard on are merely lies? You will take power, and keep it?"

"No!" Tila insisted. "There needs to be a leader who can oversee the changes that must occur. This lady has the support of many Naridan lowborn who are tired of the nobility's high-handed ways, as well as the trust of the officers commanding the rebel army, and at least some understanding with the chiefs and captains who hold sway with the Tjakorshi now The Golden is dead. She's the only natural choice for that role. Once the plan can be implemented properly, we can allow the country to select its own leaders. With luck, this lady's efforts will persuade people she should retain her influence. If not . . ."

She sighed.

"If not, at least she will have tried."

"And if the power goes to someone who should not have it?" Natan asked.

Tila shrugged. "The country won't have to wait for them to die, like they do with bad monarchs."

"Ouch."

"This lady did not mean *you*," Tila said, exasperated. "You haven't been a *bad* ruler, you've just been . . . less interested than you might have been, at times."

"This king has been trying to change that," Natan pointed out, somewhat defensively.

"Yes, this lady knows," Tila agreed. "To be honest, that's almost more frustrating, because this lady's one opportunity to change things has come just as you've taken more responsibility. She can't let that stop her, though. You have no heir, so Narida will be thrown into turmoil when you die. Nari bless us, that will be many years from now, but it's still true. We need a robust system in place before then, so the country no longer relies on Nari's bloodline. Even if these changes have little real impact on the lives of the lowborn now, fending off a civil war down the line will be worth it."

"And in order to bring this about, you threaten civil war now?" Natan asked. "If this king refuses your propositions, your army will attack. Even if you were bluffing, and this king knows you are not, the others who follow you will not be."

"There were two armies in the middle of annihilating each

other, and then the victors would probably continue to depre-
date the middlelands anyway!" Tila snapped. "This lady had
the choice of leaving them to it, or aiming them at something
else that not only had the potential to benefit a lot of people,
but *might* mean no more Naridans had to die at all!"

Natan sighed, and they walked on for a few more steps in
silence. Then he spoke again.

"You never had any intention of letting Tyrun take the
throne. You would have fought tooth and nail to prevent it.
Why do you expect the thanes to react any differently, when
you threaten their power?"

"Tyrun would have been replacing one divine ruler with
another, on the basis of nothing more than his own say-so,"
Tila said wearily. "We're not raising up a new nobility, we're
creating a new *system*. Any thane can still hold power, so long
as he can persuade people he's the best person to have it."

They had nearly reached the gate posts now, and were about
as far from their companions as they could be without leaving
the grounds entirely. Natan reached up as though to scrub his
hand through his hair, an old habit he usually only indulged
when they were alone, but paused when his fingers encountered the arrangement of crown and veil that sat atop his head.

"So far as this king can see, it is not an unworkable plan," he
said, lowering his hand once more. "It would require support
from the country as a whole, of course. And there is still the
matter of the Raiders. They wish to live near the sea, apparently, but it is our coastal towns who have suffered the most
at their hands. Black Keep was an anomaly of circumstance,
which could have failed if any number of variables had altered
slightly."

"There are probably fewer towns than there were," Tila said
bluntly. "Let them break apart, find their own piece of land,
and make them aware that any raiding of their neighbours

will result in the attention of the army. It may work out. Some of the southern lands are eager for more hands in any case. It won't be ideal, but nor was what they were doing before. So long as they don't go back to the areas they ravaged with The Golden, it might be feasible."

"This king feels you may be overestimating people's ability to compare the problems of what might be, with the reality of what is in front of them," Natan muttered, "but he cannot argue with your logic. There seems little hope of the Raiders putting back to sea, and killing them would be impractical at best, so we must make the best of it." He tapped his index fingers together a few times. Tila knew him well enough to realise he was musing over his next words, and she was proven correct.

"This king must ask for your promise on something."

"Speak, and this lady will answer you," Tila replied. She was not going to commit herself to a promise when she had not heard the details, king or no king, brother or no brother.

"This king has always trusted you to do what you think is right," Natan said slowly, "but that is not the same thing as trusting you to tell him the truth. He must know: *are* you telling the truth? Is the plan you have presented truly your intention? Or is this yet another scheme within a scheme; a lie you put forward as a plausible explanation for your actions, and which may not be completely at odds with your interests, but which mainly serves to conceal your true motives and goals?"

Tila opened her mouth to protest that of course she was telling him the truth, then stopped. It was a fair question. She had been playing different angles for so long that it was second nature. You never put everything into one scheme: she had learned that long ago from Yakov. You always worked towards a goal, but there were many different paths that could take you there, and if one suddenly looked less promising, you changed course to another.

However, she found that she had an answer to her brother's question.

"The plan is this lady's honest intention," she said. "She has obviously considered what she might do if it does not work, but this is the goal. If our stated aims for the future of Narida work as intended, they will not be serving any hidden purpose for her."

Natan nodded. "This king needed to hear you say it." He breathed out, a long, quiet breath, and they took a few more steps together before he spoke again.

"Have you considered Mother?"

"She will not approve," Tila conceded. The thought of her mother's expression was an uncomfortable one, but discomfort was the least of Tila's worries. "And of course, she could identify this lady, if she chose."

"This king might be able to persuade her otherwise," Natan said. "Nothing is certain, of course. Does anyone else know about you?"

"No." But of course, that was not true. "Well, Alazar, but—"

"*Alazar?!*" Her brother's voice was practically a yelp, and Tila looked around quickly to make sure that no one at the house thought she had just stuck a knife in him. "You told *Alazar*?"

"This lady didn't *tell* him; we stumbled together in the battle and he . . . recognised her." Which was not entirely true, but close enough. "But he wanted no involvement, and disappeared. He's intelligent enough to realise that poking his head up and making trouble for this lady is unlikely to end well for him, or his husband. So long as this lady doesn't become sufficiently tyrannical to prod his conscience into action, he'll probably lay low and stay out of her way." She sighed. "You can consider that another check on this lady's ambition, if you want: if she abuses power badly enough, Alazar of White Hill will undoubtedly appear to reveal her true identity, and ruin things." Natan simply grunted, and Tila decided to add something else. "He killed The Golden. The story works better if The Golden and Tyrun slew each other, but that isn't what happened. Alazar defeated it, one-to-one."

"Well, good for him," Natan muttered sulkily.

"This may be the last conversation we have, you know," Tila said urgently. They were beginning to circle back towards the manor house now, and it would not be long before they would have to avoid anything that might cast suspicion. One way or another, things could never be the same between them again.

"Yes," Natan agreed, and Tila was about to scold him for his terseness until she heard the choke of emotion in his voice. It eased her heart a little to know the prospect affected him too, even as it wounded her in a different way.

As for her mother . . . Would Tila even be able to speak to her? What reason would the leader of revolutionaries have to share yeng with the Queen Mother? That was a prospect that cut deep. "This lady wanted to be honest with you. You had asked for it, after all."

"This king understands," Natan replied. "Thank you, for everything. Everything you have done for him, and for Narida. It would be a worse place without your influence."

"Your sister loves you," Tila said, and his insistence on language be damned. "No matter what else has happened, or will happen, that remains true."

"And your brother loves you as well," Natan murmured. "Now, let us see if we can finish this."

That was easier said than done, of course, given the thanes' continued refusal to engage with the revolutionaries' plan on its own merits. The sun was sinking towards the treetops, and Tila's stomach was twisting with the twin aches of desperation and frustration, when Natan spoke up once more.

"We have been over this backwards and forwards, and we are scarcely any closer to an agreement," he stated baldly. "The rebels seek what they consider to be justice," he waved a hand at Tila and her fellow Naridans, "and land of their own –" He motioned in the direction of the Tjakorshi. "– but their proposal is unacceptable to the thanes of the land."

The thanes, drawn up beside his throne, nodded in weary agreement.

"And nor," Natan continued, "is it acceptable to this king."

Tila's breath caught in her throat. She had been so sure! After his performance of not recognising her in order to not expose her, his statement about how he considered the plan to be workable on its own merits, his question about whether this was her true intention . . . Had he not believed her, after all? Or had a couple of months of responsibility really convinced him that he did indeed have a divine right to rule, and that no one else could be trusted with it?

No one said anything out loud, but there was a subtle shift in posture as Natan's words made their presence felt among those assembled. Darel Blackcreek looked shocked and disappointed. Benel and Toren's faces had gone blank, the universal expressions of soldiers who had heard someone more important say something which spelled bad news for everyone. The thanes looked smug; the Tjakorshi, as Tajen finished interpreting, rolled their eyes as though they had known this entire affair was pointless all along.

Saana Sattistutar sat forward with an intense expression in her grey eyes. She was not looking at Natan, but at everyone else in turn.

She's expecting a fight to break out, Tila realised, as the

Brown Eagle clan's chief's hand strayed towards the blackstone axe that hung from her belt. *She's waiting to see who's going to move first.*

And suddenly, Tila realised that Sattistutar might not be wrong. Perhaps it had been reckless to organise this meeting. Benel and Toren had their metaphorical backs against a wall, Broadfield was a fanatic of sorts, and the Tjakorshi might just see Tila's promises of a place to live disappearing in front of their eyes, and take matters into their own hands. It would only take one person deciding that Natan's life was the substantial obstacle standing between them and what they wanted, and then acting on that realisation, for everything to fall apart.

Tila's entire body was tense, but not the sort of tension where muscles were ready to act: it was the rigidity of uncertainty, and fear. It was one thing to plan for the possibility of a war, while issuing instructions that the God-King was not to be harmed, and quite another to realise that someone nominally on your side might be about to draw his sword and aim it for your brother's chest. If First Captain Benel unsheathed his weapon, Tila did not know what she would do. Would she try to bring him down? Throw herself in front of him? Or sit where she was and watch him try to kill her brother, for the good of the country?

Her eyes met Sattistutar's, and saw only certainty there. Tila had no idea what the other woman was going to do, but she was fairly sure that Sattistutar herself knew, and in that moment Tila greatly envied her.

"This proposal seeks to remove power from the thanes of Narida, whose families were first granted that power by the divine order of a God-King," Natan continued. "In some cases, that lineage goes back to companions of Nari Himself. Worthy though the aims of the revolutionaries undoubtedly are, the decisions of mere men and women cannot override the word of our god, this king's divine ancestor. Only a royal command, issued by a descendant of Nari, could do such a thing."

The thanes nodded in agreement. Saana Sattistutar, Tila noticed, narrowed her eyes at Natan. Then she sat back again, and folded her hefty arms.

"Therefore," Natan said, "it shall be this king who issues that command."

There was a moment of silence, while everyone's brains caught up with their ears, and then all of the thanes – bar Darel Blackcreek – burst out in protest.

"SILENCE!" Natan thundered, in what Tila recognised as his best impression of their father. For a wonder, it worked. "This king accepts the basic proposals put forward, but he will not step aside for an interim government composed of those who happen to command a force of warriors. He will issue the necessary edicts, in line with these plans and advised by those present today, and he solemnly swears that he will abdicate his throne in favour of the person selected by the country, whomever that may be."

"But *Your Majesty*—" Kyrel Strongway blurted.

"This is this king's final word on the matter!" Natan said firmly. "Either accept his decision, or declare yourself a traitor and a rebel as well! Albeit one with a markedly smaller force at his disposal," he added, somewhat snidely.

For a moment, Tila honestly thought Strongway was going to declare his defiance and march away. Then, however, he sank sullenly back into his chair. The proposals allowed thanes to keep some of their wealth and land, varying depending on how much they had: Kyrel Strongway would remain a rich man by the standards of most, so long as he did not decide to make a stand on the basis of pride, and risk losing it all.

"Any thane may of course put himself – or herself," Natan

continued, nodding in the direction of Yarmina Darkspur, "forward for selection. Which is what this king will be doing."

Tila blinked in shock. "What?"

Her brother's veiled face turned towards her. "The people should be given the opportunity to choose: that is the basis of your proposals, is it not? If Naridans believe that this king is truly destined to rule this land, all they have to do is select him as their representative, and then others to select him in turn, until he becomes the head of your People's Assembly." He spread his hands. "Surely even the thanes can take no issue with this process, if there is the possibility of this king being returned to power after all. Albeit for an initial term not exceeding five years."

Her brother's plan was . . . annoying, Tila decided, but not necessarily unreasonable. He *did* have the right to stand for representation, under their proposals: she just never assumed he would bother. And it was certainly true that shouts about overriding divine right to rule could be muffled a bit by pointing out that he still *could* rule, if the people chose him to.

"Those would seem to be acceptable compromises," she said, looking across at her companions. The Tjakorshi did not care about such small details: Natan's acceptance of the plan meant an acceptance of their right to make their homes in selected parts of Narida, which was their main concern. Benel and Toren were nodding slowly, Barstan Broadfield looked like he could barely believe that Tyrun's dream of doing away with the systems of nobility was coming true, and Sebiah Wousewold . . . Well, he looked as neutrally thoughtful as he ever had at an Inner Council meeting, which at least meant that he was not objecting. He too would remain comparatively wealthy, which he had perhaps decided was a reasonable trade. Besides, Tila suspected that Wousewold would find a way to make himself useful to whoever ended up in power.

"Perhaps the Lord of Scribes would care to organise the appropriate documents for this king to sign, so as to make these declarations official over the coming days?" Natan asked, as though reading her mind. "Traitor or not, you have appropriate experience in such matters."

"Of course, Divine Majesty," Wousewold replied, bowing smoothly in his seat.

Something abruptly occurred to Tila.

"Divine Majesty," she said cautiously. "If you are intending to stand for representation ... in which district would you intend to do so?"

"Why, Idramar of course, since the timescales set out here should allow for its people to return," Natan replied. "It is, after all, the one area of Narida with no thane other than the God-King, and this king has spent the majority of his life there." He tilted his head. "Why? Did you have intentions to stand there yourself?"

Tila sat back in her chair. It had been a while since she had last had one of her headaches, but she could feel one building now.

It was shaping up to be a blinder.

Saana

J oy and grief twined through Saana's heart in equal measure.
Joy, because her daughter had come back to her. So too
had others from her town who had disappeared into the north
at different times, and for different reasons: Darel, Inkeru,
Otim and his arsehole sons; even old Osred had managed to
survive the rigours of travel with The Golden's forces.

Grief, because others had not. The loss of Tsolga Hornsounder
was a hard blow to take. Infuriating although the old woman
could be at times, her presence was the sort of reassuring con-
stant you did not think about until it was no longer there. It
was as though one of the sky's brightest stars had winked out,
providing one less waymark by which to navigate.

And then there was Daimon.

Saana could not say for sure that she had loved him. She had
liked him, that was certainly true; she had respected him, all
the more so as she became more familiar with Narida and its
ways, and realised how unusual his behaviour had been; and
she had enjoyed spending time with him when they were both
naked. Perhaps if you put all those things together, they could
add up to love? She was not sure. What she could definitely say
was that she missed him, a great deal. Life without Daimon was
as though the sun had dimmed, just a little bit. Things could
continue, but would never be quite the same.

She cursed him, at first, when she learned that he met his death challenging The Golden to single combat. She angrily asked the sky how he could be so *foolish*. Then, when she had the chance to speak to Darel about it, she learned Daimon's logic: that perhaps without The Golden to lead them, his horde would fall apart. And had that not happened? Once the draug was killed, the captains and chiefs took stock and realised that compromise was their best option. It just had not happened in time to save Daimon's life.

Daimon took one last risk with his own life, in an attempt to save other people's. The gamble did not come off this time, but it was simply his nature to do such things. That was who Saana had married.

"Chief Saana?"

Saana looked up. The rest of the Black Keep council – or such of it as was left – were looking at her from around the table. Darel's grand plans for Narida had been set in motion, but for the moment Yarmina Darkspur was still a thane, and she had allowed them to use a chamber in her castle to meet.

"Sorry," Saana muttered. "Darel is remaining with the God-King, for now, to help make sure everything goes smoothly. By the time he comes back to us, he may no longer be a thane. So . . . " She spread her hands to encompass them all. "We should get used to making decisions."

"S'man still can't believe the God-King agreed," Nalon said. The faintly stunned expression had not left his face since he heard the news. "It's . . . Well, it's hilarious is what it is, but . . . "

"Black Keep has always been a long way from Idramar and the God-Kings," Osred said. He needed to put some weight back on his old bones, but otherwise the steward was looking reasonably healthy. "We will honour Nari, no matter whether a descendant of his sits on a throne. So long as the person selected to represent us is one of us, and knows our ways, we will be fine."

"How are you defining 'one of us'?" Esser the witch asked through Nalon, once he had finished translating Osred's words.

"Well, not Darkspur or Tainbridge," Osred replied, as though it was obvious, and Saana smiled. The steward had come to accept Tjakorshi as belonging, but would not countenance being governed by Naridans from other thanedoms. There was probably something very profound about Naridan thinking in that, but she did not have the time or inclination to consider it further at the moment.

"Esser's made a good point, though," Sagel the guard said, nodding in the direction of the witch. "We all know there have been . . . problems, at times. If people don't select someone who understands everyone, we could end up back where we started, or near enough."

Aftak grunted. "This priest isn't sure that *anyone* can understand everyone."

"Well, as near as," Sagel replied, a trifle testily. "They're going to need to speak both languages."

"And be trusted and respected in both communities," Inkeru put in, through Nalon.

"And preferably have some understanding of the Smoking Valley," Osred added. "We should not allow changes in our own land to damage our relationship with them."

Saana looked from one face to another, with a growing sense of uneasiness. "If any of you are suggesting Zhanna, then Darel's laws say she is too young—"

"No, not Zhanna!" Sagel said, with a laugh. "Don't get s'man wrong, he's got nothing against her, but . . . no."

"Someone whose *child* went to the Smoking Valley, and who fulfilled the other criteria, would still be very suitable," Osred said gently.

"Each person will make their own choice, of course," Aftak said. "But this priest, for one, intends to encourage others to make the choice he thinks will be best for us all."

Every face was looking at Saana.

She was chosen for a role once before, when she was made chief of the Brown Eagle Clan. She had been young, and extremely surprised. She never had any idea that others might see her as a leader: certainly not when compared to Black Kal, the previous chief. She only later understood that perhaps that had been the point. Black Kal was a strong chief, but eager for raids and glory that had cost the clan a lot of blood, including his own. People wanted someone less likely to get them and their children killed, and a solid, dependable mother with a young daughter of her own, who could use an axe but did not make her living by it, seemed a good choice.

It looked like she was, once more, being put forward for a role she had never expected.

She smiled at them. "This man agrees with your points."

Faint smiles and nods, all around the table.

Saana widened her own smile. "Nalon would indeed be the perfect fit."

Nalon's eyes swivelled in his head like a cornered prey animal as, one by one, every face turned towards him instead. Finally, he sprang up to his feet and backed towards the door.

"You've got to be *fucking* kidding!" he shouted, then opened the door and fled through it.

Saana fell off her chair laughing.

Black Keep looked good under the sun.

The damage from the great wave could still be seen everywhere Saana looked, but the town was beginning to come back together. The settlements farther inland had sent food and labour to assist, and although Black Keep had obviously taken a battering, much more was habitable than when she left. By the time the workers returned after the harvest, their home should be ready to accommodate them again.

That was assuming they all returned, of course. More than one former resident of Black Keep seemed to like Darkspur surroundings, and perhaps the notion of returning to a repaired shell of what had once been their home, with few possessions left to call their own, held less appeal than making a new one. Yarmina was using the time left in her authority to encourage people to settle in her land, making up for the losses it had suffered when the great wave had washed away so many of their able-bodied men: and of course, Darkspur was far enough from the coast that further great waves were nothing to worry about.

That was not Saana's choice, though. She passed under the last bough of the Downwoods and brought her dragon to a halt – and what a strange notion *that* would have been, even a year ago – and looked out towards the glistening strip of water to the east. She had travelled far from the sea in the past months, but could not imagine staying away from it. She had never even been a great sailor, but there was something reassuring about just being near the ocean: the fact it was constantly changing, yet always remained more or less the same. Perhaps there was a lesson in that.

"Thinking about home?" Zhanna asked, following Saana's gaze eastwards. She was on her own dragon, her remaining hand holding the reins with a casual ease. Saana still felt a stab of guilt and pain whenever she saw her daughter's truncated left arm, but she did her best not to show it, in case Zhanna mistook it as disgust or disdain. They had faced a lot of challenges since coming to Narida, and allowing Zhanna to spread her wings had certainly done both of them good in many ways, but conversations were still sometimes difficult. There always seemed to be the possibility of prickly misunderstandings. Perhaps there always would be. Perhaps it was simply better to accept that, rather than resent the argumentative person her daughter had turned into, and make things worse.

"This is home," Saana said, and realised that she meant it.

"You don't miss Koszal?"

"A bit," Saana admitted. "But I don't think I'd go back, even now The Golden is dead."

"The broken clans think the mountain spirits ruined the land, anyway," Zhanna said. "They're pretty certain The Golden was right about that much." She looked thoughtful. "I wonder if it would be possible to go and find out."

Saana opened her mouth to reject the notion outright – the storms! The krayk! The risk of finding nothing, of running out of fresh water and slowly dying of thirst! – but shut it again.

"Just promise me you won't go unless you can find an *experienced* captain and crew willing to risk it," she said gently. "Trekking into the mountains with Amonhuhe is one thing: going head-to-head with the Dark Father in his own domain is something else entirely."

Zhanna gaped at her. "I never said *I* wanted to go!"

Saana chuckled. "You didn't have to. I know you well enough to know you want to go *everywhere*. It's just a case of where you're going to pick first."

"Well, I might go back to Darkspur for a while, soon," Zhanna said thoughtfully. "I like Yarmina, and I think she could use a friend. She doesn't have many, and I don't know if she'll be selected when the time comes. It might be that too many people dislike her because of her mother. That'll be hard for her."

Yarmina had been obviously uncomfortable around Saana ever since Zhanna had arrived at Darkspur the first time, even when they travelled north together; to answer the God-King's summons, in Yarmina's case, and find out exactly what her husband had walked into, in Saana's. Some people might have put that down to guilt over Yarmina being the reason Saana's daughter now had one less hand than before, but Saana had seen how Yarmina looked at Zhanna, and had her own suspicions about exactly how "friendly" Yarmina wanted to get.

She opened her mouth to say something . . . and closed it once more. Saana had made a vow to Daimon on matters of this sort, and she would not break it. More importantly, Zhanna was an adult now, and could make her own decisions. Saana might not have changed her mind about certain things that Naridans considered perfectly normal, but she did not have to share her opinions.

I can't control what I think, but I can control what I say. Father Krayk help me, I am an adult as well, I should be able to manage that.

"Right now, though," Zhanna continued, pointing at the castle that was still their home, at least for the moment, "I want to go there, and find a bed."

"And on that, we can agree," Saana said, and kicked her heels into her mount's flanks. The dragon grunted in vague acknowledgment of her wishes, and began to plod forwards once more.

Saana had lost a lot, bringing her clan across the ocean in search of a new home. In some ways, she had lost more than she would have thought possible. In other ways, she had gained more than she could have ever imagined.

But . . . I didn't expect this to be easy, did I?

Epilogue

In a tavern in Torgallen, three figures sit around a table. Each has a mug in front of them, from which they take the occasional pull. There is tension in the air: much of the Western Army disappeared eastwards under the command of Marshal Taladhar Torgallen, and now word is trickling back that it joined a rebellion which has failed, or possibly not failed.

One of the two smaller figures takes another drink, and speaks.

"S'man still thinks we should try Morlith."

"Nari's teeth, Mar," the larger figure groans. "You're not going to make your husband go through that bloody pass again, are you?"

"What's wrong with the Torgallen Pass?" the third figure asks. She sounds slightly surprised.

" . . . Bad memories," the larger figure says, after an uncomfortable moment or two.

"Oh. *Ohhh*. Yes, s'woman remembers now. So, uh, what makes you think we should go to Morlith?" she asks, changing the subject. "Although s'woman's still not quite sure why she's still with you, seeing as how since meeting you she's been thrown in prison once and nearly killed on multiple occasions."

"No one asked you to run into that battle," the bigger man says, taking a pull of his drink. "In fact, this sar distinctly remembers telling you *not*—"

"We're not talking about *that*," the woman interrupts him. "Marin. Why Morlith?"

"Morlith's pretty stable," the smaller man replies. "Nari only knows what's going to happen here, and even if we weren't half a world away from Kiburu ce Alaba, s'man and his husband didn't exactly make friends last time we were in East Harbour, so that's probably out. There are other cities, of course, but it still might be better not to risk it."

"Are there any cities you've been in which *don't* want to arrest you when you go back?"

"This one," the larger man grunts. "So far."

"We're not getting any younger," the smaller man says. "S'man would like to see Morlith while his legs will still carry him round it. He has some of the language, it's as good a place to earn a living as anywhere else—"

"You call thievery 'earning'?" the woman demands.

"S'man is a scholar!"

"Tell her about your secret society."

"*Laz!*"

"What secret—"

"Never mind that! Never mind anything this great hairy thundertooth says!"

"'Great Hairy Thundertooth' is also what he calls this sar's—"

"*Notlisteningnotlisteningnotlistening!*"

There is a brief pause while all three speakers compose themselves.

"*Anyway*," the smaller man says, "it's a well-known fact that medicine holds more appeal if it's thought to come from farther away. That could benefit you, you know."

"Wonderful. So instead of suspicious locals thinking s'woman is a witch, they can think of her as a *foreign* witch."

"It's a different land, with different gods," the smaller man says, and his tone is suddenly more serious. "And different . . . everything else, for that matter. After what we've seen here, s'man has to admit that holds a temptation of its own."

There is another pause, pregnant with memories of burning buildings, and public executions, and a young man with an otherworldly air and something ageless behind his eyes.

"Fuck it," the woman says, after a while. "Why not? S'woman's never even spoken to someone who's been to Morlith. It'll be completely new." She laughs, but there is a hollow edge to it. "Honestly, how much worse can she fuck everything up by going there?"

"S'man's not entirely sure if 'that's the spirit' is an appropriate response to that," the smaller man replies, "but you get the general sentiment."

"Tell your husband one thing," the larger man says to the smaller. "Tell him that this is not because of what Tolkar said about Morlith stealing all the magic."

" . . . This is definitely mostly not about what Tolkar said about Morlith stealing all the magic."

"Nari's *teeth*, Mar."

"He was almost certainly not telling the truth, you know that?" the woman asks. "Almost certainly," she adds, more quietly, and to herself.

"Yes, s'man knows," the smaller man agrees, sounding livelier once more. "But what if he *was*? There's a whole *empire* on the other side of the Catseye Mountains: there could be *anything* there! S'man just wants to see it, whatever it is. Stolen magic or not."

The big man sighs, and sets his mug down.

"Don't do that face."

"What face?"

"That one, the face you're doing now."

"The face that looks like a constipated rat?" the woman puts in.

"You know you can't say no to this face, Laz."

"Yes, yes, your husband knows," the larger man grumbles good-naturedly. "Fine. Let's go and accidentally make enemies in a completely new country, for a change. But if they *are* 'stealing all the magic' – whatever that means – you are *not* to try to steal any back, you understand?"

"No promises!"

In the other corner of the tavern, an old man has his back to the trio. His bearded lips quirk into a smile, and he raises his own mug with swollen-knuckled hands.

THE END

... POSSIBLY

Acknowledgements

Well, this has been a hell of a ride.

I've wanted to write fantasy since I was a child. I *started* to write fantasy many times, but never got beyond the first chapter or two. I had all sort of ideas for how the story was going to go, back in the 90s, but it never panned out. Even when I started writing properly, and got an agent, and got interest from publishers, my first published work was space opera. I felt that I wasn't 'ready' for my epic fantasy; that I did not yet have the skills as an author to do justice to the ideas that had been kicking around in my head for twenty years or more.

However, sometimes you've just got to take the plunge. Once the Keiko series had stopped, I started looking at my fantasy ideas properly, spread over however many notebooks and various corners of my brain. Most things had changed since my initial attempts when I was a teenager, although some elements and characters remained in one form or another: Marin and Alazar are survivors of my first ideas, for example, as is Nari the God-King. Daimon and Saana, the Tjakorshi, the City of Islands – all of that was new. The story I was telling now was not the one of 'glorious' epic battles that my teenage self had imagined, but one about understanding people who are different from you, and trying to *stop* the fighting.

And then, of course, the pandemic happened.

The Black Coast was originally due to come out in the summer of 2020, but got pushed back to February 2021. Because of how publishing timescales work, that meant I was delivering the manuscript of *The Godbreaker* only a month or so after the release of the first book in the series. It was a little nerve-wracking to be finishing up the final instalment of what I had always envisaged as my magnum opus at the same time as reactions to the first part were just starting to come in, but perhaps it was better that way. Gratifyingly, it seemed that certain parts of the world-building, the cultures and the general message struck home hard with some people. Whether this series goes on to greater recognition, or is largely forgotten, I know (because they told me) that some people I'd never met absolutely fell in love with it, and that means a huge amount to me. And so, of course, I want to thank the people who helped make this possible, and brought my childhood dream of being 'a fantasy author' to some form of fruition.

Firstly, my editor Jenni at Orbit UK, and all of her team. Jenni has been a pleasure to work with throughout this series, and has great insight and suggestions (as well as excellent taste in cartoons. ADVENTURE!). Nazia, while terrifying, has been exactly the sort of publicist any author could hope for, and can at least be pacified with doughnuts. Thanks must similarly be extended to Michael and the team at Solaris, who handled the US distribution. Both publishing houses had to deal with the impacts of the pandemic, shipping delays, paper shortages, and goodness knows what else (possibly badgers?), and the fact that these books came out anything less than utterly haphazardly is due entirely to their hard work and dedication.

No author acknowledgements would be complete without referencing their agent, and I have two to thank – Rob, who initially got me the deal, and Alex, who has since taken over and seen it through.

I want to give fulsome thanks to Stewart and Jamie, my two enduring and most helpful beta-readers; to David Rawlings of London Longsword for his help and advice, and waving swords at his webcam for me; to Nye Redman-White, who helped me make the languages and names distinct and characterful; and also to Tej Turner, who gave me a useful little piece of information relating to *The Splinter King*, and whom I forgot to thank in the acknowledgments for that novel.

I would like to thank all the bloggers and reviewers who said such nice things about *The Black Coast* and *The Splinter King*: I hope you like this one just as much.

Most importantly as always, I want to thank my wife Janine. Not only is she the best and most important thing in my life, but she managed and supervised two different teams of workers at the same time in the health and social care sector right through the teeth of the pandemic, which is something society as a whole should be thankful for, and did it even though her husband had left that organisation and spent all that time writing stories in our spare bedroom.

And finally, I must thank the people who have read these novels. Time seems a more precious resource than ever in the world today; thank you for giving me some of yours.

May the blessings of Nari and the Hundred be upon you all, and may Father Krayk not call your name for a long time to come . . .

extras

orbitbooks.net

about the author

Mike Brooks was born in Ipswich, Suffolk and now lives in Nottingham with his wife, cats, snakes and a collection of tropical fish. He worked for a homelessness charity for over fifteen years, before deciding that he preferred making up stories for a living. When not writing, he plays guitar with his punk band and DJs wherever anyone will tolerate him. He is the author of three science fiction novels, *Dark Run*, *Dark Sky* and *Dark Deeds*, and various works for Games Workshop's Black Library

Find out more about Mike Brooks and other Orbit authors by registering for the free monthly newsletter at orbitbooks.net.

if you enjoyed

THE GODBREAKER

look out for

THE UNBROKEN

by

C. L. Clark

EVERY EMPIRE DEMANDS REVOLUTION.

Touraine is a soldier. Stolen as a child and raised to kill and die for the empire, her only loyalty is to her fellow conscripts. But now, her company has been sent back to her homeland to stop a rebellion, and the ties of blood may be stronger than she thought.

Luca needs a turncoat. Someone desperate enough to tiptoe the bayonet's edge between treason and orders. Someone who can sway the rebels toward peace, while Luca focuses on what really matters: getting her uncle off her throne.

Through assassinations and massacres, in bedrooms and war rooms, Touraine and Luca will haggle over the price of a nation. But some things aren't for sale.

1

Change

A sandstorm brewed dark and menacing against the Qazāli horizon as Lieutenant Touraine and the rest of the Balladairan Colonial Brigade sailed into El-Wast, capital city of Qazāl, foremost of Balladaire's southern colonies.

El-Wast. City of marble and sandstone, of olives and clay. City of the golden sun and fruits Touraine couldn't remember tasting. City of rebellious, uncivilized god-worshippers. The city where Touraine was born.

At a sudden gust, Touraine pulled her black military coat tighter about her body and hunched small over the railing of the ship as it approached land. Even from this distance, in the early-morning dark, she could see a black Balladairan standard flapping above the docks. Its rearing golden horse danced to life, sparked by the reflection of the night lanterns. Around her, pale Balladairan-born sailors scrambled across the ship to bring it safely to harbor.

El-Wast, for the first time in some twenty-odd years. It took the air from the lieutenant's chest. Her white-knuckle grip on the rail was only partly due to the nausea that had rocked her on the water.

"It's beautiful, isn't it?" Tibeau, Touraine's second sergeant and best friend, settled against the rail next to her. The wooden rail shifted under his bulk. He spoke quietly, but Touraine could hear the awe and longing in the soft rumble of his voice.

Beautiful wasn't the first thing Touraine thought as their ship sailed up the mouth of the River Hadd and gave them a view of El-Wast. The city was surprisingly big. Surprisingly bright. It was surprisingly ... civilized. A proper city, not some scattering of tents and sand. Not what she had expected at all, given how Balladairans described the desert colonies. From this angle, it didn't even look like a desert.

The docks stretched along the river like a small town, short buildings nestled alongside what were probably warehouses and workers' tenements. Just beyond them, a massive bridge arced over shadowed farmland with some crop growing in neat rows, connecting the docks to the curve of a crumbling wall that surrounded the city. The Mile-Long Bridge. The great bridge was lined with the shadows of palm trees and lit up all along with the fuzzy dots of lanterns. In the morning darkness, you could easily have mistaken the lanterns for stars.

She shrugged. "It's impressive, I guess."

Tibeau nudged her shoulder and held his arms out wide to take it all in. "You guess? This is your home. We're finally back. You're going to love it." His eyes shone in the reflection of the lanterns guiding the Balladairan ship into Crocodile Harbor, named for the monstrous lizards that had supposedly lived in the river centuries ago.

Home. Touraine frowned. "Love it? Beau, we're not on leave." She dug half-moons into the soft, weather-worn wood of the railing and grumbled, "We have a job to do."

Tibeau scoffed. "To police our own people."

The thunk of approaching boots on the deck behind them stopped Touraine from saying something that would keep Tibeau from speaking to her for the rest of the day. Something like *These aren't my people*. How could they be? Touraine had barely been toddling in the dust when Balladaire took her.

"You two better not be talking about what I think you're talking about," Sergeant Pruett said, coming up behind them with her arms crossed.

"Of course not," Touraine said. She and Pruett let their knuckles brush in the cover of darkness.

"Good. Because I'd hate to have to throw you bearfuckers overboard."

Pruett. The sensible one to Tibeau's impetuousness, the scowl to his smile. The only thing they agreed on was hating Balladaire for what it had done to them, but unlike Tibeau, who was only biding his time before some imaginary revolution, Pruett was resigned to the conscripts' fate and thought it better to keep their heads down and hate Balladaire in private.

Pruett shoved her way between the two of them and propped her elbows on the railing. Her teeth chattered. "It's cold as a bastard here. I thought the deserts were supposed to be hot."

Tibeau sighed wistfully, staring with longing at some point beyond the city. "Only during the day. In the real desert, you can freeze your balls off if you forget a blanket."

"You sound . . . oddly excited about that." Pruett looked askance at him.

Tibeau grinned.

Home was a sharp topic for every soldier in the Balladairan Colonial Brigade. There were those like Tibeau and Pruett, who had been taken from countries throughout the broken Shālan Empire when they were old enough to already have memories of family or the lack thereof, and then there were those like Touraine, who had been too young to remember anything but Balladaire's green fields and thick forests.

No matter where in the Shālan Empire the conscripts were

originally from, they all speculated on the purpose of their new post. There was excitement on the wind, and Touraine felt it, too. The chance to prove herself. The chance to show the Balladairan officers that she deserved to be a captain. Change was coming.

Even the Balladairan princess had come with the fleet. Pruett had heard from another conscript who had it from a sailor that the princess was visiting her southern colonies for the first time, and so the conscripts took turns trying to spot the young royal on her ship.

The order came to disembark, carried by shouts on the wind. Discipline temporarily disappeared as the conscripts and their Balladairan officers hoisted their packs and tramped down to Crocodile Harbor's thronged streets.

People shouted in Balladairan and Shālan as they loaded and unloaded ships, animals in cages and animals on leads squawked and bellowed, and Touraine walked through it all in a daze, trying to take it in. Qazāl's dirt and grit crunched beneath her army-issued boots. Maybe she *did* feel a spark of awe and curiosity. And maybe that frightened her just a little.

With a *wumph*, Touraine walked right into an odd tan horse with a massive hump in the middle of its back. She spat and dusted coarse fur off her face. The animal glared at her with large, affronted brown eyes and a bubble of spit forming at the corner of its mouth.

The animal's master flicked his long gray-streaked hair back off his smiling face and spoke to Touraine in Shālan.

Touraine hadn't spoken Shālan since she was small. It wasn't allowed when they were children in Balladaire, and now it sounded as foreign as the camel's groan. She shook her head.

"Camel. He spit," the man warned, this time in Balladairan. The camel continued to size her up. It didn't look like it was coming to any good conclusion.

Touraine grimaced in disgust, but beside her, Pruett snorted. The other woman said something short to the man in Shālan before turning Touraine toward the ships.

"What did you say?" Touraine asked, looking over her shoulder at the glaring camel and the older man.

"'Please excuse my idiot friend.'"

Touraine rolled her eyes and hefted her pack higher onto her shoulders.

"Rose Company, Gold Squad, form up on me!" She tried in vain to gather her soldiers in some kind of order, but the noise swallowed her voice. She looked warily for Captain Rogan. If Touraine didn't get the rest of her squad in line, that bastard would take it out on all of them. "Gold Squad, form up!"

Pruett nudged Touraine in the ribs. She pointed, and Touraine saw what kept her soldiers clumped in whispering groups, out of formation.

A young woman descended the gangway of another ship with the support of a cane. She wore black trousers, a black coat, and a short black cloak lined with cloth of gold. Her blond hair, pinned in a bun behind her head, sparked like a beacon in the night. Three stone-faced royal guards accompanied her in a protective triangle, their short gold cloaks blown taut behind them. Each of them had a sword on one hip and a pistol on the other.

Touraine looked from the princess to the chaos on the ground, and a growing sense of unease raised the short hairs on the back of her neck. Suddenly, the crowd felt more claustrophobic than industrious.

The man with the camel still stood nearby, watching with interest like the other dockworkers. His warm smile deepened the lines in his face, and he guided the animal's nose to her, as if she wanted to pat it. The camel looked as unenthusiastic at the prospect as Touraine felt.

"No." Touraine shook her head at him again. "Move, sir. Give us this space, if you please."

He didn't move. Probably didn't understand proper Balladairan. She shooed him with her hands. Instead of reacting with annoyance or confusion, he glanced fearfully over her shoulder.

She followed his gaze. Nothing there but the press of the crowd, her own soldiers either watching the princess or drowsily taking in their new surroundings in the early-morning light. Then she saw it: a young Qazāli woman weaving through the crowd, gaze fixed on one blond point.

The camel man grabbed Touraine's arm, and she jerked away.

Touraine was a good soldier, and a good soldier would do her duty. She didn't let herself imagine what the consequences would be if she was wrong.

"Attack!" she bellowed, fit for a battlefield. "To the princess!"

The Qazāli man muttered something in Shālan, probably a curse, before he shouted, too. A warning to his fellow. To more of them, maybe. Something glinted in his hands.

Touraine spared only half a glance toward the princess. That was what the royal guard was for. Instead, she launched toward the camel man, dropping her pack instead of swinging it at him. *Stupid, stupid.* Instinct alone saved her life. She lifted her arms just in time to get a slice across her left forearm instead of her throat.

She drew her baton to counterattack, but instead of running in the scant moment he had, the old man hesitated, squinting at her.

"Wait," he said. "You look familiar." His Balladairan was suddenly more than adequate.

Touraine shook off his words, knocked the knife from his hand, and tripped him to the ground. He struggled against her with wiry strength until she pinned the baton against his throat. That kept him from saying anything else. She held him there, her teeth bared and his eyes wide while he strained for breath. Behind her, the camel man's companions clashed with the other soldiers. A young woman's high-pitched cry. *The princess or the assassin?*

The old man rasped against the pressure of the baton. "Wait," he started, but Touraine pressed harder until he lost the words.

Then the docks went silent. The rest of the attackers had been taken down, dead or apprehended. The man beneath her realized it, too, and all the fight sagged out of him.

When they relieved her, she stood to find herself surrounded. The three royal guards, alert, swords drawn; a handful of fancy-looking if spooked civilians; the general — *her* general. General Cantic. And, of course, the princess.

Heat rose to her face. Touraine knew that some part of her should be afraid of overstepping; she'd just shat on all the rules and decorum that had been drilled into the conscripts for two decades. But the highest duty was to the throne of Balladaire, and not everyone could say they had stopped an assassination. Even if Touraine was a conscript, she couldn't be punished for that. She hoped. She settled into the strength of her broad shoulders and bowed deeply to the princess.

"I'm sorry to disturb you, Your Highness," Touraine said, her voice smooth and low.

The princess quirked an eyebrow. "Thank you" — the princess looked to the double wheat-stalk pins on Touraine's collar — "Lieutenant . . . ?"

"Lieutenant Touraine, Your Highness." Touraine bowed again. She peeked at the general out of the corner of her eye, but the older woman's lined face was unreadable.

"Thank you, Lieutenant Touraine, for your quick thinking."

A small shuffling to the side admitted a horse-faced man with a dark brown tail of hair under his bicorne hat. Captain Rogan sneered over Touraine before bowing to the princess.

"Your Highness, I apologize if this Sand has inconvenienced you." Before the princess could respond, Rogan turned to Touraine and spat, "Get back to your squad. Form them up like they should have been."

So much for taking her chance to rise. So much for duty. Touraine sucked her teeth and saluted. "Yes, sir."

She tightened her sleeve against the bleeding cut on her left arm and went back to her squad, who stood in a tight clump a few yards away from the old man's camel. The beast huffed with a sound like a bubbling kettle, and a disdainful glob of foamy spittle dripped from its slack lips. Safe enough to say she had made an impression on the locals.

And the others? Touraine looked back for another glimpse at the princess and found the other woman meeting her gaze. Touraine tugged the bill of her field cap and nodded before turning away, attempting to appear as unruffled as she could.

When Touraine returned to her squad, Pruett looked uncertain as Rogan handed the older man off to another officer, who led him and the young woman away. "I told you to be careful about attracting attention."

Touraine smiled, even though her arm stung and blood leaked into her palm. "Attention's not bad if you're the hero."

That did make Pruett laugh. "Ha! Hero. A Sand? I guess you think the princess wants to wear my shit for perfume, too."

Touraine laughed back, and it was tinged with the same frustration and bitterness that talk of their place in the world always was.

This time, when she called for her squad to form up, they did. Gold Squad and the others pulled down their field caps and drew close their coats. The wind was picking up. The sun was rising. The Qazāli dock-workers bent their backs into their work again, but occasionally they glanced – nervous, scared, suspicious, hateful – at the conscripts. At Rogan's order, she and the conscripts marched to their new posts.

Change was coming. Touraine aimed to be on the right side of it.